Great

French

Short

Novels

GREAT
FRENCH
SHORT
NOVELS

EDITED WITH AN INTRODUCTION BY **F. W. DUPEE**

THE DIAL PRESS   NEW YORK 1952

Contents

Introduction

To an entire generation of Americans—those who wrote and read serious books—almost anything in the French language sounded fine enough to be engraved on a monument or daring enough to be turned into English and circulated in limited editions to elude the censorship. That, of course, was the generation of the Teens and Twenties. It was the generation represented by Eliot and Pound in poetry and criticism, by Dreiser and Lewis in fiction, by all who sought to free our writing, on the one hand from narrowly puritan and patriotic obsessions, on the other hand from its long dependence on English writing. In this liberating process appeal was made to other literatures besides the French—to the Russian, the Scandinavian, the German. But the French, as the most experimental of them all, had a special exemplary value. And although the impact of French poetry on our poetry was considerable, the impact of French novels on our novels was even greater, for the obvious reason that a prose art is more accessible to foreigners than a verse art. Thus the French realists tended to replace Dickens and Hawthorne as our models; and for many an American it came to be true, as it was for the man in Pound's poem, that "his Penelope was Flaubert."

Such men are rare today. The French influence continues but in a special way. The young Southern writer, author of intensely local novels, who declared recently in an interview that his mas-

ters were Faulkner and Proust, suggests the extent to which the
authority of French fiction has been modified by the growth of
a tradition, both native and modern, in American fiction. And this
tradition, seizing on certain traits that once seemed peculiarly
French, has made them very much its own. The preoccupation
with sex, for example. It is to be doubted that any American
today, if he were to converse with a group of French writers in
Paris, would think of writing home as Henry James in 1875 wrote
home to Howells after a session with Flaubert and his fellow
novelists:

> As editor of the austere *Atlantic* it would startle you to hear
> some of their projected subjects. The other day Edmond de
> Goncourt (the best of them) said he had been working very
> well on his novel—he had got upon an episode that greatly
> interested him, and into which he was going very far. Flau-
> bert: "What is it?" E. de G.: "A whorehouse *de province*."

The small-town brothel is now a stock subject of American
novels which are sold in drugstores, read in respectable homes
and studied in colleges. And just as the license to deal openly,
even aggressively, with sex has been naturalized among our
novelists, so has the privilege, which once seemed pre-eminently
French, of writing stories well, with attention to form, method,
and serious ideas.

Yet there remains a great deal in French fiction which we perhaps need not and very likely cannot appropriate. There is a
surviving strangeness which is all the more compelling because it
is not to be rubbed off. The two civilizations, the French and the
American, are very different; they are, in fact, ideal opposites;
and that is the main source of the fascination which each has had
for the other.

Thus our novels have acquired much of the French *intensity*
but they do not have the same reason for being intense. They are
intense today with the feeling that certain old values have been
lost or betrayed, values which have to do mostly with the land
and the family. In the importance we continue to give to those

entities, if only by exasperated indirection, we remain close, not
to the French but to the English spirit. For the English spirit the
end of experience is the harmonious private life, an achieved
serenity, the reunion of families, the act of retirement, the return
to nature. As poetry is made, according to Wordsworth, out of
emotion recollected in tranquillity, so in Matthew Arnold's view
poetry is read in order to promote a similar state of mind in the
reader; and Henry James's severest charge against Flaubert was
that he lacked serenity. To be sure, English writers are far from
actually *shunning* the world of politics and society, as American
writers are so often inclined to do; they only put it firmly in what
they judge to be its place. And how pervasive the great English
spirit is! Even James Joyce, Irish in his birth and his subject,
Continental in his method of storytelling, pays essential tribute
to that spirit in his humorous domesticity and quietism. And
surely it was with some expectation of restoring freshness and
force to the traditional ideas of home and nature that D. H.
Lawrence suffered and wrote.

American novelists, as it is perhaps needless to observe, have a
subject of their own. This subject consists in the search for
identity and meaning within the newness and largeness and
changeableness of our country. Who are we? who am I?—these
are the overwhelming questions with us. But the pursuit of answers tends to lead backward and inward—the words are meant
in no unfavorable sense—toward primal states of filial and natural
innocence. In our literature, we are the least worldly of peoples.
We hark back to the original forest, the long river, the unlimited
sea; we seek our spiritual parents in such primitive beings as
Huck's Jim and Ishmael's Queequeg and Ike McCaslin's Sam
Fathers. The most considerable work of the American present,
the novels of Faulkner, have many implications; but in one sense
they are a long elegiac epic on the breaking-up of families and the
violating of the wilderness.

Neither of the great Anglo-Saxon preoccupations plays any
large part in French fiction or in French letters generally. Nature
has there an immense force in reference to the animal in man.

But the appeal of the land is either lyrical or consolatory or simply economic; and those writers who, like George Sand, celebrate it in any comprehensive way, are exceptional. Far from being different from the city in kind, the French countryside is normally thought of as a festive extension of city life, a kind of pleasance or super backyard. If only in relation to the city, the country has then a distinct value; but the life of the small town is highly equivocal. To be confined to it is to fail of anything like entire self-realization. The failure is moderate for the heroine of *The Old Maid*, Balzac's story in this volume, because Balzac felt a sympathy, nearly always clothed in irony, with the conservativism of provincial life; but for Flaubert's Emma Bovary the failure is of course deadly. Indeed Flaubert's novel might be considered as the savage French equivalent of *Cranford*, Mrs. Gaskell's idyll of English village experience.

The family, on the other hand, is certainly omnipresent in French fiction, as it is of course in French society. But there is a difference. As the boudoir may be said to open into the drawing room, so the house opens into the street. Domestic experience debouches into that sphere of public enterprise, the World (*le monde*), which is the arena of decisive experience for the French imagination. The family is very important at the beginning of life and retains a kind of practical minimal value at all times. But it does not define the end of existence. That end lies in the active life, the life of politics in the broadest sense of the word. Passive and contemplative as he was, Proust insisted—and he was only following Montaigne—that "the Society man is a man of action." He also demonstrated it in his novel of the *beau monde*, *Remembrance of Things Past*, where all the major characters are furiously preoccupied with their passions and their careers.

If it is arrested for any reason, the impulse to action turns in upon itself, assumes the form of energetic manias, and produces those ever-present types, the libertine, the miser, the avenger, the bovarist. When, on the other hand, the impulse to action is carried to its extreme of fulfillment, it leads out of the world entirely, towards states of absolute freedom. The consummation lies in acts of martyrdom rather than in acts of retirement; the return is not to nature but to the spirit. Like Roland in the old French epic, the hero aspires finally to hand his gauntlet up to God or to render up his soul to some other object of faith. Even dandyism, that minor nineteenth-century cult of the gentleman, is enlivened by comparable ambitions. Nor has the aspiring spirit ceased to live in French fiction down to our own difficult day. Indeed the present crisis of the world, and of France in particular, has only served to rekindle the active impulse in the French novel. In the hands of Gide, Malraux and Sartre, that novel is hero-haunted as perhaps never before.

The intensity of French fiction is thus very special in its origins and it can prove by turns fascinating and exhausting to foreign readers. The hero generally inhabits, as Cocteau says of one of his characters, "the zone of ecstasy"—and not only the hero but the villain, and not only the duchess but her maid. Together they make up a highly surcharged world which hovers between extremes of success and failure, *splendeur et misère, grandeur et servitude*. It is as if the Christian melodrama of salvation and damnation, together with the élan of feudal imperialism, chivalry and the Crusades, had somehow survived the ages of doubt and democracy. And in a sense they did survive, for the French Revolution and the Napoleonic wars of conquest reanimated the old ambitions.

Its ultimate preoccupation with the spirit makes for a bracing atmosphere of human equality in the French novel, an equality which is surpassed only by that of the classic Russian novel. To be sure, distinctions of class and wealth figure importantly in the definition of character and the intensification of drama; they are the perennial materials of French fiction. Yet the duchess and her maid have equal claims on the author's imagination. To him each is fully and richly realizable in her own right and on her own ground. Among Anglo-Saxon writers this equality does not prevail in the same degree. In neither England nor America have writers constituted so independent and professionally proud a caste as they have in France; in both of those countries they tend to be drawn into the moral orbit of one or other social class. For the English novelist, the maid (or governess or valet or footman or gamekeeper or bastard) must be assimilated or domesticated or naturalized to some established standard of conduct and manners, although the standard is not necessarily aristocratic and the duchess is by no means the arbiter. Among American writers the reverse situation pertains. The standard is generally popular (or populist), and the man or woman of wealth and position is imagined with difficulty by our novelists.

The morality of the French novel is similarly free of *parti pris*. It is rarely a morality of judgment. In a good many English novels the mystery of a person's birth is second in interest only to the mystery of his real character. One reads on to discover not merely whether so-and-so is of noble or humble descent but whether so-and-so is a gentleman or a cad, a lady or an adventuress. Such questions are of course worked out with the highest delicacy, humanity and humor by the great English novelists, with their benign paternal sense of responsibility to the social family. For better or worse, French novelists feel a very different kind of responsibility toward their society. That society is not, in any case, as we have said, a projection of the family; and it is assumed by the novelist to profit more from a morality of ideas than from a morality of judgment. The great effort of the French novelist is to inquire, to define, to formulate. He must know all, must receive from his characters a total confession; and in the end he does not judge, he absolves. His relation to his audience is not paternal but priestly; often, to be sure, he is like the *de*frocked priest, the questioner, the tempter.

There is, however, another and quite indispensable constituent of the experience embodied in French novels. This is the skeptical and analytical impulse, which is the reverse side of the national habit of ambition. Ambitions are rarely realized, heroes frequently fail, and the French mind, addressing itself to the causes of the failure, produces its characteristic moral psychology. This rueful wisdom of man is the entire subject of the many writers of essays, pensées and maxims in that language; but it is also conspicuous in the novelists. Thus French novels at their best come to be distinguished on the one hand by a brilliant intelligibility as to their general import, and on the other hand by a continuous play of pertinent reflection. Even a writer of unassuming fantastic tales like Barbey d'Aurevilly has this double virtue to perfection. His ideas are not great but they are clear and they express themselves in highly appropriate inventions, while his comment is pointed and sage. It is Barbey who writes, in the story printed hereafter, "My dear fellow, you must search pretty deeply for the beginnings of my story, as you would for a bullet over which the flesh has formed; for oblivion is like the flesh of living things which forms over events and prevents you from seeing anything, or even suspecting the place after a certain time." This power of vivid generalization is not of course exclusively French but it is perhaps pre-eminently French, and it is something about which the American novel in particular has long been reticent.

It should be added that the short novels or long stories in this volume were not selected because they seemed to the editor to conform to his idea of French fiction. They were chosen for the reason that they seemed good in themselves and that they were not readily available in other collections or in good English renderings. Hasty and awkward translations have been the curse of the French novel in English; to look closely into the matter, as the editor has naturally done, is to discover monstrous crimes against the spirit both of the originals and of English idiom. It is hoped that no such renderings appear in this volume; and where existing translations were inadequate, as in the case of *Rameau's Nephew* and *The Legend of Saint Julian*, new ones have been made specially for this collection, that of the former by Jacques Barzun, that of the latter by the editor. An attempt was also made to represent at least a fraction of the more famous French novelists, although one author, Barbey d'Aurevilly, was included precisely because he is a good writer who has no fame at all outside of France. The choice proved more difficult in the modern period where the selective effects of time have not yet operated and where the work of some of the best-known writers is either perfectly available or else reserved by their American publishers. Nevertheless, between Morand's brilliant forgotten story and Malraux's great forgotten story, the modern period can scarcely be said to suffer misrepresentation here.

F. W. Dupee

May, 1952

Rameau's Nephew

DENIS DIDEROT

Denis Diderot

The father of DENIS DIDEROT (1713-1783) was a maker of cutlery in the small town of Langres and all his life Diderot was proud of his artisan antecedents. A brilliant youth, he went to school to the Jesuits, who trained him strictly and thoroughly in the expectation that he would join their order. But in Paris, where he settled as a young man, he absorbed the new liberal thought which then issued chiefly from England (Locke, Shaftesbury); and far from joining the Jesuits he became one of their most effective enemies. As an editor of the Encyclopaedia, to which he gave some twenty years of his life, he assumed the central role in the Enlightenment and worked with his fellow "Philosophes" to rid the world of irrational and oppressive orthodoxies.

Through their efforts the man of letters became a great force and they all led eventful and paradoxical lives. The established society was split apart, morally and socially, in such a way that a writer could be at once a bohemian adventurer and a profoundly serious man, courted by great ladies and hunted by the police, banned by the censorship at home and subsidized by kings abroad. Diderot was all these things; he was the Enlightenment incarnate.

His central position rested partly on his organizing genius, partly on the "indescribable vivacity" (as one acquaintance put it) of his personality and conversation, but chiefly on his general powers of mind, which even today are not fully explored and appreciated. As a man of letters his fame has always been less than that of two of his fellow Philosophers, Voltaire and Rousseau, who published solid and influential works like *Candide* and *The New Héloïse*. Experimental in form, daring in substance, much of Diderot's best writing circulated in manuscript during his lifetime and for many years after. *Rameau's Nephew*, written about 1761, was not formally published in France till 1821, although Goethe, one of Diderot's admirers, had long since translated it into German. Yet Diderot is generally admitted to have been more original than Voltaire and more various and benign in his thought than Rousseau. It was possible for him to criticize accepted ideas without replacing them by large vague brooding absolutes of his own. The natural world, in particular, he revered as a living and all-embracing force rather than as some abstract totality or some convenient point of reference in the philosophers' long quarrel with civilization. At the same time Diderot united an endless capacity for speculation with a fine care for fact and method. He wrote a great deal on a vast variety of topics; and many later developments, from the theory of impressionism in the arts to the theory of the unconscious in psychology, were foreshadowed in his thought. As a student of human conduct he was, like Montaigne before him and Gide after him, a principled relativist, a moral immoralist. He called himself "the weathercock of Langres."

With his relish for the drama of ideas, Diderot found the dialogue an especially congenial form of expression; indeed he made the dialogue live as few have been able to do since Plato. *Rameau's Nephew* is a dialogue which, by reason of the intensity with which characters and situations are created in it, is veritably a novel; and it has had a considerable influence on novelists. Of the two speakers, the "I" is doubtless Diderot himself on his rational side and the "He" is conceivably a partial portrait of another historical person, one Jean-François Rameau, nephew of the great French composer Jean-Philippe Rameau. But it has long been believed that the dialogue was essentially, as one critic expressed it, "Diderot's conversation with himself." The "I" is Diderot in his capacity as a conscientious man, a rationalist, a philosopher; the "He" is Diderot the scapegrace and artist. Finally, *Rameau's Nephew* dramatizes the eternal rivalry between theory, which is necessarily limited, and experience, which is by definition inexhaustible. The Nephew begins by resembling that old butt of satire and comedy, the parasite; he ends by seeming as various and contradictory as life itself.

Rameau's Nephew

DENIS DIDEROT

[TRANSLATOR'S NOTE: Dozens of persons are named in this dialogue, most of them contemporaries of the speakers. They fall into three general classes and the context usually discloses the character or profession of the person named; it is seldom necessary to know more than this in order to understand the point of the reference. In the first class are well-known musicians, artists and writers, notably: Lully ("The Florentine"), Rameau, (uncle of Diderot's interlocutor), Pergolese, Locatelli, Duni, Philidor (also a famous chess player), Jomelli, Galuppi, Alberti, etc.; Greuze the painter; Voltaire, Racine, and other writers: Marivaux, Helvétius, Thyard de Bissy, Crébillon fils, Fontenelle, Quinault, D'Alembert, etc. More about them can be found in appropriate biographical dictionaries, but it should perhaps be pointed out that Voltaire appears here exclusively as a poet and dramatist, the author of *Mohammed, Merope, Tancred* and other tragedies.

The second class comprises men such as Palissot, La Morlière, Poinsinet, Baculard d'Arnaud, Le Brun, La Porte, Robbé, David, Fréron, and others linked with them in the dialogue. They are the hangers-on of literature, booksellers or journalists, and sometimes professional spongers. An exception must be made for Duhamel, who was a writer of textbooks on practical subjects, and for Briasson, who was the distributing agent of the great *Encyclopédie* edited by Diderot and D'Alembert.

The third class consists of financiers, judges, and other officials.

[Translation Copyright, 1952, by Jacques Barzun]

To it belong D'Argenson, one-time foreign minister and friend of Voltaire's; Maupeou, Chancellor of France and protégé of Mme. Du Barry; Bouret, one of the Farmers-General or wealthy tax collectors; Villemorien, colleague and son-in-law of the preceding; Samuel Bernard, multi-millionaire banker to Louis XIV and Louis XV; Bertin, of the Treasury Department.

It should be sufficiently clear that the women's names preceded by "La" (though sometimes without this particle) e.g. Clairon, Dangeville, Guimard, Deschamps, Lemierre, Arnould, and Hus were actresses of the time and usually courtesans as well. The various noblemen and Abbés referred to were fashionable or semi-fashionable figures whom Diderot uses as embodiments of current morals and manners.]

Rain or shine, it is my regular habit every day about five to go and take a walk around the Palais-Royal. I can be seen, all by myself, dreaming on d'Argenson's bench. I discuss with myself questions of politics, love, taste, or philosophy. I let my mind rove wantonly, give it free rein to follow any idea, wise or mad, that may come uppermost; I chase it as do our young libertines on the track of a courtesan whose face is wind-blown and smiling, whose eye sparkles and whose nose turns up. The youth drops one and picks up another, pursuing all and clinging to none: my ideas are my trollops.

If the weather is cold or rainy, I take shelter in the Regency Café, where I entertain myself by watching chess being played. Paris is the world center, and this café is the Paris center, for the finest skill at this game. It is there that one sees the clash of the profound Légal, the subtle Philidor, the staunch Mayot; that one sees the most surprising strokes and that one hears the stupidest remarks. For although one may be a wit and a great chess player, like Légal, one may also be a great chess player and a fool, like Foubert and Mayot.

One day I was there after dinner, looking hard, saying little, and listening the least amount possible, when I was accosted by one of the oddest characters in this country, though God has not stinted us. The fellow is a compound of elevation and abjectness, of good sense and lunacy. The ideas of decency and depravity must be strangely scrambled in his head, for he shows without ostentation the good qualities that nature has bestowed upon him, just as he does the bad ones without shame. For the rest, he is endowed with a strong constitution, a special warmth of imagination, and an unusual power of lung. If you ever meet him and are not held by his originality, you will either stuff your fingers into your ears or run away. Lord, what lungs!

No one is more unlike him than he himself. Sometimes he is thin and wan like a patient in the last stages of consumption; you could count his teeth through his skin; he looks as if he had been days without food or had just come out of a Trappist monastery. The next month, he is sleek and fat as if he ate regularly at a banker's or had shut himself up in a Bernardine convent. Today his linen is filthy, his clothes torn to rags, his shoes falling apart, and he hangs his head furtively; one is tempted to hail him and toss him a coin. Tomorrow he is powdered, curled, well dressed; he holds his head high, shows himself off—you would almost take him for a man of quality. He lives from day to day, jolly or sad according to luck. His first care on arising in the morning is to ascertain where he will dine; after dinner he ponders supper. Night brings its own worries—whether to return on foot to the garret where he sleeps (unless the landlady has taken back the key from impatience at receiving no rent); or whether to repair to a suburban tavern and await the dawn over a crust of bread and a mug of beer. When he hasn't as much as six cents in his pocket, as sometimes happens, he falls back on a cab-driving friend of his, or the coachman of a noble lord, who gives him a shakedown in a stable, alongside the horses. The next morning he still has bits of his mattress in his hair. If the weather is mild, he perambulates all night up and down the Cours-la-reine or the Champs-Elysées.

Daybreak sees him back in town, all dressed from yesterday for today and from today perhaps for the remainder of the week.

I have no great esteem for such eccentrics. Some people take them on as regular acquaintances or even friends. But for my part it is only once a year that I stop and fall in with them, largely because their character stands out from the rest and breaks that tedious uniformity which our education, our social conventions, and our customary good manners have brought about. If such a character makes his appearance in some circle, he is like a grain of yeast that ferments and restores to each of us a part of his native individuality. He shakes and stirs us up, makes us praise or blame, smokes out the truth, discloses the worthy and unmasks the rascals. Then, then the sensible man keeps his ears open and sorts out his company.

I knew my man from quite a while back. He used to frequent a house to which his talent had given him entrée. There was an only daughter; he swore to the father and mother that he would marry her. They shrugged it off, laughed in his face, told him he was crazy. But I lived to see it happen. He asked me for a few dollars, which I gave him. He had somehow made his way into a few good families, where he could always dine provided he would not speak without asking permission first. He kept quiet and ate with fury. He was remarkable to see under that restraint. If he had the inclination to break the treaty and open his mouth, at the first word all the guests would shout "Rameau!" Then rage would glow in his eyes and he fell to eating with greater fury still. You wanted to know his name and now you know it. He is the nephew of the famous musician who delivered us from the plainsong of Lully that we had intoned for over a century, and who wrote so much visionary gibberish and apocalyptic truth about the theory of music—writings that neither he nor anyone else ever understood. We have from him a number of operas in which one finds harmony, snatches of song, disconnected ideas, clatter, flights, triumphal processions, spears, apotheoses, murmurings, endless victories, and dance tunes that will last for all time. Having eliminated "the Florentine" in public favor, he will be eliminated by

the Italian virtuosos—as he himself foresaw with grief, rancor, and
depression of spirits. For no one, not even a pretty woman who
wakes up to find a pimple on her nose, feels so vexed as an author
who threatens to survive his own reputation—witness Marivaux
and the younger Crébillon.

He accosts me: Ha ha! So there you are, master Philosopher!
And what are you up to among all these idlers? Do you waste your
time, too, pushing wood? (That is the contemptuous way of
describing chess and checkers.)

MYSELF: No, but when I have nothing better to do, I enjoy
watching those who push well.

HE: In that case you don't enjoy yourself very often. Apart
from Légal and Philidor, the others don't know what they're
doing.

MYSELF: What of M. de Bissy?

HE: Oh that one is to chess what Mlle. Clairon is to acting:
they know about their respective playing all that can be
learned.

MYSELF: I see you're hard to please. You forgive nothing but
sublime genius.

HE: True: in chess, checkers, poetry, eloquence, music
and other nonsense of that kind, what's the use of mediocrity?

MYSELF: Not much, I admit. But it takes a crowd to cultivate
the game before one man of genius emerges. He is one out of
many. But let it go. It's an age since I've seen you. I don't
think about you very much when I don't see you but I'm always glad when I do. What have you been doing?

HE: What you and I and the rest do, namely, good and
evil, and also nothing. And then I was hungry and I ate when
I had the chance. After eating I was thirsty and I have occasionally drunk. Meanwhile my beard grew and when grown
I had it shaved.

MYSELF: There you were wrong. A beard is all you lack to be
a sage.

HE: Right you are. My forehead is broad and wrinkled; I have glowing eyes, a beaky nose, spacious cheeks, thick black brows, a clean-cut mouth, curved-out lips and a square jaw. Cover this ample chin with a flowing beard and I assure you it would look splendid in bronze or marble.

MYSELF: Side by side with Caesar, Marcus Aurelius, and Socrates.

HE: No. I should like it better between Diogenes and Phryne. I am as cheeky as the one and often visit the sisters of the other.

MYSELF: Are you still in good health?

HE: Usually, yes, but not so well today.

MYSELF: How is that? You have a paunch like Silenus and a face like—

HE: A face like the belly's sworn enemy. That's because the spleen which is wasting my dear uncle seems to fatten his dear nephew.

MYSELF: Speaking of the uncle, do you ever see him?

HE: I see him pass in the street.

MYSELF: Doesn't he do anything for you?

HE: If he ever has done anything for anybody, it must be without knowing it. He is a philosopher after his own heart: he thinks of no one but himself; the rest of the universe is to him a tinker's dam. His wife, his daughter may die as soon as they please. Provided the parish bells that toll for them continue to sound the intervals of the twelfth and the seventeenth, all will be well. It's lucky for him and that's what I envy especially in men of genius. They are good for only one thing —apart from that, zero. They don't know what it is to be citizens, fathers, mothers, cousins, friends. Between you and me, one should try to be like them in every way, but without multiplying the breed. The world needs men, but men of genius, no; I say, no! No need of them. They are the ones who change the face of the earth. In the smallest things, stupidity is so common and powerful that it is not changed without fracas. What results is partly the reformer's vision, partly the old status quo—whence two gospels, the dress of a harle-

quin. The wisdom of the monk Rabelais is the true wisdom
for his peace of mind and ours: to do one's duty as it comes,
always speak well of the Superior, and let the world wag. It
must be all right since the majority is content with it. If I
knew history, I would prove to you that evil has always come
here below from a few men of genius; but I don't know any
history because I don't know anything at all. The devil take
me if I've ever learnt a single thing and if, having learnt nothing, I am worse off. One day I was at table with one of the
King's Ministers who has brains enough for ten. Well, he
showed us as plain as two and two make four that nothing is
more useful to the nations of the earth than lies, nothing more
harmful than the truth. I don't quite recall his proofs but it
followed very clearly that men of genius are poisonous and
that if at birth a child bore the mark of this dangerous gift of
nature, he should be either smothered or thrown to the dogs.

MYSELF: And yet those people who are so down on genius all
pretend to have some?

HE: I'm sure they think so inside, but they don't dare
admit it.

MYSELF: From modesty! So you developed from then on an un-
dying hatred of genius?

HE: And will never get over it.

MYSELF: But I remember the time when you were in despair at
the thought of being a common man. You'll never be happy
if the pros and cons weigh with you equally. You should make
up your mind and stick to it. I agree with you that men of
genius are usually odd, or—as the saying goes, "great wits
are sure to madness near allied"; but that doesn't change the
truth that ages without genius are despised. Men will continue
to honor the nations where genius thrived. Sooner or later
they put up statues to them and call them benefactors of the
race. With all due respect to the sublime minister you were
quoting, I believe that although a lie may serve for a while, it
is harmful in the long run; and contrariwise, truth necessarily
is best in the long run, even though it may do harm at the

moment. From which I incline to think that the man of genius who denounces a common error or who establishes a general truth always deserves our veneration. Such a man may fall a victim to prejudice or existing law; but there are two kinds of laws—those based on equity, which are universally true, and those based on caprice, which owe their force only to blindness or local necessity. These last cast odium on their violator for only a brief moment, an odium which time transfers to the judges and the peoples who carried out the law. Which of the two, Socrates or the judge who made him drink hemlock, is today the dishonored man?

HE: A great comfort to Socrates! Was he any the less convicted? any the less put to death? Was he less of an agitator? In violating a bad law, did he not encourage fools to despise the good ones? Wasn't he in any case a queer and troublesome citizen? A while ago you yourself were not far from marking down the man of genius too!

MYSELF: Listen, my dear fellow. A society should not tolerate any bad laws, and if it had only good ones it would never find itself persecuting men of genius. I never agreed that genius went with evil nor evil with genius. A fool is more often a knave than a genius is. And even if the latter is difficult to get on with, irritating and irritable—add wicked, if you like— what do you infer from it?

HE: That he should be drowned.

MYSELF: Gently, dear fellow. Look and tell me—I shan't take your uncle as an example. He is a hard man, brutal, inhuman, miserly, a bad father, bad husband, and bad uncle. But no one has proved that he is a genius who has advanced his art to such a point that ten years from now we shall still discuss his works. Take Racine instead—there was a genius and his reputation as a man was none too good. Take Voltaire—

HE: Don't press the point too far: I am a man to argue with you.

MYSELF: Well, which would you prefer—that he should have been a good soul, at one with his cash register, like Briasson, or with his yardstick, like Barbier; legitimately getting his wife with child annually—a good husband, good father, good uncle, good neighbor, fair trader and nothing more; or that he should have been deceitful, disloyal, ambitious, envious, and mean like the author of *Andromaque, Britannicus, Iphigénie, Phèdre,* and *Athalie?*

HE: For himself I daresay it would have been better to be the former of the two.

MYSELF: That is even truer—infinitely—than you think.

HE: There you go, you fellows! If we say anything good, it's like lunatics or people possessed—you say it's by accident. It's only people like you who really know what you are saying. I tell you, master Philosopher, I know what I say and know it as well as you know what you say.

MYSELF: Let's find out: why better for Racine?

HE: Because all those mighty works of his did not bring him in twenty thousand francs, and if he had been a good silk merchant rue St. Denis or St. Honoré, a good grocer or apothecary in a large way of business, he would have amassed a huge fortune, in the course of doing which there is no pleasure he would have failed to enjoy. From time to time he would have given a dollar to a poor buffoon like me and I would have made him laugh besides procuring for him an occasional young girl to distract him a little from eternally living with his wife. We would have eaten excellent meals at his table, played high, drunk excellent wines, coffee, liqueurs; we would have had delightful picnics—you can see I knew perfectly well what I was saying—but let me finish: it would have been better for those around him.

MYSELF: Unquestionably. Provided he hadn't used unworthily the riches acquired in legitimate trade, and had kept from his house all the gamblers, parasites, sycophants, idlers, and debauchees, as well as ordered his shopboys to beat up the officious gentlemen who would help husbands to a little distraction from habitually living with their wives.

HE: Beat up, my good sir, beat up! No one is beaten up in

a well-ordered city. The profession is respectable; many people, even persons of title, are in it. And what in hell do you think money is for, if not to have good board, good company, pretty women, every kind of pleasure and every sort of amusement? I'd rather be a beggar than own a fortune without these enjoyments. But to come back to Racine. The fellow was of use only to people he did not know, at a time when he had ceased to live.

MYSELF: Granted. But compare the good and the evil. A thousand years from now he will draw tears, will be admired of men all over the earth, will inspire compassion, human kindness, love. People will wonder who he was, from what country, and France will be envied. As against this, he brought suffering on a few persons who are dead and in whom we take no interest. We have nothing more to fear from his vices or his errors. It would no doubt have been preferable if nature had bestowed upon him the virtues of a good man as well as the talents of a great one. He is a tree which has stunted a few trees in his vicinage and blighted the plants growing at his feet; but his topmost branch reached the sky and his boughs spread afar. He afforded shade to those past, present, and future who come to rest close to his majestic trunk. He bore fruit of exquisite savor and that will not perish. Again, it would be desirable if Voltaire had the sweetness of Duclos, the ingenuity of Abbé Trublet, the rectitude of Abbé d'Olivet; but as that cannot be, consider the really interesting side of the problem; forget for a moment the point we occupy in time and space, and project your vision into future time and remote places. Think of the welfare of our species and supposing that we are not generous enough, let us thank nature for knowing her business better than we. If you throw cold water on Greuze's head, you will extinguish his talent together with his vanity. If you make Voltaire less restive under criticism, he will not delve into the soul of Merope and will no longer move you.

HE: But if nature is as powerful as it is wise, why not make
them as good as they are great?

MYSELF: Don't you see that if you argue this way you upset the
general order of things? If everything here below were excellent, nothing would be excellent.

HE: You are right. The important point is that you and I
should exist, and that we should be you and I. Outside of that,
let everything carry on as it may. The best order, for me, is
that in which I had to exist—and a fig for the most perfect
world if I am not of it. I'd rather *be*—and be even a silly
logic-chopper—than not be at all.

MYSELF: There is nobody who thinks otherwise and yet who
fails to attack the scheme of things, blind to the fact that in
doing so he repudiates his own existence.

HE: True enough.

MYSELF: So let's accept things as they are, find out their worth
and their cost, and forget whatever we do not know well
enough to assess it. It perhaps is neither good nor bad, but
only necessary, as so many good people think.

HE: I don't follow all that you're preaching to me. Apparently it's philosophy and I tell you I will have no truck with
it. All I know is that I'd be quite well pleased to be somebody
else, on the chance of being a genius, a great man. I have to
admit it. Something tells me I'd like it. I have never heard anybody praised without the praise making me secretly furious.
I am full of envy. When I hear something discreditable about
their private lives, I listen with pleasure: it brings me closer to
them; makes me bear my mediocrity more easily. I say to
myself: to be sure, you would never have been able to write
Mohammed, but then neither would I have praised Maupeou.
So I have been and I still am vexed at being mediocre. Yes, it
is true, I am both mediocre and vexed. I have never heard the
overture to *Les Indes Galantes*, nor the singing of "*Profonds
abîmes du Ténare, Nuit, éternelle nuit*," without thinking
painfully: these are things I shall never achieve. I was obviously jealous of my uncle, and if at his death were found

some grand pieces for harpsichord, I would not hesitate to remain myself and be him too.

MYSELF: If that's all that's troubling you, it isn't worth it.

HE: It's nothing, just a passing shadow.

Then he started to sing the overture of *Les Indes Galantes* and the air *"Profonds abîmes,"* adding:

The whatever-it-is inside me speaks and says to me: "Rameau, you'd give a great deal to have composed those two pieces; if you had done two, you would surely have done two more; and after a certain number you would be played and sung everywhere. You would walk about with head erect, your mind would bear witness to your own merit. Other people would point you out and say—'That's the man who wrote those lovely gavottes.'" (And he sang the gavottes. Then with the appearance of a man deeply moved by a rush of happiness, he added with a moist eye, while rubbing his hands together:) "You would have a real mansion" (measuring its breadth with his arms), "a good bed" (he made as if to recline carelessly on it), "good wine" (tasting it with a smack of tongue against palate), "a good carriage and pair" (raising his foot to climb in), "pretty women" (whom he seized by the breast and gazed at voluptuously). "A hundred loungers would come and flatter you daily." (He thought he saw them around him—Palissot, Poinsinet, the Frérons father and son, La Porte. He heard them, preened himself, agreed with what they said, smiled at them, ignored them, despised them, sent them off, recalled them—then continued): "Thus you would be told at breakfast that you are a great man, you would read in *Three Centuries of French Literature* that you are a great man, by nightfall you would be convinced that you are a great man, and the great Rameau would fall asleep to the soft hum of praise buzzing in his ears even while asleep. He would look sated, his chest would rise and fall with bliss, he would snore like a great man."

In saying this, he collapsed softly on the bench, closed his eyes and imitated the blissful sleep he was imagining. Having enjoyed this felicity of restfulness for a few moments, he awoke, stretched, yawned, rubbed his eyes and looked about him for dull flatterers who might linger.

MYSELF: You think, then, that a happy mortal snores in his sleep?

HE: Think so! When a wretch like me is back in his garret for the night and I have stuck myself within covers, I am shriveled up, my chest is tight and my breath uneasy—it is a sort of feeble plaint that can hardly be heard; whereas a financier makes the whole house resound and astonishes the entire street. But what grieves me today is not that I sleep meanly and snore wretchedly.

MYSELF: That's sad enough.

HE: What's happened to me is far worse.

MYSELF: What is it?

HE: You've always taken an interest in me because I'm a good fellow whom you despise at bottom but who amuses you—

MYSELF: I don't deny it.

HE: —so I'm going to tell you.

Before he begins he gives a mighty sigh and puts both his hands to his head; then he recovers his composure and says: "You know that I am an ignoramus, a fool, a lunatic, a lazy, impudent, greedy good-for-nothing—what we Burgundians call 'one ne'er-do-weel' —a blackguard, in short—"

MYSELF: What a eulogy!

HE: Gospel truth from beginning to end, not a word out of place. Let's not argue about it; no one knows me better than I and I haven't said all I thought.

MYSELF: Don't let me annoy you: I accept everything you say.

HE: Well, I used to live with people who had taken a liking to me precisely because I had all these qualities to a rare degree.

MYSELF: Strange! Until now I had thought that one hid them from oneself, or that one forgave oneself while condemning them in others.

HE: Hide them from oneself! Who can? You may be sure
that when Palissot is alone and reflects upon himself he tells
himself different. In tête-à-tête with his colleague he and the
other confess that they're a pair of prize scoundrels. Despise
defects in others! My people were fairer than to do that and
my character was a pleasure to them. I was treated like a king.
They missed every moment I was away from them. I was
their dear Rameau, pretty Rameau, *their* Rameau—the jester,
the buffoon, the lazy dog, the saucy rogue, the great greedy
boob. Not one of these epithets went without a smile, a chuck
under the chin, a pat on the back, a cuff, a kick. At table it
was a choice morsel tossed to me; elsewhere a liberty I could
take with no consequence—for am I not a person of no consequence? Anyone can do what he pleases with me, about
me, in front of me. I never get on my high horse. Ah, the
little gratuities that came my way! What a consummate ass I
am to have lost all that! I have lost it all because for once in
my life I showed common sense. I promise you, never again!
MYSELF: What was it all about?
HE: Rameau, Rameau, you got caught in a piece of folly—
the folly of possessing a little good taste, a little wit, a little
sense. Rameau my friend, that will teach you to stay the way
God made you, the way your patrons wanted you. Failing
which, they took you by the shoulder and put you out the
front door. They said: "Faker, beat it and don't come back.
It wants to be sensible, does it? Beat it! Good sense, we have
more of that than we know what to do with." You went, biting your fingernails: it's your tongue you should have bitten
off first. You thought of this too late and here you are, in the
gutter, penniless, and nowhere to go. You were being fed like
a fatted calf, well housed; now you'll be lucky to have your
garret back. You had a bed; now the loose straw awaits you
between the coachman of M. de Soubise and Robbé, the grub
street hack. Instead of sweet silent sleep, as you had it, one
ear will be filled with the neighing and stamping of horses,
the other with the far worse noise of a thousand harsh verses.

Wretch, idiot, lunatic at the mercy of a million damnable fiends!

MYSELF: But can't you mend your misfortune? Did you commit so unpardonable a crime? Were I in your place, I'd go back to my patrons: you must be more indispensable than you think.

HE: Oh, I'm convinced that without me around to make them laugh, they're bored stiff.

MYSELF: That's why I'd go back. I wouldn't give them time to get used to my absence, or to take up some decent amusement. Who knows, they might come to like it!

HE: That's not what I'm afraid of: it couldn't happen.

MYSELF: Well then, some other genius may take your place.

HE: With difficulty.

MYSELF: Granted. Just the same, I'd go back as you are—my face fallen, my eyes wandering, unbuttoned and unkempt—in the really tragic attire in which you are. I'd throw myself at the feet of the goddess and without once getting up, I'd say in a weak sobbing voice: "Forgive, my lady, forgive! I am a wretch, a monster, the victim of a dreadful accident, for you know very well I am not subject to suffering from common sense. I promise it will never happen again."

What is amusing is that while I was saying this, he was acting it out in pantomime. He was prostrate at my feet, his face on the ground, and seemed to be clutching in both his hands the tip of a slipper. He was crying and sobbing out words: "I swear it, your highness, I promise, never will I do it again, never, never, never." Then suddenly jumping up, he said in a perfectly sober, serious way:

HE: You're right, of course. I can see it's the better way. She's a good woman. M. Vieillard says she is, and I know well enough that she is so. But still, to go and humiliate myself before the little bitch, to cry mercy at the feet of a second-rate actress who is invariably hissed off the stage! I, Rameau, son of M. Rameau, apothecary at Dijon, a man of substance who has never crooked the knee to anyone, I, Rameau, who can be seen pacing the Palais-Royal upright and with arms akimbo ever since M. Carmontelle depicted him bent and with his hands behind his back! I who have composed keyboard works that no one plays but which may be the only works of today posterity will like, I (in short) would go and—no, my dear sir, impossible! (And putting his right hand on his heart he added): I feel something here which swells in pride and says to me: "Rameau, you will do no such thing. A certain dignity attaches to the nature of man that nothing must destroy. It stirs in protest at the most unexpected times, yes, unexpected, for there are days when I could be as vile as required without its costing me anything. On those days, for a penny I'd kiss the arse of the little Hus."

MYSELF: But see here, she's pretty, kind, plump, and white-skinned, and that's an act of humility that even a prouder man than you could condescend to.

HE: Let's be clear about this—there's kissing and kissing, literal and metaphorical. Consult that old Bergier who kisses the arse of the Duchess de La Marck, both literally and metaphorically—a case in which the two species disgust me equally.

MYSELF: If my suggestion does not seem expedient to you, then at least be courageous enough to be poor.

HE: It's very hard to be poor while there are so many wealthy fools to sponge on. And then contempt for oneself—that's unbearable!

MYSELF: Do you ever feel self-contempt?

HE: Do I! How many times have I not exclaimed, "Rameau, ten thousand fine tables are set every day in Paris—ten to a score of covers laid there, and not one for you. Purses overflow with gold, right and left, and not a coin rolls toward you. A thousand witlings without talent or merit, a thousand creatures without charm, a thousand schemers, are well dressed and you must go naked. Are you then so stupid? Can't you lick boots like the rest? Haven't you learned to lie, swear, forswear, promise, perform, or cheat like anyone else? Can't

you walk on all fours too? Can't you help my lady's affair as
well as another and carry my lord's *billet-doux* equally well?
Could you not, like the next fellow, encourage this young
man to address that young miss and persuade missy to hear
him? Is it that you're incapable of imparting to a daughter of
our bourgeoisie the fact that she is badly dressed, and that
earrings, rouge, lace, or a dress *à la polonaise* will make her
into a new woman? Tell her that those tiny feet were never
made to tread the pavement, that there is a handsome young
man who is rich and wears gold lace on his coat, owns a coach
and four, and is served by six tall footmen, has seen her, finds
her adorable and has in consequence lost the power of eating
and sleeping and will surely die of it.—But what will father
say?—To be sure, your father; he'll be a little cross at first.—
And mamma, who says I must be an honest girl because
nothing in the world is more important?—An old wives' tale
which doesn't mean anything.—And my father confessor?—
stop seeing him, or if you insist on favoring him with an
account of your pastimes, all it will cost you is the price of a
few pounds of coffee and sugar.—But he's severe and has
already refused me absolution for having sung 'Come into my
nook.'—That's because you gave him nothing, but when he
sees you in a lace dress. . . .—Shall I have a lace dress?—Undoubtedly, many dresses, and diamond earrings.—Diamond!—
Yes.—Like those of the marquise who buys gloves in our
shop?—Just so, and a fine carriage with dapple grays, two
footmen, a Negro boy, and a courier to go before. Rouge,
patches, a train carried behind you . . .—For a ball?—At balls,
at the play, at the Opera. (Already her heart is aflutter, so
you begin to play with a slip of paper.)—What's that?—
Nothing.—But what is it?—It's a note.—To whom?—To
you, if you want to know.—Can't you tell that I do? (She
reads it)—A meeting, it can't be done.—It can, when you go
to mass.—Mamma always goes with me. But perhaps he could
come here, early. I'm up first and behind the counter . . . He
comes, he is liked; one evening the damsel disappears, and I

am paid my two thousand dollars. You see, poor fool, you
are skilled in this art and you lack food and drink! Aren't
you ashamed of yourself?" I can call to mind a crowd of
knaves not fit to hold a candle to me and who were well-to-
do; I was in buckram while they went in silks, leaning on
gold-headed sticks, their fingers bejeweled with the cameo
likeness of Plato or Aristotle. Who were they? Music masters,
originally; today a kind of nobility.

It used to give me courage, uplift my soul, sharpen my
mind. I felt equal to anything. But the mood did not last,
apparently, because up to now I haven't managed to make my
way. However that may be, those are my thoughts when I
soliloquize. You can embroider them as you like, provided
you agree that I do know what self-contempt is like, that
torment of the soul due to neglect of the talents entrusted us
by Providence. It's the cruelest form of remorse. Better a
man had never been born.

I listened to him, and while he was acting the procurer and
the girl being seduced, his soul divided between opposite motives,
I hardly knew whether to burst with laughter or with indignation.
I was in pain: a dozen times laughter kept my anger down; a dozen
times my deepening anger had to end in a shout of laughter. I was
overcome by so much cunning and baseness, by notions so exact
and at the same time so false, by so complete a perversion of
feeling, by such turpitude and such frankness, both equally un-
common. He noticed the conflict raging within me. "What's the
matter?" he asked.

MYSELF: Nothing.

HE: You seem upset.

MYSELF: And so I am.

HE: But what do you advise me to do?

MYSELF: To talk of something else. Unhappy man, to have
fallen so low!

HE: I admit it. But don't let my condition weigh on you
too much. My purpose in confiding in you was not to cause
you pain. I've saved a little money at my patrons'. As you

know I had everything I wanted, absolutely everything and they gave me an allowance for my casual expenses.

Once more he beat his forehead with his fists, bit his lip and turned up his eyes to the ceiling like one distracted, adding: "But the deal is concluded. I have some savings and time having gone by, it's that much gained."

MYSELF: You mean lost?

HE: No, no, gained. One gets richer by the minute: one day less to live is the same as one banknote more. The important thing is to keep the bowels moving freely. *O stercus pretiosum!* That is the great aim of life in all social conditions. At the last all are equally rich: Samuel Bernard, who by dint of stealing, swindling, and fraud leaves twenty-seven millions in gold is no different from Rameau who leaves nothing, Rameau who will have a shroud from public charity to be buried in. The dead man hears no bells toll. A hundred priests making themselves hoarse in the church are wasted on him—as is the long procession of burning candles. His soul is not walking in step with the leader of the service. To rot under marble or to rot in bare earth is still to rot. To have around your bier the Blue Boys or the Red Boys or nobody is all one. Just look at my wrist. It was stiff as anything; the ten fingers were like so many rods stuck in a wooden palm; the tendons were old catgut more brittle and stiff than that which moves a turner's wheel. But I so thoroughly pulled and broke and worked them—ah, you won't eh? But I say you will and they will, it works—

Saying which, he had seized with his right hand the fingers and wrist of his left and was bending them this way and that, until the tips touched the forearm and the joints cracked and I was afraid they would be dislocated.

MYSELF: Be careful, you will maim yourself.

HE: Never fear, they're used to it. For the last ten years I've shown 'em worse than that. In spite of their bloody stubbornness they've had to learn to find their places on the keys and on the strings; so that now it works, it works.

By now he has the stance of a violinist; he hums an allegro by
Locatelli, his right arm moves an imaginary bow, his left hand
fingers the strings. If he plays out of tune he stops and adjusts
the peg, tries the string with his thumb and takes up the piece
where he left off. His foot beats time and he sways and twists
from top to toe as you have often seen, at the concerts of sacred
music, a Ferrari, Chiabrau, or other virtuoso in the like convulsions. It causes me the same distress by suggesting the same torture, for is it not a painful thing to witness the torments of someone who is busy depicting pleasure? Draw a curtain between such
a man and myself if he absolutely must exhibit a victim on the
rack.

In the midst of this agitation and these cries, there occurred a
passage of slow held notes, one of those harmonious moments
when the bow moves slowly across several strings at once. His
face took on an ecstatic expression, his voice grew mild, he listened
to himself in rapture, certain as he was that the chords were
sounding in his ears and mine. Then putting his instrument under
his left arm, holding it with that hand and letting the bow arm
fall, he said: "Well, what do you think of it?"

MYSELF: Marvelous!

HE: I'm in form, I think; it sounds nearly as good as the
      others—

And immediately he sat down at the keyboard.

MYSELF: I beg you to desist, for your sake and mine.

HE: No, not while I have you here; you must hear me. I
      don't want to be praised on no evidence. You will be more
      assured in your encomiums and they may bring me a pupil.

MYSELF: I know so few people: you are going to tire yourself
      for nothing.

As I saw I was being useless in my compassion for the man
(for the violin sonata had put him in a sweat), I made up my mind
to let him go ahead. So there he is, seated at the keyboard with
bent legs, staring at the ceiling as if he read his notes there, singing, improvising, performing a piece by Alberti or Galuppi—I
don't remember which. His voice went like the wind and his

fingers flew over the keys, leaping from treble to bass, dropping the accompaniment to stress the melody. On his face successive emotions could be read as they passed: tenderness, anger, bliss, sorrow. One could distinguish piano from forte and I am sure that a cleverer man than I could have recognized the piece by the tempo and dynamics, by the grimaces and the phrases that he let forth from time to time. But what was strangest was that every so often he would stumble and grope around, as if making a mistake and being annoyed at his fingers' forgetfulness.

"Now you've seen for yourself," said he straightening up and wiping the drops of sweat from his face, "that we too can correctly use a tritone, an augmented fifth, and that the handling of dominant progressions is familiar to us. Those enharmonic modulations about which the dear uncle has made so much fuss are by no means superhuman: we manage, we manage."

MYSELF: You've taken a great deal of trouble to show me that you are very talented, but I was ready to take you at your word.

HE: Very talented? Oh, no! I know my trade more or less and that's more than enough. I ask you, does one in this country need to know the subject one teaches?

MYSELF: No more than to know what one learns!

HE: Quite right, you know, quite right. Now, master Philosopher, cross your heart and tell me true, wasn't there a time when you were not so well off as you are today?

MYSELF: I'm not so very well off now.

HE: Still you wouldn't be going to the Luxembourg gardens, in summer—you remember?

MYSELF: Let's forget it; of course I remember.

HE: In a shaggy gray coat.

MYSELF: Yes, yes.

HE: Worn through on one side, the cuffs ragged and your black woolen stockings mended up the seam with white thread.

MYSELF: All right—whatever you say.

HE: Well, what were you doing in the Avenue of Sighs?

MYSELF: Cutting a rather poor figure.

HE: Once outside you would dash about the streets?

MYSELF: No doubt.

HE: You used to give lessons in mathematics.

MYSELF: Without knowing the first thing about it—is that what you're getting at?

HE: Just so.

MYSELF: I learned by teaching others and I turned out some good pupils.

HE: Perhaps so. But music isn't like algebra or geometry. Now that you are an important person—

MYSELF: Not so important.

HE: —and have feathered your nest—

MYSELF: Very few feathers.

HE: You have tutors for your daughter.

MYSELF: Not yet. Her mother attends to her education, for one must have peace in the house.

HE: Peace in the house! That's only for the master or the servants and it's better to be the master—I've had a wife, God rest her soul. But sometimes when she piped up I'd get on my high horse and thunder at her, like God himself saying "Let there be light." And there was light. As a result, during those four years we didn't squabble more than ten times all told. How old is your child?

MYSELF: What has that to do with it?

HE: How old is your child?

MYSELF: Damn it, leave my child and her age alone and let's go back to the tutors she should have.

HE: Lord, may I never meet anyone more pigheaded than a philosopher! Would it be possible by dint of humble supplications to ascertain from His Excellency the Philosopher the approximate age of his honorable daughter?

MYSELF: Let's say about eight.

HE: Eight! Then she should have been touching the keys for four years.

MYSELF: But perhaps I am not especially concerned to include in her education a study that takes up so much time and is of so little use.

HE: What then will you teach her, if you please?

MYSELF: To think straight, if I can—a rare thing among men, and still rarer among women.

HE: Oh, let her think as wildly as she likes if she is only pretty, lively, and well-dressed.

MYSELF: Since nature has been so unkind to her as to endow her with a delicate constitution and a sensitive soul, and has exposed her to the same troubles as if she had a strong body and a heart of bronze, I'll try to teach her how to bear life with courage.

HE: Oh, let her cry, suffer, simper, and throw fits like the rest, if only she is pretty, lively, and well-dressed. And I say, no dancing?

MYSELF: No more than one needs to curtsey, know how to stand, walk, and enter a room.

HE: No singing?

MYSELF: No more than one needs to enunciate clearly.

HE: No music?

MYSELF: If I knew of a good teacher and theorist I'd let him come for two hours a day for a year or two, no more.

HE: And in place of these essentials that you omit, what?

MYSELF: I put in grammar, mythology, history, geography, a little drawing, and a great deal of ethics.

HE: How easy it would be for me to prove to you the futility of all those things in the world as we know it! Did I say futility? I should perhaps say the danger. But I limit myself for the moment to one question: won't she need a master or two?

MYSELF: Of course.

HE: There we are, then, you'll expect those masters to know grammar, mythology, history, geography, and morals and to give lessons in them. Twaddle, my dear philosopher, twaddle: if they knew those subjects well enough to teach them, they wouldn't teach them.

MYSELF: Why not?

HE: Because they would have spent their whole life learning them. A man must have gone deep into art or science to
master the elements. Classic works are written only by white-
haired practitioners. The darkness of the beginnings lights up
only toward the middle or the end. Ask your friend D'Alembert, the dean of mathematicians, whether he would be too
good to teach its rudiments. Not before thirty or forty years
of application did my uncle begin to see the glimmer of his
musical theories.

MYSELF: Oh you master crackpot! (I broke out) How does it
come about that in your silly head some very sound ideas are
all muddled up with extravagant ones?

HE: Who the devil can tell? Chance sows them there and
there they grow; which would tend to show that until one
knows everything one knows nothing worth knowing, ignorant of the origin of this, the purpose of that and the place of
either. What should come first? Can one teach without
method? And where does method come from? I tell you,
master Philosopher, I have an idea physics will always be a
puny science, a drop of water picked up from the great
ocean on the point of a pin, a grain of dust from the Alps.
Take the causes of phenomena—what about them? Really, it
would be as well to know nothing as to know so little and so
poorly. That's the conclusion I had reached when I took up
music teaching. What are you thinking about?

MYSELF: I'm thinking that everything you've just said is more
specious than solid. Let's drop it. You've been teaching, you
say, composition and thoroughbass?

HE: Yes.

MYSELF: And you were entirely ignorant of both?

HE: Not really. That's why others were worse than I,
namely those who thought they knew something. I at least
never spoiled the minds or the hands of children. When they
went from me to a good master, having learnt nothing they
had nothing to unlearn, which was time and money saved.

MYSELF: What did you do actually?

HE: What they all do. I'd arrive and hurl myself into a
chair. "Whew! What wretched weather! Dreadful walking!"
I would gossip about this and that: "Mlle. Lemierre was to
play the Vestal virgin in the new opera, but she's having her
second child. Her understudy hasn't been announced. Mlle.
Arnould has just broken with her little Count; they say she's
dickering with Bertin. But the little Count found M. de
Montamy's china. At the last concert of the Friends of Music
there was an Italian girl who sang like an angel. As for that
Préville fellow, he's a rare body: you must see him in *Mercure
galant*; the scene of the riddle is killing. But la Dumesnil, poor
thing, doesn't know what she's saying or doing any of the
time. Come, now, Miss, your book."

While Miss takes her time finding the book, calls the
chambermaid and scolds whoever mislaid it, I continue:
"Clairon is really beyond making out. I hear there's an odd
marriage in the wind—Miss, er, What's-her-name, that little
thing so-and-so was keeping; he had two or three children by
her, though before him many others had . . . —No, Rameau,
you're talking rot, it can't be.—I am not and it can: they say
she *is* married. They also say that Voltaire is dead, which
makes me glad.—Why glad?—Because that means he's about
to let off a wonderful squib: he usually 'dies' a couple of
weeks beforehand. . . ."

Do you want to hear more? I would repeat a few risqué
remarks I'd heard elsewhere; we're all gossips, you know. I
acted the fool. They'd listen, laugh, exclaim "How charming!" Meanwhile the young lady's book had been found
under a chair where the lapdog or the cat had been at it. She
would sit at the keyboard and begin the noise by herself.
Then I would go nearer after having nodded my approval to
the mother.

Mother: "Not bad. It would be better with a little effort, but
effort is the last thing one thinks of. One prefers to babble,
play with ribbons, gad about, what not. You've hardly turned

your back before the book is closed—and you never scold her." Since I had to do something, I would take her hand and rearrange the fingers on the keys. I would get huffy and shout: "G, G, G, Miss, it's G!"

Mother: "Missy, have you no ear? Even I, who know nothing and can't see the book, feel instinctively that it's G. You make it extremely difficult for Mr. Rameau. I don't see how he stands it. You don't remember a thing he says and make no progress. . . ."

I would then mitigate the blows and nodding would say: "Forgive me, madam, forgive me. It *could* go better if the young lady would study a little, but she is not bad."

Mother: "If I were you, I'd keep her on the same piece for a year."—"Oh, as for that, she will stick to this until all the difficulties are overcome; and it won't take as long as you may think."—"Mr. Rameau, you're flattering her. You are much too kind, and that's the only part of the lesson she will remember and repeat to me if she sees need." The hour would go by, the pupil would present me with my fee, as graceful of arm and manner as the dancing master had managed to make her. I put it in my pocket while the mother said: "Very good, Missy; if Favillier were here he'd compliment you. . . ."
I chatted a minute more for politeness' sake and then disappeared: that's what used to be called a lesson in thorough-bass.

MYSELF: And today is it different?

HE: By God, I should say it is! I arrive, my mien is grave. I hurriedly throw off my muff. I open the clavier. I try a run. I am in a perpetual hurry. If I am kept waiting one instant, I yell as if I were being robbed. An hour hence I must be elsewhere; two hours hence at the duchess's. For dinner I'm expected at the house of a marquise—a handsome one. Dinner over there's a concert at Baron De Bagge's in the rue Neuve des Petits-Champs.

MYSELF: Whereas in fact you're not expected anywhere?

HE: Right.

MYSELF: Why resort to these vile little tricks?

HE: Why vile, if I may ask? They are part of my profession. There's nothing degrading in acting like everybody else. Did I invent these tricks? No. But I should be a clumsy oaf not to make use of them. I know well enough that if you apply to my case certain general principles of morals which they all talk about and never put into practice, it will turn out that white is black and black is white. But master Philosopher, just as there is a general grammar and exceptions in each language that you learned people call—what is it you call them?

MYSELF: Idioms?

HE: That's what I mean. Well, each profession makes exceptions to general ethics and those I'd like to call *idioms*.

MYSELF: I follow you. Fontenelle speaks and writes well even though his style is full of French idioms.

HE: Likewise the sovereign, the minister, the financier, the judge, the soldier, the writer, the lawyer, the public prosecutor, the merchant, the banker, the workman, the singing teacher, the dancing master are very respectable people even though their conduct deviates in several ways from general good behavior and is full of moral idioms. The older the profession the more the idioms; the worse the times become, the more the idioms multiply. A man is worth what his trade is worth; in the end they're equal; hence people make the trade go for as much as they can.

MYSELF: What appears clearest in all this tangle is that there are no honest trades and no honest men in them.

HE: Have it your own way. But as a compensation there are but few gougers outside their own shops. The world would get on pretty well if it weren't for a number of people who are called industrious, reliable, conscientious followers of duty, strict—or what amounts to the same thing: ever in their shops practicing their trades from morn till night and doing nothing else. Result is: they're the only ones to get rich and full of reputation.

MYSELF: By sheer strength of idiom!

HE: Exactly. I see you understand. Now an idiom that is
     common to all trades—as there are some common to all
     nations and no less common than folly—is to try to get as
     many customers as possible. The common folly is to think
     that the largest tradesman is the best. Those are two excep-
     tions to general ethics one can do nothing about. Call it
     credit or "good will," it is nothing in itself but it's worth a
     great deal in public opinion. Don't they say: "A good name
     is worth a money belt?" Yet plenty of people have a good
     name who have no money belt, and I notice that nowadays
     the money insures the name. The great thing is to have both
     and that is precisely what I am after when I employ what
     you call my vile tricks. I give lessons and give them the right
     way. The system is simple: I make people believe that I have
     more pupils than there are hours in the day—that's my idiom.

MYSELF: And you really give good lessons?

HE: Yes, or not bad, passable. The ground bass theory of
     the dear uncle has simplified everything. Formerly I swindled
     my pupil, undoubtedly. Nowadays I earn my fee at least as
     much as my colleagues.

MYSELF: Did you formerly swindle without qualms?

HE: Without qualms. They say, when one thief robs an-
     other the Devil laughs. My pupils' parents were fat with ill-
     gotten gains. They were courtiers, tax collectors, wholesalers,
     bankers, stockbrokers. I merely helped them—I and some
     others in their employ—to make restitution. In Nature all
     species live off one another; in society all classes do the same.
     We polish off one another without benefit of the law. La
     Deschamps some time since, and now la Guimard, avenges
     the King upon his tax collector; after which the dressmaker,
     the jeweler, the upholsterer, the lacemaker, the swindler, the
     lady's maid, the cook, and the saddler avenge the tax collector
     upon la Deschamps. Amid all this no one but the idiot or the
     loafer is taken advantage of without levying tribute on any-
     body else—and it serves him right. You can infer from this

that the exceptions to general ethics, or moral idioms, about which people make so much fuss under the name of mutual depredations don't amount to anything, really. When all is said and done the only thing that matters is to see straight.

MYSELF: I admire you for that.

HE: And think of poverty! The voice of conscience and honor is pretty feeble when the guts cry out. Isn't it enough that if I ever get rich I shall be bound to make restitution? I am prepared to do this in every conceivable way—through gorging, through gambling, through guzzling, and through wenching.

MYSELF: But I'm afraid you will never get rich.

HE: For my part I have a different hunch.

MYSELF: But suppose it did not work out, what then?

HE: I would act like all beggars on horseback. I'd be the most insolent ruffian ever seen. I'd remember every last thing they made me go through and pay them back with slings and arrows. I love bossing people and I would boss them. I love being praised and they will praise me. I'll have the whole troop of Villemorien's bootlickers on salary, and I'll say to them what's been said to me: "Come on, punks, entertain me." And they will. "I want decent people pulled to pieces." And they will be—if any can be found. Then too, we'll have women and when drunk we'll thee-and-thou one another. We will drink and make up stories and develop all sorts of whims and vices. It will be delightful. We'll prove that Voltaire has no genius; that Buffon is always up on stilts like the turgid declaimer he is; that Montesquieu was only a wit. We'll tell D'Alembert to stick to his ciphering and we'll kick behind and before all the little stoics like you who despise us from sour grapes, whose modesty is the prop of pride, and whose good conduct springs from lack of means. Ah, what music you'll hear from us!

MYSELF: Knowing what worthy use you would make of wealth, I see how deplorable it is that you are poor. You would cer-

tainly be doing honor to human nature, good to your compatriots and credit to yourself.

HE: I almost think you're making fun of me, master
Philosopher. But you don't even suspect whose leg it is you're
pulling; you don't seem to know that at this very moment I
represent the most important part of Town and Court. The
well-to-do of every description have either said or not said
to themselves the words I've just confided to you, and the
fact remains that the life I would lead in their position is
precisely theirs. That's where you fellows are behind the
times. You think everybody aims at the same happiness.
What an idea! Your conception presupposes a sentimental
turn of mind which is not ours, an unusual spirit, a special
taste. You call your quirks virtue, or philosophy. But virtue
and philosophy are not made for everybody. Those who can,
have it; those who can, keep it. Just imagine the universe
philosophical and wise, and tell me if it would not be devilishly dull. Listen! Hurrah for wisdom and philosophy—the
wisdom of Solomon: to drink good wines, gorge on choice
food, tumble pretty women, sleep in downy beds—outside of
that, all is vanity.

MYSELF: What! And fighting for your country?

HE: Vanity! There are no countries left. All I see from
pole to pole is tyrants and slaves.

MYSELF: What of helping your friends?

HE: Vanity! No one has any friends. And even if one had,
should one risk making them ungrateful? Look well and you
will see that's all you get for being helpful. Gratitude is a
burden and burdens are to be shuffled off.

MYSELF: To hold a position in society and discharge its duties?

HE: Vanity! What difference whether you hold a position
or not, provided you have means, since you only seek a
position in order to get wealth. Discharge one's duties—what
does that bring you?—jealousy, worries, persecution. Is that
the way to get on? On the contrary: go to court, know

people, flatter their tastes and fall in with their whims, serve
their vices and second their misdeeds—there's the secret.

MYSELF: Watch over the education of one's children?

HE: Vanity! That's a tutor's business.

MYSELF: But if a tutor imbued with your principles neglects his
duty, who will pay the penalty?

HE: Not I anyhow. Possibly, some day, my daughter's
husband or my son's wife.

MYSELF: But suppose that either or both plunge into vice and
debauchery?

HE: Then that is part of their social position.

MYSELF: If they disgrace themselves?

HE: It's impossible to disgrace yourself if you are rich.

MYSELF: Ruin themselves, then?

HE: Too bad for them.

MYSELF: It seems to me that if you overlook the conduct of
your wife, your children and your servants, you might easily
overlook your own affairs.

HE: Not so, if you will permit me: it is sometimes difficult
to procure money, hence one uses a prudent foresight.

MYSELF: You will pay little attention to your wife?

HE: None, an it please you. The best behavior toward one's
dearer half, I think, is to do what suits oneself and her. Do
you suppose company would be tolerable if everyone stuck
to his own concerns?

MYSELF: Why not? I'm never so happy in the evening as when
I'm pleased with my forenoon.

HE: Me too.

MYSELF: What makes society people so choosy about their
entertainment is that they are utterly idle.

HE: Don't you believe it: they are always on the go.

MYSELF: They never tire themselves and so can never feel
refreshed.

HE: Don't you believe it: they are constantly weary.

MYSELF: Pleasure is always their business, never a desire.

HE: All the better: desires are ever nagging.

MYSELF: They wear everything thin. Their soul gets dull, boredom masters them. Whoever should take their life in the midst of their plenty would be doing them a good turn. For they know of pleasure only that portion which soonest loses its zest. I am far from despising sensual pleasures. I have a palate too and it is tickled by a delicate wine or dish; I have eyes and a heart and I like to look at a pretty woman, like to feel the curve of her breast under my hand, press her lips to mine, drink bliss from her eyes and die of ecstasy in her arms. Sometimes a gay party with my friends, even if it becomes a little rowdy, is not displeasing to me. But I must confess that I find it infinitely sweeter to succor the unfortunate, to disentangle a bad business, to give helpful advice, to read some pleasant book, to take a walk with a man or woman who is dear to me, to spend a few instructive hours with my children, to write a page of good prose, to carry out my duties, or to tell her whom I love something tender and true which brings her arms about my neck.

I know of certain deeds which I would give all I possess to have done. Voltaire's *Mohammed* is a sublime work, but I would rather have rehabilitated the Calas family. Someone I know left home for Carthagena; he was a younger son in a country where primogeniture is the law. While abroad he learns that his elder brother, a spoiled child, has ruined his father and mother, driven them out of the castle, and left them to languish in some provincial town. What does the younger son do, who after the harsh treatment meted out by his parents had gone to seek his fortune far away? He sends them help. He winds up his affairs, comes back rich, restores his parents to their home, marries off his sisters. Ah, my dear Rameau, that man looked upon this period as the happiest in his life. He had tears in his eyes as he spoke of it and as I tell you this, I feel my heart dilate with gladness and my tongue falter with emotion.

HE: Queer people, you are!

MYSELF: And you are people to be pitied, unless you can see that one can rise above one's fate and make oneself independent of misfortune by actions such as I have described.

HE: That's a kind of happiness I would find it hard to become familiar with, it is so rarely found. Then according to you people should be decent?

MYSELF: To be happy?—Yes.

HE: Yet I see a quantity of decent people unhappy and a quantity of people happy without being decent.

MYSELF: So it seems to you.

HE: Wasn't it because I acted sensibly and frankly for one instant that tonight I don't know where to find a meal?

MYSELF: Not at all: it's because you have not always been sensible and frank; because you did not learn soon enough that the first step is to secure the means of life apart from servitude.

HE: Apart or not, my way is surely the easiest.

MYSELF: And the least assured and the least decent.

HE: But the most consistent with my nature which is idle, stupid, and crooked.

MYSELF: Granted.

HE: Since I can secure my well-being with the aid of vices natural to me, that I have acquired without labor and that I retain without effort, vices congenial to the habits of my countrymen, agreeable to the tastes of my protectors, and closer to their little needs than any virtues could be—for virtues would annoy them all day long like so many accusations—in view of all this, it would be strange indeed for me to bedevil myself like a damned soul and turn myself into what I am not; to acquire a character alien to mine, with laudable traits, no doubt (I won't argue), but difficult to maintain and make use of. It would do me no good, perhaps worse than no good, by implying a satire of the rich people in whose company paupers like me must find their livelihood.

Virtue is praised, but hated. People run away from it, for it is ice-cold and in this world you must keep your feet warm.

Besides, I would grow bad-humored, infallibly. For note how often devout people are harsh, touchy, unsociable. The reason is that they have compelled themselves to do an unnatural thing. They're in pain, and people in pain make others suffer. That's not the life for me, nor for my patrons. I must be gay, easy, jolly, droll, entertaining. Virtue earns respect and respect is inconvenient; virtue is bound to be admired, and admiration is no fun. I deal with people who are bored and I have to make them laugh. Now what is laughable is absurdity and folly. I must consequently be absurd and a fool. Even had nature not made me such, the quickest way would be to put on the appearance. Fortunately, I don't need to be a hypocrite; there are enough of them around, not counting those who deceive themselves. The Chevalier Morlière who wears his hat on one side, sniffs the air and looks at everybody over his shoulder; who drags the longest sword next to his thigh and has an insult ready for anyone unarmed; in short, who defies every man on principle, what is he really up to? He does what he can to persuade himself that he is a man of spirit, though he's a coward. Tweak his nose and he will take it mildly. If you want to make him pipe down, just raise your voice, lift your cane, or let your foot contact his buttocks. Full of surprise at finding himself a coward, he will ask you who told you of it, how you knew. Himself did not suspect it the moment before. His long and habitual aping of bravery has fooled him; so much mimicry has ended by seeming real.

And what of that woman who mortifies her flesh, who visits prisons, who attends all meetings organized for charity, who walks with lowered lids and would not dare look a man in the eye; who is continually on guard against the temptations of the senses—does any of this keep her heart from burning, her breast from sighing, her flaming desires from obsessing her? Her imagination at night rehearses the scenes of the *Portier des Chartrains* and the postures of Aretino. What then happens to her? What does her maid think when she has to get up in her shift and fly to the aid of her mistress who is suffocating? Justine, you can go back to bed, it isn't you your mistress is calling for in her fever.

And if friend Rameau himself should ever show indifference to wealth, women, good cheer, and idleness, if he should begin to stoicize, what would he be? A hypocrite. Rameau must stay what he is—a scoundrel in luck among well-heeled scoundrels; not a holier-than-thou character nor even a virtuous man eating his dry crust alone or near some other beggar. To cut it short, I want none of your kind of happiness, none of the satisfactions of a few visionaries like yourself.

MYSELF: I can see, my dear fellow, that you don't know what they are like and that you are apparently not made to find out.

HE: Thank God for that! It would only make me starve to death, die of boredom, and croak with remorse.

MYSELF: That being so, the one piece of advice I can give you is to hurry back into the place whence you so carelessly got kicked out.

HE: You want me to do that which you do not object to when it's literal, but which is a little repugnant to me when metaphorical?

MYSELF: How odd you are!

HE: Not in the least. I'm perfectly ready to be abject, but not under duress. I'm willing to lower my dignity—you're laughing!

MYSELF: Certainly. Your dignity makes me laugh.

HE: To each man his own kind. I'm willing to forget mine, but at my pleasure, not on somebody else's order. Shall it be said that at the word "Crawl!" I am to crawl? That's the worm's natural gait and it is mine too, when we are left alone, but we turn and rear, both of us, when stepped on. I was stepped on and mean to rear off. And then you have no idea of the shambles of a house I am in. Imagine a melancholy crotchety individual, a prey to vapors, wrapped up in two or three house garments, who dislikes himself and everything else besides; who can hardly be made to smile by one's utmost contortions of body and mind, who looks with a lack-luster eye on the lively twistings of my face and wit and the even livelier ones of my intellect. For between ourselves, compared to me the famous ugly Benedictine so renowned at court for his grimacing is, all boasting aside, nothing but a wooden Indian. I badger myself in vain to reach the sublimest lunacy —it's no use. Will he laugh or won't he? That's what I have to keep asking myself in the midst of my exertions. You can guess what harm so much uncertainty does to talent. My hypochondriac with his head swallowed up in a nightcap down to his eyes looks like an immovable idol with a string tied to its chin and running down beneath his chair. You wait for the string to be pulled but it is never pulled; or if the jaw drops it is only to let out some chilling word, from which you learn that you have not been understood and that your apish tricks have been wasted. That word is the answer to a question you put four days ago. The word spoken, the mastoid muscle contracts and the jaw clamps.

He then started to mimic his patron. He leaned back in a chair, his head stiff and his hat over his eyes, which were half shut. His arms hung as he moved his jaw like an automaton and said: "Yes, you are right, Miss. Be subtle there. For," he went on, "the Thing lays down the law, without appeal, morning, noon, and night—at dinner, at a café, at the gaming table, in the theatre, over supper, in bed, and God forgive me, in his mistress's arms as well. I am not by way of hearing those last sentences being handed down, but I'm fed up with the others. Gloomy, sullen, and final as fate—such is our patron.

"Opposite him is a prude who puts on important airs and to whom one manages to say that she's pretty, for she still is, despite a few spots on her face and a tendency to fat. I like curves when proportionable, but too much is too much, and matter needs motion! *Item.* She is meaner, prouder and stupider than a goose. *Item.* She strives for wit. *Item.* You have to persuade her that you think she has more of it than anybody else. *Item.* She knows

nothing and lays down the law too. *Item.* You have to applaud
her with your hands and your feet, jump for joy, and faint with
admiration: 'How beautifully put, deeply felt, shrewdly judged.
Aren't women amazing—by sheer intuition and without study,
by the light of nature—it's a miracle. Don't tell me that experience,
education and reflective thought are of any help!' And similar
absurdities amid buckets of joyful tears; ten times a day you bow
low, the forward knee bent, the other leg straight back, one arm
stretched out to the goddess. You read her wishes in her eyes, you
hang upon her lips, receive her command and—off like a flash!
Who would want to subject himself to play such a part unless it be
a poor wretch who finds in it twice or thrice a week the means
to quell the tumult of his intestines? What can one think of the
others, such as Palissot, Fréron, Poinsinet, Baculard, who are not
destitute and whose abjectness cannot be excused by the audible
pangs of a complaining stomach?"

MYSELF: I should never have thought you so fastidious.

HE: I am not. In the beginning I just watched the others
         and acted like them, better, perhaps, because I am more
         frankly impudent, a better actor, hungrier and stronger of
         lung. I must be descended direct from the famous Stentor. . . .

To give me an exact idea of his pulmonary strength, he began
to cough with violence enough to break the plate-glass windows
of the café and to arrest the chess players in mid-air.

MYSELF: But of what use is this power?

HE: Can't you guess?

MYSELF: No, I'm stupid.

HE: Suppose an argument in progress and victory uncer-
         tain. I rise and let loose my thunder, I say: "The truth is
         precisely as Mademoiselle states it. What judgment! I defy
         any of our great minds to come anywhere near it. The very
         form is impeccable!" Of course, you mustn't always back her
         up in the same way. It would be monotonous and wouldn't
         sound genuine. It would lack savor. Your only chance is to
         keep your wits about you, to be fertile. You must know how
         to prepare and establish your major keys, seize the right

instant. When, for example, opinions are divided and the debate has reached the highest pitch, no one listening and all talking at once, you should be somewhat to one side, in the corner of the room farthest from the battlefield, and your explosion should be timed after a long pause so as to crash suddenly like a bombshell among the combatants. No one has mastered this art like me. Yet my really surprising skill is in the opposite vein. I have mild notes accompanied by smiles, an infinite variety of faces expressing agreement. In these, nose, mouth, brows, and eyes participate. I have a flexibility of spine, a way of twisting it, of shrugging or sagging, of stretching out my fingers, of nodding and shutting my eyes, of being thunderstruck as if I heard a divine angel's voice come down from heaven—this it is to flatter. I don't know whether you grasp the whole force of this last attitude of mine. I did not invent it, but no one has surpassed me in performance. Just look!

MYSELF: You are right. It is unique.

HE: Can you imagine any female brain of any degree of vanity capable of resisting this?

MYSELF: No, I must admit that you have carried the art of playing the fool and abasing yourself as far as it can go.

HE: They can try what they like, any of them, they will never overtake me, not the best of them. Palissot, for example, will hardly be anything more than a good apprentice. Still, even if the part is fun to play at first, by making one laugh inwardly at the stupidity of those one fools, after a while the game loses its savor. After a number of innovations one repeats oneself, for art and wit have their limits. Only God and some few rare geniuses can keep forging ahead into novelty. Bouret may be one of those. Things are reported of him that strike me, yes me, as sublime. The trick of the lapdog, the treatise on happiness, the torches on the road to Versailles are inventions that confound and humble me. I could give up the art from self-disgust just to think of them.

MYSELF: What do you mean by the lapdog trick?

HE: Where have you been? Do you mean to tell me you
      don't know how that amazing man went about it to alienate
      from himself the affections of a little dog and attach them to
      the Keeper of the Seals who had taken a fancy to the animal?

MYSELF: Truly, I never heard of it.

HE: Well then. It is one of the greatest conceptions ever
      formed. All Europe marveled at it; every courtier envied it.
      Now you are not without guile—how would you have gone
      about it? Remember that Bouret's dog loved him. Bear in
      mind that the dog was frightened by the strange uniform of
      the Keeper of the Seals. And don't forget the problem had to
      be solved in a week. You must note all the conditions if you
      are to appreciate the elegance of the solution. Well?

MYSELF: I freely admit that in that kind of business I am
      stumped by the simplest things.

HE: Then listen (said he, tapping me on the shoulder, for
      he takes familiarities) listen and admire. He has a mask made
      to look like the Keeper of the Seals. He borrows from the
      Keeper's valet the voluminous gown, puts it and the mask on.
      He calls his dog and pats him and gives him a sweet.

          All of a sudden, the scene changes. It's no longer the
      Keeper, it's Bouret who calls his dog and whips him. Less
      than three days of this steady course make the dog flee Bouret
      the tax collector and run to Bouret the Keeper of the Seals.
      But I'm too good to you. You are a layman who doesn't
      deserve to be instructed in the miracles that go on in your
      vicinity.

MYSELF: None the less, tell me about the treatise on happiness
      and the torches on the road to Versailles.*

* During a visit of the King's to Bouret's country house, he found a
volume entitled *True Happiness*. On every page was written: "The King
paid a visit to Bouret." Again, when the King went once by night to
Versailles, he found every twenty feet a servant of Bouret's holding a
torch. Bouret made and spent 42 million francs and died owing five more
millions. *Tr.*

HE: No, no. You can ask the paving stones and they'll tell
you, and take advantage rather of the fact that I know things
nobody else knows.

MYSELF: You are right.

HE: Borrowed the gown *and wig* of the Keeper of the
Seals. I'd forgotten the wig! The idea of having a mask made
—that mask goes to my head. No wonder the man is a mil-
lionaire and enjoys the greatest respect. There are holders of
the military Cross of St. Louis who go without bread—hence
the folly of seeking the cross at the risk of life and limb. Why
not instead go after a position absolutely free of danger and
invariably rewarded. I call that aiming at true greatness. But
such paragons are discouraging; they make one despise oneself and fall into the dumps. The mask! The mask! I'd
give a finger of my right hand to have thought of the
mask.

MYSELF: But drawn as you are toward all higher things and
possessing such a ready genius, haven't you made inventions
of your own?

HE: If you please, I have. For example, that spinal expression of admiration I mentioned to you. I consider it mine,
though the jealous might dispute it. I concede that it had
been used before me, but no one had discovered how convenient it is for laughing the while at the coxcomb one is
admiring. I have, in addition, more than a hundred ways to
begin seducing a young girl, next to her mother, without
the latter's noticing it, and indeed, making her an unwitting
accomplice. I'd hardly started in my career before I gave
up the conventional ways of delivering a *billet-doux*. I have
ten ways of getting it snatched from me, and some I daresay
are new. Above all, I know the way to spur a timid youth;
I have insured the success of some who had neither brains
nor presence. Were this recorded no one could deny me a
touch of genius.

MYSELF: An unusual kind of fame.

HE: No doubt about it.

MYSELF: If I were you, I would note down some of these things. It would be a pity if they were forgotten.

HE: I agree with you. But you'd be surprised how little I think of methods and rules. The man who needs a textbook can't go far. Geniuses seldom read, and they experiment a great deal; they are their own masters. Consider Caesar, Turenne, Vauban, the Marquise de Tencin, her brother the Cardinal, and his secretary, Abbé Trublet. And then Bouret? Who ever gave Bouret lessons? Nobody. Nature creates the superior man. Do you suppose the theory of the lapdog and the mask was written down somewhere?

MYSELF: Still, when you have leisure, when the anxiety of your empty stomach or the toiling of your well-filled paunch drives away sleep—

HE: I'll think about it. Better write of great feats than perform small ones. For it uplifts the soul, fires and expands the imagination, instead of contracting it with mock-surprise (when speaking to the little Hus woman) at the applause given by a stupidly obstinate public to the simpering Dangeville and her dull acting. She walks on nearly bent over double, looks affectedly up into the eyes of her interlocutor and yet plays under his chin, taking all these goings-on for subtlety and her scampering about for gracefulness. And that bombastic Clairon!—scrawnier, stiffer, stuffier, stodgier than words can say! The witless audience claps till their hands are raw and never seems to notice that *we* are a bundle of charms (a growing bundle, to be sure, but never mind), that our skin is the finest, our eyes the handsomest, our snout the cutest—no great heart, it is true, and no sylph-like walk, but far from clumsy, in spite of what people say. And when it comes to emotional power, we can outplay every last one of them.

MYSELF: How do you mean all this—truthfully or ironically?

HE: The trouble is that this emotional power is all within. Not a glimmer of it transpires. But I give you my word she's full of it. Or if it isn't the real thing, it's very close to it.

You should see, when we're in the mood, how we deal with footmen, how the maids get slapped, how we administer kicks to the Petty Outlay Department,* whenever it fails in the respect due our person. She is a cute little devil, I tell you, full of sentiment and poise. Now you know what to make of this, don't you?

MYSELF: I confess I don't know whether you are speaking in good faith or cattily. I am a plain man and I wish you would be good enough to talk plainly and leave your "art" outside.

HE: Why, that's what we hand out to the little Hus about la Dangeville and la Clairon, except that I sprinkled in a few words here and there to tip you off. I'm willing to have you think me a scoundrel but not a fool; and only a fool or a man sunk in love could seriously retail so much nonsense.

MYSELF: How then does one muster up courage to utter it?

HE: It doesn't come easy all at once, but gradually. *Ingenii largitor venter.*

MYSELF: It must be a cruel hunger that drives you on.

HE: No doubt. Yet you may be sure that though they sound like enormities to you, they are more familiar to those who hear them than to us who offer them.

MYSELF: Is there anybody in that house with the strength of mind to agree with you?

HE: What do you mean by anybody? Mine's the opinion and the common speech of society at large.

MYSELF: Those in your circle who are not great knaves must be great fools.

HE: Fools? In that place? I promise you there is only one, and that's the man who feeds us in exchange for our deceiving him.

MYSELF: But how is it possible to be so grossly deceived? Because when all is said and done, the superior merit of Dangeville and Clairon is unquestionable.

HE: One gulps down the flattering lie and sips the bitter truth. And then we *seem* so convinced, so sincere!

*I.e. Mlle. Hus's protector Bertin, who had charge of that department.

MYSELF: Yet you must have sinned at least once against the rules of art, you must have let fall one of those wounding, bitter, truths—for I believe that in spite of the vile, abject, scoundrelly part you play, you have at bottom some delicacy of soul.

HE: I? Not a bit of it. The devil take me if I know what I am like at bottom. As a general rule, my mind is as whole as a sphere and my character fresh as a daisy. I'm never false if my interest is to speak true and never true if I see the slightest use of being false. I say whatever comes into my head—if sensible, well and good; if silly, no one minds. I take full advantage of free speech. I have never in my life thought before speaking, nor while speaking, nor after speaking. The upshot is, I offend nobody.

MYSELF: Still it did happen with those fine people you were living with, though they were so good to you.

HE: What do you expect? Accidents will happen. It was one of those bad days. Life knows no perpetual bliss. I was too happy, it could not last. Our house, as you know, receives the largest and most select society. It is a school of civilization, a return to the culture of antiquity. All the fallen poets, we pick up: we had Palissot after his *Zarès* failed, Bret after *Le Faux Généreux*, also the despised musicians, unread authors, hissed actors—in short a mob of shamefuls, of poor dull parasites at whose head I have the honor to be, myself the brave leader of a timorous band. It's I who exhort them to eat the first time they come, it's I who order their glasses refilled—they're all so diffident. A few ragged young men who don't know where to go, though presentable enough; some others, real scoundrels who cozen the master for the sake of gleaning after him in the fields of the mistress. We seem to be jolly, but actually we are all grumpy and fiercely hungry. Wolves are not more voracious nor tigers more cruel. We devour one another like wolves when the snow has long been on the ground. Like tigers we tear apart whatever succeeds. Sometimes the crowds of Bertin, Mésenge, and Villemorien join forces. It's then you should hear the noise of the menagerie! You have never seen such a collection of sullen, soured, malignant, and enraged animals. You hear nothing but the names of Buffon, Duclos, Montesquieu, Rousseau, Voltaire, D'Alembert, and Diderot. God alone knows by what adjectives they are characterized. No one shall be deemed bright if he is not as stupid as ourselves. Among that crowd was born the idea of the comedy against the *philosophes*: I supplied the plan, patterned after *The Woman Doctor, or Theology in Skirts*. And you weren't spared in it any more than the rest.

MYSELF: That's fine. Maybe it's greater honor than I deserve. I should be humiliated to find that people who malign so many good and able men were praising me.

HE: There are a lot of us and each must do his bit. When we have sacrificed the bigger beasts, we offer up the rest.

MYSELF: Insulting knowledge and virtue for a living—that is dearly earned bread!

HE: I've already told you, we're of no consequence. We insult everybody and injure nobody. Sometimes we see the heavy-going Abbé D'Olivet, the fat Abbé LeBlanc, the hypocritical Batteux—the fat one is only mean before dinner. After coffee he slumps into an armchair, his feet on the fender, and he goes to sleep like an old parrot on his perch. If the rumpus gets too loud, he yawns, stretches, rubs his eyes and asks: "What is going on, what is it? What is it?"—"We're discussing whether Piron is wittier than Voltaire."—"Let's be clear about this: it's wit you mean, not taste? Because taste, your Piron has no idea what it is."—"No idea?"—"None." Then we're off into a discussion of taste, and the boss makes a sign with his hand that he wants to be heard, because taste is what he prides himself on having. "Taste," says he, "Taste is a thing which—." I've forgotten what he said it was, and so has he.

At other times we have friend Robbé, who regales us with his shady stories, with his accounts of religious revivalists

in convulsions—actually seen by him—and with a few cantos
of a poem by him on a subject he knows thoroughly. I hate
his verse but I love to see him recite. He looks like a fanatic
and everybody around cries out: "There's a poet for you! ..."
Between ourselves, his poetry is a cacophonous noise, the
very speech of the builders of Babel. Or again, we have a visit
from a certain booby who seems base and stupid but who is as
sharp as a demon and cleverer than an old monkey. His is one
of those faces seemingly made to call forth jokes and sarcasm
but designed by God to confound people who judge by
appearance. Their mirror should have told them that it is as
easy to be intelligent and look foolish as it is to be a fool
behind a bright exterior. It's such a common piece of pol-
troonery to offer up a good man to the ridicule of others that
people never fail to pick on this fellow. He is a trap we set
for newcomers and they invariably fall into it.

(Being surprised at the justness of my madman's remarks on
men and manners, I told him so.)

HE: That, said he, is because bad company is as instructive
         as debauchery: one is indemnified for the loss of innocence
         by the loss of prejudice. In a society of bad men, they stand
         undisguised and one learns to see them as they are. And
         then I've done some reading.

MYSELF: What have you read?

HE: I keep re-reading Theophrastus, La Bruyère and
         Molière.

MYSELF: Excellent books.

HE: They're even better than people think, but who knows
         how to read them?

MYSELF: Everybody according to his capacity.

HE: I should say almost no one. Can you tell me what
         they look for in them?

MYSELF: Instruction mixed with entertainment.

HE: But what kind of instruction: that's the point!

MYSELF: The knowledge of one's duty, the love of virtue and
         the hatred of vice.

HE: Now what I find there is a compendium of what to do and what not to do. When I read *The Miser*, I say to myself: "Be as miserly as you like, but don't talk like the miser." When I read *Tartuffe*, I say: "Be a hypocrite if you choose, but don't talk like one. Keep any useful vices, but don't acquire the tone and air which would make you ridiculous. Now to avoid these one must know what they are, and the authors mentioned have given us excellent portraits. I am myself and I remain such, but I act and speak just as I ought to. Far from despising the moralists, I find profit in them, particularly those who depict morals in action. Vice offends men only from time to time; but the symptoms of vice offend day and night. It is surely better to be arrogant than to look it. The arrogant character insults you only now and then; the arrogant look insults you continually. For the rest, don't suppose that I am the only reader of my kind. My sole merit is to have accomplished systematically, through good judgment and right reason, what most other people do by instinct. Hence their reading does not make them better than I, and they remain ridiculous despite their efforts; whereas I am such only when I choose, and so surpass them by far. The same skill which saves me from ridicule, enables me on occasion to incur it with art. I recall whatever others have said, whatever I have read, and I add to all this my original contribution, which is remarkably apt.

MYSELF: It was wise of you to impart these mysteries to me, else I would have thought you self-contradictory.

HE: I'm nothing of the kind, for if it is necessary to avoid ridicule once, it is fortunately just as necessary to incur it a hundred times. There is no fitter role in high society than that of fool. For a long time the King had an appointed fool. At no time was there an appointed sage. I am Bertin's fool and that of many others—yours, possibly, this minute; or maybe you are mine. A real sage would want no fool; he who has one is no sage, and if no sage must be a fool. And were he the King himself, he may be his own fool's fool. In any event, remember that in a subject as variable as manners and morals nothing is absolutely, essentially, universally true or false—unless it be that one must be whatever self-interest requires, good or bad, wise or foolish, decent or ridiculous, honest or vicious. Had virtue chanced to lead me to fortune, I should have been as virtuous—or virtuous-seeming—as the next man. I was bidden to be ridiculous and I made myself so. As to vice, nature alone took care of that; though when I say vicious I am merely using your language. For if we really thrashed things out, we might find ourselves each calling virtue what the other calls vice and t'other way round.

At our house we also see the authors of the Opera-Comique, their actors and actresses and even oftener their managers Corbie, Moette—all people of wealth and superior merit.

And I was forgetting the great literary critics, the whole gang of penny-a-liners: *l'Avant-Coureur, les Petites Affiches, l'Année littéraire, l'Observateur littéraire, le Censeur heb-domadaire*—all of them.

MYSELF: How can that be? *L'Année littéraire* and *l'Observateur* hate each other.

HE: True, but all beggars are friends at the trough. That damned *Observateur*, the devil take him and all his sheets! It's he, that stinking, miserly, money-lending little priest who is responsible for my disgrace. He came within our ken for the first time yesterday. He arrived at the time which finds us all coming out of our lairs, the dinner hour. When the weather is bad, he's a lucky man who has the two bits to pay for a cab. One has been known to make fun of his neighbor for coming all muddy and wet through and through, who finds himself in the same condition when he gets home. One of the lot, I don't remember which, had a fearful quarrel with the Savoyard porter who has taken his stand at our door: they had deals together; the creditor wanted the debtor to pay up; the latter was in low water and couldn't, but he had to get past the other to come upstairs.

Dinner is served. They put the Abbé in the seat of honor

at the head of the table. I come in and see him. "How is that, Abbé, you're presiding? It's all right for today, but tomorrow you will please go down one cover; day after tomorrow, another cover, and so from cover to cover, to right or left, until, from having occupied the spot I held once before you, Fréron once after me, Dorat once after Fréron, and Palissot once after Dorat, you come to rest next to me, another poor bugger like you who *siedo sempre come un maestoso cazzo fra duoi coglioni.*"

The Abbé, who is a good fellow and takes everything in good part, began to laugh. Mademoiselle, struck by my remark and the accuracy of my simile, began to laugh. All those who sat to the left and right of the Abbé or whom he had displaced by one seat, began to laugh. The whole table laughed except Monsieur, who got huffy and began to use language which would have been of no consequence had we been alone: "Rameau, you are impertinent—"—"I know it, that's the condition of my being here."—"A scoundrel"—"Like the next man."—"A beggar."—"Should I be here if I weren't?"—"I'll have you turned out of doors." "After dinner I'll leave of my own accord."—"I charge you not to forget to do so."

We dined; I did not miss a mouthful. Having eaten and drunk my fill, for after all, it came to the same thing, and Messer Gaster is a person I've never treated to the sulks, I made up my mind to get ready to go. I had given my word in front of such a large group of people that I had to keep it. I took quite a while wandering around the rooms looking for my hat and stick where I knew they weren't, and hoping that the boss would burst out anew in a flood of fresh insults, that somebody would intervene and that we would end up by making friends from sheer fury of altercation. I turned and turned about, having of course no spleen to discharge; but the boss, the boss looked blacker than Homer's Apollo when he let his arrows rain down upon the Greek hosts. With his nightcap jammed lower down than usual over his eyes, he was pacing back and forth, his fist under his chin. Mademoiselle comes up to me. "Tell me," I ask her, "what is there out of the ordinary? How have I acted differently from other days?"—"I want him to go!"—"I *am* going—but I have given no ground for offense."—"I beg your pardon: we invite the Abbé and you . . ."—"It's he who offended himself by inviting the Abbé and me and so many other noodles like me."—"Come, come, dearest Rameau, just beg the Abbé's pardon."—"But I have no use for his pardon!" "Now, now, do it and everything will calm down." She takes me by the hand and drags me toward the Abbé's chair. I stretch out an arm and look down at him in wonder—who has ever begged the Abbé's pardon? "Abbé," say I, "all this is most absurd, isn't it?" And I burst out laughing and so does he. But there was the other one to deal with and that was a horse of another color. I don't recall quite how I phrased my excuse: "Sir, behold this well-known fool . . ."—"I've stood him about long enough: not another word."—"He is very sorry." "It's I who am sorry."—"It shan't happen again."— "Till the next blackguard . . ."

I don't know whether he was having one of those bad days when Mademoiselle herself is afraid to go near him and has to use kid gloves, or whether he misheard what I said, or yet whether I said the wrong thing, but it fell out worse than before. Damn it all! Doesn't he know me as I am? Doesn't he know I'm like a child and that now and then I have no control over what's inside me? And by God, come to think of it, I wouldn't have a moment's respite. You need a marionette of steel if you're going to pull the string and jerk it all day long. I have to entertain them—granted—but I must have some fun too. In the midst of this confusion there came to me a sinister idea, an arrogant idea, an idea that fills me with insolent pride, and this was that they could not get along without me. I am the irreplaceable man.

MYSELF: Yes, I rather think they need you badly, but you need them more. You won't find again, at will, a house as congenial. But they can replace one missing fool by a hundred.

HE: A hundred fools like me, master Philosopher! No, no: they are by no means so common. Dull fools, yes. But people are harder to please in folly than in talent or virtue. My species is scarce, very scarce. Now that they've lost me, what do they do? They're as sad as dogs. I am an inexhaustible store of silliness. Every minute I said things that reduced them to tears from laughter. I was worth to them a whole lunatic asylum.

MYSELF: In return for which you had the whole works: board, bed, coat, vest, pants, shoes, and pocket money.

HE: That's the rosy side, the profit. But you won't look at the reverse, the obligations. In the first place, if there was a rumor of a new play written, regardless of weather I must ferret out the author from whatever Paris attic; I must get to read the piece, and must cleverly hint that one of the parts would be ideally suited to somebody I knew.—"And who is that, pray tell?"—"Who indeed! The three graces in one, subtlety, gentility itself."—"You mean Mlle. Dangeville? Do you know her?"—"Slightly, but she's not the one I mean."—"Who, then?" I would name her in a low voice.— "That one!"—"Yes, that one," I said blushing a little, for once in a while I can feel shame and it was something to see the poet pull a long face on hearing her name; that is, when he didn't laugh in my face instead. In spite of all, I would have to drag my man to the house for dinner—willy, nilly. He'd be afraid to commit himself, would make excuses, proffer thanks. When I did not succeed in my embassy, my reception at home was a caution: they called me a clodhopper, a bungler, a fool; I was good for nothing and not worth the drink of water they let me have.

But it was even worse when she would get the part and I had to stand gallantly amid the hisses and jeers of the public (who are good judges, no matter what people say) and perform as a solitary claque, drawing on myself everybody's

astonished eyes and sometimes depriving her of her hisses.
People around me would whisper: "He's a footman in disguise—belongs to the man who sleeps with her. Will he never
stop that racket!" People can't imagine what might lead a
man to do what I did. They take it for stupidity, whereas
it's a motive that would excuse any action.

MYSELF: Including breaking the law?

HE: After a time, however, I came to be known. They
said, "That's only Rameau." All I could do to avoid the ridicule incurred by my isolated applause was to throw in a few
ironic words which gave it a contrary interpretation. You
must admit that it takes a strong interest to brave the assembled public as I did, and that I deserved more than a fiver
for each encounter.

MYSELF: Why didn't you hire help?

HE: I did now and then, and made something on it. Before
going into the torture chamber we had to burden our memory
with the brilliant passages where we must take the lead. If I
forgot or confused them, I would be blown up when I went
back: you have no idea what an earthquake it was. And then
the house was full of dogs for whose care I was responsible—
my own fault for offering to do it. I was likewise steward for
the cats, and lucky when Micou did not scratch my hand or
tear my cuff. Criquette was often subject to colic—up to me
to rub her belly. Formerly Mademoiselle suffered from
vapors, now it's nerves, not to mention other recurring in-
dispositions which no one bothers to conceal from me. Let
that pass, I'm not the one to insist on formal manners. I've
read somewhere that a King called "The Great" would lean
on the back of his mistress's chair when at stool. Familiarity
breeds contempt, and on those occasions I was treated more
familiarly than anybody. Well, I'm all for it and I used familiarity in return without their objecting. They should have
continued in that frame of mind. I have sketched the boss for
you. Mademoiselle is getting heavy; you should hear the
stories told about her.

MYSELF: I hope you don't help to spread them?

HE:　　　Why not?

MYSELF: Because it is a good deal less than right to contribute to your patrons' being mocked.

HE:　　　Isn't it far worse to take advantage of one's own philanthropy in order to revile one's protégé?

MYSELF: If the protégé weren't vile to begin with, nothing would enable his patron to vilify him.

HE:　　　And if the people in question were not ridiculous in themselves they couldn't be mocked. Is it my fault that they grow fouler with the years? Is it my fault if their disgusting habits get betrayed and mocked? When people make up their minds to keep company with the likes of me, common sense should tell them to be ready for the blackest disloyalty. When we're taken in tow, we are known for what we are—parasites whose souls are treacherous and vile. Knowing us, they can't complain. There's a tacit agreement that we'll reap benefits and return evil for good, sooner or later. Isn't that the agreement between a man and his pet monkey or parrot? Le Brun cries out that Palissot, his friend and guest, has made a squib about him. Palissot had to make the squib and Le Brun is in the wrong. Poinsinet cries out that Palissot has attributed the squib to him. Palissot had to make the attribution and Poinsinet is in the wrong. The little Abbé Rey cries out that his friend Palissot has snatched his mistress, to whom the Abbé had introduced him: this only proves he should not have introduced him, or else resigned himself to losing her. The bookseller David cries out that his partner Palissot has slept or tried to sleep with his wife; she cries out that Palissot has intimated to anyone willing to hear that he did sleep with her. Whether Palissot did or did not—a nice question, since she had to deny the fact and Palissot may have invented it— it is clear that Palissot was only acting as he must and the bookseller and his wife are in the wrong.

Helvétius may well cry out because Palissot lampoons him as a villain, though Palissot still owes him money for medical

expenses as well as food and clothing; but should Helvétius
have expected anything else from a man defiled by every
kind of infamy, a man who for fun induces a friend by false
promises to change his religion, a man who cheats his business
associates, a man who is without faith, morals, or feelings,
who seeks his fortune *per fas et nefas*, whose length of days is
measured by the number of his crimes, and who has even
represented himself on the stage as the most dangerous bully
alive—a piece of impudence unequaled in the past and not
likely to be matched in the future? Exactly—hence it is
Helvétius and not Palissot who is in the wrong.

If you take a young provincial to the zoo at Versailles,
and he is fool enough to push his hand through the bars of
the tiger's cage and lose his arm to the wild beast, which
of the two is in the wrong? The answer to all this is written
down in the tacit agreement. It's too bad for the man who
hasn't studied it or has forgotten it. How I wish I could defend under the terms of this universal and sacred compact the
people who are accused of wickedness when one should
rather accuse oneself of stupidity! Yes, my fat countess, *you*
are in the wrong when you gather about you the kind of
persons called in your circle "types," and when these "types"
play you dirty tricks or make you their accomplice to the
point of turning decent people against you. Decent people
act as they must and so do types. You have no business with
types. If Bertin lived quietly and peacefully with his mistress,
if the integrity of their character had brought them reputable
friends, if they had gathered about them men of talent and
persons renowned for virtue, if they had kept for a choice,
enlightened company the hours taken from the pleasure of
being together and loving each other in their quiet retreat,
do you suppose they would be the theme of stories, good or
bad? What has befallen them is only what they deserved.
They've been punished for their brashness and we are the
predestined instruments of Providence, now and forevermore,
to mete out justice to the Bertins of the moment. Likewise

our counterparts among our descendants will see justice done to the Mésenges and Bertins to come. And while we carry out these just decrees against them, you who depict us for what we are carry out the same decrees against us. What would you think of us if with our shameful conduct we laid claim to public regard? You would think us mad. Why then call sane people who expect good from debased characters or creatures born vicious? Everything in the world gets its due. There are two attorneys-general—the one at your beck and call, who prosecutes offenders against society. The other is Nature. It knows all the vices that escape the law. Give yourself over to debauchery with women and you die of dropsy; live fast and you end consumptive. Open your door to riff-raff, consort with them, and you get betrayed, mocked, and despised. The simplest thing is to concede the justice of all this and say to oneself: "It is all for the best." Turn over a new leaf and amend your ways—or else stay as you are and abide by the terms of the contract aforesaid.

MYSELF: You are right.

HE: To come back to those "good stories," I do not make them up; I content myself with repeating them. They say that a few days ago, about five o'clock in the morning, a furious randan broke out; all the servants' bells ringing, and the incoherent shouts of a man being smothered: "Help, help . . . murder!" The cries came from the boss's apartment. Help arrives, he is saved. It was our fat creature who had lost her head completely—as often happens in such circumstances—and by raising herself on her hands kept collapsing to the tune of two or three hundred pounds on the Petty Outlay Department, with all the momentum imparted by furious desire. Rescuing him was a job, but what a devilishly queer notion to put a tiny hammer under a huge anvil.

MYSELF: Enough of your naughtiness, will you! Let's talk of something else. I've had a question on the tip of my tongue since we started chatting.

HE: Why hold it back?

MYSELF: I was afraid to be inquisitive.

HE: After what I've told you, I can't imagine what secret I could withhold from you.

MYSELF: You are in no doubt about the opinion I have of you?

HE: No doubt at all. You think me the most abject and contemptible of men. And so I am in my own eyes—sometimes. Not often. I congratulate myself on my vices more often than blame myself. But your contempt does not vary.

MYSELF: Just so. But then why show yourself to me in all your turpitude?

HE: First, because you know a good deal of it to start with, and I stand to gain more than I lose by confessing the rest.

MYSELF: How is that, tell me?

HE: If there's one realm in which it's essential to be sublime, it's in wickedness. You spit on ordinary scum, but you can't deny a kind of respect to a great criminal: his courage amazes, his ferocity overawes. People especially admire consistency.

MYSELF: But this admirable consistency, you haven't reached it yet. I find you now and again weak in principle. You don't seem to know if your wickedness comes from nature or from study, nor whether you have pursued your studies far enough.

HE: I grant you that. But I've done my best. Haven't I with due modesty acknowledged superiors in my kind? Haven't I spoken of Bouret with the deepest admiration? To my mind, Bouret is the greatest man on earth.

MYSELF: You come right after Bouret?

HE: No.

MYSELF: Then it must be Palissot?

HE: Yes, but not Palissot by himself.

MYSELF: And who is worthy of sharing second place with him?

HE: The Renegade from Avignon.

MYSELF: I've never heard of him. He must be a remarkable man.

HE: He is that.

MYSELF: The lives of great men always interest me.

HE: I should hope so. This great man lived with a good
and decent descendant of the tribe of Abraham, which as you
know was guaranteed to equal the number of the stars in
heaven.

MYSELF: With a Jew?

HE: With a Jew. He had earned, first his host's compassion,
then his good will, finally his entire trust. For as always
happens, we are so sure of the effect of our kindness that we
seldom hide our secret from those on whom we have showered benefits. How can you expect to do away with ingrati-
tude when you expose men to the temptation of being
ungrateful with impunity? This is a sound proposition which
our Jew failed to ponder. He therefore confided to the
renegade the truth that he could not conscientiously eat pig.
You will be amazed to hear all that an inventive mind was
able to make of that secret. For a few months the renegade
was full of kindness. When he deemed his Jew entirely won
over, devoted, convinced of possessing the best friend in the
world—observe the man's circumspection: no haste, he lets
the fruit ripen before shaking the branch; too much eagerness
might ruin his project. Observe that greatness is usually the
result of a natural equilibrium among opposite qualities.

MYSELF: Spare me your reflections and get on with your story.

HE: Impossible. There are days when I am compelled to reflect. It's a disease I have to give in to. Where was I?

MYSELF: The intimate friendship between the Jew and the
renegade.

HE: Ah yes, the fruit was ripe. But you're not listening.
What's on your mind?

MYSELF: I was thinking of the unevenness of your style—now
elevated, now colloquial.

HE: Can the style of the vice-ridden be otherwise? . . . He
comes home one night to his host with a petrified air, his
voice broken, his face pale as death, and shaking in every

limb. "What's wrong?"—"We are done for!" "How, done
for?"—"Ruined, I tell you; it's hopeless."—"Explain yourself."—"Just a second, till I catch my breath."—"Yes, yes do,"
says the Jew instead of saying "you're a thorough scoundrel.
I don't know what you're about to say, but you're a scoundrel
and pretending to be terrified."

MYSELF: Why should he have said such a thing?

HE: Because he was lying and had overdone it. It's perfectly clear to me—and don't interrupt. "We're done for,
done for, it's hopeless." Can't you sense make-believe in the
repetition of "done for"? "An informer has denounced us to
the Holy Inquisition, you as a Jew and I as a renegade—a
loathsome renegade." Do you see how the traitor blithely
goes in for the foulest expression? It takes more courage than
you'd think to call oneself by one's right name. You have no
idea how painful it is to achieve.

MYSELF: I have no idea, I'm sure. And this loathsome renegade?

HE: Was lying. Very adroitly lying. The Jew takes fright,
pulls out his beard by the roots, rocks in anguish, sees the
police at his door, himself wearing the *san benito* and his
autodafé in readiness. "My dear, dear friend, my only friend,
what shall we do?"—"What to do? Why, show ourselves,
affect the greatest self-assurance, behave as usual. The pro-
cedure of the court is secret but slow. We must use the time
to sell and dispose of everything you own. I shall go and
charter a ship, or have a third party do it—yes, that would be
better—and we'll stow your money in the hold; for it's your
money they're after. Then you and I will sail and find in other
climes the right to worship our God, and so follow the law of
Abraham and of our own conscience. The main thing in our
present state of danger is to do nothing rash . . ." No sooner
said than done. The ship is chartered, stored with provisions,
manned, the Jew's fortune put on board. Tomorrow at dawn
they sail; now they can sup and sleep more cheerfully. Tomorrow they flee from persecution. In the night, the renegade

gets up, takes the Jew's purse, wallet, and jewels, makes for the ship—and he is off.

You think that's the end? You're wrong. When I was told the story I guessed what I haven't yet mentioned in order to test your intelligence. You did well to be an honest man, you would have made but half a scamp. Up to this point the renegade is not much more than that—a contemptible cur whom no one would wish to emulate. The stroke of genius in his evil-doing is that he himself was the informer who denounced his good friend the Jew to the Inquisition, which seized him that morning and made a bonfire of him a few days later. Such is the way the renegade came to peacefully enjoy the wealth of the accursed descendant of those who crucified our Lord.

MYSELF: I hardly know which I loathe more, the dreadfulness of your renegade or the way in which you speak of him.

HE: Precisely what I was saying to you: the atrociousness of the deed lifts you beyond contempt and it accounts for my sincerity with you. I wanted you to know how far I excelled in my art and to make you admit by main strength that I am at least original in my vileness. I want you to consider me in the great tradition of the master scoundrels— Then I can exclaim: "*Vivat Mascarillus, fourbum imperator!*"

Whereupon he began to sing an extraordinary kind of fugue. At one moment the melody was solemn and majestic, at other times gay and lightsome. Now he imitated the bass, now one of the upper parts. With his arms and outstretched neck he indicated the held notes, and so composed and performed in his own honor a song of triumph, from which it was clear that he understood good music far better than good morals.

As for me I hardly knew whether I should come or go, laugh or get angry. I stayed, wanting to turn the conversation to some subject that would expel from my soul the horror that filled it. I was beginning to find almost unbearable the presence of a man who could discuss a dreadful deed, an abominable crime, in the way a connoisseur in poetry or painting discusses the fine points of a work of art—or as a moralist or an historian points out the merit of an heroic action. I felt gloom overwhelming me. He noticed and asked:

HE: What is wrong, are you unwell?

MYSELF: Somewhat. It will pass off.

HE: You look disturbed like a man pursued by dark fancies.

MYSELF: Just so.

After a moment when neither spoke but during which he walked about whistling and singing, I began again in order to bring him back to a discussion of his talent. I said:

MYSELF: What are you doing these days?

HE: Nothing.

MYSELF: That must be very fatiguing.

HE: I was light-headed enough to begin with, but I went to hear the music of Duni and our other young composers and that finished me.

MYSELF: So you like this new genre?

HE: No doubt about it.

MYSELF: You manage to find beauty in these new-fangled melodies?

HE: Do I manage! Ye gods! Don't doubt for a moment that I do! What declamation! What truth of expression!

MYSELF: Every imitative art finds its models in Nature. What is the musician's model when he fashions a melody?

HE: Let's begin with a more general question: what is a melody?

MYSELF: I confess that is beyond me. We are all alike, really, we remember words, which we think we understand from the frequent and even correct use we make of them. But our minds contain only vague notions. When I utter the word "melody," I have no clearer idea than you and most of your colleagues when you say: "reputation, blame, honor, vice, virtue, modesty, decency, shame, ridicule."

HE: A melody is a vocal or instrumental imitation using the sounds of a scale invented by art—or inspired by nature,

as you prefer; it imitates either physical noises or the accents
of passion. You can see that by changing a few words in this
definition it would exactly fit painting, eloquence, sculpture
or poetry.

Now to come to your question. What is the musician's
model? It is declamation if the model is alive and a thinking
being; it is physical noise if the model is inanimate. Consider
declamation as one line, and song as another which twists
snake-like about the former. The more the declamation,
which is the prototype of song, is vivid and true, the more
the song shaped upon it will intersect it at many points. The
truer the melody, the more beautiful it will be—and that is
what our younger musicians have so well understood. When
one hears "I am but a poor wretch" one recognizes the complaint of a miser. Were he not singing he would be using
the same inflections to address the earth in which he has buried
his gold, saying "O earth, receive my treasure." And that
young girl who feels her heart going pit-a-pat, who blushes,
is upset and begs my lord to let her go—could she express
herself otherwise than as she does? One finds in these new
works every type of character, an infinite variety of utterance. Take it from me, it's sublime. Go, go and hear the piece
in which the youth feels the hand of death and sings "My
heart is gone." Listen to his song, listen to the orchestra and
then tell me what difference exists between the form of this
air and the sighs of the dying. You will discover that the
melodic line exactly coincides with the curve of spoken
utterance.

I say nothing of meter, which is another condition of
melody; I dwell on expressiveness. Nothing is more self-
evident than the maxim I read somewhere: *Musices semina-
rium accentus:* accent is the source of melody. From this you
can infer how difficult and how important it is to know how
to handle recitative. There is no beautiful air from which one
cannot make a beautiful recitative, and no beautiful recitative
from which an able composer cannot make a beautiful air. I

would not guarantee that a good reciter will sing well, but I
should be surprised if a good singer did not know how to recite well. You must believe all I have been saying, for it's true.

MYSELF: I should like nothing better than to believe you, if I
were not prevented by a small difficulty.

HE: The difficulty is?

MYSELF: Only this, that if the new music is sublime, it follows
that the music of the divine Lully, of Campra, of Destouches,
of Mouret, and—be it said between us—of your dear uncle,
must be a trifle dull.

HE (coming close and answering in my ear): I shouldn't like
to be overheard, for there are hereabouts plenty of people
who know me—but it *is* dull. Not that I worry myself much
about the dear uncle—if 'dear' has to come into it. He is made
of stone: he could see my tongue hanging out a foot long
and he would not give me a glass of water. But try as he will
—with the octave, the leading note—*Tum-tum-ta-ta-tum*,
toot-toot-toot-, *tra-la-toot*—even though he makes a racket
like the very devil, some people are beginning to catch on;
they will no longer take banging for music—and certainly
not *his* banging. The police should forbid any person, of
whatever rank, to have Pergolese's *Stabat Mater* performed.
That *Stabat* should have been burned by the public hangman.
Yes, these confounded *bouffons* with their *Serva Padrona* and
their *Tracallo* have given us a stout kick in the butt.

Formerly a *Tancred*, an *Issé*, an *Europe galante*, *Les Indes*,
Castor, *Les Talents lyriques* would run for five or six months.
The run of Lully's *Armide* was endless. Nowadays they
tumble on one another's heels like jackstraws. That's why the
managers, Rebel and Francoeur, cry out to heaven. They say
all is lost: "they are ruined; if these fair ground musicians are
allowed to keep on, our national music is done for; the so-
called Royal Academy—the Opera—might as well shut up
shop." And there is some truth in it. The old fogies who have
been going there every Friday for thirty or forty years no
longer have a good time. They are bored, they yawn without

knowing why. They ask themselves and can't answer. They
should ask *me*. As things are going now, Duni's prophecy will
come true, and I'm willing to give up living in four or five
years if, after *The Painter in Love with his Model* you find as
much as an alley cat in our celebrated Opera house.

The good souls! They've already abandoned their symphonies to hear the Italian ones. They thought they could
accustom their ears to these new instrumental pieces without
changing their taste as regards the vocal—as if symphonies
were not in relation to songs (except for the greater freedom
afforded by the range of instruments and the dexterity of
the fingers) what songs are to declamation; as if the violin did
not ape the singer, who in turn will become the ape of the
violin when acrobatics will have replaced beauty. The first
one who played Locatelli was the apostle of the new music.
Next! Next! We shall all become accustomed to the imitation of passionate accents or of natural phenomena by means
of voices and instruments—which is the whole extent of
music's purpose. D'you think we'll also keep our taste for
flights, dreams, glories, triumphs, and victories? Not so you
can notice it, Joe! Did anyone imagine that the public could
learn to weep or laugh at tragic or comic scenes when
"musicated," to respond to the tones of fury, hatred, and
jealousy, the true plaints of love, the irony and pleasantries
of the Italian or French theatre, and that in spite of all this
the public would continue to admire *Ragonde* or *Platée*.
You bet your life—go cut it with a knife! That they could
once learn how easily, softly, gently the Italian tongue, with
its natural harmony, flexible prosody, easy ellipses and in-
versions, suited the art and motion of music, the turns of
song and the measured pace of sounds—and yet would overlook the fact that French is stiff, heavy, pedantic, and monotonous? Well, well, well, they persuaded themselves that
after weeping with a mother bewailing the loss of her son,
and shuddering at the decree of a tyrant committing murder,
they would not be bored with their fairyland, their insipid

mythology, their saccharine love songs, which show the
poet's bad taste no less than the sterility of the music matched
thereto. The good souls!

It could not and cannot be. The true, the good, and the
beautiful will prevail. Their rights may at first be challenged,
but in the end they are acknowledged, and people come to
yield their admiration. Inferior things may be esteemed for a
time but the end is a great yawn. Go ahead, gentlemen, yawn
away, yawn to your heart's content, don't be afraid! The
power of nature and of the trinity which I worship will
never be overcome by the forces of darkness—the True
which is the father, engenders the Good, which is his son,
whence comes the Beautiful, which is the Holy Ghost.
Change is gradual. The foreign god takes his place humbly
next to the native idol, little by little asserts itself, and one
fine day elbows out his fellow—before you can say Jack
Robinson, there's the idol flat on its back. They say that's the
way the Jesuits introduced Christianity into India and China.
And the Jansenists can say what they like, the political method
that aims quietly and directly at the goal, without bloodshed,
martyrdom, or so much as a queue of hair cut off, is obviously
the best.

MYSELF: There is some sense in almost everything you've said.

HE: Sense? I'm glad! The devil take me if I've been making
         any special effort. I speak as it comes. I'm like the opera
         musicians when my uncle came on the scene. If I'm on the
         point, well and good. It only shows that a man of the trade
         will always speak about it more sensibly than any Academy
         or all the Duhamels in the world.

And now he paces up and down again humming in his throat
some arias from Duni's operas, occasionally raising arms and eyes
to the skies: "It's beautiful, my God, but it is beautiful—! Why?
How can a man sport a pair of ears and ask such a question?" He
was getting into a passion and beginning to sing, his voice growing louder as his passion increased. Next he gesticulated, made

faces and twisted his body, and I thought to myself: "There he goes—losing his wits and working himself up to a scene." True enough, he suddenly burst out very loud: "I am but a poor wretch ... My Lord, my Lord, I beg you to let me go! ... O Earth, receive my gold and keep my treasure safe, my soul, my life, O Earth! ... There is my little friend ... *Aspettare e non venire* ... *A Zerbina penserete ... Sempre in contrasti con te si sta. ...*" He jumbled together thirty different airs, French, Italian, comic, tragic—in every style. Now in a baritone voice he sank to the pit; then straining in falsetto he tore to shreds the upper notes of some air, imitating the while the stance, walk and gestures of the several characters; being in succession furious, mollified, lordly, sneering. First a damsel weeps and he reproduces her kittenish ways; next he is a priest, a king, a tyrant; he threatens, commands, rages. Now he is a slave, he obeys, calms down, is heartbroken, complains, laughs; never overstepping the proper tone, speech, or manner called for by the part.

All the "woodpushers" in the café had left their chess boards and gathered around us. The windows of the place were occupied from outside by passers-by who had stopped on hearing the commotion. They guffawed fit to crack the ceiling. He notices nothing, he keeps on, in the grip of mental possession, an enthusiasm so close to madness that it seems doubtful whether he will recover. He may have to be put into a cab and taken to a padded cell, still singing fragments of Jomelli's *Lamentations*. He reproduces with incredible precision, fidelity, and warmth the most beautiful passages of each scene. That magnificent recitative in which Jeremiah describes the desolation of Jerusalem, he drenches in tears which draw their like from every onlooker. His art was complete—delicacy of voice, expressive strength, true sorrow. He dwelt on the places where the musician had shown himself a master. If he left the vocal part, it was to take up the instrumental, which he abandoned suddenly to return to the voice, linking them so as to preserve the connection and unity of the whole, gripping our souls and keeping them suspended in the most singular state of being that I have ever experienced.

Did I admire him? Yes, I did admire. Was I moved to pity? I was moved. But a streak of derision was interwoven with these feelings and denatured them.

Yes, you too would have burst out laughing at the way in which he aped the different instruments. With swollen cheeks and a somber throaty sound, he would give us the horns and bassoons. For the oboes he assumed a shrill yet nasal voice, then speeded up the emission of sound to an incredible degree for the strings, for whose tones he found close analogues. He whistled piccolos and warbled traverse flutes, singing, shouting, waving about like one demented, being in himself dancer and ballerina, singer and prima donna, all of them together and the whole orchestra, the whole theatre; then redividing himself into twenty separate roles, running, stopping, glowing at the eyes like one possessed, frothing at the mouth.

The heat was stifling and the sweat, which ran down the creases of his face, mixed with the powder in his hair, dripping and marking the upper part of his coat. He would show me every conceivable thing. He wept, laughed, sighed, looked placid or melting or enraged. He was a woman in a spasm of agony, a wretched man sunk in despair, a temple being erected, birds growing silent at sunset, waters murmuring through cool and solitary places or else cascading from a mountain top, a storm, a hurricane, the anguish of those about to die, mingled with the whistling of the wind and the noise of thunder. He was night and its gloom, shade and silence—for silence itself is depictable in sound. He had completely lost his senses.

Worn out, exhausted, like a man emerging from a deep sleep or a prolonged reverie, he stood motionless, dumb, petrified. He kept looking around him like a man who has lost his way and would know where he is. He waited for returning strength and wits, wiping his face with an absent-minded gesture. Just as a man who on waking should see a large number of people around his bed and not remember or be able to conceive what he had done, he began by asking: "What is it, gentlemen? Why do you laugh? You look surprised—what is it?" Then he added: "That is what deserves to be called music. There is your musician! And yet, gentlemen, it will not do to look down on all of Lully's arias. Let anyone try a better setting of the scene 'I await the dawn' without changing the words: it can't be done. Nor must you despise certain pieces by Campra, or my uncle's works for violin, his gavottes, his military and religious processions. 'Pale torches,' 'Light more dreadful than darkness,' 'God of Tartarus and oblivion' ''—(Here his voice swelled and sustained the notes, bringing the neighbors to their windows while we stuffed our fingers into our ears.) He added: "Those are the places that call for lung power, a stout organ, a great volume of air. But before long, good-by to *L'Assomption*, *Le Carême* and *Les Rois*. They don't as yet know what to choose for setting to music, that is, what will suit a composer. True lyric poetry has yet to be born. But by dint of hearing Pergolese, The Saxon, Terradeglias, Traetta and the rest, they'll catch on."

MYSELF: Do you mean to say that Quinault, La Motte and Fontenelle didn't know their business?

HE: Not for the new style. There aren't six lines together in all their charming poems that you can put music to. They give you ingenious epigrams, sweet and delicate madrigals. But if you want to find out how empty of substance all that is for our own art—which is the most violent of all the arts, not excepting that of Demosthenes—get someone to recite these librettos to you. They will seem frigid, monotonous and dull. Nothing in them supplies a pattern for songs: I'd just as soon be asked to set the Maxims of La Rochefoucauld or the Thoughts of Pascal. We want the animal cry of the passions to dictate the melodic line, and the expressive moments must come close together. Each phrase must be short, its meaning broken off for suspense, so that the musician can make use equally of the whole or of a part, omit a word or repeat it, add a new one he needs, turn the phrase inside out like a jellyfish without destroying the sense—all of which makes lyric poetry much harder to write in French than in languages that freely use inversion and naturally afford all these advantages. "Cruel barbarian, plunge thy dagger in my breast; here I stand ready for the fatal blow. Strike! Dare! Oh, I faint, I die. A secret fire pervades my senses. Cruel love, what do you ask of me? Leave me in blissful peace as heretofore; oh, restore my reason!" Our passions have to be strong. The tenderness of the musician and the poet must be extreme . . . the aria must be the peroration of the scene. We need exclamations, interjections, suspensions, interruptions, affirmations, and negations. We call out, invoke, clamor, groan, weep, and laugh openly. No more witticisms, epigrams, neat thoughts—they are too unlike nature. And don't get it into your head that the old theatrical acting and declamation can give us a pattern to follow. Not likely! We want it more energetic, less mannered, more genuine. Simple speeches, the ordinary utterance of passion, will be all the more necessary that our French language is more monotonous, less accented. The animal cry or that of man in a passion will supply the accent. . . .

As he spoke, the crowd around us had withdrawn, whether from no longer being able to hear or from having lost interest in the subject; for in general, man is like a child and prefers being amused to being instructed. The chess players had resumed their boards and we were alone in our corner. Seated on the bench, his head resting against the wall, his arms hanging and his eyes half shut, he said:

HE: I don't know what's the matter with me; when I came here I was feeling rested and in good form. Now I am exhausted, worn out, as if I had walked thirty miles. It came upon me suddenly.

MYSELF: Should you like something to drink?

HE: With pleasure. My throat feels rough, I am a little faint and my chest hurts. This happens to me every day and I have no notion of the cause.

MYSELF: What shall you take?

HE: Whatever you say. I am not hard to please. Poverty has accustomed me to everything.

They served us beer and lemonade, of which he filled and refilled a large glass two or three times. Then, like a man restored
to life, he coughs loudly, gesticulates and begins again:

HE: Now in your opinion, master Philosopher, is it not
    a very strange thing that a foreigner, an Italian, a man named
    Duni, should be the one to teach us how to give force and
    accent to our music, and to adapt our singing to the several
    tempi, meters, intervals, and expressions without injuring
    our prosody? And yet it was nothing like drinking the ocean
    dry. All you had to do was to listen to a beggar asking for
    alms, to a man in a fury, a woman in a fit of jealousy, a lover
    in despair, a flatterer—yes, a flatterer—sweetening his voice
    and drawling out his honeyed syllables, in short, any passion
    whatsoever will do, provided it is energetic enough to supply
    the musician with a pattern. You would then have noticed
    two things: one, that long and short syllables have no fixed
    values, not even a fixed relation between them; and two, that
    passion discomposes prosody almost at will and can leap the
    largest intervals. The man who exclaims "Oh, unhappy me!"
    raises his voice on the first syllable to the highest pitch and
    sinks the rest down to the lowest, making an octave or even
    more, and giving to each sound the quantity appropriate to
    a melodic phrase without offending the ear and yet without
    retaining the longs and shorts of ordinary speech. What an
    advance since the days when we used to quote as a prodigy
    of musical expression the parenthetical remark in *Armide:*
    "Rinaldo's conqueror (if such there be)" or the "Don't hesi-
    tate, obey!" in *Les Indes galantes.* Nowadays such miracles
    make me shrug with pity. At the rate art is going, there is no
    limit to its power. Meanwhile, another drink.

He drank two, three glasses more without noticing, and would
have drowned himself like a spent swimmer had I not moved the
bottle, which he sought distractedly, not knowing what he was
about. I then said to him:

MYSELF: How is it that with such fineness of feeling, so much
    sensibility where musical beauty is concerned, you are so

blind to the beauties of morality, so insensible to the charm of virtue?

HE: It must be that virtue requires a special sense that I lack, a fiber that has not been granted me. My fiber is loose, one can pluck it forever without its yielding a note. Or else I have spent my life with good musicians and bad people, whence my ear has become very sharp and my heart quite deaf. And then there is heredity. My father's blood is the same as my uncle's; my blood is like my father's. The paternal molecule was hard and obtuse, and like a primordial germ it has affected all the rest.

MYSELF: Do you love your son?

HE: Do I love him? I am crazy about him.

MYSELF: And will you do nothing to thwart in him the effect of his accursed paternal molecule?

HE: I'll try it, but (I think) in vain. If he is fated to become a good man, trying won't do any harm. But if the molecule decides that he shall be a ne'er do well like his father, the pains I might take to make him an honest man would be very dangerous. Education would work continually at cross-purposes with the natural bent of the molecule, and he would be pulled by two contrary forces that would make him go askew down the path of life—like so many others I see who are equally clumsy in good and evil deeds. They are what we call "types," of all descriptions the worst, because it indicates mediocrity and the lowest degree of contempt. A great scoundrel is a great scoundrel; he isn't a "type." Before the molecule could recapture him and reproduce the state of perfect abjection which I have reached, it would take endless time. He would waste his best years. So at the moment I hold my hand, I simply observe him and let him come along. He is already greedy, cozening, rascally, lazy, and a liar: I am afraid he is a pedigreed beast.

MYSELF: And you will make him a musician so that the likeness can be complete?

HE: A musician! A musician! Sometimes I look at him and grind my teeth and say to myself "If you ever learn a note, I really think I'll twist your neck."

MYSELF: But why so?

HE: It leads nowhere.

MYSELF: It leads everywhere.

HE: Yes, if you excel. But who can guarantee that his child will excel? It's ten thousand to one that he will be a wretched note scraper like me. Do you know that it would be easier to find a child able to govern a kingdom than a great violinist?

MYSELF: I think on the contrary that any likely talent, even if mediocre, can lead a man to fortune, provided the country has no morals and lives on luxury and debauch. I myself once heard the following conversation take place between a sort of patron and his would-be protégé. The latter had been recommended to the former as a useful and serviceable man:

"My dear sir, what can you do?"

"I am a fairly good mathematician."

"Good enough. But after you have taught mathematics for ten or twelve years by running the streets of Paris, you will have only 300 or 400 francs a year."

"I have also studied law."

"If Puffendorf and Grotius came back to life they would starve in the gutter."

"I am well versed in geography and history."

"If there were any parents who really cared about their children's education, your fortune would be made. But such parents do not exist."

"I am a tolerable musician."

"Why didn't you say so at once? Just to show you what your gift is worth to you, let me say this: I have a daughter; come every day at seven-thirty and give her a lesson until nine. I shall pay you 250 francs a year and give you all your meals at our house. The rest of the day is yours to dispose of for your profit."

HE: And what happened?

MYSELF: If the man had been clever he would have grown rich
—which is all you seem to care about.

HE: No doubt. Gold, gold is everything; and everything,
without gold, is nothing. Therefore, instead of having my
son's head stuffed with grand maxims which he would have
to forget under pain of being a pauper, this is what I do
whenever I have a gold piece—not often, to be sure: I plant
myself in front of him, draw the piece from my pocket,
show it to him with admiring looks, raise my eyes to heaven,
kiss the gold in front of him, and to show him still more
forcibly the importance of the sacred coin, I stammer out
the names and point out with the finger all the things one
can buy with it—a beautiful gown, a beautiful hat, a good
cake; next I put the coin in my pocket, parade before him
proudly, pull up my coat tails and strike my waistcoat where
the money lies. Thus do I make him understand that it is
from that coin I draw the self-assurance he beholds.

MYSELF: Nothing could be better. But what if some day, being
deeply persuaded of the value of money, he should . . .

HE: I follow you! One must shut one's eyes to that. There
is no principle of conduct wholly without drawbacks. At the
worst, one goes through a bad half hour, then all is over.

MYSELF: Yet in spite of your wise and courageous views, I continue to think it would be a good thing to make him a musician. I know of no better way to approach the rich, to serve
their vices, and to turn one's own to advantage.

HE: True. But I have projects even more certain of success.
Ah, if I only had a daughter! But no man can do as he likes,
he must take what he gets and do the best he can with it. For
which purpose one must not, like most fathers, stupidly give
children who are destined to live in Paris the education of
ancient Sparta. One might as well plot their ruin. If the native
training is bad, the fault lies with the manners and customs of
my country, and not with me. Whoever be responsible, I
want my child happy, or what amounts to the same thing,
honored, rich, powerful. I know the easiest ways to accom-

plish this, and I mean to teach them to my son early in life. If you wise men blame me, the majority (and success itself) will absolve me. He will have gold—it's I who tell you so, I guarantee it—and if he has a great deal, he will lack nothing, not even your admiration and respect.

MYSELF: You might be wrong about the latter.

HE: If so, he can do without, like many other people.

There was in all he said much that one thinks to oneself, and acts on, but that one never says. This was in fact the chief difference between my man and rest of us. He admitted his vices, which are also ours: he was no hypocrite. Neither more nor less detestable than other men, he was franker than they, more logical, and thus often profound in his depravity. I was appalled to think of what his child would become under such a tutor. It was clear that if he was brought up on a system so exactly framed on our actual behavior, he would go far—unless he was prematurely cut off on the way.

HE: Never you fear! The important thing that a good father must do is not so much to give his child vices that will bring him wealth and foolish traits that will make him a favorite of the great—everybody does as much: not systematically like me, but by casual precept and example. No, what is more difficult is to teach him the golden art by which he can avert disgrace, shame, and the penalties of the law. These last are dissonances in the harmony of society, which one must know how to use, prepare, and resolve. Nothing is duller than a progression of common chords. One wants some contrast, which breaks up the clear white light and makes it iridescent.

MYSELF: Very good. Thanks. Your comparison brings me back from morals to music. I digressed in spite of myself, for to speak frankly, I much prefer you as musician than as moralist.

HE: And yet I am only second-rate in music, whereas I am a superior moralist.

MYSELF: I rather doubt this; but even were it so, I am an honest man and your principles do not suit me.

HE: So much the worse for you. Oh, if I only had your talent!

MYSELF: Leave my talent alone; let's go back to yours.

HE: If I could express myself as you do! But my vocabulary is a damned mongrel—half literary and well-bred, half guttersnipe.

MYSELF: Don't think I speak well. I can only tell the truth and, as you know, that doesn't always go down.

HE: It's not for telling the truth that I envy you your gifts. Just the opposite—it's to tell lies. If I only knew how to throw together a book, how to turn a dedication, intoxicate some fool with praises and make my way among women!

MYSELF: As for all that, you know much more about it than I do; I am not even fit to be your pupil.

HE: Oh, what abilities you are letting go to waste, not even suspecting what they're worth!

MYSELF: I reap whatever I sow, no more, no less.

HE: If that were true, you wouldn't be wearing these coarse clothes—linen coat, woollen stockings, thick-soled shoes and superannuated wig.

MYSELF: Granted. One must be terribly clumsy if one isn't rich after sticking at nothing to acquire wealth. But there are people like me, you see, who don't consider wealth the most important thing in the world—queer people.

HE: Very queer. No one is born that way. It's an acquired idea; it's unnatural.

MYSELF: Unnatural for man?

HE: Just unnatural. Everything that lives, man included, seeks its well-being at the expense of whoever withholds it. I'm sure that if I let my little savage grow up without saying a word to him, he would of his own accord want to be richly dressed, magnificently fed, liked by men and loved by women, and concentrate on himself all the goods of life.

MYSELF: If your little savage were left to himself and to his native blindness, he would in time join the infant's reasoning to the grown man's passions—he would strangle his father and sleep with his mother.

HE: Which only proves the need of a good education. There's no argument. But what is a good education if it is not one that leads to all the enjoyments without trouble or danger?

MYSELF: I am almost with you there, but let's not go into it.

HE: Why not?

MYSELF: Because I think we are only superficially in agreement, and that if we look into the question of troubles and dangers, we shall no longer be at one.

HE: And what's the harm of that?

MYSELF: Let it go, I say. What I know on the subject I shan't be able to teach you. You will have an easier time teaching me what you know about music, of which I am ignorant. Dear Rameau, let us talk music; and tell me how it is that with your remarkable power for understanding, remembering and rendering the most beautiful works of the great masters, with your contagious enthusiasm for them and for conveying them, you have never done anything that amounts to anything.

Instead of answering me, he started nodding with his head and uplifting a finger heavenward, cried out: "My star! my star! When Nature fashioned Leo, Vinci, Pergolese, Duni, she smiled on them. She put on a grave imposing mien when she made my dear uncle Rameau, who for a dozen years was called 'the great Rameau,' though soon nobody will have heard of him. But when she slapped together his nephew, she made a face, then another face, and still another." As he said these words he was making all sorts of faces depicting contempt, disdain, irony; he seemed to be kneading a ball of dough within his fingers.

This done, he made a gesture as if throwing the outlandish creation far from him and said: "That is how nature made me and threw me down among other idols, some with fat wrinkled bellies, others with short necks and popping, apoplectic eyes. Still others with wry necks. Some were stringy, bright of glance and beaky-nosed—all burst out laughing on seeing me and I putting my fists on my hips burst out laughing on seeing them, for lunatics and fools entertain one another; they seek one another out and are mutually drawn. If on arriving here below I hadn't found the saying ready made which tells you that 'a dolt's money is the patrimony of the man with wits' I would have invented it. I felt that nature had put my estate in the keeping of those idols and I devised a thousand ways to recover it."

MYSELF: I know those ways. You told me about them and I duly admired them. But, given your large choice of means, why didn't you try fashioning a work of art?

HE: That is the remark a man of the world made to Abbé Le Blanc. The Abbé had said: "Mme. de Pompadour took me in hand and brought me as far as the doors of the Academy. There she withdraws her hand, I fall down and break both my legs." The man of the world replied: "Well, Abbé, all you need to do is break in the doors with your head." To which the Abbé retorted: "I tried it and do you know what came of it?—a large bump right there."

This little tale told, my man started pacing again, his head lowered, looking pensive and worried. He sighed, wept, seemed in despair, raised his eyes and hands to heaven, struck his forehead with his fist with a violence fit to break his knuckles or his skull, then added: "It seems to me nevertheless that I have something there, but I knock in vain, I worry it but nothing comes out." Whereupon he started again to shake his pate and to redouble his blows on his skull, saying: "Either there's nobody at home or they refuse to answer."

The next minute he put on a look of pride, raised his head, put his right hand over his heart, took a pace forward and said: "But I feel, yes, I do feel. . . ."

He was aping a man who grows angry, indignant, who softens, commands, and implores. He improvised speeches full of anger, compassion, hatred, and love, sketching every passionate character with astonishing accuracy and subtlety. Then he went on: "Isn't that about right? It's coming, I should say. It only shows the value of having a midwife who knows how to prod and bring on the labor pains so as to bring out the child. When I take my pen by myself, intending to write, I bite my nails and belabor my brow but—no soap, the god is absent. Though I had convinced myself that I had genius, at the end of the first line I am informed that I'm a fool. But how in the name of sense can one feel, think, rise to heights, and speak with vigor while frequenting people such as those I must frequent to live—in the midst of gossip and the meaningless words that one says and hears: 'It was lovely out today. Have you heard Mlle. Marmosette? She plays like an angel. Monsieur So-and-so has the handsomest pair of dapple grays you ever saw. As for Madame X, she is really beginning to fade. Why does she think that at forty-five she can still do her hair that way. The young one is plastered with diamonds which certainly don't cost her much.—You mean which cost her a great deal?—On the contrary.—Where have you seen her? At Goldoni's *Harlequin's Child*. They did the grieving scene as never before. The Punchinello has voice but no art, no soul. Madame Z has given birth to twins—that way each father will have his own. . . .' Do you suppose that things like these, repeated over and over every day, kindle the mind and lead to great ideas?"

MYSELF: No, of course not. It would be better to shut oneself up in a garret, eat a dry crust, drink plain water and try to find oneself.

HE: That may be, but I haven't the courage. Why sacrifice one's well-being to a chancy success? And what about my name?—to be called Rameau is extremely embarrassing. Talent isn't like noble blood which is transmitted and grows in luster by being handed down from grandfather to great grandson without the ancestor's forcing any abilities on the descendant. The old line branches out into a huge spread of fools, but no matter. That's not true of talent. In order to get as much fame as one's father one has to be much more able than he. One must have inherited his sinew. I've lacked sinew —though my wrist is limber, the bow scrapes, and the pot boils. It isn't fame but it's food.

MYSELF: If I were in your place, I wouldn't take it all for granted, I'd try.

HE: You think I haven't tried? I was hardly fifteen when I first said to myself: "What's the matter, Rameau, you're dreaming. What are you dreaming about? You'd like to have accomplished some thing for the whole universe to marvel at. Then all you have to do is to spit on your hands and wiggle your fingers. One, two, three, and the thing is done." Later in life, I repeated the words of my youth; today I do it still and I stand near the statue of Memnon.

MYSELF: What does that mean, the statue of Memnon?

HE: I should think it's clear enough. Around the statue of Memnon there were an infinity of others, all equally struck by the rays of the sun. But Memnon's was the only one to give forth a sound. Who's a poet?—Voltaire. Who else? Voltaire. Name a third one: Voltaire. A fourth? Voltaire. As for musicians, there is Rinaldo of Capua, Hasse, Pergolese, Alberti, Tartini, Locatelli, Terradeglias; there's my uncle and there is the little felllow Duni, who looks like nothing at all but who can feel, by God, who is full of melody and expression. The others around this handful of Memnons are so many donkeys' ears, one pair to a stick. And we're so poor, so beggarly, it's to cry a-mercy. Ah, master Philosopher, poverty is a dreadful thing. I can see her squatting, open-mouthed to catch a few drops of the icy water that flows out of the sieve of the Danaides. I don't know whether she sharpens the wits of a philosopher, but she surely chills the brain of a poet. You can't sing under that sieve—and yet he's a lucky man who can hide under it. I had a place there and wasn't capable of holding it. It had happened to me before. I've traveled in Bohemia, Germany, Switzerland, Holland, Flanders, to the ends of the earth.

MYSELF: Under the sieve?

HE: Under it. He was a rich and free-handed Jew who loved music and my wit. I played music as Providence permitted. I played the fool. I had all I wanted. My Jew was a man who knew his law and lived by it punctiliously—sometimes with friends and invariably with strangers. It led him into a bad pass which I must tell you about because it is amusing.

There was in Utrecht a charming courtesan. My man fell for the Christian girl and despatched a messenger to her with a sizable letter of credit. The singular creature refuses his offer. He was in despair. The messenger says: "Why be so upset? If you want to sleep with a pretty woman, nothing is easier, and even with a prettier one than the one you're after. For the same price you can have my wife." The bargain is struck. The messenger keeps the letter of credit and my Jew sleeps with the fellow's wife. The letter of credit reaches maturity; the Jew lets it be protested and brings a countersuit. "Never," he thinks, "will the fellow admit in court how he obtained possession of the letter, and I shan't have to pay." At the trial he cross-examines the messenger. "This letter of credit, how did you come by it?"—"I had it from you."—"Was it for a loan?"—"No."—"Was it for services rendered?"—"No. You're off the point. The letter is mine, you signed it, and you'll pay it."—"I did not sign it."—"You're calling me a forger?"—"Either you or someone whose agent you are."—"Well, I'm a coward, but you're a swindler. Take it from me, don't force my hand. I'll tell the whole story. I'll lose my honor but you'll go down with me." The Jew made light of the threat and at the next hearing the messenger told everything. They were both castigated. The Jew was condemned to pay and the sum applied to the relief of the poor. It was then I left him and came back to this country.

What could I do? I had to do something or starve. All sorts of projects buzzed in my head. One day I was all for joining a traveling troupe, being equally fit or unfit for the footlights and the orchestra. The next I thought of having a set of pictures painted and put up in a public place, where I would have shouted: "That's his birthplace; there he is leaving his father the apothecary; now he enters the capital looking for

his uncle's house; you see him on his knees before his uncle,
who shows him the door. He joins the household of a Jew,
etc." The day after I would get up resolved to take up with a
band of street singers, and that might not have been the worst
of my ideas. We could have gone to serenade my uncle under
his own windows and made him turn up his toes with vexa-
tion. But I decided on something else. . . .

There he stopped, taking in succession the pose of a man holding a violin and turning the pegs to tune it up, and the pose of a
poor wretch who is worn out with fatigue, who faints and falters
in the legs, who is ready to give up the ghost if one does not throw
him a piece of bread. He showed his extreme need by pointing a
finger at his half-open mouth. Then he said: "You understand.
They would toss me the loaf and we were three or four starve-
lings to wrangle for a share of it. Go and have grand conceptions,
create beauty, on such a diet!"

MYSELF: It is indeed hard.

HE: From tumble to tumble I had fallen you know where.
           I lived there like a rat in a cheese. I left, and now we'll have
           to squeeze the guts again, go back to the gesture of the gaping
           mouth. Nothing is stable in this world. Today at the top of
           the heap, tomorrow at the bottom. Accursed circumstance
           guides us and does it very badly.

Then drinking what was left in one of the bottles and addressing
his neighbor, he said: "Sir, a pinch of snuff, for kindness' sake.
You have a mighty handsome snuff box. You are not a musician?
No? So much the better for you, for they're all poor buggers, a
pitiable lot. Fate has decreed that I should be one, while in Montmartre there may be in a windmill, a miller, or a miller's helper
who has never heard anything but the click of the ratchet but
who would have found the most enchanting melodies. To the
mill, Rameau! To the mill, that's the place for you!"

MYSELF: Whatever a man tries, nature destined him for that.

HE: Then she makes some very odd blunders. I can't for
           myself see from those heights where everything comes to the
           same thing—the man who prunes a tree with his shears and

the slug that eats off the leaves being just two insects each doing his duty. You go and perch on the epicycle of Mercury, and like Réaumur, who classifies the flies into seamstresses, surveyors, and reapers, you classify mankind into carpenters, builders, roofers, dancers, and singers: that's your affair, I shan't meddle with it. I am in *this* world and here I stay. But if it is natural to be hungry—I always come back to hunger, for it's with me an ever-present sensation—I find that it is no part of good order to be sometimes without food. What a hell of an economy! Some men replete with everything while others, whose stomachs are no less importunate, whose hunger is just as recurrent, have nothing to bite on. The worst of it is the constrained posture in which need holds you. The needy man doesn't walk like the rest, he crawls, twists, cringes. He spends his life choosing and performing positions.

MYSELF: What kind of "positions"?

HE: Go ask Noverre the choreographer. The world numbers more positions than his art can reproduce.

MYSELF: So you too, if I may use your expression—or rather that of Montaigne—are perched on the epicycle of Mercury and considering the different pantomimes of humankind.

HE: No, I tell you, no. I am far too clumsy to rise so high. I yield to Aeolus and his winds the kingdom of the clouds. I crawl on the earth, look about me, and take my positions. Or else I entertain myself watching others take theirs. I am good at pantomime, as you shall see.

Thereupon he began to smile, to ape a man admiring, a man imploring, a man complying. His right foot forward, the left behind, his back arched, head erect, open-mouthed, his arms are stretched out toward some object. He waits for a command, receives it, flies like an arrow, returns. The order was carried out; he is giving a report. Attentive, nothing escapes him. He picks up what is dropped, places pillow or stool under feet, holds a salver, brings a chair, opens a door, shuts a window, draws curtains, gazes at master and mistress. He is motionless, arms hanging, legs parallel; he listens and tries to read faces. Then he says: "There you have my pantomime; it's about the same as the flatterer's, the courtier's, the footman's, and the beggar's."

This man's vagaries, like the tales of Abbé Galiani and the extravaganzas of Rabelais, have often plunged me in deep reverie. Those are three storehouses from which I have drawn some absurd masks that I have then projected on the faces of the gravest figures. I seem to see Pantaloon in a prelate, a satyr in a presiding judge, a porker in a friar, an ostrich in a king's minister, and a goose in his under-secretary.

MYSELF: According to you (I went on) there are innumerable wretches in this world, for I hardly know anyone who doesn't use at least a few of your dance steps.

HE: You are right. In the whole country only one man walks—the King. Everybody else takes a position.

MYSELF: The King? Even he might have something to say about that. Don't you suppose that from time to time he finds near him a little foot, a little nose, a little curl that makes him perform a bit of pantomime? Whoever stands in need of another is needy and takes a position. The King takes a position before his mistress, and before God he dances his pantomime steps. The minister trips it too, as courtiers, flatterers, footmen and beggars do before him. The crowd of self-seekers dance all your positions in a hundred ways, each viler than the next, in front of the minister. The noble Abbé, in furred cape and cloak, dances attendance once a week at least before the official who appoints to benefices. Really, what you call the beggar's pantomime is what makes the world go round. Every man has his Bertin and his little Hus.

HE: It's very consoling to me.

While I spoke he mimicked in killing fashion the positions of the figures I enumerated. For the little Abbé, for example, he held his hat under his arm and his breviary in the left hand. With the right he lifted the train of his cloak, stepping forward with his head a little to one side, eyes lowered, and giving the very image of the hypocrite. I thought I was seeing the author of *The Refuta-*

tion petitioning the Bishop of Orleans. When he came to the courtiers and self-seekers, he crawled like a worm—the image of Bouret before the Auditor-General.

MYSELF: Your performance is unsurpassable. But there is one human being who is exempted from the pantomime. That is the philosopher who has nothing and asks for nothing.

HE: And where does the creature hide? If he has nothing, he must be suffering; if he asks for nothing, he will get nothing—and so will always suffer.

MYSELF: No. Diogenes made fun of his wants.

HE: But a man needs clothes.

MYSELF: He went naked.

HE: Wasn't it ever cold in Athens?

MYSELF: Not so often as here.

HE: But people had to eat.

MYSELF: No doubt.

HE: At whose expense?

MYSELF: At Nature's. Whom does the savage beg from? The earth, the animals and fishes, the trees and plants and roots and streams.

HE: An inferior menu.

MYSELF: But abundant.

HE: And badly served.

MYSELF: Yet it's the one whose leavings appear on all our tables.

HE: You have to admit that our cooks, pastrymen, confectioners, and caterers add a little of their own. If your Diogenes stuck to his austere diet, his organs must have been exceedingly docile.

MYSELF: You are wrong. The Cynic's costume was that of our monks and equally virtuous. The Cynics were the Carmelites and Cordeliers of Athens.

HE: I've caught you then! Diogenes must have danced a pantomime, if not in front of Pericles, at least in front of Lais and Phryne?

MYSELF: Wrong again. The others paid dear the same courtesan who gave herself to him for pleasure.

HE: What if the courtesan was busy and the Cynic in haste?

MYSELF: He went back to his tub and did without.

HE: Do you advise me to do the same?

MYSELF: I'll stake my life, it is better than to crawl, eat dirt and prostitute yourself.

HE: But I want a good bed, good food, cool clothes in summer, plenty of rest, money, and other things that I would rather owe to kindness than earn by toil.

MYSELF: That is because you are a lazy, greedy lout, a coward and a rotting soul.

HE: I believe I told you so myself.

MYSELF: The good things of life have their worth, no doubt, but you overlook the price of what you give up for them. You dance, you have danced, and you will keep on dancing the vilest pantomime.

HE: True enough. But it's cost me little and it won't cost me anything more. For which reason I should be quite wrong to take up another position, which would cause me trouble and which I could not hold. But from what you tell me I see that my poor dear little wife was a kind of philosopher. She had the courage of a lion. Sometimes we had no bread and no money and had already sold all our clothes. I would throw myself across the foot of the bed and rack my wits to find someone who would lend us a fiver that I'd never repay. She, gay as a lark, would sing and accompany herself at the clavier. She had the throat of a nightingale; I'm sorry you never heard her. When I took part in some musical evening I took her with me and on the way I would say: "Come, my lady, get yourself admired, display your talents and your charms, overwhelm, captivate." She would sing, overwhelm, captivate. Alas! I lost her, the poor thing. Besides her talents, she had a tiny mouth the width of a finger, a row of pearls for teeth, and then eyes, feet, a skin, cheeks, breasts, legs like a doe, thighs and buttocks for a sculptor. Sooner or later she would have had a Chief tax collector at least. Her walk, her rump, ye gods, what a rump!"

At once he imitated his wife's walk, taking little steps, perking his nose up in the air, flirting with a fan, swinging his hips. It was the caricature of our little coquettes, laughable and true. Then resuming his speech, he said: "I used to take her everywhere—to the Tuileries, the Palais-Royal, the Boulevards. She could not possibly have stayed with me. When she went across the street in the morning, hatless and in her smock, you would have stopped just to look at her and you could have held her waist with both thumbs and forefingers without squeezing her. Those who followed her and watched her trot along on her little feet or who gauged that rich rump outlined in her thin petticoats would hasten their pace. She let them come up then turned on them two big dark and glowing eyes that stopped them in their tracks. For the right side of the medal fully matched the reverse. But alas! I lost her and all my hopes of fortune went with her. I had taken her for no other reason, I had told her my plans. She was too intelligent not to see that they were assured of success and too sound of judgment not to agree with their aim."

At which he began to sob and choke as he said: "No, no, I never shall get over it. Ever since, I've taken minor orders and wear a skullcap."

MYSELF: From grief?

HE: If you like. But really in order to carry my soup plate upon my head. . . . But let's see what time it is, because I am going to the Opera.

MYSELF: What's on the program?

HE: Dauvergne's *Les Troqueurs*. The music has some fine things in it. Too bad he wasn't the first to write them. Among the dead there are always a few to annoy the living. Can't be helped. *Quisque suos non patimur manes.* But it's half-past five; I hear the bell ringing vespers for me and Abbé Canaye. Farewell, master Philosopher, isn't it true that I am ever the same?

MYSELF: Alas! Yes, unfortunately.

HE: Here's hoping this ill fortune lasts me another forty years. He laughs best who laughs last.

Vanina Vanini

STENDHAL

Stendhal

STENDHAL (1783-1842), whose real name was Marie-Henri Beyle, was born at Grenoble into a solid and affectionate middle-class family. He early left home to pursue an eventful career as soldier, diplomat, lover, haunter of Paris drawing rooms and Italian ruins, critic, travel-writer, theorist of sex, biographer and autobiographer. But it is for his long novels *(The Red and the Black, The Charterhouse of Parma, Lucien Leuwen)* that he is chiefly known.

Stendhal professed to write for "the happy few" in his own time but predicted that he would be widely read a century later. This has proved to be true: his once small though enviable audience (it included Balzac, Taine, Goethe, Nietzsche, Tolstoy and Henry James) has grown to vast proportions. On modern French writers in particular, his influence has been great. The traits that once seemed uniquely, even eccentrically, Stendhalian—the dry tone, the confessional frankness, the love of surprise and mystification, the compound of extravagant incident and realistic observation—have come to be almost the national idiom of literary France.

But it is not merely to his odd infectious manner that Stendhal owes his fame. He was a great original, and thus has rekindled the French imagination as Blake and Lawrence have rekindled the English imagination. Neither a romantic nor a realist, but a living fusion of both tendencies, he has helped writers, and men generally, to escape from doctrinaire extremes and become more nearly whole again. In his genius, moreover, the old French tension between enthusiasm and skepticism, love for the spirit and love for the world, received one of its classic expressions. He had fought proudly in the wars of the Empire; but where Vigny and so many others repudiated Napoleon, Stendhal continued to revere him even after Waterloo, as he revered Byron, Rousseau and other exceptional individuals. Set apart by his cult of heroes, cheered and nourished by it, he lived on into the years of the Restoration and the bourgeois monarchy, watching the pursuit of glory and liberty give way before the pursuit of conformity, money and party politics. This was a personal misfortune for Stendhal but it made him a novelist. By studying the heroic temperament in relation to social actuality, he became a great observer of behavior in general, the magnanimous as well as the mean; and in *The Red and the Black* (1831), the older adventure-novel turns decisively into the psychological novel as we know it today.

But the interest of Stendhal's novels is more than psychological, more than social or historical. Dense as they are with the particulars of time and place, they have a way of opening suddenly, blithely, into infinity. For Stendhal's protagonists, neither power nor riches nor the glory of serving some libertarian cause is in the end sufficient. Their physical lives are usually short but their moral life-expectancy is high: they seek the kind of absolute freedom which must finally make them martyrs. Yet they are too proud to be self-righteous; and they are worldly enough to be entirely human. All heroes are tempted, and we are in the habit of saying that it is on their bad or weak side that they are tempted and by virtue of their good or strong side that they are saved. But Stendhal's heroes are all of a piece; it is in their entire being that they are tempted and by their entire being that they are saved. They are as much themselves when escaping from prisons or climbing out of boudoir windows as they are when seeking freedom by way of martyrdom.

Vanina Vanini is essential Stendhal even though it is an early work (1827) and a brief one. The plebeian Missirilli, the high-born Vanina, the pride that alternately brings them together and drives them apart—these are intensely characteristic of Stendhal. His way here of dealing with improbable comic-opera situations is also peculiar to himself. There is no large compelling atmosphere of sensuous and historical detail. The portrait of Roman society is brilliant but simple. Stendhal carries conviction by means of an impassioned factuality. Like *The Charterhouse of Parma*, this story is laid in Italy under the Austrian domination. Believing that Italy could still produce heroes of passion and action, as France no longer could, or could but rarely, Stendhal admired Italy and knew it well. It was the scene of many of his own adventures in war, love, politics and archaeology. We don't doubt him when he says of Missirilli in this story, "He loved as people love for the first time at nineteen and in Italy."

Vanina Vanini

STENDHAL

It was a spring evening in 182—. All Rome was astir: the Duca di B——, the famous banker, was giving a ball in his new palazzo on the Piazza di Venezia. All the most sumptuous treasures that the arts of Italy, the luxury of Paris and London can furnish had been collected for the adornment of this palace. The gathering was immense. The fair, retiring beauties of noble England had intrigued for the honor of being present at this ball; they arrived in crowds. The most beautiful women of Rome vied with them for the prize of beauty. A girl whom her sparkling eyes and ebon tresses proclaimed of Roman birth entered, escorted by her father; every eye followed her. A singular pride was displayed in her every gesture.

One could see the foreigners who entered the room struck by the magnificence of this ball. "None of the courts of Europe," they were saying, "can compare with this."

Kings have not a palace of Roman architecture: they are obliged to invite the great ladies of their courts; the Duca di B—— invites only lovely women. This evening he had been fortunate in his invitations; the men seemed dazzled. Amid so many remarkable women it was hard to decide which was the most beautiful: the award was for some time undetermined; but at length Principessa Vanina Vanini, the girl with the raven hair and fiery eye, was proclaimed queen of the ball. Immediately the foreigners and the young Romans, deserting all the other rooms, crowded into the room in which she was.

Her father, Principe Don Asdrubale Vanini, had wished her to dance first of all with two or three Sovereign Princes from Germany. She then accepted the invitations of certain extremely handsome and extremely noble Englishmen; their starched manner irritated her. She appeared to find more pleasure in teasing young Livio Savelli, who seemed deeply in love. He was the most brilliant young man in Rome, and a Prince to boot; but, if you had given him a novel to read, he would have flung the book away after twenty pages, saying that it made his head ache. This was a disadvantage in Vanina's eyes.

Towards midnight a report ran through the ballroom, which caused quite a stir. A young carbonaro, in detention in the Castel Sant' Angelo, had escaped that evening, with the help of a disguise, and, with an excess of romantic daring, on coming to the outermost guardroom of the prison, had attacked the soldiers there with a dagger; but he had been wounded himself, the *sbirri* were pursuing him through the streets, following the track of his blood, and hoped to recapture him.

While this story was going round, Don Livio Savelli, dazzled by the charms and the success of Vanina, with whom he had just been dancing, said to her as he led her back to her seat, being almost mad with love:

"Why, in heaven's name, what sort of person could please you?"

"This young carbonaro who has just made his escape," was Vanina's reply; "he at least has done something more than take the trouble to be born."

Principe Don Asdrubale approached his daughter. He is a wealthy man who for the last twenty years has kept no accounts with his steward, who lends him his own income at a high rate of interest. If you should pass him in the street, you would take him for an elderly actor; you would not notice that his fingers were loaded with five or six enormous rings set with huge diamonds. His two sons became Jesuits, and afterwards died insane.

He has forgotten them, but it vexes him that his only daughter, Vanina, declines to marry. She is already nineteen, and has refused the most brilliant suitors. What is her reason? The same that led Sulla to abdicate, her *contempt for the Romans.*

On the day after the ball, Vanina remarked that her father, the most casual of men, who never in his life had taken the trouble to carry a key, was very careful in shutting the door of a little stair which led to an apartment on the third floor of the palazzo. The windows of this apartment looked on to a terrace planted with orange trees. Vanina went out to pay some calls in Rome; on her return, the main door of the palazzo was blocked with the preparations for an illumination, the carriage drove in through the courtyards at the back. Vanina raised her eyes, and saw with astonishment that one of the windows of the apartment which her father had so carefully closed was now open. She got rid of her companion, climbed up to the attics of the palazzo and after a long search succeeded in finding a small barred window which overlooked the orange tree terrace. The open window which she had observed from below was within a few feet of her. Evidently the room was occupied; but by whom? Next day, Vanina managed to secure the key of a small door which opened on to the terrace planted with orange trees.

She stole on tiptoe to the window, which was still open. It was screened by a sunblind. Inside the room was a bed, and somebody in the bed. Her first impulse was to retire; but she caught sight of a woman's gown flung over a chair. On looking more closely at the person in the bed, she saw that this person was fair, and evidently quite young. She had no longer any doubt that it was a woman. The gown flung over the chair was stained with blood; there was blood also on the woman's shoes placed beneath a table. The stranger moved in the bed; Vanina saw that she had been wounded. A great bandage stained with blood covered her bosom; this bandage was fastened with ribbons only; it was not a surgeon's hand that had so arranged it. Vanina noticed that every day, about four o'clock, her father shut himself up in his own rooms, and then went to visit the stranger; presently he came

downstairs and took his carriage to call upon the Contessa Vitelleschi. As soon as he had left the house, Vanina went up to the
little terrace, from which she could see the stranger. Her compassion was strongly aroused towards this young woman who
was in such a plight; she tried to imagine what could have befallen
her. The blood-stained gown that lay on the chair appeared to
have been stabbed with a dagger. Vanina could count the rents in
it. One day she saw the stranger more distinctly: her blue eyes
were fastened on the ceiling; she seemed to be praying. Presently
tears welled in those lovely eyes; the young Princess could hardly
refrain from addressing her. Next day, Vanina ventured to hide
on the little terrace before her father came upstairs. She saw Don
Asdrubale enter the stranger's room; he was carrying a small
basket in which were provisions. The Prince appeared ill at ease,
and said but little. He spoke so low that, although the window
stood open, Vanina could not overhear his words. He soon left.

"That poor woman must have very terrible enemies," Vanina
said to herself, "for my father, who is so careless by nature, not
to dare to confide in anyone and to take the trouble to climb a
hundred and twenty steps every day."

One evening, as Vanina was cautiously extending her head
towards the stranger's window, their eyes met, and she was discovered. Vanina fell on her knees, crying:

"I love you, I am your devoted servant."

The stranger beckoned to her to come in.

"How can I apologize to you?" cried Vanina; "how offensive
my foolish curiosity must appear to you! I swear to keep your
secret, and, if you insist on it, I will never come again."

"Who would not be delighted to see you?" said the stranger.
"Do you live in this palazzo?"

"Certainly," replied Vanina. "But I see that you do not know
me: I am Vanina, Don Asdrubale's daughter."

The stranger looked at her with an air of surprise, then went
on:

"Please let me hope that you will come to see me every day;
but I should prefer the Prince not to know of your visits."

Vanina's heart beat violently; the stranger's manner seemed to her most distinguished. This poor young woman had doubtless given offense to some powerful man; possibly in a moment of jealousy she had killed her lover. Vanina could not conceive any common reason for her trouble. The stranger told her that she had received a wound in the shoulder, which had penetrated her breast and gave her great pain. Often she found her mouth filled with blood.

"And you have no surgeon!" cried Vanina.

"You know that in Rome," said the stranger, "the surgeons have to furnish the police with an exact report of all the injuries that they treat. The Prince is kind enough to dress my wounds himself with the bandage you see here."

The stranger refrained with the most perfect taste from any commiseration of her accident; Vanina loved her madly. One incident, however, greatly surprised the young Princess, which was that in the middle of a conversation which was certainly most serious the stranger had great difficulty in suppressing a sudden impulse to laughter.

"I should be happy," Vanina said to her, "to know your name."

"I am called Clementina."

"Very well, dear Clementina, tomorrow at five I shall come to see you."

Next day Vanina found her new friend in great pain.

"I am going to bring you a surgeon," said Vanina as she embraced her.

"I would rather die," said the stranger. "Would you have me compromise my benefactors?"

"The surgeon of Monsignor Savelli-Catanzara, the Governor of Rome, is the son of one of our servants," Vanina answered firmly; "he is devoted to us, and in his position has no fear of anyone. My father does not do justice to his loyalty; I am going to send for him."

"I do not want any surgeon!" cried the stranger with a vivacity which surprised Vanina. "Come and see me, and if God is to call me to Himself, I shall die happy in your arms."

On the following day the stranger was worse.

"If you love me," said Vanina as she left her, "you will see a surgeon."

"If he comes, my happiness is at an end."

"I am going to send to fetch him," replied Vanina.

Without saying a word, the stranger seized hold of her, and took her hand, which she covered with kisses. A long silence followed; tears filled the stranger's eyes. At length she let go Vanina's hand, and with the air of one going to her death, said to her:

"I have a confession to make to you. The day before yesterday, I lied when I said that my name was Clementina; I am an unhappy carbonaro . . ."

Vanina in her astonishment thrust back her chair, and presently rose.

"I feel," went on the carbonaro, "that this confession is going to make me forfeit the one blessing which keeps me alive; but I should be unworthy of myself were I to deceive you. My name is Pietro Missirilli; I am nineteen; my father is a poor surgeon at Sant' Angelo in Vado, I myself am a carbonaro. Our *venuta* was surprised; I was brought, in chains, from the Romagna to Rome. Cast into a dungeon lighted day and night by a lamp, I lay there for thirteen months. A charitable soul conceived the idea of helping me to escape. I was dressed as a woman. As I was leaving the prison and passing by the guard at the outer gate, one of them cursed the carbonari; I dealt him a blow. I swear to you that it was not a piece of vain bravado, but simply that I was not thinking. Pursued by night through the streets of Rome after that act of folly, stabbed with bayonet wounds, I had begun to lose my strength, I entered a house the door of which stood open, I heard the soldiers coming in after me, I sprang into a garden; I fell to the ground within a few feet of a woman who was walking there."

"Contessa Vitelleschi! My father's mistress," said Vanina.

"What! Has she told you?" cried Missirilli. "However that may be, this lady, whose name must never be uttered, saved my life.

As the soldiers were coming into her house to seize me, your father took me away in his carriage. I feel very ill: for some days this bayonet wound in my shoulder has prevented me from breathing. I am going to die, and in despair, since I shall not see you again."

Vanina had listened with impatience; she swiftly withdrew from the room. Missirilli read no pity in those lovely eyes, but only the signs of a proud nature which had been deeply offended.

When it was dark, a surgeon appeared; he was alone. Missirilli was in despair; he was afraid that he would never see Vanina again. He questioned the surgeon, who bled him and made no reply. A similar silence on each of the days that followed. Pietro's eyes never left the window on the terrace by which Vanina used to enter; he was very miserable. Once, about midnight, he thought he could see someone in the dark on the terrace: was it Vanina?

Vanina came each night to press her face against the panes of the young carbonaro's window.

"If I speak to him," she said to herself, "I am lost! No, I must never see him again!"

Having come to this resolution, she recalled, in spite of herself, the affection that she had formed for this young man when she had so stupidly taken him for a woman. After so pleasant an intimacy, must she then forget him? In her most reasonable moments, Vanina was alarmed by the change that was occurring in her ideas. Ever since Missirilli had told her his name, all the things of which she was in the habit of thinking were, so to speak, wrapped in a veil of mist, and appeared to her now only at a distance.

A week had not gone by before Vanina, pale and trembling, entered the young carbonaro's room with the surgeon. She had come to tell him that he must make the Prince promise to let his place be taken by a servant. She was not in the room for ten seconds; but some days later she came back again with the surgeon, from a sense of humanity. One evening, although Missirilli was much better, and Vanina had no longer the excuse

of being alarmed for his life, she ventured to come unaccompanied. On seeing her, Missirilli was raised to a pinnacle of
joy, but he was careful to conceal his love; whatever happened,
he was determined not to forget the dignity befitting a man.
Vanina, who had come into the room blushing a deep crimson,
and dreading amorous speeches, was disconcerted by the noble
and devoted, but by no means tender friendliness with which he
greeted her. She left without his making any attempt to detain
her.

A few days later, when she returned, the same conduct, the
same assurances of respectful devotion and eternal gratitude. So
far from being occupied in putting a check on the transports of
the young carbonaro, Vanina asked herself whether she alone
were in love. This girl, hitherto so proud, was bitterly aware of
the full extent of her folly. She made a pretence of gaiety, and
even of coldness, came less frequently, but could not bring herself
to abandon her visits to the young invalid.

Missirilli, burning with love, but mindful of his humble birth
and of what he owed to himself, had made a vow that he would
not stoop to talk of love unless Vanina were to spend a week
without seeing him. The pride of the young Princess contested
every inch of ground.

"After all," she said to herself at length, "if I see him, it is for
my own sake, to please myself, and I will never confess to him
the interest that he arouses in me."

She paid long visits to Missirilli, who talked to her as he might
have done had there been a score of persons present. One evening,
after she had spent the day hating him, and promising herself
that she would be even colder and more severe with him than
usual, she told him that she loved him. Soon there was nothing
left that she could withhold from him.

Great as her folly may have been, it must be admitted that
Vanina was sublimely happy. Missirilli no longer thought of
what he believed to be due to his dignity as a man; he loved
as people love for the first time at nineteen and in Italy. He felt
all the scruples of "impassioned love," going so far as to confess

to this haughty young Princess the stratagem which he had
employed to make her love him. He was astounded by the fullness
of his happiness. Four months passed rapidly enough. One day
the surgeon set his patient at liberty. "What am I to do now?"
thought Missirilli; "lie concealed in the house of one of the most
beautiful people in Rome? And the vile tyrants who kept me for
thirteen months in prison without ever allowing me to see the
light of day will think they have disheartened me! Italy, thou
art indeed unfortunate, if thy sons forsake thee for so slight a
cause!"

Vanina never doubted that Pietro's greatest happiness lay in remaining permanently attached to herself; he seemed only too
happy; but a saying of General Bonaparte echoed harshly in the
young man's heart and influenced the whole of his conduct with
regard to women. In 1796, as General Bonaparte was leaving
Brescia, the municipal councilors who were escorting him to the
gate of the city told him that the Brescians loved freedom more
than any of the Italians.

"Yes," he replied, "they love to talk about it to their mistresses."

Missirilli said to Vanina with a visible air of constraint:

"As soon as it is dark, I must go out."

"Be careful to come in again before daybreak; I shall be waiting
for you."

"By daybreak I shall be many miles from Rome."

"Very well," said Vanina coldly, "and where are you going?"

"To the Romagna, to have my revenge."

"As I am rich," Vanina went on with perfect calmness, "I hope
that you will let me supply you with arms and money."

Missirilli looked at her for some moments without moving a
muscle; then, flinging himself into her arms:

"Soul of my life," he said to her, "you make me forget everything, even my duty. But the nobler your heart is, the better you
must understand me."

Vanina wept freely, and it was agreed that he should not leave
Rome until the following night.

"Pietro," she said to him on the morrow, "you have often told me that a well-known man, a Roman Prince, for instance, with plenty of money at his disposal, would be in a position to render the utmost services to the cause of freedom, should Austria ever be engaged abroad, in some great war."

"Undoubtedly," said Pietro in surprise.

"Very well, you have a stout heart; all you lack is an exalted position: I have come to offer you my hand and an income of two hundred thousand lire. I undertake to obtain my father's consent."

Pietro fell at her feet; Vanina was radiant with joy.

"I love you passionately," he told her; "but I am a humble servant of the Fatherland; the more unhappy Italy is, the more loyal I should be to her. To obtain Don Asdrubale's consent, I shall have to play a sorry part for many years. Vanina, I decline your offer."

Missirilli made haste to bind himself by this utterance. His courage was failing him.

"My misfortune," he cried, "is that I love you more than life itself, that to leave Rome is for me the most agonizing torture. Oh, that Italy were set free from the barbarians! With what joy would I set sail with you to go and live in America."

Vanina's heart was frozen. The refusal of her hand had dealt a blow to her pride; but presently she threw herself into Missirilli's arms.

"Never have you seemed so adorable," she cried; "yes, my little country surgeon, I am yours forever. You are a great man, like our ancient Romans."

All thoughts of the future, every depressing suggestion of common sense vanished; it was a moment of perfect love. When they were able to talk reasonably:

"I shall be in the Romagna almost as soon as you," said Vanina. "I am going to have myself sent to the baths of la Porretta. I shall stop at the villa we have at San Niccolò, close to Forlì. . . ."

"There I shall spend my life with you!" cried Missirilli.

"My lot henceforward is to dare all," Vanina continued with

a sigh. "I shall ruin myself for you, but no matter. . . . Will you be able to love a girl who has lost her honor?"

"Are you not my wife," said Missirilli, "and the object of my lifelong adoration? I shall know how to love and protect you."

Vanina was obliged to go out, on social errands. She had barely left Missirilli before he began to feel that his conduct was barbarous.

"What is the *Fatherland*?" he asked himself. "It is not a person to whom we owe gratitude for benefits received, or who may suffer and call down curses on us if we fail him. The *Fatherland* and *Freedom* are like my cloak, a thing which is useful to me, which I must purchase, it is true, when I have not acquired it by inheritance from my father; but after all I love the Fatherland and Freedom because they are both useful to me. If I have no use for them, if they are to me like a cloak in the month of August, what is the good of purchasing them, and at an enormous price? Vanina is so beautiful! She has so singular a nature! Others will seek to attract her; she will forget me. What woman is there who has never had more than one lover? Those Roman Princes, whom I despise as citizens, have so many advantages over me! They must indeed be attractive! Ah, if I go, she will forget me, and I shall lose her forever."

In the middle of the night, Vanina came to see him; he told her of the uncertainty in which he had been plunged, and the criticism to which, because he loved her, he had subjected that great word "Fatherland." Vanina was very happy.

"If he were absolutely forced to choose between his country and me," she told herself, "I should have the preference."

The clock of the neighboring church struck three, the time had come for a final leave-taking. Pietro tore himself from the arms of his mistress. He had begun to descend the little stair, when Vanina, restraining her tears, said to him with a smile:

"If you had been nursed by some poor woman in the country, would you do nothing to show your gratitude? Would you not seek to repay her? The future is uncertain, you are going on a journey through the midst of your enemies: give me three days out of gratitude, as if I were a poor woman, and to pay me for the care I have taken of you."

Missirilli stayed. At length he left Rome. Thanks to a passport bought from a foreign embassy, he returned in safety to his family. This was a great joy to them; they had given him up for dead. His friends wished to celebrate his home-coming by killing a carabiniere or two (such is the title borne by the police in the Papal States).

"We must not, when it is not necessary, kill an Italian who knows how to handle arms," said Missirilli; "our country is not an island, like happy England: it is soldiers that we need to resist the intervention of the Sovereigns of Europe."

Some time later Missirilli, hard pressed by the carabinieri, killed a couple of them with the pistols which Vanina had given him. A price was set on his head.

Vanina did not appear in the Romagna: Missirilli imagined himself forgotten. His vanity was hurt; his thoughts began to dwell upon the difference in rank which divided him from his mistress. In a moment of weakness and regret for his past happiness it occurred to him that he might return to Rome to see what Vanina was doing. This mad idea was beginning to prevail over what he believed to be his duty when one evening the bell of a church in the mountains sounded the Angelus in a singular fashion, and as though the ringer were thinking of something else. It was the signal for the assembling of the *venuta* of carbonari which Missirilli had joined on his arrival in Romagna. That night, they all met at a certain hermitage in the woods. The two hermits, drugged with opium, knew nothing of the use to which their little dwelling was being put. Missirilli, who arrived in great depression, learned there that the leader of the *venuta* had been arrested, and that he, a young man not twenty years old, was about to be elected leader of a *venuta* which included men of fifty and more, who had taken part in all the conspiracies since Murat's expedition in 1815. On receiving this unexpected honor, Pietro felt his heart beat violently. As soon as he was alone, he determined to give no more thought to the young Roman who

had forgotten him, and to devote his whole mind to the duty of
*freeing Italy from the barbarians.**

Two days later, Missirilli saw in the reports of arrivals and departures which were supplied to him, as leader of the *venuta*, that
the Principessa Vanina had just arrived at her villa of San Niccolò.
The sight of that name caused him more uneasiness than pleasure.
It was in vain that he imagined himself to be proving his loyalty
to his country by undertaking not to fly that very evening to the
villa of San Niccolò; the thought of Vanina, whom he was neglecting, prevented him from carrying out his duty in a reasonable
manner. He saw her next day; she loved him still as in Rome.
Her father, who wished her to marry, had delayed her departure.
She brought him two thousand sequins. This unexpected assistance
served admirably to accredit Missirilli in his new office. They had
daggers made for them in Corfu; they won over the Legate's
private secretary, whose duty it was to pursue the carbonari. Thus
they obtained a list of the clergy who were acting as spies for
the government.

It was at this time that the organization was completed of one
of the least senseless conspiracies that have been planned in unhappy Italy. I shall not enter here into irrelevant details. I shall
merely say that if success had crowned the attempt, Missirilli
would have been able to claim a good share of the glory. At a
signal from him, several thousands of insurgents would have risen,
and awaited, armed, the coming of their superior leaders. The
decisive moment was approaching when, as invariably happens,
the conspiracy was paralyzed by the arrest of the leaders.

Immediately on her arrival in Romagna, Vanina felt that his
love of his country would make her young lover forget all other
love. The young Roman's pride was stung. She tried in vain to
reason with herself; a black melancholy seized her: she found
herself cursing freedom. One day when she had come to Forlì

---

* *Liberar l'Italia de' barbari*: the words used by Petrarch in 1350, and
since then repeated by Julius II, Machiavelli and Conte Alfieri. *Author's
note.*

to see Missirilli, she was powerless to check her grief, which until then her pride had managed to control.

"Truly," she said to him, "you love me like a husband; that is not what I have a right to expect."

Soon her tears flowed; but they were tears of shame at having so far lowered herself as to reproach him. Missirilli responded to these tears like a man preoccupied with other things. Suddenly it occurred to Vanina to leave him and return to Rome. She found a cruel joy in punishing herself for the weakness that had made her speak. After a brief interval of silence, her mind was made up; she would feel herself unworthy of Missirilli if she did not leave him. She rejoiced in the thought of his pained surprise when he should look around for her in vain. Presently the reflection that she had not succeeded in obtaining the love of the man for whom she had done so many foolish things moved her profoundly. Then she broke the silence, and did everything in the world to wring from him a word of love. He said, with a distracted air, certain quite tender things to her; but it was in a very different tone that, in speaking of his political enterprises, he sorrowfully exclaimed:

"Ah, if this attempt does not succeed, if the government discovers it again, I give up the struggle."

Vanina remained motionless. For the last hour, she had felt that she would never look upon her lover again. The words he had now uttered struck a fatal spark in her mind. She said to herself:

"The carbonari have had several thousands from me. No one can doubt my devotion to the conspiracy."

Vanina emerged from her musings only to say to Pietro:

"Will you come and spend the night with me at San Niccolò? Your meeting this evening can do without you. Tomorrow morning, at San Niccolò, we can take the air together; that will calm your agitation and restore the cool judgment you require on great occasions."

Pietro agreed.

Vanina left him to make ready for the journey, locking the door, as usual, of the little room in which she had hidden him.

She hastened to the house of one of her former maids who had left her service to marry and keep a small shop in Forlì. On reaching the house, she wrote in haste on the margin of a Book of Hours which she found in the woman's room, an exact indication of the spot at which the *venuta* of carbonari was to assemble that evening. She concluded her denunciation with the words: "This *venuta* is composed of nineteen members; their names and addresses are as follows." Having written this list, which was quite accurate except that the name of Missirilli was omitted, she said to the woman, on whom she could rely:

"Take this book to the Cardinal Legate; make him read what is written in it, and give you back the book. Here are ten sequins; if the Legate ever utters your name, your death is certain; but you will save my life if you make the Legate read the page I have just written."

All went well. The Legate's fear prevented him from standing upon his dignity. He allowed the humble woman who asked to speak with him to appear before him with only a mask, but on condition that her hands were tied. In this state the shopkeeper was brought into the presence of the great personage, whom she found entrenched behind an immense table, covered with a green cloth.

The Legate read the page in the Book of Hours, holding it at a distance, for fear of some subtle poison. He gave it back to the woman, and did not have her followed. In less than forty minutes after she had left her lover, Vanina, who had seen her former maid return, appeared once more before Missirilli, imagining that for the future he was entirely hers. She told him that there was an extraordinary commotion in the town; patrols of carabinieri were to be seen in streets along which they never went as a rule.

"If you will take my advice," she went on, "we will start this very instant for San Niccolò."

Missirilli agreed. They proceeded on foot to the young Princess's carriage, which, with her companion, a discreet and well-rewarded confidant, was waiting for her half a league from the town.

Having reached the San Niccolò villa, Vanina, disturbed by the thought of what she had done, multiplied her attentions to her lover. But when speaking to him of love she felt that she was playing a part. The day before, when she betrayed him, she had forgotten remorse. As she clasped her lover in her arms, she said to herself:

"There is a certain word which someone may say to him, and once that word is uttered, then and for all time, he will regard me with horror."

In the middle of the night, one of Vanina's servants came boldly into her room. This man was a carbonaro, and she had never known it. So Missirilli had secrets from her, even in these matters of detail. She shuddered. The man had come to inform Missirilli that during the night, at Forlì, the houses of nineteen carbonari had been surrounded and they themselves arrested as they were returning from the *venuta*. Although taken unawares, nine of them had escaped. The carabinieri had managed to convey ten to the prison of the citadel. On their way in, one of these had flung himself down the well, which was deep, and had killed himself.

Vanina lost countenance; happily Pietro did not observe her; he could have read her crime in her eyes. . . . "At the present moment," the servant went on, "the Forlì garrison is lining all the streets. Each soldier is close enough to the next to be able to speak to him. The inhabitants cannot cross from one side of the street to the other except at the places where there is an officer posted."

After the man had left them, Pietro remained pensive for a moment only.

"There is nothing to be done for the present," he said finally.

Vanina was half dead; she trembled under her lover's gaze.

"Why, what is the matter with you?" he asked her.

Then his thoughts turned to other things, and he ceased to look at her. Towards midday she ventured to say to him:

"And so another *venuta* has been surprised; I hope that you are going to be undisturbed now for some time."

"Quite undisturbed," replied Missirilli with a smile which made her shudder.

She went to pay a necessary call upon the parish priest of San Niccolò, who might perhaps be a spy of the Jesuits. On returning to dine at seven o'clock, she found the little room in which her lover had been concealed empty. Beside herself with alarm, she ran over the whole house in search of him. In despair, she returned to the little room, and it was only then that she saw a note; she read:

"I am going to give myself up to the Legate; I despair of our cause; heaven is against us. Who has betrayed us? Evidently the wretch who flung himself down the well. Since my life is of no use to poor Italy, I do not wish that my comrades, seeing that I alone have not been arrested, should imagine that I have sold them. Farewell; if you love me, try to avenge me. Destroy, crush the scoundrel who has betrayed us, even if he should be my own father."

Vanina sank down on a chair, half unconscious, and plunged in the most agonizing grief. She could not utter a word; her eyes were parched and burning.

At length she flung herself upon her knees:

"Great God!" she cried, "hear my vow; yes, I will punish the scoundrel who has betrayed them; but first I must set Pietro free."

An hour later, she was on her way to Rome. Her father had long been pressing her to return. During her absence, he had arranged her marriage with Principe Livio Savelli. Immediately on Vanina's arrival, he spoke to her of this marriage, in fear and trembling. Greatly to his surprise, she consented from the first. That evening, at Contessa Vitelleschi's, her father presented to her, semiofficially, Don Livio; she conversed with him freely. He was the most exquisite young man, and had the finest horses of any; but although he was admitted to have plenty of intelligence, he was regarded as so frivolous that he was held in no suspicion by the government. Vanina reflected that, by first of all turning his head, she might make a useful agent of him. As he was the nephew of Monsignor Savelli-Catanzara, Governor of Rome and Minister of Police, she supposed that the government spies would not dare to follow him.

After showing herself most kind, for some days, to the charming Don Livio, Vanina broke to him that he could never be her husband; he had, according to her, too light a mind.

"If you were not a mere boy," she told him, "your uncle's clerks would have no secrets for you. For instance, what action is being taken with regard to the carbonari who were surprised the other day at Forlì?"

Don Livio came to inform her, a few days later, that all the carbonari taken at Forlì had escaped. She let her large black eyes rest on him with a bitter smile of the most profound contempt, and did not condescend to speak to him throughout the evening. Two days later, Don Livio came to confess to her, blushing as he did so, that he had been misinformed at first.

"But," he told her, "I have secured a key to my uncle's room; I see from the papers I found there that a *congregation* (or commission) composed of the Cardinals and prelates who are most highly considered is meeting in the strictest secrecy, and discussing whether it would be better to try these carbonari at Ravenna or in Rome. The nine carbonari taken at Forlì and their leader, a certain Missirilli, who was fool enough to give himself up, are at this moment confined in the castle of San Leo.*

At the word "fool," Vanina gripped the Prince with all her strength.

"I wish," she said, "to see the official papers myself, and to go with you into your uncle's room; you must have misread what you saw."

At these words, Don Livio shuddered; Vanina asked a thing that was almost impossible; but the girl's eccentric nature intensified his love for her. A few days later, Vanina, disguised as a

* Near Rimini in Romagna. It was in this castle that the famous Cagliostro died; the local report is that he was smothered there. *Author's note.*

man and wearing a neat little jacket in the livery of the casa
Savelli, was able to spend half an hour among the most secret
documents of the Minister of Police. She started with joyful
excitement when she came upon the daily report on *Pietro Mis-*
sirilli, on remand. Her hands shook as she seized the paper. On
reading the name again, she felt as though she must faint. As they
left the palace of the Governor of Rome, Vanina permitted Don
Livio to embrace her.

"You are coming very well," she told him, "through the tests
to which I mean to subject you."

After such a compliment, the young Prince would have set fire
to the Vatican to please Vanina. That evening, there was a ball
at the French Ambassador's; she danced frequently, and almost
always with him. Don Livio was wild with joy; he must be kept
from thinking.

"My father sometimes acts oddly," Vanina said to him one day;
"this morning he dismissed two of his servants, who came to me
in tears. One asked me to find him a place with your uncle the
Governor of Rome; the other, who served as a gunner under the
French, wishes to be employed in the Castel Sant' Angelo."

"I will take them both into my service," said the young Prince
impulsively.

"Is that what I am asking you to do?" Vanina answered
haughtily. "I repeat to you word for word the request made by
these poor men; they must obtain what they have asked for,
and nothing else."

It was the hardest thing imaginable. Monsignor Catanzara was
the most serious of men, and admitted into his household only
people well known to himself. In the midst of a life filled, apparently, with every pleasure, Vanina, crushed by remorse, was
most unhappy. The slow course of events was killing her. Her
father's man of business had supplied her with money. Ought she
to fly from the paternal roof and make her way to the Romagna
to try to compass her lover's escape? Absurd as this idea was, she
was on the point of putting it into execution, when chance took
pity on her.

Don Livio said to her:

"The ten carbonari of the Missirilli *venuta* are going to be transferred to Rome, except that they will be executed in the Romagna after they have been sentenced. My uncle obtained the Pope's authority for that this evening. You and I are the only two people in Rome who know this secret. Are you satisfied?"

"You are growing into a man," replied Vanina; "you may make me a present of your portrait."

On the day before that on which Missirilli was to reach Rome, Vanina found an excuse for going to Città Castellana. It is in the prison of this town that carbonari are lodged on their way from the Romagna to Rome. She saw Missirilli in the morning, as he was leaving the prison: he was chained by himself upon a cart; he struck her as very pale but not at all despondent. An old woman tossed him a bunch of violets; Missirilli thanked her with a smile.

Vanina had seen her lover, her mind seemed to revive; she felt fresh courage. Long before this she had procured a fine advancement for the Abate Cari, Chaplain of the Castel Sant' Angelo, in which her lover was to be confined; she had chosen this worthy priest as her confessor. It is no small matter in Rome to be the confessor of a Princess, who is the Governor's niece.

The trial of the carbonari from Forlì did not take long. To be revenged for their transfer to Rome, which it had been unable to prevent, the "ultra" party had the commission which was to try them packed with the most ambitious prelates. Over this commission presided the Minister of Police.

The law against the carbonari is clear: the men from Forlì could entertain no hope; they fought for their lives nevertheless by every possible subterfuge. Not only did their judges condemn them to death, but several were in favor of cruel tortures, amputation of the right hand, and so forth. The Minister of Police, whose fortune was made (for one leaves that office only to assume the Hat), was in no need of amputated hands: on submitting the sentence to the Pope, he had the penalty commuted to some years of imprisonment for all the prisoners. The sole exception was Pietro Missirilli. The Minister regarded the young man as a dangerous fanatic, in addition to which he had already been sentenced to death as guilty of the murder of the two carabinieri whom we have mentioned. Vanina knew of the sentence and its commutation within a few minutes of the Minister's return from seeing the Pope.

On the following evening, when Monsignor Catanzara returned to his palace about midnight, his valet was not to be found; the Minister, somewhat surprised, rang several times; finally an aged and half-witted servant appeared; the Minister, losing patience, decided to undress himself. He turned the key in his door; it was a hot night: he took off his coat, and flung it in a heap upon a chair. This coat, thrown with excessive force, went beyond the chair, and fell against the muslin curtain of the window, behind which it outlined the figure of a man. The Minister sprang swiftly to his bedside and seized a pistol. As he was returning to the window, a man quite young, wearing his livery, came towards him, pistol in hand. Seeing him advance, the Minister raised his own pistol to his eye; and was about to fire. The young man said to him with a laugh:

"Why, Monsignor, do not you recognize Vanina Vanini?"

"What is the meaning of this ill-timed foolery?" replied the Minister angrily.

"Let us discuss the matter calmly," said the girl. "In the first place, your pistol is not loaded."

The Minister, taken aback, found that this was so; whereupon he took out a dagger from the pocket of his waistcoat.*

Vanina said to him with a charming little air of authority:

* A Roman prelate would doubtless be incapable of commanding an Army Corps with gallantry, as happened more than once in the case of a divisional general who was Minister of Police in Paris, at the time of the Malet conspiracy; but he would never allow himself to be held up so simply as this in his own house. He would be too much afraid of the satirical comment of his colleagues. A Roman who knows himself to be hated always goes about well armed. It has not been thought necessary to give authority for various other slight differences between Parisian and Roman habits of speech and behavior. So far from minimizing these differences, we have felt it our duty to indicate them boldly. The Romans whom we are describing have not the honor to be French. *Author's note.*

"Let us be seated, Monsignore."

And she took her seat calmly upon a sofa.

"Are you alone, tell me that?" said the Minister.

"Absolutely alone, I swear to you!" cried Vanina.

The Minister took care to verify this assurance: he made a tour of the room and searched everywhere; after which he sat down upon a chair three paces away from Vanina.

"What object could I have," said Vanina with a calm and winning air, "in attempting the life of a man of moderate views, who would probably be succeeded by some weak hothead, capable of destroying himself and other people?"

"What is your purpose then, Signorina?" said the Minister crossly. "This scene is highly improper and must not continue."

"What I am going to add," Vanina went on haughtily, suddenly forgetting her gracious manner, "concerns you rather than myself. The life of the carbonaro Missirilli must be saved: if he is executed, you shall not outlive him by a week. I have no interest in the matter; the foolish action of which you complain was planned, first of all, for my own amusement, and also to oblige one of my friends. I wished," went on Vanina, resuming her air of good breeding, "to do a service to a man of talent, who will shortly become my uncle, and ought, one would say, to enhance considerably the fame and fortune of his house."

The Minister ceased to appear angry: Vanina's beauty no doubt contributed to this rapid alteration. Monsignor Catanzara's fondness for pretty women was well known in Rome, and in her disguise as a footman of the casa Savelli, with close-fitting silk stockings, a red waistcoat, her little sky-blue jacket with its silver braid, and the pistol in her hand, Vanina was irresistible.

"My future niece," said the Minister, almost laughing, "you are doing a very foolish thing, and it will not be the last."

"I trust that so wise a person as yourself," replied Vanina, "will keep my secret, especially from Don Livio; and to bind you, my dear uncle, if you grant me the life of my friend's favorite, I will give you a kiss."

It was by continuing the conversation in this half-jocular tone, with which Roman ladies know how to discuss the most serious matters, that Vanina succeeded in giving to this interview, begun pistol in hand, the semblance of a visit paid by the young Principessa Savelli to her uncle the Governor of Rome.

Soon Monsignor Catanzara, while rejecting with lofty scorn the idea that he could let himself be influenced by fear, found himself explaining to his niece all the difficulties that he would meet in trying to save Missirilli's life. As he talked, the Minister strolled up and down the room with Vanina; he took a decanter of lemonade that stood on the mantelpiece and poured some of the liquid into a crystal glass. Just as he was about to raise it to his lips, Vanina took it from him, and, after holding it in her hand for some time, let it fall into the garden, as though by accident. A moment later the Minister took a chocolate drop from a comfit box. Vanina seized it from him, saying with a smile:

"Take care, now; everything in the room is poisoned; for your death was intended. It was I who obtained a reprieve for my future uncle, that I might not enter the house of Savelli absolutely empty-handed."

Monsignor Catanzara, greatly astonished, thanked his niece, and gave her good reason to hope for the life of Missirilli.

"Our bargain is made!" cried Vanina, "and in proof of it, here is your reward," she said, kissing him.

The Minister accepted his reward.

"You must understand, my dear Vanina," he went on, "that I myself do not like bloodshed. Besides, I am still young, though to you perhaps I may appear very old, and I may survive to a time in which blood spilled today will leave a stain."

Two o'clock was striking when Monsignor Catanzara accompanied Vanina to the little gate of his garden.

A couple of days later, when the Minister appeared before the Pope, considerably embarrassed by the action which he had to take, His Holiness began:

"First of all, I have a favor to ask of you. There is one of those carbonari from Forlì who is under sentence of death; the thought of him keeps me awake at night: the man's life must be spared."

The Minister, seeing that the Pope had made up his mind,

raised a number of objections, and ended by writing out a decree or *motu proprio*, which the Pope signed, regardless of precedent.

Vanina had thought that she might perhaps obtain her lover's reprieve, but that an attempt would be made to poison him. The day before, Missirilli had received from the Abate Cari, his confessor, several little packets of ship's biscuit, with a warning not to touch the food supplied by the State.

Having afterwards learned that the carbonari from Forlì were to be transferred to the Castle of San Leo, she decided to attempt to see Missirilli as he passed through Città Castellana; she arrived in that town twenty-four hours ahead of the prisoners; there she found the Abate Cari, who had preceded her by several days. He had obtained the concession from the jailer that Missirilli might hear mass, at midnight, in the prison chapel. This was not all: if Missirilli would consent to have his arms and legs chained together, the jailer would withdraw to the door of the chapel, in such a way as not to lose sight of the prisoner, for whom he was responsible, but to be out of hearing of anything he might say.

The day which was to decide Vanina's fate dawned at last. As soon as morning came, she shut herself up in the prison chapel. Who could describe the thoughts that disturbed her mind during that long day? Did Missirilli love her sufficiently to forgive her? She had denounced his *venuta*, but she had saved his life. When reason prevailed in her tormented brain, Vanina hoped that he would consent to leave Italy with her: if she had sinned, it was from excess of love. As four was striking, she heard in the distance, on the cobbled street, the hooves of the carabinieri's horses. The sound of each hoofbeat seemed to strike an echo from her heart. Presently she could make out the rumbling of the carts in which the prisoners were being conveyed. They stopped in the little piazza outside the prison; she saw two carabinieri lift up Missirilli, who was alone on one cart, and so loaded with irons that he could not move. "At least he is alive," she said to herself, the tears welling into her eyes, "they have not poisoned him yet." The evening was agonizing; the altar lamp, hanging at a great height, and sparingly supplied with oil by the jailer, was the only light in the dark chapel. Vanina's eyes strayed over the tombs of various great nobles of the Middle Ages who had died in the adjoining prison. Their statues wore an air of ferocity.

All sounds had long ceased; Vanina was absorbed in her somber thoughts. Shortly after midnight had struck, she thought she heard a faint sound, like the fluttering of a bat. She tried to walk, and fell half fainting against the altar rail. At that moment, two specters appeared close beside her, whom she had not heard come in. They were the jailer and Missirilli, so loaded with chains as to be almost smothered in them. The jailer opened a dark lantern which he placed on the altar rail, by Vanina's side, in such a way as to give him a clear view of his prisoner. He then withdrew to the other end of the chapel, by the door. No sooner had the jailer moved away than Vanina flung herself on Missirilli's bosom. As she clasped him in her arms, she felt only the cold edges of his chains. "To whom does he owe these chains?" was her thought. She felt no pleasure in embracing her lover. This grief was followed by another even more poignant; she fancied for a moment that Missirilli was aware of her crime, so frigid was his greeting.

"Dear friend," he said to her at length, "I regret the affection that you have formed for me; I seek in vain to discover what merit in me has been capable of inspiring it. Let us return, believe me, to more Christian sentiments, let us forget the illusions which hitherto have been leading us astray; I cannot belong to you. The constant misfortune that has dogged my undertakings is due perhaps to the state of mortal sin into which I have so often fallen. To listen only to the counsels of human prudence, why was not I arrested with my friends, on that fatal night at Forlì? Why, in the moment of danger, was I not found at my post? Why has my absence then furnished grounds for the most cruel suspicions? I had another passion besides that for the liberation of Italy."

Vanina could not get over her surprise at the change in Missirilli. Without being perceptibly thinner, he had the air of a man of thirty. Vanina attributed this change to the ill treatment which he had undergone in prison, and burst into tears.

"Ah!" she said, "the jailers promised so faithfully that they would treat you well."

The fact was that at the approach of death all the religious principles consistent with his passion for the liberation of Italy had revived in the heart of the young carbonaro. Gradually Vanina realized that the astonishing change which she had re-marked in her lover was entirely moral, and in no way the effect of bodily ill treatment. Her grief, which she had supposed to have reached its extreme limit, was intensified still further.

Missirilli was silent; Vanina seemed to be on the point of being suffocated by her sobs. He spoke, and himself also appeared slightly moved:

"If I loved any single thing in the world, it would be you, Vanina; but, thanks be to God, I have now but one object in life; I shall die either in prison or in seeking to give Italy freedom."

Another silence followed; evidently Vanina was incapable of speech: she attempted to speak, but in vain. Missirilli went on:

"Duty is cruel, my friend; but if it were not a little difficult to perform, where would be the heroism? Give me your word that you will not attempt to see me again."

So far as the chain that was wound tightly about him would allow, he made a slight movement with his wrist and held out his fingers to Vanina.

"If you will accept the advice of one who was once dear to you, be sensible and marry the deserving man whom your father has chosen for you. Do not confide in him anything that may lead to trouble; but, on the other hand, never seek to see me again; let us henceforward be strangers to one another. You have advanced a considerable sum for the service of the Fatherland; if ever it is delivered from its tyrants, that sum will be faithfully repaid to you in national bonds."

Vanina was crushed. While he was speaking, Pietro's eye had gleamed only at the moment when he mentioned the Fatherland.

At length pride came to the rescue of the young Princess;

she had brought with her a supply of diamonds and small files. Without answering Missirilli, she offered him these.

"I accept from a sense of duty," he told her, "for I must seek to escape; but I will never see you, I swear it by this latest token of your bounty. Farewell, Vanina; promise me never to write, never to attempt to see me; leave me wholly to the Fatherland, I am dead to you: farewell."

"No," replied Vanina, grown furious, "I wish you to know what I have done, led on by the love that I bear you."

She then related to him all her activities from the moment when Missirilli had left the villa of San Niccolò to give himself up to the Legate. When her tale was finished:

"All this is nothing," said Vanina: "I have done more, in my love for you."

She then told him of her betrayal.

"Ah, monster," cried Pietro, mad with rage, hurling himself upon her; and sought to crush her to the ground with his chains.

He would have succeeded but for the jailer, who came running at the sound of her cries. He seized Missirilli.

"There, monster, I will not owe anything to you," said Missirilli to Vanina, flinging at her, as violently as his chains would allow him, the files and diamonds, and he moved rapidly away.

Vanina was left speechless. She returned to Rome: and the newspapers announce that she has just been married to Principe Don Livio Savelli.

The Malacca Cane

ALFRED DE VIGNY

ALFRED DE VIGNY (1797-1863) was born at Loches of a noble
family, entered the army at the age of seventeen and published
his first poem at eighteen. With Victor Hugo, Sainte-Beuve, and
others, he was for some years active in the Romantic movement in literature, which culminated when Hugo's play, *Hernani*,
was produced in Paris in 1830. Always an aloof and lonely man,
Vigny soon retired from the scene; and it was in reference to him
that the phrase "ivory tower"—which has since had such a tiresome currency—was first applied, by Sainte-Beuve. He married
an English woman and lived mainly in the country, composing
his well-known play, *Chatterton*, and perfecting the philosophic
poems for which he is chiefly famous. His main prose works
were the historical novels *Cinq-Mars* and *Servitude et grandeur
militaires* (1835), the last-named of which contains *The Malacca
Cane*.

Large events like the French Revolution have the effect of
making people acutely conscious of time and history. Vigny belonged to what was probably the first aggregate of writers who
were intensely aware of their making up a "generation" in the
modern sense. They were, as one of them, Alfred de Musset, said,
"children of the age," spiritually disinherited by the Revolution
and the Napoleonic wars. But Vigny's response to this situation
was uniquely proud and stoical; if he had none of Stendhal's

marvelous grace and humor, he was quite without Musset's habit of self-commiseration. In fact as a man he was notoriously self-centered. It was said of him that he was "intimate with no one, not even himself"; on his election to the Academy in 1845 he made an interminable speech and, when someone afterward remarked on its lengthiness, Vigny is said to have replied, "But I assure you, my friend, I am not at all tired." As a writer he was a total unbeliever and pessimist. Yet in Vigny, the old French chivalry lived on, however much attenuated; he had an almost fanatical conviction of personal honor and of duty to class and country.

This conviction sounds all through *The Malacca Cane*, where the warrior's personal honor and human affections are shown to be in perpetual and excruciating conflict with the violent deeds and isolated life forced upon him by his bloody and specialized profession. A veteran of the Napoleonic wars, Captain Renaud recounts his life story at a moment when that age is passing irretrievably—on the eve of the July revolution of 1830, which was to end the Bourbon restoration, bring Louis-Philippe to the throne, and establish the middle class in power once for all.

The Malacca Cane is a panoramic story; it is possibly too panoramic for its small dimensions. Yet for all the vast scope of the events described, the story is constantly throwing up lucid images which serve to define and concentrate its meaning. Such are the passages recounting Renaud's enthusiastic youth, when he exchanged Napoleon for his own father; his long pining years of captivity on the British warship; his later phase of grim anonymous service in the army; and above all the strange ironic manner of his end. Such too are Napoleon's periodic appearances, first as the triumphant conqueror; then as the defiant brutal "Comedian" of the great scene with Pius VII; finally as the bloated doom-bent dictator of the later years; nor does Vigny fail to foresee a time when the small fat grandiloquent figure will become an occasion for buffoonery and the inspiration for children's toys. Meanwhile there is the endless war, which divides man from man, men from their families, country from country.

"We have had a fight on the birthday of my little Sarah," Admiral Collingwood wistfully writes home after the battle of Trafalgar; and France and England are shown as perishing of boredom in their isolation, the French shut up within their Continental fortress, the English patrolling seas where they encounter none but other Englishmen.

The Malacca Cane is the longest of three independent episodes making up the volume, *Military Servitude and Grandeur*. The original title of the story is *La Vie et la mort du Capitaine Renaud, ou la Canne de jonc*. The story is however usually referred to by its subtitle, which is also used as the title here. Except for Captain Renaud himself, most of the characters are historical. The Pope is of course that Pius VII who was formerly Cardinal Chiaramonti. Kléber, Desaix, and Casa-Bianca were famous Napoleonic officers. Kléber was assassinated at Cairo in 1800 at the conclusion of the Egyptian campaign; Casa-Bianca's son was to become celebrated as the boy who "stood on the burning deck." The words Floréal, Brumaire, Thermidor, Prairial, and Vendémiaire were the names of months in the Revolutionary calendar adopted in 1792 and discontinued in 1806.

The Malacca Cane

ALFRED DE VIGNY

1 A Memorable Night

T HE NIGHT of July 27, 1830, was silent and solemn. To me its memory is fresher than that of more frightful pictures fate has flung before my eyes.

The quiet on land and sea before a great storm has no greater majesty than had Paris before the Revolution. The boulevards were deserted. Alone, after midnight, I walked their entire length, looking and listening eagerly. The clear sky shed over the earth the white gleam of her stars, but the houses were lightless, shut and like dead. All the street lamps were broken. Groups of workmen still clustered under trees, listening to a mysterious orator who slipped them secret words in a low voice. Then they would scatter on the run and slink into narrow, black little streets. They would remain glued against alley doors, that would open like a trap and close after them. Then nothing more stirred and the city seemed to have none but dead inhabitants and pest-blighted dwellings.

At intervals I would encounter a dark, immobile mass, unrecognizable until I almost ran into it: it was a battalion of the Guard, upright, motionless, voiceless. Farther on, an artillery battery, with the fuses ready lighted over the guns, like twin stars.

One passed with impunity in front of these somber and imposing corps. One walked around them, one left them, one returned, without provoking a question, an oath, a word. They were inoffensive, ruthless and ungrudging.

As I approached one of the largest squads, an officer came forward and in an extremely courteous manner asked me if the flames that could be seen lighting up the Port of St. Denis from afar, were not incendiary. He was about to go forward with his troop to make sure. I told him the flames came from some big trees cut down and burned by tradesmen who took advantage of the trouble to destroy those ancient elms that had hidden their shops.

Then, sitting down on one of the stone benches along the boulevard, he started to draw lines and circles in the sand with a malacca cane. I recognized him by this, and at the same time he recognized my face. As I remained standing before him, he shook hands with me, and begged me to sit down beside him.

Captain Renaud was a rigid and severe man of most cultivated mind, like many who were in the Guards at that period. His character and habits were very well known to us, and those who read these reminiscences, well know on which serious face they must place his *nom de guerre*, given him by the soldiers, adopted by the officers and indifferently accepted by the man himself. Like the old families, the old regiments keep intact during peace, take on familiar habits and invent characteristic names for their children.

An old wound in the right leg had made the captain lean always on his malacca cane, which had a very remarkable head that attracted the attention of all who saw it for the first time. He kept it by him everywhere, in his hand most of the time. There was not the slightest affectation in this habit. His manner was too simple and grave. Nevertheless, one felt he had a fondness for it.

He was greatly honored in the Guard. Without ambition and wishing to be no other than he was, a Grenadier Captain, he was forever reading, spoke as little as possible and then in monosyllables. He was very tall, very pale, melancholy of face, and on his forehead between the eyebrows there was a little scar; quite a deep one. Often it used to change from bluish to black in color, and sometimes gave a ferocious look to his habitually cold and peaceable features.

The soldiers had a great liking for him, and particularly during the Spanish campaign one remarked the joy with which they went out when the detachments were commanded by the Malacca Cane. It actually was the malacca cane that commanded them. For Captain Renaud never drew his sword, not even when, at the head of his skirmishers, he would get close enough to the enemy to run the risk of hand-to-hand combat.

He was not only a man experienced in warfare, but one who had besides so keen a knowledge of the biggest political affairs in Europe during the Empire that people did not know how to account for it. Sometimes it would be attributed to profound studies, and again to high relations of long standing; his perpetual reserve prevented people from knowing how he came by it. Besides, the dominating character of the men of today is this same reserve—and the Captain carried this general trait to an extreme. Nowadays an appearance of cold politeness covers both character and actions. Therefore, I believe that few of us will recognize ourselves beneath the mad portraits that have been drawn of us. In France affectation is more ridiculous than anywhere else, and it is doubtless for this reason that, far from exhibiting by one's actions and speech the force which passions give us, each one seeks to quell within himself any display of violent emotion, a deep sorrow, or an involuntary outburst. I do not think that civilization has stirred up everything; I seem rather to see that it has enveloped all.

I like this reserve of our epoch. There is a modesty in this apparent coldness, and genuine sentiment has need of that. Disdain also enters into it—good coin that, with which to pay the things of life.

We have already lost many friends whose memory still lives among us; you remember them well, my dear brothers-in-arms. Some died in wars, others from duels, others by suicide; all of them men of honor and strong character; but headstrong beneath their simple, cold and reserved appearance. Ambition, love, gaming, hatred, jealousy—all gnawed within them, but they never talked much, or when they did, skillfully turned any direct inquiry that might touch the bleeding wound in their hearts. They never sought to make themselves remarked in drawing rooms by their tragic attitudes; and if some young woman fresh from the perusal of a novel had seen them submissive and disciplined to the customary bows and low-voiced conversations, she certainly would have disdained them; and yet they lived and died, as strong men as nature ever produced. Cato and Brutus were no different in spite of the togas that adorned them.

Our passions are as energetic as those of any period, but it is only by the sign of their fatigue that a friendly eye can discern them. The exterior appearance, the conversations, the manners, all have a certain cold dignity which is common to all and which is cast aside only by few children who wish to grow and make themselves known in spite of all.

There is no profession wherein the coldness of the forms of speech and habits contrasts more vividly with the activity of the life, than in the army. The hatred for exaggeration is a cult, and disgust is shown for any man who seeks to magnify a feeling, or to court sympathy for his suffering. I knew this, and made ready to leave Captain Renaud quickly, when he took my arm and held me back:

"Did you see the drill of the Suisses* this morning? It was very curious. They executed hollow-square fire while advancing, with perfect accuracy. Since I have been in the service I have never seen it done. It is a drill for the parade or for the opera. But in the streets of a big city it may be worth while, provided the right and left sections quickly form in front of the platoon that has just fired."

He continued tracing lines on the ground with the tip of his cane while talking. Then he got up slowly, and as he walked along the boulevard with the intention of going away from the group of officers and soldiers, I followed him. He went on talking

* Swiss mercenaries, guards of the Bourbon Kings. *Tr.*

to me, as if voluntarily, with a sort of nervous exaltation, which captivated me, and I never would have thought it of one who would be commonly called a cold man.

Taking hold of the button of my coat, he began with a very simple request.

"Would you pardon me for asking you to send me your gorget of the Royal Guard, if you have kept it? I have left mine at home and I can't send for it, nor go for it myself, because the people kill us in the streets like mad dogs. But in the three or four years since you have left the Army, you have done away with it perhaps? I too had tendered my resignation two weeks ago, for I am very weary of the Army. But day before yesterday, when I read the orders, I said: They are taking up arms! So I bundled up my uniform, my shoulder straps and my bearskin grenadier's cap, and went into the barracks to rejoin those fine fellows who are going to be killed on every corner, and who surely would have thought, at the bottom of their hearts, that I left them in the lurch in a moment of crisis. It would have been against Honor, would it not, entirely against Honor?"

"Had you foreseen the orders before your resignation?" I answered.

"My Lord, no! I have not even read them yet."

"Well then, why do you reproach yourself?"

"Only because of appearances. I don't want appearances even to be against me."

"That is admirable," I said.

"Admirable! Admirable!" Captain Renaud walked faster. Spoke faster too. "That is the phrase today. What a childish phrase! I detest admiration. It is the cause of too many bad actions. It is given too cheaply these days, and to everybody. We had better beware of admiring too lightly."

There was a pause. Then:

"Admiration is corrupted and corrupting. People should do for the doing, not for the noise it makes. Moreover I have some ideas of my own on this." He broke off brusquely and was about to leave me.

"There is something quite as fine as a great man," I said to him, "and that is a man of Honor."

He took my hand affectionately. "We share that opinion. I have put it in practice all my life. But it has cost me dear. It is not as easy as it looks!" He spoke nervously.

The sublieutenant of his company came up to ask him for a cigar. He pulled several from his pocket and gave them to him without speaking. The officers began to smoke, tramping back and forth in a silence and serenity which memory of the attending circumstances failed to break. For no one deigned to talk of the dangers of the day, nor of his duty, thoroughly realizing both the one and the other.

Captain Renaud came back to me. "Fine weather," he said to me, pointing his malacca cane at the sky. "I don't know when I'll stop seeing the same stars every night. Once I happened to imagine that I might see those of the South Sea. But I was destined not to change hemispheres. No matter! It is superb weather. The Parisians are asleep or make believe they are. None of us has eaten or drunk for twenty-four hours. That makes one's thoughts very clear. I remember a day, going into Spain, when you asked why I had advanced so little. I had no time to tell you then. But tonight I feel tempted to come back to my life that I have been going over again in memory. You like stories, I remember. And in your retired life you will like to remember us. If you care to sit down on this parapet of the boulevard with me, we will be able to talk very quietly, for it seems to me the people have stopped taking potshots at us from windows and cellar vents.

"I shall tell you only about a few periods of my life and I shall follow only my whim. I have seen much and read much, but I do not believe I should be able to write. It is not my trade, thank God! and I have never tried it. But I know how to live and I have lived the way I had resolved to (from the moment I had the courage to resolve), and that, truly, is something. Let us sit down!"

Slowly I followed. We went through the battalion to pass to

the left of these fine grenadiers. They stood upright, gravely, chins on the rifle muzzles. A few youngsters, more fatigued by the day than the others, had sat down on their knapsacks. They were all silent, and coolly busy with repairing their gear or making it more correct. Nothing indicated worry or discontent. They were in their ranks, as after a day of review, and awaited orders.

When we were seated, our old friend began and in his own fashion told me of three great epochs that gave me an understanding of his life, and explained his bizarre habits and the somberness in his character.

Nothing he told me has been lost from my memory. I will repeat it almost word for word.

2 Malta

I DO not matter, he began. At present, it is a pleasure for me to think so. But if I were somebody, I might say like Louis XIV: I loved war too well.

What are you going to do? Bonaparte had gone to my head so violently that there was no room in my brain for another thought. My father, an elderly superior officer, always in camp, was quite unknown to me. Then one day he had the fancy to take me to Egypt with him. I was twelve years old, and have remembered, since that day as if it were today, the sentiments of the whole Army and those that took hold of my own mind. Two spirits swelled the sails of our bark; the spirit of glory and the spirit of piracy. My father heeded the latter no more than the northwester that blew us along, but the former buzzed in my ears so strongly that it made me deaf to the noises of the world for a long time, except to the music of Charles XII, the cannon.

The cannon, to me, was the voice of Bonaparte. And child as I was, when it roared I would grow red with joy. I would jump for pleasure, clap my hands at it and respond to it with loud yells. These first emotions prepared the exaggerated enthusiasm that became the purpose and the folly of my life. One memorable encounter decided this sort of fatal admiration, this mad admiration for which I wanted to sacrifice too much.

The fleet weighed anchor on the thirtieth of *Floréal* in the year VI. The first day and night I spent on the bridge to bathe in the happiness of seeing the blue ocean and all our ships. I counted one hundred hulls and I could not count all of them. Our military line was a mile long, and the half circle the convoy formed was at least six miles long.

I said nothing. I saw Corsica pass by very close, trailing Sardinia in its wake, and presently Sicily arrived to our left. The *Juno*, which carried my father and me, was to reconnoiter the way and form a vanguard with three other frigates.

My father held my hand, and showed me Mount Etna all in smoke, and other rocks I will never forget. They were Favaniane and Mount Eryx. Marsala, the ancient Lilybæum, passed in its vapors. Its white houses I took for doves piercing a cloud. And one morning, it was . . . yes, it was the twenty-fourth of *Prairial*, I saw at daybreak come before me a spectacle which has dazzled me for twenty years.

Malta rose up with its fortresses, its cannon level with the water, its long walls shining in the sun like newly polished marble, and its swarm of narrow galleys were run with long red oars. One hundred and ninety-four French ships enveloped it with their huge sails and blue, red and white standards, which at that moment were hoisted on every mast. And on the Gozo and Fort Saint-Elme the religious standards were slowly lowered: It was the last militant cross to fall. Then the fleet fired five hundred salutes.

The ship *Orient* was ahead, alone, apart, grand and motionless. Before it passed the other war vessels one by one, and slowly. From a distance I saw Desaix saluting Bonaparte. We went to him on board the *Orient*. At last I saw him, for the first time.

He stood near the rail, talking to Casa-Bianca, captain of the ship (poor *Orient*). He played with the hair of a child of ten, the captain's son.

Instantly I became jealous of that child and my heart jumped

to see him touch the general's sword. My father went towards
Bonaparte and talked to him a long time. I could not see his face
yet.

Suddenly he turned and looked at me. A quiver went through
all my body at the sight of his sallow brow overhung with long
hair that seemed all wet, as if coming out of the water; at his
big gray eyes, his thin cheeks and that receding lip above his
sharp chin.

He had just been talking of me, for he said:—"Listen, *mon
brave*, you shall come to Egypt since you want to, and General
Vaubois can stay here with his four thousand men without you.
But I don't like men to take along their children. I permitted it
only to Casa-Bianca and I was wrong. You must send this one
back to France. I want him to be strong in mathematics. And if
anything happens to you out there, I will answer for him myself. I take charge of him. I shall make a good soldier out of
him."

At the same moment he stooped down and, taking me up
under the arms, he lifted me as high as his lips and kissed my
forehead. My head was turned then and there. I knew he was
my master and that he took my soul away from my father—
whom I scarcely knew for that matter, because he lived with the
Army eternally.

I thought I felt the awe of Moses, the shepherd, beholding
God in the burning bush. Bonaparte had lifted me, free, and
when his arms gently lowered me on the bridge, they put down
another slave.

The day before I would have jumped overboard if they had
taken me away from the Army. But now I let myself be taken
wherever they pleased. I left my father indifferently. And it was
forever! But we are so bred right from childhood, and it takes
so little to lead us away from our good natural sentiments. My
father was no longer my master, because I had beheld his own,
and from him alone emanated all authority on earth, it seemed
to me!

O dreams of authority and of bondage! O corrupting thought

of power, serving to seduce children! False enthusiasms! Subtle poisons, what antidote can ever be found against you?

I was dazzled, drunk! I wanted to work, and I worked unto madness! I figured day and night, and I took on the coat, the knowledge and the sallow complexion of the school.

Now and then the cannon would interrupt me, and this voice of the demigod told me of the conquest of Egypt, of Marengo, of the 18th of *Brumaire*,* the Empire . . . and the Emperor kept his word to me! As to my father, I no longer knew what had become of him, until one day this letter here reached me.

I always carry it in this old portfolio, that once was red. I reread it often to convince myself thoroughly of the uselessness of the advice one generation gives to the next, and to reflect upon the headstrong absurdity of my illusions.

The Captain here opened his uniform and drew from his breast first a handkerchief and then a small portfolio which he opened with care. We went into a still lighted café where he read to me these fragments of letters which since then have never left me.

You will soon know why.

3 *A Simple Letter*

On board the British Vessel *Culloden* before Rochefort, 1804. Sent to France with Admiral Collingwood's permission.

It is useless for you to know, my boy, how this letter will reach you, and by what means I have been able to learn of your conduct and of your present position. Suffice it to say that I am satisfied with you, but that no doubt I shall never see you again. Probably that won't trouble you much. You knew your father only at the age when memory was not yet born and when

---

* October 9, 1799, the day on which Napoleon formally established his dictatorship. *Ed.*

the heart was not yet awake. It opens later within us than people generally believe, and I have often wondered about that. But what can we do about it?—You are no worse than any other, it seems to me. So I have to be satisfied.

All I have to tell you is that I have been a prisoner of the British since *Thermidor* 14th of the year VI (or August 2nd, 1798, by the old calendar, which people say has come in vogue again these days). I had gone on board the *Orient* to try and persuade our brave Brueys to weigh anchor for Corfu. Bonaparte had already sent me his poor aide-de-camp, Julien, who was foolish enough to let the Arabs capture him. I arrived, but in vain. Brueys was obstinate as a mule. He said they were going to find the passage of Alexandria for the ships to go through. But he added a few rather proud words which showed me that at heart he was a little jealous of the land Army.

"Do they take us for ferrymen?" he asked me, "and do they believe we are afraid of the British?"

It would have been better for France had he been afraid of them. But, if he has made mistakes, he has expiated them gloriously. And I may say that I am expiating most wearily the error I made in staying on his ship when it was attacked. Brueys was first wounded in the head and in the hand. He kept on fighting till the moment when a cannon ball tore out his entrails. He had himself put in a sack of bran and died on his officers' bench.

We were distinctly aware that by ten in the evening we would blow up. What remained of the crew lowered the boats and saved themselves, with the exception of Casa-Bianca. Naturally he remained the last. But his son, a fine boy whom you have seen, I believe, came up to me and said:

"Citizen, what does Honor require me to do?"

Poor little fellow! I think he was ten years old, and babbled of Honor at such a moment! I took him on my lap into the boat, and prevented him from seeing his father blow up with the poor *Orient*, which scattered into the air like a jet of flame. We did not blow up, but we were captured, which is a great deal worse. I went to Dover under guard of a good English captain called Collingwood, who commands the *Culloden* at present. He is a brave man if ever there was one. Since 1761 when he entered the Navy he had not quit the sea more than two years, to be married and see his two daughters born. His children, of whom he talks constantly, don't know him. Nor does his wife know his splendid character except through his letters.

But I feel that the sorrow over this defeat at Aboukir has shortened my days (that have been none too long at that) for having seen such a disaster and the death of my glorious comrades. Everybody here has been touched by my great age. And because the English climate makes me cough a great deal and has re-opened all my wounds to the point of depriving me entirely of the use of one arm, good Captain Collingwood has requested and obtained—what he could not have obtained for himself to whom the shore is denied—sanction to transfer me to Sicily, where the sun is warmer and the sky clearer.

I believe I shall end there. For, seventy-eight years, seven wounds, deep sorrows, and captivity are incurable ailments. I had only my sword to leave you, my poor boy! At present I no longer possess even that, for a prisoner has no sword.

But at least there is one counsel I may give you. It is to beware of men that rise quickly, and particularly to beware of Bonaparte. As far as I know you, you will be a satellite, and you must avoid satellitism because you are French, which means being most susceptible to this contagious disease. The number of big and little tyrants it has produced is marvelous. We are fond in the extreme of swaggerers, and we give ourselves to them so wholeheartedly that we are not slow to rue it sadly by and by. The cause of this error is that we have a great need of action and are very lazy at reflection. The consequence is that we much rather give ourselves body and soul to him that undertakes to think and be responsible for us, even should we laugh afterwards at ourselves and at him.

Bonaparte is a *bon enfant*, but he is truly too much of a

charlatan. I am afraid he will be the founder among us of a new method of juggling. We have quite enough of that in France. Charlatanism is insolent and corrupting. It has set such great examples in our century and has made so much noise with drums and fife in the public square, that it has crept into every profession, and there is no man so small but he is puffed up with it.

The number of frogs that burst is uncountable. I desire very much that my son shall not be one of them.

I am glad that he has kept his word to me "to take charge of you," as he said he would. But do not trust in him too much. A little time after my sad departure from Egypt, I was told of this scene which passed at a certain dinner. I will tell it to you so that you may think of it often.

Being at Cairo, on *Vendémiaire* 1st, year VII, Bonaparte, as a member of the Institute, gave orders for a civic festival to be held on the anniversary of the establishment of the Republic. The garrison of Alexandria celebrated the fête around Pompey's columns on which was hoisted the Tricolor flag. Cleopatra's needle was illuminated but rather badly, and the troops of upper Egypt celebrated the fête as best they could between the columns, the caryatids of Thebes, on the knees of the Colossus of Memnon, at the feet of the statues of Tâma and Châma. In Cairo the first army corps maneuvered, held its races, and set off fireworks.

The Commander in Chief had invited to the dinner the entire staff, the sages and the Kiaya of the Pasha, as well as the Emir, the members of the Divan and the Agas. They were gathered around a table with five hundred covers spread in the lower hall of the house Bonaparte occupied on the Place El-Béquier. The liberty cap and the crescent were entwined almost loverlike. The Turkish and French colors formed a cradle and a most agreeable carpet, on which the Koran and the table of the Rights of Man were happily united.

After the guests had dined well—with their fingers—on chicken and rice seasoned with saffron, pastries and fruit, Bonaparte, who had not spoken, suddenly cast a keen glance upon them all.

Kléber, who was lying beside him because he could not fold his long legs Turkish fashion, nudged Abdallah Menou, his neighbor on the other side, with his elbow, and said in his half-German accent:

"Look, here's Ali-Bonaparte getting ready to give us one of his speeches!"

He called him that because at the fête of Mohamet the general had amused himself by wearing the Oriental costume, and at the moment when he declared himself the protector of all religion, they had pompously given him the title of "The Prophet's son-in-law" and called him Ali-Bonaparte.

Kléber had not yet finished speaking and was still running his fingers through his heavy white hair when little Bonaparte was already on his feet. And raising his glass to his meager chin and huge neckcloth, he said in a brusque, clear, jerky voice:

"Let us drink to the year Three Hundred of the French Republic!"

Kléber burst out laughing upon Menou's shoulder nearly making him spill his glass over an old Aga. Bonaparte glared at them sideways, frowning.

Surely, my boy, he was right! For in the presence of a Commander in Chief a Division Commander must not behave indecently, even though the rascal be called Kléber. But they were not altogether wrong either, for at the present moment Bonaparte calls himself Emperor, and you are his page.

Captain Renaud took the letter from my hand, saying:

I had actually just been appointed page to the Emperor in 1804. Ah, what a terrible year that was! What events did it bring! How I would have watched it if I had known enough to watch anything at the time! But I had no eyes to see, no ears to hear other than the deeds of the Emperor, the voice of the Emperor, the gestures of the Emperor, the very footsteps of the Emperor! His approach intoxicated me, his presence magnetized me. The glory of being attached to that man seemed to me the greatest thing in the world and never did a lover feel the power of his mistress with keener and more overwhelming emotions than those which the sight of Napoleon gave me each day.

The admiration for a Military Chief becomes a passion, a fanaticism, a frenzy, which makes slaves of us, madmen, blind men! This poor letter I just gave you to read only filled in my spirit the place of what schoolboys call a "lecture." I felt nothing but the impious relief of a child that finds deliverance from the natural authority and believes itself free, because it has chosen the chain which the impulse of the moment rivets round its neck.

Outside of that, some native sense of decency made me preserve this sacred writing, and its authority over me has grown in the same measure that my dreams of heroic thraldom dwindled. It has been kept on my heart always and has ended by sending invisible roots into it, the moment good sense had lifted from my eyes the veil that covered them before. Tonight I could not help rereading it with you, and I scorn myself to contemplate how slow has been the curve my thoughts have followed before returning to the simplest and most solid basis of a man's conduct.

You shall see to what little it was reduced. But, sir, I truly think such a return suffices a man's life. It has taken me a great deal of time to find the source of the true Greatness that a man may possess in the almost barbarous profession of Arms.

Here Captain Renaud was interrupted by an old sergeant of Grenadiers, who posted himself at the door of the café, carrying his weapon, as do the noncommissioned officers, and pulling out a letter written on gray glazed paper from under the strap of his rifle. The Captain rose quietly and opened the order he received.

"Tell Béjaud to copy this on the order book," he said to the sergeant.

"The sergeant-major has not returned from the Arsenal," said the man, in a voice soft as a girl's, lowering his eyes, and without even deigning to say how his comrade had been killed.

"Let the mess-sergeant take his place," said the Captain without asking a question. And he signed his order on the sergeant's book, using his back for a desk.

He coughed slightly, and resumed quietly.

4   An Unknown Dialogue

MY POOR father's letter, and his death, of which I was informed shortly after, made a strong impression on me, all intoxicated though I was and dizzy with the noise of my spurs—an impression strong enough to give a jolt to my blind ardor. I began to examine more closely and more calmly what was supernatural in the splendors that intoxicated me. For the first time I asked myself of what consisted this ascendancy we allowed to be exercised over us, by men of action clad with absolute power. I even dared to make some inward effort to draw a limit to this voluntary yielding of so many men to one single man. This first shake-up made me half open an eyelid, and I was audacious enough to look the dazzling eagle square in the face. The eagle that had picked me up when I was a mere child, and whose talons gripped my loins.

I was not slow to find occasions for examining him more closely, and to spy out the spirit of the great man in the obscure actions of his private life.

They had dared to create pages, as I have told you. But we wore officers' uniforms, while awaiting the green livery with red breeches we would have to put on at the coronation. We acted as equerries, secretaries or aides-de-camp until then, according to the will of the master who accepted whatever he laid his hands on. Already he took pleasure in filling his anterooms, and as the craving to dominate pursued him everywhere, he could not keep from exercising it in the smallest matters, and he tormented those about him with the untiring infliction of his will.

He amused himself with my timidity. He played with my terror and my respectfulness. Sometimes he would call me brusquely. Then, when he saw me enter, pale and stammering, he would amuse himself by making me talk for a long while to see my astonishment and confuse my ideas.

Sometimes, while I was taking down his dictation, he would suddenly pull my ear—a way he had—and ask some irrelevant question on some common science like geometry or algebra, proposing the simplest child's problem. At the time it seemed to me as if lightning were striking me. I knew a thousand times over whatever he quizzed me on. I knew more about it than he believed, sometimes even more than himself, but his eye would paralyze me.

When he was outside the room I could breathe again. The blood began to circulate in my veins and memory would return, and with it inexpressible shame. Rage would take me and I would write down what I should have answered. Then I would roll around on the floor and cry out and want to kill myself.

"What!" I would ask myself, "is there really a head wise enough to be sure of everything and hesitate before no one? Men who daze themselves by action on all things, and whose assurance crushes others by making them believe that the key to all knowledge and all power, the key for which one does not cease to look, is in their pockets and they have but to open them in order to bring forth the light and infallible authority!" Nevertheless, I felt that this was a false and usurped force. I revolted and shouted:

"He lies! His attitude, his voice, his gesture, are only an actor's pantomime, a miserable parade of sovereignty. He must know its vanity! He cannot possibly believe in himself so sincerely! He forbids all of us to lift the veil but he must see himself naked through it. And what does he see? A poor ignoramus like ourselves, and underneath it all a feeble creature!"

Yet I did not know how to see to the bottom of this disguised soul. Power and glory defended him on all points. I turned about it without succeeding in surprising a single thing; and the ever armed porcupine rolled in front of me, offering on all sides none but prickly points. One day, however, hazard, master of us all, pushed them apart for an instant, and between these spikes and darts, let out an instant of light. (Perhaps it was the only time in all his life.) One day he did encounter a stronger force than himself and he drew back for an instant before an ascendancy greater than his own. I witnessed it and felt myself avenged.

This is how it came about.

We were at Fontainebleau. The Pope had just arrived. The Emperor had awaited him impatiently for his coronation, and had received him in a carriage, which they entered from either side at the same instant; apparently etiquette had been neglected; but indeed it had been deeply calculated so as not to cede or grasp a thing; an Italian ruse.

He came back to the palace, where everything was in an uproar. I had left several officers in the room ahead of the Emperor's room, and had remained alone in his. I was gazing at a long table which had a Roman mosaic top instead of a marble one. An enormous stack of letters and petitions overloaded it.

I had often seen Bonaparte enter here and subject these letters to a strange test. He did not take them up in their order, nor haphazard. But when their number irritated him, he would pass his hat over the table from left to right and from right to left, like a mower, and so scatter them until five or six were left which he would then open.

This scornful game had moved me singularly. All these letters of mourning and distress rejected and flung on the floor as by an angry wind; the useless pleas of widows and orphans having no chance of help any more than the flying papers swept by the consular hat; all these sobbing pages, wet with the tears of mothers, draggling haphazardly under his boots; on which he walked as he walked on his dead of the battlefields, represented the present fate of France, like a sinister lottery. No matter how

great the rude, indifferent hand that drew the lots, I thought
it was not just to yield up to the whim of his fist so many obscure
fortunes which perhaps might have been as great as his own
some day, if some support were given them.

I felt my heart rise in revolt against Bonaparte. But shame-
fully, like the slave's heart that it was. I considered these abandoned letters. Cries of unheeded grief rose from their profaned
folds. And taking them up to read them, throwing them away
again, I myself judged between these unfortunates and the Master
to whom they had given themselves, and who would be planting
himself this very day more solidly than ever upon their heads.

In my hand was one of these scorned petitions. Then the
drums announced the immediate arrival of the Emperor. You
know that, even as the flash of a cannon is seen almost before
hearing the detonation, so Napoleon was always seen simultaneously with the clamor announcing his approach—so quick were
his steps and so hastily did he seem to live and fling his actions
one upon another. When he entered the palace court on horseback, his escorts had difficulty in following him, and the sentries
had no time to snatch up their arms before he had already dis-
mounted and bounded up the stairway.

This time he had left the Pope's carriage and returned alone,
ahead and at a gallop. I heard his heels clatter the same instant
I heard the drums. I barely had time to jump in the alcove,
where stood a big bed of state that no one used, and which was
fortified by a princely balustrade, and fortunately more than half
closed by curtains embroidered with bees.

The Emperor was much excited. He walked into the room
alone like one who awaits something impatiently. In a twinkling
he had paced its length three times. Then he approached the
window and started to thrum a march on it with his nails. A
carriage rolled into the courtyard. He stopped drumming,
stamped his foot two or three times as if impatient at the sight
of something that was being done slowly, and then he rushed to
the door to open it for the Pope.

Pius VII entered alone. Bonaparte hurriedly shut the door

after him, with the promptitude of a jailer. I felt greatly terrified to find myself a third in such company. But I remained voiceless, motionless, looking and listening with all the power of my senses.

The Pope was tall of stature. His face was long, yellow, ailing, but full of a holy nobility and limitless goodness. His black eyes were large and fine, his mouth half open with a benevolent smile to which his firm chin gave an expression of keen and quick spirituality. This smile smacked not of political harshness but wholly of Christian kindness. A white cap covered his long black hair which was shot with silver. On his bent shoulders he wore carelessly a long, red velvet cape and his robe swept his feet.

He entered slowly with the quiet, careful step of an elderly woman. He sat down, eyes lowered, on one of the great Roman armchairs, gilded and loaded with eagles, and awaited what the other Italian had to say to him.

Ah! my dear sir! Such a scene! Such a scene! I can see it still.

It was not the genius of the man it showed me, but his character. And if his great spirit did not unfold, his heart at least flashed forth.

Bonaparte, then, was not as yet what you have since seen him to be. He did not have that financier's belly, that puffed sickly face, those gouty legs and all that infirm fat which art has unfortunately seized upon to make a "type" of him according to modern expression, and which has handed him down to the masses, that almost popular and grotesque form which fits him to become a child's toy and will leave him perhaps some day fabulous and deformed like *Polichinelle*. He was not that way at all at the time, but supple, nervous, quick, keen and active, convulsive in his gestures, sometimes graceful, always careful of his manners. His chest was flat and sunken between the shoulders, and his face was still as I had seen it in Malta, melancholy and sharp-featured.

He never stopped pacing up and down the room after the Pope had entered. He began to roam around the armchair, like a prudent hunter, and stopped suddenly in front of it in the stiff, motionless attitude of a corporal. He took up the sequel to some conversation broached in the carriage, but interrupted by the arrival, and which he wanted to rush through.

"I repeat, Holy Father, I am not at all strong-minded and I am not fond of arguers and idealists. I assure you that, in spite of my old Republicans, I shall attend mass."

He snapped these last words at the Pope brusquely, like a censer waved at his face, and stopped to watch the effect, thinking that the more or less impious circumstances preceding this interview should give this sudden and keen avowal an extraordinary value. The Pope lowered his eyes and put his two hands on the eagle heads that formed the arms of his chair. By this attitude, like a Roman statue, he seemed to say clearly: I resign myself in advance to hearing all the profanities he may be pleased to make me hear.

Bonaparte made the round of the room about the armchair, which stood in the center. By the look he cast sideways upon the old pontiff, I could see that he was pleased neither with himself nor with his adversary, and that he reproached himself for having reopened this conversation so quickly. So he began to talk more circumspectly, always circling the room, casting sidelong glances into the long mirrors of the apartment, where the grave countenance of the Holy Father was reflected, and peering sharply at the Holy Father's profile whenever he passed close, but never looking him full in the face, for fear of seeming too anxious about the impression his words were making.

"There is something," he said, "which continues to weigh on my heart, Holy Father. It is that you consent to the coronation in the same manner as the other time to the *Concordat*—as if you were forced to it. You have the air of a martyr before me. You sit there as if resigned, as if offering your woes to Heaven. But really, that is not your position. You are no prisoner, by God! You are free as the air!"

Pius VII smiled sadly and looked him in the face. He felt the prodigious in the demands of this despotic character. To it, as to all spirits of the same nature, it was not sufficient to make itself obeyed, unless in obeying people showed an ardent desire to do what he commanded.

"Yes," resumed Bonaparte more forcefully, "you are perfectly free. You may return to Rome; the way is open, no one holds you back."

The Pope sighed and raised his right hand and lifted his eyes to Heaven without answering. Then he lowered his wrinkled brow very slowly and fell to contemplating the gold cross hung about his neck.

Bonaparte continued talking, turning about more slowly. His voice became mild and his smile very gracious.

"Holy Father, if the gravity of your character did not prevent me, I should say that you are really a little ungrateful. You do not seem to remember enough the good services France has rendered you. The Conclave of Venice which elected you Pope was inspired by my Italian campaign and by a word I said about you—it looks a little that way to me! Austria was not treating you very well at the time, which distressed me very much. Your Holiness was compelled, I believe, to return to Rome by sea, because it was impossible to cross Austrian territory."

He broke off to await the response of Pius VII. But his silent host only bowed his head almost imperceptibly and remained as if plunged in a dejection which prevented him from listening.

Then Bonaparte pushed with his foot a chair close to the Pope's armchair. I trembled, for in picking this seat, his shoulder had grazed the curtain of the alcove where I was hidden.

"It was really as a Catholic," he continued, "that it distressed me. I never have had the time to study much theology, but I still attach a great faith to the power of the Church. It has a marvelous vitality, Holy Father. Voltaire has upset things a little, but I don't like him, and I am going to turn loose against him an old, unfrocked, oratorian monk. You will be satisfied, all right. Come, you and I might do a great many things in the future, if you cared to."

He assumed an air of innocence and of most caressing youth-fulness.

"I don't know, but for all my crying, I can't see really why you should have any repugnance against taking your seat at Paris for always! Why, I will leave the Tuileries to you, if you want. You already will find your Monte-Cavalol room there awaiting you. I hardly ever stay there. Don't you see clearly, Padre, that the real capital of the world is here? I will do anything you want. To begin with, I am a better child than people believe. Provided war and tiresome politics be left to me, you may arrange the Church any way you please. I will be your soldier altogether. Look, it would be truly splendid. We would have our Councils like Constantine and Charlemagne. I will open them, and close them. Next I will put into your hands the real keys of the World, and as our Lord has said: 'I am come with the sword. And I shall keep the sword.' I shall only bring it to you for your blessing after each success of our arms."

He bent forward slightly when he uttered these words.

The Pope, who until then had remained motionless, like an Egyptian statue, slowly raised his bowed head and smiled sorrow-fully. He lifted his eyes and said, with a quiet sigh, as if confiding his thought to his invisible guardian angel:

"Commediante!"

Bonaparte bounded from his chair like a wounded leopard. A veritable fury possessed him, one of his yellow rages. First he paced without speaking, gnawing his lips till they bled. He no longer circled around his prey with sharp glances and stealthy tread. He moved straight and strong, lengthwise, widthwise through the room. He stamped his feet roughly and clattered his spurred heels. The room quivered. The curtains shuddered, the way trees do when thunder approaches. Something big and terrible was going to happen, I thought. My hair hurt me, and in spite of myself I passed my hand through it. I looked at the Pope. He did not budge. But both his hands tightly gripped the eagles' heads on the arms of his chair.

The storm burst all of a sudden.

"Comedian? I? Ah! I shall give you comedies that will make all of you weep like women and children. Comedian! Ah! you are wrong if you think you can try your insolent composure on me! My playhouse is the world! The part I play is the part of master and creator! For actors I have the whole lot of you, Pope, Kings, Nations! And the string on which you dance is Fear! Comedian! Ah! You have to be bigger than you are to dare applaud or hiss me, *Signor Chiaramonti!* Do you realize you would be nothing but a poor curate if I wanted it? You and your tiara, France would sneer at you if I did not keep my face straight when bowing to you!

"Only four years ago, no one dared speak aloud of Christ. And who would have dared discuss the Pope, if you please? Comedian! Ah! gentlemen, you quickly feel at home with us! You are ill-tempered because I have not been silly enough to sign the disapprobation of Gallican liberties, like Louis XIV! But you don't put it over on me that way! It is I that hold you in my hands. It is I that drag you from the South to the North like marionettes. It is I that make believe you count for something, because you represent an old idea I want to revive. And you haven't the sense to see it and to act as if you didn't notice it. Not at all! You must be told everything! You must have your nose rubbed into things to understand them. And you really think people have use for you, and you stick up your head and drape yourself in your woman's petticoats! But understand well that petticoats do not awe me in the least, and that if you continue, you! I will treat them the way Charles XII did those of the Grand Vizier: I will rip them with one kick of my spurs."

He kept still. I dared not breathe. I craned my neck, when I no longer heard his roaring voice, to see if the poor old man were not dead with fright. But I saw the same serenity in his attitude, the same serenity on his face! A second time he lifted his eyes to the ceiling and after uttering another deep sigh he smiled bitterly and said:

"*Tragediante!*"

At that moment Bonaparte was down the room, leaning on

the marble chimney that was as tall as himself. He darted off like an arrow, rushing upon the old man. I believed he was going to kill him. But he stopped short. From the table he snatched up a Sèvres vase, painted with the castle of Saint-Angelo and the Capitol. He flung it down against the andirons, and crushed the pieces under his feet. Then suddenly he sat down and remained profoundly silent, formidably motionless.

I was relieved. I felt that sober thought had returned to him and that his brain had regained mastery over his seething blood. He became sad, his voice was dull and gloomy and from his first word I gathered that he was himself, and that this Proteus quelled by two words, was showing his true self.

"Miserable life!" he said first. Then he mused, and tore the brim of his hat, without speaking for another minute. Emerged from his musings he went on, as if talking to himself:

"It's true! Tragedian or Comedian. It is all a part, all a masquerade for me, long since and for all time. Such weariness! Such littleness. To pose! Always to pose! Full face for this party, in profile for that individual, according to their notion. To appear the way they like me to be, and to guess correctly their imbecile's dreams! To keep them all between hope and fear. To dazzle them with data and bulletins, with prestige of distances and prestige of names. To be master of them all and not to know what to do with it. Upon my word, that's all! And after all that, to be bored the way I am, it is too much!"

He huddled into the armchair and crossed his legs. "Truly, I am enormously bored! The moment I sit down, I die of ennui. I could not hunt around Fontainebleau for three days without perishing with dullness. I must keep going and make people keep going. If I knew how, I'd like to be hanged, by gad. I am speaking plainly to you. I have plans enough for the life of forty Emperors; I make one every morning and one every night. I have a tireless imagination. But I would not have time to fulfill two before I should be used up body and soul. For our poor lamp does not burn long. And frankly, if all my plans should be put through, I would not swear the world would be much happier for it. But it would be more beautiful, and a majestic unity would be reigning over it. I am not a philosopher, and I know only our Secretary of Florence* who had common sense. I see nothing in certain theories. Life is too short to stop and theorize. As soon as I have thought, I act! After I am gone, people will find plenty of explanations for my actions to raise me higher if I succeed, and belittle me if I fail. The paradoxes about it are all ready. They abound in France. I make them keep still while I am alive, but afterwards we shall see. No matter! My business is to succeed, and I understand that. I shall write my Iliad with deeds, day by day."

At this point he rose with a promptness that was almost gay, something alert and alive. He was natural and himself at that moment. He did not think at all of showing off the way he did afterwards in his dialogues of Saint Helena. He never thought of idealizing himself and did not set forth his person in a manner to realize the finest philosophical conceptions. He was his true self, his inner self exteriorized.

He came back close to the Holy Father, who had not stirred, and walked in front of him. Then blazing up, half laughing in irony, he uttered the following, or very nearly. It is all intermixed with trivial and imposing words as was his wont, and delivered with the inconceivable volubility, the rapid expression of this quick and facile genius, which divined everything at once without effort.

"Birth is everything! Those that come into the world poor and naked are always desperate. This turns into action or into suicide, according to the people's characters. When they have courage, like me, to put their hands on everything, they raise the devil. What do you expect? We have to live. We must find our place and make our little hole. I have shaped mine like a cannon ball. So much the worse for those that were in front of me. Some are content with little, others never have enough. What can you do about it? Everybody eats according to his appetite. And I was very hungry! Look here, Holy Father, at Toulon I did not have the price of a pair of epaulettes. Instead, I had on my

* Machiavelli. *Ed.*

shoulders a mother and God knows how many brothers. All that
is fixed at present, all right enough I hope. Josephine had married
me, as if out of pity, and we are going to crown her in the face of
Raguideau, her notary, who said I had only my sword and my
cloak. My word, he was not wrong! Imperial cloak, crown, what
does it all amount to? Is it mine? Masquerade costume! Actor's
mummery! I shall put it on for an hour and have enough of it.
Then I will put on my little officer's coat again and jump on my
horse. Always to horse; all my life on horseback! I could not sit
down a whole day without running the risk of being thrown out
of my armchair. Am I really to be envied? What?

"I'll tell you, Holy Father! There are only two kinds of people
in the world: those who possess and those who earn.

"The former lie low. The latter keep stirring. Because I have
learned that young, and at the right moment, I shall go far.
That's all! There are only two men have arrived beginning after
forty: Cromwell and Jean-Jacques! If you had given the one a
farm and the other twelve hundred francs and his servant, they
would have neither preached, nor commanded nor written. There
are artisans in building, in colors, in forms and in words. I am
an artisan in battles. It's my trade. At thirty-five I have already
manufactured eighteen of them; their names are *victories*. My
work must be paid. To pay for it with a throne is not too high a
price. Besides, I keep on working always. You will see a good
many more. You will see all dynasties date from mine, newcomer
though I am, and elected. Elected like you, Holy Father, and
drawn from among the masses. On that point we can shake
hands."

And, approaching, he held his white, brusque hand out to the
withered and timid hand of the good Pope. Softened, perhaps by
the good-natured tone of this last move of the Emperor's, perhaps by a secret reversion of thought to his own fate and the
gloomy prospect of Christian society, Pius VII gave him the tips
of his fingers, that still trembled, with the air of a grandmother
who makes up with a child she has been grieved to have scolded
too harshly. He sadly shook his head the while, and I saw a tear-

drop from his beautiful eyes, that rolled quickly down his livid, withered cheek. It seemed to me like the last farewell of dying Christianity, abandoning the earth to selfishness and hazard.

Bonaparte gave a furtive look at the tear he had wrung from this poor soul, and I even surprised, on one side of his mouth, a quick twitch which resembled a smile of triumph. At the moment this all-powerful nature appeared to me less lofty and less fine than that of his saintly opponent. It made me blush, behind my curtains, for all my past enthusiasm. I felt an entirely new sadness in discovering how the highest political greatness could become small through the heartless tricks of its vanity, its miserable pitfalls and its cunning baseness.

I saw that he had wanted nothing of his prisoner, and that it was a silent joy he had gained for himself by not failing in this interview. Having allowed himself to be surprised into anger, he had made his captive flinch under the emotion born of fatigue, fear and all the weaknesses that bring an inexplicable emotion to the eyelid of an elderly man.

Bonaparte had wished to have the last word and, without adding another, he left the room as brusquely as he had entered. I did not see whether he saluted the Pope. I do not think he did.

5   A Man of the Sea

As soon as the Emperor had left the apartment, two ecclesiastics came to the Pope and led him away, supporting him under either arm, dejected, tearful and trembling.

I stayed until night in the alcove, where I had overheard this discourse. My thoughts were confused and it was not the terror of this scene which predominated. I was overcome by what I had seen. And knowing now to what evil passes personal ambition may cause genius to stoop, I felt hatred against this passion which had blighted, under my very eyes, the most brilliant of tyrants, he who would probably give his name to the century for having retarded its progress ten years.

I felt the folly of devoting oneself to a single man, since despotic authority cannot fail to corrupt the feeble heart. But I knew no idea to which to devote myself henceforth. I have told you that I was only eighteen at the time, and I possessed within me but the vaguest instinct of good, truth, and beauty, but obstinate enough to stick forever to their research. That is the only thing I respect in myself.

I judged it was my duty to keep still about what I had witnessed. But I had reason to believe that my temporary disappearance from the Emperor's suite had been discovered, for this is what happened to me. In the Master's manner towards me I noticed no change whatever. Only I spent less time near him, and the close study of his character I had wanted to make was suddenly cut short. One morning I received orders to start instantly for the camp at Boulogne and, on my arrival, orders to embark upon one of the flat-bottomed boats that were being tried out at sea.

I left with less regret than I would have felt if this trip had been announced to me prior to the Fontainebleau scene. I breathed when leaving that old palace and its forest, and this involuntary relief made me feel that my satellitism had received its deathblow. At first this new discovery saddened me, and I trembled for the dazzling illusion which had made a duty of my blind devotion. The great egoist had revealed himself before me. But in proportion to the distance between us when I went away from him, I began to consider him in his exploits more than in his personality. And by this view of him, he regained over me a part of the magical power by which he fascinated the world.

Nevertheless, it was rather the gigantic conception of war, which henceforth appeared to me, than that of the man who represented it in such redoubtable fashion. And at this view I felt an extreme intoxication for the glory of battles renew itself within me. It silenced my grief for the master who ordered the battles, and it made me look with pride upon the perpetual labors of the men, all of whom appeared to me to be only his humble workers.

The conception was actually Homeric and fit to take in schoolboys with its dazzle of multiple activities. But something false was mixed up in it, nevertheless, and revealed itself to me vaguely, not distinctly as yet. I felt the need of a clearer view than mine to make me discover the foundation of it all. I began to learn to measure my Captain. I needed now to sound war!

A new event taught me my second lesson. For I received three harsh lessons in my life, and I am telling them to you after having meditated upon them every day. They were violent shocks for me and the last of them succeeded in overthrowing the idol of my soul.

The conspicuous demonstration of conquest of, and debarkation in, England, the memories of William the Conqueror freshly evoked, the discovery of Cæsar's camp at Boulogne, the sudden concourse of nine hundred vessels in that seaport, under the protection of a battle fleet of five hundred sails constantly advertised —all these tricks, as well as those of the establishment of training camps at Dunkirk and Ostend, Calais, Montreuil and Saint-Omer under the command of four field marshals; the military throne whence fell the first stars of the Legion of Honor; the reviews, the festivities, the partial attacks; all this glitter, when reduced to its simplest expression, as the language of geometry puts it, had only three ends: To worry England! To hush up Europe! To concentrate and enthuse the Army!

Those three points attained, Bonaparte dropped piece by piece the artificial machine that he had set playing at Boulogne. When I arrived that machine was whirling in the emptiness as that at Marly. The generals still went through the motions of simulated ardor, but their hearts were not in it. Some hapless ships continued to be launched, scorned by the English who would sink them ever and anon. I was given a command on one of these craft, the very day after my arrival.

That day, one single English frigate stood out at sea. She tacked with majestic leisure. She came, she went, she put about, she keeled over and righted herself, preened, glided, stopped and played in the sun like a swan at its ablutions. The miserable flat-boat, of newfangled and bad design, had greatly risked itself

before with four other similar boats. And we were very proud of
our audacity, launched as we had been since morning, when we
suddenly discovered the peaceful antics of the frigate. Seen from
shore, they no doubt would have appeared most graceful and
poetic to us; or if only she had amused herself indulging in her
frolics between England and ourselves! But she was, on the contrary, between us and France. The coast of Boulogne was more
than a mile off. That set us thinking.

We did the best we could with our bad sails and our worse
oars, and, while we were floundering about, the peaceable frigate
continued taking her seabath and describing a thousand pleasing
scrools about us. She played riding school, changing her paces
like a well-trained horse, tracing letters S and Z on the water in
the most amiable fashion.

We noticed that she let us pass before her several times without
firing one gunshot, and she even drew her cannon inside suddenly
and shut all her portholes. At first I believed this to be a most
peaceful maneuver, and I could make nothing of this courtesy.

But a rough old sailor nudged me and said: "Something bad is
afoot." And actually, after having let us run before her like a
mouse before a cat, that amiable and pretty frigate made for us
full tilt, without deigning to fire. She rammed us with her bows
like a horse with its chest—broke us, crushed us, sank us, and joyously passed on over us, leaving a few boats to fish out the prisoners. I was among them, the tenth. We had been two hundred
when we started.

The pretty frigate was called the *Naïade*. But, not to lose the
French habit of playing on words, you may be sure that we did
not fail to call her the "Noyade"* afterwards.

The bath I had taken had been so rigorous that they were on
the point of throwing me back into the sea for dead, when an
officer, in looking through my wallet, found my father's letter
you have just read, and on it Collingwood's signature. He made
them give me closer care. They discovered signs of life and when

---

* *Noyer* is French for "to drown." *Ed.*

I came to, I was not on board the graceful *Naïade*, but on the *Victoire*.

I asked who was in command of this other ship. They answered me laconically: "Lord Collingwood."

I thought he must be the son of the one my father knew. But when I was brought before him I was undeceived. It was the man himself!

I could not contain my surprise when he told me, with an altogether paternal kindness, that he had not expected to be the keeper of the son, after having been the father's custodian, but that he hoped to fare no worse because of it. That he had been present during my father's last moments and that, having learned my name, he had wanted to have me on board his ship. He spoke to me in the best of French, with a brooding tenderness, the impression of which has never left my memory. He offered to let me stay aboard his ship on parole if I would promise never to make any attempt at flight. I gave my word of honor unhesitatingly, after the manner of young men of eighteen, being much better off aboard the *Victory* than on some tub.

Amazed to see nothing to justify the prejudices against the English that had been inculcated in us, I became acquainted quite readily with the ship's officers. My ignorance of the sea and of their language amused them a great deal, and they found diversion in teaching me both, all the more courteously because their Admiral treated me like his son.

Nevertheless, a great sadness overwhelmed me whenever I saw the white coasts of Normandy from afar, and I would turn away so as not to weep. I resisted the desire I had to cry, because I was young and brave. But later, the moment my will no longer watched over my heart, the moment I lay down and slept, tears would come to my eyes in spite of myself and drench my cheeks and the cover of my bed to the point of waking me.

One night particularly. Another French brig had been taken. I had seen it perish at a distance without its having been possible to save a single one of the crew. In spite of the delicacy and reserve of the officers, I had to hear the cries and hurrahs of the sailors who joyfully saw the expedition vanish and the sea swallow up, bit by bit, the avalanche which threatened to crush their country. All day I had withdrawn and hidden in the quarters Lord Collingwood had given me near his own, as if the better to signify his protection. When night came I went up on deck alone.

More than ever I felt the enemy all about me and I reflected with great bitterness upon my career cut short so soon. Already I had been a prisoner of war for one month and Admiral Collingwood, treating me with such great good will in public, had spoken to me in private only once, the first day I had come aboard his ship. He was kind but cold and in his manner, as well as in that of the British officers, there was a point where all effusion ceased and where the policy of stiff formality presented itself like a barrier in every way. It was in this that life among foreigners made itself felt.

I thought of this with a kind of terror while considering my abject position, which might last until the end of the war. And the sacrifice of my youth, lost utterly in the shameful uselessness of the prisoner, seemed inevitable.

The frigate ran swiftly, under full sail, and I could not feel her go. I leaned my two hands on a rope and my forehead on my hands and, bowed like this, I gazed into the waters of the ocean. Their green and somber depths gave me a sort of dizziness. The silence of the night was unbroken save by English shouts.

For an instant I hoped the ship might take me far from France, so I would no longer see, the next day, those straight, white coasts cut into the kindly, cherished soil of my poor country.

In this way, I thought, I would be freed from the perpetual desire this view gave me, and I would at least no longer suffer the torture of being unable even to think of escaping without dishonor. A torture of Tantalus, by which an avid thirst of country must devour me for a long, long time. I was overwhelmed with loneliness and I wished for some swift occasion when I should be killed. I dreamed of bringing about my death quickly and in the grave and splendid manner of the ancients. I imagined an heroic end, worthy of those that had been the subject of so many dis-

cussions among us pages and warriors' children, the object of so
much envy among my companions.

I fell into those musings which, at eighteen, resemble more a
continuation of action and of battle than serious meditation, when
someone gently touched my arm and, facing about, I saw standing
behind me the good Admiral Collingwood.

His night glass was in his hand and he was in full dress uniform,
with the severe British regimentals. He placed one hand on my
shoulder in fatherly fashion, and I noticed a look of deep brooding in his big black eyes and on his forehead. His white hair, half
powdered, fell quite unheeded over his ears. Through the even
quiet of his voice and manner there ran an undertone of sadness,
which struck me that evening particularly, and which filled me
from the first with greater respect and attentiveness towards him.

"Already you are sad, my boy," he said to me. "I have a few
little things to say to you. Would you like to chat a bit with me?"

I stammered a few vague phrases of appreciation and politeness
which probably did not make sense, for he did not listen to them,
and sat down on a bench, holding me by the hand. I was standing
before him.

"You have been a prisoner only a month," he went on, "and
I have been one for thirty-three years. Yes, my young friend, I
am a prisoner of the Sea. She guards me on all sides; waves, forever waves. I see only them, I hear only them. My hair was
whitened under their foam, and my back was bowed a little beneath their spray. I have passed so little time in England that I
know it only by the charts. My country is an ideal being, which
I have merely glimpsed, but which I serve like a slave and which
grows the more severe with me the more I grow necessary to it.
It is the common lot, and to have such chains is what we should
desire most. But sometimes they are very heavy."

He broke off a moment and we were both silent. For I would
not have dared say a word, seeing that he was about to go on:

"I have reflected a great deal," he spoke again, "and I have
questioned myself about my duty when I had you come on board
my ship. I might have let you be taken to England. But there

you might have fallen upon misery from which I can always
protect you, or upon despair from which also I hope to save you.
I felt a very sincere friendship for your father and I shall give him
a proof of it now. If he sees me, he will be satisfied with me, will
he not?"

The Admiral was silent again and pressed my hand. He even
bent forward in the darkness and looked at me closely to see how
I took his words. But I was too much stupefied to answer him. He
went on more quickly:

"I have written already to the Admiralty to have you sent back
to France at the first exchange of prisoners. But that might take
a long time," he added, "and I won't hide it from you. For, beside
the fact that Bonaparte does not lend himself readily to this pro-
cedure, few of us are being taken prisoners. Meanwhile, let me
tell you that I should be glad to see you study the language of
your enemies. You see that we know yours. If you care to, we
will study together, and I will lend you Shakespeare and Captain
Cook. Do not distress yourself, you will be free before I am, for
if the Emperor does not make peace, I shall be prisoner for the
rest of my life."

This tone of kindliness by which he associated himself with me,
established a comradeship between us in his floating prison, made
me suffer for him. I felt that in this life of sacrifice and isolation,
he had need of doing good to console himself secretly for the
harshness of his mission of endless battling.

"Milord," I told him, "before teaching me the words of a new
language, teach me the thoughts by which you have attained this
perfect serenity, this evenness of spirit which resembles happiness
and which hides an eternal weariness. . . . Forgive me for what I
am about to say to you, but I fear that this virtue is only perpetual dissembling."

"You deceive yourself," he rejoined; "the sense of duty ends by
dominating the spirit to such extent as to enter into our character
and to become one of its principal traits, just as healthy nourish-
ment, perpetually taken may change the volume of our blood and
become one of the elements of our constitution. More than any

man, perhaps, I have proven to what point self may come to be easily forgotten. But to lay aside man completely is impossible, and there are matters to which our hearts cling more closely than we might want."

Here he broke off and took his long glass. He rested it on my shoulder to observe a distant light which glided along the horizon, and knowing at once by its motion what it was, he said:

"Fishing boats!" He came close to me, sitting on the deck of the ship. I perceived that he had been wanting for quite a while to tell me something that he did not broach. Then, suddenly:

"You never speak to me of your father. I am astonished that you do not ask me about him, about his sufferings, his words, his wishes!"

And as the night was very clear, I saw again that I was being closely observed by those big black eyes.

"I was afraid of being indiscreet," I answered, embarrassed.

He pressed my arm, as if to prevent my saying more.

"That is not it, my child, that is not it!"

And he shook his head, doubtfully and kindly.

"I have found few occasions to talk with you, Milord."

"Still less," he interrupted. "You would have talked to me about that every day, if you had cared to."

I noticed some agitation and a little of reproach in his accent. That was what he had at heart. I bethought myself of another foolish reply to justify myself. Nothing makes us so silly as false excuses.

"Milord, the humiliating sense of being a captive engrosses me more than you can think." And I remember I believed, when saying this, that I took on an air of dignity and a manner like Regulus, fit to give him a great respect for me.

"Ah, poor boy, poor child!—poor boy," he called me—"You are not right. You don't go down into yourself. Search well, and you will find an indifference for which you are not responsible as much as is the military destiny of your poor father."

He had opened up the way to Truth, and I let her start.

"I certainly did not know my father," I said. "I barely saw him once, at Malta."

"There is the truth!" he exclaimed. "There is the cruelty, my friend! Some day my two daughters will speak like that. They will say: *'We do not know our father!'* Sarah and Mary will say it! And yet, I love them with an ardent and tender heart, I bring them up from afar, I watch them from my ship, I write them every day, I direct their studies, their work, I send them thoughts and sentiments, I receive in exchange their childish confidences. I rebuke them, I calm down, I make up with them. I know all they do! I know what day they have gone to church in too fine dresses. I give their mother instructions about them continually. I can see in advance who will love them, who will woo them, who will marry them. Their husbands shall be my sons. I am making pious, simple women of them. No one can be more a father than I am. . . . Well, it counts for nothing. For they don't see me."

He spoke these last words in a moved voice, beneath which I felt tears. . . . After a moment's silence he went on:

"Yes, Sarah has never sat on my lap since she was two years old, and I held Mary in my arms only when her eyes had not yet opened. Yes, it is right that you have been indifferent about your father and that they will grow so about me some day. One doesn't love an invisible person.

"What is their father to them? A letter each day. A more or less chilly counsel. Nobody loves advice; they love a being. And a being they do not see, does not exist; they do not love him. And when he is dead, he is no more absent than he already was, —and they do not weep for him."

He choked, and stopped. Not wishing to pursue this sentiment of grief before a stranger, he moved away. He walked about awhile and paced the deck, back and forth. At first I was greatly moved at the sight of this, and it was remorse he made me feel for not having felt enough what a father means. To this evening I owed the first good, natural, sane emotion my heart had experienced. By these profound regrets, by this insurmountable grief amidst the most brilliant military splendor, I understood all I had lost through not knowing the love of home, which could leave in a great heart such poignant regrets. I understood all the artificiality there was in our barbaric, brutal education, in our insatiable need of dazzling activity.

As by a sudden revelation of the heart I saw that here was an adorable and regrettable life from which I had been violently snatched. A true life of paternal love in exchange for which a false life had been built for me, made up of hatred and all manner of puerile vanities. I understood that there was but one thing more beautiful than home, one thing to which this might be offered up in sanctity: it was that other home, the country! And while the brave old man who was moving away from me wept because he was good, I put my head in my two hands and wept because thus far I had been so wicked.

After a few minutes the Admiral returned to me:

"I must tell you," he resumed in a firmer tone, "that we shall not delay pulling closer to France. I am placed an eternal sentinel before your seaports. I have only one word to add, and I wanted it to be between ourselves. Remember that you are here on parole, and that I shall not watch you at all. But, my child, the more time goes by, the greater will be your trial. You are still very young. If temptation should become too strong for your courage to resist, come to me when you are afraid of succumbing, and do not hide from me. I may save you from a dishonorable deed which some officers have committed to the detriment of their reputations. Remember, it is permitted to break the chain of a galley slave if you can, but never your word of honor."

He left me upon these last words, pressing my hand.

I do not know, sir, whether you have noticed in life that the revolutions which take place in our souls often depend on one day, one hour, one memorable and unforeseen conversation which shakes us and drops a new seed into us that sprouts slowly and of which the remainder of our actions are merely the sequel and the natural outgrowth. Such were for me the afternoon at Fontainebleau and the night on the British vessel.

Admiral Collingwood left me a prey to a new conflict. That within me which had been only a profound weariness, an immense and youthful impatience to be doing, became an ungovernable need of country, a homesickness! To see how suffering had at length preyed upon a man always separated from the mother country, made me feel a great rush for knowing and adoring mine. I conjured up passionate ties, which in fact did not await me at all. I imagined I had a family and fell to musing about parents I had barely known and which I reproached myself for having not cherished enough. While in fact, accustomed to count me for naught, they had lived in their coldness and egoism, perfectly indifferent to my abandoned and ruined existence.

In this way even the good in me turned bad. In this way, the sage advice the brave Admiral had believed it his duty to give me, had come to me completely enveloped with his own emotion which spoke to me louder than himself. His troubled voice had touched me more than the wisdom of his words. And while he believed he was tightening my chain, he had more keenly roused in me the unbridled desire to break it.

It goes this way nearly always with all written or spoken advice.

Experience, only, and the reasoning which springs from our own reflections, are able to teach us. Look, you who have to do with it, look at the uselessness of literature. Of what use is it? Whom do you convert? And by whom are you ever understood, if you please? Nearly always you make the cause *against* which you are pleading, succeed. See, there is one of you who makes *Clarissa* the most beautiful of epic poems on the virtue of woman; then what happens? Someone takes the other side, the side of Lovelace, whom she outshines by her virginal splendor, which the rape itself has not tarnished, of Lovelace, who goes on his knees to implore the forgiveness of his sacred victim, and cannot unbend that soul, whose body had failed to drag it down in its fall; everything is all wrong in your teachings. You are of no use whatever but to stir up vices which, proud of the

way you paint them, come to admire themselves in your picture
and think themselves beautiful.

True, it does not matter to you; but my simple and splendid
Collingwood had actually made a friend of me, and my conduct
was not a matter of indifference to him. Hence he took much
pleasure at first in seeing me devoted to serious and constant
study. In my habitual reserve and my silence he also found something sympathetic to English stolidity, and he grew accustomed
to open his heart to me on many an occasion and to confide
matters to me that were not without importance. After a while
I was looked upon as his secretary and his relative, and I spoke
English well enough not to seem a stranger any longer.

Nevertheless it was a cruel life I was leading and I found the
gloomy days at sea very long. For whole years we never stopped
roaming around France and ceaselessly I saw sketched upon the
horizon the coasts of this land which Hugo Grotius has called:
"The most beautiful Kingdom next to that of Heaven." Then we
would put to sea again and for whole months there would be
nothing about me but fogs and mountains of water. When a
ship passed near us or far from us, it would be English. None
other was permitted to give itself up to the winds, and the ocean
no longer heard a word that was not English. The English themselves were dejected and complained that the ocean, these days,
had become a desert where they encountered one another
eternally, and Europe a fortress which was closed to them.

Sometimes my wooden prison would come so close to shore
that I could make out men and children on the beach. Then my
heart would beat fast, and an inward rage devour me with such
violence that I would hide in the hold so as not to succumb to
the desire to jump in and swim for it. But when I had come
back to the indefatigable Collingwood I would be ashamed of
my childish weaknesses, I could never tire admiring how with
so profound a melancholy he united such aggressive courage.
This man, who had known nothing but war and waves these forty
years, never ceased to apply himself to the study of them as to
an inexhaustible science. When one ship gave out, he climbed

on board another, like a pitiless horseman. He used them and killed them under him. He wore out seven with me. He passed the nights fully dressed, sitting on his cannons, all the time figuring out the art of keeping his vessel stockstill, a sentry, in the same spot at sea, without anchoring, despite wind and current. He was forever training his crews, watching out over them and for them. This man had enjoyed no riches whatever. And though he was called a Peer of England, he loved his pewter soup bowl like any sailor. Then, returning to his cabin, he became the family father again and wrote to his daughters not to play the fine lady; to read, not novels, but tales of travel, essays and Shakespeare as often as they pleased. He wrote:

"We have had a fight on the birthday of my little Sarah"— after the battle of Trafalgar which I had the grief to see him win, and the plans of which he had drawn with his friend, Nelson, whom he succeeded.

Sometimes he felt his health giving way. He would ask England for relief. But the inexorable answered him: 'Stay at sea,' and offered him some dignity, or a gold medal for each fine action. His breast was overloaded with them. Again he wrote:

"Since I have left my country, I have not spent ten days in any port. My eyes are weakening. When I shall be able to see my children, the sea will have made me blind. I lament that out of so many officers it is so difficult to find me a substitute of superior ability." England replied: 'You will stay at sea, always at sea.' And at sea he remained until his death.

This life, Roman and imposing, crushed me by its simplicity, when I had contemplated it only one day in its grave and thoughtful resignation. I scorned myself a great deal, I, who was nothing as a citizen, nothing as a father, nor as a son, nor as a public man, for complaining when he did not complain. He had never let himself be fathomed despite himself but once, and I, useless child —I an ant among ants that crowded around the feet of the Sultan of France—I reproached myself for my secret desire to return and offer myself up to the hazard of his whims and to become again one of the grains of the dust he would be kneading with blood.

The meeting with this true citizen, devoted, not—as I had been—to one man, but to country and duty, was a fortunate one for me. For I learned, in this severe school, that that is the veritable greatness we must henceforward seek amidst arms and how high—if well understood—it lifts our profession above all others. It may keep worthy of admiration the memory of some of us, no matter what the future of war and armies may be.

No man ever possessed to any higher degree this inward peace born of the sense of sacred duty, and the modest carefreeness of the soldier to whom it matters little if his name be famous, provided the public weal prospers. One day I saw him write:

"To maintain the independence of my country is the foremost will of my life and I would rather my body be added to the rampart of the country than dragged in futile pomp through an idle mob. To England are due my life and my strength. Do not speak of my last wound, it might be believed that I glorify myself because of my danger."

His melancholy was profound, but full of greatness. It did not keep him from perpetual activity and he gave me the measure of what an intelligent fighting man should be, professing, not for ambition's but for art's sake, the Art of War. The man who judges it loftily and often scorns it like Montecuccoli, who retired after Turenne's death, because he no longer deigned to take the part against an ordinary player.

But I was still too young to comprehend all the merits of this character and what appealed to me most was the ambition to hold, in my own country, a rank similar to his. When I saw the Kings of southern Europe beg his protection, and even Napoleon stir with the hope that Collingwood might be in the Indian Ocean, I came to calling down even in my prayers for the chance to escape and I pressed the ambition which I always nursed nearly to the point of breaking my parole. Yes, I went as far as that.

One day, the ship, the *Ocean*, which bore us, put into Gibraltar. I went ashore with the Admiral, and walking alone through the town I met an officer of the 7th Hussars who had been made a prisoner in the Spanish campaign and taken to Gibraltar with four of his comrades. They had the town for a prison, but they were closely watched.

I had known this officer in France. We were pleased to meet again, and in situations very nearly similar. It had been so long since a Frenchman had spoken French to me that I thought him eloquent, although he was perfectly silly. After a quarter of an hour we revealed our situations to each other. Right away he told me frankly that he intended to escape with his comrades. That they had found an excellent opportunity and that he would not let himself be told twice to follow them. He urged me strongly to do likewise. I answered him that he was very lucky for being watched. But that I, who was not, could not escape without dishonor and that he, his companions and myself were not in the same boat. That seemed too fine a point to him.

"My word!" he said to me, "I am no hairsplitter, and if you care to I shall send you a bishop who will tell you his opinion on it. But in your place I would go. I can see but two things—being free—or not. Do you know that your promotion has been lost during the five years that you have been dragging around in that English tub? The lieutenants of your day are already colonels."

Thereupon his companions came up and took me along into a very bad looking house where they drank sherry, and there they cited so many captains become generals, and sublieutenants become viceroys, that my head turned, and I promised them to be in the same spot, the day after the next at midnight.

We were to be taken from there in a small yawl they had hired from honest smugglers who would take us aboard a French vessel chartered to take wounded of our Army to Toulon. The project seemed an admirable one to me. And my fine companions, having made me drink off glass after glass to quiet the whisperings of my conscience, ended their discourse with a victorious argument. They swore by their own heads that I might have, at the strictest, some regard for a brave man who had treated me well, but that everything confirmed their certainty that a Britisher was not a man.

I returned on board the *Ocean* quite thoughtful, and went to sleep. When I awakened and saw my position clearly, I asked myself if my fellow patriots had not been making fun of me. Nevertheless, the desire for liberty and an ever keen ambition, aroused since my childhood, drove me to the escape, despite the shame I felt for being false to my oath. I passed the entire day with the Admiral without daring to look him in the face, and I endeavored to find him inferior and narrow-minded.

At table I spoke quite loud and arrogantly about Napoleon's greatness. I became exalted, I bragged of his universal genius which divined the laws while making the codes, and the future while shaping events. I dwelt insolently upon the superiority of this genius, compared to the mediocrity of the talents of the tacticians. I hoped to be contradicted. But contrary to my expectation, I met among the British officers still more admiration for the Emperor than I could show for this implacable enemy of theirs.

Lord Collingwood, especially, emerged from his gloomy silence and his continuous meditations. He praised him in terms so just, so forceful, so exact, and made his officers view, at the same time, the greatness of the Emperor's prevision, the magic quickness of his execution, the firmness of his orders, the sureness of his judgment, his penetration in negotiations, his clearness of ideas in councils, his greatness in battle, his calm in danger, his constancy in preparing enterprises, his pride in the stature given to France, and in reality all the qualities that composed the great man, that I asked myself what history could ever add to this eulogy. I was floored. For I had tried to rouse my ire against the Admiral in the hope of hearing him proffer unjust charges.

Wickedly, I had wanted to put him in the wrong and that one ill-considered or insulting phrase on his part might serve to justify the disloyalty I contemplated. But he seemed, on the contrary, to be doing his utmost to redouble his kindness. And as his assiduity made the others suppose I had some new sorrow

for which it was right to console me, they were all more attentive and indulgent towards me than ever. It disgusted me and I
left the table.

The next day the Admiral took me to Gibraltar again, to my
misfortune. We had to spend a week there.

The evening of the escape arrived.

My head whirled. I deliberated all the time. I allowed specious
motives and I became dizzy with their falsity. A violent conflict
raged within me. But while my spirit wrenched and wrestled
with itself, my body followed all alone the road of flight, as if
it were the arbiter betwixt ambition and honor.

Without being aware of it myself, I had made a bundle of my
clothes, and I went on my way from the house in Gibraltar
where we were, to the meeting place, when suddenly I stopped
short and felt that it was impossible.

There is something poisonous in a shameful deed which can
be tasted by a gallant man when his lips touch the rim of the
beaker of perdition. He cannot even sip of it without being ready
to die of it.

When I realized what I was about to do, that I was going to
break my parole, such a terror took hold of me that I believed
I had gone mad. I ran to the beach and from the fatal hovel as
from a pesthouse, not daring to turn and look at it. I jumped in
and swam, and during the night I boarded our ship, the *Ocean*,
my floating prison. I climbed aboard transported, clutching the
ropes. Arriving on deck, I gripped the mainmast, and clung to
it passionately, as if to a refuge which guarded me against
dishonor. And at the same time, the sense of the greatness of my
sacrifice tearing my heart, I fell to my knees and, resting my head
against the iron girders of the big mast, burst into tears like a
child.

The skipper of the *Ocean* found me in this state and believed,
or pretended to believe, I was ill. He had me carried to my cabin.
I begged him to place a sentinel at my door to prevent my going
out. They shut me in, and I breathed to be relieved at last from
the torture of being my own jailer. The next day, at daylight,

I saw we were out at sea, and I calmed down a bit for losing sight of land, the object of all the miserable temptation of my situation. I thought of it more resignedly when my little door opened and the good Admiral entered alone.

"I have come to say good-bye," he began, looking less grave than usual. "You are leaving for France tomorrow morning."

"Oh, my God. Is it to test me that you tell me that, Milord?"

"That would be a very cruel game, my boy," he rejoined. "Already I have been very wrong towards you. I should have left you a prisoner on the *Northumberland* and given you back your word. Then you might have plotted against your keepers without remorse, and used your wits without scruple to make your escape. You have suffered more, having had more freedom. But thank God! you resisted an opportunity yesterday, which would have dishonored you. It would have meant shipwreck in the harbor, since for two weeks past I have been negotiating for your exchange and Admiral Rosily has just secured it. I trembled for you yesterday for I knew of the project of your comrades. I have let them escape for your sake, lest in arresting them they would arrest you. And what could we have done to hide that? You would have been lost, my boy, believe me, you would have been badly received by Napoleon's old braves. They have the right to be testy as to honor."

I was so confused that I did not know how to thank him. He saw my embarrassment and, hastening to cut short the poor phrases in which I tried to stammer that I regretted it, he continued:

"Come, come, none of what we call French compliments. We are satisfied with each other, that's all. And your people have, I believe, a proverb that says: *There is no beautiful prison.* Let me die in mine, my friend. I am used to mine, I have jolly well had to be. But it won't last much longer. I feel my legs shaking under me and getting thin. For the fourth time I have asked Lord Mulgrave to be retired, and he has again refused me. He writes that he does not know how to replace me. When I am dead, they shall have to find some one nevertheless, and it would do no harm to take precautions. I am to remain on sentry in the Mediterranean. But you, my boy, don't lose time. There is a sloop that will take you. I have only one thing to suggest to you, that is to devote yourself to a principle rather than to a man. The love of your country is one big enough to fill a whole heart and keep busy an entire intelligence."

"Alas! Milord," I answered, "there are times when it is not easy to know what the country wishes. I am going to ask it of mine!"

Once again we said good-by and with a full heart I left this worthy man. I learned of his death shortly after. He died out at sea, the way he had lived for forty-nine years, without complaining, without glorying and without having seen his two daughters again. Alone and somber like one of those old hounds of Ossian's that guard eternally the coasts of England amidst the waves and the fogs.

At his school I had learned all that the exiles of war may suffer and all that the sense of duty may quell in a great soul. Thoroughly imbued with this example and grown more serious by my sufferings and the sight of his, I went to Paris to present myself, with my prison experience, to the all-powerful master I had left.

6   The Reception

WHEN CAPTAIN RENAUD broke off, I looked at my watch. It was two hours after midnight. He got up and we went among the Grenadiers. Deep silence reigned everywhere. A good many had sat down on their knapsacks and fallen asleep there. We sat down ourselves a few steps away, on the parapet, and he continued his story after having relighted his cigar at a soldier's pipe. Not a house showed a sign of life.

The moment I arrived in Paris, I wanted to see the Emperor. I had the opportunity at a play at Court, to which one of my old comrades, now a colonel, took me. It was down there, at the Tuileries. We sat down in a small box, opposite the Imperial box, and we waited. Only the Kings were in the hall as yet. Each of these, in a first tier box, had his court around him, and before him in the galleries were his aides-de-camp and his generals. The Kings of Westphalia, Saxony and Wurttemberg, all the princes of the Rhine Federation were placed in the same row. Murat, King of Naples, shaking his black hair curled like a mane and casting leonine glances, stood near them, talking loud and fast. Higher up was the King of Spain, and alone, shoved aside, the Russian Ambassador, Prince Kourakim, with diamond epaulettes. In the pit the crowds of generals, dukes, princes, colonels and senators. Everywhere above, the bare arms and shoulders of the ladies of the Court.

The box surmounted with the eagle was still empty. We never took our eyes off it. After a little while the Kings rose and remained standing. The Emperor entered the box alone, walking rapidly, threw himself quickly into his chair and gazed in front of him. Then he remembered that the entire hall was on its feet and awaiting a glance. He bobbed his head twice, brusquely and with bad grace, turned quickly and allowed the Queens and Kings to sit down. His chamberlains, dressed in red, stood up behind him. Occasionally he talked to them without looking at them, holding out his hand to receive a gold box, which one of them handed him and took back again. Crescentini sang *Las Horaces*, with the voice of a seraph coming out of a hectic, wrinkled face. The orchestra was soft and weak, by order of the Emperor. He wanted, perhaps, like the Lacedemonians to be soothed rather than excited by the music. He ogled in front of him, and very often in my direction. I recognized his large grayish-green eyes, but I did not like the yellow fat which had swallowed up his severe features. He put his left hand over his left eye to see better, as was his wont. I felt he had recognized me. He jerked around, looked at nothing save the stage, and soon went out. He walked rapidly through the corridor, and his fat legs bulging in white silk stockings, his puffy figure in the green

coat, almost made him unrecognizable to me. He stopped short
in front of me, and speaking to the colonel who presented me,
instead of addressing his words to me direct:

"Why have I not seen him anywhere? Still a lieutenant?"

"He has been a prisoner since 1804."

"Why did he not escape?"

"I was on parole," I murmured.

"I don't like prisoners," he said. " 'Twere better to be killed."
He turned his back on me. We remained without stirring, lined
up. And when all his suite had filed past:

"*Mon cher*," the colonel said to me, "you can see readily that
you were an imbecile. You have lost your promotion and you are
not liked any the better for it."

7   *The Russian Guard*

Is IT possible?" I said, stamping my foot. When I hear such
stories I applaud the fact that the officer in me has been dead
these several years. There remains only the solitary and independent scribe who considers what is to become of his freedom,
and who does not want to defend it against his old friends.

And I believed I saw in Captain Renaud traces of indignation
at the memory of what he was relating to me. But he smiled
quietly and with a contented expression.

He resumed:

It was all very simple. That colonel was the finest chap in the
world. But there are men who are, to use the celebrated phrase,
braggarts of crimes and of hardheartedness. He wanted to mal-
treat me because the Emperor had set the example; gross flattery
of the Guard Corps.

But how fortunate it was for me. From that day on, I began
to esteem myself inwardly, to have confidence in myself, to make
my character become purer, form itself, round itself out, become
firmer. From that day on I realized clearly that events go for
naught, that the inward man is everything. I placed myself well

above my judges. Finally my consciousness began to make itself felt. I resolved to lean on it alone, and to regard public judgments, glittering rewards, rapid fortunes, reputations of the bulletin, like so many ridiculous boastings, like a game of chance with which it was not worth busying oneself.

Very soon I plunged into the war, amid unknown ranks of the infantry of the line, the infantry of battle, in which the peasants of the army were mowed down by the thousand at a time, similar to, equal to, the wheat of a fat field of the Beauce. There I hid myself like a friar in his cell. And down in this mob of the Army marching on foot like the privates, carrying a knapsack and eating their bread, I went through the great wars of the Empire as long as the Empire stood.

Ah! If you knew how comfortable I felt amidst these unheard of hardships! How I loved this obscurity and what savage joys the great battles gave me! The beauty of war lies among the privates, in camp life, in the mud of the marching and the camping. I avenged myself on Bonaparte in serving my country, owing nothing to Napoleon. And when he passed before my regiment, I hid myself lest he show me favors. Experience had made me measure dignities and power at their true value. I no longer aspired to a thing except to take from each victory of our arms that portion of pride which would be my due according to my own feeling. I wanted to be a citizen where it was still permitted to be one, and that in my own way. At one time my services remained unnoticed, at another they were raised above their merit, and I never stopped keeping them dark, with all my power, fearing above all that my name would be too loudly mentioned. The crowd was so big that obscurity came easy, and in 1814 I still was only a lieutenant in the Imperial Guard, when I received this wound you see on my forehead, and which causes me more trouble tonight than ordinarily.

At this Captain Renaud passed his hand over his forehead and as it appeared that he wanted to keep silent I pressed him to go on, with enough insistence to make him give in.

He leaned his head on the knob of his malacca cane and continued:

Here is a singular thing: I have never told all this, and this evening I like to tell it. Bah! No matter! I like to let myself go with an old comrade. For you it will be the subject for serious reflection when you have nothing better to do. It is not unworthy of that, it seems to me. You will think me very weak or very mad; but it's all the same. Until the happening I am going to tell you about and of which I put off the telling in spite of myself, because it pains me—though it is a common enough happening to others —my love of the glory of arms had become wise, grave and utterly pure, as should be the simple and single sense of duty. But from that day on, other thoughts again came to cast a shadow on my life.

It was in 1814. It was the beginning of the year and the end of that dark war in which our poor army defended the Empire and the Emperor, and in which France looked upon the battle in dismay. Soissons had just surrendered to the Prussian Bülow. The armies of Silesia and of the North had effected their junction there. Macdonald had left Troyes and abandoned the basin of the Yonne to establish his line of defense from Nogent to Monterreau with thirty thousand men.

We were to attack Rheims, which the Emperor wanted to retake. The weather was dark and it rained continuously. The day before we had lost a superior officer who was convoying the prisoners. The Russians had surprised and killed him the preceding night, and set their comrades free. Our colonel, who was what they call a *dur à cuire*, wanted to get even. We were near Epernay and we turned the heights surrounding it. Night fell and, after spending the whole day getting ourselves together, we passed by a fine white château with towers, called Boursault, when the colonel called me. He took me aside, while the guns were being stacked, and said in his old, hoarse voice:

"You see a barn up there, don't you, on that steep hill yonder, where that big loafer of a Russian sentry is strutting, with his bishop's hat?"

"Yes, yes," I answered, "I can see the grenadier and the barn perfectly."

"Well, you are an old hand, you ought to know that yonder is the point the Russians took day before yesterday, and which bothers the Emperor most this particular quarter of an hour. He has told me it is the key to Rheims and perhaps it is. At any rate we are going to play a trick on Woronzoff. At eleven tonight you'll take two hundred of your 'boys,' and you will surprise the watch set in that barn. But, lest an alarm is raised, you will put that through with the bayonet."

He took, and offered me, a pinch of snuff, and throwing the rest away, little by little, the way I am doing here, he said to me, pronouncing a word to each grain of snuff thrown to the winds:

"You understand all right that I will be there, back of you, with my column. You'll hardly have lost sixty men; you will have the six guns they have placed there. . . . You will turn them upon Rheims. . . . At eleven . . . half-past eleven . . . the position will be ours. And we will sleep till three . . . to rest a little . . . from that little affair at Craonne . . . which had no flies on it . . . as they say."

"Very well," I told him. And I went with my second in command, to make some little preparation for our evening's party. The essential thing, as you see, was to make no noise. I made an inspection of the rifles and had the cartridges taken out of all the loaded ones, with the wad-hook. Next I walked around with my sergeants a bit, while waiting for the hour.

At ten-thirty I made them put their overcoats over their uniforms and hide their rifles under the coats; for whatever you do, as you may notice tonight, the bayonet always shows. And though it was dark as it is now, I did not trust to it. I had noticed the narrow lanes, bordered with hedges, that led to the Russian sentry post, and up them I sent the most determined gang of rascals I have ever commanded. Two of them are still there, in the ranks. They were there and remember it well.

They knew the Russians' custom and how to capture them. The sentries we met going up disappeared without noise, like reeds that are bent to the ground with the hands. The one before the rifles required more care. He stood stock-still, rifle at his heel, chin on the muzzle. The poor devil rocked back and forth like a man falling asleep from weariness and about to topple over. One of my grenadiers took him in his arms, squeezing him till he choked, and two others gagged and dropped him in the underbrush. I came on slowly and I could not help myself—I admit it—against a certain emotion I had never felt at other moments of battle. It was the shame of attacking sleeping men. There they were, rolled in their overcoats, under a dark lantern. My heart beat violently. But suddenly, on the instant of action, I feared this was only a weakness; one that resembled cowardice. I feared I had known fear this once!

And so, taking my sword from under my arm, I went in first, brusquely, setting the example to my grenadiers. I flung them a gesture they understood. They threw themselves first upon the weapons, next upon the men, like wolves on the flock. Oh, it was a dumb and horrible butchery! The bayonet pierced, the butt crushed, the knee smothered, the hand strangled. Every cry was silenced beneath the feet of our soldiers before it was barely uttered. No head lifted but received the death blow.

As I went in I had struck at random, one terrific blow straight ahead of me, at something black which I pierced through and through. An old officer, a large and strong man, white hair bristling on his head, rose up like a phantom. He saw what I had done and uttered a horrible cry, and struck a violent sword thrust at my face. The next instant he fell dead under the bayonets.

I, too, went down beside him, dizzy with the blow between my eyes. And underneath me I heard the dying, tender voice of a child, that lisped: "Papa."

Then I understood the thing I had done. I contemplated it with frenzied care. I saw one of those fourteen-year-old officers so numerous in the Russian armies that invaded us at the time, and who were trained in this terrible school. His long curly hair fell to his breast, as blond, as silky as a woman's, and his head was bent as if he only just had fallen asleep again. His rosy lips, open like those of a newborn babe, still seemed moist with his mother's milk and his big, blue, half-open eyes were beautifully shaped, candid, caressing, feminine. I lifted him by one arm and his head fell on my bloody cheek, as if he were nestling his head between his mother's neck and shoulders, to get warm. He seemed to huddle on my breast to escape his murderers. The filial tenderness, the confidence and peacefulness of sweet sleep rested on his dead face and he seemed to be saying: "Let us sleep in peace!"

"Was that an enemy?" I cried out! Whatever fatherly feeling God has put into the bowels of any man was touched and trembling within me. I hugged the poor infant to my breast. Then I felt pressing against me the hilt of my sword which had trans-fixed the heart and killed the sleeping seraph.

I wanted to hang my head on his, but my blood smirched him with big blotches. I felt the wound in my head—and I remem-bered it had been struck by his father. Shamefacedly I looked beside me and I saw nothing but a tangle of corpses my grenadiers were pulling by the legs to throw outside, only taking their cartridges away from them.

At that moment the colonel entered, followed by his column. I heard their tread and their weapons.

"Bravo! my dear sir," he said to me, "you pulled this off quickly. But are you wounded?"

"Look at this," I said. "What difference is there between me and a murderer?"

"Why, by God, my dear fellow, what do you expect? It is our trade!"

"Correct," I answered, and rose to take my command again. The child fell back in the folds of his mantle in which I wrapped him, and his little hand, adorned with heavy rings, dropped a malacca cane. It fell into my hand, as if it were being given to me. I took it. I resolved that henceforth I would carry no other weapon, no matter what might be my danger. I did not have the heart to draw my cutthroat sword out of his breast.

Hurriedly I left the den that reeked with blood, and when I came outside, I found the strength to wipe off my red, wet forehead. My grenadiers stood in line. Each one was coolly cleaning off his bayonet on the grass, and refastening the flintlock of his rifle. My sergeant-major, followed by the quartermaster, passed along the ranks, the roll in his hand and calling it by the light of a candle stuck in the muzzle of his gun, like a torch. He was serenely mustering the men. I leaned against a tree, where the surgeon-major came to bandage my forehead. A heavy March rain, falling on my bare head, did me some good. I could not help sighing deeply.

"I am tired of war," I said to the surgeon.

"So am I," said a grave voice which I recognized.

I raised the bandage over my eyebrows and saw before me, not Napoleon the Emperor, but Bonaparte the soldier. He was alone, on foot, brooding. He stood before me, his boots sunk in the mud, his coat torn; the rain streamed from the rim of his hat. He felt his last days were come, and looked about him at his last soldiers.

He considered me attentively. "I have seen you somewhere, *grognard*," he said.

By this last word I knew that he was saying merely a banal phrase. I knew my face had aged more than my years, and the hardship, whiskers and wound disguised me quite.

"I have seen you everywhere, without being seen," I answered.

"Do you want promotion?"

"It is pretty late."

He crossed his arms and did not answer a while. Then:

"You are right. Three more days, and you and I will quit the service."

He turned his back on me and mounted his horse again, which had been held a few steps away. That same moment the head of our column had attacked and we were being shelled. One shell fell in front of our company. A few drew back upon a first impulse, and then hesitated, ashamed. Bonaparte alone went towards the bomb, that smoked and sputtered before his horse, and made it sniff the smoke. All remained silent and stock-still. The bomb burst, and hurt no one.

The grenadiers realized the terrible lesson Napoleon had given them. I felt, besides that, something that smacked of despair. France was failing him, and for a moment he had doubted his old heroes. I felt I was too much avenged, and he too much punished for his faults by so great a desertion. I rose with difficulty, and stumbling towards him I grasped and wrung the hand he held out to several among us. He did not recognize me at all, but to me it meant a tacit reconciliation between the most obscure and the most illustrious of the men of our century.

The charge was sounded, and next day, at sunrise, Rheims was retaken by us. But so was Paris a few days later, by others!

Captain Renaud remained silent a long time after this tale and hung his head. I did not want to interrupt his musing. I regarded this fine man with veneration, and while he spoke I had followed attentively the slow transformations in this good and simple soul, always repressed within its self-immolation, always crushed by an invincible power, but winning through to find rest in humblest and most austere duty.

His obscure existence appeared to me as beautiful inwardly as the brilliant life of any man of action whosoever.

Each wave of the sea adds a film of white to the beauties of a pearl; each billow labors slowly to make it more perfect; each puff of foam that floats upon it leaves it a mysterious hue, half golden, half translucent, through which the inward ray that emanates from its heart may be only divined.

Quite in the same manner this man's character had been formed in vast upheavals, in the depths of darkest and perpetual trials. I knew that as long as the Emperor lived he had considered it a duty never to serve in the Army, respecting what he called common decency, despite all the entreaties of his friends. And afterwards, freed by Napoleon's death from the bond of his old promise to a master who knew him no more, he had returned to command, in the Royal Guards, the remnants of his Old Guard.

As he never spoke about himself, no one had ever thought of him and he had had no promotion. He worried little about that. It was his custom to say that unless one is a general at twenty-five, the age when one's imagination can be given scope, it were better to remain a simple captain to live with the soldiers as a family father, as a prior of a monastery.

"Look," he said to me after this spell of rest, "watch our old grenadier Poirier, with his somber, squinting eyes, his bald head and the sword slashes on his cheek. The Marshals of France used to stop and admire him when he presented arms for them at the King's door. Look at Beccaria with his profile of a Roman veteran, at Fréchou with his white whiskers, at that whole first row, all decorated, with three chevrons on their sleeves! What would they have said, those old friars of the ancient Army, if I had failed them this morning, I who still commanded them a fortnight ago? It would have been different if I had taken on fireside habits of ease or another profession several years ago.

"Why, look how still everything is in Paris tonight, still as the air," he added, rising with me. "Here is day breaking. No doubt they will begin smashing street lamps again, and tomorrow we'll go back to quarters. Probably in a few days I shall retire, to a little corner of land I own somewhere in France where there is a little tower in which I will finish up my studies on Polybius, Turenne, Folard and Vauban, to amuse myself. Nearly all my comrades were killed in the Great Army, or have died since. It has been a long time since I have talked with anybody, and you know by what road I have come to hate war, while waging it energetically all the time."

Thereupon he wrung my hand heartily while again asking me for the gorget he needed, if mine were not rusted and if I could find it at my home. Then he called me back and said:

"Look here, as it is not altogether impossible they will again fire on us from some window, I beg of you to keep for me this portfolio full of old letters. They interest me, me alone, and you will burn them if we do not see each other again.

"Several of our old comrades have happened along and we have begged them to return to their homes. We are not fighting a Civil War. We are as serene as firemen whose duty it is to put out a fire. Explanations will follow; that does not concern us."

And he left me, smiling.

8   A Marble

Two weeks after this conversation, which the Revolution itself had not made me forget, I was thinking alone about his modest heroism and disinterestedness, both so rare! I tried to forget the pure blood that had been shed, and I reread in the history of America how, in 1783, the victorious Anglo-American Army, after having delivered the country and laid down arms, was on the point of revolting against Congress which, too poor to pay it, was getting ready to disband it. Washington, generalissimo and conqueror, had but to say a word or nod his head to be Dictator. He did what only he had the power to accomplish: he disbanded the Army and gave in his resignation.

I had laid down the book and I compared this serene greatness to our restless ambition. I was sad and recalled all the warlike, pure spirits, without false brilliance, without charlatanism, who have loved power and command only for the public weal, who have guarded it without pride and have neither turned it against the country nor converted it into gold. I thought of all the men who have waged war with the intelligence of its worth. I thought of Collingwood and his resignation, and finally of that obscure Captain Renaud, when I saw coming in a tall man dressed in a long blue cape which was in pretty bad condition. By his white mustache and the scars on his bronzed face, I recognized one of the grenadiers of his company. I asked him if the Captain was still alive, and the emotion of this good fellow showed me something disastrous had happened. The grenadier sat down, wiped his forehead, and after a little fussing and a little time, he told me what had happened to the Captain.

During the two days of July 28 and 29, Captain Renaud had

not done a thing but march in column along the streets at the head
of his grenadiers. He would place himself in front of the first
section of his column, and walk on peaceably amid a hail of
stones and rifle shots that came from cafés, balconies and windows. If he stopped, it was to close up the ranks opened by
those that had fallen, and to look if his left guides were keeping
their distances and abreast their files. He had not drawn his
sword, and marched, cane in hand. At first his orders had come
to him promptly. But, either because the aides-de-camp were
killed on their way, or because the general staff did not send
them, he was left, during the night of the 28th to the 29th, on
the Place de la Bastille, without other instructions than to fall
back upon Saint-Cloud and destroy the barricades on his way.
This he did without firing a shot.

Arrived at the Jéna Bridge he stopped to call the roll of his
company. Fewer men were missing with his than with all the
other companies of the Guard that had been detached. And his
men also were less tired. He had known the trick of letting them
rest to good purpose in the shade during those sizzling days,
and of finding for them in the abandoned barracks the food which
the hostile houses refused them. The aspect of his column was
such that he had found each barricade deserted, and had only
to take the trouble to demolish it.

There he was standing on the Jéna Bridge covered with dust,
stamping his feet. He was looking towards the barrier to see if
anything might trouble the passing of his detachment and told
off the scouts to send ahead. There wasn't a soul in the Champ-
de-Mars except two masons who seemed asleep, lying on their
bellies, and a little boy of about fourteen who ran barefoot and
played castanets with two bits of broken pottery. He rattled
them from time to time on the parapet of the bridge. In this way
he came playing up to the stone on which Renaud stood. The
Captain at this moment was pointing out the heights of Passy with
his cane. The child came close to him, looking at him with big,
startled eyes, and pulling a horse pistol from his blouse, he took
it in both hands and pointed it at the Captain's breast. Renaud

deflected the pistol with his cane but the child had fired and the bullet hit up in the thigh. The Captain fell to a sitting posture without saying a word and regarded this singular enemy with pity. He saw this young boy holding his weapon with both hands all the time, utterly frightened by what he had done. The grenadiers at the moment were leaning gloomily on their rifles. They disdained lifting a hand against this queer little one. Some of them lifted their Captain, others just took the child by the arm and led him forward to the man he had wounded.

The boy burst into tears, and when he saw the blood streaming from the Captain's wound over his white trousers, he was so scared of the butchery that he fainted. The man and the boy were taken to a little house near Passy at the same time. They were there still.

The column, led by the lieutenant, had continued on its way to Saint-Cloud, and four grenadiers, after having doffed their uniforms, had remained in this little hospitable house to nurse their old commander.

One of them (the one who was talking to me) had obtained work as a gunsmith's helper in Paris, the others as fencing masters. Bringing their day's wages to the Captain, they had kept him from lacking care till that day. His leg had been amputated. But the fever had been high and bad, and fearing dangerous complications, he had sent for me.

There was no time to lose. I went immediately with the worthy soldier who had told me these details with moist eyes and trembling voice, but without a murmur of indignation or accusation. He only repeated: "It is a great misfortune for us."

The wounded man had been carried into a small shopkeeper's. She was a widow living alone in her little shop in a side street of the village of Passy, with some young children. She had not been afraid of compromising herself a single moment, and no one had thought of bothering her on the subject. On the contrary, the neighbors had offered their aid in caring for the wounded man. The doctors who had been called in had not thought him fit to be moved after the operation. So she had kept him and spent several nights by his bedside.

When I came in, she went ahead of me with an air of gratitude and shyness that pained me. I felt how much embarrassment she had hidden out of natural goodness and benevolence. She was very pale, and her eyes were red and tired. She went back and forth to a tiny rear shop which I noticed from the door, and I saw, by the way she hurried, that she was setting the little sick-chamber to rights with a sort of coquettishness, in order that I, the stranger, might find it fitting. Therefore I took pains to go in very slowly, giving her all the time she needed.

"You see, sir, he has suffered a great deal!" she said opening the door to me.

Captain Renaud was sitting up in a little bed with serge curtains set in a corner of the room. Several bolsters propped up his body. He was thin as a rail and on his cheekbones were two fiery red spots. The wound on his forehead was black. I saw he did not have long to live. His smile, too, told me so.

He gave me his hand and motioned me to sit down. At his right a young boy was holding a glass of sweetened water which he stirred with a spoon. He rose and gave me his chair. Renaud, from his bed, took him by the tip of the ear, and told me softly in a weakened voice:

"Look, *mon cher*, let me introduce my conqueror!"

I shrugged my shoulders, and the poor child lowered his eyes and reddened. I saw a big tear rolling down his cheek.

"Come! Come!" the Captain said, passing his hand over the boy's hair, "it is not his fault. Poor boy! He had met two men who had given him brandy to drink and paid him, and sent him to fire the pistol at me. He did it just as he might have thrown a marble at the milestone I stood on. Did you not, Jean?"

And Jean began to tremble and took on an expression of such heartbreaking grief that I was touched. I looked at him more closely; he was a very handsome lad.

"It was a marble all right enough, too," said the young shop-keeper. "Look sir!" And she showed me an agate marble, as big

as the heaviest lead bullet, and with which they had loaded the
large caliber pistol that lay there.

"No more than that is necessary to cut down a Captain's leg,"
joked Renaud.

"You must not let him talk much," timidly ventured the young
tradeswoman.

Renaud did not hear her:

"Yes, *mon cher*, I have not enough leg left to make a wooden
leg stick to it."

I pressed his hand without answering. It was humiliating to
see that, to kill a man who had seen and suffered so much, whose
breast was bronzed by twenty campaigns and ten wounds, im-
mune to ice and fire, passed by of bayonet and lance, the mere
jumping up of one of these frogs from the gutters of Paris,
that are called *gamins*, had sufficed.

Renaud answered my thought. He leaned his cheek on the
bolster, and taking my hand said:

"We are at war! He is no more a murderer than I myself was
at Rheims. When I killed the Russian lad, perhaps I, too, was a
murderer? In the great Spanish War, the men that knifed our
sentries did not believe they were assassins, and being at war,
they probably were not. The Catholics and the Huguenots
murdered each other, or did they not? Of how many murders
does a big battle consist? That is one of those questions where
our reason fails and knows not what to say. It is war that is
wrong, not we. I assure you that this little fellow is very nice
and very gentle. He reads and writes very well already. He is a
foundling. He was a cabinetmaker's apprentice. He has not left
my room these two weeks, and he loves me very much, poor lad.
He shows aptness for figures. Something can be made of him."

As he spoke with greater difficulty and came close to my ear,
I bent over, and he gave me a little piece of folded paper
which he asked me to look through. I recognized a brief will,
in which he left a kind of poor little farm he owned to the
woman who had taken him in, and after her, to Jean, whom she
was to bring up upon condition that he should never be a soldier.

He stipulated the sum to be paid for his substitute and gave his little piece of land to his four old grenadiers for a shelter. The execution of all this he gave in charge to a notary in his district.

When I had the paper in my hands he seemed calmer and ready for a rest. Then he shivered, and reopening his eyes he begged me to take and keep his malacca cane. After this he dozed off again. His old grenadier shook his head and took his hand. I took the other, and felt it was icy. He said his feet were cold, and Jean lay down and leaned his young body on the bed to warm him.

Captain Renaud began plucking the blankets with his hands, saying he could not feel them any more, which is a fatal sign. His voice was hollow. With difficulty he lifted one hand to his forehead, looked at Jean attentively and said again:

"Strange! This lad here resembles the Russian child!" Then he shut his eyes, and pressing my hand with recurring presence of mind:

"You see, it is the brain that is touched now. It's the end."

His look was different and calmer. We understood this struggle of a strong spirit which judged itself against the pain that made it stray. And this spectacle on this miserable truckle-bed seemed full of solemn majesty. He reddened again and spoke very loud:

"They were fourteen years old . . . both of them. . . . Who knows but it is this young spirit returned in the other's young body to avenge himself? . . ."

Again he shivered. He grew pale and looked at me peacefully, tenderly:

"Tell me! . . . Could you shut my mouth? I am afraid to talk . . . it weakens . . . I don't want to talk any more . . . I am thirsty."

They gave him a few spoonfuls of water, and he said:

"I have done my duty. That thought does good. . . ."

And he added:

"If the country is better for all that has been done, we have nothing to say. But you will see. . . ."

Thereupon he dozed off and slept for about half an hour.

After that, a woman came to the door timidly and motioned that the surgeon had come. I left on tiptoe to speak with him and as I went into the little garden with him, and stopped beside a well to question him, we heard a loud cry. We ran in only to draw the sheet over the head of this honest man, who was no more.

The Old Maid

HONORÉ DE BALZAC

Honoré de Balzac

Honoré de balzac (1799-1850) was born at Tours in a region
of many historical and literary associations, Rabelais (among
others) having flourished there and commemorated the countryside in his tales of Gargantua and Pantagruel. Balzac's father was
a plebeian who had recently prospered, his mother was a cultivated
woman of a well-to-do family. But Balzac's childhood and youth
were hard. His parents were coldhearted, his schools were like
prisons. He spent long years turning out commercial romances
before he began, about 1829, to become a serious novelist; and in
addition to writing he practiced law for a while and started a
printing business which ended in financial disaster.

He seems to have acquired a taste for hardship, which he carried over into his later years of success. It was an irrational but
no doubt necessary part of his genius. He wrote incessantly, often
working the whole night through; he was a tireless promoter of
business enterprises which turned out badly; he bought large
houses and quantities of furnishings and works of art, only to live
in and among them like a hermit. And although he loved several
women, he was primarily attached to a Polish countess, Evelina
Hanska, whom he rarely saw and was not able to marry until he
was fifty years old. Five months after the marriage Balzac died.

His novels were very numerous and embraced a good many
aspects of French life, past and present. That their interest was

not strictly local and historical was, however, recognized in Balzac's lifetime, for example by Baudelaire, who described him as a "visionary." It seems to have been perceived by Balzac himself, when he decided to assemble his mature work under the ambitious general title of The Human Comedy. This was in 1842, and what he had written hitherto (except the early potboilers) and what he wrote afterward, entered the Comedy in one or other of its departments, which he called Scenes of Country Life, Scenes of Parisian Life, Philosophical Studies, etc.

By reason of their greater mastery, certain other novelists, notably the author of *Don Quixote*, had perhaps better claim to a general title which invites comparison with *The Divine Comedy* of Dante. Balzac was not a writer in whom, as in Dante or Cervantes, the qualities of experience, mind and art worked together with consistent harmony, although he had all three qualities to a high degree. Frequently dull, he is sometimes even ludicrous, especially when he is trying to be wise and witty in the traditional French manner. He had little wit, although he had great resources of humor (which are generally overlooked by critics); and on occasion he seems more knowing than wise. Yet there is in Balzac a prodigious imagination for human relationships. His men and women are defined by their relations to family, friends and lovers; to their social class, their profession and their political tendency; to their region, town, house, furnishings and clothes. They are defined but not *con*fined by such considerations; nor are they brought together in the merely plausible fashion of a more doctrinaire or more unimaginative realism. Balzac often relates them to one another by *juxtaposition,* uniting under one roof or in a single business or intrigue people of the most differing status and character. Out of these juxtapositions come his explosive insights into human behavior, insights which do after all justify his ambitious title, The Human Comedy.

His genius, however, is not only for the forms that life takes in a given time and place but also for undifferentiated life itself. This appears partly in his portraits of vivid and aspiring young people, such as Suzanne in *The Old Maid*, although in this depart-

ment of portraiture he had not Stendhal's grace. He is most himself with men and women in whom the energy of life expresses
itself by way of worldly ambition, people who contain the whole
potential of their class (e. g. du Bousquier in *The Old Maid*).
Not less memorable are those other characters whose force is
somehow blocked in its flow and who consequently acquire fierce
and destructive manias: the misers, the libertines, the avengers.

Among Balzac's arrested and obsessed figures there are several
spinsters, the most famous being the vengeful Cousine Bette in
the long novel of that title. Mlle. Cormon, the heroine of *The
Old Maid*, is not vengeful; indeed, by reason of the pity as well
as the laughter that Balzac invokes in her behalf, she is very
appealing; and not least when, after her long ordeal of enforced
chastity and her terrible disappointment, she falls in a faint and,
carried to her room by the masterful du Bousquier, her body
suddenly bursts out of her corset: "the jewel [is] shaken violently
out of its case." Mlle. Cormon is also, as Balzac says, "the very
incarnation of the life of the provinces"; and the life of the
provinces, as it is recreated here with engaging care, is shown to
be both a retarding and a conserving force like the old maid herself. The story begins slowly; there is more of detailed portraiture
than there is of action; but when the action comes it seems in-
separable from the portraiture, and no detail is wasted.

The Old Maid (La Vieille Fille) was first published in 1836,
then linked with another story under the joint title, *The Rivalries
of a Country Town (Les Rivalités en province)* and finally
brought into the Comedy among the *Scènes de la vie de province*.

The Old Maid

PLENTY OF people must have come across at least one Chevalier
de Valois in the provinces; there was one in Normandy, another
was extant at Bourges, a third flourished at Alençon in the year
1816, and the South very likely possessed one of its own. But we
are not here concerned with the numbering of the Valois tribe.
Some of them, no doubt, were about as much of Valois as Louis
XIV was a Bourbon; and every chevalier was so slightly acquainted with the rest that it was anything but politic to mention
one of them when speaking to another. All of them, however,
agreed to leave the Bourbons in perfect tranquillity on the throne
of France, for it is a little too well proven that Henri IV succeeded to the crown in default of heirs male in the Orléans, otherwise the Valois branch; so that if any Valois exist at all, they must
be descendants of Charles of Valois, Duke of Angoulême, and
Marie Touchet; and even there the direct line was extinct (unless
proof to the contrary is forthcoming) in the person of the Abbé
de Rothelin. As for the Valois Saint-Remy, descended from Henri
II, they likewise came to an end with the too famous Lamothe-
Valois of the Diamond Necklace affair.

Every one of the chevaliers, if information is correct, was, like
the chevalier of Alençon, an elderly noble, tall, lean, and without
fortune. The Bourges chevalier had emigrated, the Touraine
Valois went into hiding during the Revolution, and the Alençon

chevalier was mixed up in the Vendean war, and implicated to
some extent in Chouannerie.* The last-named gentleman spent
the most part of his youth in Paris, where, at the age of thirty, the
Revolution broke in upon his career of conquests. Accepted as a
true Valois by persons of the highest quality in his province, the
Chevalier de Valois d'Alençon (like his namesakes) was remarkable for his fine manners, and had evidently been accustomed to
move in the best society.

He dined out every day and played cards of an evening, and
thanks to one of his weaknesses, was regarded as a great wit; he
had a habit of relating a host of anecdotes of the times of Louis
XV, and those who heard his stories for the first time thought
them passably well narrated. The Chevalier de Valois, moreover,
had one virtue: he refrained from repeating his own good sayings,
and never alluded to his conquests, albeit his smiles and airs were
delightfully indiscreet. The old gentleman took full advantage of
the old-fashioned Voltairean noble's privilege of staying away
from mass, but his irreligion was very tenderly dealt with out of
regard for his devotion to the Royalist cause.

One of his most remarked graces (Molé must have learned it of
him) was his way of taking snuff from an old-fashioned snuff-box
with a portrait of a lady on the lid. The Princess Goritza, a lovely
Hungarian, had been famous for her beauty toward the end of the
reign of Louis XV; and the chevalier could never speak without
emotion of the foreign great lady whom he loved in his youth, for
whom he had fought a duel with M. de Lauzun.

But by this time the chevalier had lived fifty-eight years, and if
he owned to but fifty of them, he might safely indulge himself in
that harmless deceit. Thin, fair-complexioned men, among other
privileges, retain their youthfulness of shape which in men, as in
women, contributes as much as anything to stave off any appearance of age. And, indeed, it is a fact that all the life, or rather, all
the grace, which is the expression of life, lies in the figure. Among
the chevalier's personal traits, mention must be made of the por-

* The Royalist rising in Vendée. *Tr.*

tentous nose with which nature had endowed him. It cut a pallid
countenance sharply into two sections which seemed to have
nothing to do with each other; so much so, indeed, that only one-
half of his face would flush with the exertion of digestion after
dinner; all the glow being confined to the left side, a phenomenon
worthy of note in times when physiology is so much occupied
with the human heart. M. de Valois' health was not apparently
robust, judging by his long, thin legs, lean frame, and sallow complexion; but he ate like an ogre, alleging, doubtless by way of
excuse for his voracity, that he suffered from a complaint known
in the provinces as a "hot liver." The flush on his left cheek confirmed the story; but in a land where meals are developed on the
lines of thirty or forty dishes, and last for four hours at a stretch,
the chevalier's abnormal appetite might well seem to be a special
mark of the favor of Providence vouchsafed to the good town.
That flush on the left cheek, according to divers medical authorities, is a sign of prodigality of heart; and, indeed, the chevalier's
past record of gallantry might seem to confirm a professional dictum for which the present chronicler (most fortunately) is in
nowise responsible. But in spite of these symptoms, M. de Valois
was of nervous temperament, and in consequence long-lived; and
if his liver was hot, to use the old-fashioned phrase, his heart was
not a whit less inflammable. If there was a line worn here and
there in his face, and a silver thread or so in his hair, an experienced eye would have discerned in these signs and tokens the
stigmata of desire, the furrows traced by past pleasure. And, in
fact, in his face, the unmistakable marks of the crow's foot and
the serpent's tooth took the shape of the delicate wrinkles so
prized at the court of Cytherea.

Everything about the gallant chevalier revealed the "ladies'
man." So minutely careful was he over his ablutions that it was a
pleasure to see his cheeks; they might have been brushed over
with some miraculous water. That portion of his head which the
hair refused to hide from view shone like ivory. His eyebrows,
like his hair, had a youthful look, so carefully was their growth
trained and regulated by the comb. A naturally fair skin seemed

to be yet further whitened by some mysterious preparation; and while the chevalier never used scent, there was about him, as it were, a perfume of youth which enhanced the freshness of his looks. His hands, that told of race, were as carefully kept as if they belonged to some coxcomb of the gentler sex; you could not help noticing those rose-pink neatly-trimmed fingernails. Indeed, but for his lordly superlative nose, the chevalier would have looked like a doll.

It takes some resolution to spoil this portrait with the admission of a foible; the chevalier put cotton wool in his ears, and still continued to wear earrings—two tiny Negroes' heads set with brilliants. They were of admirable workmanship, it is true, and their owner was so far attached to the singular appendages that he used to justify his fancy by saying that his "sick headaches had left him since his ears were pierced." He used to suffer from sick headaches. The chevalier is not held up as a flawless character; but even if an old bachelor's heart sends too much blood to his face, is he never therefore to be forgiven for his adorable absurdities? Perhaps (who knows?) there are sublime secrets hidden away beneath them. And besides, the Chevalier de Valois made amends for his Negroes' heads with such a variety of other and different charms that society ought to have felt itself sufficiently compensated. He really was at great pains to conceal his age and to make himself agreeable.

First and foremost, witness the extreme care which he gave to his linen, the one distinction in dress which a gentleman may permit himself in modern days. The chevalier's linen was invariably fine and white, as befitted a noble. His coat, though remarkably neat, was always somewhat worn, but spotless and uncreased. The preservation of this garment bordered on the miraculous in the opinion of those who noticed the chevalier's elegant indifference on this head; not that he went so far as to scrape his clothes with broken glass (a refinement invented by the Prince of Wales), but he set himself to carry out the first principles of dress as laid down by Englishmen of the very highest and finest fashion, and this with a personal element of coxcombry which Alençon was scarcely capable of appreciating. Does the world owe no esteem to those that take such pains for it? And what was all this labor but the fulfillment of that very hardest of sayings in the Gospel, which bids us return good for evil? The freshness of the toilet, the care for dress, suited well with the chevalier's blue eyes, ivory teeth, and bland personality; still, the superannuated Adonis had nothing masculine in his appearance, and it would seem that he employed the illusion of the toilet to hide the ravages of other than military campaigns.

To tell the whole truth, the chevalier had a voice singularly at variance with his delicate fairness. So full was it and sonorous, that you would have been startled by the sound of it unless, with certain observers of human nature, you held the theory that the voice was only what might be expected of such a nose. With something less of volume than a giant double-bass, it was a full, pleasant baritone, reminding you of the hautboy among musical instruments, sweet and resonant, deep and rich.

M. de Valois had discarded the absurd costume still worn by a few antiquated Royalists, and frankly modernized his dress. He always appeared in a maroon coat with gilt buttons, loosely-fitting breeches with gold buckles at the knees, a white sprigged vest, a tight stock, and a collarless shirt; this being a last vestige of eighteenth-century costume, which its wearer was the less willing to relinquish because it enabled him to display a throat not unworthy of a lay abbé. Square gold buckles of a kind unknown to the present generation shone conspicuous upon his patent-leather shoes. Two watch chains hung in view in parallel lines from a couple of fobs, another survival of an eighteenth-century mode which the old boy did not disdain to copy in the time of the Directory. This costume of a transition period, reuniting two centuries, was worn by the chevalier with the grace of an old-world marquis, a grace lost to the French stage since Molé's last pupil, Fleury, retired from the boards and took his secret with him.

The old bachelor's private life, seemingly open to all eyes, was in reality inscrutable. He lived in a modest lodging (to say the

least of it) up two sets of stairs in a house in the rue du Cours, his
landlady being the laundress most in request in Alençon—which
fact explains the extreme elegance of the chevalier's linen. Ill luck
was so to order it that Alençon one day could actually believe
that he had not always conducted himself as befitted a man of his
quality, and that in his old age he privately married one Césarine,
the mother of an infant which had the impertinence to come
without being called.

"He gave his hand to her who for so long had lent her hand
to iron his linen," said a certain M. du Bousquier.

The sensitive noble's last days were the more vexed by this unpleasant scandal, because, as shall be shown in the course of this
present Scene, he had already lost a long-cherished hope for
which he had made many a sacrifice.

Mme. Lardot's two rooms were let to M. le Chevalier de Valois
at the moderate rent of a hundred francs per annum. The worthy
gentleman dined out every night, and only came home to sleep;
he was therefore at charges for nothing but his breakfast, which
always consisted of a cup of chocolate with butter and fruit, according to the season. A fire was never lighted in his rooms except
in the very coldest winters, and then only while he was dressing.
Between the hours of eleven and four M. de Valois took his walks
abroad, read the newspapers, and paid calls.

When the chevalier first settled in Alençon, he magnanimously
owned that he had nothing but an annuity of six hundred livres
paid in quarterly installments by his old man of business, with
whom the certificates were deposited. This was all that remained
of his former wealth. And every three months, in fact, a banker
in the town paid him a hundred and fifty francs remitted by one
M. Bordin of Paris, the last of the *procureurs du Châtelet*.* These
particulars everybody knew, for the chevalier had taken care to
ask his confidant to keep the matter a profound secret. He reaped
the fruits of his misfortunes. A cover was laid for him in all the
best houses in Alençon; he was asked to every evening party. His

* Fiduciary agent. *Tr.*

talents as a card player, a teller of anecdotes, a pleasant and well-bred man of the world were so thoroughly appreciated that an evening was spoiled if the connoisseur of the town was not present. The host and hostess and all the ladies present missed his little approving grimace. "You are adorably well dressed," from the old bachelor's lips, was sweeter to a young woman in a ballroom than the sight of her rival's despair.

There were certain old-world expressions which no one could pronounce so well. "My heart," "my jewel," "my little love," "my queen," and all the dear diminutives of the year 1770 took an irresistible charm from M. de Valois' lips; in short, the privilege of superlatives was his. His compliments, of which, moreover, he was chary, won him the goodwill of the elderly ladies; he flattered everyone down to the officials of whom he had no need.

He was so fine a gentleman at the card table that his behavior would have marked him out anywhere. He never complained; when his opponents lost he praised their play; he never undertook the education of his partners by showing them what they ought to have done. If a nauseating discussion of this kind began while the cards were making, the chevalier brought out his snuffbox with a gesture worthy of Molé, looked at the Princess Goritza's portrait, took off the lid in a stately manner, heaped up a pinch, rubbed it to a fine powder between finger and thumb, blew off the light particles, shaped a little cone in his hand, and by the time the cards were dealt he had replenished the cavities in his nostrils and replaced the princess in his waistcoat pocket—always on the left-hand side.

None but a noble of the Gracious as distinguished from the Great Century could have invented such a compromise between a disdainful silence and an epigram which would have passed over the heads of his company. The chevalier took dull minds as he found them, and knew how to turn them to account. His irresistible evenness of temper caused many a one to say: "I admire the Chevalier de Valois!" Everything about him, his conversation and his manner, seemed in keeping with his mild appearance. He was careful to come into collision with no one, man or woman. Indulgent with deformity as with defects of intellect, he listened patiently (with the help of the Princess Goritza) to tales of the little woes of life in a country town; to anecdotes of the under-cooked egg at breakfast, or the sour cream in the coffee; to small grotesque details of physical ailments; to tales of dreams and visitations and wakings with a start. The chevalier was an ex-quisite listener. He had a languishing glance, a stock attitude to denote compassion; he put in his "Ohs" and "Poohs" and "What-did-you-dos?" with charming appropriateness. Till his dying day no one ever suspected that while these avalanches of nonsense lasted, the chevalier in his own mind was rehearsing the warmest passages of an old romance, of which the Princess Goritza was the heroine. Has anyone ever given a thought to the social uses of extinct sentiment?—or guessed in how many indirect ways love benefits humanity?

Possibly this listener's faculty sufficiently explains the chevalier's popularity; he was always the spoiled child of the town, although he never quitted a drawing room without carrying off about five livres in his pocket. Sometimes he lost, and he made the most of his losses, but it very seldom happened. All those who knew him say with one accord that never in any place have they met with so agreeable a mummy, not even in the Egyptian museum at Turin. Surely in no known country of the globe did parasite appear in such a benignant shape. Never did selfishness in its most concentrated form show itself so inoffensive, so full of good offices, as in this gentleman; the chevalier's egoism was as good as another man's devoted friendship. If any person went to ask M de Valois to do some trifling service which the worthy chevalier could not perform without inconvenience, that person never went away without conceiving a great liking for him, and departed fully convinced that the chevalier could do nothing in the matter, or might do harm if he meddled with it.

To explain this problematical existence the chronicler is bound to admit, while Truth—that ruthless debauchee—has caught him by the throat, that latterly, after the three sad, glorious July Days Alençon discovered that M. de Valois' winnings at cards amounted to something like a hundred and fifty crowns every quarter, which amount the ingenious chevalier intrepidly remitted to himself as an annuity, so that he might not appear to be without resources in a country with a great turn for practical details. Plenty of his friends—he was dead by that time, please to remark—plenty of his friends denied this *in toto*; they maintained that the stories were fables and slanders set in circulation by the Liberal party, and that M. de Valois was an honorable and worthy gentleman. Luckily for clever gamblers, there will always be champions of this sort for them among the onlookers. Feeling ashamed to excuse wrongdoing, they stoutly deny that wrong had been done. Do not accuse them of wrongheadedness; they have their own sense of self-respect, and the Government sets them an example of the virtue which consists in burying its dead by night without chanting a Te Deum over a defeat. And suppose that M. de Valois permitted himself a neat stratagem that would have won Gramont's esteem, a smile from Baron de Fœneste, and a shake of the hand from the Marquis de Moncade, was he any the less the pleasant dinner guest, the wit, the unvarying card player, the charming retailer of anecdotes, the delight of Alençon? In what, moreover, does the action, lying, as it does, outside the laws of right and wrong, offend against the elegant code of a man of birth and breeding? When so many people are obliged to give pensions to others, what more natural than of one's own accord to allow an annuity to one's own best friend? But Laïus is dead.

After some fifteen years of this kind of life, the chevalier had amassed ten thousand and some odd-hundred francs. When the Bourbons returned, he said that an old friend of his, M. le Marquis de Pombreton, late a lieutenant in the Black Musketeers, had returned a loan of twelve hundred pistoles with which he emigrated. The incident made a sensation. It was quoted afterward as a set-off against droll stories in the *Constitutionnel* of the ways in which some *émigrés* paid their debts. The poor chevalier used to blush all over the right side of his face whenever this noble trait in the Marquis de Pombreton came up in conversation. At the time everyone rejoiced with M. de Valois; he used to consult capitalists

as to the best way of investing this wreck of his former fortune;
and, putting faith in the Restoration, invested it all in Government stock when the Funds had fallen to fifty-six francs twenty-
five centimes. MM. de Lenoncourt, de Navarreins, de Verneuil,
de Fontaine, and La Billardière, to whom he was known, had obtained a pension of a hundred crowns for him from the privy
purse, he said, and the cross of St. Louis. By what means the old
chevalier obtained the two solemn confirmations of his title and
quality, no one ever knew; but this much is certain, the cross of
St. Louis gave him brevet rank as a colonel on a retiring pension,
by reason of his services with the Catholic army in the West.

Besides the fiction of the annuity, to which no one gave a
thought, the chevalier was now actually possessed of a genuine
income of a thousand francs. But with this improvement in his
circumstances he made no change in his life or manners; only—
the red ribbon looked wondrous well on his maroon coat; it was
a finishing touch, as it were, to this portrait of a gentleman. Ever
since the year 1802 the chevalier had sealed his letters with an
ancient gold seal, engraved roughly enough, yet not so badly but
that the Castérans, d'Esgrignons, and Troisvilles might see that
he bore the arms of France impaled with his own, to wit, *France
per pale, gules two bars gemelles, a cross of five mascles conjoined
or, on a chief sable a cross pattee argent over all;* with a knight's
casquet for crest and the motto—VALEO. With these noble arms
the so-called bastard Valois was entitled to ride in all the royal
coaches in the world.

Plenty of people envied the old bachelor his easy life, made up
of boston, trictrac, reversis, whist, and piquet; of good play, dinners well digested, pinches of snuff gracefully taken, and quiet
walks abroad. Almost all Alençon thought that his existence was
empty alike of ambitions and cares; but where is the man whose
life is quite as simple as they suppose who envy him?

In the remotest country village you shall find human mollusks,
rotifers inanimate to all appearance, which cherish a passion for
lepidoptera or conchology, and are at infinite pains to acquire
some new butterfly, or a specimen of *Concha Veneris.* And the

chevalier had not merely shells and butterflies of his own, he cherished an ambitious desire with a pertinacity and profound strategy worthy of a Sixtus V. He meant to marry a rich old maid; in all probability because a wealthy marriage would be a steppingstone to the high spheres of the Court. *This* was the secret of his royal bearing and prolonged abode in Alençon.

Very early one Tuesday morning in the middle of spring in the year '16 (to use his own expression), the chevalier was just slipping on his dressing gown, an old-fashioned green silk damask of a flowered pattern, when, in spite of the cotton in his ears, he heard a girl's light footstep on the stairs. In another moment someone tapped discreetly three times on the door, and then, without waiting for an answer, a very handsome damsel slipped like a snake into the old bachelor's apartment.

"Ah, Suzanne, is that you?" said the Chevalier de Valois, continuing to strop his razor. "What are you here for, dear little jewel of mischief?"

"I have come to tell you something which perhaps will give you as much pleasure as annoyance."

"Is it something about Césarine?"

"Much I trouble myself about your Césarine," she pouted, half careless, half in earnest.

The charming Suzanne, whose escapade was to exercise so great an influence on the lives of all the principal characters in this story, was one of Mme. Lardot's laundry girls. And now for a few topographical details:

The whole first floor of the house was given up to the laundry. The little yard was a drying ground where embroidered handkerchiefs, collarettes, lawn slips, cuffs, frilled shirts, cravats, laces, embroidered petticoats, all the fine washing of the best houses in the town, in short, hung out along the lines of hair rope. The chevalier used to say that he was kept informed of the progress of the receiver-general's wife's flirtations by the number of slips thus brought to light; and the amount of frilled shirts and cambric cravats varied directly with the petticoats and collarettes. By this system of double entry, as it were, he detected all the assignations in the town; but the chevalier was always discreet, he never let fall an epigram that might have closed a house to him. And yet he was a witty talker! For which reason you may be sure that M. de Valois' manners were of the finest, while his talents, as so often happens, were thrown away upon a narrow circle. Still, for he was only human after all, he sometimes could not resist the pleasure of a searching side glance which made women tremble, and nevertheless they liked him when they found out how profoundly discreet he was, how full of sympathy for their pretty frailties.

Mme. Lardot's forewoman and factotum, an alarmingly ugly spinster of five-and-forty, occupied the rest of the third floor with the chevalier. Her door on the landing was exactly opposite his; and her apartments, like his own, consisted of two rooms, looking respectively upon the street and the yard. Above, there was nothing but the attics where the linen was dried in winter. Below lodged Mme. Lardot's grandfather. The old man, Grévin by name, had been a privateer in his time, and had served under Admiral Simeuse in the Indies, now he was paralyzed and stone deaf. Mme. Lardot herself occupied the rooms beneath her forewoman, and so great was her weakness for people of condition that she might be said to be blind where the chevalier was concerned. In her eyes, M. de Valois was an absolute monarch, a king that could do no wrong; even if one of her own work-girls had been said to be guilty of finding favor in his sight, she would have said, "He is so amiable!"

And so, if M. de Valois, like most people in the provinces, lived in a glass house, it was secret as a robber's cave so far as he at least was concerned. A born confidant of the little intrigues of the laundry, he never passed the door—which always stood ajar—without bringing something for his pets—chocolate, bonbons, ribbons, laces, a gilt cross, and the jokes that grisettes love. Wherefore the little girls adored the chevalier. Women can tell by instinct whether a man is attracted to anything that wears a petticoat; they know at once the kind of man who enjoys the mere sense of their presence, who never thinks of making blundering demands of repayment for his gallantry. In this respect woman-kind has a canine faculty; a dog in any company goes straight to the man who respects animals. The Chevalier de Valois in his poverty preserved something of his former life; he was as unable to live without some fair one under his protection as any great lord of a bygone age. He clung to the traditions of the *petite maison*.* He loved to give to women, and women alone can receive gracefully, perhaps because it is always in their power to repay.

In these days, when every lad on leaving school tries his hand at unearthing symbols or sifting legends, is it not extraordinary that no one has explained that portent, the Courtesan of the eighteenth century? What was she but the tournament of the sixteenth in another shape? In 1550 the knights displayed their prowess for their ladies; in 1750 they displayed their mistresses at Long-champs; today they run their horses over the course. The noble of every age has done his best to invent a life which he, and he only, can live. The pointed shoes of the fourteenth century are the red heels of the eighteenth; the parade of a mistress was one fashion in ostentation; the sentiment of chivalry and the knight-errant was another.

The Chevalier de Valois could no longer ruin himself for a mistress, so for bonbons wrapped in bank bills he politely offered a bag of genuine cracknels; and to the credit of Alençon, be it said, the cracknels caused far more pleasure to the recipients than M. d'Artois' presents of carriages or silver-gilt toilet sets ever gave to the fair Duthé. There was not a girl in the laundry but recognized the chevalier's fallen greatness and kept his familiarities in the house a profound secret.

In answer to questions, they always spoke gravely of the Chevalier de Valois; they watched over him. For others he became a venerable gentleman, his life was a flower of sanctity. But at home they would have lighted on his shoulders like parakeets.

The chevalier liked to know the intimate aspects of family

* Little house: place of a mistress' installation. *Tr.*

life which laundresses learn; they used to go up to his room of a morning to retail the gossip of the town; he called them his "gazettes in petticoats," his "living feuilletons." M. Sartine himself had not such intelligent spies at so cheap a rate nor yet so loyal in their rascality. Remark, moreover, that the chevalier thoroughly enjoyed his breakfasts.

Suzanne was one of his favorites. A clever and ambitious girl with the stuff of a Sophie Arnould in her, she was besides as beautiful as the loveliest courtesan that Titian ever prayed to pose against a background of dark velvet as a model for his Venus. Her forehead and all the upper part of her face about the eyes were delicately molded; but the contours of the lower half were cast in a commoner mold. Hers was the beauty of a Norman, fresh, plump, and brilliant-complexioned, with that Rubens fleshiness which should be combined with the muscular development of the Farnese Hercules. This was no Venus de' Medici, the graceful feminine counterpart of Apollo.

"Well, child," said the chevalier, "tell me your adventures little or big."

The chevalier's fatherly benignity with these grisettes would have marked him out anywhere between Paris and Pekin. The girls put him in mind of the courtesans of another age, of the illustrious queens of opera of European fame during a good third of the eighteenth century. Certain it is that he who had lived for so long in a world of women now as dead and forgotten as the Jesuits, the buccaneers, the abbés, and the farmers-general, and all great things generally—certain it is that the chevalier had acquired an irresistible good humor, a gracious ease, an unconcern, with no trace of egoism discernible in it. So might Jupiter have appeared to Alcmena—a king that chooses to be a woman's dupe, and flings majesty and its thunderbolts to the winds that he may squander Olympus in follies, and "little suppers," and feminine extravagance; wishful, of all things, to be far enough away from Juno.

The room in which the chevalier received company was bare enough, with its shabby bit of tapestry to do duty as a carpet, and very dirty, old-fashioned easy chairs; the walls were covered with a cheap paper, on which the countenances of Louis XVI and his family, framed in weeping willow, appeared at intervals among funeral urns, bearing the *sublime testament* by way of inscription, amid a whole host of sentimental emblems invented by royalism under the Terror; but in spite of all this, in spite of the old, flowered green silk dressing gown, in spite of its owner's air of dilapidation, a certain fragrance of the eighteenth century clung about the Chevalier de Valois as he shaved himself before the old-fashioned toilet glass covered with cheap lace. All the graceless graces of his youth seemed to reappear; he might have had three hundred thousand francs' worth of debts to his name and a chariot at his door. He looked a great man, great as Berthier in the Retreat from Moscow issuing the order of the day to battalions which were no more.

"Monsieur le Chevalier," Suzanne replied archly, "it seems to me that I have nothing to tell you—you have only to look!"

So saying, she turned and stood sideways to prove her words by ocular demonstration; and the chevalier, deep old gentleman, still holding his razor across his chin, cast his right eye downward upon the damsel, and pretended to understand.

"Very good, my little pet, we will have a little talk together presently. But you come first, it seems to me."

"But, Monsieur le Chevalier, am I to wait till my mother beats me and Madame Lardot turns me away? If I do not go to Paris at once, I shall never get married here, where the men are so ridiculous."

"These things cannot be helped, child! Society changes, and women suffer just as much as the nobles from the shocking confusion which ensues. Topsy-turvydom in politics ends in topsy-turvy manners. Alas! woman soon will cease to be woman" (here he took the cotton-wool out of his ears to continue his toilet). "Women will lose a great deal by plunging into sentiment; they will torture their nerves, and there will be an end of the good old ways of our time, when a little pleasure was desired without blushes, and accepted without more ado, and the vapors" (he polished the earrings with the Negroes' heads)—"the vapors were only known as a means of getting one's way; before long they will take the proportions of a complaint only to be cured by an infusion of orange blossoms." (The chevalier burst out laughing.) "Marriage, in short," he resumed, taking a pair of tweezers to pluck out a gray hair, "marriage will come to be a very dull institution indeed, and it was so joyous in my time. The reign of Louis XIV and Louis XV (bear this in mind, my child) saw the last of the finest manners in the world."

"But, Monsieur le Chevalier," urged the girl, "it is your little Suzanne's character and reputation that are at stake, and you are not going to forsake her, I hope!"

"What is all this?" cried the chevalier, with a finishing touch to his hair; "I would sooner lose my name!"

"Ah!" said Suzanne.

"Listen to me, little masquerader." He sat down in a large, low chair, a *duchesse*, as it used to be called, which Mme. Lardot had picked up somewhere for her lodger. Then he drew the magnificent Suzanne to him till she stood between his knees; and Suzanne submitted—Suzanne who held her head so high in the streets and had refused a score of overtures from admirers in Alençon, not so much from self-respect as in disdain of their pettiness. Suzanne so brazenly made the most of the supposed consequences of her errors that the old sinner, who had fathomed so many mysteries in persons far more astute than Suzanne, saw the real state of affairs at once. He knew well enough that a grisette does not laugh when disgrace is really in question, but he scorned to throw down the scaffolding of an engaging fib with a touch.

"We are slandering ourselves," said he, and there was an inimitable subtlety in his smile. "We are as well conducted as the fair one whose name we bear; we can marry without fear. But we do not want to vegetate here; we long for Paris, where charming creatures can be rich if they are clever, and we are not a fool. So we should like to find out whether the City of Pleasure has young Chevaliers de Valois in store for us, and a carriage and diamonds and an opera box. There are Russians and English and Austrians that are bringing millions to spend in Paris, and some of that money mamma settled on us as a marriage portion when she gave us our good looks. And beside, we are patriotic; we should like to help France to find her own money in these gentlemen's pockets. Eh! eh! my dear little devil's lamb, all this is not bad. The neighbors will cry out upon you a little at first, perhaps, but success will make everything right. The real crime, my child, is poverty; and you and I both suffer for it. As we are not lacking in intelligence, we thought we might turn our dear little reputation to account to take in an old bachelor, but the old bachelor, sweetheart, knows the alpha and omega of woman's wiles; which is to say, that you would find it easier to put a grain of salt upon a sparrow's tail than to persuade me, the Chevalier de Valois, to believe that I have had any share in your affair.

"Go to Paris, my child, go at the expense of a bachelor's vanity; I am not going to hinder you, I will help you, for the old bachelor, Suzanne, is the cashbox provided by nature for a young girl. But do not thrust me into the affair. Now, listen, my queen, understanding life so well as you do—you see, you might do me a good deal of harm and give me trouble; harm, because you might spoil my marriage in a place where people are so particular; trouble on your account, because you will get yourself in a scrape for nothing, a scrape entirely of your own invention, sly girl; and you know, my pet, that I have no money left, I am as poor as a church mouse. Ah! if I were to marry Mademoiselle Cormon, if I were rich again, I would certainly rather have you than Césarine. You were always fine gold enough to gild lead, it seemed to me; you were made to be a great lord's love; and as I knew you were a clever girl, I am not at all surprised by this trick of yours, I expected as much. For a girl, this means that you burn your boats. It is no common mind, my angel, that can do it; and for that reason you have my esteem," and he bestowed confirmation upon her cheek after the manner of a bishop, with two fingers.

"But, Monsieur le Chevalier, I do assure you that you are mis-

taken, and——" she blushed, and dared not finish her sentence, at
a glance he had seen through her, and read her plans from beginning to end.

"Yes, I understand, you wish me to believe you. Very well, I
believe. But take my advice and go to Monsieur du Bousquier.
You have taken Monsieur du Bousquier's linen home from the
wash for five or six months, have you not? Very good. I do not
ask to know what has happened between you; but I know *him*,
he is vain, he is an old bachelor, he is very rich, he has an income
of two thousand five hundred livres, and spends less than eight
hundred. If you are the clever girl that I take you for, you will
find your way to Paris at his expense. Go to him, my pet, twist
him round your fingers, and of all things be supple as silk, and
make a double twist and a knot at every word; he is just the man
to be afraid of a scandal; and if he knows that you can make him
sit on the stool of repentance—— In short, you understand,
threaten to apply to the ladies of the charitable fund. He is ambitious besides. Well and good, with a wife to help him there
should be nothing beyond a man's reach; and are you not handsome enough and clever enough to make your husband's fortune?
Why, plague take it, you might hold your own with a court
lady."

The chevalier's last words let the light into Suzanne's brain;
she was burning with impatience to rush off to du Bousquier;
but as she could not hurry away too abruptly, she helped the
chevalier to dress, asking questions about Paris as she did so.
As for the chevalier, he saw that his remarks had taken effect,
and gave Suzanne an excuse to go, asking her to tell Césarine
to bring up the chocolate that Mme. Lardot made for him every
morning, and Suzanne forthwith slipped off in search of her prey.

And here follows du Bousquier's biography. He came of an old
Alençon family in a middle rank between the burghers and the
country squires. On the death of his father, a magistrate in the
criminal court, he was left without resource, and, like most
ruined provincials, betook himself to Paris to seek his fortune.
When the Revolution broke out, du Bousquier was a man of

affairs; and in those days (in spite of the Republicans, who are all up in arms for the honesty of their government) the word "affairs" was used very loosely. Political spies, jobbers, and contractors, the men who arranged with the syndics of communes for the sale of the property of *émigrés*, and then bought up land at low prices to sell again—all these people, like ministers and generals, were men of affairs.

From 1793 to 1799 du Bousquier held contracts to supply the army with forage and provisions. During those years he lived in a splendid mansion; he was one of the great capitalists of the time; he went shares with Ouvard; kept open house and led the scandalous life of the times. A Cincinnatus, reaping where he had not sowed, and rich with stolen rations and sacks of corn, he kept *petites maisons* and a bevy of mistresses, and gave fine entertainments to the directors of the Republic. Citizen du Bousquier was one of Barras' intimates; he was on the best of terms with Fouché, and hand in glove with Bernadotte. He thought to be a minister of State one day, and threw himself heart and soul into the party that secretly plotted against Bonaparte before the battle of Marengo. And but for Kellermann's charge and the death of Desaix, du Bousquier would have played a great part in the State. He was one of the upper members of the permanent staff of the promiscuous government which was driven by Napoleon's luck to vanish into the side-scenes of 1793.

The victory unexpectedly won by stubborn fighting ended in the downfall of this party; they had placards ready printed, and were only waiting for the First Consul's defeat to proclaim a return to the principles of the Mountain.

Du Bousquier, feeling convinced that a victory was impossible, had two special messengers on the battlefield, and speculated with the larger part of his fortune for a fall in the Funds. The first courier came with the news that Mélas was victorious; but the second arriving four hours afterward, at night, brought the tidings of the Austrian defeat. Du Bousquier cursed Kellermann and Desaix; the First Consul owed him millions, he dared not curse him. But between the chance of making millions on the one hand, and stark ruin on the other, he lost his head. For several days he was half idiotic; he had undermined his constitution with excesses to such an extent that the thunderbolt left him helpless. He had something to hope from the settlement of his claims upon the Government; but in spite of bribes, he was made to feel the weight of Napoleon's displeasure against army contractors who speculated on his defeat. M. de Fermon, so pleasantly nicknamed *"Fermons la caisse,"* left du Bousquier without a penny. The First Consul was even more incensed by the immorality of his private life and his connection with Barras and Bernadotte than by his speculations on the Bourse; he erased M. du Bousquier's name from the list of receivers-general, on which a last remnant of credit had placed him for Alençon.

Of all his former wealth, nothing now remained to du Bousquier save an income of twelve hundred francs from the Funds, an investment entirely due to chance, which saved him from actual want. His creditors, knowing nothing of the results of his liquidation, only left him enough in consols to bring in a thousand francs per annum; but their claims were paid in full after all, when the outstanding debts had been collected, and the Hôtel de Beauséant, du Bousquier's town house, sold beside. So, after a close shave of bankruptcy, the sometime speculator emerged with his name intact. Preceded by a tremendous reputation due to his relations with former heads of government departments, his manner of life, his brief day of authority, and final ruin through the First Consul, the man interested the city Alençon, where Royalism was secretly predominant. Du Bousquier, exasperated against Bonaparte, with his tales of the First Consul's pettiness, of Josephine's lax morals, and a whole store of anecdotes of ten years of revolution, seen from within, met with a good reception.

It was about this period of his life that du Bousquier, now well over his fortieth year, came out as a bachelor of thirty-six. He was of medium height, fat as became a contractor, and willing to display a pair of calves that would have done credit to a gay and gallant attorney. He had strongly marked features; a flattened nose with tufts of hair in the equine nostrils; bushy black brows,

and eyes beneath them that looked out shrewd as M. de Talleyrand's own, though they had lost something of their brightness.
He wore his brown hair very long, and retained the side whiskers
(*nageoires*, as they were called) of the time of the Republic. You
had only to look at his fingers, tufted at every joint, or at the
blue knotted veins that stood out upon his hands, to see the
unmistakable signs of a very remarkable muscular development;
and, in truth, he had the chest of the Farnese Hercules, and
shoulders fit to bear the burden of the national debt; you never
see such shoulders nowadays. His was a luxuriant virility admirably
described by an eighteenth-century phrase which is scarcely intelligible to-day; the gallantry of a bygone age would have
summed up du Bousquier as a "payer of arrears"—*un vrai payeur
d'arrèrages*.

Yet, as in the case of the Chevalier de Valois, there were
sundry indications at variance with the ex-contractor's general
appearance. His vocal powers, for instance, were not in keeping
with his muscles; not that it was the mere thread of a voice which
sometimes issues from the throats of such two-footed seals; on
the contrary, it was loud but husky, something like the sound
of a saw cutting through damp, soft wood; it was, in fact, the
voice of a speculator brought to grief. For a long while du
Bousquier wore the costume in vogue in the days of his glory:
the boots with turned-down tops, the white silk stockings, the
short cloth breeches, ribbed with cinnamon color, the blue coat,
the Robespierre vest.

His hatred of the First Consul should have been a sort of passport into the best Royalist houses of Alençon; but the seven or
eight families that made up the local Faubourg Saint-Germain,
into which the Chevalier de Valois had the entrance, held aloof.
Almost from the first, du Bousquier had aspired to marry one
Mlle. Armande, whose brother was one of the most esteemed
nobles of the town; he thought to make this brother play a great
part in his own schemes, for he was dreaming of a brilliant
return match in politics. He met with a refusal, for which he
consoled himself with such compensation as he might find

among some half-score of retired manufacturers of Point d'Alençon lace, owners of grass lands or cattle, or wholesale linen merchants, thinking that among these chance might put a good match in his way. Indeed, the old bachelor had centered all his hopes on a prospective fortunate marriage, which a man, eligible in so many ways, might fairly expect to make. For he was not without a certain financial acumen, of which not a few availed themselves. He pointed out business speculations as a ruined gambler gives hints to new hands; and he was expert at discovering the resources, chances, and management of a concern. People looked upon him as a good administrator. It was an often-discussed question whether he should not be mayor of Alençon, but the recollection of his Republican jobberies spoiled his chances and he was never received at the prefecture.

Every successive government, even the government of the Hundred Days, declined to give him the coveted appointment, which would have assured his marriage with an elderly spinster whom he now had in his mind. It was his detestation of the Imperial Government that drove him into the Royalist camp, where he stayed in spite of insults there received; but when the Bourbons returned, and still he was excluded from the prefecture, that final rebuff filled him with a hatred deep as the profound secrecy in which he wrapped it. Outwardly, he remained patiently faithful to his opinions; secretly, he became the leader of the Liberal party in Alençon, the invisible controller of elections; and, by his cunningly devised maneuvers and underhand methods, he worked no little harm to the restored Monarchy.

When a man is reduced to live through his intellect alone, his hatred is something as quiet as a little stream; insignificant to all appearance, but unfailing. This was the case with du Bousquier. His hatred was like a Negro's, so placid, so patient, that it deceives the enemy. For fifteen years he brooded over a revenge which no victory, not even the Three Days of July, 1830, could sate.

When the chevalier sent Suzanne to du Bousquier, he had his own reasons for so doing. The Liberal and the Royalist divined

each other, in spite of the skillful dissimulation which hid their
common aim from the rest of the town.

The two old bachelors were rivals. Both of them had planned
to marry the Demoiselle Cormon, whose name came up in the
course of the chevalier's conversation with Suzanne. Both of
them, engrossed by their idea and masquerading in indifference,
were waiting for the moment when some chance should deliver
the old maid to one or other of them. And the fact that they were
rivals in this way would have been enough to make enemies of
the pair even if each had not been the living embodiment of a
political system.

Men take their color from their time. This pair of rivals is a
case in point; the historic tinge of their characters stood out in
strong contrast in their talk, their ideas, their costume. The one,
blunt and energetic, with his burly abrupt ways, curt speech, dark
looks, dark hair, and dark complexion, alarming in appearance,
but impotent in reality as insurrection, was the Republic personified; the other, bland and polished, elegant and fastidious, gaining
his ends slowly but surely by diplomacy, and never unmindful of
good taste, was the typical old-world courtier. They met on the
same ground almost every evening. It was a rivalry always courteous and urbane on the part of the chevalier, less ceremonious on
du Bousquier's, though he kept within the limits prescribed by
Alençon, for he had no wish to be driven ignominiously from the
field. The two men understood each other well; but no one else
saw what was going on. In spite of the minute and curious interest which provincials take in the small details of which their lives
are made up, no one so much as suspected that the two men were
rivals.

M. le Chevalier's position was somewhat the stronger; he had
never proposed for Mlle. Cormon, whereas du Bousquier had
declared himself after a rebuff from one of the noblest families,
and had met with a second refusal. Still, the chevalier thought so
well of his rival's chances that he considered it worth while to
deal him a *coup de Jarnac*, a treacherous thrust from a weapon as
finely tempered as Suzanne. He had fathomed du Bousquier; and,

as will shortly be seen, he was not mistaken in any of his conjectures.

Suzanne tripped away down the rue du Cours, along the rue
de la Porte de Séez and the rue du Bercail to the rue du Cygne,
where du Bousquier, five years ago, had bought a small countrified
house built of the gray stone of the district, which is used like
granite in Normandy or Breton schist in the West. The sometime forage contractor had established himself there in more
comfort than any other house in the town could boast, for he had
brought with him some relics of past days of splendor; but provincial manners and customs were slowly darkening the glory
of the fallen Sardanapalus. The vestiges of past luxury looked
about as much out of place in the house as a chandelier in a barn.
Harmony, which links the works of man or of God together, was
lacking in all things large or small. An ewer with a metal lid, such
as you only see on the outskirts of Brittany, stood on a handsome
nest of drawers; and while the bedroom floor was covered with a
fine carpet, the window-curtains displayed a flower pattern only
known to cheap, printed cottons. The stone mantelpiece, daubed
over with paint, was out of all keeping with a handsome clock
disgraced by a shabby pair of candlesticks. Local talent had made
an unsuccessful attempt to paint the doors in vivid contrasts of
startling colors; while the staircase, ascended by all and sundry
in muddy boots, had not been painted at all. In short, du Bousquier's house, like the time which he represented, was a confused
mixture of grandeur and squalor.

Du Bousquier was regarded as well-to-do, but he led the para-
sitical life of the Chevalier de Valois, and he is always rich enough
that spends less than his income. His one servant was a country
bumpkin, a dull-witted youth enough; but he had been trained,
by slow degrees to suit du Bousquier's requirements until he had
learned, much as an orangutan might learn, to scour floors, black
boots, brush clothes, and to come for his master of an evening
with a lantern if it was dark and a pair of sabots if it rained. On
great occasions, du Bousquier made him discard the blue-checked

cotton blouse with loose sagging pockets behind, which always bulged with a handkerchief, a clasp knife, apples, or "stickjaw taffy." Arrayed in a regulation suit of clothes, he accompanied his master to wait at table, and overate himself afterward with the other servants. Like many other mortals, René had only stuff enough in him for one vice, and his was gluttony. Du Bousquier made a reward of this service, and in return his Breton factotum was absolutely discreet.

"What, have you come our way, miss?" René asked when he saw Suzanne in the doorway. "It is not your day; we have not got any linen for Madame Lardot."

"Big stupid!" laughed the fair Suzanne, as she went up the stairs, leaving René to finish a porringer full of buckwheat bannocks boiled in milk.

Du Bousquier was still in bed, ruminating his plans for fortune. To him, as to all who have squeezed the orange of pleasure, there was nothing left but ambition. Ambition, like gambling, is inexhaustible. And, moreover, given a good constitution, the passions of the brain will always outlive the heart's passions.

"Here I am!" said Suzanne, sitting down on the bed; the curtain rings grated along the rods as she swept them sharply back with an imperious gesture.

"*Quésaco*, my charmer?" asked du Bousquier, sitting upright.

"Monsieur," Suzanne began, with much gravity, "you must be surprised to see me come in this way; but, under the circumstances, it is no use my minding what people will say."

"What is all this about?" asked du Bousquier, folding his arms.

"Why, do you not understand?" returned Suzanne. "I know" (with an engaging little pout), "I know how ridiculous it is when a poor girl comes to bother a man about things that you think mere trifles. But if you really knew me, monsieur, if you only knew all that I would do for a man, if he cared about me as I could care about you, you would never repent of marrying me. It is not that I could be of so much use to you *here*, by the way; but if we went to Paris, you should see how far I could bring a man of spirit with such brains as yours, and especially just now, when they are re-making the Government from top to bottom, and the foreigners are the masters. Between ourselves, does this thing in question really matter after all? Is it not a piece of good fortune for which you would be glad to pay a good deal one of these days? For whom are you going to think and work?"

"For myself, to be sure!" du Bousquier answered most brutally.

"Old monster! you shall never be a father!" said Suzanne, with a ring in her voice which turned the words to a prophecy and a curse.

"Come, Suzanne, no nonsense; I am dreaming still, I think."

"What more do you want in the way of reality?" cried Suzanne, rising to her feet. Du Bousquier scrubbed his head with his cotton nightcap, which he twisted round and round with a fidgety energy that told plainly of prodigious mental ferment.

"He actually believes it!" Suzanne said within herself. "And his vanity is tickled. Good Lord, how easy it is to take them in!"

"Suzanne! What the deuce do you want me to do? It is so extraordinary—— I that thought—— The fact is—— But, no, no, it can't be——"

"Do you mean that you cannot marry me?"

"Oh, as to that, no. I am not free."

"Is it Mademoiselle Armande or Mademoiselle Cormon, who have both refused you already? Look here, Monsieur du Bousquier, it is not as if I was obliged to get gendarmes to drag you to the registrar's office to save my character. There are plenty that would marry me, but I have no intention whatever of taking a man that does not know my value. You may be sorry some of these days that you behaved like this; for if you will not take your chance today, not for gold, nor silver, nor anything in this world will I give it you again."

"But, Suzanne—are you sure——?"

"Sir, for what do you take me?" asked the girl, draping herself in her virtue. "I am not going to put you in mind of the promises you made, promises that have been the ruin of a poor girl, when all her fault was that she looked too high and loved too much."

But joy, suspicion, self-interest, and a host of contending emo-

tions had taken possession of du Bousquier. For a long time past
he had made up his mind that he would marry Mlle. Cormon; for,
after long ruminations over the Charter, he saw that it opened
up magnificent prospects to his ambition through the channels of
a representative government. His marriage with that mature spinster would raise his social position very much; he would acquire
a great influence in Alençon. And here this wily Suzanne had
conjured up a storm, which put him in a most awkward dilemma.
But for that private hope of his, he would have married Suzanne
out of hand, and put himself openly at the head of the Liberal
party in the town. Such a marriage meant the final renunciation
of the best society, and a drop into the ranks of the wealthy
tradesmen, storekeepers, rich manufacturers, and graziers, who,
beyond a doubt, would carry him as their candidate in triumph.
Already du Bousquier caught a glimpse of the Opposition benches.
He did not attempt to hide his solemn deliberations; he rubbed
his hand over his head, made a wisp of the cotton nightcap, and
a damaging confession of the nudity beneath it. As for Suzanne,
after the wont of those who succeed beyond their utmost hopes,
she sat dumfounded. To hide her amazement at his behavior, she
drooped like a hapless victim before her seducer, while within
herself she laughed like a grisette on a frolic.

"My dear child, I will have nothing to do with hanky-panky of
this sort."

This brief formula was the result of his cogitations. The ex-
contractor to the Government prided himself upon belonging to
that particular school of cynic philosophers which declines to be
"taken in" by women and includes the whole sex in one category
as suspicious characters. Strong-minded men of this stamp, weaklings are they for the most part, have a catechism of their own
in the matter of womankind. Every woman, according to them,
from the Queen of France to the milliner, is at heart a rake, a
hussy, a dangerous creature, not to say a bit of a rascal, a liar in
grain, a being incapable of a serious thought. For du Bousquier
and his like, woman is a maleficent *bayadère** that must be left

* Indian dancing girl. *Tr.*

to dance, and sing, and laugh. They see nothing holy, nothing great in woman; for them she represents, not the poetry of the senses, but gross sensuality. They are like gluttons who mistake the kitchen for the dining room. On this showing, a man must be a consistent tyrant, unless he means to be enslaved. And in this respect, again, du Bousquier and the Chevalier de Valois stood at opposite poles.

As he delivered himself of the above remark, he flung his night-cap to the foot of the bed, much as Gregory the Great might have flung down the candle while he launched the thunders of an excommunication; and Suzanne learned that the old bachelor wore a false front.

"Bear in mind, Monsieur du Bousquier, that by coming here I have done my duty," she remarked majestically. "Remember that I was bound to offer you my hand and to ask for yours; but, at the same time, remember that I have behaved with the dignity of a self-respecting woman; I did not lower myself so far as to cry like a fool; I did not insist; I have not worried you at all. Now you know my position. You know that I cannot stay in Alençon. If I do, my mother will beat me; and Madame Lardot is as high and mighty over principles as if she washed and ironed with them. She will turn me away. And where am I to go, poor work-girl that I am? To the hospital? Am I to beg for bread? Not I. I would sooner fling myself into the Brillante or the Sarthe. Now, would it not be simpler for me to go to Paris? Mother might find some excuse for sending me, an uncle wants me to come, or an aunt is going to die, or some lady takes an interest in me. It is just a question of money for the traveling expenses and—you know what——"

This news was immeasurably more important to du Bousquier than to the Chevalier de Valois, for reasons which no one knew as yet but the two rivals, though they will appear in the course of the story. At this point, suffice it to say that Suzanne's fib had thrown the sometime forage contractor's ideas into such confusion that he was incapable of thinking seriously. But for that bewilderment, but for the secret joy in his heart (for a man's own vanity is a swindler that never lacks a dupe), it must have struck him that any honest girl, with a heart still unspoiled, would have died a hundred deaths rather than enter upon such a discussion or make a demand for money. He must have seen the look in the girl's eyes, seen the gambler's ruthless meanness that would take a life to gain money for a stake.

"Would you really go to Paris?" he asked.

The words brought a twinkle to Suzanne's gray eyes, but it was lost upon du Bousquier's self-satisfaction.

"I would indeed, sir."

But at this du Bousquier broke out into a singular lament. He had just paid the balance of the purchase money for his house; and there was the painter, and the glazier, and the bricklayer, and the carpenter. Suzanne let him talk; she was waiting for the figures. Du Bousquier at last proposed three hundred francs, and at this Suzanne, with an assumption of dignity, got up as if to go.

"Eh, what! Where are you going?" du Bousquier cried uneasily. "A fine thing to be a bachelor," he said to himself. "I'll be hanged if I remember doing more than rumple the girl's collar; and hey presto! on the strength of a joke she takes upon herself to draw a bill upon you, point-blank!"

Suzanne meanwhile began to cry. "Monsieur," she said, "I am going to Madame Granson, the treasurer of the Maternity Fund; she pulled one poor girl in the same strait out of the water (as you may say) to my knowledge."

"Madame Granson?"

"Yes. She is related to Mademoiselle Cormon, the lady patroness of the society. Asking your pardon, some ladies in the town have started a society that will keep many a poor creature from making away with her child, like that pretty Faustine of Argentan did; and paid for it with her life at Mortagne just three years ago."

"Here, Suzanne," returned du Bousquier, holding out a key, "open the desk yourself. There is a bag that has been opened, with six hundred francs still left in it. It is all I have."

Du Bousquier's chopfallen expression plainly showed how little good will went with his compliance.

"An old thief!" said Suzanne to herself. "I will tell tales about his false hair!" Mentally she compared him with that delightful old Chevalier de Valois; he had given her nothing, but he understood her, he had advised her, he had the welfare of his grisettes at heart.

"If you are deceiving me, Suzanne," exclaimed the object of this unflattering comparison, as he watched her hand in the drawer, "you shall——"

"So, monsieur, you would not give me the money if I asked you for it?" interrupted she with queenly insolence.

Once recalled to the ground of gallantry, recollections of his prime came back to the ex-contractor. He grunted assent. Suzanne took the bag and departed, first submitting her forehead to a kiss which he gave, but in a manner which seemed to say, "This is an expensive privilege; but it is better than being browbeaten by counsel in a court of law as the seducer of a young woman accused of child-murder."

Suzanne slipped the bag into a pouch-shaped basket on her arm, execrating du Bousquier's stinginess as she did so, for she wanted a thousand francs. If a girl is once possessed by a desire, and has taken the first step in trickery and deceit, she will go to great lengths. As the fair laundress took her way along the rue de Bercail, it suddenly occurred to her that the Maternity Fund under Mlle. Cormon's presidency would probably make up the sum which she regarded as sufficient for a start, a very large amount in the eyes of an Alençon grisette. And beside, she hated du Bousquier, and du Bousquier seemed frightened when she talked of confessing her so-called strait to Mme. Granson. Wherefore Suzanne determined that whether or not she made a centime out of the Maternity Fund, she would entangle du Bousquier in the inextricable undergrowth of the gossip of a country town. There is something of a monkey's love of mischief in every grisette. Suzanne composed her countenance dolorously and betook herself accordingly to Madame Granson.

Mme. Granson was the widow of a lieutenant-colonel of artillery who fell at Jena. Her whole yearly income consisted of a
pension of nine hundred francs for her lifetime, and her one
possession beside was a son whose education and maintenance
had absorbed every penny of her savings. She lived in the rue du
Bercail, in one of the cheerless first-floor apartments through
which you can see from back to front at a glance as you walk
down the main street of any little town. Three steps, rising pyramid fashion, brought you to the level of the house door, which
opened upon a passageway and a little yard beyond, with a
wooden-roofed staircase at the farther end. Mme. Granson's
kitchen and dining room occupied the space on one side of the
passage, on the other side a single room did duty for a variety of
purposes, for the widow's bedroom among others. Her son, a
young man of three-and-twenty, slept upstairs in an attic above
the second floor. Athanase Granson contributed six hundred
francs to the poor mother's housekeeping. He was distantly related to Mlle. Cormon, whose influence had obtained him a little
post in the registrar's office, where he was employed in making
out certificates of births, marriages, and deaths.

After this, anyone can see the little chilly, yellow-curtained
parlor, the furniture covered with yellow Utrecht velvet, and
Mme. Granson going round the room, after her visitors had left,
to straighten the little straw mats put down in front of each chair,
so as to save the waxed and polished red brick floor from contact
with dirty boots; and, this being accomplished, returning to her
place beside her work table under the portrait of her lieutenant-
colonel. The becushioned armchair, in which she sat at her sew-
ing, was always drawn up between the two windows, so that she
could look up and down the rue du Bercail and see every one
that passed. She was a good sort of woman, dressed with a homely
simplicity in keeping with a pale face, beaten thin, as it were,
by many cares. You felt the stern soberness of poverty in every
little detail in that house, just as you breathed a moral atmosphere
of austerity and upright provincial ways.

Mother and son at this moment were sitting together in the

dining room over their breakfast—a cup of coffee, bread and butter, and radishes. And here, if the reader is to understand how gladly Mme. Granson heard Suzanne, some explanation of the secret hopes of the household must be given.

Athanase Granson was a thin, hollow-cheeked young man of medium height, with a white face in which a pair of dark eyes, bright with thought, looked like two marks made with charcoal. The somewhat worn contours of that face, the curving line of the lips, a sharply turned-up chin, a regularly cut marble fore-head, a melancholy expression caused by the consciousness of power on the one hand and of poverty on the other—all these signs and characteristics told of imprisoned genius. So much so, indeed, that anywhere but at Alençon his face would have won help for him from distinguished men, or from the women that can discern genius incognito. For if this was not genius, at least it was the outward form that genius takes; and if the strength of a high heart was wanting, it looked out surely from those eyes. And yet, while Athanase could find expression for the loftiest feeling, an outer husk of shyness spoiled everything in him, down to the very charm of youth, just as the frost of penury dis-heartened every effort. Shut in by the narrow circle of provincial life, without approbation, encouragement, or any way of escape, the thought within him was dying out before its dawn. And Athanase, beside, had the fierce pride which poverty intensifies in certain natures, the kind of pride by which a man grows great in the stress of battle with men and circumstance, while at the outset it only handicaps him.

Genius manifests itself in two ways—either by taking its own as soon as it finds it, like a Napoleon or a Molière, or by patiently revealing itself and waiting for recognition. Young Granson belonged to the latter class. He was easily discouraged, ignorant of his value. His turn of mind was contemplative, he lived in thought rather than in action, and possibly, to those who cannot imagine genius without the Frenchman's spark of enthusiasm, he might have seemed incomplete. But Athanase's power lay in the world of thought. He was to pass through successive phases of

emotion, hidden from ordinary eyes, to one of those sudden resolves which bring the chapter to a close and set fools declaring
that "the man is mad." The world's contempt for poverty was
sapping the life in Athanase. The bow, continually strung tighter
and tighter, was slackened by the enervating close air of a solitude
with never a breath of fresh air in it. He was giving way under
the strain of a cruel and fruitless struggle. Athanase had that in
him which might have placed his name among the foremost names
of France; he had known what it was to gaze with glowing eyes
over Alpine heights and fields of air whither unfettered genius
soars, and now he was pining to death like some caged and starved
eagle.

While he had worked on unnoticed in the town library, he
buried his dreams of fame in his own soul lest they should injure
his prospects; and he carried beside another secret hidden even
more deeply in his heart, the secret love which hollowed his
cheeks and sallowed his forehead.

Athanase loved his distant cousin, that Mlle. Cormon, for
whom his unconscious rivals du Bousquier and the Chevalier de
Valois were laying an ambush. It was a love born of self-interest.
Mlle. Cormon was supposed to be one of the richest people in the
town; and he, poor boy, had been drawn to love her partly
through the desire for material welfare, partly through a wish
formed times without number to gild his mother's declining years,
and partly also through cravings for the physical comfort necessary to men who live an intellectual life. In his own eyes, his love
was dishonored by its very natural origin; and he was afraid of
the ridicule which people pour on the love of a young man of
three-and-twenty for a woman of forty. And yet his love was
quite sincere. Much that happens in the provinces would be improbable upon the face of it anywhere else, especially in matters
of this kind.

But in a country town there are no unforeseen contingencies;
there is no coming and going, no mystery, no such thing as
chance. Marriage is a necessity, and no family will accept a man
of dissolute life. A connection between a young fellow like

Athanase and a handsome girl might seem a natural thing enough
in a great city; in a country town it would be enough to ruin a
young man's chances of marriage, especially if he were poor; for
when the prospective bridegroom is wealthy an awkward business
of this sort may be smoothed over. Between the degradation of
certain courses and a sincere love, a man that is not heartless can
make but one choice if he happens to be poor; he will prefer the
disadvantages of virtue to the disadvantages of vice. But in a
country town the number of women with whom a young man
can fall in love is strictly limited. A pretty girl with a fortune is
beyond his reach in a place where everyone's income is known
to a farthing. A penniless beauty is equally out of the question. To
take her for a wife would be "to marry hunger and thirst," as the
provincial saying goes. Finally, celibacy has its dangers in youth.
These reflections explain how it has come to pass that marriage
is the very basis of provincial life.

Men in whom genius is hot and unquenchable, who are forced
to take their stand on the independence of poverty, ought to
leave these cold regions; in the provinces thought meets with the
persecution of brutal indifference, and no woman cares, or dares,
to play the part of a sister of charity to the worker, the lover of
art or sciences.

Who can rightly understand Athanase's love for Mlle. Cormon?
Not the rich, the sultans of society, who can find seraglios at
their pleasure; not respectability, keeping to the track beaten
hard by prejudice; nor yet those women who shut their eyes to
the cravings of the artist temperament, and, taking it for granted
that both sexes are governed by the same laws, insist upon a system
of reciprocity in their particular virtues. The appeal must, perhaps, be made to young men who suffer from the repression of
young desires just as they are putting forth their full strength;
to the artist whose genius is stifled within him by poverty till it
becomes a disease; to power at first unsupported, persecuted, and
too often unfriended till it emerges at length triumphant from the
twofold agony of soul and body.

These will know the throbbing pangs of the cancer which was

gnawing Athanase. Such as these have raised long, cruel debates within themselves, with the so high end in sight and no means of attaining it. They have passed through the experience of abortive effort; they have left the spawn of genius on the barren sands. They know that the strength of desire is as the scope of the imagination; the higher the leap, the lower the fall; and how many restraints are broken in such falls? These, like Athanase, catch glimpses of a glorious future in the distance; all that lies between seems but a transparent film of gauze to their piercing sight; but of that film which scarcely obscures the vision, society makes a wall of brass. Urged on by their vocation, by the artist's instinct within them, they too seek times without number to make a steppingstone of sentiments which society turns in the same way to practical ends. What! when marriages in the provinces are calculated and arranged on every side with a view to securing material welfare, shall it be forbidden to a struggling artist or man of science to keep two ends in view, to try to insure his own subsistence that the thought within him may live?

Athanase Granson, with such ideas as these fermenting in his head, thought at first of marriage with Mlle. Cormon as a definite solution of the problem of existence. He would be free to work for fame, he could make his mother comfortable, and he felt sure of himself—he knew that he could be faithful to Mlle. Cormon. But soon his purpose bred a real passion in him. It was an unconscious process. He set himself to study Mlle. Cormon; then familiarity exercised its spell, and at length Athanase saw nothing but beauties—the defects were all forgotten.

The senses count for so much in the love of a young man of three-and-twenty. Through the heat of desire woman is seen as through a prism. From this point of view it was a touch of genius in Beaumarchais to make the page Cherubino in the play strain Marcellina to his heart. If you recollect, moreover, that poverty restricted Athanase to a life of great loneliness, that there was no other woman to look at, that his eyes were always fastened upon Mlle. Cormon, and that all the light in the picture was concentrated upon her, it seems natural, does it not, that he should love her? The feeling hidden in the depths of his heart could but grow stronger day by day. Desire and pain and hope and meditation, in silence and repose, were filling up Athanase's soul to the brim; every hour added its drop. As his senses came to the aid of imagination and widened the inner horizon, Mlle. Cormon became more and more awe-inspiring, and he grew more and more timid.

The mother had guessed it all. She was a provincial, and she frankly calculated the advantages of the match. Mlle. Cormon might think herself very lucky to marry a young man of twenty-three with plenty of brains, a likely man to do honor to his name and country. Still the obstacles, Athanase's poverty and Mlle. Cormon's age, seemed to her to be insurmountable; there was nothing for it that she could see but patience. She had a policy of her own, like du Bousquier and the Chevalier de Valois; she was on the lookout for her opportunity, waiting, with wits sharpened by self-interest and a mother's love, for the propitious moment.

Of the Chevalier de Valois, Mme. Granson had no suspicion whatsoever; du Bousquier she still credited with views upon the lady, albeit Mlle. Cormon had once refused him. An adroit and secret enemy, Mme. Granson did the ex-contractor untold harm to serve the son to whom she had not spoken a word. After this, who does not see the importance of Suzanne's lie once confided to Mme. Granson? What a weapon put into the hands of the charitable treasurer of the Maternity Fund! How demurely she would carry the tale from house to house when she asked for subscriptions for the chaste Suzanne!

At this particular moment Athanase was pensively sitting with his elbow on the table, balancing a spoon on the edge of the empty bowl before him. He looked with unseeing eyes round the poor room, over the walls covered with an old-fashioned paper only seen in wine-saloons, at the window curtains with a chessboard pattern of pink-and-white squares, at the red-brick floor, the straw-bottomed chairs, the painted wooden sideboard, the glass door that opened into the kitchen. As he sat facing his mother and with his back to the fire, and as the fireplace was almost opposite the door, the first thing which caught Suzanne's eyes was his pale face, with the light from the street window falling full upon it, a face framed in dark hair, and eyes with the gleam of despair in them, and a fever kindled by the morning's thoughts.

The grisette surely knows by instinct the pain and sorrow of love; at the sight of Athanase, she felt that sudden electric thrill which comes we know not whence. We cannot explain it; some strong-minded persons deny that it exists, but many a woman and many a man has felt that shock of sympathy. It is a flash, lighting up the darkness of the future, and at the same time a presentiment of the pure joy of love shared by two souls, and a certainty that this other too understands. It is more like the strong, sure touch of a master hand upon the clavier of the senses than anything else. Eyes are riveted by an irresistible fascination, hearts are troubled, the music of joy rings in the ears and thrills the soul; a voice cries, "It is he!" And then—then very likely, reflection throws a douche of cold water over all this turbulent emotion, and there is an end of it.

In a moment, swift as a clap of thunder, a broadside of new thoughts poured in upon Suzanne. A lightning flash of love burned the weeds which had sprung up in dissipation and wantonness. She saw all that she was losing by blighting her name with a lie, the desecration, the degradation of it. Only last evening this idea had been a joke, now it was like a heavy sentence passed upon her. She recoiled before her success. But, after all, it was quite impossible that anything should come of this meeting; and the thought of Athanase's poverty, and a vague hope of making money and coming back from Paris with both hands full, to say: "I loved you all along"—or fate, if you will have it so—dried up the beneficent dew. The ambitious damsel asked shyly to speak for a moment with Mme. Granson, who took her into her bedroom.

When Suzanne came out again she looked once more at Athanase. He was still sitting in the same attitude. She choked back her tears.

As for Mme. Granson, she was radiant. She had found a terrible weapon to use against du Bousquier at last; she could deal him a deadly blow. So she promised the poor victim of seduction the support of all the ladies who subscribed to the Maternity Fund. She foresaw a dozen calls in prospect. In the course of the morning and afternoon she would conjure down a terrific storm upon the elderly bachelor's head. The Chevalier de Valois certainly foresaw the turn that matters were likely to take, but he had not expected anything like the amount of scandal that came of it.

"We are going to dine with Mademoiselle Cormon, you know, dear boy," said Mme. Granson; "take rather more pains with your appearance. It is a mistake to neglect your dress as you do; you look so untidy. Put on your best frilled shirt and your green cloth coat. I have my reasons," she added, with a mysterious air. "And beside, there will be a great many people; Mademoiselle Cormon is going to the Prébaudet directly. If a young man is thinking of marrying, he ought to make himself agreeable in every possible way. If girls would only tell the truth, my boy, dear me! you would be surprised at the things that take their fancy. It is often quite enough if a young man rides by at the head of a company of artillery, or comes to a dance in a suit of clothes that fits him passably well. A certain way of carrying the head, a melancholy attitude, is enough to set a girl imagining a whole life; we invent a romance to suit the hero; often he is only a stupid young man, but the marriage is made. Take notice of Monsieur de Valois, study him, copy his manners; see how he looks at ease; he has not a constrained manner, as you have. And talk a little; anyone might think that you knew nothing at all, *you* that know Hebrew by heart."

Athanase heard her submissively, but he looked surprised. He rose, took his cap, and went back to his work.

"Can mother have guessed my secret?" he thought, as he went round by the rue de Val-Noble where Mademoiselle Cormon lived, a little pleasure in which he indulged of a morning. His head was swarming with romantic fancies.

"How little she thinks that going past her house at this moment is a young man who would love her dearly, and be true to her, and never cause her a single care, and leave her fortune entirely in her own hands! Oh me! what a strange fatality it is that we two should live as we do in the same town and within a few paces of each other, and yet nothing can bring us any nearer! How if I spoke to her tonight?"

Meanwhile Suzanne went home to her mother, thinking the while of poor Athanase, feeling that for him she could find it in her heart to do what many a woman must have longed to do for the one beloved with superhuman strength; she could have made a steppingstone of her beautiful body if so he might come to his kingdom the sooner.

And now we must enter the house where all the actors in this Scene (Suzanne excepted) were to meet that very evening, the house belonging to the old maid, the converging point of so many interests. As for Suzanne, that young woman with her well-grown beauty, with courage sufficient to burn her boats, like Alexander, and to begin the battle of life with an uncalled-for-sacrifice of her character, she now disappears from the stage after bringing about a violently exciting situation. Her wishes, moreover, were more than fulfilled. A few days afterward she left her native place with a stock of money and fine clothes, including a superb green rep gown and a green bonnet lined with rose color, M. de Valois' gifts, which Suzanne liked better than anything else, better even than the Maternity Society's money. If the chevalier had gone to Paris while Suzanne was in her heyday, she would assuredly have left all for him.

And so this chaste Susanna, of whom the elders scarcely had more than a glimpse, settled herself comfortably and hopefully in Paris, while all Alençon was deploring the misfortunes with which the ladies of the Charitable and Maternity Societies had manifested so lively a sympathy.

While Suzanne might be taken as a type of the handsome Norman virgins who furnish, on the showing of a learned physician, one-third of the supply devoured by the monster, Paris,

she entered herself, and remained in those higher branches of
her profession in which some regard is paid to appearances. In
an age in which, as M. de Valois said, "woman has ceased to be
a woman," she was known merely as Mme. du Val-Noble; in
other times she would have rivaled an Imperia, a Rhodope, a
Ninon. One of the most distinguished writers of the Restoration
took her under his protection, and very likely will marry her
some day; he is a journalist, and above public opinion, seeing that
he creates a new one every six years.

In almost every prefecture of the second magnitude there is
some salon frequented not exactly by the cream of the local
society, but by personages both considerable and well considered.
The host and hostess probably will be among the foremost
people in the town. To them all houses are open; no entertainment, no public dinner is given but they are asked to it; but in
their salon you will not meet the *gens à château*—lords of the
manor, peers of France living on their broad acres, and persons
of the highest quality in the department, though these are all on
visiting terms with the family, and exchange invitations to dinner
and evening parties. The mixed society to be found there usually
consists of the lesser noblesse resident in the town, with the clergy
and judicial authorities. It is an influential assemblage. All the wit
and sense of the district is concentrated in its solid, unpretentious
ranks. Everybody in the set knows the exact amount of his neighbor's income, and professes the utmost indifference to dress and
luxury, trifles held to be mere childish vanity compared with the
acquisition of a *mouchoir à bœufs*—a pocket handkerchief of some
ten or a dozen acres, purchased after as many years of pondering
and intriguing and a prodigious deal of diplomacy.

Unshaken in its prejudices whether good or ill, the coterie
goes on its way without a look before or behind. Nothing from
Paris is allowed to pass without a prolonged scrutiny; innovations
are ridiculous, and bonds and cashmere shawls alike objectionable.
Provincials read nothing and wish to learn nothing; for them
science, literature, and mechanical invention are as the things
that is not. If a prefect does not suit their notions, they do their

best to have him removed; if this cannot be done, they isolate him. So will you see the inmates of a beehive wall up an intruding snail with wax. Finally, of the gossip of the salon, history is made. Young married women put in an appearance there occasionally (though the card table is the one resource) that their conduct may be stamped with the approval of the coterie and their social status confirmed.

Native susceptibilities are sometimes wounded by the supremacy of a single house, but the rest comfort themselves with the thought that they save the expense entailed by the position. Sometimes it happens that no one can afford to keep open house, and then the bigwigs of the place look about them for some harmless person whose character, position, and social standing offer guarantees for the neutrality of the ground, and alarm nobody's vanity or self-interest. This had been the case at Alençon. For a long time past the best society of the town has been wont to assemble in the house of the old maid before mentioned, who little suspected Mme. Granson's designs on her fortune, or the secret hopes of the two elderly bachelors who have just been unmasked.

Mlle. Cormon was Mme. Granson's fourth cousin. She lived with her mother's brother, a sometime vicar-general of the bishopric of Séez; she had been her uncle's ward and would one day inherit his fortune. Rose-Marie-Victoire Cormon was the last representative of a house which, plebeian though it was, had associated and often allied itself with the noblesse, and ranked among the oldest families in the province. In former times the Cormons had been intendants of the duchy of Alençon, and had given a goodly number of magistrates to the bench, and several bishops to the church. M. de Sponde, Mlle. Cormon's maternal grandfather, was elected by the noblesse to the States-General; and M. Cormon, her father, had been asked to represent the Third Estate, but neither of them accepted the responsibility. For the last century, the daughters of the house had married into the noble families of the province, in such sort that the Cormons were grafted into pretty nearly every genealogical tree in the duchy. No burgher family came so near being noble.

The house in which the present Mlle. Cormon lived had never passed out of the family since it was built by Pierre Cormon in the reign of Henri IV; and of all the old maid's worldly possessions, this one appealed most to the greed of her elderly suitors; though, so far from bringing in money, the ancestral home of the Cormons was a positive expense to its owner. But it is such an unusual thing, in the very center of a country town, to find a house handsome without, convenient within, and free from mean surroundings, that all Alençon shared the feeling of envy.

The old mansion stood exactly halfway down the rue du Val-Noble, *The Val-Noble*, as it was called, probably because the Brillante, the little stream which flows through the town, has hollowed out a little valley for itself in a dip of the land thereabout. The most noticeable feature of the house was its massive architecture, of the style introduced from Italy by Marie de' Medici; all the cornerstones and facings were cut with diamond-shaped bosses, in spite of the difficulty of working in the granite of which it is built. It was a two-storied house with a very high-pitched roof, and a row of dormer windows, each with its carved tympanum standing picturesquely enough above the lead-lined parapet with its ornamental balustrade. A grotesque gargoyle, the head of some fantastic bodyless beast, discharged the rain water through its jaws into the street below, where great stone slabs, pierced with five holes, were placed to receive it. Each gable terminated in a leaden finial, a sign that this was a burgher's house, for none but nobles had a right to put up a weathercock in olden times. To the right and left of the yard stood the stables and the coach house; the kitchen, laundry, and woodshed. One of the leaves of the great gate used to stand open; so that passers-by, looking in through the little low wicket with the bell attached, could see the parterre in the middle of a spacious paved court, and the low-clipped privet hedges which marked out miniature borders full of monthly roses, clove gilliflowers, scabious, lilies, and Spanish broom; as well as the laurel bushes and pomegranates and myrtles which grew in tubs put out of doors for the summer.

The scrupulous neatness and tidiness of the place must have struck any stranger and furnished him with a clue to the old maid's character. The mistress' eyes must have been unemployed, careful, and prying; less, perhaps, from any natural bent, than for want of any occupation. Who but an elderly spinster, at a loss how to fill an always empty day, would have insisted that no blade of grass should show itself in the paved courtyard, that the wall-copings should be scoured, that the broom should always be busy, that the coach should never be left with the leather curtains undrawn? Who else, from sheer lack of other employment, could have introduced something like Dutch cleanliness into a little province between Perche, Normandy, and Brittany, where the natives make boast of their crass indifference to comfort? The chevalier never climbed the steps without reflecting inwardly that the house was fit for a peer of France; and du Bousquier similarly considered that the Mayor of Alençon ought to live there.

A glass door at the top of the flight of steps gave admittance to an antechamber lighted by a second glass door opposite, above a corresponding flight of steps leading into the garden. This part of the house, a kind of gallery floored with square red tiles, and wainscoted to elbow-height, was a hospital for invalid family portraits; one here and there had lost an eye or sustained injury to a shoulder, another stood with a hole in the place where his hat should have been, yet another had lost a leg by amputation. Here cloaks, clogs, overshoes, and umbrellas were left; everybody deposited his belongings in the antechamber on his arrival, and took them again on his departure. A long bench was set against either wall for the servants who came of an evening with their lanterns to fetch home their masters and mistresses, and a big stove was set in the middle to mitigate the icy blasts which swept across from door to door.

This gallery, then, divided the first floor into two equal parts. The staircase rose to the left on the side nearest the courtyard, the rest of the space being taken up by the great dining room, with its windows looking out upon the garden, and a pantry beyond, which communicated with the kitchen. To the right lay the drawing room, lighted by four windows, and a couple of smaller rooms beyond it, a boudoir which gave upon the garden, and a room which did duty as a study and looked into the court-yard. There was a complete suite of rooms on the second floor, beside the Abbé de Sponde's apartments; while the attic story, in all probability roomy enough, had long since been given over to the tenancy of rats and mice. Mlle. Cormon used to report their nocturnal exploits to the Chevalier de Valois and marvel at the futility of all measures taken against them.

The garden, about half an acre in extent, was bounded by the Brillante, so called from the mica spangles which glitter in its bed; not, however, in the Val-Noble for the manufacturers and dyers of Alençon pour all their refuse into the shallow stream before it reaches this point; and the opposite bank, as always happens wherever a stream passes through a town, was lined with houses where various thirsty industries were carried on. Luckily, Mlle. Cormon's neighbors were all of them quiet tradesmen—a baker, a fuller, and one or two cabinet makers. Her garden, full of old-fashioned flowers, naturally ended in a terrace, by way of a quay, with a short flight of steps down to the water's edge. Try to picture the wallflowers growing in blue-and-white glazed jars along the balustrade by the river, behold a shady walk to right and left beneath the square-clipped lime trees, and you will have some idea of a scene full of unpretending cheerfulness and sober tranquillity; you can see the views of homely humble life along the opposite bank, the quaint houses, the trickling stream of the Brillante, the garden itself, the linden walks under the garden walls, and the venerable home built by the Cormons. How peace-ful, how quiet it was! If there was no ostentation, there was nothing transitory, everything seemed to last forever there.

The first-floor rooms, therefore, were given over to social uses. You breathed the atmosphere of the Province, ancient, unalterable Province. The great square-shaped drawing room, with its four doors and four windows, was modestly wainscoted with carved panels, and painted gray. On the wall, above the single oblong mirror on the mantel, the Hours, in monochrome, were ushering in the Day. For this particular style of decoration, which used to infest the spaces above doors, the artist's invention devised the eternal Seasons which meet your eyes almost anywhere in central France, till you loathe the detestable Cupids engaged in reaping, skating, sowing seeds, or flinging flowers about. Every window was overarched with a sort of baldachin with green damask curtains drawn back with cords and huge tassels. The tapestry-covered furniture, with a darn here and there at the edges of the chairs, belonged distinctly to that period of the eighteenth century when curves and contortions were in the very height of fashion; the frames were painted and varnished, the subjects in the medallions on the backs were taken from La Fontaine. Four card tables, a table for piquet, and another for backgammon filled up the immense space. A rock-crystal chandelier, shrouded in green gauze, hung suspended from the prominent crossbeam which divided the ceiling, the only plastered ceiling in the house. Two branched candle sconces were fixed into the wall above the mantel, where a couple of blue Sèvres vases stood on either side of a copper-gilt clock which represented a scene taken from "Le Déserteur"—a proof of the prodigious popularity of Sedaine's work. It was a group of no less than eleven figures, four inches high; the deserter emerging from jail escorted by a guard of soldiers, while a young person, swooning in the foreground, held out his reprieve. The hearth and fire irons were of the same date and style. The more recent family portraits—one or two Rigauds and three pastels by Latour—adorned the handsome wainscot panels.

The study, paneled entirely in old lacquer work, red and black and gold, would have fetched fabulous sums a few years later; Mlle. Cormon was as far as possible from suspecting its value; but if she had been offered a thousand crowns for every panel, she would not have parted with a single one. It was a part of her system to alter nothing, and everywhere in the provinces the belief in ancestral hoards is very strong. The boudoir, never used, was hung with the old-fashioned chintz so much run after nowadays by amateurs of the "Pompadour style," as it is called.

The dining room was paved with black-and-white stone; it had not been ceiled, but the joists and beams were painted. Ranged round the walls, beneath a flowered trellis, painted in fresco, stood the portentous, marble-topped sideboards, indispensable in the warfare waged in the provinces against the powers of digestion. The chairs were cane-seated and varnished, the doors of unpolished walnut wood. Everything combined admirably to complete the general effect, the old-world air of the house within and without. The provincial spirit had preserved all as it had always been; nothing was new or old, young or decrepit. You felt a sense of chilly precision everywhere.

Any tourist in Brittany, Normandy, Maine, or Anjou must have seen some houses more or less like this in one or other provincial town; for the Hôtel de Cormon was in its way a very pattern and model of burgher houses over a large part of France, and the better deserves a place in this chronicle because it is at once a commentary on the manners of the place and the expression of its ideas. Who does not feel, even now, how much the life within the old walls was one of peaceful routine?

For such library as the house possessed you must have descended rather below the level of the Brillante. There stood a solidly clasped oak-bound collection, none the worse, nay, rather the better, for a thick coating of dust; a collection kept as carefully as a cider-growing district is wont to keep the products of the presses of Burgundy, Touraine, Gascony, and the South. Here were works full of native force, and exquisite qualities, with an added perfume of antiquity. No one will import poor wines when the cost of carriage is so heavy.

Mlle. Cormon's whole circle consisted of about a hundred and fifty persons. Of these, some went into the country, some were ill, others from home on business in the department, but there was a faithful band which always came, unless Mlle. Cormon gave an evening party in form; so also did those persons who were bound either by their duties or old habit to live in Alençon itself. All these people were of ripe age. A few among them had traveled, but scarcely any of them had gone beyond the province, and one or two had been implicated in Chouannerie. People could begin to speak freely of the war, now that rewards had come to the heroic defenders of the good cause. M. de Valois had been concerned in the last rising, when the Marquis de Montauran lost his life, betrayed by his mistress; and Marche-à Terre, now peacefully driving a grazier's trade by the banks of the Mayenne, had made a famous name for himself. M. de Valois, during the past six months, had supplied the key to several shrewd tricks played off upon Hulot the old Republican, commander of a demi-brigade stationed at Alençon from 1798 till 1800. There was talk of Hulot yet in the countryside.

The women made little pretense of dress, except on Wednesdays, when Mlle. Cormon gave a dinner party, and last week's guests came to pay their "visit of digestion." On Wednesday evening the rooms were filled. Guests and visitors came in gala dress; here and there a woman brought her knitting or her tapestry work, and some young ladies unblushingly drew patterns for point d'Alençon, by which they supported themselves. Men brought their wives, because there were so few young fellows there; no whisper could pass unnoticed, and therefore there was no danger of love-making for maid or matron. Every evening at six o'clock the lobby was filled with articles of dress, with sticks, cloaks, and lanterns. Every one was so well acquainted, the customs of the house were so primitive, that if by any chance the Abbé de Sponde was in the lime-tree walk, and Mlle. Cormon in her room, neither Josette the maid nor Jacquelin the man thought it necessary to inform them of the arrival of visitors. The first comer waited till someone else arrived; and when they mustered players sufficient for whist or boston, the game was begun without waiting for the Abbé de Sponde or mademoiselle. When it grew dark, Josette or Jacquelin brought lights as soon as the bell rang, and the old abbé out in the garden, seeing the

drawing-room windows illuminated, hastened slowly toward the
house. Every evening the piquet, boston, and whist tables were
full, giving an average of twenty-five or thirty persons, including
those who came to chat; but often there were as many as thirty
or forty, and then Jacquelin took candles into the study and the
boudoir. Between eight and nine at night the servants began to
fill the antechamber; and nothing short of a revolution would
have found anyone in the salon at ten o'clock. At that hour the
frequenters of the house were walking home through the streets,
discussing the points made, or keeping up a conversation begun
in the drawing room. Sometimes the talk turned on a pocket
handkerchief of land on which somebody had an eye, sometimes
it was the division of an inheritance and disputes among the
legatees, or the pretensions of the aristocratic set. You see exactly
the same thing at Paris when the theaters disgorge.

Some people who talk a great deal about poetry and understand nothing about it are wont to rail at provincial towns
and provincial ways; but lean your forehead on your left hand,
as you sit with your feet on the firedogs, and rest your elbow
on your knee, and then—if you have fully realized for yourself
the level, pleasant landscape, the house, the interior, the folk
within it and their interests, interests that seem all the larger
because the mental horizon is so limited (as a grain of gold is
beaten thin between two sheets of parchment)—then ask yourself what human life is. Try to decide between the engraver of
the hieroglyphic birds on an Egyptian obelisk, and one of these
folk in Alençon playing boston through a score of years with
du Bousquier, M. de Valois, Mlle. Cormon, the president of the
Tribunal, the public prosecutor, the Abbé de Sponde, Mme.
Granson, and all the rest. If the daily round, the daily pacing of
the same track in the footsteps of many yesterdays, is not exactly
happiness, it is so much like it that others, driven by dint of storm-
tossed days to reflect on the blessings of calm, will say that it is
happiness indeed.

To give the exact measure of the importance of Mlle. Cormon's
salon, it will suffice to add that du Bousquier, a born statistician,

computed that its frequenters mustered among them a hundred and thirty-one votes in the electoral college, and eighteen hundred thousand livres of income derived from lands in the province. The town of Alençon was not, it is true, completely represented there. The aristocratic section, for instance, had a salon of their own, and the receiver-general's house was a sort of official inn kept, as in duty bound, by the Government, where everybody who was anybody danced, flirted, fluttered, fell in love, and supped. One or two unclassified persons kept up the communications between Mlle. Cormon's salon and the other two, but the Cormon salon criticized all that passed in the opposed camps very severely. Sumptuous dinners gave rise to unfavorable comment; ices at a dance caused searchings of heart; the women's behavior and dress and any innovations were much discussed.

Mlle. Cormon being, as it were, the style of the firm and figurehead of an imposing coterie, was inevitably the object of any ambition as profound as that of the du Bousquier or the Chevalier de Valois. To both gentlemen she meant a seat in the Chamber of Deputies, with a peerage for the chevalier, a receiver-general's post for du Bousquier. A salon admittedly of the first rank is every whit as hard to build up in a country town as in Paris. And here was the salon ready made. To marry Mlle. Cormon was to be lord of Alençon. Finally, Athanase, the only one of the three suitors that had ceased to calculate, cared as much for the woman as for her money.

Is there not a whole strange drama (to use the modern cant phrase) in the relative positions of these four human beings? There is something grotesque, is there not, in the idea of three rival suitors eagerly pressing about an old maid who never so much as suspected their intentions, in spite of her intense and very natural desire to be married? Yet, although things being so, it may seem an extraordinary thing that she should not have married before, it is not difficult to explain how and why, in spite of her fortune and her three suitors, Mlle. Cormon was still unwed.

From the first, following the family tradition, Mlle. Cormon
had always wished to marry a noble, but between the years
1789 and 1799 circumstances were very much against her. While
she would have wished to be the wife of a person of condition,
she was horribly afraid of the Revolutionary Tribunal; and these
two motives weighing about equally, she remained stationary,
according to a law which holds equally good in esthetics or
statics. At the same time, the condition of suspended judgment is
not unpleasant for a girl, so long as she feels young and thinks
that she can choose where she pleases. But, as all France knows,
the system of government immediately preceding the wars of
Napoleon produced a vast number of widows; and the number of
heiresses was altogether out of proportion to the number of eligible men. When order was restored in the country, in the time of
the Consulate, external difficulties made marriage as much of a
problem as ever for Rose-Marie-Victoire. On the one hand, she
declined to marry an elderly man; and, on the other, dread of
ridicule and circumstances put quite young men out of the question. In those days heads of families married their sons as mere
boys, because in this way they escaped the conscription. With
the obstinacy of a landed proprietor, mademoiselle would not
hear of marrying a military man; she had no wish to take a
husband only to give him back to the Emperor, she wished to
keep him for herself. And so, between 1804 and 1815, it was
impossible to compete with a younger generation of girls, too
numerous already in times when cannon shot had thinned the
ranks of marriageable men.

Again, apart from Mlle. Cormon's predilection for birth, she
had a very pardonable craze for being loved for her own sake.
You would scarcely believe the lengths to which she carried
this fancy. She set her wits to work to lay snares for her admirers, to try their sentiments; and that with such success that
the unfortunates one and all fell into them, and succumbed in
the whimsical ordeals through which they passed unawares. Mlle.
Cormon did not study her suitors, she played the spy upon them.
A careless word or a joke, and the lady did not understand jokes

very well, was excuse enough to dismiss an aspirant as found wanting. This had neither spirit nor delicacy; that was untruthful and not a Christian; one wanted to cut down tall timber and coin money under the marriage canopy; another was not the man to make her happy; or, again, she had her suspicions of gout in the family, or took fright at her wooer's antecedents. Like mother church, she would fain see a priest without blemish at her altar. And then Rose-Marie-Victoire made the worst of herself and was as anxious to be loved, with all her factitious plainness and imaginary faults, as other women are to be married for virtues which they have not and for borrowed beauty. Mlle. Cormon's ambition had its source in the finest instincts of womanhood. She would reward her lover by discovering to him a thousand virtues after marriage, as other women reveal the many little faults kept hitherto strenuously out of sight. But no one understood. The noble girl came in contact with none but commonplace natures, with whom practical interests came first; the finer calculations of feeling were beyond their comprehension.

She grew more and more suspicious as the critical period so ingenuously called "second youth" drew nearer. Her fancy for making the worst of herself with increasing success frightened away the latest recruits; they hesitated to unite their lot with hers. The strategy of her game of blindman's bluff (the virtues to be revealed when the finder's eyes were opened) was a complex study for which few men have inclination; they prefer perfection ready-made. An ever-present dread of being married for her money made her unreasonably distrustful and uneasy. She fell foul of the rich, and the rich could look higher; she was afraid of poor men, she would not believe them capable of that disinterestedness on which she set such store; till at length her rejections and other circumstances let in an unexpected light upon the minds of suitors thus presented for her selection like dried peas on a seedman's sieve. Every time a marriage project came to nothing, the unfortunate girl, being gradually led to despise mankind, saw the other sex at last in a false light. Inevitably, in her inmost soul, she grew misanthropic, a tinge of bitterness was infused into her conversation, a certain harshness into her expression. And her manners became more and more rigid under the stress of enforced celibacy; in her despair she sought to perfect herself. It was a characteristic and a noble vengeance. She would polish and cut for God the rough diamond rejected by men.

Before long public opinion was against Mlle. Cormon. People accept the verdict which a woman passes upon herself if, being free to marry, she fails to fulfill expectations, or is known to have refused eligible suitors. Everyone decides that she has her own reasons for declining marriage, and those reasons are always misinterpreted. There was some hidden physical defect or deformity, they said; but she, poor girl, was pure as an angel, healthy as a child, and overflowing with kindness. Nature had meant her to know all the joys, all the happiness, all the burdens of motherhood.

Yet in her person Mlle. Cormon did not find a natural auxiliary to gain her heart's desire. She had no beauty, save of the kind so improperly called "the devil's"; that full-blown freshness of youth which, theologically speaking, the devil never could have possessed; unless, indeed, we are to look for an explanation of the expression in the devil's continual desire of refreshing himself. The heiress' feet were large and flat; when, on rainy days, she crossed the wet streets between her house and St. Leonard's, her raised skirt displayed (without malice, be it said) a leg which scarcely seemed to belong to a woman, so muscular was it, with a small, firm, prominent calf like a sailor's. She had a figure for a wet nurse. Her thick, honest waist, her strong, plump arms, her red hands; everything about her, in short, was in keeping with the round, expansive contours and portly fairness of the Norman style of beauty. Wide-open, prominent eyes of no particular color, gave to a face, by no means distinguished in its round outlines, a sheepish, astonished expression not altogether inappropriate, however, in an old maid: even if Rose had not been innocent, she must still have seemed so. An aquiline nose was oddly assorted with a low forehead, for a feature of that type is almost invariably found in company with a lofty brow. In spite of thick, red lips, the sign of great kindliness of nature, there were evidently so few ideas behind that forehead that Rose's heart could scarcely have been directed by her brain. Kind she must certainly be, but not gracious. And we are apt to judge the defects of goodness very harshly, while we make the most of the redeeming qualities of vice.

An extraordinary length of chestnut hair lent Rose Cormon such beauty as belongs to vigor and luxuriance, her chief personal characteristics. In the time of her pretensions she had a trick of turning her face in three-quarters profile to display a very pretty ear, gracefully set between the azure-streaked white throat and the temple, and thrown into relief by thick masses of her hair. Dressed in a ball gown, with her head poised at this angle, Rose might almost seem beautiful. With her protuberant bust, her waist, her high health, she used to draw exclamations of admiration from Imperial officers. "What a fine girl!" they used to say.

But, as years went on, the stoutness induced by a quiet, regular life distributed itself so unfortunately over her person, that its original proportions were destroyed. No known variety of corset could have discovered the poor spinster's hips at this period of her existence; she might have been cast in one uniform piece. The youthful proportions of her figure were completely lost; her dimensions had grown so excessive that no one could see her stoop without fearing that, being so top-heavy, she would certainly overbalance herself; but nature had provided a sufficient natural counterpoise, which enabled her to dispense with all adventitious aid from "dress improvers." Everything about Rose was very genuine.

Her chin developed a triple fold, which reduced the apparent length of her throat, and made it no easy matter to turn her head. She had no wrinkles, she had creases. Wags used to assert that she powdered herself, as nurses powder babies, to prevent chafing of the skin. To a young man, consumed, like Athanase, with suppressed desires, this excessive corpulence offered just the kind of physical charm which could not fail to attract youth. Youthful imaginations essentially intrepid, stimulated by appetite, are prone to dilate upon the beauties of that living expanse. So does the plump partridge allure the epicure's knife. And, indeed, any debt-burdened young man of fashion in Paris would have resigned himself readily enough to fulfilling his part of the contract and making Mademoiselle Cormon happy. Still the unfortunate spinster had already passed her fortieth year!

At this period of enforced loneliness, after the long, vain struggle to fill her life with those interests that are all in all to woman, she was fortifying herself in virtue by the most strict observance of religious duties; she had turned to the great consolation of well-preserved virginity. A confessor, endowed with no great wisdom, had directed Mademoiselle Cormon in the paths of asceticism for some three years past, recommending a system of self-scourging calculated, according to modern doctors, to produce an effect the exact opposite of that expected by the poor priest, whose knowledge of hygiene was but limited. These absurd practices were beginning to bring a certain monastic tinge to Rose Cormon's face; with frequent pangs of despair, she watched the sallow hues of middle age creeping across its natural white and red; while the trace of down about the corners of her upper lip showed a distinct tendency to darken and increase like smoke. Her temples grew shiny. She had passed the turning-point, in fact. It was known for certain in Alençon that Mademoiselle Cormon suffered from heated blood. She inflicted her confidence upon the Chevalier de Valois, reckoning up the number of foot baths that she took and devising cooling treatment with him. And that shrewd observer would end by taking out his snuffbox, and gazing at the portrait of the Princess Goritza as he remarked: "But the real sedative, my dear young lady, would be a good and handsome husband."

"But whom could one trust?" returned she.

But the chevalier only flicked away the powdered snuff from the creases of his paduasoy vest. To anybody else the proceeding would have seemed perfectly natural, but it always made the poor old maid feel uncomfortable.

The violence of her objectless longings grew to such a height that she shrank from looking a man in the face, so afraid was she that the thoughts which pierced her heart might be read in her eyes. It was one of her whims, possibly a later development of her former tactics, to behave almost ungraciously to the possible suitors toward whom she still felt herself attracted, so afraid was she of being accused of folly. Most people in her circle were utterly incapable of appreciating her motives, so noble throughout; they explained her manner to her coevals in single blessedness by a theory of revenge for some past slight.

With the beginning of the year 1815 Rose Cormon had reached the fatal age, to which she did not confess. She was forty-two. By this time her desire to be married had reached a degree of intensity bordering on monomania. She saw her chances of motherhood fast slipping away forever; and, in her divine ignorance, she longed above all things for children of her own. There was not a soul found in Alençon to impute a single unchaste desire to the virtuous girl. She loved love, taking all for granted, without realizing for herself what love would be—a devout Agnès, incapable of inventing one of the little shifts of Molière's heroine.

She had been counting upon chance of late. The disbanding of the Imperial troops and the reconstruction of the King's army were sending a tide of military men back to their native places, some of them on half pay, some with pensions, some without, and all of them anxious to find some way of amending their bad fortune, and of finishing their days in a fashion which would mean the beginning of happiness for Mlle. Cormon. It would be hard indeed if she could not find a single brave and honorable man among all those who were coming back to the neighborhood. He must have a sound constitution in the first place, he must be of suitable age, and a man whose personal character would serve as a passport to his Bonapartist opinions; perhaps he might even be willing to turn Royalist for the sake of gaining a lost social position.

Supported by these mental calculations, Mlle. Cormon maintained the severity of her attitude for the first few months of the year; but the men that came back to the town were all either too old or too young, or their characters were too bad, or their opinions too Bonapartist, or their station in life was incompatible with her position, fortune, and habits. The case grew more and more desperate every day. Officers high in the service had used their advantages under Napoleon to marry, and these gentlemen now became Royalists for the sake of their families. In vain had she put up prayers to heaven to send her a husband that she might be happy in Christian fashion; it was written, no doubt, that she should die virgin and martyr, for not a single likely-looking man presented himself.

In the course of conversation in her drawing room of an evening, the frequenters of the house kept the police register under tolerably strict supervision; no one could arrive at Alençon but they informed themselves at once as to the newcomer's mode of life, quality, and fortune. But, at the same time, Alençon is not a town to attract many strangers; it is not on the highroad to any large city; there are no chance arrivals; naval officers on their way to Brest do not so much as stop in the place.

Poor Mlle. Cormon at last comprehended that her choice was reduced to the natives. At times her eyes took an almost fierce expression, to which the chevalier would respond with a keen glance at her as he drew out his snuffbox to gaze at the Princess Goritza. M. de Valois knew that, in feminine jurisprudence, fidelity to an old love is a guarantee for the new. But Mlle. Cormon, it cannot be denied, was not very intelligent. His snuffbox strategy was wasted upon her.

She redoubled her watchfulness, the better to combat the "evil one," and with devout rigidness and the sternest principles she consigned her cruel sufferings to the secret places of her life.

At night, when she was alone, she thought of her lost youth, of her faded bloom, of the thwarted instincts of her nature; and while she laid her passionate longings at the foot of the cross, together with all the poetry doomed to remain pent within her, she vowed inwardly to take the first man that was willing to marry her, just as he was, without putting him to any proof whatsoever. Sounding her own dispositions, after a series of vigils, each more trying than the last, in her own mind she went so far as to espouse a sub-lieutenant, a tobacco smoker to boot; nay, he was even head over ears in debt. Him she proposed to transform with care, submission, and gentleness into a pattern for mankind. But only in the silence of night could she plan these imaginary marriages, in which she amused herself with playing the sublime part of guardian angel; with morning, if Josette found her mistress' bedclothes turned topsy-turvy, mademoiselle had recovered her dignity; with morning, after breakfast, she would have nothing less than a solid landowner, a well-preserved man of forty—a young man, as you may say.

The Abbé de Sponde was incapable of giving his niece assistance of any sort in schemes for marriage. The good man, aged seventy or thereabout, referred all the calamities of the Revolution to the design of a providence prompt to punish a dissolute church. For which reasons M. de Sponde had long since entered upon a deserted path to heaven, the way trodden by the hermits of old. He led an ascetic life, simply, unobtrusively; hiding his deeds of charity, his constant prayer and fasting from all other eyes. Necessity was laid upon all priests, he thought, to do as he did; he preached by example, turning a serene and smiling face upon the world, while he completely cut himself off from worldly interests. All his thoughts were given to the afflicted, to the needs of the church, and the saving of his own soul. He left the management of his property to his niece. She paid over his yearly income to him; and, after a slight deduction for his maintenance, the whole of it went in private almsgiving or in donations to the church.

All the abbé's affections were centered upon his niece, and she looked upon him as a father. He was a somewhat absent-minded father, however, without the remotest conception of the rebellion of the flesh; a father who gave thanks to God for maintaining his beloved daughter in a state of virginity; for from his youth up he had held, with St. John Chrysostom, that "virginity is as much above the estate of marriage as the angels are above man."

Mlle. Cormon was accustomed to look up to her uncle; she did not venture to confide her wishes for a change of condition to him; and he, good man, on his side was accustomed to the ways of the house, and perhaps might not have relished the introduction of a master into it. Absorbed in thoughts of the distress which he relieved, or lost in fathomless inner depths of prayer, he was often unconscious of what was going on about him; frequenters of the house set this down to absent-mindedness; but while he said little, his silence was neither unsociable nor ungenial. A tall, spare, grave, and solemn man, his face told of kindly feeling and a great inward peace. His presence in the house seemed, as it were, to consecrate it. The abbé entertained a strong liking for that elderly skeptic the Chevalier de Valois. Far apart as their lives were, the two grand wrecks of the eighteenth-century clergy and noblesse recognized each other by generic signs and tokens; and the chevalier, for that matter, could converse with unction with the abbé, just as he talked like a father with his grisettes.

Some may think that Mlle. Cormon would leave no means untried to gain her end; that among other permissible feminine artifices, for instance, she would turn to her toilettes, wear low-cut bodices, use the passive coquetry of a display of the splendid equipment with which she might take the field. On the contrary, she was as heroic and steadfast in her high-necked gown as a sentry in his sentry box. All her dresses, bonnets, and finery were made in Alençon by two hunchbacked sisters, not wanting in taste. But in spite of the entreaties of the two artists, Mlle. Cormon utterly declined the adventitious aid of elegance; she must be substantial throughout, body and plumage, and possibly her heavy-looking dresses became her not amiss. Laugh who will at her, poor thing. Generous natures, those who never trouble themselves about the form in which good feeling shows itself but admire it wherever they find it, will see something sublime in this trait. Perhaps some slight-natured feminine critic may begin to carp, and say that there is no woman in France so simple but that she can angle for a husband, that Mlle. Cormon is one of those abnormal creatures which common sense forbids us to take for a type; that the best or the most babyish unmarried woman that has a mind to hook a gudgeon can put forward some physical charm wherewith to bait her line. But when you begin to think that the sublime Apostolic Roman Catholic is still a power in Brittany and the ancient duchy of Alençon, these criticisms fall to the ground. Faith and piety admit no such subtleties. Mlle. Cormon kept to the straight path, preferring the misfortune of a maidenhood infinitely prolonged to the misery of untruthfulness, to the sin of small deceit. Armed with self-discipline, such a girl cannot make a sacrifice of a principle; and therefore love (or self-interest) must make a very determined effort to find her out and win her.

Let us have the courage to make a confession, painful in these days when religion is nothing but a means of advancement for some, a dream for others; the devout are subject to a kind of moral ophthalmia, which, by the especial grace of providence, removes a host of small earthly concerns out of the sight of the pilgrim of eternity. In a word, the devout are apt to be dense in a good many ways. Their stupidity, at the same time, is a measure of the force with which their spirits turn heavenward; albeit the skeptical M. de Valois maintained that it is a moot point whether stupid women take naturally to piety or whether piety, on the other hand, has a stupefying effect upon an intelligent girl.

It must be borne in mind that it is the purest orthodox goodness, ready to drink rapturously of every cup set before it, to submit devoutly to the will of God, to see the print of the divine finger everywhere in the clay of life—that it is Catholic virtue stealing like hidden light into the innermost recesses of this history that alone can bring everything into right relief and widen its significance for those who yet have faith. And, again, if the stupidity is admitted, why should the misfortunes of stupidity be less interesting than the woes of genius in a world where fools so overwhelmingly preponderate?

To resume: Mlle. Cormon's divine girlish ignorance of life was an offense in the eyes of the world. She was anything but observant, as her treatment of her suitors sufficiently showed. At this very moment, a girl of sixteen who had never opened a novel in her life might have read a hundred chapters of romance in Athanase's eyes. But Mlle. Cormon saw nothing all the while; she never knew that the young man's voice was unsteady with emotion which he dared not express, and the woman who could invent refinements of high sentiment to her own undoing could not discern the same feelings in Athanase.

Those who know that qualities of heart and brain are as independent of each other as genius and greatness of soul will see nothing extraordinary in this psychological phenomenon. A complete human being is so rare a prodigy that Socrates, that pearl among mankind, agreed with a contemporary phrenologist that he himself was born to be a very scurvy knave. A great general may save his country at Zurich, and yet take a commission from contractors; a banker's doubtful honesty does not prevent him from being a statesman; a great composer may give the world divine music, and yet forge another man's signature; and a woman of refined feeling may be excessively weak-minded. In short, a devout woman may have a very lofty soul, and yet have no ears to hear the voice of another noble soul at her side.

The unaccountable freaks of physical infirmity find a parallel in the moral world. Here was a good creature making her preserves and breaking her heart till she grew almost ridiculous, because, forsooth, there was no one to eat them but her uncle and herself. Those who sympathized with her for the sake of her good qualities, or, in some cases, on account of her defects, used to laugh over her disappointments. People began to wonder what would become of so fine a property with all Mlle. Cormon's savings, and her uncle's to boot.

It was long since they began to suspect that at bottom, and in spite of appearances, Mlle. Cormon was "an original." Originality is not allowed in the provinces; originality means that you have ideas which nobody else can understand, and in a country town people's intellects, like their manner of life, must all be on a level. Even in 1804 Rose's matrimonial prospects were considered so problematical, that "to marry like Mlle. Cormon" was a current saying in Alençon, and the most ironical way of suggesting Such-an-one would never marry at all.

The necessity to laugh at someone must indeed be imperious in France if anyone could be found to raise a smile at the expense of that excellent creature. Not merely did she entertain the whole town, she was charitable, she was good; she was incapable of saying a spiteful word; and more than that, she was so much in unison with the whole spirit of the place, its manners and its customs, that she was generally beloved as the very incarnation of the life of the province; she had imbibed all its prejudices and made its interests hers; she had never gone beyond its limits, she adored it; she was imbedded in provincial tradition. In spite of her eighteen thousand livres per annum, a tolerably large income for the neighborhood, she accommodated herself to the ways of her less wealthy neighbors. When she went to her country house, the Prébaudet, for instance, she drove over in an old-fashioned wicker cariole hung with white leather straps and fitted with a couple of rusty weatherbeaten leather curtains which scarcely closed it in. The equipage, drawn by a fat, broken-winded mare, was known all over the town. Jacquelin, the manservant, cleaned it as carefully as if it had been the finest carriage from Paris. Mademoiselle was fond of it; it had lasted her a dozen years, a fact which she was wont to point out with the triumphant joy of contented parsimony. Most people were grateful to her for forbearing to humiliate them by splendor which she might have flaunted before their eyes; it is even credible that if she had sent for a calèche from Paris, it would have caused more talk than any of her "disappointments." After all, the finest carriage in the world, like the old-fashioned cariole, could only have taken her to the Prébaudet; and in the provinces they always keep the end in view, and trouble themselves very little about the elegance of the means, provided that they are sufficient.

To complete the picture of Mlle. Cormon's household and

domestic life, several figures must be grouped round Mlle. Cormon and the Abbé de Sponde. Jacquelin, and Josette, and Mariette, the cook, ministered to the comfort of uncle and niece.

Jacquelin, a man of forty, short and stout, dark-haired and
ruddy, with a countenance of the Breton sailor type, had been
in service in the house for twenty-two years. He waited at table,
groomed the mare, worked in the garden, cleaned the abbé's shoes,
ran errands, chopped firewood, drove the cariole, went to the
Prébaudet for corn, hay, and straw, and slept like a dormouse in
the antechamber of an evening. He was supposed to be fond
of Josette, and Josette was six-and-thirty. But if she had married
him, Mlle. Cormon would have dismissed her; and so the poor
lovers were fain to save up their wages in silence, and to wait
and hope for mademoiselle's marriage, much as the Jews look
for the advent of the Messiah.

Josette came from the district between Alençon and Mortagne;
she was a fat little woman. Her face, which reminded you of
a mud-bespattered apricot, was not wanting either in character or
intelligence. She was supposed to rule her mistress. Josette and
Jacquelin, feeling sure of the event, found consolation, pre-
sumably, by discounting the future. Mariette, the cook, had likewise been in the family for fifteen years; she was skilled in
cookery of the country and the preparation of the most esteemed
provincial dishes.

Perhaps the fat, old bay mare, of the Normandy breed, which
Mlle. Cormon used to drive to the Prébaudet, ought to count for
a good deal, for the affection which the five inmates of the house
bore the animal amounted to mania. Penelope, for that was her
name, had been with them for eighteen years; and so well was she
cared for, so regularly tended, that Jacquelin and mademoiselle
hoped to get quite another ten years of work out of her. Penelope
was a stock subject and source of interest in their lives. It seemed
as if poor Mlle. Cormon, with no child of her own, lavished
all her maternal affection upon the lucky beast. Almost every
human being leading a solitary life in a crowded world will sur-

round himself with a make-believe family of some sort, and
Penelope took the place of dogs, cats, or canaries.

These four faithful servants—for Penelope's intelligence had
been trained till it was very nearly on a par with the wits of the
other three, while they had sunk pretty much into the dumb,
submissive jog-trot life of the animal—these four retainers
came and went and did the same things day after day, with
the unfailing regularity of clockwork. But, to use their own
expression, "they had first eaten their white bread." Mlle. Cormon
suffered from a fixed idea upon the nerves; and, after the wont
of such sufferers, she grew fidgety and hard to please, not by
force of nature, but because she had no outlet for her energies.
She had neither husband nor children to fill her thoughts, so
they fastened upon trifles. She would talk for hours at a stretch
of some inconceivably small matter, of a dozen serviettes, for
instance, lettered Z, which somehow or other had been put
before O.

"Why, what can Josette be thinking about?" she cried. "Has
she no notion what she is doing?"

Jacquelin chanced to be late in feeding Penelope one afternoon, so every day for a whole week afterward mademoiselle inquired whether the horse had been fed at two o'clock. Her narrow
imagination spent itself on small matters. A layer of dust forgotten by the feather duster, a slice of scorched toast, an omission
to close the blinds on Jacquelin's part when the sun shone in
upon the furniture and carpets—all these important trifles produced serious trouble, mademoiselle lost her temper over them.
Nothing was the same as it used to be. The servants of old days
were so changed that she did not know them. They were spoilt.
She was too good to them, and so forth and so forth. One day
Josette gave her mistress *The Christian's Day* instead of *The
Easter Fortnight*. The whole town heard of the mistake before night. Mademoiselle had been obliged to get up and come
out of church, disturbing whole rows of chairs and raising the
wildest conjectures, so that she was obliged afterward to give all
her friends a full account of the mishap.

"Josette," she said mildly, when she had come the whole way home from St. Leonard's, "this must never happen again."

Mlle. Cormon was far from suspecting that it was a very fortunate thing for her that she could vent her spleen in petty squabbles. The mind, like the body, requires exercise; these quarrels were a sort of mental gymnastics. Josette and Jacquelin took such unevennesses of temper as the agricultural laborer takes the changes of the weather. The three good souls could say among themselves that "It is a fine day," or "It rains," without murmuring against the powers above. Sometimes in the kitchen of a morning they would wonder in what humor mademoiselle would wake, much as a farmer studies the morning mists. And of necessity Mlle. Cormon ended by seeing herself in all the infinitely small details which made up her life. Herself and God, her confessor and her washing days, the preserves to be made, the services of the church to attend, and the uncle to take care of —all these things absorbed faculties that were none of the strongest. For her the atoms of life were magnified by virtue of an optical process peculiar to the selfish or the self-absorbed. To so perfectly healthy a woman, the slightest symptom of indigestion was a positively alarming portent. She lived, moreover, under the ferule of the system of medicine practiced by our grandsires; a drastic purgative dose fit to kill Penelope, taken four times a year, merely gave Mlle. Cormon a fillip.

What tremendous ransackings of the week's dietary if Josette, assisting her mistress to dress, discovered a scarcely visible pimple on shoulders that still boasted a satin skin! What triumph if the maid could bring a certain hare to her mistress' recollection, and trace the accursed pimple to its origin in that too heating article of food! With what joy the two women would cry: "It is the hare beyond a doubt!"

"Mariette overseasoned it," mademoiselle would add; "I always tell her not to overdo it for my uncle and me, but Mariette has no more memory than——"

"Than the hare," suggested Josette.

"It is the truth," returned mademoiselle; "she has no more memory than the hare; you have just hit it."

Four times in a year, at the beginning of each season, Mlle. Cormon went to spend a certain number of days at the Pré-baudet. It was now in the middle of May, when she liked to see how her apple trees had "snowed," as they say in the cider country, an allusion to the white blossoms strewn in the orchards in the spring. When the circles of fallen petals look like snow-drifts under the trees, the proprietor may hope to have abundance of cider in the autumn. Mlle. Cormon estimated her barrels, and at the same time superintended any necessary after-winter repairs, planning out work in the garden and orchard, from which she drew no inconsiderable supplies. Each time of year had its special business.

Mademoiselle used to give a farewell dinner to her faithful inner circle before leaving, albeit she would see them again at the end of three weeks. All Alençon knew when the journey was to be undertaken. Anyone that had fallen behindhand immediately paid a call, her drawing room was filled; everybody wished her a prosperous journey, as if she had been starting for Calcutta. Then, in the morning, all the tradespeople were standing in their doorways; everyone, great and small, watched the cariole go past, and it seemed as if everybody learned a piece of fresh news when one repeated after another, "So Mademoiselle Cormon is going to the Prébaudet."

One would remark: "She has bread ready baked, she has!"

And his neighbor would return: "Eh! my lad, she is a good woman; if property always fell into such hands as hers, there would not be a beggar to be seen in the countryside."

Or another would exclaim: "Halloo! I should not wonder if our oldest vines are in flower, for there is Mademoiselle Cormon setting out for the Prébaudet. How comes it that she is so little given to marrying?"

"I should be quite ready to marry her, all the same," a wag would answer. "The marriage is half made—one side is willing, but the other isn't. Pooh! the oven is heating for Monsieur du Bousquier."

"*Monsieur du Bousquier?* She has refused him."

At every house that evening people remarked solemnly: "Mademoiselle Cormon has gone."

Or perhaps: "So you have let Mademoiselle Cormon go!"

The Wednesday selected by Suzanne for making a scandal chanced to be this very day of leave-taking, when Mlle. Cormon nearly drove Josette to distraction over the packing of the parcels which she meant to take with her. A good deal that was done and said in the town that morning was like to lend additional interest to the farewell gathering at night. While the old maid was busily making preparations for her journey; while the astute chevalier was playing his game of piquet in the house of Mlle. Armande de Gordes, sister of the aged Marquis de Gordes and queen of the aristocratic salon, Mme. Granson had sounded the alarm bell in half a score of houses. There was not a soul but felt some curiosity to see what sort of figure the seducer would cut that evening; and to Mme. Granson and the Chevalier de Valois it was an important matter to know how Mlle. Cormon would take the news, in her double quality of marriageable spinster and lady president of the Maternity Fund. As for the unsuspecting du Bousquier, he was taking the air on the parade. He was just beginning to think that Suzanne had made a fool of him; and this suspicion only confirmed the rules which he had laid down with regard to womankind.

On these high days the cloth was laid about half-past three in the Cormon house. Four o'clock was the state dinner hour in Alençon, on ordinary days they dined at two, as in the time of the Empire; but then, they supped!

Mlle. Cormon always felt an inexpressible sense of satisfaction when she was dressed to receive her guests as mistress of her house. It was one of the pleasures which she most relished, be it said without malice, though egoism certainly lay beneath the feeling. When thus arrayed for conquest, a ray of hope slid across the darkness of her soul; a voice within her cried that nature had not endowed her so abundantly in vain, that surely some enterprising man was about to appear for her. She felt the younger for the wish and the fresher for her toilet; she looked at her stout figure with a certain elation; and afterward, when she went downstairs to submit drawing room, study, and boudoir to an awful scrutiny, this sense of satisfaction still remained with her. To and fro she went, with the naïve contentment of the rich man who feels conscious at every moment that he is rich and will lack for nothing all his life long. She looked round upon her furniture, the eternal furniture, the antiquities, the lacquered panels, and told herself that such fine things ought to have a master.

After admiring the dining room, where the space was filled by the long table with its snowy cloth, its score of covers symmetrically laid; after going through the roll call of a squadron of bottles ordered up from the cellar, and making sure that each bore an honorable label; and finally, after a most minute verification of a score of little slips of paper on which the abbé had written the names of the guests with a trembling hand—it was the sole occasion on which he took an active part in the household, and the place of every guest always gave rise to grave discussion— after this review, Mlle. Cormon in her fine array went into the garden to join her uncle; for at this pleasantest hour of the day he used to walk up and down the terrace beside the Brillante, listening to the twittering of the birds, which, hidden closely among the leaves in the lime-tree walk, knew no fear of boys or sportsmen.

Mlle. Cormon never came out to the abbé during these intervals of waiting without asking some hopelessly absurd question, in the hope of drawing the good man into a discussion which might interest him. Her reasons for so doing must be given, for this very characteristic trait adds the finishing touch to her portrait.

Mlle. Cormon considered it a duty to talk; not that she was naturally loquacious, for, unfortunately, with her dearth of ideas and very limited stock of phrases, it was difficult to hold forth at any length; but she thought that in this way she was fulfilling the social duties prescribed by religion, which bids us be agreeable to our neighbor. It was a duty which weighed so much upon her mind that she had submitted this case of conscience out of the *Child's Guide to Manners* to her director, the Abbé Couturier. Whereupon, so far from being disarmed by the penitent's humble admission of the violence of her mental struggles to find something to say, the old ecclesiastic, being firm in matters of discipline, read her a whole chapter out of St. François de Sales on the "Duties of a Woman in the World"; on the decent gayety of the pious Christian female, and the duty of confining her austerities to herself; a woman, according to this authority, ought to be amiable in her home and to act in such sort that her neighbor never feels dull in her company. After this, Mlle. Cormon, with a deep sense of duty, was anxious to obey her director at any cost. He had bidden her to discourse agreeably, so every time the conversation languished she felt the perspiration breaking out over her with the violence of her exertions to find something to say which should stimulate the flagging interest. She would come out with odd remarks at such times. Once she revived, with some success, a discussion on the ubiquity of the apostles (of which she understood not a syllable) by the unexpected observation that "You cannot be in two places at once unless you are a bird." With such conversational cues as these, the lady had earned the title of "dear, good Mademoiselle Cormon" in her set, which phrase, in the mouth of local wits, might be taken to mean that she was as ignorant as a carp, and a bit of a "natural"; but there were plenty of people of her own caliber to take the remark literally, and reply: "Oh, yes, Mademoiselle Cormon is very good."

Sometimes (always in her desire to be agreeable to her guests and fulfill her duties as a hostess) she asked such absurd questions that everybody burst out laughing. She wanted to know, for example, what the government did with the taxes which it had been receiving all these years; or how it was that the Bible had not been printed in the time of Christ, seeing that it had been written by Moses. Altogether she was on a par with the English country gentleman, a member of the House of Commons, who made the famous speech in which he said: "I am always hearing of Posterity; I should very much like to know what Posterity has done for the country."

On such occasions, the heroic Chevalier de Valois came to the rescue, bringing up all the resources of his wit and tact at the sight of the smiles exchanged by pitiless smatterers. He loved to give to woman, did this elderly noble; he lent his wit to Mlle. Cormon by coming to her assistance with a paradox, and covered her retreat so well, that sometimes it seemed as if she had said nothing foolish. She once owned seriously that she did not know the difference between an ox* and a bull. The enchanting chevalier stopped the roars of laughter by saying that oxen could never be more than uncles to the bullocks. Another time, hearing much talk of cattle breeding and its difficulties—a topic which often comes up in conversation in the neighborhood of the superb du Pin stud—she so far grasped the technicalities of horse breeding as to ask: "Why, if they wanted colts, they did not serve a mare twice a year?" The chevalier drew down the laughter upon himself.

"It is quite possible," said he. The company pricked up its ears.

"The fault lies with the naturalists," he continued; "they have not found out how to breed mares that are less than eleven months in foal."

Poor Mlle. Cormon no more understood the meaning of the words than the difference between the ox and the bull. The chevalier met with no gratitude for his pains; his chivalrous services were beyond the reach of the lady's comprehension. She saw that the conversation grew livelier; she was relieved to find that she was not so stupid as she imagined. A day came at last when she settled down in her ignorance, like the Duc de Brancas; and the hero of *Le Distrait*, it may be remembered, made himself so comfortable in the ditch after his fall that, when the people came to pull him out, he asked what they wanted with him. Since a somewhat recent period Mlle. Cormon had lost her

* Draught oxen are emasculated. *Tr.*

fears. She brought out her conversational cues with a self-possession akin to that solemn manner—the very coxcombry of stupidity—which accompanies the fatuous utterances of British patriotism.

As she went with stately steps toward the terrace, therefore, she was chewing the cud of reflection, seeking for some question which should draw her uncle out of a silence which always hurt her feelings; she thought that he felt dull.

"Uncle," she began, hanging on his arm, and nestling joyously close to him (for this was another of her make-believes, "If I had a husband, I should do just so!" she thought); "uncle, if everything on earth happens by the will of God, there must be a reason for everything."

"Assuredly," the Abbé de Sponde answered gravely. He loved his niece, and submitted with angelic patience to be torn from his meditations.

"Then if I never marry at all, it will be because it is the will of God?"

"Yes, my child."

"But still, as there is nothing to prevent me from marrying to-morrow, my will perhaps might thwart the will of God."

"That might be so, if we really knew God's will," returned the subprior of the Sorbonne. "Remark, my dear, that you insert an *if*."

Poor Rose was bewildered. She had hoped to lead her uncle to the subject of marriage by way of an argument *ad omnipotentem*. But the naturally obtuse are wont to adopt the remorseless logic of childhood, which is to say, they proceed from the answer to another question, a method frequently found embarrassing.

"But, uncle," she persisted, "God cannot mean women never to marry; for if He did, all of them ought to be either unmarried or married. Their lots are distributed unjustly."

"My child," said the good abbé, "you are finding fault with the church, which teaches that celibacy is a more excellent way to God."

"But if the church was right, and everybody was a good Catholic, there would soon be no more people, uncle."

"You are too ingenious, Rose; there is no need to be so ingenious to be happy."

Such words brought a smile of satisfaction to poor Rose's lips and confirmed her in the good opinion which she began to conceive of herself. Behold how the world, like our friends and enemies, contributes to strengthen our faults. At this moment guests began to arrive, and the conversation was interrupted. On these high festival occasions, the disposition of the rooms brought about little familiarities between the servants and invited guests. Mariette saw the president of the Tribunal, a triple expansion glutton, as he passed by her kitchen.

"Oh, Monsieur du Ronceret, I have been making cauliflower *au gratin* on purpose for you, for mademoiselle knows how fond you are of it. 'Mind you do not fail with it, Mariette,' she said; 'Monsieur le Président is coming.' "

"Good Mademoiselle Cormon," returned the man of law. "Mariette, did you baste the cauliflowers with gravy instead of stock? It is more savory." And the president did not disdain to enter the council chamber where Mariette ruled the roast, nor to cast an epicure's eye over her preparations, and give his opinion as a master of the craft.

"Good day, madame," said Josette, addressing Mme. Granson, who sedulously cultivated the waiting-woman. "Mademoiselle has not forgotten you; you are to have a dish of fish."

As for the Chevalier de Valois, he spoke to Mariette with the jocularity of a great noble unbending to an inferior—

"Well, dear *cordon bleu*, I would give you the cross of the Legion of Honor if I could; tell me, is there any dainty morsel for which one ought to save one's self?"

"Yes, yes, Monsieur de Valois, a hare from the Prébaudet; it weighed fourteen pounds!"

"That's a good girl," said the chevalier, patting Josette on the cheek with two fingers. "Ah! weighs fourteen pounds, does it?"

Du Bousquier was not of the party. Mlle. Cormon treated him

hardly, faithful to her system before described. In the very bottom of her heart she felt an inexplicable drawing toward this man of fifty, whom she had once refused. Sometimes she repented of that refusal, and yet she had a presentiment that she should marry him after all, and a dread of him which forbade her to wish for the marriage. These ideas stimulated her interest in du Bousquier. The Republican's herculean proportions produced an effect upon her which she would not admit to herself; and the Chevalier de Valois and Mme. Granson, while they could not explain Mlle. Cormon's inconsistencies, had detected naïve, furtive glances, sufficiently clear in their significance to set them both on the watch to ruin the hopes which du Bousquier clearly entertained in spite of a first check.

Two guests kept the others waiting, but their official duties excused them both. One was M. du Coudrai, registrar of mortgages; the other, M. Choisnel, had once acted as land steward to the Marquis de Gordes. Choisnel, the notary of the old noblesse, was received everywhere among them with the distinction which his merits deserved; he had beside a not inconsiderable private fortune. When the two latecomers arrived, Jacquelin, the manservant, seeing them turn to go into the drawing room, came forward with: " 'They' are all in the garden."

The registrar of mortgages was one of the most amiable men in the town. There were but two things against him—he had married an old woman for her money in the first place, and in the second it was his habit to perpetrate outrageous puns, at which he was the first to laugh. But, doubtless, the stomachs of the guests were growing impatient, for at first sight he was hailed with that faint sigh which usually welcomes last-comers under such circumstances. Pending the official announcement of dinner, the company strolled up and down the terrace by the Brillante, looking out over the stream with its bed of mosaic and its water-plants, at the so picturesque details of the row of houses huddled together on the opposite bank; the old-fashioned wooden balconies, the tumble-down window sills, the balks of timber that shored up a story projecting over the river, the cabinetmaker's workshop, the tiny gardens where odds and ends of clothing were hanging out to dry. It was, in short, the poor quarter of a country town, to which the near neighborhood of the water, a weeping willow drooping over the bank, a rosebush or so, and a few flowers had lent an indescribable charm, worthy of a landscape painter's brush.

The chevalier meanwhile was narrowly watching the faces of the guests. He knew that his firebrand had very successfully taken hold of the best coteries in the town; but no one spoke openly of Suzanne and du Bousquier and the great news as yet. The art of distilling scandal is possessed by provincials in a supreme degree. It was felt that the time was not yet ripe for open discussion of the strange event. Everyone was bound to go through a private rehearsal first. So it was whispered—

"Have you heard?"

"Yes."

"Du Bousquier?"

"And the fair Suzanne."

"Does Mademoiselle Cormon know anything?"

"No."

"Ah!"

This was gossip *piano*, presently destined to swell into a *crescendo* when they were ready to discuss the first dish of scandal.

All of a sudden the chevalier confronted Mme. Granson. That lady had sported her green bonnet, trimmed with auriculas; her face was beaming. Was she simply longing to begin the concert? Such news is as good as a gold mine to be worked in the monotonous lives of these people; but the observant and uneasy chevalier fancied that he read something more in the good lady's expression —to wit, the exultation of self-interest! At once he turned to look at Athanase, and detected in his silence the signs of profound concentration of some kind. In another moment the young man's glance at Mlle. Cormon's figure, which sufficiently resembled a pair of regimental kettledrums, shot a sudden light across the chevalier's brain. By that gleam he could read the whole past.

"Egad!" he said to himself, "what a slap in the face I have laid myself out to get!"

He went across to offer his arm to Mlle. Cormon, so that he might afterward take her in to dinner. She regarded the chevalier with respectful esteem; for, in truth, with his name and position in the aristocratic constellations of the province, he was one of the most brilliant ornaments of her salon. In her heart of hearts, she had longed to be Mme. de Valois at any time during the past twelve years. The name was like a branch for the swarming thoughts of her brain to cling about—he fulfilled all her ideals as to the birth, quality, and externals of an eligible man. But while the Chevalier de Valois was the choice of heart and brain and social ambition, the elderly ruin, curled though he was like a St. John of a procession-day, filled Mlle. Cormon with dismay; the heiress saw nothing but the noble; the woman could not think of him as a husband. The chevalier's affectation of indifference to marriage, and still more his unimpeachable character in a house-ful of work-girls, had seriously injured him, contrary to his own expectations. The man of quality, so clear-sighted in the matter of the annuity, miscalculated on this subject; and Mlle. Cormon her-self was not aware that her private reflections upon the too well-conducted chevalier might have been translated by the remark: "What a pity that he is not a little bit of a rake!"

Students of human nature have remarked these leanings of the saint toward the sinner, and wondered at a taste so little in ac-cordance, as they imagine, with Christian virtue. But, to go no further, what nobler destiny for a virtuous woman than the task of cleansing, after the manner of charcoal, the turbid waters of vice? How is it that nobody has seen that these generous creatures, confined by their principles to strict conjugal fidelity, must naturally desire a mate of great practical experience? A reformed rake makes the best husband. And so it came to pass that the poor spinster must sigh over the chosen vessel, offered her as it were in two pieces. Heaven alone could weld the Chevalier du Valois and du Bousquier in one.

If the significance of the few words exchanged between the

chevalier and Mlle. Cormon is to be properly understood, it is necessary to put other matters before the reader. Two very serious questions were dividing Alençon into two camps, and, moreover, du Bousquier was mixed up in both affairs in some mysterious way. The first of these debates concerned the curé. He had taken the oath of allegiance in the time of the Revolution, and now was living down orthodox prejudices by setting an example of the loftiest goodness. He was a Cheverus on a smaller scale, and so much was he appreciated that when he died the whole town wept for him. Mlle. Cormon and the Abbé de Sponde belonged, however, to the minority, to the church sublime in its orthodoxy, a section which was to the Court of Rome as the Ultras were shortly to be to the Court of Louis XVIII. The abbé, in particular, declined to recognize the church that had submitted to force and made terms with the Constitution-nels. So the curé was never seen in the salon of the Maison Cormon, and the sympathies of its frequenters were with the officiating priest of St. Leonard's, the aristocratic church in Alençon. Du Bousquier, that rabid Liberal under a Royalist's skin, knew how necessary it is to find standards to rally the discontented, who form, as it were, the back-shop of every opposition, and therefore he had already enlisted the sympathies of the trading classes for the curé.

Now for the second affair. The same blunt diplomatist was the secret instigator of a scheme for building a theater, an idea which had only lately sprouted in Alençon. Du Bousquier's zealots knew not their Mahomet, but they were the more ardent in their defense of what they believed to be their own plan. Athanase was one of the very hottest of the partisans in favor of the theater; in the mayor's office for several days past he had been pleading for the cause which all the younger men had taken up.

To return to the chevalier. He offered his arm to Mlle. Cormon, who thanked him with a radiant glance for this attention. For all answer, the chevalier indicated Athanase by a meaning look.

"Mademoiselle," he began, "as you have such well-balanced judgment in matters of social convention, and as that young man is related to you in some way——"

"Very distantly," she broke in.

"Ought you not to use the influence which you possess with him and his mother to prevent him from going utterly to the bad? He is not very religious as it is; he defends that perjured priest; but that is nothing. It is a much more serious matter; is he not plunging thoughtlessly into opposition without realizing how his conduct may affect his prospects? He is scheming to build this theater; he is the dupe of that Republican in disguise, du Bousquier——"

"Dear me, Monsieur de Valois, his mother tells me that he is so clever, and he has not a word to say for himself; he always stands planted before you like a 'statute'——"

"Of limitations," cried the registrar. "I caught that flying. I present my *devoars* to the Chevalier de Valois," he added, saluting the latter with the exaggeration of Henri Monnier as "Joseph Prudhomme," an admirable type of the class to which M. du Coudrai belonged.

M. de Valois, in return, gave him the abbreviated patronizing nod of a noble standing on his dignity; then he drew Mlle. Cormon farther along the terrace by the distance of several flower-pots, to make the registrar understand that he did not wish to be overheard.

Then, lowering his voice, he bent to say in Mlle. Cormon's ear: "How can you expect that lads educated in these detestable Imperial Lyceums should have any ideas? Great ideas and a lofty love can only come of right courses and nobleness of life. It is not difficult to foresee, from the look of the poor fellow, that he will be weak in his intellect and come to a miserable end. See how pale and haggard he looks!"

"His mother says that he works far too hard," she replied innocently. "He spends his nights, think of it! in reading books and writing. What good can it possibly do a young man's prospects to sit up writing at night?"

"Why, it exhausts him," said the chevalier, trying to bring the lady's thoughts back to the point, which was to disgust her with Athanase. "The things that went on in those Imperial Lyceums were something really shocking."

"Oh yes," said the simple lady. "Did they not make them walk out with drums in front? The masters had no more religion than heathens; and they put them in uniform, poor boys, exactly as if they had been soldiers. What notions!"

"And see what comes of it," continued the chevalier, indicating Athanase. "In my time, where was the young man that could not look a pretty woman in the face? Now, *he* lowers his eyes as soon as he sees you. That young man alarms me, because I am interested in him. Tell him not to intrigue with Bonapartists, as he is doing, to build this theater; if these little youngsters do not raise an insurrection and demand it (for insurrection and constitution, to my mind, are two words for the same thing), the authorities will build it. And tell his mother to look after him."

"Oh, she will not allow him to see these half-pay people or to keep low company, I am sure. I will speak to him about it," said Mlle. Cormon; "he might lose his situation at the mayor's office. And then what would they do, he and his mother? It makes one shudder."

As M. de Talleyrand said of his wife, so said the chevalier within himself at that moment, as he looked at the lady—

"If there is a stupider woman, I should like to see her. On the honor of a gentleman, if virtue makes a woman so stupid as this, is it not a vice? And yet, what an adorable wife she would make for a man of my age! What principle! What ignorance of life!"

Please to bear in mind that these remarks were addressed to the Princess Goritza during the manipulation of a pinch of snuff.

Mme. Granson felt instinctively that the chevalier was talking of Athanase. In her eagerness to know what he had been saying, she followed Mlle. Cormon, who walked up to the young man in question, putting out six feet of dignity in front; but at that very moment Jacquelin announced that "Mademoiselle was served," and the mistress of the house shot an appealing glance at the chevalier. But the gallant registrar of mortgages was beginning to see a something in M. de Valois' manner, a glimpse of the barrier which the noblesse were about to raise between themselves and the bourgeoisie; so, delighted with a chance to cut out the chevalier, he crooked his arm, and Mlle. Cormon was obliged to take it. M. de Valois, from motives of policy, fastened upon Mme. Granson.

"Mademoiselle Cormon takes the liveliest interest in your dear Athanase, my dear lady," he said, as they slowly followed in the wake of the other guests, "but that interest is falling off through your son's fault. He is lax and Liberal in his opinions; he is agitating for this theater; he is mixed up with the Bonapartists; he takes the part of the Constitutionnel curé. This line of conduct may cost him his situation. You know how carefully his majesty's government is weeding the service. If your dear Athanase is once cashiered, where will he find employment? He must not get into bad odor with the authorities."

"Oh, Monsieur le Chevalier," cried the poor startled mother, "what do I not owe you for telling me this! You are right; my boy is a tool in the hands of a bad set; I will open his eyes to his position."

It was long since the chevalier had sounded Athanase's character at a glance. He saw in the depths of the young man's nature the scarcely malleable material of Republican convictions; a lad at that age will sacrifice everything for such ideas if he is smitten with the word Liberty, that so vague, so little comprehended word which is like a standard of revolt for those at the bottom of the wheel for whom revolt means revenge. Athanase was sure to stick to his opinions, for he had woven them, with his artist's sorrows and his embittered views of the social framework, into his political creed. He was ready to sacrifice his future at the outset for these opinions, not knowing that he, like all men of real ability, would have seen reason to modify them by the time he reached the age of six-and-thirty, when a man has formed his own conclusions of life, with its intricate relations and interdependences. If Athanase was faithful to the op-

position in Alençon, he would fall into disgrace with Mlle. Cormon. Thus far the chevalier saw clearly.

And so this little town, so peaceful in appearance, was to
the full as much agitated internally as any congress of diplo-
mats, when craft and guile and passion and self-interest are met
to discuss the weightiest questions between empire and empire.

Meanwhile the guests gathered about the table were eating
their way through the first course as people eat in the provinces,
without a blush for an honest appetite; whereas, in Paris, it
would appear that our jaws are controlled by sumptuary edicts
which deliberately set the laws of anatomy at defiance. We eat
with the tips of our teeth in Paris, we filch the pleasures of the
table, but in the provinces things are taken more naturally; possibly existence centers a little too much about the great and
universal method of maintenance to which God condemns all
His creatures. It was at the end of the first course that Mlle.
Cormon brought out the most celebrated of all her conversational cues; it was talked of for two years afterward; it is quoted
even now, indeed, in the lower bourgeois strata of Alençon
whenever her marriage is under discussion. Over the last entrée
but one, the conversation waxed lively and wordy, turning, as
might have been expected, upon the affair of the theater and the
curé. In the first enthusiasm of royalism in 1816, those extremists,
who were afterward called *les jésuites du pays*, or country
Jesuits, were for expelling the Abbé François from his cure. M.
de Valois suspected du Bousquier of supporting the priest and
instigating the intrigues; at any rate, the noble chevalier piled
the burdens on du Bousquier's back with his wonted skill; and
du Bousquier, being unrepresented by counsel, was condemned
and put in the pillory. Among those present, Athanase was the
only person sufficiently frank to stand up for the absent, and he
felt that he was not in a position to bring out his ideas before
these Alençon magnates, of whose intellects he had the meanest
opinion. Only in the provinces nowadays will you find young
men keeping a respectful countenance before people of a certain
age without daring to have a fling at their elders or to contra-

dict them too flatly. To resume: On the advent of some delicious *canards aux olives*, the conversation first decidedly flagged, and then suddenly dropped dead. Mlle. Cormon, emulous of her own poultry, invented another *canard* in her anxiety to defend du Bousquier, who had been represented as an arch-concoctor of intrigue, and a man to set mountains fighting.

"For my own part," said she, "I thought that Monsieur du Bousquier gave his whole attention to childish matters."

Under the circumstances, the epigram produced a tremendous effect. Mlle. Cormon had a great success; she brought the Princess Goritza face downward on the table. The chevalier, by no means expecting his Dulcinea to say anything so much to the purpose, could find no words to express his admiration; he applauded after the Italian fashion, noiselessly, with the tips of his fingers.

"She is adorably witty," he said, turning to Mme. Granson. "I have always said that she would unmask her batteries some day."

"But when you know her very well, she is charming," said the widow.

"All women, madame, have *esprit* when you know them well."

When the Homeric laughter subsided, Mlle. Cormon asked for an explanation of her success. Then the chorus of scandal grew to a height. Du Bousquier was transformed into a bachelor Father Gigogne; it was he who filled the Foundling Hospital; the immorality of his life was laid bare at last; it was all of a piece with his Paris orgies, and so forth and so forth. Led by the Chevalier de Valois, the cleverest of conductors of this kind of orchestra, the overture was something magnificent.

"I do not know," said he, with much indulgence, "what there could possibly be to prevent a du Bousquier from marrying Mademoiselle Suzanne whatever-it-is, what do you call her? Suzette! I only know the children by sight, though I lodge with Mme. Lardot. If this Suzon is a tall, fine-looking forward sort of girl with gray eyes, a slender figure, and little feet—I have not paid much attention to these things, but she seemed to me to be very insolent and very much du Bousquier's superior in the matter of manners. Beside, Suzanne has the nobility of beauty; from that point of view, she would certainly make a marriage beneath her. The Emperor Joseph, you know, had the curiosity to go to see the du Barry at Luciennes. He offered her his arm; and when the poor courtesan, overcome by such an honor, hesitated to take it: 'Beauty is always a queen,' said the Emperor. Remark that the Emperor Joseph was an Austrian German," added the chevalier; "but, believe me, that Germany, which we think of as a very boorish country, is really a land of noble chivalry and fine manners, especially toward Poland and Hungary, where there are——" Here the chevalier broke off, fearing to make an allusion to his own happy fortune in the past; he only took up his snuffbox and confided the rest to the princess who had smiled on him for thirty-six years.

"The speech was delicately considerate for Louis XV," said du Ronceret.

"But we are talking of the Emperor Joseph, I believe," returned Mlle Cormon, with a knowing little air.

"Mademoiselle," said the chevalier, seeing the wicked glances exchanged by the president, the registrar, and the notary, "Madame du Barry was Louis XV's Suzanne, a fact known well enough to us scapegraces, but which young ladies are not expected to know. Your ignorance shows that the diamond is flawless. The corruptions of history have not so much as touched you."

At this the Abbé de Sponde looked graciously upon M. de Valois and bent his head in laudatory approval.

"Do you not know history, mademoiselle?" asked the registrar.

"If you muddle up Louis XV and Suzanne, how can you expect me to know your history?" was Mlle. Cormon's angelic reply. She was so pleased! The dish was empty and the conversation revived to such purpose that everybody was laughing with their mouths full at her last simple but ingenuous observation.

"Poor young thing!" said the Abbé de Sponde. "When once trouble comes, that love divine called charity is as blind as the pagan love, and should see nothing of the causes of the trouble. You are president of the Maternity Society, Rose; this child will need help; it will not be easy for her to find a husband."

"Poor child!" said Mlle. Cormon.

"Is du Bousquier going to marry her, do you suppose?" asked the president of the Tribunal.

"It would be his duty to do so if he were a decent man," said Mme. Granson; "but, really, my dog has better notions of decency——"

"And yet Azor is a great forager," put in the registrar, trying a joke this time as a change from a pun.

They were still talking of du Bousquier over the dessert. He was the butt of uncounted playful jests, which grew more and more thunder-charged under the influence of wine. Led off by the registrar, they followed up one pun with another. Du Bousquier's character was now "ap-parent"; he was not a father of the church, nor a reverend father, nor yet a conscript father, and so on and so on, till the Abbé de Sponde said: "In any case, he is not a foster-father," with a gravity that checked the laughter.

"Nor a heavy father," added the chevalier.

The church and the aristocracy had descended into the arena of word-play without loss of dignity.

"Hush!" said the registrar, "I can hear du Bousquier's boots creaking; he is in over shoes over boots, and no mistake."

It nearly always happens that when a man's name is in everyone's mouth, he is the last to hear what is said of him; the whole town may be talking of him, slandering him or crying him down, and if he has no friends to repeat what other people say of him, he is not likely to hear it. So the blameless du Bousquier, du Bousquier who would fain have been guilty, who wished that Suzanne had not lied to him, was supremely unconscious of all that was taking place. Nobody had spoken to him of Suzanne's revelations; for that matter, everybody thought it indiscreet to ask questions about the affair, when the man most concerned sometimes possesses secrets which compel him to keep silence. So when the people adjourned for coffee to the drawing room, where several evening visitors were already assembled, du Bousquier wore an irresistible and slightly fatuous air.

Mlle. Cormon, counseled by confusion, dared not look toward the terrible seducer. She took possession of Athanase and administered a lecture, bringing out the oddest assortment of the commonplaces of Royalist doctrines and edifying truisms. As the unlucky poet had no snuffbox with a portrait of a princess on the lid to sustain him under the shower bath of foolish utterances, it was with a vacant expression that he heard his adored lady. His eyes were fixed on that enormous bust, which maintained the absolute repose characteristic of great masses. Desire wrought a kind of intoxication in him. The old maid's thin, shrill voice became low music for his ears; her platitudes were fraught with ideas.

Love is an utterer of false coin; he is always at work transforming common copper into gold louis; sometimes, also, he makes his seeming douzains* of fine gold.

"Well, Athanase, will you promise me?"

The final phrase struck on the young man's ear; he woke with a start from a blissful dream.

"What, mademoiselle?" returned he.

Mlle. Cormon rose abruptly and glanced across at du Bousquier. At that moment he looked like the brawny fabulous deity whose likeness you behold upon Republican three-franc pieces. She went over to Mme. Granson and said in a confidential tone:

"Your son is weak in his intellect, my poor friend. That lyceum has been the ruin of him," she added, recollecting how the Chevalier de Valois had insisted on the bad education given in those institutions.

Here was a thunderbolt! Poor Athanase had had his chance of flinging fire upon the dried stems heaped up in the old maid's heart, and he had not known it! If he had but listened to her, he

* Old French sou. *Tr.*

might have made her understand; for in Mlle. Cormon's present highly wrought mood a word would have been enough, but the very force of the stupefying cravings of lovesick youth had spoiled his chances; so sometimes a child full of life kills himself through ignorance.

"What can you have been saying to Mademoiselle Cormon?" asked his mother.

"Nothing."

"Nothing? I will have this cleared up," she said, and put off serious business to the morrow; du Bousquier was hopelessly lost, she thought, and the speech troubled her very little.

Soon the four card tables received their complement of players. Four persons sat down to piquet, the most expensive amusement of the evening, over which a good deal of money changed hands. M. Choisnel, the attorney for the crown, and a couple of ladies went to the red-lacquered cabinet for a game of trictrac. The candles in the wall sconces were lighted, and then the flower of Mlle. Cormon's set blossomed out about the fire, on the settees, and above the tables. Each new couple, on entering the room, made the same remark to Mlle. Cormon: "So you are going to the Prébaudet tomorrow?"

"Yes, I really must," she said, in answer to each.

All through the evening the hostess wore a preoccupied air. Mme. Granson was the first to see that she was not at all like herself. Mlle. Cormon was thinking.

"What are you thinking about, cousin?" Mme. Granson asked at last, finding her sitting in the boudoir.

"I am thinking of that poor girl. Am I not patroness of the Maternity Society? I will go now to find ten crowns for you."

"*Ten crowns!*" exclaimed Mme. Granson. "Why, you have never given so much to anyone before!"

"But, my dear, it is so natural to have a child."

This improper cry from the heart struck the treasurer of the Maternity Society dumb from sheer astonishment. Du Bousquier had actually gone up in Mlle. Cormon's opinion!

"Really," began Mme. Granson, "du Bousquier is not merely a

monster—he is a villain into the bargain. When a man has spoiled
somebody else's life, it is his duty surely to make amends. It
should be his part rather than ours to rescue this young person;
and when all comes to all, she is a bad girl, it seems to me,
for there are better men in Alençon than that cynic of a du
Bousquier. A girl must be shameless indeed to have anything to
do with him."

"Cynic? Your son, dear, teaches you Latin words that are quite
beyond me. Certainly I do not want to make excuses for Monsieur
du Bousquier; but explain to me why it is immoral for a woman
to prefer one man to another?"

"Dear cousin, suppose now that you were to marry my
Athanase; there would be nothing but what was very natural in
that. He is young and good-looking; he has a future before him;
Alençon will be proud of him some day. But—everyone would
think that you took such a young man as your husband for the
sake of greater conjugal felicity. Slanderous tongues would say
that you were making a sufficient provision of bliss for yourself.
There would be jealous women to bring charges of depravity
against you. But what would it matter to you? You would be
dearly loved—loved sincerely. If Athanase seemed to you to be
weak of intellect, my dear, it is because he has too many ideas.
Extremes meet. He is as clean in his life as a girl of fifteen; *he*
has not wallowed in the pollutions of Paris. Well, now change the
terms, as my poor husband used to say. It is relatively just the
same situation as du Bousquier's and Suzanne's. But what would
be slander in your case is true in every way of du Bousquier.
Now do you understand?"

"No more than if you were talking Greek," said Rose Cormon, opening wide eyes and exerting all the powers of her understanding.

"Well, then, cousin, since one must put dots on all the *i*'s, it is
quite out of the question that Suzanne should love du Bousquier.
And when the heart counts for nothing in such an affair——"

"Why, really, cousin, how should people love if not with
their hearts?"

At this Mme. Granson thought within herself, as the chevalier had thought—

"The poor cousin is too innocent by far. This goes beyond the permissible——" Aloud she said: "Dear girl, it seems to me that a child is not conceived of spirit alone."

"Why, yes, dear, for the Holy Virgin——"

"But, my dear, good girl, du Bousquier is not the Holy Ghost."

"That is true," returned the spinster; "he is a man—a man dangerous enough for his friends to recommend him strongly to marry."

"You, cousin, might bring that about——"

"Oh, how?" cried the spinster, with a glow of Christian charity.

"Decline to receive him until he takes a wife. For the sake of religion and morality, you ought to make an example of him under the circumstances."

"We will talk of this again, dear Madame Granson, when I come back from the Prébaudet. I will ask advice of my uncle and the Abbé Couturier," and Mlle. Cormon went back to the large drawing room. The liveliest hour of the evening had begun.

The lights, the groups of well-dressed women, the serious and magisterial air of the assembly, filled Mlle. Cormon with pride in the aristocratic appearance of the rooms, a pride in which her guests all shared. There were plenty of people who thought that the finest company of Paris itself was no finer. At that moment du Bousquier, playing a rubber with M. de Valois and two elderly ladies, Mme. du Coudrai and Mme. du Ronceret, was the object of suppressed curiosity. Several women came up on the pretext of watching the game, and gave him such odd, albeit furtive, glances that the old bachelor at last began to think that there must be something amiss with his appearance.

"Can it be that my toupet is askew?" he asked himself. And he felt that all-absorbing uneasiness to which the elderly bachelor is peculiarly subject. A blunder gave him an excuse for leaving the table at the end of the seventh rubber.

"I cannot touch a card but I lose," he said; "I am decidedly too unlucky at cards."

"You are lucky in other respects," said the chevalier, with a knowing look. Naturally, the joke made the round of the room, and everyone exclaimed over the exquisite breeding shown by the Prince Talleyrand of Alençon.

"There is no one like Monsieur de Valois for saying such things," said the niece of the curé of St. Leonard's.

Du Bousquier went up to the narrow mirror above "The Deserter," but he could detect nothing unusual.

Toward ten o'clock, after innumerable repetitions of the same phrase with every possible variation, the long antechamber began to fill with visitors preparing to embark; Mlle. Cormon convoying a few favored guests as far as the steps for a farewell embrace. Knots of guests took their departure, some in the direction of the Brittany road and the château, and others turning toward the quarter by the Sarthe. And then began the exchange of remarks with which the streets had echoed at the same hour for a score of years. There was the inevitable: "Mademoiselle Cormon looked very well this evening."

"Mademoiselle Cormon? She looked strange, I thought."

"How the abbé stoops, poor man! And how he goes to sleep— did you see? He never knows where the cards are now; his mind wanders."

"We shall be very sorry to lose him."

"It is a fine night. We shall have a fine day tomorrow."

"Fine weather for the apples to set."

"You beat us tonight; you always do when Monsieur de Valois is your partner."

"Then how much did he win?"

"Tonight? Why, he won three or four francs. He never loses."

"Faith, no. There are three hundred and sixty-five days in the year, you know; at that rate, whist is as good as a farm for him."

"Oh! what bad luck we had tonight!"

"You are very fortunate, monsieur and madame, here you are at your own doorstep, while we have half the town to cross."

"I do not pity you; you could keep a gig if you liked, you need not go afoot."

"Ah! monsieur, we have a daughter to marry (that means one wheel), and a son to keep in Paris, and that takes the other."

"Are you still determined to make a magistrate of him?"

"What can one do? You must do something with a boy, and besides, it is no disgrace to serve the King."

Sometimes a discussion on cider or flax was continued on the way, the very same things being said at the same season year after year. If any observer of human nature had lived in that particular street, their conversation would have supplied him with an almanac. At this moment, however, the talk was of a decidedly Rabelaisian turn; for du Bousquier, walking on ahead by himself, was humming the well-known tune *"Femme sensible, écoute-tu le ramage?"* without a suspicion of its appropriateness. Some of the party held that du Bousquier was uncommonly longheaded, and that people judged him unjustly. President du Ronceret inclined toward this view since he had been confirmed in his post by a new royal decree. The rest regarded the forage contractor as a dangerous man of lax morals, of whom anything might be expected. In the provinces, as in Paris, public men are very much in the position of the statue in Addison's ingenious fable. The statue was erected at a place where four roads met; two cavaliers coming up on opposite sides declared, the one that it was white, the other that it was black, until they came to blows, and both of them lying on the ground discovered that it was black on one side and white on the other, while a third cavalier coming up to their assistance affirmed that it was red.

When the Chevalier de Valois reached home, he said to himself: "It is time to spread a report that I am going to marry Mademoiselle Cormon. The news shall come from the d'Esgrignon's salon; it shall go straight to the bishop's palace at Séez, and come back through one of the vicars-general to the curé of St. Leonard's. He will not fail to tell the Abbé Couturier, and in this way Mademoiselle Cormon will receive the shot well under the water line. The old Marquis d'Esgrignon is sure to ask the Abbé

de Sponde to dinner to put a stop to gossip which might injure
Mademoiselle Cormon if I fail to come forward; or me, if she
refuses me. The abbé shall be well and duly entangled; and after
a call from Mademoiselle de Gordes, in the course of which the
grandeur and the prospects of the alliance will be put before
Mademoiselle Cormon, she is not likely to hold out. The abbé
will leave her more than a hundred thousand crowns; and as for
her, she must have put by more than a hundred thousand livres
by this time; she has her house, the Prébaudet, and some fifteen
thousand livres per annum. One word to my friend the Comte
de Fontaine, and I am Mayor of Alençon, and deputy; then, once
seated on the right-hand benches, the way to a peerage is cleared
by a well-timed cry of '*Clôture*,' or 'Order.' "

When Mme. Granson reached home, she had a warm explanation with her son. He could not be made to understand the connection between his political opinions and his love. It was the
first quarrel which had troubled the peace of the poor little household.

Next morning, at nine o'clock, Mlle. Cormon, packed into the
cariole with Josette by her side, drove up the rue Saint-Blaise
on her way to the Prébaudet, looking like a pyramid above an
ocean of packages. And the event which was to surprise her there
and hasten on her marriage was unseen as yet by Mme. Granson,
or du Bousquier, or M. de Valois, or by Mlle. Cormon herself.
Chance is the greatest artist of all.

On the morrow of mademoiselle's arrival at the Prébaudet,
she was very harmlessly engaged in taking her eight-o'clock
breakfast, while she listened to the reports of her bailiff and
gardener, when Jacquelin, in a great flurry, burst into the dining
room.

"Mademoiselle," cried he, "Monsieur l'Abbé has sent an express
messenger to you; that boy of Mother Grosmort's has come with
a letter. The lad left Alençon before daybreak, and yet here he
is! He came almost as fast as Penelope. Ought he to have a glass
of wine?"

"What can have happened, Josette? Can uncle be——"

"He would not have written if he was," said the woman, guessing her mistress' fears.

Mlle. Cormon glanced over the first few lines.

"Quick! quick!" she cried. "Tell Jacquelin to put Penelope in. Get ready, child, have everything packed in half an hour, we are going back to town," she added, turning to Josette.

"Jacquelin!" called Josette, excited by the expression of Mlle. Cormon's face. Jacquelin on receiving his orders came back to the house to expostulate.

"But, mademoiselle, Penelope has only just been fed."

"Eh! what does that matter to me? I want to start this moment."

"But, mademoiselle, it is going to rain."

"Very well. We shall be wet through."

"The house is on fire," muttered Josette, vexed because her mistress said nothing, but read her letter through to the end, and then began again at the beginning.

"Just finish your coffee at any rate. Don't upset yourself! See how red you are in the face."

"Red in the face, Josette!" exclaimed Mlle. Cormon, going up to the mirror; and as the quicksilvered sheet had come away from the glass, she beheld her countenance doubly distorted. "Oh, dear!" she thought, "I shall look ugly! Come, come, Josette, child, help me to dress. I want to be ready before Jacquelin puts Penelope in. If you cannot put all the things into the chaise, I would rather leave them here than lose a minute."

If you have fully comprehended the degree of monomania to which Mlle. Cormon had been driven by her desire to marry, you will share her excitement. Her worthy uncle informed her that M. de Troisville, a retired soldier from the Russian service, the grandson of one of his best friends, wishing to settle down in Alençon, had asked for his hospitality for the sake of the abbé's old friendship with the mayor, his grandfather, the Vicomte de Troisville of the reign of Louis XV. M. de Sponde, in alarm, begged his niece to come home at once to help him to entertain the guest and to do the honors of the house; for as there had been

some delay in forwarding the letter, M. de Troisville might be
expected to drop in upon him that very evening.

How was it possible after reading that letter to give any attention to affairs at the Prébaudet? The tenant and the bailiff, beholding their mistress' dismay, lay low and waited for orders. When
they stopped her passage to ask for instructions, Mlle. Cormon,
the despotic old maid, who saw to everything herself at the
Prébaudet, answered them with an "As you please," which struck
them dumb with amazement. This was the mistress who carried
administrative zeal to such lengths that she counted the fruit
and entered it under headings, so that she could regulate the
consumption by the quantity of each sort!

"I must be dreaming, I think," said Josette, when she saw her
mistress flying upstairs like some elephant on which God should
have bestowed wings.

In a little while, in spite of the pelting rain, mademoiselle was
driving away from the Prébaudet, leaving her people to have
things all their own way. Jacquelin dared not take it upon himself
to drive the placid Penelope any faster than her usual jog trot
pace; and the old mare, something like the fair queen after whom
she was named, seemed to take a step back for every step forward. Beholding this, mademoiselle bade Jacquelin, in a vinegar
voice, to urge the poor astonished beast to a gallop, and to use
the whip if necessary, so appalling was the thought that M. de
Troisville might arrive before the house was ready for him. A
grandson of an old friend of her uncle's could not be much
over forty, she thought; a military man must infallibly be a
bachelor. She vowed inwardly that, with her uncle's help, M. de
Troisville should not depart in the estate in which he entered the
Maison Cormon. Penelope galloped; but mademoiselle, absorbed
in dresses and dreams of a wedding night, told Jacquelin again
and again that he was standing still. She fidgeted in her seat,
without vouchsafing any answer to Josette's questions, and talked
to herself as if she was revolving mighty matters in her mind.

At last the cariole turned into the long street of Alençon,
known as the rue Saint-Blaise if you come in on the side of

Mortagne, the rue de la Porte de Séez by the time you reach the sign of the Three Moors, and lastly as the rue du Bercail, when it finally debouches into the highway into Brittany. If Mlle. Cormon's departure for the Prébaudet made a great noise in Alençon, anybody can imagine the hubbub caused by her return on the following day, with the driving rain lashing her face. Everybody remarked Penelope's furious pace, Jacquelin's sly looks, the earliness of the hour, the bundles piled up topsy-turvy, the lively conversation between mistress and maid, and, more than all things, the impatience of the party.

The Troisville estates lay between Alençon and Mortagne. Josette, therefore, knew about the different branches of the family. A word let fall by her mistress just as they reached the paved street of Alençon put Josette in possession of the facts, and a discussion sprang up in the course of which the two women settled between themselves that the expected guest must be a man of forty or forty-two, a bachelor, neither rich nor poor. Mademoiselle saw herself Vicomtesse de Troisville.

"And here is uncle telling me nothing, knowing nothing, and wanting to know nothing! Oh, so like uncle! He would forget his nose if it was not fastened to his face."

Have you not noticed how mature spinsters, under these circumstances, grow as intelligent, fierce, bold, and full of promises as a Richard III? To them, as to clerics in liquor, nothing is sacred.

In one moment, from the upper end of the rue Saint-Blaise to the Porte de Séez, the town of Alençon heard of Mlle. Cormon's return with aggravating circumstances, heard with a mighty perturbation of its vitals and trouble of the organs of life public and domestic. Cook-maids, storekeepers, and passers-by carried the news from door to door, then, without delay, it circulated in the upper spheres, and almost simultaneously the words: "Mademoiselle Cormon has come back," exploded like a bomb in every house.

Meanwhile Jacquelin climbed down from his wooden bench in front, polished by some process unknown to cabinetmakers,

and with his own hands opened the great gates with the rounded
tops. They were closed in Mlle. Cormon's absence as a sign of
mourning; for when she went away her house was shut up, and
the faithful took it in turn to show hospitality to the Abbé de
Sponde. (M. de Valois used to pay his debt by an invitation to
dine at the Marquis d'Esgrignon's.) Jacquelin gave the familiar
call to Penelope standing in the middle of the road; and the
animal, accustomed to this maneuvering, turned into the courtyard, steering clear of the flower bed, till Jacquelin took the
bridle and walked round with the chaise to the steps before the
door.

"Mariette!" called Mlle. Cormon.

"Mademoiselle?" returned Mariette, engaged in shutting the
gates.

"Has the gentleman come?"

"No, mademoiselle."

"And is my uncle here?"

"He is at church, mademoiselle."

Jacquelin and Josette were standing on the lowest step of the
flight, holding out their hands to steady their mistress' descent
from the cariole; she, meanwhile, had hoisted herself upon the
shaft, and was clutching at the curtains, before springing down
into their arms. It was two years since she had dared to trust
herself upon the iron step of double strength, secured to the
shaft by a fearfully made contrivance with huge bolts.

From the height of the steps, mademoiselle surveyed her courtyard with an air of satisfaction.

"There, there, Mariette, let the great gate alone and come
here."

"There is something up," Jacquelin said to Mariette as she came
past the chaise.

"Let us see now, child, what is there in the house?" said Mlle.
Cormon, collapsing on the bench in the long antechamber as if
she were exhausted.

"Just nothing at all," replied Mariette, hands on hips. "Mademoiselle knows quite well that Monsieur l'Abbé always dines

out when she is not at home; yesterday I went to bring him back from Mademoiselle Armande's."

"Then where is he?"

"Monsieur l'Abbé? He is gone to church; he will not be back till three o'clock."

"Uncle thinks of nothing! Why couldn't he have sent you to market? Go down now, Mariette, and, without throwing money away, spare for nothing, get the best, finest, and daintiest of everything. Go to the coach office and ask where people send orders for pâtés. And I want crayfish from the brooks along the Brillante. What time is it?"

"Nine o'clock all but a quarter."

"Oh dear, oh dear; don't lose any time in chattering, Mariette. The visitor my uncle is expecting may come at any moment; pretty figures we should cut if he comes to breakfast."

Mariette, turning round, saw Penelope in a lather, and gave Jacquelin a glance which said: "Mademoiselle means to put her hand on a husband this time."

Mlle. Cormon turned to her housemaid. "Now, it is our turn, Josette; we must make arrangements for Monsieur de Troisville to sleep here tonight."

How gladly those words were uttered; "We must arrange for Monsieur de Troisville" (pronounced Tréville) "to sleep here to-night!" How much lay in those few words! Hope poured like a flood through the old maid's soul.

"Will you put him in the green chamber?"

"The bishop's room? No," said mademoiselle, "it is too near mine. It is very well for his lordship, a holy man."

"Give him your uncle's room."

"It looks so bare; it would not do."

"Lord, mademoiselle, you could have a bed put up in the boudoir in a brace of shakes; there is a fireplace there. Moreau will be sure to find a bedstead in his warehouse that will match the hangings as nearly as possible."

"You are right, Josette. Very well; run round to Moreau's and ask his advice about everything necessary; I give you authority.

If the bed, Monsieur de Troisville's bed, can be set up by this evening, so that Monsieur de Troisvile shall notice nothing, supposing that Monsieur de Troisville should happen to come in while Moreau is here, I am quite willing. If Moreau cannot promise that, Monsieur de Troisville shall sleep in the green chamber, although Monsieur de Troisville will be very near me."

Josette departed; her mistress called her back.

"Tell Jacquelin all about it," she exclaimed in a stern and awful voice; "let *him* go to Moreau. How about my dress? Suppose Monsieur de Troisville came and caught me like this without uncle here to receive him! Oh, uncle, uncle! Come, Josette, you shall help me to dress."

"But how about Penelope?" the woman began imprudently. Mlle. Cormon's eyes shot sparks for the first and last time in her life.

"It is always Penelope! Penelope this, Penelope that! Is Penelope mistress here?"

"She is all of a lather, and she has not been fed."

"Eh! and if she dies, let her die——" cried Mlle. Cormon—"so long as I am married," she added in her own mind.

Josette stood stockstill a moment in amazement, such a remark was tantamount to murder, then, at a sign from her mistress, she dashed headlong down the steps into the yard.

"Mademoiselle is possessed, Jacquelin!" were Josette's first words.

And in this way, everything that occurred throughout the day led up to the great climax which was to change the whole course of Mlle. Cormon's life. The town was already turned upside down by five aggravating circumstances which attended the lady's sudden return, to wit—the pouring rain; Penelope's panting pace and sunk flanks covered with foam; the earliness of the hour; the untidy bundles; and the spinster's strange, scared looks. But when Mariette invaded the market to carry off everything that she could lay her hands on; when Jacquelin went to inquire for a bedstead of the principal upholsterer in the rue Porte de Séez, close by the church; here, indeed, was material on which to build the gravest conjecture! The strange event was discussed on the parade and the promenade; everyone was full of it, not excepting Mlle. Armande, on whom the Chevalier de Valois happened to be calling at the time.

Only two days ago Alençon had been stirred to its depths by occurrences of such capital importance that worthy matrons were still exclaiming that it was like the end of the world! And now, this last news was summed up in all houses by the inquiry: "What can be happening at the Cormons'?"

The Abbé de Sponde, skillfully questioned when he emerged from St. Leonard's to take a walk with the Abbé Couturier along the parade, made reply in the simplicity of his heart, to the effect that he expected a visit from the Vicomte de Troisville, who had been in the Russian service during the Emigration, and now was coming back to settle in Alençon. A kind of labial telegraph, at work that afternoon between two and five o'clock, informed all the inhabitants of Alençon that Mlle. Cormon at last had found herself a husband by advertisement. She was going to marry the Vicomte de Troisville. Some said that "Moreau was at work on a bedstead already." In some places the bed was six feet long. It was only four feet at Mme. Granson's house in the Rue du Bercail. At President du Ronceret's, where du Bousquier was dining, it dwindled into a sofa. The tradespeople said that it cost eleven hundred francs. It was generally thought that this was like counting your chickens before they were hatched.

Farther away, it was said that the price of carp had gone up. Mariette had swooped down upon the market and created a general scarcity. Penelope had dropped down at the upper end of the rue Saint-Blaise; the death was called in question at the receiver-general's; nevertheless, at the prefecture it was known for a fact that the animal fell dead just as she turned in at the gate of the Hôtel Cormon, so swiftly had the old maid come down upon her prey. The saddler at the corner of the Rue de Séez, in his anxiety to know the truth about Penelope, was hardy enough to call in to ask if anything had happened to

Mlle. Cormon's chaise. Then from the utmost end of the rue Saint-Blaise to the furthermost parts of the rue du Bercail, it was known that, thanks to Jacquelin's care, Penelope, dumb victim of her mistress' intemperate haste, was still alive, but she seemed to be in a bad way.

All along the Brittany road the Vicomte de Troisville was a penniless younger son, for the domains of Perche belonged to the marquis of that ilk, a peer of France with two children. The match was a lucky thing for an impoverished *émigré*; as for the vicomte himself, that was Mlle. Cormon's affair. Altogether the match received the approval of the aristocratic section on the Brittany road; Mlle. Cormon could not have put her fortune to a better use.

Among the bourgeoisie, on the other hand, the Vicomte de Troisville was a Russian general who had borne arms against France. He was bringing back a large fortune made at the court of St. Petersburg. He was a "foreigner," one of the "Allies" detested by the Liberals. The Abbé de Sponde had maneuvered the match on the sly. Every person who had any shadow of a right of entrance to Mlle. Cormon's drawing room vowed to be there that night.

While the excitement went through the town, and all but put Suzanne out of people's heads, Mlle. Cormon herself was not less excited; she felt as she had never felt before. She looked round the drawing room, the boudoir, the cabinet, the dining room, and a dreadful apprehension seized upon her. Some mocking demon seemed to show her the old-fashioned splendor in a new light; the beautiful furniture, admired ever since she was a child, was suspected, nay, convicted, of being out of date. She was shaken, in fact, by the dread that catches almost every author by the throat when he begins to read his own work aloud to some exigent or jaded critic. Before he began, it was perfect in his eyes; now the novel situations are stale; the finest periods turned with such secret relish are turgid or halting; the metaphors are mixed or grotesque; his sins stare him in the face. Even so, poor Mlle. Cormon shivered to think of the smile on M. de Troisville's lips when he looked round that drawing room, which looked like a bishop's drawing room, unchanged for one possessor after another. She dreaded his cool survey of the ancient dining room; in short, she was afraid that the picture might look the older for the ancient frame. How if all these old things should tinge her with the age? The bare thought of it made her flesh creep. At that moment she would have given one-fourth of her savings for the power of renovating her house at a stroke of a magic wand. Where is the general so conceited that he will not shudder on the eve of an action? She, poor thing, was between an Austerlitz and a Waterloo.

"Madame la Vicomtesse de Troisville," she said to herself, "what a fine name! Our estates will pass to a good house, at any rate."

Her excitement fretted her. It sent a thrill through every fiber of every nerve to the least of the ramifications and the papillæ so well wadded with flesh. Hope tingling in her veins set all the blood in her body in circulation. She felt capable, if need was, of conversing with M. de Troisville.

Of the activity with which Josette, Mariette, Jacquelin, Moreau, and his assistants set about their work, it is needless to speak. Ants rescuing their eggs could not have been busier than they. Everything, kept so neat and clean with daily care, was starched and ironed, scrubbed, washed, and polished. The best china saw the light. Linen damask cloths and serviettes docketed A B C D emerged from the depths where they lay shrouded in triple wrappings and defended by bristling rows of pins. The rarest shelves of that oak-bound library were made to give account of their contents; and finally, mademoiselle offered up three bottles of liqueurs to the coming guest, three bottles bearing the label of the most famous distiller of oversea—Mme. Amphoux, name dear to connoisseurs.

Mlle. Cormon was ready for battle, thanks to the devotion of her lieutenants. The munitions of war, the heavy artillery of the kitchen, the batteries of the pantry, the victuals, provisions for the attack, and body of (p)reserves, had all been brought up in array. Orders were issued to Jacquelin, Mariette, and Josette to wear their best clothes. The garden was raked over. Mademoiselle only regretted that she could not come to an understanding with the nightingales in the trees, that they might warble their sweetest songs for the occasion. At length, at four o'clock, just as the abbé came in, and mademoiselle was beginning to think that she had brought out her daintiest linen and china and made ready the most exquisite of dinners in vain, the crack of a postilion's whip sounded outside in the Val-Noble.

"It is *he*!" she thought, and the lash of the whip struck her in the heart.

And indeed, heralded by all this tittle-tattle, a certain post-chaise, with a single gentleman inside it, had made such a prodigious sensation as it drove down the rue Saint-Blaise and turned into the rue du Cours, that several small urchins and older persons gave chase to the vehicle, and now were standing in a group about the gateway of the Hôtel Cormon to watch the postilion drive in. Jacquelin, feeling that his own marriage was in the wind, had also heard the crack of the whip and was out in the yard to throw open the gates. The postilion (an acquaintance) was on his mettle, he turned the corner to admiration and came to a stand before the flight of steps. And, as you can understand, he did not go until Jacquelin had duly and properly made him tipsy.

The abbé came out to meet his guest, and in a trice the chaise was despoiled of its occupant, robbers in a hurry could not have done their work more nimbly; then the chaise was put into the coach house, the great door was closed, and in a few minutes there was not a sign of M. de Troisville's arrival. Never did two chemicals combine with a greater alacrity than that displayed by the house of Cormon to absorb the Vicomte de Troisville. As for mademoiselle, if she had been a lizard caught by a shepherd, her heart could not have beat faster. She sat heroically in her low chair by the fireside; Josette threw open the door, and the Vicomte de Troisville, followed by the Abbé de Sponde, appeared before her.

"This is Monsieur le Vicomte de Troisville, niece, a grandson of an old schoolfellow of mine. Monsieur de Troisville, my niece, Mademoiselle Cormon."

"Dear uncle, how nicely he puts it," thought Rose-Marie-Victoire.

The Vicomte de Troisville, to describe him in a few words, was a du Bousquier of noble family. Between the two men there was just that difference which separates the gentleman from the ordinary man. If they had been standing side by side, even the most furious Radical could not have denied the signs of race about the vicomte. There was all the distinction of refinement about his strength, his figure had lost nothing of its magnificent dignity. Blue-eyed, dark-haired, and olive-skinned, he could not have been more than six-and-forty. You might have thought him a handsome Spaniard preserved in Russian ice. His manner, gait, and bearing, and everything about him, suggested a diplomatist, and one that has seen Europe. He looked like a gentleman in his traveling dress.

M. de Troisville seemed to be tired. The abbé rose to conduct him to his room, and was overcome with astonishment when Rose opened the door of the boudoir, now transformed into a bedroom. Then uncle and niece left the noble visitor leisure to attend to his toilet with the help of Jacquelin, who brought him all the luggage he needed. While M. de Troisville was dressing, they walked on the terrace by the Brillante. The abbé, by a strange chance, was more absent-minded than usual, and Mlle. Cormon no less preoccupied, so they paced to and fro in silence. Never in her life had Mlle. Cormon seen so attractive a man as this Olympian vicomte. She could not say to herself, like a German girl, "I have found my ideal!" but she felt that she was in love from head to foot. "The very thing for me," she thought. On a sudden she fled to Mariette, to know whether dinner could be put back a little without serious injury.

"Uncle, this Monsieur de Troisville is very pleasant," she said when she came back again.

"Why, my girl, he has not said a word as yet," returned the abbé, laughing.

"But one can tell by his general appearance. Is he a bachelor?"

"I know nothing about it," replied her uncle, his thoughts full of that afternoon's discussion with the Abbé Couturier on Divine Grace. "Monsieur de Troisville said in his letter that he wanted to buy a house here. If he were married, he would not have come alone," he added carelessly. It never entered his head that his niece could think of marriage for herself.

"Is he rich?"

"He is the younger son of a younger branch. His grandfather held a major's commission, but this young man's father made a foolish marriage."

"Young man!" repeated his niece. "Why, he is quite five-and-forty, uncle, it seems to me." She felt an uncontrollable desire to compare his age with hers.

"Yes," said the abbé. "But to a poor priest at seventy, a man of forty seems young, Rose."

By this time all Alençon knew that M. le Vicomte de Troisville had arrived at the Cormon house.

The visitor very soon rejoined his host and hostess, and began to admire the Brillante, the garden, the house, and surroundings.

"Monsieur l'Abbé," he said, "to find such a place as this would be the height of my ambition."

The old maid wished to read a declaration in the speech. She lowered her eyes.

"You must be very fond of it, mademoiselle," continued the vicomte.

"How could I help being fond of it? It has been in our family since 1574, when one of our ancestors, an Intendant of the Duchy of Alençon, bought the ground and built the house. It is laid on piles."

Jacquelin having announced that dinner was ready, M. de Troisville offered his arm. The radiant spinster tried not to lean too heavily upon him; she was still afraid that he might think her forward.

"Everything is quite in harmony here," remarked the vicomte as they sat down to table.

"Yes, the trees in our garden are full of birds that give us music for nothing. Nobody molests them; the nightingales sing there every night," said Mlle. Cormon.

"I am speaking of the inside of the house," remarked the vicomte; he had not troubled himself to study his hostess particularly, and was quite unaware of her vacuity. "Yes, everything contributes to the general effect; the tones of color, the furniture, the character of the house," added he, addressing Mlle. Cormon.

"It costs a great deal, though," replied that excellent spinster, "the taxes are something enormous." The word "contribute" had impressed itself on her mind.

"Ah! then are the taxes high here?" asked Monsieur de Troisville, too full of his own ideas to notice the absurd non sequitur.

"I do not know," said the abbé. "My niece manages her own property and mine."

"The taxes are a mere trifle if people are well-to-do," struck in Mlle. Cormon, anxious not to appear stingy. "As to the furniture, I leave things as they are. I shall never make any changes here; at least I shall not, unless I marry, and in that case everything in the house must be arranged to suit the master's taste."

"You are for great principles, mademoiselle," smiled the vicomte; "somebody will be a lucky man."

"Nobody ever made me such a pretty speech before," thought Mlle. Cormon.

The vicomte complimented his hostess upon the appointments of the table and the housekeeping, admitting that he had thought that the provinces were behind the times, and found himself in most delectable quarters.

"*Delectable*, good Lord! what does it mean?" thought she. "Where is the Chevalier de Valois to reply to him? De-lect-able? Is it made up of several words? There! courage; perhaps it is Russian, and if so I am not obliged to say anything." Then she added aloud, her tongue loosed by an eloquence which almost every human creature can find in a great crisis, "We have the most brilliant society here, Monsieur le Vicomte. You will be able to judge for yourself, for it assembles in this very house; on some of our acquaintances we can always count; they will have heard of my return no doubt, and will be sure to come to see me. There is the Chevalier de Valois, a gentleman of the old court, a man of infinite wit and taste; then there is Monsieur le Marquis d'Esgrignon and Mademoiselle Armande, his sister"—she bit her lip and changed her mind—"a—a remarkable woman in her way. She refused all offers of marriage so as to leave her fortune to her brother and his son."

"Ah! yes; the d'Esgrignons, I remember them," said the vicomte.

"Alençon is very gay," pursued mademoiselle, now that she had fairly started off. "There is so much going on; the receiver-general gives dances; the prefect is a very pleasant man; his lordship the bishop occasionally honors us with a visit——"

"Come!" said the vicomte, smiling as he spoke, "I have done well, it seems, to come creeping back like a hare (*un lièvre*) to die in my form."

"It is the same with me," replied mademoiselle; "I am like a creeper (*le lierre*), I must cling to something or die."

The vicomte took the saying thus twisted for a joke, and smiled.

"Ah!" thought his hostess, "that is all right, *he* understands me."

The conversation was kept up upon generalities. Under pressure of a strong desire to please, the strange, mysterious, indefinable workings of consciousness brought all the Chevalier de Valois' tricks of speech uppermost in Mlle. Cormon's brain. It fell out, as it sometimes does in a duel, when the devil himself seems to take aim; and never did duelist hit his man more fairly and squarely than the old maid. The Vicomte de Troisville was too well mannered to praise the excellent dinner, but his silence was panegyric in itself! As he drank the delicious wines with which Jacquelin plied him, he seemed to be meeting old friends with the liveliest pleasure; for your true amateur does not applaud, he enjoys. He informed himself curiously of the prices of land, houses, and sites; he drew from mademoiselle a long description of the property between the Brillante and the Sarthe. He was amazed that the town and the river lay so far apart, and showed the greatest interest in local topography. The abbé sat silent, leaving all the conversation to his niece. And, in truth, mademoiselle considered that she interested M. de Troisville; he smiled graciously at her, he made far more progress with her in the course of a single dinner than the most ardent of her former wooers in a whole fortnight. For which reasons, you may be certain that never was guest so cosseted, so lapped about with small attentions and observances. He might have been a much-loved lover, newly come home to the house of which he was the delight.

Mademoiselle forestalled his wants. She saw when he needed bread, her eyes brooded over him; if he turned his head, she adroitly supplemented his portion of any dish which he seemed to like; if he had been a glutton, she would have killed him. What a delicious earnest of all that she counted upon doing for her lover! She made no silly blunders of self-depreciation this time! She went gallantly forward, full sail, and all flags flying; posed as the queen of Alençon, and vaunted her preserves. Indeed, she fished for compliments, talking about herself as if her trumpeter were dead. And she saw that she pleased the vicomte, for her wish to please had so transformed her that she grew almost feminine. It was not without inward exultation that she heard footsteps while they sat at dessert; sounds of going and coming in the antechamber and noises in the drawing room; and knew that the usual company was arriving. She called the attention of her uncle and M. de Troisville to this fact as a proof of the affection in which she was held, whereas it really was a symptom of the paroxysm of curiosity which convulsed the whole town. Impatient to show herself in her glory, she ordered coffee and the liqueurs to be taken to the drawing room, whither Jacquelin went to display to the élite of Alençon the splendors of a Dresden china service, which only left the cupboard twice in a twelvemonth. All these circumstances were noted by people disposed to criticize under their breath.

"Egad!" cried du Bousquier, "nothing but Madame Amphoux's liqueurs, which only come out on the four great festival days!"

"Decidedly, this match must have been arranged by corre-

spondence for a year past," said M. le Président du Ronceret.
"The postmaster here has been receiving letters with an Odessa
postmark for the last twelve months."

Mme. Granson shuddered. M. le Chevalier de Valois had eaten
a heavy dinner, but he felt the pallor spreading over his left cheek;
felt, too, that he was betraying his secret, and said: "It is cold today, do you not think? I am freezing."

"It is the neighborhood of Russia," suggested du Bousquier.
And the chevalier looked at his rival as who should say: "Well
put in!"

Mlle. Cormon was so radiant, so triumphant, that she looked
positively handsome, it was thought. Nor was this unwonted
brilliancy wholly due to sentiment; ever since the morning the
blood had been surging through her veins; the presentiments of a
great crisis at hand affected her nerves. It needed a combination
of circumstances to make her so little like herself. With what joy
did she not solemnly introduce the vicomte to the chevalier, and
the chevalier to the vicomte; all Alençon was presented to M. de
Troisville, and M. de Troisville made the acquaintance of all
Alençon. It fell out, naturally enough, that the vicomte and the
chevalier, two born aristocrats, were in sympathy at once; they
recognized each other for inhabitants of the same social sphere.
They began to chat as they stood by the fire. A circle formed
about them listening devoutly to their conversation, though it was
carried on *sotto voce*. Fully to realize the scene, imagine Mlle.
Cormon standing with her back to the chimney piece, busy preparing coffee for her supposed suitor.

M. DE VALOIS. "So Monsieur le Vicomte is coming to settle
here, people say."

M. DE TROISVILLE. "Yes, monsieur. I have come to look for a
house." (*Mlle. Cormon turns, cup in hand.*) "And I must have a
large one"—(*Mlle. Cormon offers the cup of coffee*)—"to hold
my family." (*The room grows dark before the old maid's eye.*)

M. DE VALOIS. "Are you married?"

M. de TROISVILLE. "Yes, I have been married for sixteen years.
My wife is the daughter of the Princess Scherbelloff."

Mlle. Cormon dropped like one thunderstruck. Du Bousquier, seeing her reel, sprang forward and caught her in his arms. Somebody opened the door to let him pass out with his enormous burden. The melted Republican, counseled by Josette, summoned up his strength, bore the old maid to her room, and deposited her upon the bed. Josette, armed with a pair of scissors, cut the stay-laces, drawn outrageously tight. Du Bousquier, rough and ready, dashed cold water over Mlle. Cormon's face and bust, which broke from its bounds like the Loire in flood. The patient opened her eyes, saw du Bousquier, and gave a cry of alarmed modesty. Du Bousquier withdrew, leaving half a dozen women in possession, with Mme. Granson at their head, Mme. Granson beaming with joy.

What had the Chevalier de Valois done? True to his system, he had been covering the retreat.

"Poor Mademoiselle Cormon!" he said, addressing M. de Troisville, but looking round the room, quelling the beginnings of an outbreak of laughter with his haughty eyes. "She is dreadfully troubled with heated blood. She would not be bled before going to the Prébaudet (her country house), and this is the result of the spring weather."

"She drove over in the rain this morning," said the Abbé de Sponde. "She may have taken a little cold, and so caused the slight derangement of the system to which she is subject. But she will soon get over it."

"She was telling me the day before yesterday that she had not had a recurrence of it for three months; she added at the time that it was sure to play her a bad turn," added the chevalier.

"Ah! so you are married!" thought Jacquelin, watching M. de Troisville, who was sipping his coffee.

The faithful manservant made his mistress' disappointment his own. He guessed her feelings. He took away the liqueurs brought out for a bachelor, and not for a Russian woman's husband. All these little things were noticed with amusement.

The Abbé de Sponde had known all along why M. de Troisville had come to Alençon, but in his absent-mindedness he had said nothing about it; it had never entered his mind that his niece could take the slightest interest in that gentleman. As for the vicomte, he was engrossed by the object of his journey; like many other married men, he was in no great hurry to introduce his wife into the conversation; he had had no opportunity of saying that he was married; and beside, he thought that Mlle. Cormon knew his history. Du Bousquier reappeared, and was questioned without mercy. One of the six women came down, and reported that Mlle. Cormon was feeling much better and that her doctor had come; but she was to stay in bed, and it appeared that she ought to be bled at once. The drawing room soon filled. In Mlle. Cormon's absence, the ladies were free to discuss the tragicomic scene which had just taken place; and duly they enlarged, annotated, embellished, colored, adorned, embroidered, and bedizened the tale which was to set all Alençon thinking of the disappointed old maid on the morrow.

Meanwhile, Josette upstairs was saying to her mistress, "That good Monsieur du Bousquier! How he carried you upstairs! What a fist! Really, your illness made him quite pale. He loves you still."

And with this final phrase, the solemn and terrible day came to a close.

Next day, all morning long, the news of the comedy, with full details, circulated over Alençon, raising laughter everywhere, to the shame of the town be it said. Next day, Mlle. Cormon, very much the better for the bloodletting, would have seemed sublime to the most hardened of those who jeered at her if they could but have seen her noble dignity and the Christian resignation in her soul, as she gave her hand to the unconscious perpetrator of the hoax, and went in to breakfast. Ah! heartless wags, who were laughing at her expense, why could you not hear her say to the vicomte—

"Madame de Troisville will have some difficulty in finding a house to suit her. Do me the favor of using my house, monsieur, until you have made all your arrangements."

"But I have two girls and two boys, mademoiselle. We should put you to a great deal of inconvenience."

"Do not refuse me," said she, her eyes full of apprehension and regret.

"I made the offer, however you might decide, in my letter; but you did not take it," remarked the abbé.

"What, uncle! did you know?——"

Poor thing, she broke off. Josette heaved a sigh, and neither M. de Troisville nor the uncle noticed anything.

After breakfast, the Abbé de Sponde, carrying out the plan agreed upon overnight, took the vicomte to see houses for sale and suitable sites for building. Mlle. Cormon was left alone in the drawing room.

"I am the talk of the town, child, by this time," she said, looking piteously at Josette.

"Well, mademoiselle, get married."

"But, my girl, I am not at all prepared to make a choice."

"Bah! I should take Monsieur du Bousquier if I were you."

"Monsieur de Valois says that he is such a Republican, Josette."

"Your gentlemen don't know what they are talking about; they say that he robbed the Republic, so he can't have been at all fond of it," said Josette, and with that she went.

"That girl is amazingly shrewd," thought Mlle. Cormon, left alone to her gnawing perplexity.

She saw that the only way of silencing talk was to marry at once. This last so patently humiliating check was enough to drive her to extreme measures; and it takes a great deal to force a feeble-minded human being out of a groove, be it good or bad. Both the old bachelors understood the position of affairs, both made up their minds to call in the morning to make inquiries, and (in their own language) to press the point.

M. de Valois considered that the occasion demanded a scrupulous toilet; he took a bath, he groomed himself with unusual care, and for the first time and the last Césarine saw him applying "a suspicion of rouge" with incredible skill.

Du Bousquier, rough-and-ready Republican that he was, inspired by dogged purpose, paid no attention to his appearance; he hurried round and came in first. The fate of men, like the destinies of empires, hangs on small things. History records all such principal causes of great failure or success—a Kellermann's charge at Marengo, a Blücher coming up at the battle of Waterloo, a Prince Eugène slighted by Louis XIV, a curé on the battlefield of Denain; but nobody profits by the lesson to be diligently attentive to the little trifles of his own life. Behold the results. The Duchesse de Langeais in *The Thirteen** entering a convent for want of ten minutes' patience; Judge Popinot in *The Commission in Lunacy* putting off his inquiries as to the Marquis d'Espard till tomorrow; Charles Grandet coming home by way of Bordeaux instead of Nantes—and these things are said to happen by accident and mere chance! The few moments spent in putting on that suspicion of rouge wrecked M. de Valois' hopes. Only in such a way could the chevalier have succumbed. He had lived for the Graces, he was foredoomed to die through them. Even as he gave a last look in the mirror, the burly du Bousquier was entering the disconsolate old maid's drawing room. His entrance coincided with a gleam of favor in the lady's mind, though in the course of her deliberations the chevalier had decidedly had the advantage.

"It is God's will," she said to herself when du Bousquier appeared.

"Mademoiselle, I trust you will not take my importunity in bad part; I did not like to trust that great stupid of a René to make inquiries, and came myself."

"I am perfectly well," she said nervously; then, after a pause, and in a very emphatic tone, "Thank you, Monsieur du Bousquier, for the trouble that you took and that I gave you yesterday——"

She recollected how she had lain in du Bousquier's arms, and the accident seemed to her to be a direct order from heaven. For the first time in her life a man had seen her with her belt wrenched

---

* This and the following are references to stories and characters of Balzac. *Ed*.

apart, her stay-laces cut, the jewel shaken violently out of its case.

"I was so heartily glad to carry you that I thought you a light weight," said he.

At this Mlle. Cormon looked at du Bousquier as she never looked at any man in the world before; and thus encouraged, the ex-contractor for forage flung a side glance that went straight to the old maid's heart.

"It is a pity," added he, "that this has not given me the right to keep you always." (She was listening with rapture in her face.) "You looked dazzling as you lay swooning there on the bed; I never saw such a fine woman in my life, and I have seen a good many. There is this about a stout woman, she is superb to look at, she has only to show herself, she triumphs."

"You mean to laugh at me," said the old maid; "that is not kind of you, when the whole town is perhaps putting a malicious and bad construction on things that happened here yesterday."

"It is as true as that my name is du Bousquier, mademoiselle. My feelings toward you have never changed; your first rejection did not discourage me."

The old maid lowered her eyes. There was a pause, a painful ordeal for du Bousquier. Then Mlle. Cormon made up her mind and raised her eyelids; she looked up tenderly at du Bousquier through her tears.

"If this is so, monsieur," she said, in a tremulous voice, "I only ask you to allow me to lead a Christian life, do not ask me to change any of my habits as to religion, leave me free to choose my spiritual directors, and I will give you my hand," holding it out to him as she spoke.

Du Bousquier caught the plump, honest hand that held so many francs, and kissed it respectfully.

"But I have one thing more to ask," added Mlle. Cormon, suffering him to kiss her hand.

"It is granted, and if it is impossible, it shall be done," (a reminiscence of Beaujon).

"Alas!" began the old maid, "for love of me you must burden

your soul with a sin which I know is heinous; falsehood is one of
the seven deadly sins; but still you can make confession, can you
not? We will both of us do penance." They looked tenderly at
each other at those words.

"Perhaps," continued Mlle. Cormon, "after all, it is one of those
deceptions which the church calls venial——"

"Is she going to tell me that she is in Suzanne's plight?" thought
du Bousquier. "What luck!——" Aloud he said, "Well, mademoiselle?"

"And you must take it upon you——"

"What?"

"To say that this marriage was agreed upon between us six
months ago."

"Charming woman!" exclaimed the forage-contractor, and by
his manner he implied that he was prepared to make even this
sacrifice; "a man only does thus for the woman he has worshiped
for ten years."

"In spite of my severity?" asked she.

"Yes, in spite of your severity."

"Monsieur du Bousquier, I have misjudged you." Again she held
out her big, red hand, and again du Bousquier kissed it.

At that very moment the door opened, and the betrothed
couple, turning their heads, perceived the charming but too tardy
chevalier.

"Ah! fair queen," said he, "so you have risen?"

Mlle. Cormon smiled at him, and something clutched at her
heart. M. de Valois, grown remarkably young and irresistible,
looked like Lauzun entering La Grande Mademoiselle's apartments.

"Ah! my dear du Bousquier!" he continued, half laughingly,
so sure was he of success. "Monsieur de Troisville and the Abbé
de Sponde are in front of your house, looking it over like a pair of
surveyors."

"On my word," said du Bousquier, "if the Vicomte de Troisville wants it, he can have it for forty thousand francs. It is of no
use whatever to me. Always, if mademoiselle has no objection,

that must be ascertained first. Mademoiselle, may I tell? Yes? Very well, *my dear chevalier*, you shall be the first to hear"— Mlle. Cormon dropped her eyes—"of the honor and the favor that mademoiselle is doing me; I have kept it a secret for more than six months. We are going to be married in a very few days, the contract is drawn up, we shall sign it tomorrow. So, you see, that I have no further use for my house in the Rue du Cygne. I am quietly on the lookout for a purchaser; and the Abbé de Sponde, *who knew this*, naturally took Monsieur du Troisville to see it."

There was such a color of truth about this monstrous fib that the chevalier was quite taken in by it. *My dear chevalier* was a return for all preceding defeats; it was like the victory won at Pultowa by Peter the Great over Charles XII. And thus du Bousquier enjoyed a delicious revenge for hundreds of pinpricks endured in silence; but in his triumph he forgot that he was not a young man, he passed his fingers through the false toupet, and— it came off in his hand!

"I congratulate you both," said the chevalier, with an agreeable smile; "I wish that you may end like the fairy stories, 'They lived very happily and had a fine—*family of children*!'" Here he shaped a cone of snuff in his palm before adding mockingly, "But, monsieur, you forgot that—er—you wear borrowed plumes."

Du Bousquier reddened. The false toupet was ten inches awry. Mlle. Cormon raised her eyes to the face of her betrothed, saw the bare cranium, and bashfully looked down again. Never toad looked more venomously at a victim than du Bousquier at the chevalier.

"A pack of aristocrats that look down on me!" he thought. "I will crush you all some of these days."

The Chevalier de Valois imagined that he had regained all the lost ground. But Mlle. Cormon was not the woman to understand the connection between the chevalier's congratulation and the allusion to the false toupet; and, for that matter, even if she had understood, her hand had been given. M. de Valois saw too clearly that all was lost. Meantime, as the two men stood without speaking, Mlle. Cormon innocently studied how to amuse them.

"Play a game of reversis," suggested she, without any malicious intention.

Du Bousquier smiled, and went as future master of the house for the card table. Whether the Chevalier de Valois had lost his head, or whether he chose to remain to study the causes of his defeat and to remedy it, certain it is that he allowed himself to be led like a sheep to the slaughter. But he had just received the heaviest of all bludgeon blows; and a noble might have been excused if he had been at any rate stunned by it. Very soon the worthy Abbé de Sponde and M. de Troisville returned, and at once Mlle. Cormon hurried into the antechamber, took her uncle aside, and told him in a whisper of her decision. Then, hearing that the house in the Rue du Cygne suited M. de Troisville, she begged her betrothed to do her the service of saying that her uncle knew that the place was for sale. She dared not confide the fib to the abbé, for fear that he should forget. The falsehood was destined to prosper better than if it had been a virtuous action. All Alençon heard the great news that night. For four days the town had found as much to say as in the ominous days of 1814 and 1815. Some laughed at the idea, others thought it true; some condemned, others approved the marriage. The bourgeoisie of Alençon regarded it as a conquest, and they were the best pleased.

The Chevalier de Valois, next day, among his own circle, brought out this cruel epigram: "The Cormons are ending as they began; stewards and contractors are all on a footing."

The news of Mlle. Cormon's choice went to poor Athanase's heart; but he showed not a sign of the dreadful tumult surging within. He had heard of the marriage at President du Ronceret's while his mother was playing a game of boston. Mme. Granson, looking up, saw her son's face in the glass; he looked white, she thought, but then he had been pale ever since vague rumors had reached him in the morning. Mlle. Cormon was the card on which Athanase staked his life, and chill presentiments of impending catastrophe already wrapped him about. When intellect and imagination have exaggerated a calamity till it becomes a burden too heavy for shoulders and brow to bear, when some long-cherished hope fails utterly, and with it the visions which enable a man to forget the fierce vulture-cares gnawing at his heart; then, if that man has no belief in himself, in spite of his powers; no belief in the future, in spite of the Power Divine—he is broken in pieces. Athanase was a product of education under the Empire. Fatalism, the Emperor's creed, spread downward to the lowest ranks of the army, to the very schoolboys at their desks. Athanase followed Mme. du Ronceret's play with a stolidity which might so easily have been taken for indifference, that Mme. Granson fancied she had been mistaken as to her son's feelings.

Athanase's apparent carelessness explained his refusal to sacrifice his so-called "Liberal" opinions. This word, then recently coined for the Emperor Alexander, proceeded into the language, I believe, by way of Mme. de Staël through Benjamin Constant.

After that fatal evening the unhappy young man took to haunting one of the most picturesque walks along the Sarthe; every artist who comes to Alençon sketches it from that point of view, for the sake of the water-mills, and the river gleaming brightly out among the fields, between the shapely well-grown trees on either side. Flat though the land may be, it lacks none of the subdued peculiar charm of French landscape; for in France your eyes are never wearied by glaring Eastern sunlight nor saddened by too continual mist. It is a lonely spot. Dwellers in the provinces care nothing for beautiful scenery, perhaps because it is always about them, perhaps because there is a sense lacking in them. If there is such a thing as a promenade, a mall, or any spot from which you see a beautiful view, it is sure to be the one unfrequented part of the town. Athanase liked the loneliness, with the water like a living presence in it, and the fields just turning green in the warmth of the early spring sunlight. Occasionally someone who had seen him sitting at a poplar foot, and received an intent gaze from his eyes, would speak to Mme. Granson about him.

"There is something the matter with your son."

"I know what he is about," the mother would say with a satisfied air, hinting that he was meditating some great work.

Athanase meddled no more in politics; he had no opinions; and
yet, now and again, he was merry enough, merry at the expense
of others, after the wont of those who stand alone and apart in
contempt of public opinion. The young fellow lived so entirely
outside the horizon of provincial ideas and amusements that he
was interesting to few people; he did not so much as rouse curiosity. Those who spoke of him to his mother did so for her sake,
not for his. Not a creature in Alençon sympathized with Athanase;
the Sarthe received the tears which no friend, no loving woman
dried. If the magnificent Suzanne had chanced to pass that way,
how much misery might have been prevented—the two young
creatures would have fallen in love.

And yet Suzanne certainly passed that way. Her ambition had
been first awakened by a sufficiently marvelous tale of things
which happened in 1799; an old story of adventures begun at the
sign of the Three Moors had turned her childish brain. They used
to tell how an adventuress, beautiful as an angel, had come from
Paris with a commission from Fouché to ensnare the Marquis de
Montauran, the Chouan leader sent over by the Bourbons; how
she met him at that very inn of the Three Moors as he came back
from his Mortagne expedition; and how she won his love, and
gave him up to his enemies. The romantic figure of this woman,
the power of beauty, the whole story of Marie de Verneuil and
the Marquis de Montauran, dazzled Suzanne, till, as she grew
older, she too longed to play with men's lives. A few months after
her flight, she could not resist the desire to see her native place
again, on her way to Brittany with an artist. She wanted to see
Fougères, where the Marquis de Montauran met his death; and
thought of making a pilgrimage to the scenes of stories told to
her in childhood of that war in the West, so little known even
yet. She wished, beside, to revisit Alençon with such splendor in
her surroundings, and so completely metamorphosed, that nobody should know her again. She intended to put her mother beyond the reach of want in one moment, and, in some tactful way,

to send a sum of money to poor Athanase—a sum which for genius in modern days is the equivalent of a Rebecca's gift of horse and armor to an Ivanhoe of the Middle Ages.

A month went by. Opinions as to Mlle. Cormon's marriage fluctuated in the strangest way. There was an incredulous section which strenuously denied the truth of the report, and a party of believers who persistently affirmed it. At the end of fourteen days, the doubters received a severe check. Du Bousquier's house was sold to M. de Troisville for forty-three thousand francs. M. de Troisville meant to live quite quietly in Alençon; he intended to return to Paris after the death of the Princess Scherbelloff, but until the inheritance fell in he would spend his time in looking after his estates. This much appeared to be fact. But the doubting faction declined to be crushed. Their assertion was that, married or not, du Bousquier had done a capital stroke of business, for his house only stood him in a matter of twenty-seven thousand francs. The believers were taken aback by this peremptory decision on the part of their opponents. "Choisnel, Mademoiselle Cormon's notary, had not heard a word of marriage settlements," added the incredulous.

But on the twentieth day the unshaken believers enjoyed a signal victory over the doubters. M. Lepresseur, the Liberal notary, went to Mlle. Cormon's house, and the contract was signed. This was the first of many sacrifices which Rose made to her husband. The fact was that du Bousquier detested Choisnel; he blamed the notary for Mlle. Armande's refusal in the first place, as well as for his previous rejection by Mlle. Cormon, who, as he believed, had followed Mlle. Armande's example. He managed Mlle. Cormon so well, that she, noble-hearted woman, believing that she had misjudged her future husband, wished to make reparation for her doubts, and sacrificed her notary to her love. Still she submitted the contract to Choisnel, and he—a man worthy of Plutarch—defended Mlle. Cormon's interests by letter. This was the one cause of delay.

Mlle. Cormon received a good many anonymous letters. She was informed, to her no small astonishment, that Suzanne was as

honest a woman as she was herself; and that the seducer in the
false toupet could not possibly have played the part assigned to
him in such an adventure. Mlle. Cormon scorned anonymous letters; she wrote, however, to Suzanne with a view to gaining light
on the creeds of the Maternity Society. Suzanne probably had
heard of du Bousquier's approaching marriage; she confessed to
her stratagem, sent a thousand francs to the Fund, and damaged the
forage-contractor's character very considerably. Mlle. Cormon
called an extraordinary meeting of the Maternity Charity, and
the assembled matrons passed a resolution that henceforward the
Fund would give help after and not before misfortunes befell.

In spite of these proceedings, which supplied the town with
titbits of gossip to discuss, the banns were published at the church
and the mayor's office. It was Athanase's duty to make out the
needful documents. The betrothed bride had gone to the Prébaudet, a measure taken partly by way of conventional modesty,
partly for general security. Thither du Bousquier went every
morning, fortified by atrocious and sumptuous bouquets, returning in the evening to dinner.

At last, one gray rainy day in June, the wedding took place;
and Mlle. Cormon and the Sieur du Bousquier, as the incredulous
faction called him, were married at the parish church in the sight
of all Alençon. Bride and bridegroom drove to the mayor's office,
and afterward to the church, in a calèche—a splendid equipage
for Alençon. Du Bousquier had it sent privately from Paris. The
loss of the old cariole was a kind of calamity for the whole town.
The saddler of the Porte de Séez lost an income of fifty francs per
annum for repairs; he lifted up his voice and wept. With dismay
the town of Alençon beheld the luxury introduced by the Maison
Cormon; every one feared a rise of prices all round, an increase
of house rent, an invasion of Paris furniture. There were some
whose curiosity pricked them to the point of giving Jacquelin ten
sous for a nearer sight of so startling an innovation in a thrifty
province. A pair of Normandy horses likewise caused much concern.

"If we buy horses for ourselves in this way, we shall not sell them long to those that come to buy of us," said du Ronceret's set.

The reasoning seemed profound, stupid though it was, insofar as it prevented the district from securing a monopoly of money from outside. In the political economy of the provinces the wealth of nations consists not so much in a brisk circulation of money as in hoards of unproductive coin.

At length the old maid's fatal wish was fulfilled. Penelope sank under the attack of pleurisy contracted forty days before the wedding. Nothing could save her. Mme. Granson, Mariette, Mme. du Coudrai, Mme. du Ronceret—the whole town, in fact—noticed that the bride came into church with the left foot foremost, an omen all the more alarming because the word Left even then had acquired a political significance.

The officiating priest chanced to open the mass-book at the *De profundis*. And so the wedding passed off, amid presages so ominous, so gloomy, so overwhelming, that nobody was found to augur well of it. Things went from bad to worse. There was no attempt at a wedding party; the bride and bridegroom started out for the Prébaudet. Paris fashions were to supplant old customs! In the evening Alençon said its say as to all these absurdities; some persons had reckoned upon one of the usual provincial jollifications, which they considered they had a right to expect, and these spoke their minds pretty freely. But Mariette and Jacquelin had a merry wedding, and they alone in all Alençon gainsaid the dismal prophecies.

Du Bousquier wished to spend the profit made by the sale of his house on restoring and modernizing the Cormon place. He had quite made up his mind to stay for some months at the Prébaudet, whither he brought his Uncle de Sponde. The news spread dismay through Alençon; everyone felt that du Bousquier was about to draw the country into the downward path of domestic comfort. The foreboding grew to a fear one morning when du Bousquier drove over from the Prébaudet to superintend his workmen at the Val-Noble; and the townspeople beheld a tilbury, harnessed to a new horse, and René in livery by his master's side. Du Bousquier had invested his wife's savings in the Funds which stood at sixty-seven francs fifty centimes. This was the first act of the new administration. In the space of one year, by constantly speculating for a rise, he made for himself a fortune almost as considerable as his wife's. But something else happened in connection with this marriage to make it seem yet more inauspicious, and put all previous overwhelming portents and alarming innovations into the background.

It was the evening of the wedding day. Athanase and his mother were sitting in the salon by the little fire of brushwood (or *régalades*, as they say in the patois), which the servant had lighted after dinner.

"Well," said Mme. Granson, "we will go to President du Ronceret's tonight, now that we have no Mademoiselle Cormon. Goodness me! I shall never get used to calling her Madame du Bousquier; that name makes my lips sore."

Athanase looked at his mother with a sad constraint; he could not smile, and he wanted to acknowledge, as it were, the artless thoughtfulness which soothed the wound it could not heal.

"Mamma," he began—it was several years since he had used that word, and his tones were so gentle that they sounded like his child's voice—"mamma, dear, do not let us go out just yet; it is so nice here by the fire!"

It was a supreme cry of mortal anguish; the mother heard it but did not understand.

"Let us stay, child," she said. "I would certainly rather talk with you and listen to your plans than play at boston and perhaps lose my money."

"You are beautiful tonight; I like to look at you. And beside, the current of my thoughts is in harmony with this poor little room, where we have been through so much trouble—you and I."

"And there is still more in store for us, poor Athanase, until your work succeeds. For my own part, I am used to poverty; but, oh, my treasure, to look on and see your youth go by while you have no joy of it! Nothing but work in your life! That thought is like a disease for a mother. It tortures me night and morning.

I wake up to it. Ah, God in heaven! what have I done? What sin of mine is punished with this?"

She left her seat, took a little chair, and sat down beside Athanase, nestling close up to his side, till she could lay her head on her child's breast. Where a mother is truly a mother, the grace of love never dies. Athanase kissed her on the eyes, on the gray hair, on the forehead, with the reverent love that fain would lay the soul where the lips are laid.

"I shall never succeed," he said, trying to hide the fatal purpose which he was revolving in his mind.

"Pooh! you are not going to be discouraged? Mind can do all things, as you say. With ten bottles of ink, ten reams of paper, and a strong will, Luther turned Europe upside down. Well, and you are going to make a great name for yourself; you are going to use to good ends the powers which he used for evil. Did you not say so? Now *I* remember what you say, you see; I understand much more than you think; for you still lie so close under my heart, that your least little thought thrills through it, as your slightest movement did once."

"I shall not succeed *here*, you see, mamma, and I will not have you looking on while I am struggling and heartsore and in anguish. Mother, let me leave Alençon; I want to go through it all away from you."

"*I* want to be at your side always," she said proudly. "Suffering alone! *you* without your mother! your poor mother that would be your servant if need were, and keep out of sight for fear of injuring you, if you wished it, and never accuse you of pride! No, no, Athanase, we will never be parted!"

Athanase put his arms about her and held her with a passionate, tight clasp, as a dying man might cling to life.

"And yet I wish it," he said. "If we do not part, it is all over with me. The double pain—yours and mine—would kill me. It is better that I should live, is it not?"

Mme. Granson looked with haggard eyes into her son's face.

"So this is what you have been brooding over! They said truth. Then are you going away?"

"Yes."

"But you are not going until you have told me all about it, and
without giving me any warning? You must have some things to
take with you, and money. There are some louis d'ors sewed into
my petticoat; you must have them."

Athanase burst into tears.

"That was all that I wanted to tell you," he said after a while.
"Now, I will see you to the president's house."

Mother and son went out together. Athanase left Mme. Granson
at the door of the house where she was to spend the evening. He
looked long at the shafts of light that escaped through chinks in
the shutters. He stood there glued to the spot, while a quarter of
an hour went by, and it was with almost delirious joy that he
heard his mother say: "Grand independence of hearts."

"Poor mother, I have deceived her!" he exclaimed to himself as
he reached the river.

He came down to the tall poplar on the bank where he had
been wont to sit and meditate during the last six weeks. Two
big stones lay there; he had brought them himself for a seat. And
now, looking out over the fair landscape lying in the moonlight,
he passed in review all the so glorious future that should have
been his. He went through cities stirred to enthusiasm by his
name; he heard the cheers of crowded streets, breathed the incense
of banquets, looked with a great yearning over that life of his
dreams, rose uplifted and radiant in glorious triumph, raised a
statue to himself, summoned up all his illusions to bid them farewell in a last Olympian carouse. The magic could only last for a
little while; it fled, it had vanished forever. In that supreme moment he clung to his beautiful tree as if it had been a friend; then
he put the stones, one in either pocket, and buttoned his overcoat.
His hat he had purposely left at home. He went down the bank to
look for a deep spot which he had had in view for some time; and
slid in resolutely, trying to make as little noise as possible. There
was scarcely a sound.

When Mme. Granson came home about half-past nine that

night, the maid-of-all work said nothing of Athanase, but handed her a letter. Mme. Granson opened it and read—

"I have gone away, my kind mother; do not think hardly of me." That was all.

"A pretty thing he has done!" cried she. "And how about his linen and the money? But he will write, and I shall find him. The poor children always think themselves wiser than their fathers and mothers." And she went to bed with a quiet mind.

The Sarthe had risen with yesterday's rain. Fishers and anglers were prepared for this, for the swollen river washes down the eels from the little streams on its course. It so happened that an eel-catcher had set his lines over the very spot where poor Athanase had chosen to drown himself, thinking that he should never be heard of again; and next morning, about six o'clock, the man drew out the newly dead body.

One or two women among Mme. Granson's few friends went to prepare the poor widow with all possible care to receive the dreadful yield of the river. The news of the suicide, as might be expected, produced a tremendous sensation. Only last evening the poverty-stricken man of genius had not a single friend; the morning after his death scores of voices cried: "I would so willingly have helped him!" So easy is it to play a charitable part when no outlay is involved. The Chevalier de Valois, in the spirit of revenge, explained the suicide. It was a boyish, sincere, and noble passion for Mlle. Cormon that drove Athanase to take his own life. And when the chevalier had opened Mme. Granson's eyes, she saw a multitude of little things to confirm this view. The story grew touching; women cried over it.

Even before Mme. du Bousquier came back to town, her obliging friend, Mme. du Ronceret, went to fling a dead body down among the roses of her new-wedded happiness, to let her know what a love she had refused. Ever so gently Mme. President squeezed a shower of drops of wormwood over the honey of the first month of married life. And as Mme. du Bousquier returned, it so happened that she met Mme. Granson at the corner of the Val-Noble, and the look in the heartbroken mother's eyes cut her to the quick. It was a look from a woman dying of grief, a thousand curses gathered up into one glance of malediction, a thousand sparks in one gleam of hate. It frightened Mme. du Bousquier; it boded ill and invoked ill upon her.

Mme. Granson had belonged to the party most opposed to the curé; she was a bitter partisan of the priest of St. Leonard's; but on the very evening of the tragedy she thought of the rigid orthodoxy of her own party, and she shuddered. She herself laid her son in his shroud, thinking all the while of the Mother of the Saviour; then, with a soul quivering with agony, she betook herself to the house of the perjured priest. She found him busy, the humble good man, storing the hemp and flax which he gave to poor women and girls to spin, so that no worker should ever want work, a piece of wise charity which had saved more than one family that could not endure to beg. He left his hemp at once and brought his visitor into the dining room, where the stricken mother saw the frugality of her own housekeeping in the supper that stood waiting for the curé.

"Monsieur l'Abbé," she began. "I have come to entreat you——"

She burst into tears, and could not finish the sentence.

"I know why you have come," answered the holy man, "and I trust to you, madame, and to your relative Madame du Bousquier to make it right with his lordship at Séez. Yes, I will pray for your unhappy boy; yes, I will say masses; but we must avoid all scandal, we must give no occasion to ill-disposed people to gather together in the church. I myself, alone, and at night——"

"Yes, yes, as you wish, if only he is laid in consecrated ground!" she said, poor mother; and taking the priest's hand in hers, she kissed it.

And so, just before midnight, a bier was smuggled into the parish church. Four young men, Athanase's friends, carried it. There were a few little groups of veiled and black-clad women, Mme. Granson's friends, and some seven or eight lads that had been intimate with the dead. The bier was covered with a pall, torches were lit at the corners, and the curé read the office for the dead, with the help of one little choir boy whom he could trust. Then the suicide was buried, noiselessly, in a corner of the churchyard, and a dark wooden cross with no name upon it marked the grave for the mother. Athanase lived and died in the shadow.

Not a voice was raised against the curé; his lordship at Séez was silent; the mother's piety redeemed her son's impious deed.

Mme. Granson, by the riverside, whither she had gone to see the place where her son had drowned himself, saw a woman at some distance—a woman who came nearer, till she reached the fatal spot, and exclaimed—

"Then this is the place!"

One other woman in the world wept there as the mother was weeping, and that woman was Suzanne. She had heard of the tragedy on her arrival that morning at the Three Moors. If poor Athanase had been alive, she might have done what poor and generous people dream of doing, and the rich never think of putting in practice; she would have inclosed a thousand francs with the words: "Money lent by your father to a comrade who now repays you." During her journey Suzanne had thought of this angelic way of giving. She looked up and saw Mme. Granson.

"I loved him," she said; then she hurried away.

Suzanne, true to her nature, did not leave Alençon till she had changed the bride's wreath of orange flowers to water lilies. She was the first to assert that Mme. du Bousquier would be Mlle. Cormon as long as she lived. And with that one jibe she avenged both Athanase and the dear Chevalier de Valois.

Alençon beheld another and more piteous suicide. Athanase was promptly forgotten by a world that willingly, and indeed of necessity, forgets its dead as soon as possible; but the poor Chevalier's existence became a kind of death-in-life, a suicide continued morning after morning during fourteen years. Three months after du Bousquier's marriage, people remarked, not without astonishment, that the chevalier's linen was turning yellow, and his hair irregularly combed. M. de Valois was no more, for a disheveled M. de Valois could not be said to be himself. An ivory tooth here and there deserted from the ranks, and no student of human nature could discover to what corps they belonged, whether they were native or foreign, animal or vegetable; nor whether, finally, they had been extracted by old age, or were merely lying out of sight and out of mind in the chevalier's dressing-table drawer. His cravat was wisped, careless of elegance, into a cord. The Negroes' heads grew pale for lack of soap and water. The lines on the chevalier's face deepened into wrinkles and darkened as his complexion grew more and more like parchment; his neglected nails were sometimes adorned with an edge of black velvet. Grains of snuff lay scattered like autumn leaves in the furrows of his vest.

Hitherto the chevalier's nose had made a peculiarly elegant appearance in public; never had it been seen to distill a drop of amber, to let fall a dark wafer of moist rappee; but now, with a snuff-bedabbled border about the nostrils, and an unsightly stream taking advantage of the channel hollowed above the upper lip, that nose, which no longer took pains to please, revealed the immense trouble that the chevalier must have formerly taken with himself.

Latterly the chevalier's witticisms had been few and far between; the anecdotes went the way of the teeth, but his appetite continued as good as ever; out of the great shipwreck of his hopes he saved nothing but his digestion; and while he took his snuff feebly, he dispatched his dinner with an avidity alarming to behold. You may mark the extent of the havoc wrought in his ideas in the fact that his colloquies with the Princess Goritza grew less and less frequent. He came to Mlle. Armande's one day with a false calf in front of his shins. The bankruptcy of elegance was something painful, I protest; all Alençon was shocked by it. It scared society to see an elderly young man drop suddenly into his dotage, and from sheer depression of spirits pass from fifty to ninety years. And beside, he had betrayed his secret. He had been waiting and lying in wait for Mlle. Cormon. For ten long years, persevering sportsman that he was, he had been stalking the game, and then he had missed his shot.

He became a man of the worst character. The Liberal party laid all du Bousquier's foundlings on the chevalier's doorstep, while the Faubourg Saint-Germain of Alençon boastingly accepted them; laughed and cried: "The dear chevalier! What else could he do?" Saint-Germain pitied the chevalier, took him to its bosom, and smiled more than ever upon him; while an appalling amount of unpopularity was drawn down upon du Bousquier's head.

But the especial result of the marriage was a more sharply marked division of parties in Alençon. The Maison d'Esgrignon represented undiluted aristocracy; for the Troisvilles on their return joined the clique. The Maison Cormon, skillfully influenced by du Bousquier, was not exactly Liberal, nor yet resolutely Royalist, but of that unlucky shade of opinion which produced the 221 members, so soon as the political struggle took a definite shape, and the greatest, most august, and only real power of kingship came into collision with that most false, fickle, and tyrannical power which, when wielded by an elective body, is known as the power of Parliament.

The third salon, the salon du Ronceret, out-and-out Radical in its politics, was firmly but secretly allied with the Maison Cormon.

With the return from the Prébaudet, a life of continual suffering began for the Abbé de Sponde. He kept all that he endured locked within his soul, uttering not a word of complaint to his niece; but to Mlle. Armande he opened his heart, admitting that, taking one folly with another, he should have preferred the chevalier.

"Mademoiselle," the old abbé said as the thin tears fell from his faded old eyes, "the lime tree walk, where I have been used to meditate these fifty years, is gone. My dear lime trees have all been cut down! Just as I am nearing the end of my days the Republic has come back again in the shape of a horrible revolution in the house."

"Your niece must be forgiven," said the Chevalier de Valois.

"Republicanism is a youthful error; youth goes out to seek for liberty, and finds tyranny in its worst form—the tyranny of the impotent rabble. Your niece, poor thing, has not been punished by the thing wherein she sinned."

"What is to become of me in a house with naked women dancing all over the walls? Where shall I find the lime tree walks where I used to read my breviary?"

Like Kant, who lost the thread of his ideas when somebody cut down the fir tree on which he fixed his eyes as he meditated, the good abbé pacing up and down the shadowless alleys could not say his prayers with the same uplifting of soul. Du Bousquier had laid out an English garden!

"It looked nicer," Mme. du Bousquier said. Not that she really thought so, but the Abbé Couturier had authorized her to say and do a good many things that she might please her husband.

The Abbé de Sponde was the first to see the unhappiness which lay beneath the surface of his dear child's married life. The old dignified simplicity which ruled their way of living was gone; du Bousquier gave two balls every month in the course of the first winter. The venerable house—oh, to think of it!—echoed with the sound of violins and worldly gaiety. The abbé, on his knees, prayed while the merriment lasted.

The politics of the sober salon underwent a gradual change for the worse. The Abbé de Sponde divined du Bousquier; he shuddered at his nephew's dictatorial tone. He saw tears in his niece's eyes when the disposal of her fortune was taken out of her hands; her husband left her only the control of the linen, the table, and such things as fall to a woman's lot.

Does anyone know how much it costs to give up the delicious exercise of authority? If the triumph of will is one of the most intoxicating of the great man's joys, to have one's own way is the whole life of narrow natures. No one but a cabinet minister fallen into disgrace can sympathize with Mme. du Bousquier's bitter pain when she saw herself reduced to a cipher in her own house.

But these beginnings were the roses of life. Every concession was counseled by poor Rose's love for her husband, and at first du

Bousquier behaved admirably to his wife. He was very good to her; he brought forward sufficient reasons for every encroachment. The room, so long left empty, echoed with the voices of husband and wife in fireside talk. And so, for the first few years of married life, Mme. du Bousquier wore a face of content, and that little air of emancipation and mystery often seen in a young wife after a marriage of love. She had no more trouble with "heated blood." This countenance of hers routed scoffers, gave the lie to gossip concerning du Bousquier's impotence, and put observers of human nature at fault.

Rose-Marie-Victoire was so afraid lest she should lose her husband's affection or drive him from her side by setting her will against his, that she would have made any sacrifice, even of her uncle if need be. And the Abbé de Sponde, deceived by Mme. du Bousquier's poor foolish little joys, bore his own discomforts the more easily for the thought that his niece was happy.

At first Alençon shared this impression. But there was one man less easy to deceive than all the rest of Alençon put together. The Chevalier de Valois had taken refuge on the sacred mount of the most aristocratic section, and spent his time with the d'Esgrignons. The perpetrator of puns had been already brought low, and he meant to stab du Bousquier to the heart.

The poor abbé, knowing as he did the cowardliness of his niece's first and last love, shuddered as he guessed his nephew's hypocritical nature and the man's intrigues. Du Bousquier, be it said, put some constraint upon himself; he had an eye to the abbé's property, and had no wish to annoy his wife's uncle in any way, yet he dealt the old man his deathblow.

If you can translate the word Intolerance by Firmness of Principle; if you can forbear to condemn in the old Roman Catholic vicar-general that stoicism which Scott has taught us to revere in Jeanie Deans' puritan father; if, finally, you can recognize in the Roman church the nobility of a *Potius mori quam fœdari* which you admire in a Republican—then you can understand the anguish that rent the great Abbé de Sponde when he saw the apostate in his nephew's drawing room; when he was

compelled to meet the renegade, the backslider, the enemy of the
church, the aider and abettor of the Oath to the Constitution. It
was du Bousquier's private ambition to lord it over the countryside; and as a first proof of his power, he determined to reconcile
the officiating priest of St. Leonard's with the curé of Alençon.
He gained his object. His wife imagined that peace had been
made where the stern abbé saw no peace, but surrender of principle. M. de Sponde was left alone in the faith. The bishop came
to du Bousquier's house, and appeared satisfied with the cessation of hostilities. The Abbé François' goodness had conquered
everyone—everyone except the old Roman of the Roman church,
who might have cried with Cornélie: "Ah, God! what virtues you
make me hate!" The Abbé de Sponde died when orthodoxy ex-
pired in the diocese.

In 1819 the Abbé de Sponde's property raised Mme. du Bousquier's income from land to twenty-five thousand livres without
counting the Prébaudet or the house in the Val-Noble. About the
same time du Bousquier returned the amount of his wife's savings (which she had made over to him) and instructed her to
invest the money in purchases of land near the Prébaudet, so that
the estate, including the Abbé de Sponde's adjoining property,
was one of the largest in the department. As for du Bousquier,
he invested his money with the Kellers, and made a journey to
Paris four times a year. Nobody knew the exact amount of his
private fortune, but at this time he was supposed to be one of
the wealthiest men in the department of the Orne. A dexterous
man, and the permanent candidate of the Liberal party, he always
lost his election by seven or eight votes under the Restoration.
Ostensibly he repudiated his connection with the Liberals, offering himself as a Ministerial-Royalist candidate; but although he
succeeded in gaining the support of the Congrégation and of the
magistrature, the repugnance of the administration was too strong
to be overcome.

Then the rabid Republican, frantic with ambition, conceived
the idea of beginning a struggle with the royalism and aristocracy
of the country, just as they were carrying all before them. He

gained the support of the clergy by an appearance of piety very skillfully kept up; always going with his wife to mass, giving money to the convents, and supporting the confraternity of the Sacred Heart; and whenever a dispute arose between the clergy and the town, or the department, or the State, he was very careful to take the clerical side. And so, while secretly supported by the Liberals, he gained the influence of the church; and as a Constitutional-Royalist kept close beside the aristocratic section, the better to ruin it. And ruin it he did. He brought about an industrial revolution; and his detestation of certain families on the highroad to Brittany rapidly increased the material prosperity of the province.

And so he paved the way for his revenge upon the *gens à châteaux* in general, and the d'Esgrignons in particular; some day, not so very far distant, he would plunge a poisoned blade into the very heart of the clique. He found capital to revive the manufacture of point d'Alençon and to increase the linen trade. Alençon began to spin its own flax by machinery. And while his name was associated with all these interests, and written in the hearts of the masses, while he did all that Royalty left undone, du Bousquier risked not a centime of his own. With his means, he could afford to wait while enterprising men with little capital were obliged to give up and leave the results of their labors to luckier successors. He posed as a banker. A Laffitte on a small scale, he became a sleeping partner in all new inventions, taking security for his money. And as a public benefactor he did remarkably well for himself. He was a promoter of insurance companies, a patron of new public conveyances; he got up memorials for necessary roads and bridges. The authorities, being left behind in this way, regarded this activity in the light of an encroachment; they blundered, and put themselves into the wrong, for the prefecture was obliged to give way for the good of the country.

Du Bousquier embittered the provincial noblesse against the court nobles and the peerage. He helped, in short, to bring it to pass that a very large body of Constitutional-Royalists supported the *Journal des Débats* and M. de Chateaubriand in a contest with the throne. It was an ungrateful opposition based on ignoble motives which contributed to bring about the triumph of the bourgeoisie and the press in 1830. Wherefore du Bousquier, like those whom he represented, had the pleasure of watching a funeral procession of Royalty* pass through their district without a single demonstration of sympathy for a population alienated from them in ways so numerous that they cannot be indicated here.

Then the old Republican, with all that weight of masses on his conscience, hauled down the white flag above the town hall amid the applause of the people. For fifteen years he had acted a part to satisfy his vendetta, and no man in France beholding the new throne raised in August, 1830, could feel more intoxicated than he with the joy of revenge. For him, the succession of the younger branch meant the triumph of the Revolution; for him, the hoisting of the tricolor flag was the resurrection of the Mountain; and *this* time the nobles should be brought low by a surer method than the guillotine, in that its action should be less violent. A peerage for life only; a National Guard which stretches the marquis and the grocer from the corner store on the same camp bed; the abolition of entail demanded by a bourgeois barrister; a Catholic church deprived of its supremacy; in short, all the legislative inventions of August, 1830, simply meant for du Bousquier the principles of 1793 carried out in a more ingenious manner.

Du Bousquier has been receiver-general of taxes since 1830. He relied for success upon his old connections with Égalité Orléans (father of Louis Philippe) and M. de Folmon, steward of the dowager duchess. He is supposed to have an income of eighty thousand livres. In the eyes of his fellow countrymen, *Monsieur* du Bousquier is a man of substance, honorable, upright, obliging, unswerving in his principles. To him, Alençon owes her participation in the industrial movement which makes her, as it were, the first link in a chain which some day perhaps may bind Brittany to the state of things which we nickname "modern civilization." In 1816 Alençon boasted but two carriages, properly

* Charles X on his way to England. *Tr.*

speaking; ten years afterward, calèches, coupés, landaus, cabri-
olets, and tilburies were rolling about the streets without causing
any astonishment. At first the townsmen and landowners were
alarmed by the rise of prices, afterward they discovered that the
increased expenditure produced a corresponding increase in their
incomes.

Du Ronceret's prophetic words: "Du Bousquier is a very strong
man," were now taken up by the country. But, unfortunately for
du Bousquier's wife, the remark is a shocking misnomer. Du
Bousquier, the husband, is a very different person from du Bousquier the public man and politician. The great citizen, so liberal
in his opinions, so easy-humored, so full of love for his country,
is a despot at home, and has not a particle of love for his wife.
The Cromwell of the Val-Noble is profoundly astute, hypocritical, and crafty; he behaves to those of his own household as he
behaved to the aristocrats on whom he fawned, until he could cut
their throats. Like his friend Bernadotte, he has an iron hand in
a velvet glove. His wife gave him no children. Suzanne's epigram
and the Chevalier de Valois' insinuations were justified; but the
Liberals and Constitutional-Royalists among the townspeople,
the little squires, the magistrature, and the "clericals" (as the
Constitutionnel used to say), all threw the blame upon Mme. du
Bousquier. M. du Bousquier had married such an elderly wife,
they said; and beside, how lucky it was for her, poor thing, for
at her age bearing a child meant such a risk. If, in periodically
recurrent despair, Mme. du Bousquier confided her troubles with
tears to Mme. du Coudrai or Mme. du Ronceret:

"Why you must be mad, dear!" those ladies would reply. "You
do not know what you want; a child would be the death of you."

Men like M. du Coudrai, who followed du Bousquier's lead because they fastened their hopes to his success, would prompt their
wives to sing du Bousquier's praises; and Rose must listen to
speeches that wounded like a stab.

"You are very fortunate, dear, to have such a capable husband;
some men have no energy, and can neither manage their own

property nor bring up their children; you are spared these troubles."

Or, "Your husband is making you queen of the district, fair lady. *He* will never leave you at a loss; he does everything in Alençon."

"But I should like him to take less trouble for the public and rather——"

"My dear Mme. du Bousquier, you are very hard to please; all the women envy you your husband."

Unjustly treated by a world which condemned her without a hearing, she found ample scope for the exercise of Christian virtues in her inner life. She who lived in tears always turned a serene face upon the world. For her, pious soul, was there not sin in the thought which was always pecking at her heart—"I loved the Chevalier de Valois, and I am du Bousquier's wife?" Athanase's love rose up like a remorse to haunt her dreams.

The Chevalier de Valois was the malignant artificer of her misfortune. He had it on his mind to snatch his opportunity and undeceive Mme. du Bousquier as to one of her articles of faith; for the chevalier, a man of experience, saw through du Bousquier the married man, as he had seen through du Bousquier the bachelor. But it was not easy to take the astute Republican by surprise. His salon, naturally, was closed to the Chevalier de Valois, as to all others who discontinued their visits to the Maison Cormon at the time of his marriage. And beside, du Bousquier was above the reach of ridicule; he possessed an immense fortune, he was king of Alençon; and as for his wife, he cared about her much as Richard III might have cared for the loss of the horse with which he thought to win the battle. To please her husband, Mme. du Bousquier had broken with the Maison d'Esgrignon, but sometimes, when he was away at Paris for a few days, she paid Mlle. Armande a visit.

Two years after Mme. du Bousquier's marriage, just at the time of the abbé's death, Mlle. Armande went up to her as she came out of church. Both women had been to St. Leonard's to hear a mourning mass said for M. de Sponde; and Mlle. Armande, a generous-natured woman, thinking that she ought to try to comfort the weeping heiress, walked with her as far as the parade. From the parade, still talking of the beloved and lost, they came to the forbidden Hôtel d'Esgrignon, and Mlle. Armande drew Mme. du Bousquier into the house by the charm of her talk. Perhaps the poor brokenhearted woman loved to speak of her uncle with someone whom her uncle had loved so well. And beside, she wished to receive the old marquis' greetings after an interval of nearly three years. It was half-past one o'clock; the Chevalier de Valois had come to dinner, and with a bow he held out both hands.

"Ah! well, dear, good, and well-beloved lady," he said tremulously, "*we* have lost our sainted friend. Your mourning is ours. Yes; your loss is felt as deeply here as under your own roof—more deeply," he added, alluding to du Bousquier.

A funeral oration followed, to which every one contributed his phrase; then the chevalier, gallantly taking the lady's hand, drew it under his arm, pressed it in the most adorable way, and led her aside into the embrasure of a window.

"You are happy, at any rate?" he asked with a fatherly tone in his voice.

"Yes," she said, lowering her eyes.

Hearing that "Yes," Mme. de Troisville (daughter of the Princess Scherbelloff) and the old Marquise de Castéran came up; Mlle. Armande also joined them, and the group took a turn in the garden till dinner should be ready. Mme. du Bousquier was so stupid with grief that she did not notice that a little conspiracy of curiosity was on foot among the ladies.

"We have her here, let us find out the answer to the riddle," the glances exchanged among them seemed to say.

"You should have children to make your happiness complete," began Mlle. Armande, "a fine boy like my nephew now—"

Tears came to Mme. du Bousquier's eyes.

"I have heard it said that it was entirely your own fault if you had none," said the chevalier, "that you were afraid of the risk."

"*I!*" she cried, innocently; "I would endure a hundred years in hell to have a child."

The subject thus broached, Mme. la Vicomtesse de Troisville and the dowager Marquise de Castéran steered the conversation with such exceeding tact that they entangled poor Rose until, all unsuspectingly, she revealed the secrets of her married life. Mlle. Armande laid her hand on the chevalier's arm, and they left the three matrons to talk confidentially. Then Mme. du Bousquier's mind was disabused with regard to the deception of her marriage; and as she was still "a natural," she amused her confidantes with her irresistible naïveté. Before long the whole town was in the secret of du Bousquier's maneuvers, and knew that Mlle. Cormon's marriage was a mockery; but after the first burst of laughter, Mme. du Bousquier gained the esteem and sympathy of every woman in it. While Mlle. Cormon rushed unsuccessfully at opportunities of establishing herself, everyone had laughed; but people admired her when they knew the position in which she was placed by the severity of her religious principles. "Poor, dear Mademoiselle Cormon!" was replaced by "poor Madame du Bousquier!"

In this way the chevalier made du Bousquier both ridiculous and very unpopular for a while, but the ridicule died down with time; the slander languished when everybody had cut his joke; and beside, it seemed to many persons that the mute Republican had a right to retire at the age of fifty-seven. But if du Bousquier previously hated the Maison d'Esgrignon, this incident so increased his rancor that he was pitiless afterward in the day of vengeance. Mme. du Bousquier received orders never to set foot in that house again; and by way of reprisals, he inserted the following paragraph in the *Orne Courier*, his own new paper:

A REWARD of Funds to bring in a thousand francs will be paid to any person who shall prove that one M. de Pombreton existed either before or after the Emigration.

Though Mme. du Bousquier's happiness was essentially negative, she saw that her marriage had its advantages. Was it not better to take an interest in the most remarkable man in the place than to live alone? After all, du Bousquier was better than the dogs, cats, and canaries on which old maids center their affections; and his feeling for his wife was something more genuine and disinterested than the attachment of servants, confessors, and legacy hunters. At a still later period she looked upon her husband as an instrument in God's hands to punish her for the innumerable sins which she discovered in her desires for marriage; she regarded herself as justly rewarded for the misery which she had brought on Mme. Granson, and for hastening her own uncle's end. She felt the strongest aversion for the conduct and opinions of the man she had married, and yet it was her duty to take a tender interest in him; and if, as often happened, du Bousquier ate her preserves, or thought that the dinner was good, she was in the seventh heaven. She saw that his comfort was secured even in the smallest details.

Did du Bousquier go on a journey, she fidgeted over his traveling cloak and his linen; she took the most minute precautions for his material comfort. If he was going over to the Prébaudet, she began to consult the weatherglass twenty-four hours beforehand. A sleeping dog has eyes and ears for his master, and so it was with Mme. du Bousquier; she used to watch the expression of her husband's face to read his wishes. And if that burly personage, vanquished by duty-prescribed love, caught her by the waist and kissed her on the forehead, exclaiming: "You are a good woman!" tears of joy filled the poor creature's eyes. It is probable that du Bousquier felt it incumbent upon him to make compensations which won Rose-Marie-Victoire's respect; for the church does not require that an assumption of wifely devotion should be carried quite so far as Mme. du Bousquier thought necessary. And yet when she listened to the rancorous talk of men who took Constitutional Royalism as a cloak for their real opinions, the woman of saintly life uttered not a word. She foresaw the downfall of the church, and shuddered. Very occasionally she would hazard some foolish remark, promptly cut in two by a look from du Bousquier. The timid sheep walked in the way marked out by the shepherd; never leaving the bosom of the church, practicing austerities, without a thought of the devil, his pomps and works.

And so, within herself, she united the purest Christian virtues, and du Bousquier truly was one of the luckiest men in the kingdom of France and Navarre.

"She will be a simpleton till her last sigh," said the cruel ex-registrar (now cashiered). But, all the same, he dined at her table twice a week.

The story would be singularly incomplete if it omitted to mention a last coincidence: the Chevalier de Valois and Suzanne's mother died at the same time.

The chevalier died with the Monarchy in August, 1830. He went to Nonancourt to join the funeral procession; piously making one of the King's escort to Cherbourg, with the Troisvilles, Castérans, d'Esgrignons, Verneuils, and the rest. He had brought with him his little hoard of savings and the principal which brought him in his annual income, some fifty thousand francs in all, which he offered to a faithful friend of the elder branch to convey to his majesty. His own death was very near, he said; the money had come to him through the King's bounty; and, after all, the property of the last of the Valois belonged to the Crown. History does not say whether the chevalier's fervent zeal overcame the repugnance of the Bourbon who left his fair kingdom of France without taking one centime into exile; but the King surely must have been touched by the old noble's devotion; and this much is at least certain—Césarine, M. de Valois' universal legatee, inherited scarcely six hundred livres of income at his death. The chevalier came back to Alençon, brokenhearted and spent with the fatigue of the journey, to die just as Charles X set foot on foreign soil.

Mme. du Val-Noble and her journalist protector, fearing reprisals from the Liberals, were glad of an excuse to return incognito to the village where the old mother died. Suzanne attended the sale of the chevalier's furniture to buy some relic of her first good friend, and ran up the price of the snuffbox to the enormous amount of a thousand francs. The Princess Goritza's portrait alone was worth that sum. Two years afterward, a young man of fashion, struck with its marvelous workmanship, obtained it of

Suzanne for his collection of fine eighteenth-century snuffboxes; and so the delicate toy which had been the confidante of the most courtly of love affairs, and the delight of an old age till its very end, is now brought into the semipublicity of a collection. If the dead could know what is done after they are gone, there would be a flush at this moment on the chevalier's left cheek.

If this history should inspire owners of sacred relics with a holy fear, and set them drafting codicils to provide for the fate of such precious souvenirs of a happiness now no more, by giving them into sympathetic hands; even so an enormous service would have been rendered to the chivalrous and sentimental section of the public; but it contains another and a much more exalted moral. Does it not show that a new branch of education is needed? Is it not an appeal to the so enlightened solicitude of Ministers of Public Instruction to create chairs of anthropology, a science in which Germany is outstripping us?

Modern myths are even less understood of the people than ancient myths, eaten up with myths though we may be. Fables crowd in upon us on every side, allegory is pressed into service on all occasions to explain everything. If fables are the torches of history, as the humanist school maintains, they may be a means of securing empires from revolution, if only professors of history will undertake that their interpretations thereof shall permeate the masses in the departments. If Mlle. Cormon had had some knowledge of literature; if there had been a professor of anthropology in the department of the Orne; if (a final if) she had read her Ariosto, would the appalling misfortune of her marriage have befallen her? She would, perhaps, have found out for herself why the Italian poet makes his heroine Angelica prefer Medoro (a suave Chevalier de Valois) to Orlando, who had lost his mare, and could do nothing but work himself into a fury.* Might not Medoro be taken as an allegorical figure as the courtier of woman's sovereignty, whereas Orlando is revolution personified, an undisciplined, furious, purely destructive force, incapable of pro-

* Aristo's *Orlando Furioso. Tr.*

ducing anything? This is the opinion of one of M. Ballanche's pupils; we publish it, declining all responsibility.

As for the tiny Negroes' heads, no information of any kind concerning them is forthcoming. Mme. du Val-Noble you may see any day at the opera. Thanks to the primary education given to her by the Chevalier de Valois, she looks almost like a woman who makes a necessity of virtue, while in truth she only exists by virtue of necessity.

Mme. du Bousquier is still living, which is to say, is it not, that her troubles are not yet over? At sixty, when women can permit themselves to make admissions, talking confidentially to Mme. du Coudrai, whose husband was reinstated in August, 1830, she said that the thought that she must die without knowing what it was to be a wife and mother was more than she could bear.

Happiness in Crime

JULES BARBEY D'AUREVILLY

Jules Barbey D'Aurevilly

J ULES BARBEY D'AUREVILLY (1808-1888) was a poor, hard-
worked, eccentric and rather solitary man. He lived so long and
survived so many changes in politics and literature that he seemed
to his fellow writers of Paris, where he chiefly lived, to go on and
on like time itself. He had, however, two good causes for feeling
and showing pride. One was his distinguished birth, for he came
of an authentically noble though obscure family of Norman landowners. Another was his mastery of a fine elaborate prose, which
in turn reflected his entire style of life. Like other writers of the
time, he defied the growing sobriety of male attire by wearing
fancy dress. Sometimes he appeared in the lace and ruffles of an
eighteenth-century gentleman, sometimes in the burnous of an
Arab chieftain. There is an old photograph of him in his burnous,
which Peter Quennell describes as follows: "From beneath its
peaked hood, his eyes flash out at the photographer cold and
bright and deep-set. His nose is a curved beak, between sharp
imperious lines. His long mustaches are pulled down to form a
haughty circumflex—mustaches that look as if they should be
either gnawed or twisted. . . ."

A youth when French Romanticism was in its prime, Barbey
continued to bear its chalice proudly through a host of foes. The
rise of science, skepticism, democracy and the naturalistic novel
only intensified his faith in ideal beauty, the aristocratic principle

343

and the Church. In respect to his religion, however, he was, as Sainte-Beuve said of Chateaubriand, "an Epicurean Catholic," and more of a Satanist than a Theist. His special "saint" was the very secular George Brummel, founder of nineteenth-century dandyism; and one of Barbey's principal efforts, a book called *Du Dandyism et de Georges Brummel*, turned that Englishman's code into a veritable cult of self, a proud philosophy of personal freedom. Such a faith, Barbey wrote, "may outlast the search for happiness in others, in women for example . . . may outlast, indeed, the entirety of what are called illusions." Dandyism aspires to set up nothing less than "a new type of aristocracy . . . based on the most precious, the most indestructible, of the human faculties and on divine gifts that labor and wealth have no power of conferring." In short, the true dandy, as distinguished from the mere fop, loves and cultivates in himself "whatever is best in human pride."

Barbey's was a genuine if obviously limited faith and he was a fine though minor writer. A work of his old age (1874), *Happiness in Crime (Le Bonheur dans le crime)* is from the best-known of his volumes, *Les Diaboliques*. It is notable for the consistency with which it pursues its amoral theme. Crime here fails to issue in the usual remorse and punishment, and the story is without any denouement save that supplied by the doctor-narrator's vivid concluding reflections. As he says, "When I looked at these happy beings, I understood the seriousness of the joke of my old comrade Broussais, when he said about conscience: 'I have been dissecting for thirty years and have never found a trace of that little beast.' " Like Broussais's remark, *Happiness in Crime* is a kind of serious joke.

Happiness in Crime

JULES BARBEY D'AUREVILLY

"In these pleasant days, when a man relates a true story it is to be supposed that the Devil dictated it."

ONE MORNING last autumn, I was walking in the zoological gardens with Doctor Torty, one of my oldest friends. When I was still a child, Doctor Torty was practicing in the town of V., but after thirty years of that agreeable exercise and when all his old patients were dead—his *tenants*, as he called them, who brought him more than the tenants do to their landlords in the best part of Normandy—he had not cared to look for any others, but, being already old and glad to be independent, like a horse that has always felt the bit, and has ended by breaking it, he came to amuse himself in Paris, and lived in the neighborhood of the Jardin des Plantes—in the rue Cuvier, I think. He never practiced medicine then, except for his own pleasure, but that was very often, for he was a doctor to the finger tips, clever in his profession and a great observer in many other cases besides physiological or pathological ones.

Have you ever met Doctor Torty? He was one of those bold and vigorous minds that you might call "unmittened," for the good and proverbial reason that "a cat in mittens catches no mice," and this wary old mouser had caught a good many, and wanted to catch still more. I liked him very much, and, I think for those sides of his character which most displeased others. In fact, few people did like this brusque and original old doctor when they were well, but, when once they were ill, those who disliked him the most salaamed to him as the savages did to Robinson Crusoe's gun, but not for the same reason—because it could kill them—but quite a contrary reason—because he could cure them.

Had it not been for that important consideration, the Doctor would never have made twenty thousand francs a year in a small, devout, and aristocratic town, the chief people of which would have shown him the outside of their carriage gates if they had been prompted solely by their opinions and antipathies. He reasoned about this very calmly, and even joked about it, during his thirty years' "lease" at V. "They had," he said, "to choose between me and Extreme Unction, and, devout as they were, they preferred me to the sacramental oil."

As you see, the Doctor did not trouble to restrain himself. His wit was rather profane. He was a true disciple of Cabanis in medical philosophy, and, like his old comrade Chaussier belonged to that terrible school of materialistic doctors, and, like Dubois— the first one—was distinguished by a cynical contempt for all things, and called duchesses, and the maids of honor of the Empress, "my good woman"—treating them with no more respect than if they had been fishwives.

To give you an idea of his cynical humor, I may mention that he said one night at the club, as he gazed at the table with its snowy white napery, laid with covers for a hundred and twenty guests: "I made them all!"

Moses could not have been prouder when he showed the rod with which he had struck the rock.

But what could you expect, Madame? He had not the bump of respect, and even declared that where that bump existed on other men's heads, there was a hole in his.

He was old, being more than seventy, but square-built, robust, and wiry, with a sarcastic face under his light chestnut, shiny, short wig, and penetrating eyes that never needed glasses. He dressed nearly always in gray, or that shade of brown which was long called "Moscow smoke," and looked very unlike the Paris doctors, stiff in their white cravats like their dead patients in their winding sheets.

He was quite a different sort of man. His doeskin gloves and
thick-soled boots gave him something of the look of a horseman—
as indeed he was, for he had ridden every day for thirty years
over roads which would have broken a centaur in half. His strong
legs, which had never felt a twinge of rheumatism, were bowed
like a postilion's. He might have been called a French provincial
Leatherstocking, and, like Fenimore Cooper's hero, he laughed at
the laws of society and had not replaced them by the idea of God.
Such a close observer could not fail to be a misanthrope—and he
was. But he was not a misanthrope like Alceste.* He never displayed any virtuous indignation, nor was he ever angry. No, he
simply despised man as quietly as he took a pinch of snuff, and had
not even as much pleasure in the scorn as he had in the pinch.
Such was, in short, the character of Doctor Torty, with whom
I was then walking.

The day was one of those bright, clear autumn days which
prevent the swallows from leaving. Noon had just sounded from
Notre-Dame, and the deep boom of the bell sounded in long
trills over the river. The red foliage of the trees had shaken off
the blue fog which envelops them on October mornings, and the
sun was agreeably warm on our backs, as the Doctor and I
stopped to look at the famous black panther, which died the
following winter of lung disease—just as though it had been a
young girl.

All round us was the usual public of the zoological gardens,
soldiers and nursemaids, who love to stroll round the cages and
throw nutshells and orange peel at the sleepy animals. The
panther, before whose cage we had arrived, was of that particular
species which comes from the island of Java, the country where
nature is most luxuriant, and seems itself like some great tigress
untamable by man. In Java the flowers have more brilliancy and
perfume, the fruits more taste, the animals more beauty and
strength, than in any other country in the world.

Lying gracefully with its paws stretched out in front, its head
up, and its emerald eyes motionless, the panther was a splendid
specimen of the savage products of the country. Not a touch of

* In Molière's comedy Le Misanthrope. Ed.

yellow sullied its black velvet skin—of a blackness so deep and dull that the sunlight was absorbed by it as water is absorbed by a sponge. When you turned from this ideal form of supple beauty— of terrific force in repose—of silent and royal disdain—to the human creatures who were timidly gazing at it, open-eyed and open-mouthed, it was not the human beings who had the superiority over the animal. The latter was so much the superior that the comparison was humiliating.

I had just whispered this remark to the Doctor, when two persons made their way through the group, and planted themselves just in front of the panther.

"Yes," said the Doctor, "but look now, and you will see that the equilibrium between the species is restored."

They were a man and a woman, both tall, and I guessed at a glance that they both belonged to the upper ranks of society. Neither was young, but both were handsome. The man might have been forty-seven or more, and the woman upwards of forty. They had therefore, as sailors say, "crossed the line"—that fatal line more terrible than the equator. But they appeared to care very little, and showed no signs of melancholy.

The man, in a tightly fitting black coat, resembled, in his haughty but effeminate bearing, one of the *minions* of Henry III, and, to make the resemblance more complete, he wore his hair short, and in his ears were dark-blue sapphire earrings, which reminded one of the two emeralds which Sbogar wore in the same place. Except for this ridiculous detail—as the world would have called it—and which showed a disdain for the tastes and opinions of the time, he was simply a dandy in the sense in which Brummell understood the word, that is to "be not remarkable," and he would have passed unnoticed had it not been for the woman he had on his arm.

In fact, this woman attracted more attention than the man who accompanied her, and held it longer. She was as tall as he was. Her head was nearly on a level with his. And as she was dressed entirely in black, she made one think of the black Isis of the Egyptian Museum, by her shape, her mysterious pride, and her strength. For, strange to say, in this handsome couple it was the woman who had the muscles, and the man who possessed the nerves.

I could see only her profile, but the profile is either the greatest peril of beauty or its most astonishing manifestation. Never had I seen a purer or more noble outline. Of her eyes I could not judge, fixed as they were upon the panther, which, no doubt, received therefrom a magnetic and disagreeable impression, for, though motionless before, it became yet more rigid, and, without moving its head or even its whiskers, it slowly dropped its eyelids over its emerald eyes—as a cat will do when dazzled by a strong light—and seemed unable to meet the fixed glance of the woman.

"Ah, ah! Panther against panther," the Doctor murmured in my ear; "but the satin is stronger than the velvet."

The satin was the woman, who wore a dress of that gleaming material—a dress with a long train. The Doctor was right. Black, supple, as powerfully muscular, and as royal in bearing—quite as beautiful in her own way, and with a charm still more disquieting —this woman, this unknown person, resembled a human panther opposed to the brute panther whom she had conquered; and the animal no doubt felt it when it had closed its eyes.

But the woman—if she was one—was not content with her triumph. She was wanting in generosity. She wished that her rival should see that it was humiliated, and should open its eyes on purpose to see it. Without saying a word, she undid the twelve buttons of the violet glove which fitted so closely her magnificent arm, took off the glove, and, daringly putting her hand between the bars of the cage, flicked the panther's muzzle with it. The panther made but one movement—but such a movement!—and snapped its teeth like lightning. A cry went up from the little group around. We thought her hand must be bitten off at the wrist. But it was only the glove. The panther had swallowed it. The terrible beast, deeply insulted, had opened its eyes to their full size, and its nostrils quivered with anger.

"Fool!" said the man, seizing the beautiful hand which had just escaped this terrible bite.

You know how that word "fool" is sometimes said. That was how he said it, as he passionately kissed her hand.

And as he was on the same side as we were, she turned slightly to look at him, and I saw her eyes—eyes which fascinated tigers, and were at present fascinated by eyes which were two large black diamonds expressing all the pride of life, and adoration of love.

Those eyes were, and told, a whole poem. The man had not released the arm which had just felt the feverish breath of the panther, and, holding it to his heart, led the woman to the broad walk of the garden, indifferent to the murmurs and exclamations of the people—still somewhat excited by the incident—and walked quietly along it. They passed close to the Doctor and me, but their faces were turned towards each other, and they were pressing so close together that it seemed as though they wished to make one body of the two, and see nothing but themselves. They were both, as one could see when they passed, of those superior beings who do not even perceive that their feet touch the ground, and who pass through the world in a cloud, like the immortals of Homer.

Such people are rare in Paris, and we therefore stopped to watch this splendid couple—the woman allowing the long train to trail in the dust, like a peacock disdainful of its plumage.

They looked superb as they passed along, under the rays of the midday sun, in all the majesty of their mutual embrace. We watched them to the gate, where a carriage, the horses resplendent in plated harness, was waiting for them.

"They forget the universe," I said to the Doctor.

"Oh, a lot they care for the universe!" he replied in his sarcastic voice. "They see nothing in all creation, and, what is worse, they even pass close to their doctor without noticing him."

"What, you, Doctor!" I cried. "Then you can tell me who they are, my dear Doctor."

The Doctor made a long pause, in order to produce an effect—the cunning old man!

"Well!" he said quietly, "they are Philemon and Baucis—that's all."

"Rather a proud-looking Philemon and Baucis," I replied, "and not much resembling those of antiquity. But that is not their name, Doctor. What *is* their name?"

"What!" replied the Doctor; "in the fashionable society in which you mix, you have never heard the Comte and Comtesse Serlon de Savigny held up as the models of conjugal love?"

"No," I replied; "in the fashionable world in which I mix, we do not talk much about conjugal love."

"Hum! Hum! that is very probable," said the Doctor—more in answer to his own thoughts than to mine. "In that society—which is also theirs—one passes over a good many things that are more or less proper. But, besides having another reason for not going into society, they live nearly all the year in their old château at Savigny, in the Cotentin. Some reports about them circulated in the Faubourg Saint-Germain, but as the nobility all hang together, they are never mentioned there now."

"What were these reports? You interest me greatly, Doctor. The château of Savigny is not very far from the town of V., where you used to practice, Doctor, so you must know something about them."

"Oh, those reports!" said the Doctor, pensively taking a pinch of snuff. "They were believed to be false. It all passed over. But although marriages of inclination, and the happiness which springs from them, are the ideals of all mothers in the country, who are generally virtuous and romantic, they did not talk very much—at least those I knew—to their daughters about this particular one."

"And yet you called them Philemon and Baucis, Doctor."

"Baucis! Baucis! Hum!" interrupted Doctor Torty, crooking his first finger and passing it over his long parrot-like nose (one of his gestures); "don't you think that woman looks less like Baucis than Lady Macbeth?"

"Doctor—my dear and adorable Doctor," I continued as coax-

ingly as I could, "you will tell me all you know about the Comte
and Comtesse de Savigny—won't you?"

"The doctor is the confessor in these times," said the Doctor,
in a mock-serious manner. "He has replaced the priest, sir, and,
like the priest, is obliged to keep the secrets of confession."

He looked at me mischievously, for he knew my respect and
regard for the Catholic religion, of which he was the enemy. He
winked, and thought he had caught me.

"And he is going to keep it—as the priest does!" he cried with
a cynical laugh. "Come along with me where we can talk."

He led me to the broad walk which runs between the zoological
gardens and the Boulevard de l'Hôpital; we sat down on one of
the benches, and he began.

"My dear fellow, you must search pretty deeply for the beginning of my story, as you would for a bullet over which the flesh
has formed; for oblivion is like the flesh of living things which
forms over events and prevents you from seeing anything, or even
suspecting the place after a certain time.

"It was in the first years after the Restoration. A regiment of
the Guards passed through the town of V., and, being obliged,
for some military reason or other, to stay there two days, the
officers determined to give an assault of arms in honor of the
town. As a matter of fact, the town fully deserved that the officers of the Guards should do it that honor. It was, as they said
then, more royalist than the King. Considering its size (for it
contained barely five or six thousand souls), it teemed with
nobility. More than thirty young men belonging to the best
families of the place were then serving either in the Life Guards
or the Prince's Regiment, and the officers then passing through V.
knew them nearly all. But the principal reason which induced the
officers to give this assault of arms was the fighting reputation of
V. The Revolution of 1789 had taken away from the nobles the
right to wear their swords, but at V. they proved that if they no
longer wore them, they knew how to use them.

"The assault given by the officers was a brilliant success.

"It brought together all the best swordsmen of the district, and even some amateurs who belonged to a younger generation, and who had not much cultivated, as they did in former days, an art so difficult and complicated as fencing; and all showed such enthusiasm for the glorious weapon of our forefathers that an old fencing instructor of the regiment, who had served his time three or four times over, and whose arm was covered with good-conduct stripes, thought that it would be a good idea to open a school of arms at V. and end his days there; and the Colonel, to whom he broached the subject, approved of the plan, and gave him his discharge.

"The idea was quite a stroke of genius on the part of the fencing master, whose name was Stassin, but who was more generally known as 'Old Straight-thrust.'

"For a long time past there had been no properly conducted fencing school at V. This had long been a subject of regret amongst the nobility, who were obliged to teach their own sons, or else have recourse to some friend who had left the army, and who was perhaps not a good swordsman, or did not know how to teach.

"The inhabitants of V. pride themselves on being very particular. They really possessed the sacred fire. It was not enough to be able to kill their man—they wished to kill him neatly and scientifically according to the principles of art. They were most particular about a graceful attitude, and had a profound contempt for those strong but awkward swordsmen who might be dangerous antagonists in a duel, but who were not fencers in the strict sense of the word.

" 'Old Straight-thrust' had been a good man in his youth, and was so still. When quite a young man, he had beaten all the other instructors in the camp, and had carried off the prize—a pair of silver-mounted foils and masks—and in fact was one of those swordsmen who are exceptionally endowed by nature, and cannot be produced by art. He was, naturally, the admiration of all V., and soon was something more. The sword is a great leveler. In the days of the old monarchy, kings ennobled their fencing master. Louis XV—if I recollect rightly—gave his master, Danet (who has left us a book on fencing), four of his fleurs-de-lis, between two crossed swords, as his coat of arms. These country gentlemen, who were stuffed full of monarchical ideas, very soon looked upon the old fencing master as an equal, and as though he had been one of themselves.

"So far, Stassin, otherwise known as 'Old Straight-thrust,' was to be congratulated on his good fortune; but, unfortunately, the red-morocco heart on the white-leather padded jacket, which the old fencing master put on when he gave a lesson, was not the only one he possessed.

"He had, underneath that one, another heart which sought for an affinity amongst all the young women of V. A soldier's heart is always made of gunpowder, it would seem; and when age has dried the powder, it catches fire all the more readily. Most of the women of V. are pretty, so there were plenty of sparks everywhere, ready for the dry powder of the fencing master, and his history was that of a great many other old soldiers. After having knocked about in all the countries of Europe, and chucked under the chin, or taken round the waist, all the girls whom the Devil had put in his road, the old soldier of the First Empire committed his last folly by marrying, when he was past fifty, and with all the necessary formalities and sacraments—at the municipality and the church—a working-girl from V. Of course, she— I know the working-girls of that country, I have attended enough of them in childbirth!—presented him at the end of nine months, day by day, with a child; and that child, who was a girl, is no other, my dear fellow, than the woman with the air of a goddess who has just passed, brushing us insolently with her robe, and taking no more notice of us than though we had not been there."

"The Comtesse de Savigny!" I cried.

"Yes, the Comtesse de Savigny herself! Ah, you must not look at the origin of women any more than of nations; you should never look into anyone's cradle. I remember having seen at Stockholm that of Charles XII, which looked like a horse's manger, was roughly colored in red, and did not stand level on its four legs. Yet that was what that tempest of a man came out of. Besides, all cradles are sewers, of which you are obliged to change the linen several times a day, and that is never poetical for those who believe in poetry, but when the child is no longer there."

And to strengthen his dictum, the Doctor, at this point of his story, struck his thigh with one of his doeskin gloves, which he held by the middle finger, and the noise the doeskin made against his thigh proved to one who knows something about music that the Doctor was not deficient in muscle.

He waited, but I did not contradict his statements, and, seeing that I said nothing, he continued:

"Like all old soldiers, who are even fond of other people's children—'Old Straight-thrust' doted on his. There was nothing astonishing in that. When a man who is already old has a child, he loves it more than as though he were young, for vanity, which doubles everything, doubles also the paternal instinct. All the fellows I have known who became fathers late in life, adored their offspring, and were as comically proud of it as though it were a wonderful action. Nature, who was laughing at them, had persuaded them in their hearts that they were young again. I know of only one happiness more intoxicating, one pride more droll; and that is when an old man, instead of one child, makes two at once. 'Old Straight-thrust' had not the paternal pride of being the father of twins, but it is certain that his child was big enough to make two ordinary ones. His daughter—you have seen her, and know whether she turned out as well as she promised—was a wonderful child, both for strength and beauty.

"The first care of the old fencing master was to look out for a godfather amongst the noblemen who continually haunted his school, and he chose, from amongst them all, the Comte d'Avice, the oldest of all the wielders of the foil, and who, during the emigration, had himself been a fencing master in London, at ever so many guineas a lesson.

"Comte d'Avice de Sortoville, in Beaumont, who was already a knight of St. Louis and a captain of dragoons before the Revolution—and who was at least seventy years of age—could still 'button' the young fellows in fine style. He was a mischievous old rascal, and some of his jokes were rather ferocious. Thus, for instance, he would pass the blade of his foil through the flame of a candle, and when he had rendered it so hard that it would not bend, and would smash your breastbone or your ribs, he would call it his 'rascal-driver.'

"He was very fond of 'Old Straight-thrust,' and treated him familiarly. 'The daughter of a man like you,' he said, 'should be named after the sword of an illustrious warrior. Call her Haute Claire.'

"And that was the name that was given her. The parish priest of V. made rather a grimace at this unaccustomed name, which had never been heard at the font of his church, but as the sponsor was the Comte d'Avice, and there will always be, in spite of the liberals and their tricks, indestructible ties between the nobility and the clergy, and as, on the other hand, there is a saint named Claire in the Roman calendar, the name of Oliver's sword was given to the child without the town of V. being greatly disturbed thereby.

"Such a name seemed to augur a destiny. The old fencing master, who loved his profession almost as much as his daughter, resolved to teach her, and to leave her his talent as a marriage portion. But a poor pittance considering modern fashions—which the old instructor could not foresee.

"As soon as the child could stand, he began to teach her exercises, and as the little girl was solidly built, with joints like thin steel, he developed her in such an amazing manner that at ten years old she seemed to be fifteen, and could hold her own with the foils against her father, or the best fencers of the town of V. Little Hauteclaire Stassin was talked about everywhere, and later she became Mademoiselle Hauteclaire Stassin. It was more especially, as you may suppose, amongst the young ladies of the town—into whose society, however well he might stand with their father, the daughter of Stassin, called 'Old Straight-thrust,' could not decently enter—that there was an incredible (or rather a perfectly credible) curiosity about her, mixed with spite and envy. Their fathers and brothers spoke of her with astonishment and admiration before them, and they wished to inspect closely this female St. George whose beauty was said to equal her skill in fencing. They saw her only at a distance. I was then living at V., and I was often a witness of this burning curiosity. 'Old Straight-thrust,' who had, during the Empire, served in the Hussars, and who had made a good deal of money with his fencing school, had bought a horse in order that he might give lessons in riding to his daughter, and as all the year round he had young horses to break in for some of his pupils, he often rode with Hauteclaire along the roads which surround the town.

"I met them many times when returning from my professional visits, and in these meetings I was able to judge of the extreme interest which this fine tall young woman had aroused amongst the other young women of the district. I was always riding about the roads at that time, and I frequently saw young ladies in carriages going to make calls at some of the neighboring châteaux. Well! you should have seen with what haste, and I may say with what imprudence, they rushed to the carriage windows whenever Mademoiselle Hauteclaire Stassin was seen on the road, riding alongside her father. But their trouble was useless, and the next day when I called on their mothers they would tell me that they had seen nothing but the figure of the young woman, her face being more or less concealed beneath a thick, blue veil.

"Mademoiselle Hauteclaire Stassin was known only to the men of V. Foil in hand, and her face hidden by the mask, which she seldom removed, she hardly ever left the fencing school, and often gave lessons in place of her father, who was beginning to grow feeble. She rarely showed herself in the street, and though she went to Mass every Sunday, both at church and in the street she was as much masked as she was in the school. Was there conceit or affectation in thus hiding herself from the public gaze? It is very possible; but who knows?—who can say?—And was not this young woman, who dropped the mask only for the veil, as impenetrable in character as she was in face?—as events well proved!

"You will understand, my dear fellow, that I am obliged to

pass rapidly over the details of this period in order to arrive at the moment when my story really begins. Mademoiselle Hauteclaire was then about seventeen. 'Old Straight-thrust' had become a stout old bourgeois. He had lost his wife, and he himself was morally killed by the Revolution of July, which sent all the nobles grieving off to their châteaux, and emptied the fencing school. Moreover, the gout, which was not afraid of the old master's challenges, had attacked him, and was taking him as fast as possible to the cemetery. To a doctor knowing anything of diagnosis there was no doubt about that; it was easy enough to see, and I gave him a short time to live.

"One morning there was brought to the fencing school—by the Vicomte de Taillebois and Chevalier de Mesnilgrand—a young man who, after being educated in some distant place, had returned to inhabit his ancestral château, his father having recently died. This was the Comte Serlon de Savigny, the suitor (as they said in the town) of Mademoiselle Delphine de Cantor. The Comte de Savigny was certainly one of the most distinguished of the swell youth of the locality. There are none of them left now. He had heard much of the famous Hauteclaire Stassin, and wanted to see this miracle. He found her to be what she was, a beautiful young girl, looking provokingly attractive in her silk hose, which showed off the shape of a form like the Pallas of Velletri, and the black morocco jacket tightly fitting her supple and strong figure —one of those figures which the Circassian women obtain by confining their daughters in a leather belt, which the development of the body breaks.

"Hauteclaire Stassin was as serious as a Clorinda.

"He watched her give her lesson, and asked if he might be permitted to cross swords with her. But the Comte de Savigny was not the Tancred of the situation. Mademoiselle Hauteclaire Stassin bent her foil into a semicircle ever so many times on the heart of the handsome Serlon, and she was not touched once.

" 'I cannot touch you, Mademoiselle,' he said courteously.

" 'Is that an omen?'

"Was the young man's conceit overcome by love?

"From that time, the Comte de Savigny went every day to the fencing school of 'Old Straight-thrust' to take a lesson.

"The Comte's château was only a few leagues distant, and he could easily ride or drive into the town without remark, for though the slightest thing was enough to provoke scandal, the love of fencing explained all. Savigny took no one into his confidence. He even avoided taking his lesson at the same time as the other young men of the town. He was a young man who was not wanting in cunning. What passed between him and Hauteclaire, if anything passed at all, no one knew or suspected. His marriage with Mademoiselle Delphine de Cantor had been arranged by the two families years before, and was too far advanced for either party to be able to draw back. They were married three months after his return, and he took the opportunity of spending a month in V. near his fiancée, with whom he passed all his days in the orthodox manner, but whom he left in the evening that he might take his fencing lesson.

"Like everybody else in the town, Mademoiselle Hauteclaire heard the banns of Comte de Savigny and Mademoiselle de Cantor proclaimed at the parish church of V., but neither her attitude nor her face betrayed that she took any interest whatever in those public declarations. It is true that no one was on the lookout, no liaison between Savigny and the fair Hauteclaire being suspected. The marriage having been celebrated, the Comtesse went to live quietly in her château, but her husband did not give up his usual habits, and came to town every day. Many of the other gentlemen of the locality did the same, however.

"Time went on. 'Old Straight-thrust' died. The school was shut for a short time, and then opened again. Mademoiselle Hauteclaire Stassin announced that she would keep the school open, and, so far from having fewer pupils than before her father's death, it had more. Men are all the same. Anything strange displeases them, if it is done by another man; but if it is done by anyone in petticoats, they rather like it. A woman who does what a man does, though she may not do it half so well, will always have a marked advantage over a man, especially in France. But what Mademoiselle Hauteclaire Stassin did, she did better than a man. She was more skillful than her father. As a professor she could demonstrate admirably, and her swordplay was splendid. She had coups which were irresistible—those coups which are not learned any more than the wrist-work of a violin-player, and cannot be taught to anyone.

"I used to fence a little in those days, as everyone else round me did, and I must confess that some of her passes were simply wonderful. Amongst other things, she had a way of disengaging from carte to tierce, which was like magic. It was not a foil that hit you, it was a bullet. Parry as rapidly as a man would, his blade only cut the air, even when she had warned him that she was about to disengage, and he was infallibly hit on the shoulder or breast, without his blade being able even to meet hers. I have seen swordsmen become quite wild at this coup, which they called sleight of hand, and ready to swallow their foil in fury. If she had not been a woman, they would have tried to pick a quarrel with her about that coup. A man would have had twenty duels on his hands.

"But apart from this phenomenal talent, so little suited for a woman, this poor young girl, who had no resource but her foil, and mixed with all the rich young men of the town—amongst whom there were some sad scapegraces, and some conceited asses —without her reputation suffering at all, was an interesting person.

"Nothing was said about Mademoiselle Hauteclaire Stassin concerning either Savigny or anyone else. 'It seems that she is an honest woman,' said all the respectable folks—as though they had been talking of an actress.

"I myself—as I have been talking about myself—who prided myself on my powers of observation, was of the same opinion as all the town concerning the virtue of Hauteclaire. I sometimes went to the fencing school, both before and after the marriage of Monsieur de Savigny, and I never saw anything but a grave young woman performing her business simply. She had, I ought to say, a commanding air, and made everybody treat her with

respect, and she was not familiar with anyone. Her face was
extremely haughty, and had not then that passionate expression
with which you have been so struck, but it showed neither cha-
grin, nor preoccupation, nor anything of a nature to suggest in the
most distant manner the astonishing circumstance which, in the
atmosphere of the quiet and plodding little town, had the same
effect as the report of a cannon, and broke the windows.

" 'Mademoiselle Hauteclaire Stassin has disappeared?'

"She had disappeared! How? Why? Where had she gone?
No one knew; but what was certain was that she had disappeared.
First there was an outcry, followed by silence, but the silence
did not last long. Tongues began to wag. They had been long
kept in—like the water in a millstream which, when the flood-
gates are opened, rushes out and makes the wheel spin round
furiously—and now began to chatter about this unexpected disappearance which nothing could explain, for Mademoiselle Hauteclaire had disappeared without saying a word or leaving a word
to or for anybody. She had disappeared as people disappear when
they wish really to disappear—not leaving behind them some
trifling trace which others can seize to explain their disappearance.
She had disappeared in the most complete manner. She had not
done 'a moonlight flit,' as it is termed, for she had not left a single
debt behind her.

"The neighbors' tongue-mill had nothing to grind, but it turned
all the same, and ground her reputation to bits.

"All that was known about her was told, retold, powdered, and
sifted. How, and with whom, had this proud and reserved girl
run away? Who had carried her off?—for it was certain that
someone had carried her off. No reply could be given. It was
enough to drive any little town mad, and V. became mad. There
were motives for its indignation. Only fancy what the town had
lost. Firstly, it lost its time in guessing about a girl it thought
it knew and did not know, because it had not judged her capable
of disappearing 'like that.' Then it had lost the girl herself, who
ought to have grown old or married, like all the other girls of
the town, but never have moved off the chessboard of life in a

country town. And finally, in losing Mademoiselle Stassin (who was now spoken of only as 'that Stassin woman'), the town had lost a school of arms, celebrated through all the country round, the ornament and honor of the town, and a feather in its cap.

"All these losses were very hard to bear, and were so many reasons comprised in one for throwing all the mud that supposition would allow upon the irreproachable Hauteclaire. And the mud *was* thrown. Except a few old gentlemen who were too grand to indulge in gossip, and who, like her godfather, the Comte d'Avice, had known her as a child, and who, if they thought about the matter at all, regarded it as very natural that she had found a better shoe for her foot than a fencing sandal, not a soul defended the disappearance of Hauteclaire Stassin. She had offended the self-conceit of all; and the youngest were the most bitter against her, because she had not run away with one of them.

"That was for a long time their great grief and their great anxiety. With whom had she run away? Many of the young men went every year to spend a month or two of the winter in Paris, and two or three of them declared they had seen and recognized her there—at the theater—or on horseback in the Champs Elysées—alone or in company—but they were not quite sure. They could affirm nothing. It might have been she, or it might not have been. But it showed how much she was thought about, this girl they had all so much admired, and who in disappearing had thrown consternation into this sword-loving town, of which she was the leading *artiste*—the *diva*—the star. When that star was extinguished—in other words, after the disappearance of the celebrated Hauteclaire—the town of V. fell into that state of lethargy which is the normal condition of all country towns which have not a center of activity towards which all castes and passions converge. The love of arms grew weak, and without the youthful swordsmen the town was dull. The young nobles who used to ride into the town every day to fence, exchanged the foil for the gun. They became sportsmen, and remained on their own estates, or in their woods—the Comte de Savigny like all the others. He came to V. less and less frequently, and when I did meet him occasionally, it was at the house of his wife's parents, who were patients of mine.

"Only, as I did not suspect at that time that he was in any way connected with the disappearance of Hauteclaire, I had no reason to speak to him about it—indeed, people had got tired of talking of it by that time—nor did he ever speak to me of Hauteclaire, or the occasions when we had met at the fencing school, or even make the slightest allusion to her."

"I can hear your little wooden shoes coming," I said to the Doctor, using an expression current in the district about which he was talking, and which is also my native country. "It was he who had abducted her."

"Oh, no! not at all," replied the Doctor. "Better than that. But you would never guess what it was.

"Besides, in the country especially, an elopement is not very easily kept secret, and, moreover, the Comte de Savigny had never since his marriage left the château of Savigny.

"He lived there, as everybody knew, along with his wife, in what appeared to be a perpetual honeymoon—and as everything is remarked and talked about in the country, remarks were made about Savigny, and he was cited as one of those husbands who are so rare they ought to be burned (provincial humor) and their ashes thrown over the others. Heaven only knows how long I myself should have been duped by this reputation, if it had not happened—more than a year after the disappearance of Hauteclaire Stassin—that I was suddenly called one day to the château of Savigny, the lady of the house having been taken ill.

"I started at once, and on my arrival was taken to the Comtesse, who was in reality suffering from one of those vague and complicated diseases which are more dangerous than a severe attack of some ordinary malady. She was one of those women of good family who are worn out, elegant, distinguished, and proud, and whose pale faces and pinched forms seem to say, 'I am conquered by the era, like all my race. I die, but I despise you,' and, devil take me! plebeian as I am, though it is not very philosophic, if I can help admiring that spirit!

"The Comtesse was lying on a couch in a kind of parlor with white walls and black beams, very large, very high, and decorated with a profusion of old furniture which did honor to the taste of the old Counts of Savigny. A solitary lamp lighted this vast apartment, and its light, rendered more mysterious by the green shade which veiled it, fell on the Comtesse, whose face was flushed with fever. She had been ill some days, and Savigny—in order to watch her the better—had had a small bed placed by the side of the couch of his well-beloved better half. But the fever was not to be taken off, and had become worse in spite of all his attention, and therefore he had sent for me. He was standing there, with his back to the fire, looking so gloomy and disturbed as to make me believe that he passionately loved his wife, and believed her to be in danger. But the disturbed expression on his face was not for her, but for another, whom I did not suspect to be at the château de Savigny, and the sight of whom amazed me beyond measure. It was Hauteclaire."

"The devil! That was risky!" I said to the Doctor.

"So risky," he replied, "that I thought I must be dreaming when I saw her. The Comtesse had requested her husband to ring for her maid, who had been told, before my arrival, to prepare a drink I had ordered—and some seconds later the door opened.

" 'Eulalie, where is the tisane I asked for?' said the Comtesse impatiently.

" 'Here it is, Madame,' replied a voice that I seemed to recognize, and it had no sooner struck my ear than I saw emerge from the shadow which enveloped the greater part of the room, and advance into the circle of light thrown by the lamp round the bed, Hauteclaire Stassin—yes, Hauteclaire, herself!—holding in her beautiful hands a silver waiter, on which smoked the bowl for which the Comtesse had asked. Such a sight was enough to take away my breath! Eulalie!

"Fortunately, the name of Eulalie pronounced so naturally, told me all, and was like a blow with a hammer of ice which restored the coolness I had lost, and enabled me to resume my attitude as doctor and observer.

"Hauteclaire had become Eulalie, and lady's maid to the Comtesse de Savigny! Her disguise—if such a woman can be disguised—was complete. She wore the costume of the girls of V. and their headdress, which resembles a helmet, and their long corkscrew curls falling each side of the cheeks—those corkscrews which the preachers of those days called serpents in order to try and disgust the pretty girls with them—which they never succeeded in doing.

"Her eyes were cast down, and she looked beautiful, reserved, and dignified, which only proves that those vipers of women can do whatever they like with their confounded bodies whenever it is to their interest to do so. Having recovered myself, like a man who bites his lips in order to prevent a cry of surprise escaping him, I had a desire to show this impudent woman that I recognized her, and whilst the Comtesse drank her potion, and her face was hidden by the bowl, I fixed my eyes on Eulalie's eyes, but hers—as mild as a fawn's that evening—were firmer than those of the panther she has just stared down. She never winked.

"The hands which held the platter trembled almost imperceptibly, but that was all. The Comtesse drank very slowly, and when she had finished—

" 'Very good! Take it away,' she said.

"And Hauteclaire-Eulalie walked away with that tournure that I should have recognized amongst all the twenty thousand daughters of Ahasuerus. I will own that I did not look at the Comte de Savigny for a minute, for I felt what a look from me would mean at such an instant; but when I did venture to do so, I found his gaze fixed upon me, and his face turned from an expression of terrible anxiety to one of deliverance.

"He saw that *I knew*, but he saw also that *I did not intend to know*, and he breathed more freely. He was sure of my impenetrable discretion, which he explained probably (but I did not care about that) by my interest as a doctor to retain such a good customer as he was, whilst really it was only the interest I took as an observer, who did not want the doors of a house where such interesting events were going on, to be closed against him.

"So I returned with my finger on my lips, well resolved not to breathe a word to a single person, or give anyone any cause to suspect. Ah, what pleasure it is to be an observer, what impersonal and solitary pleasures one enjoys, and which I promised myself in this quiet corner of the country, in this old château, to which as a doctor I could come whenever I liked!

"Glad to be delivered from his anxiety, Savigny had said to me: 'Come every day, Doctor, until further orders.'

"I could therefore study with as much interest as though it had been a disease, the mystery of a situation which no one would have deemed credible if they had been informed of it. And as, from the very first day, this mystery had aroused my ratiocinative faculties, which are the blind man's stick to the *savant*, and especially to the doctor, in their curious researches. I began immediately to reason out the situation in order that I might understand it. How long had it existed? Did it date from the disappearance of Hauteclaire? That was more than a year ago—had Hauteclaire Stassin been lady's maid to the Comtesse de Savigny all that time? How was it that no one had ever seen what I had seen so easily and so quickly? All these questions jumped on my horse with me, and rode along with me to V., accompanied by many others which I picked up on the road.

"The Comte and Comtesse de Savigny, who were believed to adore each other, lived, it is true, remote from all society. But still a visitor might drop in at the château at any time. It is true that if the visitor were a man, Hauteclaire need not appear; and if the visitor were a lady, the ladies of V. had not seen (sufficiently to be able to recognize) a girl who hardly ventured out of the school of arms, and who, when seen at a distance on horseback or in church, wore purposely a thick veil—for Hauteclaire (as I have said) had always possessed that pride of the very proud, who are offended at too much curiosity, and the more they are gazed at, the more they try to hide themselves. As for the servants of Monsieur de Savigny, with whom she was obliged to live, if

they did not come from V. they would not know her—and perhaps not even if they did.

"Thus did I reply, as I trotted along, to the first questions
which suggested themselves, and, before I got out of the saddle,
I had constructed a whole edifice of suppositions, more or less
plausible, to explain what, to anyone but a reasoner like me,
would have been inexplicable. Perhaps the only thing that I
could not explain well, was that the wonderful beauty of Hauteclaire had not been an obstacle to her entering the service of the
Comtesse de Savigny, who loved her husband, and might therefore be jealous. But the patrician ladies of V., quite as proud as
the wives of Charlemagne's paladins, could not suppose (a grave
mistake, but they had never read *Le Mariage de Figaro*) that the
prettiest lady's maid could be for their husbands any more than
the handsomest lackey was to them—and so I ended by saying
to myself, as I took my foot out of the stirrup, that the Comtesse
de Savigny had every reason to believe that she was loved, and
that rascal Savigny was quite capable of keeping up the illusion."

"Hum!" I said skeptically—for I could not keep from interrupting—"all that is very fine, my dear Doctor, but the situation
was a terribly imprudent one all the same."

"Certainly!" replied this experienced student of human nature;
"but suppose the imprudence made the situation? There are some
passions which are only excited by imprudence, and without the
dangers they provoke they would never exist. In the sixteenth
century, which was about as passionate an age as could be, the
most prolific cause of love was the danger of love. A man stood
a chance of being poniarded as he left the arms of his mistress,
or a husband put poison in his wife's sleeve, which you kissed
and made a fool of yourself over in all the usual ways; and so far
from putting a stop to love, this incessant danger only rendered
it the more irresistible. In our tame modern customs, where the
law has replaced passion, it is evident that the article of the Code
which applies to the husband who is capable of having—as the
law coarsely puts it—'introduced a concubine into the conjugal
domicile,' is an ignoble danger enough, but for noble natures this

danger seems all the more grand, and Savigny, in exposing himself to it, perhaps found the only anxious pleasure which really intoxicates strong minds.

"The next day, as you may imagine," continued Doctor Torty, "I was at the château early, but neither that day nor the following ones did I see anything but what was absolutely normal and regular. Neither on the part of the invalid, nor on that of the Comte, nor even on that of the false Eulalie, who performed her duties as naturally as though she had been brought up to them, did I remark anything which could give me information concerning the secret I had surprised. What was certain was that the Comte de Savigny and Hauteclaire Stassin were playing the most abominably impudent comedy with all the ease of consummate actors, and that they had agreed together to play it. But that of which I was not so certain, and which I wanted to know first, was whether the Comtesse was really their dupe, and, in case she were, whether it were possible that she should long be so.

"It was upon the Comtesse, therefore, that I concentrated my attention. I had no trouble in seeing her, as she was my patient, and therefore, on account of her illness, the focus of my observations. She was, as I have told you, a true lady of V., knowing nothing but this—that she was noble, and that outside the nobility there was nothing worthy of regard. The appreciation of their nobility is the only passion of the women of V., of the upper class—and of all classes that have not deep passions. Mademoiselle Delphine de Cantor had been educated by the Benedictine nuns, and, not being at all inclined to religion, had been horribly bored, and had left the nunnery to bore herself still more at home until she married the Comte de Savigny, whom she loved, or thought she loved, with all the readiness of young girls who are bored to love the firstcomer presented to them.

"She was one of those pale women with soft flesh but hard bones, of the color of milk with which bran has been mixed; for the little freckles which covered her skin were certainly darker than her hair, which was a very pale gold. When she stretched out her white arm, veined with opalescent blue, and a small aristocratic wrist, in which the pulse was normally languid, she gave me the idea that she had been created specially to become a victim—to be crushed under the feet of the haughty Hauteclaire, who had bowed herself before her to the extent of becoming her servant.

"But this idea, which arose the first moment you looked at her, was contradicted by the chin which finished off this thin face—a chin like that of Fulvia on the Roman medals, out of place amongst ordinary features—and also by a forehead obstinately projecting under her colorless hair. It was a puzzle to express an opinion about her; but, at any rate, it was impossible that the present situation could last long without an explosion. With a view to that future explosion, I set to work to sound this little woman, who could not long remain a secret to her doctor. He who confesses the body, soon holds the heart. If there were moral or immoral causes for the actual sufferings of the Comtesse, she might try to conceal her impressions and thoughts, but she would have at last to reveal them.

"That is what I said to myself; but I turned and re-turned my medical screws in vain. It was evident to me, after some days, that she had not the least suspicion of the complicity of her husband and Hauteclaire in the domestic crime of which the house was the silent and desired theater. Was it want of sagacity on her part? or the dumbness of jealousy? With the false Eulalie who waited on her, she was imperious but gentle. That sounds contradictory, but it is not—it is true. She gave her orders briefly, but she never raised her voice, like a woman who was made to be obeyed, and is sure of being obeyed—and she was, admirably. Eulalie slipped noiselessly about the room, and her attentions stopped just short of the point at which they would have become tiresome, and everything was done with a readiness and a knowledge of the character of her mistress which showed good will and intelligence.

"I even went so far as to speak to the Comtesse about Eulalie, who was always near her when I paid my visits, and the sight of whom gave me a chill up my back—as though I had seen a serpent stealthily approaching a sleeping woman. One day when the Comtesse had sent her to fetch something or other, and she had stolen out of the room noiselessly, I took advantage of the opportunity to ask a question which might give me some light on the matter.

" 'What a velvety footfall!' I said, as I watched her leave. 'You have a maid, Madame, who does her work well. May I ask where you found her? Does she come from V.?'

" 'Yes, she serves me very well,' replied the Comtesse with indifference, looking at herself in a little hand mirror, framed in green velvet and surrounded by peacock's feathers, and speaking in that impertinent tone which was a proof that she took no interest in the subject. 'I am highly satisfied with her. She did not come from V., but I could not tell you where she does come from—I know nothing about her. Ask Monsieur de Savigny if you want to know, Doctor, for he brought her to me soon after we were married. She had been in the service, he told me, of an old lady, a cousin of his, who had died, and she could not find another place. I trusted in him, and I was not disappointed. She is perfect as a lady's maid. I do not believe she has a single fault.'

" 'I know of one,' I said with affected gravity.

" 'Ah! what is that?' she replied languidly, without any interest in what she was saying, and still attentively studying her pale lips in the little hand mirror.

" 'She is pretty,' I said; 'she is really much too pretty to be a lady's maid. One of these days you will have someone run away with her.'

" 'Do you think so?' she replied, still looking at herself, and utterly indifferent to what I said.

" 'And perhaps it will be a man of your own station who will fall in love with her. She is pretty enough to turn the head of a duke.'

"I weighed my words before uttering them, for I wanted to sound her, and see how much she knew—if she knew nothing, I could do no more.

" 'There is no duke at V.,' replied the Comtesse, and her forehead remained as smooth as the glass she held in her hand. 'Besides, all women of that sort,' she added, raising one eyebrow, 'leave you when they like to suit their own convenience. Eulalie does her work well, but if I showed any affection for her she would, no doubt, abuse it, so I do nothing of the sort.'

"There was no further mention made of Eulalie that day. The Comtesse was completely deceived. Who would not have been, for that matter? Even I—though I had seen Hauteclaire so many times at only a sword's length between us, in her father's fencing school—was almost tempted at times to believe in Eulalie. Savigny, though he ought to have acted as well as she did, was far less at home in this acted lie, but she lived and moved in this atmosphere of deceit as easily and naturally as a fish does in the water. She must certainly have been in love, and very deeply in love, to do what she did do, and have given up all the advantages of a life which flattered her vanity by making her the cynosure of all eyes in a little town—for her the whole universe—where sooner or later she might have found amongst the young men, her admirers and adorers, one who would marry her for love, and take her into that good society of which she knew only the men. Her lover certainly staked less than she did. His devotion was less than hers. His pride, as a man, must have suffered greatly at not being able to spare his mistress the indignity of such a humiliating position. It seemed out of keeping with the impetuous character generally ascribed to Savigny. If he loved Hauteclaire enough to sacrifice his young wife for her, he might have gone to live with her in Italy—that was often done at that time—without all the abominations of a shameful and concealed concubinage. Was his love less than hers? Did he suffer Hauteclaire to love him more than he loved her? Was it she who had broken down the guard of the conjugal domicile? And did he, finding the experience hazardous and interesting, allow himself to be tempted by this new kind of Potiphar's wife?

"All that I could see or hear did not teach me much concerning Savigny and Hauteclaire. Accomplices in adultery of some sort they certainly were—but what was behind that? What was the

position of these two persons in regard to one another? That
was a problem I wanted to solve. Savigny's conduct to his wife
was irreproachable, but when Hauteclaire-Eulalie was there, I
could see, out of the corner of my eye, certain precautions which
denoted that his mind was not at ease. When, in the course of
my daily visits, he asked for a book or a paper, or some other
article, he had a way of taking it from the hands of the lady's
maid which would have revealed his secret to any other woman
but this little schoolgirl, brought up by the Benedictine nuns,
whom he had married. You could see that he was afraid lest
his hand should touch that of Hauteclaire, as though, if he did
touch it by chance, he would be obliged to take it. Hauteclaire
did not display this embarrassment and these precautions.

"Women are all temptresses, ready to tempt God or the Devil,
and she seemed pleased to risk desire and danger at the same time.

"Once or twice my visit took place at dinner time, and Savigny
always took his dinner by his wife's bedside.

"Hauteclaire waited at table, the other servants never entering
the Comtesse's apartment. In order to place the dishes on the
table, she was obliged to lean over Savigny's shoulder, and, in
doing so, her dress touched his neck or ears, and I noticed that
the Comte turned pale, and glanced at his wife to see if she were
looking. By Jove! I was young then, and the disturbance of the
molecules in the organization, which is called the violence of
emotion, seemed to me the only thing worth living for. I thought
to myself that it must be strangely delightful to enjoy a mysterious concubinage with a sham servant, under the eyes of an
abused wife who might guess the truth.

"But, except for the paleness and the ill-suppressed emotion
of Savigny, I saw nothing of the tragedy they were playing, and
the inevitable catastrophe in which it must end. What were they
doing? I wanted to learn the secret of their romance. The
problem worried me so much that from observing I took to
spying, which is only observation at any price. Ah, our tastes soon
deprave us. In order to know that of which I was ignorant, I
allowed myself to commit meannesses which were unworthy and

which I knew to be so, and yet did them. It is the being accustomed to sound, my dear fellow. I tried every means. When, in my visits to the château, I put my horse in the stable, I questioned the servants—without appearing to do so, of course. I spied—oh, I won't spare to use the word—solely for my own curiosity. But the servants were all as much deceived as the Comtesse.

"They honestly took Hauteclaire for one of themselves, and all my curiosity would have been wasted had it not been for chance, which, as usual, did more than all my schemes, and taught me more than all my spying.

"For more than two months I had been attending the Comtesse, whose health did not improve, for she showed more and more all the symptoms of that debility which is so common now, and which the medical men of this enervated age call anemia. Savigny and Hauteclaire continued to play with the same consummate art the difficult comedy which my arrival at the château had not disconcerted. Nevertheless, it seemed to me that the actors were getting tired. Savigny had grown thin, and I heard it said at V.: 'What a good husband Monsieur de Savigny is! He has quite changed since his wife's illness. How nice it must be to be loved like that!'

"The impassive beauty of Hauteclaire was spoiled by the weary look in her eyes—not the look caused by weeping, for she had never cried in all her life—but a look as though she had sat up too much. The leanness of Savigny, and the wearied eyes, might have been due to some other cause than the life they were leading. There were many things in that land of subterranean volcanoes which might have caused the symptoms.

"I had remarked these telltale signs on their faces, and had asked myself the meaning without being able to give a reply, when one day, returning from my rounds, I passed by Savigny. My intention had been to call as usual, but a difficult accouchement had kept me very late, and when I passed the château it was too late for a visit. I did not even know what time it was. My hunting watch had stopped. But the moon, which had

already begun to descend, marked midnight passed on the vast
dial, and its crescent was below the summits of the fir trees of
Savigny, behind which it was about to disappear.

"Have you ever been to Savigny?" asked the Doctor, breaking
off his story and turning to me. I nodded.

"Yes? Well, then you know that you are obliged to pass
through the wood, and along the walls of the château, which you
must double like a cape, in order to get to the high road which
leads directly to V. Suddenly, in this thick wood, in which you
could not see a ray of light, nor hear the slightest sound, there
fell on my ears a noise which I took to be that of beating clothes
—some poor woman, I thought, who was occupied all day in the
fields, had taken advantage of the moonlight to wash her clothes
at some tank or ditch. It was only as I neared the château that
with these regular beats there mingled another sound which
enlightened me as to the nature of the first. It was the clashing of
crossed swords. You know how plainly you can hear in the night,
when the least sounds become distinct, and there was no mistake
about its being the sound of iron on iron. An idea crossed my
mind, and when I emerged from the pine wood before the
château, which was bathed in the moonlight, and one of the
windows of which was open, I said:

" 'Hallo! so that is their way of making love!'

"It was evident that Savigny and Hauteclaire were fencing, at
that hour of the night. I could hear the foils as plainly as though
I had seen them. What I had taken for the noise of beating
clothes was the stamping of the feet, or *appels*, of the fencers.
The open window was in the pavilion which, of all the four, was
the farthest removed from the chamber of the Comtesse. The
sleeping château, white and gloomy in the moonlight, looked
dead. All the rest of the house was dark, but in this one room the
Venetian shutters had been closed, and through them streaks of
light came, and it was from this room that the noise of the clashing
of foils proceeded. As the night was warm—it was in July—they
had opened the window, which led on to the balcony.

"I had drawn up my horse at the edge of the wood, to listen to their combat, which appeared to be a lively one, and I was interested in this assault at arms between lovers who had first loved with weapons in their hands, and who continued to love one another after the click of the foils had ceased.

"The blinds were pushed to one side, and I had only just time to back my horse into the shadow of the trees, when Savigny and Hauteclaire came out and leaned over the iron rail of the balcony. I could see them wonderfully well. The moon had fallen below the wood, but the light of a candelabrum that J could see in the room behind them, showed up their figures. Hauteclaire was dressed—if it may be called dressed—as I had seen her often when giving her lessons at V., in a leather jacket, like a cuirass, and her legs, in the tightly fitting silk hose, showed all their muscular beauty. Savigny wore an almost similar costume. Both were lithe and robust, and they looked, in the lighted square of the window, like two beautiful statues of Youth and Strength. You have just admired, in this garden, the proud beauty of both, which time has not yet destroyed. Well, that will help to give you an idea of the magnificent couple I perceived on the balcony, their tightly fitting clothes making them appear bare. They were leaning on the balcony and talking, but so low that I could not hear what they said, but their attitude told me enough. Savigny had thrown one arm round that Amazonian waist, which seemed well fitted to resist—but did nothing of the kind.

"And at the same instant the proud Hauteclaire threw her arms round Savigny's neck, and they thus formed the celebrated and voluptuous group by Canova, which everyone recollects, and thus they remained mouth to mouth long enough to drink a whole bottleful of kisses. That lasted for quite sixty beats of my pulse, which went faster than at present, and which this sight caused to beat even faster still.

" 'Oh! oh!' I said to myself when they had returned into the room and closed the heavy curtains, and I had emerged from my hiding place. 'One of these days they will have to confide in me. It will not be only themselves they will have to hide!' From the sight of their caresses, and this familiarity, I deduced, as a doctor would, the consequences. But their ardor defeated my prophecy. You know that there are persons who love too much" —the cynical old doctor used another word—"and consequently never have any children.

"The next morning I went to Savigny. I found Hauteclaire, now become Eulalie again, seated in the embrasure of one of the windows of the long corridor which led to her mistress' room, with a quantity of linen and other stuff before her, and which she was engaged in cutting and mending—she, the fencer of the previous night. Could anyone suspect it? I thought, as I noticed that graceful form which I had seen almost bare the previous night, and which not even the petticoat and the white apron could altogether hide.

"I passed her without speaking, for I spoke to her as little as possible, not wishing to seem to know what I did know, and which might have been remarked in my voice or look. I felt that I was not such an actor as she was, and I distrusted myself.

"Generally when I passed along this corridor, where she was always at work when she was not attending to the Comtesse, she heard me coming, and was so certain as to who it was that she never raised her head, which remained bowed under the starched cap, or the Norman headdress she sometimes wore, and which resembled that of Isabella of Bavaria—and with her eyes bent on her work, and her cheeks hidden by the blue-black corkscrew curls which framed her pale oval face, she offered to my gaze only a gracefully curved neck, covered by thick curls. In Hauteclaire, it was the animal which was paramount. No other woman had the same kind of beauty. Men—who say everything when alone together—had often remarked it. At V., when she gave her fencing lessons, the men used to call her, between themselves, Mademoiselle Esau. The Devil teaches women what they are— or they would teach it to the Devil if he did not know.

"Hauteclaire, though not much of a coquette, had a habit, when she was listening to anyone, of rolling round her fingers the long curls which adorned her neck, and which had rebelled against the

comb that smoothed her chignon. One of these curls was sufficient to trouble a man's spirit, as the Bible says. She knew well
the effect they caused. But now that she was a lady's maid, I
had never once seen her indulge in this gesture, even when looking at Savigny.

"My parenthesis has been rather long, my dear fellow, but
anything which enables you to understand Hauteclaire Stassin is
of importance to my story. On that day she was obliged to rise
and show her face, for the Comtesse rang and ordered her to
bring me pen and paper, which I needed to write out a prescrip-
tion. She came, with a steel thimble still on her finger, for she
had not had time to take it off, and she had stuck the threaded
needle in her tempting breast, where there were already many
others. Even these steel needles suited this confounded girl,
who was made for steel, and in the Middle Ages would have worn
a cuirass.

"When I had finished, I raised my eyes and looked at her,
and saw in her face marks of the fatigue of the previous night.

"Savigny, who was not there when I arrived, suddenly appeared. He looked much more fatigued than she did. He spoke
to me about the health of the Comtesse, who was no better. He
seemed impatient and annoyed that this was so. His tone was
bitter and violent. He walked to and fro as he spoke. I looked
at him coolly, thinking that this Napoleonic tone was rather too
much. 'But if I should cure your wife,' I thought to myself,
'you would not be able to practice fencing and—love-making—
all night with your mistress,' I could have recalled him to the
reality and politeness which he had forgotten, by putting under
his nose—if I had so liked—the smelling salts of a sharp reply.
I contented myself with looking at him. He was more interesting
to me than ever, for it was evident that he was acting a part more
than ever."

The Doctor stopped again. He plunged his big finger and
thumb into his silver snuffbox, and took a pinch of rappee. He,
in his turn, appeared so interesting to me that I made no observa-

tion, and he continued his story, after having taken his pinch and passed his bent finger over his hooky nose.

"Oh, he was really impatient—but it was not because the wife to whom he was so persistently faithless, did not get well. Confound it! a man who made a concubine of his servant in his own house, could scarcely be angry that his wife was not cured of an illness. If she had been cured, would not his adultery have been more difficult?

"Did he imagine it would not be such a long affair? And, as I have since thought, the idea of ending it came to him, or her, or both of them—since neither the disease nor the doctor would finish—perhaps, at that moment."

"What, Doctor! Then they——?"

I did not finish my sentence: the idea that the Doctor had suggested cut short my words.

He bent his head and looked at me as tragically as the statue of the Commander when he accepts the supper.

"Yes!" he said slowly in a low voice, in answer to my thought. "At least, some days later, everybody heard with horror that the Comtesse had been poisoned, and was dead."

"Poisoned!" I cried.

"By her lady's maid, Eulalie, who had mistaken one bottle for another, and given her mistress some copying ink instead of a medicine I had prescribed. After all, such a mistake was possible. But I knew that Eulalie was Hauteclaire. I had seen them both forming Canova's group on the balcony. Society had not seen what I had seen. Society was at first under the impression that a terrible accident had occurred. But when—two years after this catastrophe—they learned that Comte Serlon de Savigny had publicly married Stassin's daughter—for the secret had to come out as to who the sham Eulalie was—and that she occupied the hardly cold bed of the Comte's first wife, Mademoiselle Delphine de Cantor, oh, then no end of suspicions were muttered, as though people were afraid to say what they thought. But, in reality, no one knew. They knew about his marriage, which caused the Comte de Savigny to be pointed at and shunned as though he had the pest. That was quite enough, though. You know what a disgrace it is—or rather it was—for things have much changed in that district—to say of a man: 'He has married his servant!' That disgrace rested on him like a stain. As to the horrible rumors of a suspected crime, they were buzzed about, and died away. But there was one person, however, who knew and was sure."

"And that must have been you, Doctor!" I interrupted.

"It was I, as a matter of fact," he continued, "but not I only. If I alone had known it, I should never have had but vague glimmerings of the truth that would have been worse than ignorance. I should never have been certain, and," he said, laying the stress of absolute certainty on each word, "*I am!*

"And listen to how it is that I am!" he added, pressing my knee between his bony fingers. But his story "nipped" me even more than the crablike claws of his strong hand.

"You may well suppose," he continued, "that I was the first to hear that the Comtesse had been poisoned. Whether they were guilty or not, they were obliged to send for the family doctor. They did not stop to have a horse saddled. A groom came at full gallop on a barebacked horse to me at V. and I followed him at the same pace to Savigny. When I arrived—had that been calculated?—it was not possible to counteract the effects of the poison. Serlon, his face grief-stricken, met me in the courtyard, and, as I got out of the saddle, said, as though he were frightened at his own words:

"'A servant made a mistake.' (He took care not to say Eulalie, whom everybody named next day.) 'But, Doctor, can it be possible that copying-ink is a poison?'

"'That depends entirely on what it is made of,' I replied.

"He took me to the Comtesse, who was worn out with pain, and whose contracted face resembled a ball of white thread that had fallen into some green dye.

"She looked awful. She smiled at me horribly with her black lips, and with that kind of smile which seems to say to a man: 'I know well what you think.' I glanced quickly round the room to see if Eulalie was there. I should have liked to see her face at that moment. She was not there.

"Brave as she was, was she afraid of me? Ah, at that time, I was—certain.

"The Comtesse made an effort when she saw me, and raised herself on her elbow.

" 'Ah, there you are, Doctor,' she said; 'but you come too late. I am dying. It is not the doctor you should have sent for, Serlon, but the priest. Send for him at once, and leave me alone for two minutes with the Doctor. I wish it.'

"She said that 'I wish it' as I had never heard her speak before —but like a woman who had that chin and forehead I have mentioned.

" 'Even me?' said Savigny, feebly.

" 'Even you,' she replied. And she added almost caressingly, 'You know, my dear, that women are sometimes too modest to speak before those they love.'

"Hardly had he left than a terrible change came over her. From mild she became ferocious.

" 'Doctor,' she said in a voice that teemed with hate, "my death is not an accident, it is a crime! Serlon loves Eulalie, and she has poisoned me. I did not heed you when you told me that girl was too pretty to be a lady's maid. I was wrong. He loves that wretched, that abominable woman, who has killed me. He is more guilty than she is, for he loves her, and has deceived me for her sake. For some days past, the looks they exchanged across my bed have warned me. And then the horrible taste of that ink with which they poisoned me. But I drank it all to the last drop, in spite of the horrible taste, because I was glad to die. Don't talk about antidotes. I want none of your remedies. I wish to die.'

" 'Then why did you send for me, Madame la Comtesse?'

" 'Well, this is why,' she replied breathlessly. 'To tell you that they have poisoned me, and that you should give me your word of honor to keep the secret. It would make a terrible scandal. That must not be, you are my doctor, and people will believe you when you speak of this mistake they have invented—when you say that I should not have died, but might have been saved, if my health had not been so bad for a long time past. That is what you must swear, Doctor.'

"As I did not reply, she saw what was passing in my mind. I thought she loved her husband to such an extent that she wished to save him. That was the idea that occurred to my mind—a natural and vulgar idea, for there are some women so intended for love and all its self-denials, that they would not return the blow that killed them. But the Comtesse de Savigny had never appeared to me to be a woman of that sort.

" 'Oh, it is not what you imagine that makes me ask you to swear that, Doctor. Ah, no! I hate Serlon so at this moment that I could never love him again. But I am not such a coward as to forgive him. I shall leave this life jealous of him and implacable. But this does not concern Serlon, Doctor,' she continued with energy, showing me a side of her character of which I had already caught a glimpse, but the depths of which I had not penetrated. 'It concerns the Comte de Savigny. I do not want it to be known, when I am dead, that the Comte de Savigny murdered his wife. I do not want him tried at the assizes, and accused of complicity with a servant who is an adulteress and a poisoner. I do not want that stain to rest on the name of Savigny, which I bear. Oh, it is not for his sake, for he is worthy of the scaffold. I should like to torture him. But it concerns all the aristocracy of the country. If we were still what we ought to be, I should have thrown Eulalie into one of the dungeons of the château of Savigny, and there would have been no more said about her. But we are no longer masters in our own houses. We have no longer our expeditious and silent justice, and on no account would I have the scandal and publicity of yours, Doctor; and I prefer to leave them in each other's arms, happy, and freed from me, and for me to die as I am dying, than to think when I am dying that the nobility of V. should have the disgrace of counting a poisoner in its ranks.'

"She spoke with unaccustomed clearness, although her jaws

chattered as though her teeth would break. It was the aristocrat that was stronger in her than the jealous wife. She would die as befitted a daughter of V., the last aristocratic town in France. And, touched by that—perhaps more than I ought to have been —I promised and swore to do what she asked.

"And I have done so, my dear fellow. I did not save her.

"I could not save her; she obstinately refused to take any remedy.

"I said what she wished me to when she was dead, and I was believed.

"That is fully twenty-five years ago. At present everything concerning the affair is silent and forgotten. Most of her contemporaries are dead. Other generations—ignorant or indifferent —are drifting toward their tombs, and the first account of this story that I have ever given is to you.

"And if it had not been for what we have seen, I should not have told you now. It needed those two beings, unchangeably beautiful in spite of time, unchangeably happy in spite of their crime, powerful, passionate, absorbed in each other, passing through life as they did through this garden, like two angels united in the golden shadow of their four wings."

I was amazed. "But," I said, "if what you tell me is true, the happiness of these people is a terrible disorder of nature."

"It is disorder, or it is order, whichever you please," replied Doctor Torty, a confirmed atheist, and as quiet in mind as the persons of whom he was speaking, "but it is a fact. They are exceptionally happy; insolently happy. I am an old man, and I have seen, in the course of my life, much happiness which did not endure, but I have never seen but that one which was so profound and yet lasted forever.

"And yet you may believe that I have well studied and scrutinized it. I have sought for a rift in their happiness. If you will excuse the expression, I may say that I have loused it. I have searched the life of those two beings to see if there was not, in their astonishing and revolting happiness, a fault or crack however small, in some secret place, but I have never found anything but an excellent and successful joke of the Devil's against God, if there be a God or a Devil.

"After the death of the Comtesse, I remained, as you may imagine, on good terms with Savigny. As I had lent the weight of my authority to the fable they had devised to explain the poisoning, they had no interest in putting me on one side, and I had a great interest in knowing what would follow, what they would do, and what would become of them. What followed was the period of mourning of Savigny, which lasted the customary two years, and which Savigny performed in a manner to confirm the public idea that he was the most excellent of husbands, past, present, or future.

"During these two years, he saw absolutely no one, but buried himself in his château in such solitude that no one knew that he had kept at Savigny, Eulalie, the involuntary cause of the death of the Comtesse, and whom he ought in common decency to have got rid of, even if he had known she was innocent.

"The imprudence of keeping in his house such a woman after such a catastrophe, showed the senseless passion that I had always suspected in Serlon. Therefore I was not at all surprised when one day, on returning from my rounds, I met one of the servants on the road near Savigny, and on asking what was going on at the château was told that Eulalie was still there. By the indifferent tone in which he said that, I saw that none of the Comte's servants suspected that Eulalie was his mistress. 'They are playing a close game,' I said to myself. 'But why do they not leave the country? The Comte is rich. He could live in good style anywhere. Why not run away with this beautiful she-devil (in the way of she-devil, I do believe in that one) who, in order that she might hook him the better, preferred to live in her lover's house, in spite of the danger, than to be his mistress at V., in some quiet lodging where he could come and see her secretly?' There was something underneath all this I could not understand. Their infatuation, their devotion to each other, was then so great that they forgot all prudence and precaution? Hauteclaire, whom I supposed to have a stronger character than

Serlon, and to be the man of the couple—did she intend to remain in the château where she had been a servant, and where she might become mistress, and, if that caused any scandal, prepare public opinion for a yet greater scandal—her marriage with the Comte de Savigny? That idea had not occurred to me, if it had occurred to her at that period of my story. Hauteclaire Stassin, the daughter of the fencing master, 'Old Straight-thrust,' whom we had all seen giving lessons at V., Comtesse de Savigny! Impossible! The world would come to an end! For my own part, I believed that the concubinage between these two fierce animals, who had recognized at the first glance that they were of the same species, and had dared to commit adultery under the eyes of the Comtesse, would still continue.

"But a marriage impudently accomplished in the face of God and man—a challenge and defiance to outraged public opinion— I was, upon my word, a thousand miles from imagining such a thing, and when, after the two years' mourning, the event occurred, I was quite as much surprised as any of those fools who never expect anything, and who howl like a whipped dog when the unexpected does occur.

"Moreover, during those two years of mourning which Serlon observed so strictly, and which—when people saw what the end was—caused him to be so furiously taxed with hypocrisy and baseness, I did not go much to Savigny. What should I do there? They were both in good health, and until the moment, perhaps not so far off, when they would send for me in the night for an accouchement (which would require concealing also), they had no need of my services. Nevertheless, I now and then paid a visit to the Comte. Politeness mingled with curiosity. Serlon received me wherever he might be when I arrived. He did not show the least embarrassment. His kind manner had returned. He was grave. I have remarked that happy people are grave. They carry their heart like a full glass, that the least movement might cause to overflow or break. In spite of his gravity and his black clothes, there was in Serlon's eyes an unmistakable expression of immense happiness. It was no longer an expression of relief and deliverance, as on the day when he saw that I had recognized Hauteclaire but had determined *not* to recognize her. No, *parbleu!* it was really and truly happiness. Although in these ceremonious and short visits we talked only about superficial matters, his voice was not as it had been in the time of his wife. Its intonation seemed to show that he was obliged to restrain the sentiments he really felt.

"As for Hauteclaire (still Eulalie, and at the château, as the servant had told me), it was a long time before I met her. I no longer passed her in the corridor, working in the window seat, as in the days of the Comtesse. And yet the pile of linen in the same place, and the scissors, workbox, and thimble on the window sill showed that she must work there, on that chair empty now, and perhaps warm, which she perhaps had left when she heard me coming. You will remember that I was conceited enough to believe that she was afraid to meet my eye, but at present she had nothing to fear. She was not aware that the Comtesse had related that terrible secret to me. Such was her bold, proud nature that she would have braved anyone sagacious enough to divine her secret. And, in fact, when I did see her, her happiness was written on her face in such a radiant manner that you could not have effaced it if you had poured over it all the bottle of copying-ink with which she had poisoned the Comtesse.

"It was on the grand staircase of the château that I met her the first time. She was coming down as I was going up. She was gliding along rather quickly, but when she saw me she went more slowly, no doubt with the intention of showing me her face and looking me full in the eyes—but if she could make the panther close its eyes, she could not make me close mine. As she came down the staircase, her skirt floated behind her, owing to her rapid movement, and she seemed to have descended from heaven. She had a sublimely happy air. It was fifteen thousand leagues above that of Serlon. I passed her, nevertheless, without any signs of politeness, for if Louis XIV saluted the maidservants when he met them on the stairs, at least they were not poisoners. She was still dressed as a lady's maid, with a white apron; but the happy appearance of the triumphant and despotic mistress had replaced the impassiveness of the slave. That air she has never lost. You have seen her and can judge. It is more striking even than the beauty of the face upon which it shines. That superhuman air of pride in happy love, she has been able to bestow upon Serlon, who did not have it at first; and she continues after twenty years to have it still, and I have never seen it diminished or veiled for an instant on the faces of these two privileged beings. By that air they have always been able to reply victoriously to neglect, slander, or outraged public opinion, and it has caused all those who have met them to believe that the crime of which they were suspected for a short time, was an atrocious calumny."

"But you, Doctor," I interrupted, "after all that you know, you are not imposed upon by that appearance? You have followed them about everywhere, have you not? You have seen them at all sorts of times?"

"Except in their bedroom at night, and it is not there that they would lose it," replied Doctor Torty, jokingly, but wisely, "I have seen them, I believe, at all times of their life since their marriage—which took place I know not where, in order not to face the rough music which the populace of V., quite as furious in its own way as the nobility in theirs, had promised to give them. When they returned home married, and she was properly and authentically the Comtesse de Savigny, and he absolutely disgraced by marriage with his servant, they settled down in their château at Savigny. People turned their backs on them, but they did not care. But they have never wearied of each other; even now their passion is not appeased. As a doctor, I do not wish to die before I have written a treatise on teratology, and as they interest me—as strange monsters—I have not followed those who avoid them. When I saw the sham Eulalie completely a countess, she received me as though she had been one all her life. She was well aware that I remembered the white apron and the silver platter.

"'I am no longer Eulalie,' she said. 'I am Hauteclaire, happy to have been a servant for his sake.'

"I thought she had been something else as well; but as I was the only person in the district who went to Savigny when they returned there, I swallowed my pride, and ended by going there often. I may say that I continued to strive to pierce the intimacy of these two beings, so completely happy in their love. Well, you may believe me or not, as you like, my dear fellow, but I have never seen the purity of that happiness (though I was sure it was stained by a crime), I will not say dulled, not even shadowed for a single minute in a single day. The stain of a cowardly crime, which had not the courage to be a bloody one, had never sullied the blue horizon of their happiness once, so far as I can see. That is enough to knock over—is it not?—all the moralists on earth, who have invented the fine theory about vice punished and virtue rewarded.

"Neglected and solitary as they were, and seeing no one but me, for whom they did not put themselves out of the way, I being a doctor who was almost a friend, by dint of familiarity they ceased to be on their guard. They forgot me, and lived, when I was present, in the intoxication of a passion to which I have seen nothing to compare in all my life. You were the witness of it a moment ago. They passed, and they did not even perceive me, although I was at their elbow. A good part of the time I spent with them, they never saw me either. Polite and amiable, but often absent-minded, their behavior to me was such that I should never have returned to Savigny if I had not wanted to study microscopically their incredible happiness, and to discover, for my personal edification, the grain of weariness, of suffering, or—if I must speak plainly—of remorse. But there was nothing! —nothing! Love pervaded everything, and obscured their moral sense and what you call conscience, and when I looked at these happy beings, I understood the seriousness of the joke of my old comrade Broussais when he said about conscience: 'I have been dissecting for thirty years and have never found a trace of that little beast.'

"And do not imagine," continued the sarcastic old doctor, as though he had read my thoughts, "that what I am telling you is a mere theory—the proof of the doctrine which denies the existence of conscience as Broussais denied it, I believe to be true. There is no theory here. I do not pretend to ask your opinion. I relate nothing but facts, which astonished me as much as they do you. It is merely the phenomenon of continued happiness— of a soap bubble which increased in size and never burst. When happiness lasts like that, it is always surprising, but happiness in crime is astounding, and in twenty years I have never got over my amazement. The old doctor, the old observer, the old moralist —or immoralist," he added, seeing me smile, "is disconcerted by this spectacle which he has beheld so many years, and which he cannot relate in detail, for, as is well said, happiness has no history.

"No description is possible. You can no more paint happiness —that infusion of a higher life into ordinary life—than you can paint the circulation of blood in the veins. You can certify by the beating of the arteries that it *does* circulate; and, by the same reasoning, I can certify to the happiness of those incomprehensible beings, whose pulse I have been feeling for so many years. The Comte and Comtesse de Savigny, without knowing it, recreate every day that splendid chapter of "Love in Marriage" of Madame de Staël, or the still more magnificent verses of Milton's *Paradise Lost*. For my own part, I have never been very sentimental or very poetical, but the ideal which they have realized, and which I deemed impossible, has disgusted me with the best marriages I have known, and which the world called charming. I have always found these so inferior to theirs—so colorless and cold. Destiny, or their star, or chance—whatever it may be—has decreed that they shall live for themselves alone. Being rich, they have that idleness without which love cannot exist, but which often kills the love from which it necessarily springs. But their case is an exception, and idleness has not killed theirs. Love, which simplifies everything, has made their life a sublime simplification.

There are none of those important matters which are called events in the existence of those two married people, who have lived, apparently, like most rich people, far from a world of which they ask nothing, caring nothing for its esteem or its disdain.

"They have never left one another. Where one goes, the other goes. The roads round V. again saw Hauteclaire on horseback, as in the time of 'Old Straight-thrust'; but it was the Comte de Savigny who was with her, and the ladies of the district, when they passed in their carriages, now stared at her more, perhaps, than when she was the tall and mysterious young girl in the dark-blue veil, whom they could not see. Now she had raised her veil, and boldly showed the face of the servant who had known how to make a good match, and the ladies returned home indignant, but thoughtful.

"The Comte and Countess de Savigny never travel; they sometimes come to Paris, but they stay only a few days. Their life is concentrated entirely in the château of Savigny, which was the theater of a crime, of which they have perhaps forgotten the memory in the bottomless abyss of their hearts."

"Have they never had any children, Doctor?" I asked.

"Ah!" said Doctor Torty, "you fancy perhaps, that that is their curse—the revenge of Fate—what you call the vengeance or the justice of God! No, they have never had any children. I once thought they would never have any. They love one another too much. The fire which devours, consumes and does not produce. One day I said to Hauteclaire:

"'Are you not sorry not to have any children, Madame la Comtesse?'

"'I do not want any,' she said proudly. 'I should love Serlon less. Children,' she added with a kind of scorn, 'are good only for women who are unhappy.'"

And Doctor Torty finished his story abruptly with this remark, which he deemed profound.

He had interested me, and I said:

"Criminal as she may be, I am interested in this woman, Hauteclaire. Had it not been for her crime, I should have understood Serlon's love."

"And, perhaps, even with her crime," said the Doctor. "As, indeed, I do," he added boldly.

The Legend of Saint Julian the Hospitaller

GUSTAVE FLAUBERT

Gustave Flaubert

GUSTAVE FLAUBERT (1821-1880) concludes the following narrative by saying: "And that is the story of Saint Julian the Hospitaller more or less as you will find it on a church window in my part of the country." Flaubert's part of the country was Normandy, more especially the city of Rouen, where the church window was and is, and where Flaubert himself was born, the son of a local surgeon and a fine austere woman of old Norman descent. As a youth he was to travel in Italy, Egypt and the Near East; he was often to be resident at Paris, where, as the author of *Madame Bovary* and the chief of the Realists, his fame was great and his conversation much admired; but the center of his existence was always to be in Rouen and its vicinity. There, on a small estate bordering the river Seine, he did most of his writing and there he died.

His attachment to his native place represented all that was beautifully conservative in Flaubert, as well (perhaps) as something that was recessive in a morbid sense. For although he was by endowment high-spirited, handsome and strongly built (a latter-day viking, as his friends said) he came to suffer from a chronic melancholia. He owed this partly to certain shocks experienced in his early years: the sight of blood and suffering in his father's hospital, the loss of a much-loved sister and a much-loved friend. In his twenties he was attacked by a severe nervous

illness which revisited him periodically throughout his life; and
although his love affairs were impassioned they led to violent differences and he never married. On the other hand, considering
the general spirit of his times, the failure in 1848 of the revolutionary hopes in which, as a youth, he had believed in his fashion,
the corruptions and vulgarities of French life under the Second
Empire, the rise of yellow journalism, the triumph of the cliché
over personal belief, it is more useful to understand Flaubert's
melancholia as an extreme form of historical pessimism. He owed
it mainly to a willingness to let his mind serve as a kind of arena,
pitilessly open and glaring, wherein the old pieties and chivalries
of Europe came into headlong and fatal conflict with the new
commercial and bureaucratic temper. In Flaubert's mind the death
of the spirit and of art was re-enacted daily, hourly, whenever he
opened a local newspaper or a contemporary romance or looked
into some overstuffed bourgeois parlor or heard some passage of
ignorant intolerant conversation on the street. He was perhaps by
nature a universal misanthropist like Swift before him; but he had
the historical obsession of his time, he was a kind of inverted
Marxist, and so his resources of hatred came to vent themselves
on the middle class and nineteenth-century civilization.

Flaubert has been criticized for refusing to temper his despair
with philosophy and his contempt of the bourgeois with charity;
and the failure or partial failure of some of his books (*Salammbô*,
The Sentimental Education, *Bouvard and Pécuchet*) has been
offered as evidence of moral weakness. Yet even his unsuccessful
or half-successful writings have proved to be of enormous interest: *The Sentimental Education* has been rewritten many times in
all the modern languages; *Salammbô* has remained the model of
the high historical romance up to the time of Thomas Mann's
Joseph; and *Bouvard and Pécuchet*, the "epic of the cliché," lives
on in *Babbitt* and *Ulysses*. When Flaubert failed, it was because
he was a tireless experimenter in new forms of fiction rather than
because he was a misanthrope. And when he succeeded! well,
Madame Bovary is still the arch-novel for many readers, and the
Three Tales remain the perfection of their kind. Besides his

novels, Flaubert left many personal letters which, immensely rich in detail and reference, make up one of the indispensable correspondences of the time. And of the man in general it may be said that, refusing compromise, he became the great exemplary figure of the mid-century on its darker side. Many of those who have since undertaken to reconstruct human pride by way of the novel —Henry James, Joyce, Gide, Proust—have had to contend with Flaubert's image as with that of some difficult but unquestionably legitimate father.

Flaubert might have said with Swift, "I detest mankind but love Tom, Dick and Harry"; for his misanthropy was qualified by his intense devotion to family, friends (certain friends), and disciples. Most of all, of course, he gave himself to the writing of fiction, which he sought to turn into a highly conscious art. To Balzac's energy of invention he added an energy of language and form whereby the novel came to rival poetry in subtlety and resonance; and even more than Balzac, he constructed his stories according to the pattern of a human life rather than of a dramatic action, thus severing the novel's ancient tie with the stage play and setting it within the fluid temporal medium which has been its usual medium ever since. At the same time, novelist though he was, Flaubert perpetuated that genius for extravagantly symbolic invention, tending to farce, which characterizes French writing in general, whether the author is Rabelais or Proust. *Madame Bovary* is "realism" and *Saint Julian* is "fantasy," but the latter is highly circumstantial in its telling and the former is full of bizarre incidents.

To his criticism of the new society Stendhal had brought the gaiety and detachment of a man who remained in some ways firmly entrenched in the optimistic culture of the Enlightenment; Balzac, who said no to the new society in principle, was committed to it by the whole force of his aggressive and acquisitive genius; but Flaubert, repudiating it in both theory and practice, was obliged to acquire a sense of order and purpose through his own laboriously perfected art and through the exercise of an historical imagination supported by exhaustive archæological researches. In all his best work these painfully acquired values are effectively present; to them *Madame Bovary* (1857) owes its intensities of beauty and horror and the *Three Tales* (1877)—of which *Saint Julian* is one—their note of ironic idealism. For, although Emma Bovary is entirely destructive, the heroes of these tales (*Hérodias* and *The Simple Heart* are the other two) are finally affirmative: if they murder they also create. They are men and women who achieve sanctity despite the pressure of great evil within or around them—two of them are actual saints of the church, the third is Flaubert's idea of a modern and quite anonymous type of sainthood. Actually, Julian seems to have lived in Africa in the fourth century; in making a medieval figure of him Flaubert has followed those old saints' legends which, with their disregard of historical fact and their mixture of piety and sensationalism, were very popular in the middle ages. Flaubert's version is both a parody and a serious recreation of those pious tales; and among all his works it is probably the most complete parable of his own inner being and struggle.

The Legend of St. Julian the Hospitaller

GUSTAVE FLAUBERT

Julian's father and mother lived in a castle on a hillside in the deep woods. At the four corners were pointed towers roofed with lead; the walls sprang from shafts of living rock which sloped steeply to the moat's bottom. The flagstones in the courtyard were tidy as a church floor; long spouts, representing dragons with their jaws wide, spat rainwater into cisterns; and at every window on every floor bloomed basil or heliotrope in painted pots.

Outside the castle was a second enclosure fenced in with stakes and containing first an orchard, then a flower garden of intricately patterned beds, then an arbor with many bowers where you sat to take the air, finally a playing field for the sport-loving pages. At the far side of the castle were kennels, stables and barns, a bakehouse and a winepress. Beyond lay green-turfed pastures, enclosed in turn by a stout hedge of thorn.

The castle had long been at peace with the world and the portcullis was never lowered now, grass grew in the moat, and swallows nested in the rotting battlements. If there was too much sun the bowman who paced the rampart all day long would retire into his sentry-house and sleep like a monk.

There was a gleam of polished metals in the great rooms; walls were hung with tapestries against the cold; cupboards bulged

[Translation Copyright, 1952, by F. W. Dupee]

397

with linen, cellars with wine casks, coffers with bags of gold and silver coin. In the armory, among captive banners and the heads of hunted beasts, were weapons of every age and nation, from slings of the Amalekites and javelins of the Garamantes, to Saracen swords and Norman coats of mail. The great spit in the kitchen could roast an ox whole, the chapel was as splendid as a king's oratory. In a secluded corner there was even a Roman bath, although the old lord thought it a heathen device and abstained from putting it to use.

Wrapped always in a foxskin cape, he wandered about the castle, administering justice to his vassals and settling disputes among his neighbors. In winter he studied the flying snowflakes or had stories read to him. With the first fine days he rode out on his mule along country roads through fields of greening wheat, stopping every now and then to chat with the serfs and give them advice. He had many light loves, then at last took to wife a woman of the highest birth.

Pale, serious, a little proud, she wore headdresses which brushed the tops of doors and her train trailed three paces behind her. She ran her household as if it were a convent. Every morning she set the servants to their tasks, supervised the making of unguents and preserves, then turned to spinning or to embroidering altar cloths. She prayed God for a son and a son was born to her.

There was great rejoicing then. There was a feast that went on for three days and four nights while torches flared and harps sounded and the strewn greens wilted underfoot. Rare spices were eaten and fowls the size of sheep, and a dwarf entertained by emerging unexpectedly from a pie. The crowd swelled so from hour to hour that the supply of wine cups gave out at last and men took to swilling from helmets and hunting horns.

The young mother shunned the festivities, keeping quietly to her bed. One night she came suddenly awake and made out a sort of shadow in vague motion beneath her moon-streaked window. It was an old man in monk's cloth; he had a rosary at his side and a sack on his shoulder and the look and bearing of a hermit. He came toward her where she lay, and while his lips did not move, a voice spoke distinctly through them. "Be glad," it said, "be glad, O mother, for this son of yours will be a saint."

She would have cried out, but the old man rose softly into the air and glided off and out of sight along a streak of moonlight. Now the banqueters' voices grew loud in song. She heard angels' voices; and her head fell back upon the pillow, above which hung some great martyr's bone in a jeweled frame.

Next morning she questioned the servants, who denied having seen any hermit. What she herself had seen and heard then was surely a message from heaven whether it had happened in reality or in a dream. But she was careful not to speak of it for fear she should be accused of presumption.

The guests went off at daybreak and Julian's father had just seen the last of them out and was standing by the gate alone when someone emerged suddenly from the morning mist—a man with the braided beard and silver finery and intense dark stare of a gypsy. He began to speak, to stammer crazily, as if he were possessed. "Your son, your son!" he cried, and went on to speak of someone "winning a lot of glory and shedding a lot of blood," and he ended by hailing Julian's parents as "the blest family of an emperor." The excited lord tossed him a purse full of coins. The man stooped to retrieve it, the high grass covered him, and he was gone. Looking this way and that the old lord called and called again. No answer! The wind was loud, the mists of morning blew away.

He blamed the vision on his exhausted state: he had been too long without sleep. "I shall be laughed at if I speak of it," he thought but the glory promised to his son continued to excite him even though he was unsure that he had heard the prophecy aright or that he had heard anything at all.

Husband and wife kept their secrets from each other but loved their son equally and made much of him and were intensely careful of his person because they believed him to be chosen by God. He lay in his down-stuffed cradle, a dove-shaped lamp burning always just above; three nurses kept the cradle in motion; and with his blue eyes and rosy cheeks, his heavy swaddling, his embroidered gown and pearl-sewn cap, he did really resemble an infant Jesus. He cut all his teeth without crying.

When he was seven his mother taught him to sing and his father put him astride a huge battle horse to make him brave. The boy smiled with pleasure and soon was expert in the lore of battle horses. Meanwhile a learned old monk taught him Holy Writ, the Arabic numerals, the Latin alphabet and how to make dainty pictures on vellum. They worked together in a tower room high above the uproar of the castle; and when the lesson was over they came down into the garden to stroll and pause, studying the flowers.

Sometimes a train of pack animals was seen advancing through the valley below, driven by a man dressed like an Oriental. The lord, knowing the driver for a merchant, would send a servant after him; and the driver, confident of not being robbed, would consent to turn out of his road and be conducted into the great hall where he would throw open his trunks and hand around the many treasures within: the silks and velvets and perfumes and jewels, the various curios and inventions whose use was unknown in those parts. Finally he would be off, greatly enriched and quite unharmed. Or some pilgrim band would come knocking at the gate and when they had been fed and their wet clothes hung steaming by the fire they would recount the story of their travels: the errant rocking voyages by sea, the long marches over hot sands, the fury of the paynims, the Syrian caves, the Manger and the Sepulcher. Before leaving they would present the young lord with seashells such as they wore sewed to their coats in token of their travels.

There were days when the lord feasted his old companions-at-arms. They drank and talked, recalling old engagements: the fortresses stormed, the rams and catapults making their din, the terrible wounds. Julian shouted as he listened and his father was now convinced that some day he would be a conqueror. But then evening came, and seeing the noble modesty with which, after prayers, he went among the kneeling poor to distribute alms, his mother decided that he was a future archbishop.

His place in chapel was next to his parents and even when the services were very protracted he stayed quietly on his knees with hands clasped firmly and his cap beside him on the floor. One day during Mass he looked up and saw a small white mouse creep from a hole in the wall, travel the length of the first altar step, explore about uncertainly, then trot back to its hole. Thinking to see the mouse again next Sunday, he felt strangely anxious. He did see it: the mouse reappeared; and each Sunday thereafter he watched for it, more and more anxious, hating the creature, intent on destroying it. So one Sunday after Mass he closed the door and strewed crumbs along the altar steps and stood waiting by the hole, armed with a stick. Long minutes passed, a small pink snout appeared, at last the entire mouse. He struck lightly, then stood amazed when the small body no longer moved. On the floor was a single drop of blood. Hastily Julian wiped it up with his sleeve, and tossed the dead mouse outside, saying nothing to anyone.

So many small birds pecked at the seeds in the garden that he thought of making a weapon out of a hollow reed filled with dried peas. When he came upon some tree that was noisy with birds, he approached it quietly, leveled his shooter, and blew out his cheeks. Birds came raining down in such abundance that he laughed aloud, pleased with his cleverness. As he was returning one morning along the rampart he spied a fat pigeon taking the sun there. He stopped to look at it; and as the wall was breached at this point and loose stones lay at hand, he grabbed one and swung and the bird dropped heavily into the moat.

He raced down after it, tearing his flesh on the brambles, searching wildly, as keen on the hunt as a young dog. The pigeon hung quivering in a bush with its wings broken. Its obstinate life filled him with rage. He took its throat in his hands and squeezed; the bird's struggles made his heart pound and his loins crawl with a strange lust and when it finally stiffened he was close to fainting.

At supper that night his father announced that the boy was old enough to learn to hunt. He got out an ancient book treating of the art of venery, written in the form of questions and answers exchanged between some master hunter and a pupil. It told how to train dogs and falcons, set traps, know a stag by its droppings, a fox by its tracks, a wolf by its lair, how best to start and track animals, where they are apt to take cover, which winds are most favorable, what cries to employ in the chase and what rules govern the division of the quarry. When Julian was able to repeat all this by heart his father made him a present of a magnificent pack of hunting dogs. There were twenty-four Barbary greyhounds, faster than gazelles but terribly wild and apt to get out of hand. There were seventeen pairs of loud-baying deep-chested white-and-russet Breton dogs, which looked wild but were easily controlled. For hunting wild boar with their ugly tactic of doubling back on the hunter, there were forty great shaggy boarhounds; and for bison hunting there were Tartary mastiffs which stood almost as tall as a jackass. Spaniels' black coats shone like satin; beagles sang out and setters yapped in chorus. In a yard by themselves were eight growling, eye-rolling, chain-rattling bulldogs—terrible beasts that leap at men's throats and are quite unafraid of lions.

Every dog in the pack ate white bread, drank from troughs of hewn stone, and answered to some high-sounding name.

At that the dogs were probably inferior to the falcons. Spending money freely, the old lord acquired tiercelets from the Caucasus, sakers from Babylonia, gerfalcons from Germany; he had the kind of pilgrim-hawks which are only captured along the high shores of cold seas in far parts of the world. A special shed housed all the birds; there they were chained along a perch according to size, and led out every so often to stretch and play on their own strip of turf. In the shops of the castle men were busy making purse-nets, hooks, traps and snares of all kinds.

Julian's family sometimes got up large parties to go quail hunting in the fields. There the bird dogs soon began to point, then crouched motionless while the runners-in advanced with care and spread an immense net over and around them. A word from the huntsmen and the dogs barked, the quail took wing, and the ladies of the neighborhood with their husbands, children and maidservants, dashed for the net and captured the birds with ease. Or hares were started by beating on drums or foxes tumbled into pits or wolves thrust unsuspecting paws into cruel traps.

But Julian scorned these easy contrivances, preferring to hunt alone with horse and hawk. The hawk was usually a great white Scythian tararet, which perched firmly on his master's arm while they covered the plain at a gallop, a plume nodding on its leather hood and golden bells tinkling around its blue claws. When Julian loosed the jesses, letting him go, the wonderful bird shot arrow-like into the sky. Julian saw two dark specks circle and meet and vanish into the blue altitudes; then the falcon would drop dizzily from the skies, tearing at some bird in his claws, and resume his perch on the gauntlet with shaking wings. So Julian hunted heron, kites, crows and vultures.

He loved also to sound his horn and follow the dogs as they raced down the hills and jumped the streams and climbed to the next woods; and when a stag fell among them, moaning as they attacked it with their teeth, he skillfully dispatched it, then looked on with pleasure while they tore and devoured the bloody carcass.

On foggy days he hid out in the marshes to watch for geese, otter or wild duck. Three of his squires would have been waiting for him on the steps since daybreak; and even though the old monk his teacher made admonitory signs at him from his high window, Julian refused to look back. He went out in rain or storm or broiling sun, drank with his cupped hand from springs, ate wild apples as he went, snatched brief naps under trees; and reached home at midnight with burrs in his hair, mud and gore on his clothes, and the smell of game all over him. Gradually he came to resemble the wild things he hunted. He was indifferent to his mother's entreaties, cold to her kisses, and seemed to be caught in the dark toils of a dream.

He killed bears with a knife, bulls with a hatchet and wild boars with a spear. And once, with nothing but a stick, he kept off a lot of wolves which were feeding on the corpses around a gallows.

There came a winter morning when he set out before daybreak, thoroughly equipped, with his bow astride his shoulder and his quiver slung to his pommel. A couple of terriers trailed his Danish hunter, all three of them keeping step and pounding the ground in unison while the wind blew and frost collected on his coat. Toward the east the sky began to clear and in the pallid light he saw a multitude of rabbits leaping and running among their burrows. Immediately the dogs were among them, upon them, cracking their frail spines. Next he was in a stretch of woods and, spying a woodcock that perched as if frozen to a branch, with head under wing, he made at it with a backstroke of his sword and severed its two feet from its body and was off without stopping to retrieve it.

Three hours more and he was cresting a mountain so immensely high that the heavens hung blue-black around him; and there in front of him was an expanse of flat rock with a precipice beyond and a couple of wild goats standing far out on it gazing idly into the gulf. Having no arrows—he had left his horse behind—he decided to fall directly upon them; and so, barefoot, bent double, dagger in hand, he advanced painfully towards them and brought the near one down with a sudden thrust in the ribs. The other, in a panic, leaped towards the void and Julian was after it to strike it down in turn when he stumbled and fell headlong across the body of the dead goat and there he lay, arms flung wide, staring down into space.

Then he was on the flats once more, following a willow-bordered stream, and a great number of cranes were in low shuttling flight above his head. Julian cut them all down, one by one, with his whip.

Meanwhile the day grew warmer, the frost melted and the sun broke through the haze. He now saw far off, lead-gray and gleaming, a small lake, and breasting its bright still surface was some unknown beaver-like animal. Across the distance he let fly an arrow and saw the creature sink and was sorry because he could not bring home the skin.

Now he was in an avenue of great trees, and passing under them as under some triumphal arch he entered a forest that lay beyond. A deer suddenly broke cover there, a buck showed in a side road, a badger came out of a hole, a peacock spread his tail along the grass; and when he had slain them all, there suddenly was another deer, more bucks and badgers sprang up around him, more peacocks and jays and blackbirds and foxes and porcupines and polecats and lynxes—an infinity of beasts, increasing as he advanced.

They crowded round him, trembling, with eyes of mild entreaty. But Julian attacked them tirelessly, having no thought except to be upon them with arrow or sword or knife. There was only the brute fact of his existence to remind him that he had been hunting for incalculable hours in some vague country where things happened with the same ease as in our dreams.

Then he saw an astonishing thing that made him pause at last. There opened before him a steep-sided sandy-bottomed valley, a sort of natural coliseum; and it was full of stags, an army of them, which huddled close and breathed warmth on one another, the steamy cloud from a hundred nostrils rising to mingle with the morning haze. For a moment, the prospect of so much slaughter made Julian go faint with excitement; then, springing from his horse, he thrust back his sleeves and began to take aim. With the twang of the first arrow all the stags looked up as one, a diffused moan broke from them, fissures opened in their solid ranks and panic shook the whole herd. As Julian's arrows fell upon them, hemmed in as they were by the valley walls, the herd stampeded. Stags reared, pawed, locked antlers, climbed heavily on each other. And all the while they fell, bodies and antlers piling up into one vast inextricable ever-growing ever-shifting mound. So one by one, with heaving lungs and bursting bowels, they died along the sands and soon everything was still and night came down and the tree-screened sky was the color of blood.

Julian leaned against a tree and stared on the enormous massacre, trying to remember how it had been done. Then across the valley at the woods edge he saw another stag with its hind and fawn. Dark, enormous, the stag had a white beard and an intricate many-pointed growth of horn; the hind, pale as a dead leaf, grazed idly by while her spotted fawn trotted alongside, pull-

ing at her dugs. Again Julian's bow sang out. The fawn dropped.
The mother, looking up, uttered a single shattering all but human
cry. Julian, tense, exasperated, brought her down as well, with a
shot full in the breast. Seeing her fall the great stag leaped and
received Julian's arrow, his last one, between the eyes. There it
stuck fast but the stag, indifferent, came striding over the bodies
of his dead, came on and on, while Julian retreated in horror, seeing himself charged and laid flat and disemboweled. Then the
great stag halted and with burning eyes, solemn, accusing, like
some patriarch or judge, he spoke, while off in the distance a bell
tolled.

"Accurst! accurst! accurst! one day, O savage heart, you will
destroy your father and mother."

The stag dropped quietly to earth and closed his eyes and died.

Julian stood as if stunned; then a weariness swept over him,
followed by great waves of disgust and sadness. His horse was
lost, his dogs had taken to their heels, the solitude around him
seemed full of vague alarms. He fled, striking across country, following a trail at random. And there, suddenly, was the castle gate.

That night he did not sleep but lay staring into the uneven light
of the hanging lamp and saw always the great black, bearded wide-
antlered stag. The stag's words obsessed him; repeatedly he denied them. "It cannot be that I should kill them. No, no! I have no
wish to kill them." Then in a moment he thought, "But suppose
I *should* wish—" And he lay and trembled for fear the Devil
should implant that unspeakable wish in him.

Three months his mother prayed in anguish by his bed while
his father, groaning, paced the corridors. Specialists were brought
in, famous doctors and apothecaries; they said he was sick with
a miasma or with carnal desire; they prescribed drugs and more
drugs. When they questioned him, however, Julian merely shook
his head.

Growing stronger, he walked briefly in the courtyard, leaning on his father and the old monk. When he had quite recovered
he obstinately refused to hunt again. His father, hoping to bring
him around, made him a present of a fine stout Saracen sword. It

hung aloft on a pillar among other arms and trophies, and Julian had to mount a ladder to bring it down. It was very heavy and slipped from his hands and, clattering down, grazed the old lord's shoulder and slashed his mantle. Julian fainted, thinking he had killed his father.

From then on he felt a horror of weapons and went white at the sight of a bare blade. This weakness grieved his family and at last the old monk, in the name of God, honor and the ancestral dead, bade him take up again the exercises of a gentleman.

The squires amused themselves by practicing daily with javelins. Julian soon excelled at this sport and could drive his javelin into a bottle's mouth or strike the tail-feathers from a weathercock or pick out doornails at a hundred paces.

One summer evening he loitered in the arbor, now dim in the failing light; and spying beyond the arbor, against a wall, what he thought to be two white fluttering wings, surely a stork, he hurled his javelin. There was a terrible cry; it was the voice of his mother, whose bonnet with its long white fluttering ribbons stayed pinned to the wall.

Julian fled the castle and was seen there no more.

2

He fell in with a passing troop of adventuring soldiers and came to know thirst, hunger, fever, and vermin, the noise of battle, the sight of dying men. His skin browned in the wind; his arms and legs grew hard under the weight of his armor; and being strong, fearless, just and shrewd, he was soon in command of a company.

With sword aloft he waved his men into battle; he scaled fortress walls by night, hanging to knotted ropes, tugged at by the wind, while sparks of Greek fire clung to his cuirass and boiling tar and molten lead poured hissing down from the battlements. Stones crashed on his buckler, shivering it; bridges overloaded with men gave way beneath him. On one occasion he felled four-teen men with a single swing of his battle-ax; in the lists he overcame all challengers; many times he was left on the field for dead.

Yet he always walked away, thanks to the divine favor which he enjoyed now, because he had become the protector of churchmen, orphans, widows and aged men. Of aged men most of all, and seeing some old stranger on the road ahead he would call out to him to show his face, as if afraid he might kill him in error.

Desperate men flocked to his banner, runaway slaves, serfs in revolt, bastards without fortune; and soon he had an army of his own, its fame increasing with its numbers, until the world sought him out and he was able to give aid by turns to the French Dauphin, the English king, the Templars of Jerusalem, the Surena of the Parthians, the Negus of Abyssinia, the Emperor of Calcutta. He did battle with Scandinavians in fish-scale armor, with Negroes astride red asses and brandishing shields of hippopotamus hide, with East Indians the color of pale gold who waved shining swords and wore their crowns into battle. He subdued the Troglodytes and the Anthropophages. He journeyed through hot countries where men's hair took fire from the sun and they flared up like torches, through cold countries where men's arms snapped freezing from their sockets and fell heavily to earth, through fogbound countries where they marched among phantoms.

He was consulted by republics in distress, he conferred with ambassadors and obtained unexpected terms, he rebuked tyrants, delivered captive queens and set whole peoples free. It was Julian and no other who slew the Milanese serpent and the dragon of Oberbirbach.

Now the Emperor of Occitania was victorious over the Spanish Moslems and took the Caliph of Cordova's sister as his concubine and by her had a daughter whom he brought up in the Christian faith. But the Caliph, feigning a desire to be converted, arrived with a numerous escort as if on a visit to the Emperor, put his entire garrison to the sword and threw him into a dungeon where he used him cruelly to extort his treasure.

Julian hastened to his aid, destroyed the infidel army, laid siege to the town, slew the Caliph, chopped off his head and tossed it over the ramparts like a ball. Then he released the Emperor and set him on his throne again in the presence of his entire court. By way of reward the Emperor offered him money, whole basketfuls; Julian would have none of it. Did he want more?—the Emperor offered him three-quarters of his wealth and was refused again; then half his kingdom; Julian thanked him and declined. The Emperor was in tears, he saw no way of showing his gratitude. At last he slapped his brow and turned whispering to one of his attendants; a curtain was drawn and there stood a young girl.

Her great dark eyes were like two soft lights and she had a charming smile. Her curls tangled with the jewels on her half-open bodice; through her transparent tunic shone the young lines of her body, which was plump, small, finely made.

Julian was dazzled, all the more because he had been chaste till now. So he took the Emperor's daughter in marriage, with a castle which she held from her mother and, the wedding over, quitted his host after an exchange of many courtesies.

Their palace was built of white marble in the Moorish style and stood on a promontory among orange groves. There was an expanse of bright bay below, a fanlike spread of forest behind, and terraces of flowers descending to a rosy beach where small shells crackled underfoot. The sky was an unchanging blue. Trees stirred in light winds that blew, now from off the sea, now down from the steep far all-enveloping mountains.

The rooms were full of shadow yet drew soft light from encrusted walls. Tall reedlike columns supported domed vaults sculptured to represent stalactites in a cave. In the great halls were fountains, in the courts mosaics, on the walls festoons; delicate instances of architectural fancy abounded; and such was the silence everywhere that you could hear plainly the rustle of a scarf, the echo of a sigh.

Julian made war no longer but lived at ease among a tranquil people, contingents of them arriving daily to kneel before him and kiss his hand and do him homage like people of the East, while he lounged in purple dress in some deep-set window and called to mind the old hunting days. He longed to hunt again, to scour the desert after gazelle and ostrich, stalk leopards among the bamboos, strike into forests full of rhinoceros, scale impossible mountains where the eagle screamed, and wrestle with bears on icebergs in the polar sea. Sometimes, in dreams, he saw himself like our father Adam sitting in the middle of Paradise with the entire race of animals around him. He stretched forth an arm and they died. Or else they paraded before him two by two in order of size, from elephants and lions to ermines and ducks, as on the day when they entered Noah's ark. Standing in a cave's mouth, hidden, he rained darts on them, darts that never missed. More animals appeared, endless animals, until, wild-eyed, he woke at last.

There were princes among his acquaintance who invited him to hunt. He refused, thinking by such penance to turn aside the curse. He believed that the fate of his father and mother was linked in some way with the slaughtering of animals. Yet he grieved because he could not see his parents; and his other great desire, the secret one, became more and more unbearable.

His wife hoped to divert him and so engaged jugglers and dancers to perform in the castle, or traveled with him into the country in an open litter, or lay beside him in a boat while they watched the play of wandering fish in sky-clear water. She pelted him with flowers; she sat at his feet and plucked charmingly at the three strings of an old mandolin; and then, in despair, "My dear good lord, what ails you?" she asked mildly, laying a hand on his shoulder.

For a long time he refused to answer though sometimes he wept. Then one day he told her what was horribly on his mind. She fought against it, she argued well. Very probably his father and mother were dead already; and if by chance they were alive still and he should see them again, whatever could make him commit so abominable an act, what weird circumstance or impossible motive? His fears were all groundless, she said, and he should go back to hunting. Julian listened smiling but could not bring himself to yield.

One August night as they were preparing for sleep and she was already in bed and Julian was at his prayers, he heard a fox barking at a distance and, nearer by, directly under the window, soft,

stealthy, padding footfalls. Now he was at the window and looking down in the gloom on some vague prowling forms, the shadows, as it were, of animals. He was too strongly tempted. From
its hook on the wall, he seized his old quiver; and when his wife
looked at him, astonished, he said, "You see! I obey you. I shall
be back at sunrise." Suddenly she was afraid and began to speak
of accidents and injuries but Julian comforted her and left, surprised to see her so changed.

Soon afterwards a page informed her that two strangers had
come inquiring for the lord; in his absence they begged to see his
lady at once. They came in to her, an aged couple, each of them
leaning heavily on a stick, the dust of the road on their ragged
clothes. They made bold to say that they brought news of Julian's
father and mother and she leaned from her bed to listen. But first
they exchanged a glance and asked if he ever spoke of his parents,
still loved them.

"Ah, yes!" she said.

"Well, we are his parents!" they cried, and sat themselves down
because they were very tired.

She hesitated. Could it be so? They guessed her doubt and went
on to offer proof by describing a curious birthmark on Julian's
body. She leaped from bed crying to the page to bring them food.
But hungry as they looked, they ate little and she saw how their
bony fingers shook when they raised their cups. She answered
their many questions about their son but took pains to conceal
his terrible obsession. They told her that they had left their castle
when Julian failed to return, and wandered for years in search of
him, following vague clues, never losing hope. So much of their
money had gone into meeting river tolls and inn charges, princes'
exactions and those of highwaymen, that they were now quite
penniless and had to beg their way. But what of that, when they
would soon be able to take Julian in their arms! How happy he
must be to have so pretty a wife, they said; and they gazed long
at her and kissed and kissed her. The fine room made them stare;
and the old man inquired why the walls bore the Emperor of
Occitania's coat-of-arms.

"He is my father," she said.

He started, remembering what the gypsy had prophesied, while his wife called to mind the prophecy of the hermit. No doubt their son's present happiness promised some even greater, some eternal, glory to come; and the old couple sat wide-eyed in the blaze of the great candelabra on the table.

They must have been very handsome in their youth. The mother, her fine abundant hair intact, wore it in lengthy white braids along her cheek; while the father, with his great height and great beard, resembled some statue in a church. Julian's wife persuaded them not to wait up for him. She made them sleep in her own bed, tucked them away like children and drew the curtains. They were asleep soon, and outside, in the first gleams of dawn, small birds were singing.

Julian had crossed the park and come into the forest, his step eager, his senses alert to the soft grass and mild moonlit air. Shadows were deep on the moss banks under trees. At intervals there were moon-drenched clearings where he abruptly halted, thinking he was about to plunge into a woodland pond; and there were real ponds, which he mistook for clearings. Everywhere the silence was intense; there was no trace of the animals which only a moment ago had been prowling around the castle. He was now in a dense stand of trees where the gloom was especially thick. He felt the play of warm scented airs on his flesh. His feet sank among dead leaves and he stopped, leaning breathless against an oak.

Then a dark, still darker, something leaped suddenly from behind him, a wild boar, which was off before he had time to seize his bow and which he mourned the loss of as if that was a great misfortune. Leaving the woods he spied a wolf stealing along a hedge and let fly an arrow. The wolf stopped, looked briefly around at him, and went on. It trotted evenly along, keeping the same distance from him, halting at intervals; but when Julian started to take aim, it fled. Thus he covered a wide plain, then a tract of sand hills, and came out on high ground overlooking miles of country below.

He was among great flat jumbled stones, the scatterings of some old graveyard long ago abandoned to the weather. He stumbled over moldy crosses leaning sadly askew among the stones, and he trod on the bones of the dead. There was a stirring of vague shapes in the dark of the tombs, hyenas in wild-eyed panting flight. Their hooves came clattering over the stones and they closed in on Julian, sniffing, yawning, showing their gums. He drew his sword and they fled, severally, at a headlong limping gallop, kicking up a dust which finally hid them from sight.

Later, in a ravine, there was a wild bull pawing the sand and menacing him with lowered horns. Julian thrust at it with his lance but the lance sang out and fell in splinters as if it had come against some bull cast in bronze and he closed his eyes, expecting to be charged and killed. When he opened them the bull was gone.

His heart sank with shame, his strength gave way before some higher power, and striking back into the forest, he headed for home. He was in a tangle of creepers, cutting a passage with his sword, when a weasel shot between his legs; a panther, leaping, cleared his shoulder; around the trunk of an ash a snake coiled upward; from out the leaves above, a huge jackdaw eyed him; and it was as if the sky had rained down all its stars upon the forest, for everywhere around him, sparking the darkness, were the innumerable eyes of beasts—owls, squirrels, monkeys, parrots, bobcats.

Julian attacked them with arrows but the feathered shafts only showered like white butterflies among the leaves. He threw stones, but they dropped harmlessly to earth. He raged, cursed himself, made the forest loud with imprecations. Then the various animals he had just been hunting showed themselves and came round him in a narrow circle, keeping erect or going down on their haunches. There he stood in the midst of them, terrified and quite unable to move. By making a great effort he succeeded in taking a step forward. As soon as he moved, wings began to flutter in the trees, paws stirred on the ground, and the whole assemblage moved with him. He went on, the hyenas striding ahead, the wolf and the boar behind; the bull, swinging its enormous head, on his left; the snake coiling along through the grass on his right; the panther advancing at a distance with arched back and long soft-footed strides. He walked very slowly to avoid exciting them and as he went he saw porcupines, foxes, jackals, vipers and bears breaking cover around him. He began to run and they ran too. The snake hissed, the dirtier creatures slavered; he felt the boar's tusks prodding at his heels, the wolf's hairy snout nuzzling his hand. Monkeys pinched him and made faces; a weasel somersaulted over his feet; a bear knocked his cap from his head with a backswing of its paw; and the panther, after chewing placidly on an arrow, let it drop with disdain.

There was irony in their sly motions. Watching him from the corners of their eyes, they seemed to be planning some revenge; and Julian, dazed by buzzing insects and the slapping of birds' tails and the breath from many nostrils, walked like a blind man with eyes closed and arms flung out, not daring even to cry, "Have mercy!"

A cock crowed, others replied, day was breaking; and Julian made out the lines of the castle roof riding above the orange trees. Then he discovered some partridges fluttering in a stubble-field close by. He flung off his cloak and threw it over them like a net. On lifting it, however, he found only the decaying body of a bird long dead. This was the worst irony yet; he raged anew; the thirst to kill came over him and, failing beasts, he would gladly have killed men. Quickly he mounted the three terraces and with a blow of his fist swung the door wide. But on the stairs within he remembered his darling wife and his heart softened. She was no doubt asleep and he would have the pleasure of surprising her. Quietly, his sandals in his hand, he turned the knob and entered their bedroom.

The early light came dimly through leaded windows. Julian stumbled over some clothes lying on the floor; a little farther, and he knocked against a table loaded with dishes. "She must have eaten," he thought and advanced with caution towards the alcove where, in total darkness, the bed stood. He stooped to kiss his wife, bending over the two who lay there side by side in sleep. His lips touched a man's beard and he fell back, thinking he was out of his mind. He stooped over the bed again and this time his searching fingers discovered a woman's long hair. To assure himself that he had been mistaken, he felt for the beard again—and found it! found a man there, a man lying with his wife.

He was upon them in a fury, striking with his dagger, foaming, stamping, howling like a wild beast. At last he stopped. Pierced through the heart they had not so much as stirred, they were dead. He heard the rattle of death in their throats, rhythmic, prolonged, growing feebler at last, mingling then with another sound, now vague and far off, now coming steadily closer, swelling, ringing out cruelly; and he recognized in terror the belling of the great black stag.

He turned and saw in the door, candle in hand, ghostlike, the pale figure of his wife. Drawn there by sounds of violence, she took it all in with one wide glance and fled in horror, dropping her candle. Julian picked it up.

His father and mother lay face up before him with great wounds in their breasts. In their superb gentle eyes was the look of people intent on keeping a secret forever. There was blood on their white hands, the bedclothes, the floor, the ivory crucifix on the alcove wall. The glare of the newly risen sun made the whole room red as if with blood. Julian looked at the dead. He said to himself, endeavored to believe, that this thing could not be, that he must be entangled in some fearful error. To make sure of their identity he stooped close over the old man's face and saw beneath open lids two eyes, now glazed, which scorched him like fire. He then circled the bed to where, in the dark recesses of the alcove, the other body lay, the face half hidden by white hair. He lifted the head with one hand and with the other held the candle close to it while drop by drop the bed discharged its load of blood upon the floor.

At evening he came in where his wife was and speaking with a stranger's voice bade her first of all not to answer him or come near him or even look at him; then to obey, under penalty of damnation, his various commands, every one of which she must consider irrevocable.

In the death-chamber she would find written instructions for the funeral. These she must carry out to the letter. To her he made over everything he owned: castle, serfs, goods—even the clothes on his back and the sandals on his feet, which she would find presently at the stair head.

The dead were splendidly interred in an abbey church at three days' journey from the castle. A monk, his face concealed by his hood, followed the procession at a distance and to him no one dared speak. All during the Mass he lay flat on the porch floor, his arms crossed, his face in the dust.

After the burial he was seen to take the road leading to the mountains. He looked back at intervals and finally was gone.

3

He went about the world begging his way. He reached up a hand to horsemen on the roads, bent a knee to reapers in the fields, stood patiently at castle gates, and looked so grief-stricken that he was not refused. Humbly, again and again, he told his story and people fled crossing themselves. When he passed through a village where he had been before, they abused and stoned him and shut their doors in his face, although a few charitable souls put plates of food on their windowsills before banging the shutters on the unholy sight of him.

Shunned by all, he began to shun mankind himself, feeding on roots, plants and windfalls, and shellfish gathered along the beaches of the world. Sometimes, on coming over a hill, he would find himself in sight of some multitudinous jumble of roofs and spires below; from the dark maze of streets came the steady hum of human life and he would be drawn downward by a need to be with other people. No sooner was he in the streets, however, than the brutal look on people's faces, the bustle in the stores, the up-roar of shops and foundries, the callous idle talk, would begin to freeze his heart. On feast days when bells began tolling at day-break and people responded with excitement, he watched them pouring from their houses, the dancers in the public squares, the beer fountains at the crossroads, the rich bright hangings on the princely houses; and then after dark he spied through windows on the long family tables where old people sat with children in their laps. He would turn away in tears and strike back into the country.

He gazed with yearning at colts in their pastures, birds in their nests, insects among flowers; all fled at his approach. He sought out deserted places but there was the rattle of death in the blow-ing of wind, tears in the dewdrops, blood in the sun at evening, and parricide by night in his dreams. He undertook acts of mor-tification, ascended on his knees to high and holy places. But the horror in his mind corrupted the splendor of tabernacles and nul-lified the rigor of his penances. He did not curse God for having caused him to murder, but having murdered he despaired of God. The horror he felt of his own person made him risk it eagerly in dangerous enterprises. He rescued children from pits in the earth and helpless men and women from their burning houses. But the earth rejected him, the flames spared him. With the passing of time he suffered not less but more and finally he resolved to die.

One day, however, while he was staring into a spring of water to judge of its depth, he saw appear on the far side an old man with so much misery on his lean white-bearded face that Julian suddenly wept. The old man fell to weeping too; and Julian, look-ing him in the face, knew him and did not know him. "My father!" he cried and thought no more of destroying himself.

So, weighed down with memories, he traversed many lands and came at last to a river which tore along swiftly between marshy shores and had long defied anyone to cross it. Mud-bound and half concealed in the reeds lay an old boat, and on looking around Julian also discovered a pair of oars. It came over him that he might devote his life to the service of others.

He began by constructing a sort of ramp across the marsh, connecting the river's channel with solid ground. He broke his nails on enormous stones, carried them pressed against his heaving stomach, sprawled in the mud, sank into it, was nearly drowned several times. Then he set to patching up the boat from the debris of other vessels and he made himself a hut of logs and clay.

Travelers soon heard of Julian's ferry and began to flock to it. On the far side a flag was raised to summon him and Julian would leap aboard and row across for the waiting passengers. The boat was heavy to begin with and when it was loaded with men and their belongings including domestic animals that kicked and reared in alarm, it could only be managed with difficulty. He asked nothing for his trouble though some of the passengers gave him worn-out clothes or leftovers from their store of food. The ugly ones cursed him out and he reproved them gently. If they went on cursing, he was satisfied to bless them.

A small table, a stool, a bed made of dry leaves, and three earthen bowls were all the furnishings he had while a couple of holes in the wall served as windows. In front the great river rolled its turgid green flood; at the rear stretched a vast colorless barrens strewn with shallow ponds. In spring the damp soil reeked of decay; then came powerful winds driving dust before them till it roiled the water and gritted between his teeth; then came mosquitoes in endless humming biting clouds; then appalling frosts which turned the earth to stone and gave him in his chilled and exhausted state a tremendous appetite for meat. Months passed when Julian, seeing no one, sat with his eyes shut trying to revive in memory the days of his youth. A castle courtyard would rise before him with greyhounds at rest on the terraces, grooms busy in the armory, and a yellow-haired boy sitting in a bower of vines between an old man wrapped in furs and a lady in a tall bonnet. Suddenly an image of two dead bodies would intervene and he would fling himself on his bed and sob, "Ah, poor father! Poor mother, poor mother!" and, dozing off, he would continue to see them in dreams.

There came a night when he thought he heard someone calling

him in his sleep. He strained to listen but made out nothing except the river's roar. Then "Julian!" the same voice cried again, "Julian!" It reached him, amazingly, from the far shore of the broad and noisy river. "Julian!" he heard again, the voice loud, vibrant, like a church bell. With lantern alight, he stepped from the hut into a night wild with wind and rain, the river foaming white in the intense darkness.

He hesitated briefly then leapt into the boat and cast off. Instantly the waves subsided and the boat sped easily to the far shore. There a man stood waiting in a ragged coat, his face white as a plaster mask, his eyes redder than coals. Holding up his lantern Julian saw that the stranger was covered with hideous sores. He was a leper but he had the majesty of a king. The boat gave alarmingly under his weight, then rose again, and Julian began to work the oars.

At every stroke the bow slapped against a wave and was flung aloft, while dark water streamed alongside. Masses of water gathered beneath, thrusting the boat skyward, then fell away, leaving it to skitter down into some deep trough where it spun helplessly. Julian could only keep it under control by leaning far forward and then, feet powerfully braced, hands riveted to the oar handles, flinging his torso backward with a convulsive pull at the oars. Hail cut his hands, rain poured down his back, and suddenly breathless in the terrible wind, he paused, letting the boat drift with the waves. But feeling that something very great was at stake, a mission that he must not fail, he once more seized the oars and made them rattle on their pins in the loud wind. At the bow the lantern burned, its rays intercepted at intervals by the fluttering passage of storm-blown birds. But always he saw the eyes of the Leper who stood immobile at the stern. And they were a long, long time in crossing.

Arrived in the hut Julian closed the door behind them. The Leper took the stool and sat. His shroudlike dress fell to his loins; his chest, his shoulders, his lean arms were plastered with sores. There were great pained wrinkles on his forehead. Skeleton-like, he had a hole instead of a nose; his lips were blue, a steamy and malodorous exhalation pouring from them.

"I am hungry!" he said.

Julian gave him what he had, a black loaf and rind of bacon. When he had devoured them, the table, bowl and knife handle bore the same sores that he had on his body. Then he said,

"I am thirsty!"

Julian went to get the water jug and found it full of some exciting sweet-smelling liquid. It was wine—a wonderful find. The Leper reached for it and drank the jug dry at a draught.

Then he said, "I am cold."

Julian put his candle to a heap of dried fern in the middle of the floor. The Leper, on his knees, crouched by the fire, body shaking, sores running, eyes growing dim. He was weakening visibly, and in a faint voice murmured,

"Your bed!"

Julian helped him to it gently and covered him with everything he had, even the tarpaulin for his boat. The Leper groaned through his teeth, the rattle of death came faster in his chest, and with every breath he took his belly sank into his spine. At last his eyes went closed.

"My bones are like ice! Come close to me!"

And Julian, raising the tarpaulin, lay down at his side on the dry leaves. The Leper turned his head. "Take off your clothes," he commanded, "that I may have the warmth of your body." Julian flung off his clothes and lay down once more as naked as on the day he was born. Against his thigh he felt the Leper's skin, colder than a snake and rough as a file. He tried to cheer him but the other merely said in a low whisper, "I am dying. Come closer, get me warm! No! not with your hands, with your whole body."

Julian laid himself at full length upon him, mouth to mouth, breast to breast. The Leper clasped him hard and suddenly his eyes shone like stars, the hair on his head was like the rays of the sun, his breath was like the breath of the rose, there was incense in the smoke of the fern-fire, music on the water. To Julian, fainting, came a great bliss, a joy more than human; and the one who held him grew tall, grew taller, till his head and feet touched the two walls of the hut. The roof gaped, the wide firmament looked down—and Julian rose into blue altitudes face to face with Our Lord Jesus who carried him up to heaven.

And that is the story of Saint Julian the Hospitaller more or less as you will find it on a church window in my part of the country.

Captain Burle

ÉMILE ZOLA

Émile Zola

Born in Paris of a French mother and a father who was half Greek and half Italian, ÉMILE ZOLA (1840-1902) spent his childhood in the southern town of Aix-en-Provence, where Paul Cézanne, the future painter, was one of his school friends. Returning to Paris at eighteen he was soon busy writing for the newspapers. His first full-length novel, the remarkable *Thérèse Raquin*, appeared while he was still in his twenties; and thereafter he produced long and densely documented novels with a wonderful regularity, the best known of them being *Nana*, *The Dram-shop* (*L'Assomoir*), *The Debacle*, and *Germinal*.

Zola had been a vigorous reformer from the start; his final years were enlivened by his part in the Dreyfus affairs, which rocked French military, civil and social life at the turn of the century. He lived to see Dreyfus acquitted, and died shortly afterward, asphyxiated by fumes from a defective flue in his bedroom in Paris.

While he lived Zola had an immense fame that reached everywhere. Chekhov in Russia, Wells and Bennett in England, Dreiser in America, all learned from him. He was admired, partly for the sensational excitement of his stories of vice and crime and war and social violence, partly for the extremely serious theories of life and art on which his work rested. He undertook to produce another Human Comedy like Balzac's, but one based on post-

Darwinian science and attempting a more precise observation of individual and social behavior than Balzac had essayed. Most of Zola's novels deal with the fortunes of a family called the Rougon-Macquarts. And even in his novels, or especially in his novels, he was the reformer: their end was practical. Like Jean-Paul Sartre after the recent war—but with very different means—Zola sought to reconstruct the French spirit following the defeat of 1870 and the strife of the Commune; he wanted to lay the ghosts of Romantic despair and decadence; to establish life, politics and art in the Third Republic on what he conceived to be the reasonable basis provided by the biological and social sciences. In this literary-philosophic-political endeavor Zola was joined by other writers, and their tendency came to be known as Naturalism.

Zola's scientific optimism was heady and brilliant; it was also excessive. He was essentially a fine artist but he wrote too much; some of his long novels seem to have been galvanized by his mastery of a method and his encyclopaedic knowledge of society rather than by any intimate passion for life and language. His reputation was soon eclipsed; an English critic could recently dismiss his entire work as "dreary realism." But this is not at all the case; and several of the great novelists who succeeded Zola in reputation—Mann, Proust, Joyce—profited by his mastery of the epic narrative and of social reality, even though they went on from there.

Zola at his best went on from there, too. His good stories are finally effective because, like Mann and the others, he has a strong feeling for symbolic behavior and human relationships. When in *Thérèse Raquin* he makes a murderer's scar the emblem of his conscience, and when in *Germinal* he represents the coal mines as a kind of mythical underworld, he is a symbolist just as these later writers have been and as any good writer is.

Captain Burle is a case in point. The story is intense with Zola's knowledge of army life in a small garrison town during the peace-time doldrums following the great excitement and heroism of a war. Vauchamp is such a town; and the officers Burle and Laguitte are two former heroes who have grown fat and corrupt, one of them hopelessly corrupt, under peacetime conditions and the solicitations of civilian vice and graft; while Burle's mother and son suffer in their different ways from the same cause. Yet none of the adults in the story is a mere victim of historical conditions; on the contrary. Crude and foolish as he is, lame himself yet irresistibly amused at the sight of a servant girl's ugliness, Laguitte nevertheless proves capable of an act of private heroism by which he demonstrates his own moral freedom, sets his friend Burle free of guilt, and saves "the honor of the French Army." In a story that proceeds with high economy and logic, the most powerful moment is probably that at which the degraded Burle comes to sudden awareness during the duel: "At last he understood that this was an execution."

Meanwhile Zola gives form and meaning to his story by involving the characters in a pattern of eloquent relationships. Burle and Laguitte are at one in their corruption but different in their capacity to transcend it. Burle has betrayed the army and his dominating, military-minded mother, only to turn to the powerful, statuesque Mélanie whom everyone likens to a drum-major. And although Madame Burle and Mélanie never meet, they have in common the fact that both are aggrieved widows. Perhaps *Captain Burle* is only one of those genre studies that French writers accomplish so well, but art and feeling combine to give it a lasting beauty and importance.

Captain Burle

1   The Swindle

IT WAS nine o'clock. The little town of Vauchamp, dark and
silent, had just retired to bed amid a chilly November rain. In the
rue des Recollets, one of the narrowest and most deserted streets
of the district of Saint-Jean, a single window was still alight on
the third floor of an old house, from whose damaged gutters torrents of water were falling into the street. Mme. Burle was sitting
up before a meager fire of vine stocks, while her little grandson
Charles pored over his lessons by the pale light of a lamp.

The apartment, rented at one hundred and sixty francs per
annum, consisted of four large rooms which it was absolutely impossible to keep warm during the winter. Mme. Burle slept in the
largest chamber, her son Captain and Quartermaster Burle
occupying a somewhat smaller one overlooking the street, while
little Charles had his iron cot at the farther end of a spacious
drawing room with mildewed hangings which was never used.
The few pieces of furniture belonging to the captain and his
mother, furniture of the massive style of the First Empire, dented
and worn by continuous transit from one garrison town to another, almost disappeared from view beneath the lofty ceilings
whence darkness fell. The flooring of red-colored tiles was cold
and hard to the feet; before the chairs there were merely a few
threadbare little rugs of poverty-stricken aspect, and athwart

429

this desert all the winds of heaven blew through the disjointed doors and windows.

Near the fireplace sat Mme. Burle, leaning back in her old yellow velvet armchair and watching the last vine branch smoke, with that stolid, blank stare of the aged who live within themselves. She would sit thus for whole days together, with her tall figure, her long stern face and her thin lips that never smiled. The widow of a colonel who had died just as he was on the point of becoming a general, the mother of a captain whom she had followed even in his campaigns, she had acquired a military stiffness of bearing and formed for herself a code of honor, duty and patriotism which kept her rigid, desiccated, as it were, by the stern application of discipline. She seldom, if ever, complained. When her son had become a widower after five years of married life she had undertaken the education of little Charles as a matter of course, performing her duties with the severity of a sergeant drilling recruits. She watched over the child, never tolerating the slightest waywardness or irregularity, but compelling him to sit up till midnight when his exercises were not finished, and sitting up herself until he had completed them. Under such implacable despotism Charles, whose constitution was delicate, grew up pale and thin, with beautiful eyes, inordinately large and clear, shining in his white, pinched face.

During the long hours of silence Mme. Burle dwelt continuously upon one and the same idea: she had been disappointed in her son. This thought sufficed to occupy her mind, and under its influence she would live her whole life over again, from the birth of her son, whom she had pictured rising amid glory to the highest rank, till she came down to mean and narrow garrison life, the dull, monotonous existence of nowadays, that stranding in the post of a quartermaster, from which Burle would never rise and in which he seemed to sink more and more heavily. And yet his first efforts had filled her with pride, and she had hoped to see her dreams realized. Burle had only just left Saint-Cyr when he distinguished himself at the battle of Solferino, where he had captured a whole battery of the enemy's artillery with merely a hand-

ful of men. For this feat he had won the cross; the papers had
recorded his heroism, and he had become known as one of the
bravest soldiers in the army. But gradually the hero had grown
stout, embedded in flesh, timorous, lazy and satisfied. In 1870,
still a captain, he had been made a prisoner in the first encounter;
and he returned from Germany quite furious, swearing that he
would never be caught fighting again, for it was too absurd. Being
prevented from leaving the army, as he was incapable of embracing any other profession, he applied for and obtained the position
of captain quartermaster, "a kennel," as he called it, "in which he
would be left to kick the bucket in peace." That day Mme. Burle
experienced a great internal disruption. She felt that it was all
over, and she ever afterward preserved a rigid attitude with
tightened lips.

A blast of wind shook the rue des Recollets and drove the rain
angrily against the windowpanes. The old lady lifted her eyes
from the smoking vine roots now dying out, to make sure that
Charles was not falling asleep over his Latin exercise. This lad,
twelve years of age, had become the old lady's supreme hope, the
one human being in whom she centered her obstinate yearning
for glory. At first she had hated him with all the loathing she had
felt for his mother, a weak and pretty young lacemaker whom the
captain had been foolish enough to marry when he found out that
she would not listen to his passionate addresses on any other condition. Later on, when the mother had died and the father had
begun to wallow in vice, Mme. Burle dreamed again in presence
of that little ailing child whom she found it so hard to rear. She
wanted to see him robust, so that he might grow into the hero
that Burle had declined to be, and for all her cold ruggedness she
watched him anxiously, feeling his limbs and instilling courage
into his soul. By degrees, blinded by her passionate desires, she
imagined that she had at last found the man of the family. The
boy, whose temperament was gentle, dreamy, had a physical horror of soldiering, but as he lived in mortal dread of his grandmother and was extremely shy and submissive, he would echo

all she said and resignedly express his intention of entering the army when he grew up.

Mme. Burle observed that the exercise was not progressing. In fact, little Charles, overcome by the deafening noise of the storm, was dozing, albeit his pen was between his fingers and his eyes were staring at the paper. The old lady at once struck the edge of the table with her bony hand; whereupon the lad started, opened his dictionary and hurriedly began to turn over the leaves. Then, still preserving silence, his grandmother drew the vine roots together on the hearth and unsuccessfully attempted to rekindle the fire.

At the time when she had still believed in her son she had sacrificed her small income, which he had squandered in pursuits she dared not investigate. Even now he drained the household; all its resources went to the streets, and it was through him that she lived in penury, with empty rooms and cold kitchen. She never spoke to him of all those things, for with her sense of discipline he remained the master. Only at times she shuddered at the sudden fear that Burle might someday commit some foolish misdeed which would prevent Charles from entering the army.

She was rising to fetch a fresh piece of wood in the kitchen when a fearful wind fell upon the house, making the doors rattle, tearing off a shutter and whirling the water in the broken gutters like a spout against the window. In the midst of the uproar a ring at the bell startled the old lady. Who could it be at such an hour and in such weather? Burle never returned till after midnight, if he came home at all. However, she went to the door. An officer stood before her, dripping with rain and swearing savagely.

"Hell and thunder!" he growled. "What cursed weather!"

It was Major Laguitte, a brave old soldier who had served under Colonel Burle during Mme. Burle's palmy days. He had started in life as a drummer boy and, thanks to his courage rather than his intellect, had attained to the command of a battalion, when a painful infirmity—the contraction of the muscles of one of his thighs, due to a wound—obliged him to accept the post of major.

He was slightly lame, but it would have been imprudent to tell him so, as he refused to admit it.

"What, you, Major?" said Mme. Burle with growing astonishment.

"Yes, thunder," grumbled Laguitte, "and I must be confoundedly fond of you to roam the streets on such a night as this. One would think twice before sending even a parson out."

He shook himself, and little rivulets fell from his huge boots onto the floor. Then he looked round him.

"I particularly want to see Burle. Is the lazy beggar already in bed?"

"No, he is not in yet," said the old woman in her harsh voice.

The major looked furious, and, raising his voice, he shouted: "What, not at home? But in that case they hoaxed me at the café, Mélanie's establishment, you know. I went there, and a maid grinned at me, saying that the captain had gone home to bed. Curse the girl! I suspected as much and felt like pulling her ears!"

After this outburst he became somewhat calmer, stamping about the room in an undecided way, withal seeming greatly disturbed. Mme. Burle looked at him attentively.

"Is it the captain personally whom you want to see?" she said at last.

"Yes," he answered.

"Can I not tell him what you have to say?"

"No."

She did not insist but remained standing without taking her eyes off the major, who did not seem able to make up his mind to leave. Finally in a fresh burst of rage he exclaimed with an oath: "It can't be helped. As I am here you may as well know— after all, it is, perhaps, best."

He sat down before the chimney piece, stretching out his muddy boots as if a bright fire had been burning. Mme. Burle was about to resume her own seat when she remarked that Charles, overcome by fatigue, had dropped his head between the open pages of his dictionary. The arrival of the major had at first interested him, but, seeing that he remained unnoticed, he had been unable to struggle against his sleepiness. His grandmother turned toward the table to slap his frail little hands, whitening in the lamplight, when Laguitte stopped her.

"No—no!" he said. "Let the poor little man sleep. I haven't got anything funny to say. There's no need for him to hear me."

The old lady sat down in her armchair; deep silence reigned, and they looked at one another.

"Well, yes," said the major at last, punctuating his words with an angry motion of his chin, "he has been and done it; that hound Burle has been and done it!"

Not a muscle of Mme. Burle's face moved, but she became livid, and her figure stiffened. Then the major continued: "I had my doubts. I had intended mentioning the subject to you. Burle was spending too much money, and he had an idiotic look which I did not fancy. Thunder and lightning! What a fool a man must be to behave so filthily!"

Then he thumped his knee furiously with his clenched fist and seemed to choke with indignation. The old woman put the straightforward question:

"He has stolen?"

"You can't have an idea of it. You see, I never examined his accounts; I approved and signed them. You know how those things are managed. However, just before the inspection—as the colonel is a crotchety old maniac—I said to Burle: 'I say, old man, look to your accounts; I am answerable, you know,' and then I felt perfectly secure. Well, about a month ago, as he seemed queer and some nasty stories were circulating, I peered a little closer into the books and pottered over the entries. I thought everything looked straight and very well kept——"

At this point he stopped, convulsed by such a fit of rage that he had to relieve himself by a volley of appalling oaths. Finally he resumed: "It isn't the swindle that angers me; it is his disgusting behavior to me. He has gammoned me, Madame Burle. By God! Does he take me for an old fool?"

"So he stole?" the mother again questioned.

"This evening," continued the major more quietly, "I had just finished my dinner when Gagneux came in—you know Gagneux, the butcher at the corner of the Place aux Herbes? Another dirty beast who got the meat contract and makes our men eat all the diseased cow flesh in the neighborhood! Well, I received him like a dog, and then he let it all out—blurted out the whole thing, and a pretty mess it is! It appears that Burle only paid him in driblets and had got himself into a muddle—a confusion of figures which the devil himself couldn't distentangle. In short, Burle owes the butcher two thousand francs, and Gagneux threatens to inform the colonel if he is not paid. To make matters worse, Burle, just to blind me, handed me every week a forged receipt which he had squarely signed with Gagneux's name. To think he did that to me, his old friend! Ah, curse him!"

With increasing profanity the major rose to his feet, shook his fist at the ceiling and then fell back in his chair. Mme. Burle again repeated: "He has stolen. It was inevitable."

Then without a word of judgment or condemnation she added simply: "Two thousand francs—we have not got them. There are barely thirty francs in the house."

"I expected as much," said Laguitte. "And do you know where all the money goes? Why, Mélanie gets it—yes, Mélanie, a creature who has turned Burle into a perfect fool. Ah, those women! Those fiendish women! I always said they would do for him! I cannot conceive what he is made of! He is only five years younger than I am, and yet he is as mad as ever. What a woman hunter he is!"

Another long silence followed. Outside the rain was increasing in violence, and throughout the sleepy little town one could hear the crashing of slates and chimney pots as they were dashed by the blast onto the pavements of the streets.

"Come," suddenly said the major, rising, "my stopping here won't mend matters. I have warned you—and now I'm off."

"What is to be done? To whom can we apply?" muttered the old woman drearily.

"Don't give way—we must consider. If I only had the two thousand francs—but you know that I am not rich."

The major stopped short in confusion. This old bachelor, wifeless and childless, spent his pay in drink and gambled away at écarté whatever money his cognac and absinthe left in his pocket. Despite that, however, he was scrupulously honest from a sense of discipline.

"Never mind," he added as he reached the threshold. "I'll begin by stirring him up. I shall move heaven and earth! What! Burle, Colonel Burle's son, condemned for theft! That cannot be! I would sooner burn down the town. Now, thunder and lightning, don't worry; it is far more annoying for me than for you."

He shook the old lady's hand roughly and vanished into the shadows of the staircase, while she held the lamp aloft to light the way. When she returned and replaced the lamp on the table she stood for a moment motionless in front of Charles, who was still asleep with his face lying on the dictionary. His pale cheeks and long fair hair made him look like a girl, and she gazed at him dreamily, a shade of tenderness passing over her harsh countenance. But it was only a passing emotion; her features regained their look of cold, obstinate determination, and, giving the youngster a sharp rap on his little hand, she said:

"Charles—your lessons."

The boy awoke, dazed and shivering, and again rapidly turned over the leaves. At the same moment Major Laguitte, slamming the house door behind him, received on his head a quantity of water falling from the gutters above, whereupon he began to swear in so loud a voice that he could be heard above the storm. And after that no sound broke upon the pelting downpour save the slight rustle of the boy's pen traveling over the paper. Mme. Burle had resumed her seat near the chimney piece, still rigid, with her eyes fixed on the dead embers, preserving, indeed, her habitual attitude and absorbed in her one idea.

2 The Café

THE CAFÉ DE PARIS, kept by Mélanie Cartier, a widow, was situated on the Place du Palais, a large irregular square planted with meager, dusty elm trees. The place was so well known in Vauchamp that it was customary to say, "Are you coming to Mélanie's?" At the farther end of the first room, a spacious one, there was another called "the divan," a narrow apartment having sham leather benches placed against the walls, while at each corner there stood a marble-topped table. The widow, deserting her seat in the front room, where she left her little servant Phrosine, spent her evenings in the inner apartment, ministering to a few customers, the usual frequenters of the place, those who were currently styled "the gentlemen of the divan." When a man belonged to that set it was as if he had a label on his back; he was spoken of with smiles of mingled contempt and envy.

Mme. Cartier had become a widow when she was five and twenty. Her husband, a wheelwright, who on the death of an uncle had amazed Vauchamp by taking the Café de Paris, had one fine day brought her back with him from Montpellier, where he was wont to repair twice a year to purchase liqueurs. As he was stocking his establishment he selected, together with divers beverages, a woman of the sort he wanted—of an engaging aspect and apt to stimulate the trade of the house. It was never known where he had picked her up, but he married her after trying her in the café during six months or so. Opinions were divided in Vauchamp as to her merits, some declaring that she was superb, while others asserted that she looked like a drum major. She was a tall woman with large features and coarse hair falling low over her forehead. However, everyone agreed that she knew very well how to fool the sterner sex. She had fine eyes and was wont to fix them with a bold stare on the gentlemen of the divan, who colored and became like wax in her hands. She also had the reputation of possessing a wonderfully fine figure, and southerners appreciate a statuesque style of beauty.

Cartier had died in a singular way. Rumor hinted at a conjugal quarrel, a kick, producing some internal tumor. Whatever may have been the truth, Mélanie found herself encumbered with the café, which was far from doing a prosperous business. Her husband had wasted his uncle's inheritance in drinking his own absinthe and wearing out the cloth of his own billiard table. For a while it was believed that the widow would have to sell out, but she liked the life and the establishment just as it was. If she could secure a few customers the bigger room might remain deserted. So she limited herself to repapering the divan in white and gold and recovering the benches. She began by entertaining a chemist. Then a vermicelli maker, a lawyer and a retired magistrate put in an appearance; and thus it was that the café remained open, although the waiter did not receive twenty orders a day. No objections were raised by the authorities, as appearances were kept up; and, indeed, it was not deemed advisable to interfere, for some respectable people might have been worried.

Of an evening five or six well-to-do citizens would enter the front room and play at dominoes there. Although Cartier was dead and the Café de Paris had got a queer name, they saw nothing and kept up their old habits. In course of time, the waiter having nothing to do, Mélanie dismissed him and made Phrosine light the solitary gas burner in the corner where the domino players congregated. Occasionally a party of young men, attracted by the gossip that circulated through the town, would come in, wildly excited and laughing loudly and awkwardly. But they were received there with icy dignity. As a rule they did not even see the widow, and even if she happened to be present she treated them with withering disdain, so that they withdrew, stammering and confused. Mélanie was too astute to indulge in any compromising whims. While the front room remained dark, save in the corner where the few townsfolk rattled their dominoes, she personally waited on the gentlemen of the divan, showing herself amiable without being free, merely venturing in moments of familiarity to lean on the shoulder of one or another of them, the better to watch a skillfully played game of écarté.

One evening the gentlemen of the divan, who had ended by tolerating each other's presence, experienced a disagreeable surprise on finding Captain Burle at home there. He had casually entered the café that same morning to get a glass of vermouth, so it seemed, and he had found Mélanie there. They had conversed, and in the evening when he returned Phrosine immediately showed him to the inner room.

Two days later Burle reigned there supreme; still he had not frightened the chemist, the vermicelli maker, the lawyer or the retired magistrate away. The captain, who was short and dumpy, worshiped tall, plump women. In his regiment he had been nicknamed "Petticoat Burle" on account of his constant philandering. Whenever the officers, and even the privates, met some monstrous-looking creature, some giantess puffed out with fat, whether she were in velvet or in rags, they would invariably exexclaim, "There goes one to Petticoat Burle's taste!" Thus Mélanie, with her opulent presence, quite conquered him. He was lost—quite wrecked. In less than a fortnight he had fallen to vacuous imbecility. With much the expression of a whipped hound in the tiny sunken eyes which lighted up his bloated face, he was incessantly watching the widow in mute adoration before her masculine features and stubby hair. For fear that he might be dismissed, he put up with the presence of the other gentlemen of the divan and spent his pay in the place down to the last copper. A sergeant reviewed the situation in one sentence: "Petticoat Burle is done for; he's a buried man!"

It was nearly ten o'clock when Major Laguitte furiously flung the door of the café open. For a moment those inside could see the deluged square transformed into a dark sea of liquid mud, bubbling under the terrible downpour. The major, now soaked to the skin and leaving a stream behind him, strode up to the small counter where Phrosine was reading a novel.

"You little wretch," he yelled, "you have dared to gammon an officer; you deserve——"

And then he lifted his hand as if to deal a blow such as would have felled an ox. The little maid shrank back, terrified, while the amazed domino players looked, openmouthed. However, the major did not linger there—he pushed the divan door open and appeared before Mélanie and Burle just as the widow was playfully making the captain sip his grog in small spoonfuls, as if she were feeding a pet canary. Only the ex-magistrate and the chemist had come that evening, and they had retired early in a melancholy frame of mind. Then Mélanie, being in want of three hundred francs for the morrow, had taken advantage of the opportunity to cajole the captain.

"Come," she said, "open your mouth; ain't it nice, you greedy piggy-wiggy?"

Burle, flushing scarlet, with glazed eyes and sunken figure, was sucking the spoon with an air of intense enjoyment.

"Good heavens!" roared the major from the threshold. "You now play tricks on me, do you? I'm sent to the roundabout and told that you never came here, and yet all the while here you are, addling your silly brains."

Burle shuddered, pushing the grog away, while Mélanie stepped angrily in front of him as if to shield him with her portly figure, but Laguitte looked at her with that quiet, resolute expression well known to women who are familiar with bodily chastisement.

"Leave us," he said curtly.

She hesitated for the space of a second. She almost felt the gust of the expected blow, and then, white with rage, she joined Phrosine in the outer room.

When the two men were alone Major Laguitte walked up to Burle, looked at him and, slightly stooping, yelled into his face these two words: "You pig!"

The captain, quite dazed, endeavored to retort, but he had not time to do so.

"Silence!" resumed the major. "You have bamboozled a friend. You palmed off on me a lot of forged receipts which might have sent both of us to the gallows. Do you call that proper behavior? Is that the sort of trick to play a friend of thirty years' standing?"

Burle had fallen back in his chair; he was livid; his limbs shook as if with ague. Meanwhile the major, striding up and down and striking the tables wildly with his fists, continued: "So you have become a thief like the veriest scribbling cur of a clerk, and all for the sake of that creature here! If at least you had stolen for your mother's sake it would have been honorable! But, curse it, to play tricks and bring the money into this shanty is what I cannot understand! Tell me—what are you made of at your age to go to the dogs as you are going all for the sake of a creature like a grenadier!"

"*You* gamble——" stammered the captain.

"Yes, I do—curse it!" thundered the major, lashed into still greater fury by this remark. "And I am a pitiful rogue to do so, because it swallows up all my pay and doesn't redound to the honor of the French army. However, I don't steal. Kill yourself, if it pleases you; starve your mother and the boy, but respect the regimental cashbox and don't drag your friends down with you."

He stopped. Burle was sitting there with fixed eyes and a stupid air. Nothing was heard for a moment save the clatter of the major's heels.

"And not a single copper," he continued aggressively. "Can you picture yourself between two gendarmes, eh?"

He then grew a little calmer, caught hold of Burle's wrists and forced him to rise.

"Come!" he said gruffly. "Something must be done at once, for I cannot go to bed with this affair on my mind—I have an idea."

In the front room Mélanie and Phrosine were talking eagerly in low voices. When the widow saw the two men leaving the divan she moved toward Burle and said coaxingly: "What, are you going already, Captain?"

"Yes, he's going," brutally answered Laguitte, "and I don't intend to let him set foot here again."

The little maid felt frightened and pulled her mistress back by the skirt of her dress; in doing so she imprudently murmured the word "drunkard" and thereby brought down the slap which the major's hand had been itching to deal for some time past. Both women having stooped, however, the blow only fell on Phrosine's back hair, flattening her cap and breaking her comb. The domino players were indignant.

"Let's cut it," shouted Laguitte, and he pushed Burle on the pavement. "If I remained I should smash everyone in the place."

To cross the square they had to wade up to their ankles in mud. The rain, driven by the wind, poured off their faces. The captain walked on in silence, while the major kept on reproaching him with his cowardice and its disastrous consequences. Wasn't it sweet weather for tramping the streets? If he hadn't been such an idiot they would both be warmly tucked in bed instead of paddling about in the mud. Then he spoke of Gagneux—a scoundrel whose diseased meat had on three separate occasions made the whole regiment ill. In a week, however, the contract would come to an end, and the devil himself would not get it renewed.

"It rests with me," the major grumbled. "I can select anyone I choose, and I'd rather cut off my right arm than put that poisoner in the way of earning another cent."

Just then he slipped into a gutter and, half choked by a string of oaths, he gasped:

"You understand—I am going to rout up Gagneux. You must stop outside while I go in. I must know what the rascal is up to and if he'll dare to carry out his threat of informing the colonel tomorrow. A butcher—curse him! The idea of compromising oneself with a butcher! Ah, you aren't overproud, and I shall never forgive you for all this."

They had now reached the Place aux Herbes. Gagneux's house was quite dark, but Laguitte knocked so loudly that he was eventually admitted. Burle remained alone in the dense obscurity and did not even attempt to seek any shelter. He stood at a corner of the market under the pelting rain, his head filled with a loud buzzing noise which prevented him from thinking. He did not feel impatient, for he was unconscious of the flight of time. He stood there looking at the house, which, with its closed door and windows, seemed quite lifeless. When at the end of an hour the major came out again it appeared to the captain as if he had only just gone in.

Laguitte was so grimly mute that Burle did not venture to question him. For a moment they sought each other, groping about in the dark; then they resumed their walk through the somber streets, where the water rolled as in the bed of a torrent. They moved on in silence side by side, the major being so abstracted that he even forgot to swear. However, as they again crossed the Place du Palais, at the sight of the Café de Paris, which was still lit up, he dropped his hand on Burle's shoulder and said, "If you ever re-enter that hole I——"

"No fear!" answered the captain without letting his friend finish his sentence.

Then he stretched out his hand.

"No, no," said Laguitte, "I'll see you home; I'll at least make sure that you'll sleep in your bed tonight."

They went on, and as they ascended the rue des Recollets they slackened their pace. When the captain's door was reached and Burle had taken out his latchkey he ventured to ask:

"Well?"

"Well," answered the major gruffly, "I am as dirty a rogue as you are. Yes! I have done a scurrilous thing. The devil take you! Our soldiers will eat carrion for three months longer."

Then he explained that Gagneux, the disgusting Gagneux, had a horribly level head and that he had persuaded him—the major—to strike a bargain. He would refrain from informing the colonel, and he would even make a present of the two thousand francs and replace the forged receipts by genuine ones, on condition that the major bound himself to renew the meat contract. It was a settled thing.

"Ah," continued Laguitte, "calculate what profits the brute must make out of the meat to part with such a sum as two thousand francs."

Burle, choking with emotion, grasped his old friend's hands, stammering confused words of thanks. The vileness of the action committed for his sake brought tears into his eyes.

"I never did such a thing before," growled Laguitte, "but I was driven to it. Curse it, to think that I haven't those two thousand francs in my drawer, it is enough to make one hate cards. It is my own fault. I am not worth much; only, mark my words, don't begin again, for, curse it—*I* shan't."

The captain embraced him, and when he had entered the house the major stood a moment before the closed door to make certain that he had gone upstairs to bed. Then as midnight was striking and the rain was still belaboring the dark town, he slowly turned homeward. The thought of his men almost broke his heart, and, stopping short, he said aloud in a voice full of compassion:

"Poor devils! what a lot of cow beef they'll have to swallow for those two thousand francs!"

3 Again?

THE REGIMENT was altogether nonplused: Petticoat Burle had quarreled with Mélanie. When a week had elapsed it became a proved and undeniable fact; the captain no longer set foot inside the Café de Paris, where the chemist, it was averred, once more reigned in his stead, to the profound sorrow of the retired magistrate. An even more incredible statement was that Captain Burle led the life of a recluse in the rue des Recollets. He was becoming a reformed character; he spent his evenings at his own fireside, hearing little Charles repeat his lessons. His mother, who had never breathed a word to him of his manipulations with Gagneux, maintained her old severity of demeanor as she sat opposite him in her armchair, but her looks seemed to imply that she believed him reclaimed.

A fortnight later Major Laguitte came one evening to invite himself to dinner. He felt some awkwardness at the prospect of meeting Burle again, not on his own account but because he dreaded awakening painful memories. However, as the captain was mending his ways he wished to shake hands and break a crust with him. He thought this would please his old friend.

When Laguitte arrived Burle was in his room, so it was the old lady who received the major. The latter, after announcing that he had come to have a plate of soup with them, added, lowering his voice:

"Well, how goes it?"

"All right," answered the old lady.

"Nothing queer?"

"Absolutely nothing. Never away—in bed at nine—and looking quite happy."

"Ah, confound it," replied the major, "I knew very well he only wanted a shaking. He has some heart left, the dog!"

When Burle appeared he almost crushed the major's hands in his grasp, and standing before the fire, waiting for the dinner, they conversed peacefully, honestly, together, extolling the charms of home life. The captain vowed he wouldn't exchange his home for a kingdom and declared that when he had removed his braces, put on his slippers and settled himself in his armchair, no king was fit to hold a candle to him. The major assented and examined him. At all events his virtuous conduct had not made him any thinner; he still looked bloated; his eyes were bleared, and his mouth was heavy. He seemed to be half asleep as he repeated mechanically: "Home life! There's nothing like home life, nothing in the world!"

"No doubt," said the major; "still, one mustn't exaggerate— take a little exercise and come to the café now and then."

"To the café, why?" asked Burle. "Do I lack anything here? No, no, I remain at home."

When Charles had laid his books aside Laguitte was surprised to see a maid come in to lay the cloth.

"So you keep a servant now," he remarked to Mme. Burle.

"I had to get one," she answered with a sigh. "My legs are not what they used to be, and the household was going to wrack and ruin. Fortunately Cabrol let me have his daughter. You know old Cabrol, who sweeps the market? He did not know what to do with Rose—I am teaching her how to work."

Just then the girl left the room.

"How old is she?" asked the major.

"Barely seventeen. She is stupid and dirty, but I only give her ten francs a month, and she eats nothing but soup."

When Rose returned with an armful of plates Laguitte, though he did not care about women, began to scrutinize her and was amazed at seeing so ugly a creature. She was very short, very dark and slightly deformed, with a face like an ape's: a flat nose, a huge mouth and narrow greenish eyes. Her broad back and long arms gave her an appearance of great strength.

"What a snout!" said Laguitte, laughing, when the maid had again left the room to fetch the cruets.

"Never mind," said Burle carelessly, "she is very obliging and does all one asks her. She suits us well enough as a scullion."

The dinner was very pleasant. It consisted of boiled beef and mutton hash. Charles was encouraged to relate some stories of his school, and Mme. Burle repeatedly asked him the same question: "Don't you want to be a soldier?" A faint smile hovered over the child's wan lips as he answered with the frightened obedience of a trained dog, "Oh, yes, Grandmother." Captain Burle, with his elbows on the table, was masticating slowly with an absent-minded expression. The big room was getting warmer; the single lamp placed on the table left the corners in vague gloom. There was a certain amount of heavy comfort, the familiar intimacy of penurious people who do not change their plates at every course but become joyously excited at the unexpected appearance of a bowl of whipped egg cream at the close of the meal.

Rose, whose heavy tread shook the floor as she paced round the table, had not yet opened her mouth. At last she stopped behind the captain's chair and asked in a gruff voice: "Cheese, sir?"

Burle started. "What, eh? Oh yes—cheese. Hold the plate tight."

He cut a piece of Gruyère, the girl watching him with her narrow eyes. Laguitte laughed; Rose's unparalleled ugliness amused him immensely. He whispered in the captain's ear, "She is ripping! There never was such a nose and such a mouth! You ought to send her to the colonel's someday as a curiosity. It would amuse him to see her."

More and more struck by this phenomenal ugliness, the major felt a paternal desire to examine the girl more closely.

"Come here," he said, "I want some cheese too."

She brought the plate, and Laguitte, sticking the knife in the Gruyère, stared at her, grinning the while because he discovered that she had one nostril broader than the other. Rose gravely allowed herself to be looked at, waiting till the gentleman had done laughing.

She removed the cloth and disappeared. Burle immediately went to sleep in the chimney corner while the major and Mme. Burle began to chat. Charles had returned to his exercises. Quietude fell from the lofty ceiling; the quietude of a middle-class household gathered in concord around their fireside. At nine o'clock Burle woke up, yawned and announced that he was going off to bed; he apologized but declared that he could not keep his eyes open. Half an hour later, when the major took his leave, Mme. Burle vainly called for Rose to light him downstairs; the girl must have gone up to her room; she was, indeed, a regular hen, snoring the round of the clock without waking.

"No need to disturb anybody," said Laguitte on the landing; "my legs are not much better than yours, but if I get hold of the banisters I shan't break any bones. Now, my dear lady, I leave you happy; your troubles are ended at last. I watched Burle closely, and I'll take my oath that he's guileless as a child. Dash it—after all, it was high time for Petticoat Burle to reform; he was going downhill fast."

The major went away fully satisfied with the house and its inmates; the walls were of glass and could harbor no equivocal conduct. What particularly delighted him in his friend's return to virtue was that it absolved him from the obligation of verifying the accounts. Nothing was more distasteful to him than the inspection of a number of ledgers, and as long as Burle kept steady, he—Laguitte—could smoke his pipe in peace and sign the books in all confidence. However, he continued to keep one eye open for a little while longer and found the receipts genuine, the entries correct, the columns admirably balanced. A month later he contented himself with glancing at the receipts and running his eye over the totals. Then one morning, without the slightest suspicion of there being anything wrong, simply because he had lit a second pipe and had nothing to do, he carelessly added up a row of figures and fancied that he detected an error of thirteen francs. The balance seemed perfectly correct, and yet he was not mistaken; the total outlay was thirteen francs more than the various sums for which receipts were furnished. It looked queer, but he said nothing to Burle, just making up his mind to examine the next accounts closely. On the following week he detected a fresh error of nineteen francs, and then, suddenly becoming alarmed, he shut himself up with the books and spent a wretched morning poring over them, perspiring, swearing and feeling as if his very skull were bursting with the figures. At every page he discovered thefts of a few francs—the most miserable petty thefts—ten, eight, eleven francs, latterly, three and four; and, indeed, there was one column showing that Burle had pilfered just one franc and a half. For two months, however, he had been steadily robbing the cashbox, and by comparing dates the major found to his disgust that the famous lesson respecting Gagneux had only kept him straight for one week! This last discovery infuriated Laguitte, who struck the books with his clenched fists, yelling through a shower of oaths:

"This is more abominable still! At least there was some pluck about those forged receipts of Gagneux. But this time he is as contemptible as a cook charging twopence extra for her cabbages. Powers of hell! To pilfer a franc and a half and clap it in his pocket! Hasn't the brute got any pride then? Couldn't he run away with the safe or play the fool with actresses?"

The pitiful meanness of these pilferings revolted the major, and, moreover, he was enraged at having been duped a second time, deceived by the simple, stupid dodge of falsified additions. He rose at last and paced his office for a whole hour, growling aloud.

"This gives me his measure. Even if I were to thrash him to a jelly every morning he would still drop a couple of coins into his pocket every afternoon. But where can he spend it all? He is never seen abroad; he goes to bed at nine, and everything looks so clean and proper over there. Can the brute have vices that nobody knows of?"

He returned to the desk, added up the subtracted money and found a total of five hundred and forty-five francs. Where was this deficiency to come from? The inspection was close at hand, and if the crotchety colonel should take it into his head to examine a single page, the murder would be out and Burle would be done for.

This idea froze the major, who left off cursing, picturing Mme. Burle erect and despairing, and at the same time he felt his heart swell with personal grief and shame.

"Well," he muttered, "I must first of all look into the rogue's business; I will act afterward."

As he walked over to Burle's office he caught sight of a skirt vanishing through the doorway. Fancying that he had a clue to the mystery, he slipped up quietly and listened and speedily recognized Mélanie's shrill voice. She was complaining of the gentlemen of the divan. She had signed a promissory note which she was unable to meet; the bailiffs were in the house, and all her goods would be sold. The captain, however, barely replied to her. He alleged that he had no money, whereupon she burst into tears and began to coax him. But her blandishments were apparently ineffectual, for Burle's husky voice could be heard repeating, "Impossible! Impossible!" And finally the widow withdrew in a towering passion. The major, amazed at the turn affairs were taking, waited a few moments longer before entering the office, where Burle had remained alone. He found him very calm, and despite his furious inclination to call him names he also remained calm, determined to begin by finding out the exact truth.

The office certainly did not look like a swindler's den. A cane-seated chair, covered with an honest leather cushion, stood before the captain's desk, and in a corner there was the locked safe. Summer was coming on, and the song of a canary sounded through the open window. The apartment was very neat and tidy, redolent of old papers, and altogether its appearance inspired one with confidence.

"Wasn't it Mélanie who was leaving here as I came along?" asked Laguitte.

Burle shrugged his shoulders.

"Yes," he mumbled. "She has been dunning me for two hundred francs, but she can't screw ten out of me—not even tenpence."

"Indeed!" said the major, just to try him. "I heard that you had made up with her."

"I? Certainly not. I have done with the likes of her for good."

Laguitte went away, feeling greatly perplexed. Where had the five hundred and forty-five francs gone? Had the idiot taken to drinking or gambling? He decided to pay Burle a surprise visit that very evening at his own house, and maybe by questioning his mother he might learn something. However, during the afternoon his leg became very painful; latterly he had been feeling in ill-health, and he had to use a stick so as not to limp too outrageously. This stick grieved him sorely, and he declared with angry despair that he was now no better than a pensioner. However, toward the evening, making a strong effort, he pulled himself out of his armchair and, leaning heavily on his stick, dragged himself through the darkness to the rue des Recollets, which he reached about nine o'clock. The street door was still unlocked, and on going up he stood panting on the third landing, when he heard voices on the upper floor. One of these voices was Burle's, so he fancied, and out of curiosity he ascended another flight of stairs. Then at the end of the passage on the left he saw a ray of light coming from a door which stood ajar. As the creaking of his boots resounded, this door was sharply closed, and he found himself in the dark.

"Some cook going to bed!" he muttered angrily. "I'm a fool."

All the same he groped his way as gently as possible to the door and listened. Two people were talking in the room, and he stood aghast, for it was Burle and that fright Rose! Then he listened, and the conversation he heard left him no doubt of the awful truth. For a moment he lifted his stick as if to beat down the door. Then he shuddered and, staggering back, leaned against the wall. His legs were trembling under him, while in the darkness of the staircase he brandished his stick as if it had been a saber.

What was to be done? After his first moment of passion there had come thoughts of the poor old lady below. And these made him hesitate. It was all over with the captain now; when a man sank as low as that he was hardly worth the few shovelfuls of earth that are thrown over carrion to prevent them from polluting the atmosphere. Whatever might be said of Burle, however much one might try to shame him, he would assuredly begin the next day. Ah, heavens, to think of it! The money! The honor of the army! The name of Burle, that respected name, dragged through the mire! By all that was holy this could not and should not be!

Presently the major softened. If he had only possessed five hundred and forty-five francs! But he had not got such an amount. On the previous day he had drunk too much cognac, just like a mere sub, and had lost shockingly at cards. It served him right —he ought to have known better! And if he was so lame he richly deserved it too; by rights, in fact, his leg ought to be much worse.

At last he crept downstairs and rang at the bell of Mme. Burle's flat. Five minutes elapsed, and then the old lady appeared.

"I beg your pardon for keeping you waiting," she said; "I thought that dormouse Rose was still about. I must go and shake her."

But the major detained her.

"Where is Burle?" he asked.

"Oh, he has been snoring since nine o'clock. Would you like to knock at his door?"

"No, no, I only wanted to have a chat with you."

In the parlor Charles sat at his usual place, having just finished his exercises. He looked terrified, and his poor little white hands

were tremulous. In point of fact, his grandmother, before sending
him to bed, was wont to read some martial stories aloud so as
to develop the latent family heroism in his bosom. That night
she had selected the episode of the *Vengeur*, the man-of-war
freighted with dying heroes and sinking into the sea. The child,
while listening, had become almost hysterical, and his head was
racked as with some ghastly nightmare.

Mme. Burle asked the major to let her finish the reading. "Long
live the republic!" She solemnly closed the volume. Charles was
as white as a sheet.

"You see," said the old lady, "the duty of every French soldier
is to die for his country."

"Yes, Grandmother."

Then the lad kissed her on the forehead and, shivering with
fear, went to bed in his big room, where the faintest creak of the
paneling threw him into a cold sweat.

The major had listened with a grave face. Yes, by heavens!
Honor was honor, and he would never permit that wretched
Burle to disgrace the old woman and the boy! As the lad was so
devoted to the military profession, it was necessary that he should
be able to enter Saint-Cyr with his head erect.

When Mme. Burle took up the lamp to show the major out,
she passed the door of the captain's room, and stopped short,
surprised to see the key outside, which was a most unusual
occurrence.

"Do go in," she said to Laguitte; "it is bad for him to sleep so
much."

And before he could interpose she had opened the door and
stood transfixed on finding the room empty. Laguitte turned
crimson and looked so foolish that she suddenly understood everything, enlightened by the sudden recollection of several little
incidents to which she had previously attached no importance.

"You knew it—you knew it!" she stammered. "Why was I not
told? Oh, my God, to think of it! Ah, he has been stealing again
—I feel it!"

She remained erect, white and rigid. Then she added in a harsh voice:

"Look you—I wish he were dead!"

Laguitte caught hold of both her hands, which for a moment he kept tightly clasped in his own. Then he left her hurriedly, for he felt a lump rising in his throat and tears coming to his eyes. Ah, by all the powers, this time his mind was quite made up.

4 Inspection

THE REGIMENTAL inspection was to take place at the end of the month. The major had ten days before him. On the very next morning, however, he crawled, limping, as far as the Café de Paris, where he ordered some beer. Mélanie grew pale when she saw him enter, and it was with a lively recollection of a certain slap that Phrosine hastened to serve him. The major seemed very calm, however; he called for a second chair to rest his bad leg upon and drank his beer quietly like any other thirsty man. He had sat there for about an hour when he saw two officers crossing the Place du Palais—Morandot, who commanded one of the battalions of the regiment, and Captain Doucet. Thereupon he excitedly waved his cane and shouted: "Come in and have a glass of beer with me!"

The officers dared not refuse, but when the maid had brought the beer Morandot said to the major: "So you patronize this place now?"

"Yes—the beer is good."

Captain Doucet winked and asked archly: "Do you belong to the divan, Major?"

Laguitte chuckled but did not answer. Then the others began to chaff him about Mélanie, and he took their remarks good-naturedly, simply shrugging his shoulders. The widow was undoubtedly a fine woman, however much people might talk. Some of those who disparaged her would, in reality, be only too pleased to win her good graces. Then turning to the little counter and assuming an engaging air, he shouted:

"Three more glasses, madame."

Mélanie was so taken aback that she rose and brought the beer herself. The major detained her at the table and forgot himself so far as to softly pat the hand which she had carelessly placed on the back of a chair. Used as she was to alternate brutality and flattery, she immediately became confident, believing in a sudden whim of gallantry on the part of the "old wreck," as she was wont to style the major when talking with Phrosine. Doucet and Morandot looked at each other in surprise. Was the major actually stepping into Petticoat Burle's shoes? The regiment would be convulsed if that were the case.

Suddenly, however, Laguitte, who kept his eye on the square, gave a start.

"Hallo, there's Burle!" he exclaimed.

"Yes, it is his time," explained Phrosine. "The captain passes every afternoon on his way from the office."

In spite of his lameness the major had risen to his feet, pushing aside the chairs as he called out: "Burle! I say—come along and have a glass."

The captain, quite aghast and unable to understand why Laguitte was at the widow's, advanced mechanically. He was so perplexed that he again hesitated at the door.

"Another glass of beer," ordered the major, and then turning to Burle, he added, "What's the matter with you? Come in. Are you afraid of being eaten alive?"

The captain took a seat, and an awkward pause followed. Mélanie, who brought the beer with trembling hands, dreaded some scene which might result in the closing of her establishment. The major's gallantry made her uneasy, and she endeavored to slip away, but he invited her to drink with them, and before she could refuse he had ordered Phrosine to bring a liqueur glass of anisette, doing so with as much coolness as if he had been master of the house. Mélanie was thus compelled to sit down between the captain and Laguitte, who exclaimed aggressively: "I *will* have ladies respected. We are French officers! Let us drink Madame's health!"

Burle, with his eyes fixed on his glass, smiled in an embarrassed way. The two officers, shocked at the proceedings, had already tried to get off. Fortunately the café was deserted, save that the domino players were having their afternoon game. At every fresh oath which came from the major they glanced around, scandalized by such an unusual accession of customers and ready to threaten Mélanie that they would leave her for the Café de la Gare if the soldiery was going to invade her place like flies that buzzed about, attracted by the stickiness of the tables which Phrosine scoured only on Saturdays. She was now reclining behind the counter, already reading a novel again.

"How's this—you are not drinking with Madame?" the major said roughly to Burle. "Be civil at least!"

Then as Doucet and Morandot were again preparing to leave, he stopped them.

"Why can't you wait? We'll go together. It is only this brute who never knows how to behave himself."

The two officers looked surprised at the major's sudden bad temper. Mélanie attempted to restore peace and with a light laugh placed her hands on the arms of both men. However, Laguitte disengaged himself.

"No," he roared, "leave me alone. Why does he refuse to chink glasses with you? I shall not allow you to be insulted—do you hear? I am quite sick of him."

Burle, paling under the insult, turned slightly and said to Morandot, "What does this mean? He calls me in here to insult me. Is he drunk?"

With a wild oath the major rose on his trembling legs and struck the captain's cheek with his open hand. Mélanie dived and thus escaped one half of the smack. An appalling uproar ensued. Phrosine screamed behind the counter as if she herself had received the blow; the domino players also entrenched themselves behind their table in fear lest the soldiers should draw their swords and massacre them. However, Doucet and Morandot pinioned the captain to prevent him from springing at the major's throat and forcibly led him to the door. When they got him outside they succeeded in quieting him a little by repeating that Laguitte was quite in the wrong. They would lay the affair before the colonel, having witnessed it, and the colonel would give his decision. As soon as they had got Burle away they returned to the café where they found Laguitte in reality greatly disturbed, with tears in his eyes but affecting stolid indifference and slowly finishing his beer.

"Listen, Major," began Morandot, "that was very wrong on your part. The captain is your inferior in rank, and you know that he won't be allowed to fight you."

"That remains to be seen," answered the major.

"But how has he offended you? He never uttered a word. Two old comrades too; it is absurd."

The major made a vague gesture. "No matter. He annoyed me."

He could never be made to say anything else. Nothing more as to his motive was ever known. All the same, the scandal was a terrible one. The regiment was inclined to believe that Mélanie, incensed by the captain's defection, had contrived to entrap the major, telling him some abominable stories and prevailing upon him to insult and strike Burle publicly. Who would have thought it of that old fogy Laguitte, who professed to be a woman-hater? they said. So he, too, had been caught at last. Despite the general indignation against Mélanie, this adventure made her very conspicuous, and her establishment soon drove a flourishing business.

On the following day the colonel summoned the major and the captain into his presence. He censured them sternly, accusing them of disgracing their uniform by frequenting unseemly haunts. What resolution had they come to, he asked, as he could not authorize them to fight? This same question had occupied the whole regiment for the last twenty-four hours. Apologies were unacceptable on account of the blow, but as Laguitte was almost unable to stand, it was hoped that, should the colonel insist upon it, some reconciliation might be patched up.

"Come," said the colonel, "will you accept me as arbitrator?"

"I beg your pardon, Colonel," interrupted the major; "I have brought you my resignation. Here it is. That settles everything. Please name the day for the duel."

Burle looked at Laguitte in amazement, and the colonel thought it his duty to protest.

"This is a most serious step, Major," he began. "Two years more and you would be entitled to your full pension."

But again Laguitte cut him short, saying gruffly, "That is my own affair."

"Oh, certainly! Well, I will send in your resignation, and as soon as it is accepted I will fix the day for the duel."

The unexpected turn that events had taken startled the regiment. What possessed that lunatic major to persist in cutting the throat of his old comrade Burle? The officers again discussed Mélanie; they even began to dream of her. There must surely be something wonderful about her since she had completely fascinated two such tough old veterans and brought them to a deadly feud. Morandot, having met Laguitte, did not disguise his concern. If he—the major—was not killed, what would he live upon? He had no fortune, and the pension to which his cross of the Legion of Honor entitled him, with the half of a full regimental pension which he would obtain on resigning, would barely find him in bread. While Morandot was thus speaking Laguitte simply stared before him with his round eyes, persevering in the dumb obstinacy born of his narrow mind; and when his companion tried to question him regarding his hatred for Burle, he simply made the same vague gesture as before and once again repeated:

"He annoyed me; so much the worse."

Every morning at mess and at the canteen the first words were: "Has the acceptance of the major's resignation arrived?" The duel was impatiently expected and ardently discussed. The majority believed that Laguitte would be run through the body in three seconds, for it was madness for a man to fight with a paralyzed leg which did not even allow him to stand upright.

A few, however, shook their heads. Laguitte had never been a marvel of intellect, that was true; for the last twenty years, indeed, he had been held up as an example of stupidity, but there had been a time when he was known as the best fencer of the regiment, and although he had begun as a drummer he had won his epaulettes as the commander of a battalion by the sanguine bravery of a man who is quite unconscious of danger. On the other hand, Burle fenced indifferently and passed for a poltroon. However, they would soon know what to think.

Meanwhile the excitement became more and more intense as the acceptance of Laguitte's resignation was so long in coming. The major was unmistakably the most anxious and upset of everybody. A week had passed by, and the general inspection would commence two days later. Nothing, however, had come as yet. He shuddered at the thought that he had, perhaps, struck his old friend and sent in his resignation all in vain, without delaying the exposure for a single minute. He had in reality reasoned thus: If he himself were killed he would not have the worry of witnessing the scandal, and if he killed Burle, as he expected to do, the affair would undoubtedly be hushed up. Thus he would save the honor of the army, and the little chap would be able to get in at Saint-Cyr. Ah, why wouldn't those wretched scribblers at the War Office hurry up a bit? The major could not keep still but was forever wandering about before the post office, stopping the estafettes and questioning the colonel's orderly to find out if the acceptance had arrived. He lost his sleep and, careless as to people's remarks, he leaned more and more heavily on his stick, hobbling about with no attempt to steady his gait.

On the day before that fixed for the inspection he was, as usual, on his way to the colonel's quarters when he paused, startled, to see Mme. Burle (who was taking Charles to school) a few paces ahead of him. He had not met her since the scene at the Café de Paris, for she had remained in seclusion at home. Unmanned at thus meeting her, he stepped down to leave the whole sidewalk free. Neither he nor the old lady bowed, and the little boy lifted his large inquisitive eyes in mute surprise. Mme. Burle, cold and erect, brushed past the major without the least sign of emotion or recognition. When she had passed he looked after her with an expression of stupefied compassion.

"Confound it, I am no longer a man," he growled, dashing away a tear.

When he arrived at the colonel's quarters a captain in attendance greeted him with the words: "It's all right at last. The papers have come."

"Ah!" murmured Laguitte, growing very pale.

And again he beheld the old lady walking on, relentlessly rigid and holding the little boy's hand. What! He had longed so eagerly for those papers for eight days past, and now when the scraps had come he felt his brain on fire and his heart lacerated.

The duel took place on the morrow, in the barrack yard behind a low wall. The air was keen, the sun shining brightly. Laguitte had almost to be carried to the ground; one of his seconds supported him on one side, while on the other he leaned heavily, on his stick. Burle looked half asleep; his face was puffy with unhealthy fat, as if he had spent a night of debauchery. Not a word was spoken. They were all anxious to have it over.

Captain Doucet crossed the swords of the two adversaries and then drew back, saying: "Set to, gentlemen."

Burle was the first to attack; he wanted to test Laguitte's strength and ascertain what he had to expect. For the last ten days the encounter had seemed to him a ghastly nightmare which he could not fathom. At times a hideous suspicion assailed him, but he put it aside with terror, for it meant death, and he refused to believe that a friend could play him such a trick, even to set things right. Besides, Laguitte's leg reassured him; he would prick the major on the shoulder, and then all would be over.

During well nigh a couple of minutes the swords clashed, and then the captain lunged, but the major, recovering his old suppleness of wrist, parried in a masterly style, and if he had returned the attack Burle would have been pierced through. The captain now fell back; he was livid, for he felt that he was at the mercy of the man who had just spared him. At last he understood that this was an execution.

Laguitte, squarely poised on his infirm legs and seemingly turned to stone, stood waiting. The two men looked at each other fixedly. In Burle's blurred eyes there arose a supplication—a prayer for pardon. He knew why he was going to die, and like a child he promised not to transgress again. But the major's eyes remained implacable; honor had spoken, and he silenced his emotion and his pity.

"Let it end," he muttered between his teeth.

Then it was he who attacked. Like a flash of lightning his sword flamed, flying from right to left, and then with a resistless thrust it pierced the breast of the captain, who fell like a log without even a groan.

Laguitte had released his hold upon his sword and stood gazing at that poor old rascal Burle, who was stretched upon his back with his fat stomach bulging out.

"Oh, my God! My God!" repeated the major furiously and despairingly, and then he began to swear.

They led him away, and, both his legs failing him, he had to be supported on either side, for he could not even use his stick.

Two months later the ex-major was crawling slowly along in the sunlight down a lonely street of Vauchamp, when he again found himself face to face with Mme. Burle and little Charles. They were both in deep mourning. He tried to avoid them, but he now only walked with difficulty, and they advanced straight upon him without hurrying or slackening their steps. Charles still had the same gentle, girlish, frightened face, and Mme. Burle retained her stern, rigid demeanor, looking even harsher than ever.

As Laguitte shrank into the corner of a doorway to leave the whole street to them, she abruptly stopped in front of him and stretched out her hand. He hesitated and then took it and pressed it, but he trembled so violently that he made the old lady's arm shake. They exchanged glances in silence.

"Charles," said the boy's grandmother at last, "shake hands with the major."

The boy obeyed without understanding. The major, who was very pale, barely ventured to touch the child's frail fingers; then, feeling that he ought to speak, he stammered out: "You still intend to send him to Saint-Cyr?"

"Of course, when he is old enough," answered Mme. Burle.

But during the following week Charles was carried off by typhoid fever. One evening his grandmother had again read him the story of the *Vengeur* to make him bold, and in the night he had become delirious. The poor little fellow died of fright.

Open All Night

PAUL MORAND

Paul Morand

Paul Morand (1888—) was born in Paris and largely educated there. His future career as a diplomat and international writer was, however, foreshadowed by a year of study which he put in at Oxford. In 1913 he entered the diplomatic corps, serving by turns in London, Rome and Madrid. After 1919 he was in the Ministry for Foreign Affairs at Paris, where he began to write his novels and travel books. *Open All Night* (1922) was his most popular work, as it is probably his best one; but some of its quality is also found in *Tender Shoots* and *Closed All Night* as well as in Morand's many books of travel.

Open All Night delighted Morand's ambitious contemporaries, Gide and Proust, but reached a larger audience than they could reach, going through dozens of editions in many countries including the United States. Then the book slowly disappeared from people's tables. In time it came to be thought of as something frivolous and far away and typical of the youth and froth of modernism.

Open All Night will someday be read again and perhaps recognized as a small classic. Its surface is frivolous indeed, but studiously, fantastically frivolous. Morand's style is bizarre because his subject is bizarre. He is writing about the confusion of the new and the old, the good and the bad, in European society after the first world war. His startling metaphors and juxtapositions serve to make that confusion vivid and intelligible. They also help to make it seem funny, for *Open All Night* is a kind of lighthearted *The Waste Land* and was published in the same year as that poem of T. S. Eliot's. Morand's book is a comedy of manners while Eliot's is a religious tragedy. Yet both are about the failure of love within the larger crisis occasioned by the breakdown of culture.

The hero of the several episodes which comprise *Open All Night* is an anonymous young Frenchman who wanders about Europe in search of sexual adventure. Everywhere he is fascinated and baffled by the disorder of things. If ancient Barcelona "preserves the Inquisition behind its screens of electric signs," ancient Paris reverberates to the new dance music and the cult of the bicycle racer. People in general, and especially women—for *Open All Night* is in the main a gallery of feminine portraits—find themselves playing strange roles. Though conservative by instinct, the Spanish girl Remedios becomes "a mermaid in the sea of Marxism." She is fatally miscast, and so in a different way is the Baltic girl Aïno. Naturally pretty and friendly, Aïno seems designed for a robust and charming life of passion. Yet she subscribes to an absurd cult of athletic nudism and gives herself to the parallel bars while her intensely respectable mother sits by in the raw reading Fichte. Aïno is, in fact, a vestal virgin of the doctrinaire barbarism which blows across precariously established borders from the new Germany and the new Russia. "You are nothing but a cosmopolitan swine," she cries to the young Frenchman when he tries to make love to her. And there is some justice in her reproach, for the young Frenchman is eternally—and not even very successfully—on the make. Yet what Aïno says is no cry from the heart; it seems to burst from some organ or faculty engendered in her by propaganda. Thus in the long run she is no happier in her mechanical virginity than the young Frenchman is in his ironic libertinism. For although he is the ineffectual bearer of that French spirit which once helped to civilize all Europe, he is still true to it to the extent of being honest in his desires and acute in his observations.

Open All Night is composed of six episodes, each complete in itself; the three most substantial of them are reprinted here.

The Catalonian Night

PAUL MORAND

I WAS going to have a lady to travel with. Half of her already adorned the compartment in which I sat. The other half, leaning out of the window, still belonged to the Lausanne station and to a delegation of men of various nationalities, welded together by the same shadow on the platform, linked by the same wild rose in the buttonhole of each of them. Bells began to ring. Passengers ran about on the asphalt. As though at the bidding of the time-table the signal drooped like a scarlet fruit at the top of its latticed trunk. A whistle blew. The lady shook hands over the lowered window; a freckled British hand; a pulpy German hand; a Russian hand with a skin like parchment; the slim fingers of a Japanese. And lastly a young Spaniard, whose stock covered a boil on his neck, stretched out a grimy hand covered with copper rings and said:

"Good-bye, Doña Remedios!"

Then the crowd parted and through the gap a mauve star twinkled, followed by a soft flare and a cloud of smoke through which a film camera performed its bewildered duties without delay.

One by one the train broke the handclasps that anchored it and having gained its freedom, sped away. A shout went up: "Long live the International!" but it was instantly smothered by the clatter of the turntables and the velvety darkness of a tunnel.

The lady still leant rashly out of the window, waving. I pre-

467

vailed on her to stop by placing a hand on her plump shoulder, and drawing her attention to the enameled notice on which was written:

IT IS DANGEROUS TO ALLOW CHILDREN TO
LEAN OUT OF THE WINDOWS

at which she smiled, turning towards me.

Beautiful, handsome, pretty, intriguing. In that moment Fate made amends for the disappointments of so many other train departures, in which it is the woman with whom one wants to travel who remains behind on the platform, while the man who was with her sits next to one, without any indication until that moment as to which of the two was going to travel, so equally affected were they by the parting, so equally full of emotion in their fancy tweed clothes.

There was no disillusionment when the train came out of the tunnel. Under cover of a drowsiness with which I pretended to be overcome I began to study my companion's features as though they were a map, so that I should be in no danger of following the wrong road. A charming and undulating country bounded by shoes and a hat. I always envy those passport officials whose daily task is to make a record of so many human faces, cold or warm, as different from one another as the flower-like imprints of finger-tips.

In this face, with its soft curves, every feature was honestly blunt and rounded: her full lips, her forehead, her high cheekbones which, seen three-quarter face, hid her eyelids from one's gaze, cutting one's glance off slantwise in an irresistible way and sending it off in one of those theatrical exits known as "into the wings," which deceive no one but are none the less charming. Her bosom rose in a gentle slope to her rounded neck, encircled by a plain necklace of imitation pearls, and shaded by a youthful and determined chin. On her first finger shone a sapphire set in brilliants; her thin silk dress fell in a fold between her short thighs. In the mittened hands spread flat upon her knees, in her feet, so arched that they almost seemed to bulge and which did not quite reach the floor, in her hair which, when she took off her hat, seemed to be tightly stretched back to her ears where it was allowed to escape in frothy waves, so oiled that it ceased to be black and reflected every color of its surroundings, in the back hair twisted like a wrung-out cloth and glistening with brilliantine, in all these things one's memory was taken irresistibly back to Spain.

She leaned her head against the railway embroidery on the head-rest and went to sleep quite naturally. Perhaps I had hypnotized her.

When we drew level with Montreux we entered a storm which burst suddenly. Terrific thunderclaps crashed against the mountain peaks, drowning the noise of the rain. A whimper came from somewhere. My companion woke with a start and unconsciously made the sign of the cross. Taken unawares, she wore that look of a bird with ruffled plumage which southern women get when traveling. The young ones lose their composure and become wooden, while the older ones turn a lead-gray color and droop beneath the splendor of their jewels. The sky was rent like a piece of silk. With more suddenness even than a press photographer's flashlight, the lightning had fallen on the railway track. I offered to pull down the blind.

"I'm not frightened of the storm, but my dog, who is in her basket, can't bear it."

Then, as though she had been stripped by the thunder, she opened a bag and reconstructed her face behind a cloud of powder. There was a white lock amongst her black hair, like a jet of steam in a puff of coal smoke. The whimpering began again under the seat and went on until she made up her mind to take a mongrel fox terrier with fawn-colored ears out of a gilt basket on which was written "Souvenir of the Rigi." In order to put her more at her ease I opened my bag and took out a teddy bear and a red donkey. She complimented me on my menagerie. On my side I showered praises on her dog in a way which is usually only done on suburban lines.

"Trick is ugly, monsieur, but I love her because she is all I have left in the world."

"Nevertheless, the leave-takings I witnessed at the station a little while ago seemed extraordinarily warm. Having only been in Lausanne a few hours myself, I know nothing at all of a person worthy of being photographed by flashlight. Perhaps you've been giving a charity performance at the Casino?"

"I am not, monsieur, altogether an actress,"—as she finished the word, lisping slightly, her tongue appeared for a moment between her closed teeth like minute grains of rice. She favored me with a tired smile—"even though I have played a part in the most terrible judicial parody of the century. My name is Remedios Sirvent and I was the companion of Estebán Puig,* the Catalonian champion of liberty, legally assassinated at Barcelona last spring by the reactionaries of the police, the army and the church."

I had, like everyone else, taken a passing interest in that event, which some considered to be a just punishment and others a martyrdom, and which had subsequently been relegated to oblivion. Consequently I was greatly surprised at the description she gave me of the gathering at Lausanne and at the thought of which—here she beat her breast—she still thrilled.

To protest against proscriptions and to bring pressure to bear on the Spanish Government, the International Socialist Bureau had organized a monster demonstration.

The mass meeting, she explained to me, took place in the rain, on the borders of the lake, in close, serried ranks. A seething mass of humanity stretched as far as the balconies of the villas and the hotel terraces; the roofs were packed with sight-seers; souvenir cards were sold; subscription lists were filled with names; preceded by their silken streamers the delegations marched forward; anarchist contingents from Zurich and Lugano beneath their black banners; Russian social-revolutionaries, Indian nationalists, American Zionists, the General Unions of French and Belgian workers; the officials of the Independent Labour Party and of the Second International sang hymns. All the comrades were there:

* Pronounced *Pootch*, meaning "mountain" in Catalan.

Rosario, Rakovski, Vanderveld, Luxembourg, Jaurès, Burns, Thomas, Lippovici. A never-to-be-forgotten moment. What mattered it that one no longer possessed a country, when one was received as she had been received, into the heart of humanity? She would go about her duties now with renewed strength of purpose, pushing aside all obstacles in her path, striving to banish the languor which overcomes one after a great sorrow, and during which nature recruits her strength. She wanted to remain bruised, both in her opinions and in her affections, and to know no rest unless the work to which Puig had devoted his life were continued and the cause striven after. He had left her beyond the reach of need. She belonged to the lower middle class and was too much inclined by nature to a life of luxury and ease beneath a tranquil sky. But she would not drift into becoming the charming widow, preoccupied by her white rabbits and her vineyards, taking the air in her carriage in the evening in her widow's weeds. She felt the need of great international conflicts, of European upheavals, of harsh climates, propaganda voyages and lectures, to compel attention, to win the hearts of the people, to keep the memory of the dead man green and to obtain a revision of his shameful trial.

Enthusiasm radiated from her eyes, her lips and the palms of her hands, with a mixture of playfulness and childishness which was particularly attractive. Sometimes she interpreted her thoughts seriously, announcing its degeneracy to a decadent world; in her own words, "throwing the blame on it." Sometimes she started off on a frantic and confused flow of invective without, however, losing any of her charm in the process.

The idea of a new order of society enraptured her so much that beads of moisture stood out on her brow. The natural ardent charity of the Spaniard gave way before a fervor of despotism which was held in check only by her eloquence. But at the back of everything there remained the cold and austere religious sense and the respect for established rule which are the nearest kin to prayer. Her marvelous credulity was a great asset, egging her on in her course of romantic sacrilege and above all giving her the strength to be insatiable, which is usually lacking in revolutionaries of the Latin races, satisfied with so little.

"*Hombre*," she said, "my life is expressed in four words: service, knowledge, faith, love."

She enlarged upon this idea, but before explaining it, insisted on defining her position in relation to the different political parties in Spain. For my part, I listened with such good will that I fell asleep.

We were approaching the frontier.

The lightning still accompanied us, punctuated by desultory thunderclaps, like an endless argument among the mountain tops. Doña Remedios still nursed her dog which, covering its mistress' knees with its ears, gloomily surveyed her little feet adorned with beautifully chased buckles, shaped like pieces of barbaric jewelry.

The day faded, a drained lamp blackening with the last glimmer of its flame. Eau de Cologne sloshed monotonously in bottles at the bottom of bags, with the gurgling sound of subterranean springs, my companion, comfortably ensconced in the corner of that one-night traveling home, thick with smoke and smelling of hot leather, was reading *Les Samedis de Chiffonnette*.

The sound of iron-shod boots on the metal foot-warmers announced the customs examination. Doña Remedios lifted her eyes.

"Nothing to declare," she said.

A southern French custom officer, accompanied by a Swiss soldier, on whose cap one noticed with surprise the absence of the word "Lift," pointed to a parcel of some size lying in the rack.

"What have you got in that basket?" he asked.

With a gesture of mixed irritation and shyness my companion rose and lifted down a thick bunch of palms tied in a bundle by a red silk ribbon. She opened it and I saw in the midst of the foliage a plaster gentleman with empty eyes who looked like President Carnot.

"There!" she said, proudly. "That is the statue of Estebán Puig which was presented to me this afternoon by the B. I. L. (Bureau Internationale de Lausanne). Is there any duty on the memory of the dead on entering France?"

And she wiped away a tear with a lace handkerchief the size of a postage stamp.

Samuel Pacifico, professor of history at the Louis-le-Grand college, was at home to his friends every Sunday in his sixth-floor attic in the rue Saint-Jacques. Since leaving school we had always kept up the custom of visiting our old master. The author of *The History of the Working-Classes* was a timid shaggy dwarf with a network of blue veins, who smelled of the quartiers Saint-Paul, made his own shoes, and cut his own hair with a machine which he had invented himself. He used to walk down the Boulevard Saint-Michel, hugging the wall, talking to himself and scrutinizing everyone with his black and gray eyes which reminded one of a photographic plate in a yellow developer. He had preserved for us that affection which had formerly saved our lessons from drudgery, an affection we had later fostered and returned, no subsequent experience having ever again brought us the good luck of our first childhood, of finding a man who did not mind corrupting a youth which was no longer worthy of corruption. His intelligence, capable of overthrowing a nation, was entirely at the service of science. He imposed a discipline and austere habits on himself which he did not even desire for us, holding himself as it were responsible for our happiness. The Jesuits, against their inclination, took their boarders to Pacifico's classes, disapproving all the time of his infernal wit; later, at the Political Science lectures, Monsieur Laguillère-Desveaux would interrupt his polished and colorless discourse to warn us against "the anti-liberal licentiousness with which nowadays people proceed to the study of Social Science."

Pacifico never went out to dinner, never set foot in the drawing room and only crossed the Seine when he went to the Rue de la Paix to buy rings, of which he had a collection which drove women to distraction. It was the only Eastern taste he possessed. He commanded respect as having played his part in the pomps (and also in some of the shady intrigues) of the Third Republic, an active part which will never be accredited to him by History, exerting his influence on behalf of his friends, avenging them, bringing to bear a subtle pressure which ministerial cabinets rarely resisted for more than a few hours, seeking no personal advantage and having for his recreation nothing but his weekly receptions.

It would have been useless to have tried to open one of Beyle's folios in the room at the rue Saint-Jacques on Sunday evenings towards six o'clock; there would not have been room. In an atmosphere of tobacco and sealing wax one found university students in dinner jackets and ready-made ties, examination crammers with their acid-stained fingers, an unfrocked priest, a painted female lawyer or two, a few members of the communist colonies of Draveil who stole the teaspoons, and an actress from the Théâtre-Français converted to modern art, who had refused the Legion of Honor and talked of acting only for the lower classes.

Imagine my surprise when I saw my traveling companion of the previous week walk into the circular study, picking her way between the books and manuscripts. I wondered why it had not struck me that I should meet her here. This room, as unpretentious as a railway turntable on a branch line, the abode of a scholar and recluse, unknown to Paris as is indeed everything else, was it not famous to the foreigner? On crossing the frontier, on the threshold of France, the first enquiries he makes are about hotels and about this address. Wells, Unamuno, Gorki, Wedekind (Shaw simply wrote, "G. B. S., Irishman") have signed their names in the master's visitors' book. The leaders of Europe have come here to pick up hints about governing their countries. It was natural that Doña Remedios, in her turn, should continue her work close to the man who could drown his bold thoughts in wisdom in the same way that, after a war, explosives are relegated to the bottom of the sea. She sat there draped in a graduate's gown lined with white satin, rolled her big eyes, accompanied her replies with little grimaces and mechanically turned over the pages of Jaurès' *Social History of the French Revolution* as though it were a warrant for her presence there.

"We are old friends," she said, when Pacifico introduced me. "A storm brought us together."

She recalled the station, the thunder and the whining of her dog Trick.

"That journey," I said, "seems almost mythical to me now, and Switzerland has taken on a dignity which has not really been hers for a hundred years. The integrity of the air, the eloquence of the mountain torrents, the red elegy of your widowhood and that precious train of ours with its two engines which bore us through such forests of symbols and pines," (Remedios never flinched) "I shall retain all these pictures in my mind forever."

How inviting she looked, hazarding in Paris the creation of the best dressmaker of the Parallelo, all black, a pretentious hat with a feather in it, a silver fox fur, a little blood in her cheeks and a little blood on her hands, brooding on vengeance through those autumn days during which, at the bidding of the chrysanthemums, one passes so imperceptibly into winter.

Pacifico begged her to write something in his album.

"Will a quotation do?"

When she had put on her spectacles and taken up the pen, I suggested:

"Why not a thought of your own?"

She laughed and held the book out:

"It is a quotation from our Moratin."

We read—

"Being young and thoughtless she was a charming woman.

"Remedios"

My confusion made her laugh and she observed that it would be a lesson to me not to make fun of her.

"In the first place," I said, "I met you in Helvetia where one is allowed to think and besides I can assure you that in Paris abstract ideas are no longer practicable; every thought has to be expressed in anecdote."

The master took up the cudgels for Remedios and denounced me as having a purely literary turn of mind. In this way we passed the time till dinner to which we were asked to stay: for these gatherings added to their other attractions that of being far from inimical to laughter, particularly when the Collège de France made way for the younger generation which, Pacifico said, "prolonged his life." The food was good and the wines carefully chosen, our host having entrusted the care of his establishment to a housekeeper who had at one time made the bishop's palace at Toulouse the best pothouse in the Southwest Provinces.

A few of us remained that evening under the vanilla-tinted light of the gothic bronze chandelier, surrounded by the illusive pastures of the tapestries on which, facing each other, were hung portraits of Renan and Berthelot, who continued their conversation above the fumes of turkey and cabbage. Remedios presided over this family dinner with her head and shoulders proudly erect.

Pacifico held a glass of sherry to the light and then presented it to Remedios, saying:

"To your health and to the glory of Puig."

"I thank you and I take you at your word. In rushing headlong to his death, Estebán did nothing more than answer the call of the oppressed with a hero's heart."

"And now darkness is spreading over Spain once more," added Pacifico.

"So it will always be, *hombre*, each time anyone tries to goad into life a proletariat which has stagnated for centuries in monastic ignorance and barbarism," said Remedios with her thick Spanish accent. "Estebán realized the futility of violence after the attempts of 1905, and he explained to me that the problem would have to be approached from a greater distance. 'We are working for thirty, for fifty years hence,' he said. But as soon as he had revealed his plans they made away with him."

One of the guests, a professor of semasiology, asked her to explain.

Full of her subject, Remedios considered us with the challenging air of a great pianist who is about to attack the *Symphonic Variations*. But she must have seen the look I gave her, devoid of all interest and enthusiasm, for she cut out the peroration and, in a rapid voice, laid down her conclusions.

"There is nothing to say that you don't know already," she said. "To the traveler, Spain is just like any other country, with lottery tickets, watering places, life insurance, members of parliament who kiss each other on the mouth after debates, and elevators whose floors gape as soon as one sets foot in them. A picturesque cesspool. Barcelona is cast in a South American mold and there the sleeping cars bloom at the end of their stalks into hotels which are flowers of mahogany and blue velvet. One goes through the streets on metal wires, one paints as at Schwabing, one only applauds the bullfighters on their return from Buenos Aires and one constructs tiled buildings in which one can drive a motor car up to the fifth floor. Then suddenly, round a bend in the road, appears the Blessed Sacrament, that obsolete coinage which still circulates among us; the people fall on their knees (they are fined if they don't) and one sees officials in blue silk belts carrying candles, followed by officers in cassocks and field boots. The overloaded tram-cars stop, surrounded by yoked oxen and Hispano-Suiza cars, to make room for these people with their heads of Inquisitors, these mitred vultures, these mean old peasant faces issuing from priceless lace, the lackeys of a God who abandons the poor in order to fawn upon the rich. Or else, if the traveler doesn't read the papers and therefore doesn't know that a strike is imminent, he is surprised one morning on waking to see from the windows of his hotel the *guardia civil* in their yellow harness lying in ambush at the corners of the streets, waiting for the syndicated worker to issue forth. The town, haughty yesterday beneath its diadem of electric light, and distributing alms to the rest of Spain, is thenceforth as empty as the Sepulcher on the third day. The civil population is driven to work at the point of the mercenaries' rifles. Constitutional guarantees are suspended and a police of hired assassins carry out a systematic search in those evil-smelling suburbs of ours, redolent of charred bones, essence of cesspool and resin. Everything now proceeds according to an abominable routine. The civil authorities resign and martial law is declared; following a telegram which is said to come from Madrid but which in actual fact the governor always keeps in his safe, the government passes into the hands of the most backward beings that exist on the face of the earth, only equaled, perhaps, by some of the Russian governors in the Caucasian provinces. The artillery takes up its position in the public squares, machine guns are placed on the monuments. The troops shoot without orders. People are arrested in their homes, searches are carried out at all hours of the day and night, trials take place without counsel or witnesses, depositions being read out in a parody of Justice. Then one day at dawn in the moat of the fortress they kill. It's all over: Truth is veiled for another fifty years."

She took a cigar, lit it and blew a long cloud of smoke beneath the chandelier. Then she hummed a tune they play in Spain for the entrance of the bull.

"Don't let my nervous temperament worry you. In reality these memories are a consolation to me. In Paris people work well, but they forget too soon. There is no time here to think of death, which is an ordinary Spanish amusement. One ought to think of it; it helps to keep things in their proper focus. Either the present order of society must change or I must leave my bones on it. I don't want to die until the great fictions of life, religion, authority, family, which with us still retain all their evil influence, have had their emptiness exposed; nor do I want to die without having helped my brothers and sisters to rid themselves of the burden of 'pobreness,' and of the yoke of the capitalist and of the 'padrón.' Of all those who exploit the poor Catalonians are the most bitter, the most cruel and the most unjust. Oh, how wonderful it would be to exterminate them all!"

And she banged her fist on the table, not with her thumb inside her fingers, womanlike, but with it placed correctly over the fingers like a lid. Her bosom and the glasses trembled.

Suddenly her mood changed to one of gaiety and she pushed her chair away from the table, addressing herself to Pacifico:

"Thank you, foster father, for my good dinner."

"My little red child, your home is here, as they say in your country."

"For a moment," she said, "we swerve from our purpose and neglect our duty. That is the whole treacherous cunning of Paris. But tomorrow we resume our labors until the time comes for the prison gates to fly open and for the whole fabric of prolific and radiant Spain to crumble to the ground."

She was exquisite in this mood, in her ardor and her strength; in her moments of repose she seemed disconnected, with an affectation which was usually out of place, and she was generally rather ridiculous. She was at her best when thinking in capital letters and flying to extremes suited her, even though after falling under her spell one had, as a sort of self-punishment, a ready tendency to look upon her as a character in a Spanish tragicomedy. Looking at her under the chandelier, wasting her energy in extravagant phrases, a well-built woman with a firm cool body and the sturdy limbs of a well-fed shopkeeper's wife, one hesitated or even refused altogether to share her enthusiasm. But she had even less charm when she became once more a nice, simple, naturally fresh young woman. She seemed to alternate between an eagle and a hen. In any case, she was a graceful figure, without any particular genius and without any of the outward signs of adversity. Misfortune had inscribed no bitterness on her soft childish nose or on her full lips; no wrinkles furrowed her low forehead or the eyelids stretched over her wide eyes filled with a lasting but harmless fire.

I went on studying her. She had dispensed with all creeds and had freed herself from human ties and divine pledges; one did not expect less of her for that. But when all was said, what one felt most about this rebel girl was her sense of well-being, the integrity of her thoughts, her Catholic ancestry, mixed with that middle-class Spanish attitude of grateful respect towards man which is a legacy from the Moors. As we sat round her we were all conscious of these things, but we all had an inclination to put her beliefs to the test, watching for any sign of weaken-

ing, believing that hers was more a sentimental escapade into
anarchism than a true vocation.

"Remedios," said one of the guests, as we left the table, "is
an eclogue of a thoroughly domestic kind. She is a mermaid in
the sea of Marxism."

"It would be interesting to see into her future," said Pacifico,
who had leanings towards occultism.

Everyone had something to say:

"I think her end will come in days of violence, full of blood
shed in spite of her."

"She will marry a bullfighter who has retired on his wounds
and will keep a hotel in Algeciras."

"She will give lectures in the Argentine or go into the moving
pictures."

"Is she at all literary?"

"No, I believe she's quite a good girl."

From this point onwards all seriousness ceased. A friend of
Pacifico's childhood, an old gentleman with rouged cheeks who
played chess and repaired old lace, offered to tell our fortunes by
cards. But we preferred the game which consists in giving each
person a list of qualities or defects against which he has to give
himself marks ranging from 0 to 20. We were soon penciling
away on our knees. The old gentleman established himself at the
piano and played the overture to *Les Indes Galantes*. The autumn
wind blew white ash from the fire all over the carpet.

Remedios moistened her pencil with a look of perplexity and
asked the difference between sensuality and temperament, maintaining that in Spanish there was only one word for both and
that she, for her part, saw no difference between them. Pacifico,
in his precise way, got the uncompromising idea of "goodness"
changed to "niceness." Someone else pointed out that we had
forgotten "snobbishness." Some of them cheated; others, seized
with remorse, scratched out their marks, or, after a brief examination of conscience, increased them. Remedios proceeded hesitat-
ingly, india rubber in hand, full of sincerity. I asked if one could
give oneself more than twenty marks for anything.

There was no sound save that made by the housekeeper clearing the table, the creaking of the furniture and the regular ticking
of the clock. When the lists were complete, Pacifico called out
each quality or defect and each person in turn, either boldly or
sheepishly, called out the number of marks he had given himself for it.

"Man, know thyself," said Pacifico. And so we did, extraordinarily well. The younger ones were, I must admit, sometimes
rather wide of the mark, but for those who had reached a certain
age there were certainly no illusions left.

We then went on to the second part of the game, which consisted in taking one's neighbor's list and substituting for his marks
the marks we thought he really deserved.

"But you know nothing at all about me," exclaimed Remedios,
as I took possession of her moral inventory.

I answered that I could always guess and that in any case I
had drunk out of her glass in the dining car when she was not
looking.

Many days have passed since that happy Sunday. But I have
still got Remedios' list, carefully drawn up by her and corrected
by me. I give here, for what it is worth, this precious document
which, beneath its dry figures, seems to me now to be full of
admissions:

REMEDIOS

Qualities or defects	Her own ratings	My revision
Beauty	18	14
Charm	9	17
Elegance	20	8
Intelligence	2	7
Genius	3	?
Sensitiveness	8	19
Business sense	1	18
Sensuality	0	19
Temperament	2	15
Modesty	20	10

Qualities or defects	Her own ratings	My revision
Political sense	19	3
Judgment	10	10
Wit	0	20
Religious feeling	8	4
Snobbishness	7	17
Luck	0	19
Sense of Humor	1	18
Will power	16	5
Selfishness	19	4
Greed	18	18

"If you like, Remedios, we could dine together some evening, without dressing, and go to a cinema."

"I should love to. I hate being alone. I hear mysterious knockings on my shutters every evening and the ghost of a nun appears from the back of my wardrobe every time I open it to get out my nightgown."

"*Et j'ai peur de mourir quand je couche seule.*"*

"Who wrote that?"

"Mallarmé, but it should have been Baudelaire."

"Come and fetch me on Tuesday at seven o'clock at the Hôtel du Mexique in the rue Servandoni."

I had to wait for Remedios in the palm-filled hall, seated in a blue cane armchair, until the hands of the cuckoo clock pointed to a quarter to nine. Dinner, which was served on linoleum table-cloths, with an Ispahan pattern, had been cleared away for two hours. The ecclesiastic contingent of the establishment had played with the cat and read the advertisements in *La Croix* and the games of piquet were finishing. They were beginning to go to bed. At last Remedios came down, glistening with diamonds, beneath a cloak of black Liberty silk, through which one caught an intimate glimpse of full evening dress, with the key of her room and her candlestick in her hand. An elaborately cut tortoise-shell comb a foot high towered above her and knocked against the top

* "And I am afraid of dying when I sleep alone."

of the carriage. At the sight of these things I changed my mind about taking her to a cabaret and I ran my mind along the grand boulevards to try to think of a restaurant in which a cloak like this would not be out of place.

In spite of all my precautions, our entry did not pass altogether unnoticed.

"Please get it firmly into your mind that I want nothing but vegetables and a glass of water."

"Remedios, wonderful woman of a wonderful evening, do be serious. Do you like it dry or sweet?"

Between the salt cellar and the pepper pot she deposited her white gloves twisted together, a velvet bag on which the following motto was worked in diamonds:

REMEDIOS

SIN DIOS*

and a fan made of green feathers.

"I'll have some oysters," she declared with resignation, "if you will ask them to do one up in paper for me to take home to my Chinese goldfish. I should also like the outside slice of the saddle for Trick. You are dining with a woman who was rich this morning and who tonight has nothing left. I think I told you in the train—in that spontaneous impulse to make confidences which is evoked by sympathy—that by his will Estebán Puig had left me beyond the reach of need. He left me two houses let on lease at Biarritz. In point of fact, rumor attributed a much larger fortune to me. It hurt me to think of it. Buying *El Debate*, the organ of the Jesuits, at a kiosk in the Boulevard Saint-Michel this morning, I realized how much use our enemies were making of this. So I went straight to my lawyer and made him draw up a formal deed of renunciation which I signed there and then and which will be published tomorrow in *l'Humanité*. The whole of Puig's gift will pass to his Socialist Institute. Which explains why I am penniless this evening."

* Remedios The Godless.

She laughed and stirred her wine with her fork.

"No, there is nothing praiseworthy about this renunciation. It was wrong of me ever to have accepted it. I can never lose the real gifts I received from Puig. He found me, chose me and raised me to his level when I was nothing but a pupil teacher in a suburban school. He made me read, think; until the very day of his death his one desire for me was to make me a companion worthy of him. He was twenty years my senior, tall, with a head like a boulder and the eyes of a basilisk, but the lower part of his face and his hands were serene and full of wisdom. That is how he struck me when he came to my house one evening to ask me if I would take night classes for working-class children. His voice shook and seemed to issue from some secret hiding-place. He told me that he needed me. His face was as white as an altar cloth. I followed him."

The dress she was wearing fitted her closely and was cut low, her bosom swelling above it like an overflowing cup.

"Where did you get your dress?"

"At Worth's," she said, "they called it 'Eastern Night.' It can't be helped. . . . In future I shall copy the dresses in the woman's supplement of the *Vanguardia*."

She went on:

"Just think. Puig was the soul of the Socialist Institute. It was created by him in 19— on an entirely new basis of teaching, at any rate in Spain, and there (you can imagine how revolutionary it was) he gave a mixed education both in the social and sexual sense of the word. In addition he insisted on a moral and material cleanliness, teaching truth without either rewards or punishments, and knowledge without religion, making a fair distribution of mental and manual labor. In a word the system consisted of the admirable scholastic enactments of your Convention, the ideas of Lavoisier put into practice, to quote Puig, as they have never been in France. Reclus and Kropotkin helped. I've got a wonderful correspondence with them in one of my hat boxes. But to create all this was to wage the battle of light against darkness and this cannot be done with impunity. Puig was crushed. In my country one must not take the children away from the church which wants to make a saint of everyone."

She stopped talking, absorbed in her pocket mirror.

"How dark my complexion is! I wonder why?"

"A woman's complexion, Remedios, is her conscience."

"I am upsetting myself too much. Please forgive me, but I must keep on reminding myself of these things. In spite of the head-waiter who is listening to us with such awe, you must hear the exordium of Puig's funeral oration as it was delivered over his grave by Portet. It went like this: 'The reputed son of one of those innumerable gods created by man is condemned to death because he wished to be proclaimed king. He is about to die. Born, as are all gods, of ignorance and fear, he falters when face to face with death, loses confidence and cries tremulously: "Father, why hast thou forsaken me?" On the other hand, look at Puig, the son of free thought and of morality without the sanctions; he also is about to die. Does he flinch? Does he lose his freedom of thought? No! He stands stiffly erect to the end, crying as he falls: "Long live the International!" ' "

Remedios' eyes are black or gray or blue. How can one tell? Eyes are of all colors. All my pleasure suddenly collapses. With hands as clumsy as wooden splints I take her hand. On her wrist she is wearing a bracelet of graduated sapphires. I feel I want to leave the place, but everything seems to have taken root. It is all a dream. My heart aches as though someone were extracting teeth from it.

"Remedios!"

"*Por favor?*"

"As a favor let me love you."

"You would be making a great mistake if you did," she replied, shrugging her shoulders in little quick movements which had the effect of doing away entirely with her already short neck.

"It is principally to avoid it that I say it, dear remedy."

This talk of love gave the coffee back its taste and restored that equipoise which procures for us the sympathy of tradesmen and the friendship of destiny.

"The fact is that when I am not violent and weak and overcome by the withering emotion of love, my wickedness, Remedios, knows no bounds."

"Yes, I've noticed that," she replied, "and to be quite frank, for my part, I am quite certain that I shall never love anyone again. That side of my life is finished. Physical love is nothing but a magnificent debauch which time can, if necessary, replace. But when the bonds that bind two hearts are once broken, it is different."

She quoted some grossly sentimental Andalusian proverb which I have forgotten and which suddenly detracted from her beauty.

After a moment of silence she went on:

"I am going to make my living by giving Spanish lessons."

"May I be one of your pupils?"

"My first and my favorite one."

The revolving door of the restaurant turned its pink silk paddle-boards in the concave water of its glass sides. The tables were emptying. Women were going downstairs in their brightly-lined cloaks like statues in colored alcoves; men were looking anxiously for their companions or their hats.

Remedios exuded a fragrance in the warm room like wine that has been warmed. The last diners also gave forth an impression of delightful well-being. The wine clerk became god-like. A lady who was drinking with one finger in the air remarked as she finished:

"Yes, it's very good, it leaves a slight taste."

The radiators were cooling with a sound of cracking joints.

Remedios pushed aside her plate and her glass, took her lipstick and drew a *jota* on the tablecloth.

"First steps. The alphabet is A B C D E F G H I *J* . . . that's the *jota*. No, it isn't a dance, it's the first difficulty that besets you when you cross the Pyrenees."

For a moment I tried to pronounce it.

"Your progress surprises me," said Remedios, flatteringly.
"Now let's choose a phrase in which the r's and the j's are well
distributed: *el pajarito de la caja roja.*"

"What does that purring sound mean, Remedios?"

"It means: 'The little bird in the red cage.' "

"But, Remedios, that's you!"

It is late. We rise. The restaurant is empty. I love her for her
life. While she goes to the cloakroom I return to our little table
and furtively lick her spoon.

I had patiently accustomed my tongue to rolling r's on my
teeth, from which I threw them back with a sudden movement on
to the glottis in the pronunciation of a not too imperfect *jota.* On
my way to the rue Servandoni I set myself the task of repeating
a hundred times the phrase which Remedios had taught me two
days before.

At the hotel I found a note waiting for me. Remedios had left
France the day before by the Barcelona express. The red cage
was empty. All that was left was this revolting hall decorated
with lizard skins, with colored glass and with the cat which was
devouring a sort of brain pudding out of an imitation Rouen plate.
The autumn day was dying peacefully away under the canopy of
an orange-colored storm, and was being momentarily prolonged
by the coat which painters, singing at their work, were putting
on the front of the houses.

I stood in the Luxembourg like a monolith crushed beneath the
habits of two long days, suddenly crystallized into a fidelity that
was new to me. I had keyed myself up to meet Remedios again,
to beset her with childish excitements as one does to stop hic-
coughs, to ask her a thousand questions of grammar, to create
quaint fancies for her, without ever revealing to her my purpose,
which was to keep her thoughts on myself, to persuade her that
all the refinements of Paris, the atmosphere of the Seine, the
genius of the Saint-Michel fountain which overflows like a bath-
tub in which one has fallen asleep with the tap on, the statement
of the program girl offering you a program: "it cost me a franc,"

the charm of private rooms in restaurants, the broad outlook of the big stores where the remnants unroll in little waves beneath the arc-lamps of the central hall like dazzling orchids, were all nothing but different forms of love, a love in which the cafés also played their part when the hour of a quarter to eight brought its delicious relaxation with it.

By this unpremeditated departure I saw her on the contrary, freed, in more peaceful possession of herself even than before, and gone for ever from me. It was still daylight and the only stars those of the trams, when I began to realize how complete was my subjection and how sudden an end had been put to my happiness, and that this state of affairs would go on even after sunset. Why this sudden departure, leaving no trace? Was not Spain closed to her? Or had she perhaps concealed the truth from me and set out for Italy and a mad round of excitements, or for America from a desire either for self-effacement or for notoriety?

It was indeed towards Spain that she had gone, for on the following day I received a postcard from the frontier. On it were depicted the docks of Port-Vendres with a row of large casks and a view of the town hall above which rose a fort. On the back of the card were these words: *"The decree of Fate,"* the proud Spanish brevity of which was spoilt by the fact that the handwriting was that of a servant girl and by the ending: *"A greeting from Port-Vendres."* I hoped that Remedios had been unable to cross the frontier. But a few days later Pacifico told me that she had reached Barcelona.

Paris was flooded by an enervating November rain in which houses were reflected right up to the roof in the asphalt. The spray round the shades of the street lamps broke into a sort of pink dust. Along the drenched pavements the stunted trees bore the full brunt of the wind. The sound of noisy torrents beneath the roads came from the outfalls of the sewers at night. The need I felt for Remedios did not cease, nor did it even diminish. Our first meetings seemed now to have been especially arranged by destiny to ensure that at any rate our two lives should not remain

apart for ever. I went over in my mind all the circumstances of
our acquaintance. In the beginning I had loved her voice, coars-
ened by public meetings, her short hands, shorter still in their
mittens, her murderer's thumb, her adventures in which lethargy
always seemed to play a part, her escapade into anarchy; then I
had come to love the narrow limits of her ideas, the chronicle of
her sufferings, her goodness and also the perpetual amusement
afforded by her love of pleasure, her natural sense of duty and
the rebelliousness which made her swerve continually from the
path of her destiny. I conjured her up again, irresponsible, romantic, always smiling. Was it possible that our meeting was
merely one of those incidents which, judging from their results,
Remedios accused of conspiring against her peace of mind, declaring them at the same time to be inevitable? Everything began to
hold evil omens; the shape of the clouds and of coffee grounds
began to be unfavorable. The loneliness of the evenings, and even
of the mornings, too brilliant to permit me to submit to Fate and
to live sensibly, urged me to follow her. The newspapers announced grave reactionary measures in Catalonia. I could not
bear the thought that, far from my side, Remedios was perhaps
hurtling headlong towards disaster, and I in my turn took the
evening express.

.   .   .   .

I am in a circus with an arena of sand, an unbroken beach in
which the forces of sunlight and shadow hold equal sway. Above
the blue circus of the sky across which the fierce sun moves without encountering the outspread cape of a single cloud. A dense
crowd is suspended midway between these two empty circuses,
like a frame of dark wood dividing two mirrors which reflect
each other. The countless pale smudges of the closely packed faces
quiver in the heat-haze which makes individual sounds vibrate
and unite into a single harmony. Can one of these smudges, one
of these sounds, be Remedios? It is the Fiesta de la Prensa and on
the glaring posters we are promised eight Sottomayor bulls. In
the space of an hour the town has emptied itself into this Moorish
basin. I carefully scan the tiers, stripping them like a corncob. I

clear the circus of everything that is not a brilliant, eloquent
mouth, a shapely body molding a silk dress and two eyes as open
as a book. Are you there, Remedios, you precious thing, you indispensable object? Perhaps, but not recognizable, because you
are no longer that preposterous and provoking figure, that tongue
of flame which one would have picked out instantly from a gray
Parisian crowd; here you are merely one of these thousand pliant
glimmering lights, one of these bodies satiated with siestas, puffed
out with sweetmeats, swayed by religion and superstition, a Spanish woman.

One sees the *guardia civil* in their top boots, the military band
in *alpargatas*. In his box the president is holding forth to some
women who remind one of candy. He casts his gestures to the
crowd like handfuls of pennies. Piercing whistles shriek and die.
The president rises. So violently does he wave his handkerchief
that it starts the brazen notes of a trumpet into life. The trumpet
in turn sets in motion the gate of the *toril*, revealing a dark passage
at the end of which is a glimmer of blue sky.

The bull has charged into the light. Bewildered, he stops at the
edge of the shadow. His coat is dirty, his flanks are mottled. His
horns are covered with plaster from the walls. He is alone, the
single point on which the two halves of the ring are strained like
bows. He is attracted by a horse kicking against the *barrera*. He
trots towards it. It is a decrepit old gray nag. Its stomach is
patched like a poor man's coat and its legs totter beneath the
weight of the upholstered *picador* flourishing his lance. The bull
halts for a moment and bellows. His eye caught by the greasy
glitter of the steel which menaces him, he charges, muzzle to the
ground. The lance enters between his shoulders, bends like a rapier
and breaks. His horns pierce the horse's belly with a squelching
sound. The horse seems to leap; it remains suspended in the air, legs
apart, while the bull, blinded with blood, gores its stomach. Then
the horse crashes down like an old wall, burying the rider ham-
pered by his horsehair armor. From the midst of the harness and
entrails the picador's head emerges. His hat with its gaudy rosettes
has fallen off, revealing the fat face of a terrified monk, glistening

with sweat. The horse scrambles up and staggers off, shedding its bowels over the arena. Other horses are lying beside the *barrera*; the absence of saddles accentuates the prominence of their bones. Their yellow teeth show.

Remedios? Not one of those fans is cooling that beloved neck into which, in Paris, her veil used to dig so deep a furrow. No eyebrow is as plastered down as hers, which she used to smooth with a little brush made for glazing pastry. None of the women round me possess that husky voice which enthralls me so. Remedios is not here. Remedios cannot bear the sight of blood.

The bull now becomes the prey of men dressed in silver, arranged in a row like chessmen. One after the other they spread their wings, set flight and settle before the crimson horns. One sways his hips in his cape, his foolish pink stockings emerging from below the skirt thus formed. Another holds up a bright cape stained with dry blood. He drags this cape along the ground like a net and then spreads it out like a curtain. The curtain parts. Behold! A man has flashed across the sun, leaving in the bull two pairs of banderillas decorated with tin foil, a silver flower from the stem of which the blood bubbles, already turning black.

The bull is slowing up. He is now the property of the man in gold. From the crowd there begins to rise a low rumbling growl which the first clever pass will break into a thousand separate rounds. The killer is a small man. His hair resembles the patent leather of his pumps. The bull shreds the red cloth and the man's silk sleeves. He is failing, his head droops lower and lower to the earth on which he slowly slobbers. The man retires three paces, wipes the sweat from his blue and yellow face and throws off his hat with a theatrical toss of his head; he is bald. He rises up on tiptoe like a tenor. A sudden powerful stroke and a backward leap; he waits, hands on hips; a smile wrinkles his thin cheeks. He signs to the crowd to contain itself another moment. The bull retreats obliquely, his muzzle in the sand; his legs bend; he falls on his knees. His feet stiffen and his head falls backwards.

The president awards the ear.

Nothing remains in the empty arena but a trampled place with a jumble of footprints and hoofmarks round a dark stain.

Is it the aniseed-perfumed afternoon, my love-privation, or this harrowing butchery that makes me feel so sick?

.   .   .   .   .   .

My search lasted two days. At last I got Remedios' telephone number from the Socialist Institute. Her voice! She made an appointment to meet me at seven o'clock next morning at the outskirts of the town.

I tried to sleep, without success. My window looked out over a flat boulevard bedecked with palm trees. Children played there until two in the morning, digging with their spades in the electrically lit sand beneath the street lamps, enjoying themselves in the middle of the night of which other European children only know the borders. Electric signs flickered. A soap advertisement traced its crimson path across a house front and died, only to return an instant later to greet one in blue, and then in green, just as theatrical stars take each curtain call wearing a different shawl. Above this domestic conflagration the fortress of Montjuich continued its relentless vigil from the top of its rock, swept four times every minute by the lighthouse.

When three o'clock struck the square was empty. The Trente et Quarante rooms still glowed on the first floors. I caught glimpses of chandeliers and parquet floors. Some of the players came out on the balconies while the cards were being shuffled and leant their elbows on the plush-covered rails. In the streets below the cabmen were also playing cards in their carriages. With the first signs of dawn above the horizon, even the hairdressers in whose shops the customers had been suffering a kind of cosmetic trepanning, covered up their hot water apparatus, and the town entered on a brief period of rest.

A little later a taxi came to take me to the Parque de Vich where Remedios had asked me to meet her. On the Plaza de Colón the confraternity of beggars was sleeping, each member stretched out on two iron chairs. There were about a hundred of them, their faces black, their feet wrapped in evening papers, under the pachydermatous palm trees, scratching themselves even in their dreams. Among them a gentleman in a dinner jacket with a flower in his buttonhole, having decided against going home, was snoring with his mouth open.

The carriage passed through the parque *Guëll*, the quarter inhabited by rich cotton-brokers. To tell the truth I was not sure that I was yet awake. It was an endless series of villas twisted like marshmallow stalks, lit by windows which resembled chain armor, railed off by metallic seaweed and zinc creepers painted green or pale pink. Under corrugated iron roofs sagged india-rubber houses, pierced by gaping doors through which the road seemed to continue, rising in a gentle slope to the roofs. At their sides the porters' lodges bulged like tumors and chimneys rose like varicose veins at the top of walls where rabbit-fishes were fighting in thickets of wrought-iron irises. Then, the imagination of the architects having apparently come to an end, the avenues no longer existed except in their name plates, hidden in the featureless country. Here and there between the market gardens a private house still thrust up its silhouette of a mounted gun, with its burnt almond stucco, bristling with burr-stones, looking like unappetizing praline. At last the carriage came to a halt before a tiled terrace decorated with china fruits on the top of twelve staggering cromlechs. This platform must also have served as a roof, for pierced japanned pipes reminding one of pepper pots sprouted from it like trees. I penetrated along the path which wriggled like a severed worm and I reached, in spirals, the checkerboard summer house where Remedios was waiting for me, smiling among the aloes. She looked as though she had nothing on beneath her lilac dust coat from Valentin's, the rubber king. The sky was reflected in her oiled hair. She turned her great eyes to me and pursing up her lips in that barren kiss which is called a pout, she said:

"Well, *simpático*, are you satisfied?"

"It's like a dream, I adore you so."

She patted my shoulder and then my back with her hand, showing her delight at seeing me in the Spanish fashion, in one of those embraces which one still sees in classic comedy at the Théâtre-Français.

"How can I ever tell you," she said, "the sacrifice I am making in going back on my resolution? You have come at a terrible moment, when I ought to see no one, but providence. . . . This is the Parque de Vich, given to the town by a Catalonian who made his fortune in Chile. A mixture of Bagatelle and Luna Park. You must admit it is idyllic with its banks, its aloes and its powdered glass designs; in the evening a steam orchestra plays in the grotto. I am happy here; as in the well-known tango: '*I wish I were a bee, to die among the flowers.*' Instead of that one must always be fighting. Oh, yes, I don't mind admitting to you that I wasn't made for that sort of thing. I am the secretary of the Party and honorary president with Anatole France of a League of Freedom, in addition to being traveler, lecturer and propagandist. But what I really love, you know, is to be able to lunch in my dressing gown, to have a maid and keep birds, to have the hairdresser in every day, to sleep in the shelter of two strong arms, to drink my chocolate in bed, to go to the cinema at the apéritif hour, the *funcion-vermouth* as we say, to dine with my sisters amongst my nephews and nieces and to find a bowl of roses at my bedside when I go home. I have never admitted this to anyone else; take it with you as a secret to the grave. You must go now. I can't be sure I haven't been followed even though I came straight here after getting up. Take the train back to France this evening."

"I came here to see you."

She became insistent.

"There is going to be a general strike in Barcelona at any moment, perhaps even tomorrow. All foreigners will be suspect; people will be mercilessly shot. I can't say more than that."

"My only desire, Remedios, is to love you, and my only mistake is to want to seduce you. If I am plunged into danger with you it won't be from imprudence or gallantry or facetiousness on my part, but because the need of being near you keeps me here."

Having said this, I took her into my arms.

She deposited face powder and dried cosmetic on my clothes, grew sentimental and put on her spectacles.

From the summit of this calvary of ours with its border of fantastic shrubbery amongst which beds of heliotrope were laid out in the form of the insignia of the order of Alfonso XII, between the embrasures adorned with breastplates, the town appeared in the tense atmosphere, fined down like a model in an architectural exhibition. A thick haze hung over the sea and joined it to the sky. The funicular railway began to move; a dynamo purred somewhere. "You see the awakening of Barcelona," said Remedios, "with her luxurious houses, her peaceful tramways, her civic amenities, all eloquent of her industry; but you have not seen her in her hours of bloodshed, with her torn-down shutters, her twisted and broken pipes, and just beneath my window, caressed by the sun, a single blot—the body of a little girl killed as she was leaving school, stretched on the ground, her head covered with flies." When she was carried away by her subject little silver bubbles blew from her mouth and floated for a moment in the sunlight.

"Yes, *Mono*. Less than a year ago it began with a meeting of protest against the despatch of reservists to Morocco, that cancer which gnaws at the vitals of Spain. Opposite the station over there to the right, from which smoke is rising as from a cauldron, a watch was kept from the sinister windows of the *Capitanía General*. The rails had been torn up to prevent the arrival of reinforcements from Valencia and Madrid. It was a Wednesday. Paving stones were being taken up and trees taken down. At midday the sack of the convents began. The first one was that of San Martín de Provensals, if I remember rightly. Puig, who had gone out at dawn, had not returned. At midnight I ventured out. The populace was converging towards the center of the town, after rifling the armories. I found out that Puig was remaining permanently at the syndicalist headquarters.

"The churches of Maristes, San Antonio, San Pablo, the convents and the parish churches were burning one by one. Forty-nine were roasted this way. Machine guns swept the city from the top of the statue of Columbus. The infantry refused to fire. The Jesuits of Sarria, that barrack-like building over there by the gashouse, defended themselves with rifles. At length the batteries of Montjuich trained their guns on the revolutionary party. From my room I heard muffled reports, the explosion of hidden syndicalist or clerical bomb stores. Then the reinforcements arrived. General Santiago had appalling notices put up. There was a stampede and the ringleaders made for the Pyrenees. At last the detonations died down and ceased altogether. . . . Barcelona became once more as you see it there, a city of wealth and vice, the town of child prostitution, obscene photographs and 'fancy goods,' preserving the spirit of the Inquisition behind a screen of electric signs, with its fortified convents and banks, its patchwork houses with their strongroom doors and their cellars protected by bars, of which those which keep the poor from the confessionals are but gilded replicas. In the meantime Puig had been arrested and imprisoned up there.

"They had got him. They had at last laid their hands on this dangerous anarchist. No civil lawyer was allowed to cross the threshold of his cell. And yet you remember the indignation of Europe and the way in which every lover of justice had his eyes focused on that dungeon in which the greatest heart in the world was waiting without weakening for a single moment. Socrates, Christ, the Chevalier du Barreau, Bismarck, Ravachol, all the great adventurers into the realm of thought, have met their death like that. As for me, I never saw him again alive. Puig wrote to me every day, I know, but I never got his letters. I was myself placed secretly in a cabin of the *Pelayo*, that old cruiser which sleeps its crocodile sleep in the harbor basin, ready at any moment to serve as a jail.

"Look, they are decking it with flags. Today, triumphal arches of silver paper will be erected all over the town. This evening there will be a candle in every window, for the King is coming tomorrow to review the troops who are going to Tetuan. Everything is beginning all over again, and will go on until the time when . . ."

An appetizing domestic smell of chocolate rises in the morning air.

Remedios sucked her pendant with a faraway look. Then she went on speaking, as though in a dream:

"Puig was put into the chapel at six o'clock in the evening. All night long he remained awake, refusing to kneel, standing between two Brothers of Charity. . . . He died shot in the back. For another whole day he remained on view in his black deal coffin, his head swathed in bandages, his face bloodless, and a wound in his throat plugged with lime."

Suddenly she threw her arms round my neck:

"What a little ragamuffin I am, aren't I?"

I went to the window to open it but Remedios threw herself on the curtain and pulled it right across.

"Is that because of the man who is patrolling up and down outside?" I asked.

For some time I had noticed that a very tall man with a stoop and a complexion like fine porcelain framed in a beard was watching us.

"Yes, that is José Salt."

"Police?"

"No."

"Jealous?"

"It's rather sad. Salt was formerly professor of history at the Institute. He was one of Puig's most ardent supporters and served him with intelligence, envy and vanity. I in my turn took a class, as you know, and became Puig's companion. Salt fell in love with me and lost his peace of mind. He spied on us, followed us about, plagued us with anonymous letters, probably denounced us to the police, in short became such a nuisance that Puig, in spite of his gentleness and self-control, had a quarrel with him, with the result that Salt had to leave the Institute. He was in the Argentine when the trouble occurred. I found him here on my return, avoiding me, dedicating poetry to me. He is lecturing again—the preachings of a visionary which no one listens to—passes his nights in churches and takes cocaine. Yesterday he came up to me in the street and asked me to live with him; when I tried to move away he swore that tomorrow he would put a bomb inside a bouquet of the flowers I like best and throw it into the King's carriage on his return from the review."

"That is the sort of romantic application that makes anarchy intolerable. Anarchy should above all be an exact science. But Spaniards have lost all sense of the fitness of things since they have given up the study of theology."

"It is quite true, *amor simpático*. You talk like a chaffinch."

I suddenly heard my neck crack; against my lips I found teeth which were not my own. A heat greater than that of the midday sun pervaded me. I couldn't breathe; close to my eyes I saw a single shining eye which gazed at me, gave me a feeling of intense discomfort, and went out.

"What has suddenly changed me like this?" asked Remedios after the kiss. "I can assure you it isn't a 'whim' on my part—that's what you say, what you do in Paris, isn't it? No. I've no desire for pleasure left. But you were so unhappy that I couldn't resist you. That is my weak spot."

"In the first place, I am that *animal triste* . . ."

"Yes, I felt that about you when we first dined together, and you let me ask the gypsy band to play the music of Lakme. I remember:

It is that God is deserting us.

Just at the moment someone was cracking lobster claws. I felt it was my heart that was being crushed. You see, something goes on throbbing beneath all this. In France your votive offerings take the shape of election cards, academic palms and dentists' diplomas. In Spain, round the statue of the Virgin hang hearts, bunches of hearts. . . ."

"Yes, and diseased eyes, tumors and, especially at Toledo, sexual organs, all modeled in wax."

"In any case, why should I invoke the Fates when we are together again? We have been separated for so long. . . ."

"And you have got thinner," I continued flatteringly.

"Then you will love me always?"

"Of course."

"I should like you to be a cat," said Remedios, playing with my watch chain. "You would never leave me then. In the daytime you would be put into a little basket and in the evening I would take you out and you would become a man again."

Her satin blouse is covered with big childish dots and has a sailor collar with a white crêpe de Chine scarf. I feel I want to bite her toes to stop them swinging to and fro. What numberless seated ancestors she must have had to be what she is! Except for the flies we are alone in the tea shop. Half a Dutch cheese, like a severed breast, shares its glass cover with a raw ham which smells of tallow and is turning black.

"When are we going on with our lessons? The irregular verbs?"

Remedios studies the lines round my eyes. I can no longer see anything but her round powdered nose protruding from her plump face.

"I think you are hypersensitive," she explained, "and capable of very deep affection. You ought to get to know me better. Personally I am hyperneurotic."

Just the same I open the window, so that she can call for help if I try to kill her.

"You cannot often have been accused of coldness of heart," she said. "And at the same time you are not very demonstrative."

Her body is too long and from it she emits a sigh which fills the whole room.

Beyond the pavement is an imitation wharf. Barcelona is a monstrous town. All the women who go past seem to have thick eyelids and large thighs; they are followed by thin Jesuits who go along in threes, holding each other's little fingers. In the background there is the inevitable Montjuich, a sheer rock with palms growing out of its crevices like hairs and dotted with little houses clinging on like limpets. The view from the other window consists of a woman selling dyed feathers and, in the distance, the modern cathedral of Soller, with its four reinforced concrete towers and its merry-go-round organ. Remedios is dwindling. She is becoming just an ordinary companion. That display of authority by which she asserted herself in Switzerland and France has gone. Her own country tones her down. Is that the reason she no longer wanted a country of her own? She used to be the personification of glory and love. But now she has become comfortable, cheerful and docile, a kind of domestic article. She has eyes for no one but me and her looks seem to say: "After all one must live, so why not enjoy one's life?" She forgets the dead in the living, and uses her old expression: "Her sacrifice," to excuse herself. She really believes it, too; and not altogether without reason. I am only annoyed that I cannot be grateful to her for it. Or is it her spotted blouse and the white crêpe de Chine scarf that irritate me? How she used to attract me in Paris in her mourning! (There was, for instance, the silver veil she kept for interviews.) She climbed up the rue Saint-Jacques as though it were a Calvary. What a crowd of idlers were always after her! I thought, as one always does, that I had found something quite extraordinary. Today, without hypocrisy to myself, just as without any irony towards her . . .

"Let's take the funicular up to the Tibidabo this evening," she said. "I'll bring Trick and we can dine à la carte. The view stretches as far as the Palma lighthouse. I will rest my head softly on your shoulder and we will be wafted to the country of conventional dreams, in which heroism does not exist. I will bring a nightdress."

At each ear a black jet pendant quivered acquiescence.

. . . .

I had room number 217. It was a new room and smelt of glue. A black beetle crawled leisurely across the carpet. Someone had left an ace of clubs in one of the drawers. I ordered dinner for two. At that moment there was an explosion in the distance. The electric light went out and I lit three candles.

I opened the window. It looked out over a courtyard from which rose the smell of *bisque d'écrevisse* and soapsuds. I counted the flowers on the counterpane, rubbed up the tarnished bottles of my dressing case on the curtains and put my slippers away. Lastly, I placed some flowers in a waterless vase as they do on the stage.

Remedios wants me to be a cat in a little basket. She has promised to give me a cigarette case with an enameled cover representing a nude blonde female on the seashore. For some obscure reason she has had the bust of Estebán Puig with its gouged-out eyes brought to my hotel, wrapped in oilcloth. I have had to put it under my bed. What am I to do? But one must either live alone or take people as one finds them. Why do the Spanish newspapers devote the whole of their front pages to obituary notices? There is something so sinister in their daily lament.

I make new resolutions. I must be more enthusiastic. I must be more carried away, more emotional. Perhaps I should exhibit chronic ardor. How exquisite, how radiant Remedios is!

Tired of waiting for her, I dined alone. Every twenty minutes the funicular announced its arrival by a jar which made the mountain shake, followed by a noise of rushing water. Then my anxiety redoubled. I strained my ears. But Remedios was still not in that one. I dared not try to explain her lateness to myself or to think of what would happen if she did not come at all, out of fear of arousing hostile forces which would prevent her from reaching me. I wanted Remedios with all my heart and I longed to see her safe with me between these four smooth sanatorium walls. I forgot that on that very morning I would have given anything to be back in Paris.

Gradually I compelled myself to believe that Remedios would certainly not come, but that I should pass just as good a night stretched diagonally or right across the bed.

The hotel was 800 meters above the sea-level. The sounds of country life had not yet begun there and the hum of the town was too far away to reach me. Either would have lulled me into a sleep which was denied me and there was nothing left to do but wait.

I lay down fully dressed. Towards two in the morning my neighbors, who had been carrying on an excited conversation for hours without a stop, sent for a steak and a bottle of manzanilla. Then a child began to cry, heralding the dawn. Another child answered it.

I had left the door ajar and I thrilled to every sound. A hundred times I dozed for a moment. The telephone bell kept ringing in the corridor, but the floor waiter drooping beneath a red lamp paid no attention to it. The panels of the imported English furniture kept cracking all through the night. Every time I started up I saw the other pillow lying there swollen and cold, and the infinitely big room, lit only by the moon which an obliging mirror deflected on to the dusty water of a fire bucket.

Then, suddenly, I sank into sleep.

It was not until the following morning that I heard of the attack and of the arrest of Remedios.

The Six-day Night

SHE HAD been there for three nights running. She was always alone except for the dances which she never missed, but which she only danced with professional dancers or with girl friends. If anyone else asked her for a dance she refused; she refused me also, although I went there only to see her and she knew it. It was not so much her milk-white back, her jet bead dress which was a shimmering black cascade, or her excess of onyx jewelry, her long narrow eyes meeting her side locks and looking like onyxes themselves; it was rather her flat nose, the rise and fall of her bosom, her beautiful Jewish complexion like a sulphur-dusted vine, the odd fact of her being alone. And in addition to this her curious maneuverings several times each evening towards the washroom and the telephone.

She spent her money on drinks, not on tips for the headwaiter. She went from short drinks to long ones. Between the hours of midnight and three o'clock on this third evening these consisted of two glasses of champagne, six anisettes and a small decanter of brandy, to say nothing of toothpicks and green almonds.

She went upstairs to the telephone with me behind her.

"Léa speaking. Is your milk good. Everything going on all right? . . . No stitch or anything? Has he eaten yet? Ah . . . ? From the bottle?"

We seemed to know each other better in the setting of this waterless washroom polluted by dead flowers, cigarette ends, broken dolls, cocaine, assignations and *poudre Rachel*. She examined herself pitilessly in the mirror beneath the lamp, so closely that she kissed her own lips. On the mist of the breath she left there I inscribed my heart. She shrugged a shoulder.

She was wearing a bodice on which numerous Chinese officials in silver thread were discussing affairs of state on the threshold of numerous pagodas.

"Any of these to let?" I enquired, placing my finger on the door of the pagoda at each place where the pattern repeated it on her chest. She drew herself up with dignity.

"Do you often get that way?"

The attendant, who was wiping her hands on an overcoat, turned round and pleaded for me.

"Yes, you look like a gentleman," said Léa, "but when I'm tight I'm always wrong."

From the balcony, above the up-pointing bows of the fiddlers, one saw a picture of Negroes in seaside clothes chewing at nothing and quaking with a kind of religious ague. Twisted copper irises like offshoots of the "metro" illuminated views of the Seine, no longer spoilt by factories, but steeped in romance and in which nude ladies were bathing timidly. Clasped body to body in the waltzing-trough the dancers surged along. The hall emitted an aroma of oxo, addled egg, armpit and the strains of *un jour viendra*.

"Where do you live?" I asked, "I love you."

"Go on! You're kidding. Or d'you mean it?"

"Both together, as usual."

She went on inevitably:

"I seem to have seen you before somewhere."

"You are my very sister," I said, kissing her dress, "and I cannot live without you."

I must have seemed to her brazen, contemptible and utterly devoid of character. She disengaged herself.

"You seem in an awful hurry."

"I'm not really, but I always do everything quickly and badly because I'm so afraid of ceasing to want to do it too soon."

"Well, it's nearly two o'clock. I've got to clear off now."

"Not before you've told me why you disappear every other moment. Are you selling *it*?"

She opened her eyes wide like saucers.

"Not likely," she replied, "do you think I want five years?"

"Well then, what?"

"It's to get the latest news of my boy friend who's working."

"What does your friend do?"

"He's a long-distance cyclist, a six-day man. . . ."

"He's in a six-day race, see? You've never heard of Petit-mathieu? Where on earth do you come from?"

With a sweep of her arm she enveloped herself in the skins of ninety-eight white rabbits.

"I told my coachman not to wait. Get me a taxi. Tell him to go towards Grenelle."

Along the banks of the winding Seine the taxi clock kept beating like a fevered pulse. Lamps like the husks of pink pearls along the girl's dry cough, bursts of affection, resolutions on my part not to have any more nonsense after leaving the Champ-de-Mars, carts full of blue cabbages.

"I love cabs," I said. "We ought to take one of these cabs and live in it for months until we get to know its lamps, its springs, its tires by heart. To know, *for instance*, that the blinds of the Urbaine cabs only pull down halfway and that it is nice to be behind a slow horse when Paris seethes beneath its cloak of mist and one Cours-la-Reine, phosphorescent sewer outfalls, does that which depopulates the world. . . ."

Grenelle. The river sweeps beneath the yoke of the bridge. Red lights on the lovers' parapet, green ones on the businessmen's. Fourteen francs twenty-five centimes on the clock.

I enquire anxiously:

"Don't you live in Paris?"

"Idiot," she replies. "Who said anything about where I live? I am going to the Winter velodrome for the two o'clock stakes."

An underground passage led to the weighing room. The cheap carpet was rippled by draughts. When we were halfway through there was a terrific thundering overhead. The boards groaned. Then we entered a wooden circus filled to its glass roof with a fog cut by luminous cones. Under enameled shades powerful electric lamps followed the track. Léa stood imperially on tiptoe.

"Look: yellow and black. . . . The Wasps . . . the team of 'aces.' That's Van den Hoven racing now. They're gong to wake Petit-mathieu up for the two o'clock stakes."

Shrill whistles cut through the air. Then four thousand yells broke out, yells that seemed to burst from the depths of the throat, such as one only gets from a Parisian crowd.

The Australian tried to forge ahead. The sprinting began. Above the billboards I saw the drawn features and eager eyes of the populace. A band broke out. Latrich was singing. "*Hardi coco!*" was taken up in chorus. This livened matters up. The six-teen competitors passed by every twenty seconds in a compact body, keeping a watchful eye on each other.

The weighing room occupied one end of the velodrome. At each end the track turned and there it gradually banked until it was as steep as a wall which the racers in their impetus climbed almost up to the words: "THE MOST RELIABLE PETROL." The score board began to show signs of life. Figures came down and others went up.

"Fourth night, 85th hour. 2,300 kilometers 650 meters."

"Look, there he is!" said Léa, "there's my darling getting on to his machine."

So far Petitmathieu was still swinging along easily by himself, with his curled hair, his dirty neck and his eyes as treacherous as a cat's.

"Isn't he a lamb, considering it's his fourth night, the dear boy!"

The nickeled megaphone announced two stakes of a hundred francs each.

"Let's go closer, things are becoming more exciting. Look, he has seen us."

He had seen me. I was holding Léa's hand. We exchanged a look of hatred as man to man.

The noise seemed to echo in spirals that became shorter at every turn. At each bell the sixteen men seemed to shoot round the corners and be hurled into the straight again by the steep twisted turns.

"Léa," I murmured, "I wish we were 'cradled in delight,' as that old puritan Agrippa d'Aubigné says. What do you like for breakfast?"

The mob was making an inhuman din.

"You're balmy," she answered. "Go on the spree when that darling is going round and round on that track there? Not much. A fine sort of thing I'd be if I thought of anything but him during these six days and six nights."

At the finish they pounced on the stakes like carp on a crumb, the woolly Italian, the Swiss giant, the Corsican N. C. O.'s and all the Negroes amongst the fair Flemings.

"It's all over. The Australian's won. Just like our luck! Petitmathieu let himself be pocketed," said Léa. "He's going to get off; let's go and see him, the dear!"

The competitors' quarters had sprung up at the short turn of the track. Each man had his own wooden cubicle containing a curtained cot. In a slot above one of these was written: "VELOX STAND. PETITMATHIEU—VAN DEN HOVEN TEAM." A searchlight played on the innermost recesses of the cubicles so that the crowd should not miss a single action of its favorites, even during their rest. The attendants dressed in white hospital uniform bustled about with a clinking of plates amongst the petrol and grease stains, mixing embrocations with eggs and camphor on garden chairs. Dismantled machines, bicycle frames, rubber washers, pieces of black cottonwool soaking in basins. Petitmathieu was lying stretched on his back, his hands behind his head, resigning his hairy and heavily veined legs to the masseur who was patting them to make them limber.

"Do let me kiss him, Bibendum," said Léa to the manager.

Petitmathieu opened an eye.

"That's all right," he said crossly, pushing her away. "Let him get on with his job."

"You haven't shaved, you ugly old thing."

"Oh! Shut up!"

Silence fell. The racers passed by at the rail, their shadows whisking across the awning above the cubicles. Their naked legs went round like mechanical toys. Van den Hoven called out as he passed:

"Buck up! Tomorrow night's nearly here."

I made Petitmathieu's acquaintance, but he seemed to ignore my presence entirely. He was grumbling to himself. That would teach him to get up again for a bloody stake. And only a hundred-franc one at that. Stingy brutes. A lot of touts who came there with their tarts, that is, if they didn't come to steal other people's girls!

His thighs were now like wet ivory.

"Petitmathieu! Stand up there!" the mob cried relentlessly from above the Peugeot lions. But he made a sign with his hand that he had had enough.

The soiled mechanics in khaki shirts with their five days' beard were binding handlebars with pitched string, making bundles of wheels to be examined, tightening nuts.

Petitmathieu was feeling uncomfortable.

"My stomach, when are you going to do my stomach?"

The masseur pulled down the elastic belt of Petitmathieu's shorts. Below his navel was written *"4th Zouave Regiment. 1st Company"* with the motto *"all I can get."* He rubbed him with the palm of his hand.

"Put some talcum powder on my thighs."

Those who had just been relieved by their team mates got off their machines for two hours' sleep. Their managers stopped them by grasping their saddles and handlebars, undid the straps fastening their feet to the pedals and carried their charges with tender care towards their beds.

Then everything settled down for the night. In spite of the noise some of the competitors were snoring. Others got up and ragged about from bed to bed like in a barrack room. One heard the noise of bicycle pumps, followed by that of compressed air whistling through valves.

Petitmathieu remained on his back like a corpse, his hands with their square black nails and thick aluminum rings crossed on his chest. Léa sat herself at his feet and rouged her cheeks. I moved away.

From behind the partition I heard Petitmathieu talking:

"All the same, I told you to keep away from Maxim's during the race."

Léa explained that she was too nervous to stay at home by herself. She couldn't sleep. She only thought of him and of his beautiful legs working away so hard, of his beloved face with his black curly hair, his Charlie Chaplin mustache, his square jaw, his eyes fixed on the backwheel of the pacer, his scarlet sweater fastened at the neck by mother-of-pearl buttons. It wasn't the first time she had been tested. Hadn't she simply *lived* at the end of a telegraph wire all the time he was grinding round at Madison Square Garden the year before?

Crushed beneath the weight of their 95 hours of work and 2,652 kilometers 580 meters of distance the competitors were going round in Indian file to the silvery trill of bearing-balls, a Negro leading the way. Some of them had put on goggles. Now and then someone had a puncture or a chain broke. Hurriedly his sleeping comrade was awakened and seated forcibly on the saddle; still asleep he attached himself to the others. The round became monotonous as always at the end of those nights which no one ever dreams of leaving except in the case of collapse. A silence weighing tons descended on the assembly.

Léa rejoined me in the enclosure.

"Beat it, or he won't be able to sleep. He's watching us all the time. It drives him crazy to know I'm with someone and that he can't leave his bunk. He'll get so tired he'll lose his nerve.

"It isn't that he's got it in for you, he even thinks you're rather a sport, if a little half-baked," she went on. "But he's got it in for me. He won't let me go to Maxim's or dance. He's awfully touchy."

I learnt that Petitmathieu only allowed her to go to the Excelsior, the racers' café, to write letters and see people. There at any rate he knew what was going on, from his pals and from the waiters.

In vain I promised her a surprise, presents, complete discretion; I could not persuade Léa to come back with me. I only got her permission to meet her next day at the apéritif hour. I needed her. She had such sweet plump curves and her harsh voice, a delight in itself, enchanted me. All that soft skin smoothed by beauty creams, washed with ointments, all those jewels, all her hidden charms, her dyes, drugs and tenderness, were all at the disposition of those strong, hairy, pistol-like legs now resting, rolled so carefully in their blankets. The whole thing was an illogical and yet natural game into which I was intruding as a third party and which amazed and irritated me but at the same time was the only thing that gave me the strength to bear that cruel moment in which the nighthawk has to confess himself beaten.

Sunset. Grenadine. The hour flowed smoothly. A feeling of peace crept over everything in spite of the fieriness of my drink. I was waiting for Léa at the Brasserie de la Port-Maillot. She came down from Montmartre in a hired brougham, wearing an otter coat, and drank long drinks.

"This reminds me of when I first knew Petitmathieu. I rented a room by the month in the rue des Acacias."

My first words were to ask her for news of the race.

"A little tired," she said. "Backache. And colic. But the other

leading team has it too. The Australian is all in. Water on the
knee coming on. He's quit. They've hardly moved all the morning; they're just crawling along."

"And Van den Hoven?"

"Pedals like a demon all the time. But he has no head for team-
work. It's Bibendum and Petitmathieu who come out strong when
something's got to be done."

I began to realize that my pleasure at seeing Léa again was not
an unmixed one. I loved her plebeian hands, her eyelids the color
of a fifty-franc note . . . that cold heart which warmed as if by
magic to physical strength, but I could not forget the struggle
going on round and round down there.

Drawn up by the curb the cars of the spectators exhausted the
catalogue of strange shapes. There were torpedoes, yachts, bath-
tubs, airships, whilst some of them were merely hastily covered
with a champagne case. Their owners were those highly polished
and beautiful young men who stand for hours behind plate-glass
windows in the avenue des Champs-Elysées in tiled showrooms
containing nothing but a palm, a Persian prayer rug and a nickeled
chassis. They always remind me of the ladies sitting in their windows in the low quarters of Amsterdam.

The waiters hurried about between the tables, holding a black-
colored apéritif between each finger. Mechanics in overalls,
cyclists with tires wrapped round their bodies, pugilists leaving
Cuny's. Each man greeted his friends with a gesture characteristic
of his occupation. Bantamweights gave each other hearty right
hooks in the ribs, footballers slapped each other on the legs.

Léa was still pretty and elusive. The only thing which roused
her at all was a yellow and black scarf, the colors of the team,
which I had bought specially for her. She wore a large white
felt hat trimmed with a single vulture's feather and drop earrings
which reminded me of the Far West and of the ladies who
shoot over their shoulders, aiming in a mirror. I told her this. I
also told her that I was not a man like Petitmathieu with "All I
can get" for a motto, and that I had never wanted anything for
six days and six nights in my life, that the doctor forbade me cold

baths, that in matters of daily life I had always done "the correct thing" to a dreadful extent, that my heart was an object entirely distinct from myself and that very thin women with curly hair were not without their charm.

On the other hand she was enthralled when she discovered that I knew the Italian lakes and the author of "Tipperary" and that I had some autographs of Marshal Joffre. I even boasted of having in my studio an exact replica of an Arab chief's tent and of being able to play Tartini's *Devil's Trill Sonata* on the violin.

She looked at me:

"I say, you're not a bit like other people, are you?"

"Thank you, Léa. No one but a woman would say a thing like that; and yet it is above all with women that one is like everybody else."

The motoring school nearby emitted a fetid stench. In the distance a hunt could be heard in progress just beyond the fortifications, mixed with the melancholy hooting of the siren in the shadows of the scenic railway at Luna Park which is like the hull of a huge steamer abandoned on the stocks of a bankrupt shipbuilder.

. . . . . .

I had to admit to myself with some annoyance on arriving at the racetrack that evening after a dull day, that I was going there just as much for the race as for Léa; nothing had changed on the announcements. But suddenly there was an uproar. The six racers were going round in a colored ribbon in which were mixed green, yellow, white, scarlet and orange. By their nimble pedaling they devoured the track worn smooth by their tires, to the clang of the bell marking their progress.

Petitmathieu was in the saddle; he saw me and gave me a smile of recognition with his left eyelid. Then, towards the 3,421st kilometer in the 131st hour, a spurt began. The balconies groaned beneath the weight of the public surprised during their supper, their mouths full of food.

The Negro, his nose glued to his handlebars, went off like an arrow, and getting half a lap ahead, kept his lead. There was instant confusion. Those who were suffering from the effects of a fall or from aching backs and those whose wheels were buckled were left behind one by one and were soon caught up again. Led by Petitmathieu, the competitors threw themselves in the wake of the Negro who began to weaken and look round; his team mate was asleep and did not come; the crowd yelled to him to come to the rescue.

"Hey, cocky! Boot-face! Get mounted!"

A waiter let a glass of beer fall from the first tier. The Hall shook beneath the howls, the rattles and the whistles until suddenly the Negro straightened his back, brought his hands to the center of his handlebars and, coasting on his momentum, showed that he had had enough.

I made for the competitors' quarters. Petitmathieu began to dine heartily. Washed, shaved, a fine-looking lad in his cashmere dressing gown, he was gnawing away at a cutlet he held in his hand. Seated on the edge of the bed, Léa watched him chew, her eyes moist and submissive. He offered me a bowl of champagne and some whisked eggs in a tin that had once held rubber solution.

I was proud of my acquaintance with this athlete whom the program called "a Caruso of the pedal." I found myself admiring his supple legs, his faultless knees. I assured him of my warm support and spurred him on.

"I led the pack," he explained, simply. "When that happened it didn't take long to break the nigger's heart. Team work is everything."

Petitmathieu amazed me most by his calm, dining peacefully like any ordinary citizen a few minutes after that hue and cry, surrounded now by his assiduous attendants, his adoring mate beside him, propped up by cushions, with a screen decorated with wistaria behind him which gave him the appearance of being in his home.

Léa held one of his fingers tenderly and said nothing. I loved them both equally. I told them so.

We clinked glasses. Léa proposed the following toast:

> To our health which is dear to us all,
> And which is so necessary to us,
> Because with health we can earn money,
> And with money we can buy sugar,
> And with sugar we can catch flies.

Petitmathieu explained his happiness to me: "She's a regular scream. But a good girl for all that. And always ready with tempting dishes, bandages and anything else that's wanted. She's got a coachman by the month who plays the trumpet and knows all about mushrooms. Clever isn't the word for her, and what a talker! Makes a party go like anything. Between ourselves, a skin with veins in it like rivers on a map, a mane of hair down to her heels, none of those three blobs of hair women wear nowadays and which don't keep a comb busy. And what breasts! cool as an icehouse; and then going about things painstakingly while only putting half her back into it; washes her teeth after every meal, eats asparagus with special tongs and never wears stays.

"Wait till you know her a bit better," he said, "and you'll see what I mean."

The orchestra was playing a boston like the Russian mountains. From exquisite heights one was cast into the languorous valleys of the refrains. Some comedians with powdered chins came in after the theater. They wanted to dance but the mob treated them as good-for-nothings, braggarts, sausage-eaters.

I left Petitmathieu in high spirits, holding his audience, pretending to be in bed with Léa in his cubicle.

I had to give my promise that I would be back the next day for the supreme effort and that I would stay there all night.

Sixth night, 138th hour, 3,864 kilometers, 570 meters. The same monotonous spectacle. They slept as they went round, like weary squirrels. One of them touched the wheel in front and fell, dragging the others with him. One heard shouts in English, Turkish oaths, a desultory clamor caused by someone giving up the race. Then the round began again.

It was very late. The night sprints were over. The competitors circled round, their hands reversed to rest their wrists and wrapped in thick woolen shawls against the night cold.

Petitmathieu was resting in his cubicle. Van den Hoven was carrying out the humble toil of the night, leaving to his team mate the brilliant work of the last hours which was about to begin. I offered to lend a hand to Bibendum whose face was as drawn by weariness as though distorted in a spoon. In our shirtsleeves we put an inner tube into a bucket of water to find the leak in it. Léa found me doing this and reproached me for neglecting her. I shrugged my shoulders.

Many of the spectators were spending the night there. Children were sleeping lying on pink or yellow sporting papers. Orderlies from the École Militaire, private chauffeurs, workmen from les Moulineaux on their way to their factories, clerks on their way to their offices, provincial couples in mourning, yawned, kept themselves awake by playing cards and opened bottles with a pop.

"Ugéne," said someone, "pass me the atomizer."

Wrapping ourselves in blankets, our heads on sacking, we waited side by side for the dawn. Léa took my hand in hers.

"What small bones you've got. I feel I'm going to get into trouble over you," she said, like the heroine of a penny novelette. Her voice was soft and silky. "You're just the opposite of a record-breaker. You're more like a priest or a comic singer. You don't say much but you're full of life. And besides, I've always longed to be interested in someone whose health wasn't very good. A young artist, for instance, with his shirt open at the neck, veins much too blue and a fine pointed beard. . . . Take me."

"Nothing," I replied, "could have afforded me greater pleasure, even as late as yesterday. And perhaps tomorrow again. But today my whole heart is here; I am a prey to one thought only, and that is that Petitmathieu should win. I no longer belong to myself; nor do you; we have become part of the Velodrome, an incident in the race, waiting for victory. A few hours more and just think of the click of the cameras, the crowd, the special editions of the papers, the banquet with its flags and deputies. We will ourselves have contributed in our own small way to our winner getting all this."

"Dearest," said Léa, annoyed, "you're a good boy. That's nice. It's sweet of you. I love you more for that."

Disappointment turned down the corners of her mouth.

She waited. She closed her eyes. Then half dreaming she said: "I don't know how Petitmathieu will take this."

On our right, above the advertisement of Éternol varnish, through the glass roof the desolate dawn appeared, heralded by a pianola. I sang:

> Amidst the tumbled sheets at break of day,
> While cock to hoarse-voiced cock his greeting cries,
> Lovers are parted, love, flowers cast away,
> And while you sleep, sweet love, my passion dies.

The Baltic Night

THE GOTHIC porch was lit by a two hundred candle power lamp. I stood for a moment on the opposite pavement. People were going in; a few men alone and then others who had women with them. With a beating heart and in a state of mind that was far from heroic I waited until it seemed that the last person had gone in. A flight of uninviting steps led up to a door before which there were a few traces of sawdust. In the hall I was assailed by a smell of gas and stale perspiration. A small girl in pigtails read my temporary membership card—a little parchment hexagon— and I entered the men's dressing room. Shirts were hanging there, emptied of their bodies; braces were resting from their labors; boots exhibited their heels shod with little indiarubber discs; apparently the feet of Northern Europe had not escaped that wave of American exportation which, in the form of calculating machines, fly-swatters and dental floss, descended upon Eastern

Europe on the morrow of the Armistice. A nickel shoe horn twinkled in the middle of the room.

Ought I to undress? Doubtless the notices on the walls said so, but how could anyone understand those words with their toad- or insect-like faces equipped with feelers and carrying on their backs countless modification signs like pimples and small air-balloons? I removed my shoes and opened the door a little way. Though my attire would now have been eminently suitable for a mosque, it was obviously not that of the club, for there before me were two members in full dress, if one could call it that. One of them was facing me, his back resting against a balustrade. A wisp of hair as dry as lichen wandered over his head, first sparse prom-ise of the white beard which flowed down to his chest where it became confused like the tangled horsehair which one sees burst-ing from old sofas in second-hand furniture shops. Then the hair divided into two regular streaks, one on each side of his stomach, frothed up again for a moment and, meandering down his legs like ivy, finished its journey on his feet. His companion was facing him and so had his back to me. He had bristly black hair and the wires of his gold-rimmed spectacles sparkled behind his ears. He too was naked and was waggling his right big toe rhythmically up and down.

I closed the door again and sat down on a bench. The mere fact of undressing and going about naked like the others did not worry me, as from my earliest youth I had constantly been to fencing schools, athletic and swimming clubs and Turkish Baths. Besides, as I was careful to remind myself in order to gain con-fidence, I was here of my own free will, having applied for ad-mission as a foreign member to the "Diana-Bund" or "Society of Diana."

Without having to go back to the fifteenth century when sects sprang up in Bohemia (only to be massacred in the end) to fol-low the Hussite heresy which declared in favor of the return to a state of adamic nudity as a sure means of getting to Heaven, I had often heard of Teutonic Societies whose members assembled together for the sole purpose of living without clothing. I had been put on the right track in the course of reading a German magazine for the propagation of nudity, a magazine devoted to questions of esthetics and hygiene, to say nothing of eugenics. This periodical acquainted me with the fact that devotees of that new form of reciprocation, the *Nacktkultur*, existed in the Northern European countries. An advertisement in the Swedish Review *Beauty* did the rest:—

> Persons of both sexes, of Aryan descent, who wish to join a Society of which the objects are those of *Beauty*, are invited to communicate with Box 78, Poste Restante at ——. Affiliations in all Northern countries.

Happening a little later to be at ——, I wrote to the address given, enclosing a stamp for a reply, and I duly received a letter-card in which one Doctor Vulpius begged me to state categorically my reasons for wishing to join the Society, and to give him full particulars of my age, profession, etc. I sent the doctor a declaration of principles modeled on the tone of the Review, conjuring up the great civilizations of antiquity, the festivals of Sparta, the laws of Lycurgus, the Germania of Tacitus and recalling also, from the purely medical point of view, the benefits of the chemical action of the sun on the skin.

I was given an appointment for the day after next in the Prince Alexander Room on the first floor of the Café Odin where a conversazione and magic lantern display were to take place, in the course of which I should be brought before the executive committee.

It was about seven o'clock in the evening, after dinner. The café looked out over the timber wharf of the town. A few Norwegian sailing ships with frost-covered yards, the sole reminder of the recently melted snow, stretched their topmasts to the level of the double windows from which the paper gummed on them for the winter had not yet been scraped. An evening breeze tortured the waves as far as the islands which slid in a gentle slope into the sea, following the lines of the repairing-slips loaded with newly tarred boats glistening with red lead in the setting sun.

The President (whom I knew to be Doctor Vulpius) was quite blind and wore black spectacles on a wide expanse of blotchy face. Flanked by the Vice-President and the Treasuress, he was solemnly holding forth from the seat of judgment. The Treasuress was a fair woman with a face like a tortoise, obviously an officer's widow: she carried a lorgnette and was surmounted by a hat trimmed with daffodils. She favored me with a steady and calculating stare which penetrated me like a knife. Her thoughts came out and met mine halfway and I realized that my admission depended finally upon this female guardian of the gate.

I explained myself in English. My remarks were translated to a young girl who was hidden from me by a sheet of paper sticking out of her typewriter; this stenographer, in her turn, expressed herself in the local idiom. The examination lasted twenty minutes. The fact that I was a Frenchman produced more interest than sympathy and inspired anything but confidence.

"It is quite understood that you are not impelled by any curiosity of an immoral nature to enter our Society?

"We only admit amongst us persons of unimpeachable honesty who are addicted neither to alcoholic drinks nor to theosophy, who do not read loose books and who are persons of financial substance."

The assistant on his right, a man in a frock coat, of about forty years of age with a red beard and very suave manner, closed the interrogatory:—

"Do you associate with Russians? Or with Jews?"

After I had produced my passport and furnished a reference, the jury deliberated in low tones. Then the typewriter began to click.

"You will be admitted for two months as soon as you have passed the medical examination. You will be given an appointment for this. Be good enough to step into the waiting room."

I rose as the door opened. The stenographer came in; she gave me an envelope and a smile in which I read a favorable verdict. All the awkwardness was on my side. The fascination of the seriousness, the taciturnity and the unaffected actions of these people came over me in a wave. My sympathy went out to her immediately. She had blue eyes bordered with black lashes level as the edges of a fringe, a sympathetic mouth and bobbed hair full of gleaming lights. I was on the point of making advances and of breaking out into a dissertation when, with her toes turned out, she suddenly made me an adorable and extremely rapid little curtsey; it was no more than a quiver going through her from head to foot. Her hair swayed forward and trembled and then, without a word, she left the room.

The next day I passed the medical examination in the consulting room of a suburban hospital, a lazaret where refugees from Kronstadt were getting rid of their vermin. A very rapid examination, but very thorough, all contagious disease being a bar to admission (even including bad breath and worms) as well as any skin disease or physical deformity which might spoil the esthetic pleasure of the other members.

I was accepted, paid my subscription and set to work to learn the rules. My anxiety increased as I read them and reflected on this phrase: "The least infraction of the ideal of the Society, or any indecency calculated to shock the feelings of the other members, involves immediate expulsion."

Without anything on, then, except a turquoise ring on my finger, I had, with my head held high, to enter the recreation room where, twice a week, the members of the Diana-Bund stripped themselves and passed the evening in the costume of heaven. I was going to be one of them. It was not enough that the proceedings were authorized by the Police and considered natural for me to look at them quite in the same light. Certainly my apprehension diminished when I thought of my previous Northern experience, the mixed sunbaths on the German shores of the Baltic, the Swedish hydrotherapic establishments in which one is delivered over to soft feminine hands which seem to be

almost worn away by soap, and Russian bathing parties where I
had seen men and women sunburnt and naked with their arms
about each other's waists in the island water, blue as stylographic
ink. All the same, the thought of finding myself suddenly naked
in the midst of women and girls was disturbing. I half opened the
door again. In the gallery with its decoration of flags, gilded
palms and snakes in glass bottles, a third man had joined the
other two. I looked at him. He was wearing a fountain pen hung
round his neck in a sheath of black shagreen; but there could be
no question of pants or a handkerchief, even for a neophyte; the
time was getting on. I was evidently the last one to undress. With
a measured step, firmly, my fists clenched and a dryness in my
throat, I entered the hall.

The first thing I noticed was that one corner was set aside for
refreshments and there naked families in cane armchairs were par-
taking of coffee and radishes. The sight reminded me of those
Turkish Bath meals one has in the cooling room. A lady knitting
with her work resting on her stomach seemed to me like a bad
dream. I heard shouts and the sound of people calling to one another; the floor shook beneath the stamping of feet. Balls were
trundling along with a noise like thunder, scattering ninepins. I
found myself in the center of a hall surrounded by windows obscured by pinewood shutters treated with boat varnish, as is
everything in this country. Forty people of both sexes were amusing themselves. Quite a crowd of men were high-jumping, leaping over a cord which could be altered two centimeters at a
time. A nude gentleman who looked like the king of Sweden
despoiled by a revolution put the cord up one notch after each
series. I strove to concentrate my attention on these people and
to avoid looking at the opposite sex. A gymnasium was installed
at one end of the room. Solitary enthusiasts raised themselves up
and down in the sawdust or were loosening their dorsal muscles
with Indian clubs. Athletic-looking boys were hurling javelins
against mattresses; when resting they rinsed out their mouths with
iced water, spitting it out on to the floor at some distance from
them. Elderly ladies, as though the victims of some penitentiary

system, were accomplishing hexagonal shuffles of triangular jumps reminiscent of hopscotch. The sound of rings striking together attracted my attention. I lifted my eyes which up to this moment I had kept religiously lowered like a nun and I saw, suspended in the air, a curious bundle made of intertwined limbs from which pointed elbows and rounded knees were protruding. Then, the body turned; below the backbone there came a fleeting glimpse of bare pink leg, hoisted into view by the power of the wrists; a sudden effort on the part of the neck and there emerged a head framed in fair coppery hair, tied behind with a big bow of black moiré ribbon. The vision smiled and I recognized the stenographer of Doctor Vulpius, the girl who had handed me my certificate. She remained like this, on the rings, frog-like, idle, supple, completely at ease, smiling at me with her fresh irregular face of a Northern sprite. I felt a pricking sensation running under the roots of my hair. The young girl's head sank again towards the ground and her arms spread out at right angles, stretched to their full extent; round this as axis the whole body circled and came slowly upright; the legs in their turn closed, described a quarter circle and came to rest on the floor.

She stood there before me, the most beautiful figure of a young girl that could possibly be imagined. My eyes dared not leave her face. She smiled at me again and greeted me. I felt her breath on my arms. I suddenly cut the interview short and, turning my back on her brusquely, dashed to the high-jump apparatus at which some of the men were still exercising themselves, took a run and leapt on to the springboard in a sort of religious fervor. My foot caught in the cord and I measured my length on the ground. I got up with my nose grazed and my hands all torn, but with a feeling of satisfaction. I felt the urgent necessity of taking strenuous and continued exercise and of not allowing my eyes to wander towards where the girl stood. What eyes she had! I hurled myself at the trapeze, I took the parallel bars in a stride. How sweet, how inviting, the corners of her mouth! I lifted a pair of 40-lb. dumbbells. What a perfect bosom! I carried out a rapid series of leaps, one after the other, rising in the general estimation by my Aryan energy. Panting, out of training, perspiring in every pore, I was forced at length to stop. But she was still before me, an Eve with bobbed hair, before the Fall, without shyness or shame, stretching out to me a pair of arms not spoiled by knotted biceps and triceps, but covered, like those of a swimmer, with long rippling muscles which were hardly discernible. I was quite out of breath.

"My name is Aïno," she said, speaking in German. "My parents beg that you will take a glass of tea with them." I followed her. Her father, a fat man with a sort of pelt which blurred his silhouette, asked me very politely to sit down. He was the manager of the Baltika Hereditas Assurance Company. Her young brother was exercising the muscles of his fingers with spring dumbbells. Her mother kept her ample bosom imprisoned between her elbows. She was reading Fichte and gave me a hyacinth to smell. Her arms still retained their youth. Only her face and her stomach showed her age. I fumbled down my sides for my trouser pockets. I sneezed.

"You'll soon get used to going without clothes," she said. "We always do at home. In the summer we sometimes take our clothes off and go and gather strawberries, and in the winter we always break the ice for our morning dip. For the beauty of the ancients is not dead, monsieur, as the Lutherans would have us believe: it is always coming back, like the swallows which, according to our peasants, pass the winter at the bottom of the lakes."

She turned her attention to her youngest son:

"If you go on biting your nails," she said, "you will deform your hands and you'll be thrown down a deep well."

Everything went smoothly. I drank tea with lemon amongst these robust citizens who exuded respectability and a certain amount of prosperity. Coffee with milk, cucumbers and acacia fritters passed to and fro on huge trays, like offerings to Scandinavian gods. Aïno's father took a fancy to me and showed me his stomach all furrowed as the result of an extremely rare operation. He told me that his company occasionally effected insurance against appendicitis, reinsuring with Lloyds. He also spoke

to me of the nutritive values of vegetables. I looked furtively at
Aïno. Whenever I caught her eye and my feelings began to get
the better of me, I turned my attention hurriedly to some other
less perfect body, or lowered my gaze to the deformed feet of my
companions, amongst which, rather top-heavy with their big
heads, little naked children were disporting themselves, rolling
about like lion cubs. No longer fearing to be thought a Philistine,
I asked everything I wanted to know, drawing the line at nothing.
The worst, it seemed to me, was over.

But who was it who suddenly made us play round games? The
game of cat and mouse went off quite quietly. We formed ourselves into a wide circle. The cat endeavored to catch the mouse,
whose flight we impeded in every conceivable way. Great laughter and excitement. An armistice. Then the game of fox and goose
began; a sort of human chain, a playful farandole in which each
player held on to the waist of the person in front. The fox tried
to catch the goose, and the living chain writhed, broke and joined
up again, trying to protect the prey from the hunter. Aïno was
behind me. Her fingers seemed to burn their way into my hips
like red-hot irons. Laughingly she begged me not to fall back.
I avoided contact with her, but in doing so I anchored myself
more firmly to a sturdy girl in front, fair, ugly and as solid as a
bridge pile, who bent her legs in order to lower her center of
gravity and to withstand the jars better. Conscientiously enthusiastic, she abandoned herself entirely to the game, the angle made
by her body protruding towards me, cracking beneath the effort.
The recoiling movement which her attitude forced me, in my
turn, to adopt, pressed Aïno against me. At one moment in which
the struggle became particularly tense, I felt her arms go round
my waist and her whole body press against mine; her legs took
an intolerable purchase against me and her panting bosom was
crushed against my back. I shut my eyes and felt an indescribable
embarrassment come over me; in it an outrageous feeling of shame
mingled with a pleasant feeling of numbness which made me want
to stay just like that forever. But at every moment the chain was
on the point of breaking under the violence of the game. Sud-

denly I let go my hold and at the same time tore myself away from Aïno. I leapt impetuously from the crowd without daring to look behind me, bounded to the top of the stairs and made a dash for the cloakroom, where I shut myself in.

In the street a sharp icy blast like a charge of salt from a rifle cut my cheeks and I felt as light as a bird, and as though I was charged with electricity.

. . . .

Two days later I met Aïno in a confectioner's shop.

"Don't you recognize me?" she asked.

"Very nearly. If you are Aïno you've got beauty spots on your left shoulder and your right breast. But it is so difficult to tell in all those clothes."

"Why do you wear your hair like that? Nothing is more beautiful than a man who shaves his head every day. Don't you carry your private diary round your neck on a chain? What method do you employ for throwing the hammer? Do you always stoop like that when you walk?"

When I pressed her to dine with me or to meet me somewhere she said: "Tomorrow I will come and fetch you with my side-car. We will go and spend midsummer day at G———. Bring a bag with you."

We passed through the town bouncing up and down on every unevenness in the road, and threading our way with difficulty and the aid of the klaxon. Pedestrians all made way for us hurriedly. When our progress over the cobbled road was blocked by trams we swerved into the sidewalk, brushing past the effete and wornout cabs painted in brilliant hues and crushed beneath the weight of their cabmen in astrakhan caps. From beneath the yokes of the troïkas the ponies cast a fiery eye at us through their tangled forelocks. We swept past curious buildings: the High Courts of Justice, Police Courts, Greek temples dating from the earliest days of the Russian Occupation: the offices of German Shipping Companies with bearded statues of their agents, naked to the waist, masquerading as caryatids. Street sellers, buffeted by the wind, were selling all kinds of birchwood articles

—bags, bicycles, even beds; in the shops trade was being carried on in foreign goods: tinned tongues and safety razors, each fastened with yellow ribbons to a portrait of General Krabb. But the chief object in the shop windows was our own reflection; it swept along, getting itself confused with the goods inside and absorbing them by transparency. There I was in that little varnished crimson coffin out of which peered my hatless head and streaming eyes, and there beneath my cramped legs was a wheel to which our speed gave the appearance of being oval; above this uninspiring reflection of myself appeared that of Aïno in green stockinette with American cloth boots coming right up to her hips. Strained back by the wind, her short hair full of soft, bewitching lights took the edge from the somber and forbidding mask of the wire goggles which covered the upper part of the face like a snout; beneath this appeared her thick, young, confident mouth. Aïno gave her whole mind to driving the sidecar, unconscious of the fetid smell of the oil and the noise of the misfiring cylinders; cutting off the engine and my breath at the same time whenever we came to crossroads, but more often altering direction by the mere application of brakes, throwing an occasional glance between her legs at the exhaust or a smile at me beneath her elbow.

There were no suburbs. The open country began suddenly at the foot of a five-storied building. In the distance a few clouds lay on the road before us like carpets. Above the clear water of the lakes the sky was so bright that the gulls looked almost like crows. Dotted about the country were occasional wood-pulp works above which rose the posts of wireless telegraph stations. We passed through well cared for stadiums erected in clearings in the pine woods; athletes were busy getting themselves into training there. We flew along the ragged ribbon which could hardly be dignified by the name of road. I hunched myself up, straightened out my legs and supported myself on my hands to minimize the bumping. Aïno laughed joyously and the more violent jerks, which almost shot me out of my box, enraptured her. She kept up my spirits with words that were swept away by the wind. A little farther on nothing was left but endless white birches, black-edged, as though they were in mourning, their monotony broken every now and then by pools bordered by willows with their twisted gouty trunks and in which, half submerged, tree trunks were floating down towards the sawmills. What visions of safety matches!

A month earlier I had left the Champs Elysées, where the trees were already beginning to cast shadows. They were tidying up the Ambassadeurs, and the oriflammes of the Salon were in flower; burnished by tires, the asphalt flowed like a deep river towards the Place de la Concorde. I missed all those things. These endless birches! I would have given the world for one chestnut tree. At Dresden the lilac had flowered and the world was beginning to turn green; in Sweden they were removing the icebeams from the ships and thinking of launching their yachts; but here there were as yet only tiny leaves on the trees. It was as though the moving picture of Spring was being released backwards as one traveled north. Preceded by the clang of their bells the engines of the trains carried still more birches in their tenders, but in this case only their helpless bodies cut up into fuel. From their bell-mouthed smokestacks issued green and red smoke, not so beautiful as the blue smoke of coal, but wafting to us on the wind the acrid scented smell of essential vegetable oils which was delicious. The wooden ski-jumping scaffolds, laid bare by the melting of the snow, poked their frames idly into the air.

I was happy. I took Aïno's hand in mine and stroked her wrist tenderly, with the result that she cut off the engine and we stopped dead. I clasped her in my arms. She rose on her pedals, pushed her goggles on to her forehead, broke her comb and tried to tidy her hair with her fingers.

"Frenchwomen don't do that, do they? I had a girl friend once who was French. Her head was so big that she was always toppling over. Her hands couldn't hold things; something was always falling from her like fruit from a tree, a glove, a bag or something, whenever she moved."

"My friends," I replied, piqued, "order their dresses by telephone, wash themselves on the floor and never have stomach aches. But not one of them possesses your lack of eloquence, your tanned skin or that body of yours which slid in and out of those rings like a cashmere scarf through a wedding ring."

And then, so that she should not get off scot-free:

"But to me your sisters were always soap-eaters who worshiped idols with the heads of crows."

G——— consisted of a dark wooden house built on granite blocks. Only the window and door frames were white. On the door someone had scratched Russian characters.

Our two rooms were next to each other, so exactly alike with their yellow curtains, their soft birch furniture, their monumental white china stoves, their double windows between which hyacinths were growing, that I was soon unable to distinguish her room from mine. Everything was so clean that one did not even know where to put cigarette ash.

"We are going to have cold supper and then we will go to bed," she said.

"Already! Wouldn't it be better to wait till dinnertime?"

She smiled. I looked at my watch. It was eleven o'clock.

The table was loaded like a fisherman's net with all kinds of fish: salmon, trout curled round in rings, herrings, anchovies tied by the tail in bunches of six. But there was nothing to drink but milk and unfermented beer. Surreptitiously I produced a bottle of Norwegian brandy. Aïno clapped her hands, drew the cork with a hairpin and sneezed with pleasure. Filling two glasses to the brim she gave me one and took the other herself; placing herself in a position of defense, she clicked her heels and her tongue and paid me the immediate compliment of an empty glass, which she turned to me bottom first with a few conventional words which I did not hear. She had taken off her boots and put on a house smock decorated with peasant embroidery. A necklace of vegetable ivory swayed round her like a second row of teeth. We ate silently like a couple of English people. Aïno's cheeks were brilliant without any artificiality, like all Scandinavian faces into which coursing blood puts a color which fresh

air or the most fleeting glance will immediately heighten. A
second bottle added its eloquence to the first. Our heads began
to buzz.

The laws exact temperance. But the foreigner who comes to
a meal provided with a couple of bottles of benedictine is much
esteemed. The flavor of the fish is brought out if one drinks it
in bumpers. As someone once said to me: "Real success never
costs more than this," adding that at the same time it was a lot
to pay for it. My bag turned out to be a small cellar. I made various ingenious and potent cocktails; the "corpse-reviver" which I
had from the barman of the Grand Hotel in Stockholm and the
"bosom-caresser" which I learnt in Denmark. Aïno submitted to
them artlessly, contentedly and with a cold detachment that
quelled my impulse to beg her to take her smock off. She wandered round the table, plate in hand, composing symphonies in
fish, trailing her feet across the floor from her winter habit of
wearing snowshoes. As she passed by me I told her passionately
how much I wanted to kiss her nostrils. She let me do it submissively. Her skin smelt of tar and caustic soda. I took her head
between my hands and examined her features. She was mongol
in type, with the flat nose and deep-set eyes which make so many
women of her race look like pink-cheeked Chinese.

In my stupid Western way I asked her: "What will your people say?" "It's midsummer day, they will think I have stayed the
night at G———." I was touched by the frank straightforward-
ness, the primitive honesty of these people, at all those things by
which for so long we have dreamed of replacing our own
pretenses, our sordid lies, our feeble excuses. Like night in this
country, hypocrisy practically did not exist. One bathed in candor
and in the midnight sun.

"Aïno," I said, "your skin is always fresh and cool; you never
take a cruel pleasure in distrusting me; you don't ask for the
moon; you have no back hair and are quite guileless. My friends
in Paris would say: 'She is just a splendid washerwoman.' You're
a girl and yet you're not a doll. When other women are worn
out you are as fresh as ever. You stand so upright, you don'

turn your feet over when you walk and you don't wear the
carpet out in front of your mirror."

"I like Frenchmen because they never leave a woman alone."

"In my country women are quite easy to get on with if you
take them out in the afternoon, amuse them in the evening, fondle
them at night and don't bother them in the morning. But not one
of our fair-haired women is really fair, not with the fairness of
you."

"You're being disloyal to your own countrywomen."

"I love things like sunburn, bruises, grazed knees, the marks
of kisses, sunstroke and skin that preserves its whiteness at the
roots of the hair—all that *you* are, your modesty, your steadiness,
your ringless fingers. You see I have passed the age when a man
imagines that women only give way to one man—himself."

I was holding her hand, a large red hand, content in the knowledge that I had already seen Aïno naked, and certain in my own
mind that no misapprehension was possible between us, that
there could be no question of drawing back. I ought to know
whither I was bound. How unreal all that mass of sham to which
I had been accustomed seemed to me now, from the bombast of
dresses and the intriguing mechanism of veils in shaded corners,
to the chemise to which they cling as though it were a stage
property without which their conjuring tricks would fall flat.

Aïno began to give me a list of all the animals in her country,
all the creatures which live amongst the islands and in the lakes
which are so like each other that one might almost think that
the ones had been built of earth dug out of the others. The penguins on the dung-covered cliffs lined up like bottles in a chemist's shop, the sleek-looking beavers, the eagle-owls in their white
woolly coats, the seals like well-greased pieces of ordnance, the
brown bears sharpening their claws on the trees fringing the
Arctic wastes, the humped reindeer amongst the granite rocks,
all the splendors of the frost, the pomps of the thaw, the magic
of summer.

"Have you got any whiskey?" asked Aïno. "I love whiskey

and, if I can't get that, dentifrice, because they make me feel as if I were at sea."

I suddenly realized that she was drunk. But she did not make a noise or bite pieces out of her glass or take her shoes off under the table: she just sat there, chewing large tasteless watery gherkins; then she wiped her mouth on a paper napkin and kissed me on the mouth, calling me "*püppchen*." There it was. She had reached that happy state when Polish girls tell of the jewels they have stolen, German ones try to imitate poetry, when Spaniards object to such and such a kiss because "lips are made to receive Holy Communion" and American girls ask for money.

I tried to take Aïno in my arms. She made an effort to get up, collapsed, slid off her chair and remarking "I am not . . ." fell to the floor where she lay with her arms out.

I carried her to her bed. She was breathing heavily. Her clothes fell apart like the husk of a fruit, and once more my eyes fell on her bosom, firmly held to her shoulders by muscles hardened by rowing. I put a cold water bandage on her head. Her legs were open and full of shadows. . . .

"No," she said.

She forced open her eyes, closed like those of a newborn kitten, sat up, and said she wanted to be sick.

Frost-rimed stars were already coming out in the sky. The accordion seemed to catch its breath every now and then and wriggle like a bisected worm. Aïno and I kept in the bows of the ferryboat. We could hear other couples laughing together, or was it the cries of the seagulls? When we were still less than halfway to the island fragments of sentences began to come to us across the water. The tops of the pines were beginning to turn a deep purple.

Aïno had slept until midday, only getting up once to drink half a gallon of water. She fumbled in my pockets. I threatened to throw overboard a flask of Napoleon brandy which she found there. She raised her clear innocent eyes to me and her only reply was to butt me in the stomach like a goat.

I was still vexed that, protected by her stupor, she had escaped me the night before. Her silence now was like the mute reproaches of natives: "Him wicked paleface; him bring firewater." I felt some sort of explanation was needed:

"My country is the country of wine, of temperance, of sociabil . . ."

"One must never quarrel on midsummer night," she said, interrupting me.

The sun disappeared like a section of beet-root through the bars made by the tree trunks. The ferryboat arrived at the landing stage and her two anchors rattled down from her prow. It was midnight. A strange hour began, orange-tinted and streaked with red. Columns of mist rose above the water. We followed the path which seemed least littered with fishbones, paper and torn underclothing. The whole island was illuminated by bonfires, lit on enormous blocks of granite. Other fires were floating on the water.

"Let's stop here near that spring," said Aïno, "it goes so well with the view. These bonfires are supposed to incite the sun to return by force of example. The stones are merely sexual symbols."

"I like you much better when you call me 'püppchen' " I said, peevishly.

In the shadows couples were hugging each other on the ground, silently, unconscious of our presence, utterly cut off from their surroundings. We stepped over their bodies. Elsewhere noisy games were in progress, accompanied by songs and the report of firearms. Beneath the mountain ashes young girls were foretelling their future from split ears of corn. The smell of roasting pine needles and baking cakes came up to us. People were jumping into the bonfires with arms and legs outstretched, uttering their wishes out loud in the middle of the flames. Fantastic shadows strewed the ground and flickered round the fires.

I begged Aïno to talk to me about herself. She was studious by nature, she said, but she admitted that she was fanciful. The year before she had been appointed secretary to the Northern Territorial Commission and had come into close contacts with the Bolsheviks. She had a uniform with gold piping made for herself in Stockholm, and a cocked hat trimmed with vultures' feathers, which she wore on the day the treaty was signed. Feeling a sudden looseness round her waist she found that, while she was talking, I had undone her dress.

I whispered things to her, full of hidden meanings.

"I never go about naked except with my family," said Aïno.

We sat down in the middle of a clearing in the wood, amongst cows which lay on the ground and smelt of whey. All around us rose the tender sighs with which women sought to excite their large-limbed lethargic swains. With a hoarse cry someone stepped into a concealed gully and there was a sound of bones cracking like dead wood.

"What are you thinking about?" asked Aïno.

"The simple grandeur of these saturnalia stirs up my lustful, lying and inquisitive French soul. I know the New York parks which, during the hot nights in August, remain open to the public. In the damp warmth, workmen in their shirtsleeves lie down with Irish girls on the grass plots which look like cemeteries in the gloom; now and again a Neapolitan mechanic half remembers his forgotten tenor voice; the Slavs gather together and sing choruses. In Hyde Park in the winter lovers stay with their lips locked, amongst the sheep, swathed to their shoulders in mist, heedless of the clamorings of the Salvation Army, with no thought of sitting down, enthralled in each other. In Madrid, in the Recoletos, behind the motor cars drawn up before the Ritz, muleteers in black velvet fumble amongst the cambric petticoats of the girl hawkers. In Tahiti the women swim in a damp herd to the boats as they come in, and clamber on board. In Paris, in the moats of the fortifications, young couples with their hair all frizzled up . . ."

Aïno clasped her hands tightly round my neck:

"You are nothing but a cosmopolitan swine," she said.

I took her in my arms and she stayed there for the remainder of the night, that is to say, hardly ten minutes, for the sun, after a hurried dip, was beginning to clamber back over the horizon.

The Conquerors

ANDRÉ MALRAUX

André Malraux

ANDRÉ MALRAUX (1901—) once remarked that "Flaubert and Henry James are not eternal types of the writer." And Malraux himself, by combining an adventurous personal life with a brilliant career as a serious writer, has shown the possibility in our time of another kind of artist than that represented by Flaubert and James. If those writers may be said, without prejudice to their achievement, to have been studio artists, then Malraux is an artist of the barricade, the bomb and the armored plane. His subject is history seized at the moment of its formation.

A native of Paris, where his father was in business, the young Malraux attended the School of Oriental Languages in that city, becoming proficient in archaeology as well as Sanskrit and Chinese. On an archaeological expedition to Indo-China in 1923, he began to feel sympathy with the peoples of the East in their effort to free themselves from Western imperialism. Presently he entered into that protracted and uneasy relationship with communism which was to contribute so much to his adventures and his writing. At that time, the Communists were themselves involved in an uneasy coalition with the Kuomintang, and Malraux served as its associate-secretary during the Canton general strike of 1925. That action, which forms the subject of *The Conquerors*, gave strong impetus to the nationalist cause; and as the Kuomintang armies marched north upon Shanghai and Peking,

Malraux became a member of the authoritative Committee of Twelve, to which Chiang Kai-shek also belonged. When, however, the coalition broke down, in 1927, and Communists and Nationalists began to make war on one another, Malraux's active part in Chinese affairs came to an end.

For some years he was chiefly occupied with archaeological research and the writing of his novels of Asiatic upheaval. Of these *The Conquerors* (*Les Conquérants*, 1928) and *Man's Fate* (*La Condition humaine*, 1933) are the most notable. With the rise of fascism in Europe and the outbreak of the Spanish Civil War, he returned to active politics. In *Days of Wrath* (*Le Temps de mépris*, 1935) and *Man's Hope* (*L'Espoir*, 1937) he dealt with those contemporary subjects. Meanwhile he had served in the Loyalist air corps, which he helped to organize. Following the Nazi-Soviet Pact, Malraux's connection with communism was decisively terminated. He has since been its determined enemy, as well as a supporter of General de Gaulle. Enlisting in the tank corps of the French army, he saw action in the recent war, was captured by the Germans, and made his escape from a prison camp. His experiences of tank warfare account for some stirring pages in *Les Noyers de l'Altenburg* (1943). Of this work, the first installment in a projected long novel to be called *La Lutte avec l'ange*, only a fragment has so far appeared in English. More recently he completed a book he had been engaged on since his years as a practicing archaeologist. This is his *Psychology of Art*, an ambitious study of the origin and function of the visual arts.

Malraux is widely recognized as the most important writer of modern France after Proust, Valéry and Gide. His fame, however, was brightest in the 1930's when many readers everywhere had high expectations of communist policy and revolutionary literature. Yet to reread his novels today is to note the high degree of independence that prevailed in his literary relations with communism. This was especially true in the period of *The Conquerors* and *Man's Fate*, both of which are marked by an awareness of the gravely equivocal character of the movement they also in part celebrate. Given his time and kind of art, Malraux could not make decisive affirmations or rejections of communism. His art was, however, finely equipped to capture the moral texture of experience within the equivocations of the communist world. In his earlier novels there is a labyrinthine confusion of purposes, a compelling atmosphere of mixed light and shadow, exaltation and suffering. All of this stems from Malraux's feeling that communism has tremendous implications, on the one hand for heroic action in the cause of humanity, on the other hand for the cynical exploitation of human life and hope.

This is not to say that Malraux owed his relative independence to any special idealism or acumen in respect to practical politics. On the contrary, neither idealism nor acumen seems to have distinguished him in his communist phase. His relative independence may be attributed, rather, to his preoccupation with the philosophy of heroism. In some fashion of his own he has always harked back to that cult of the exceptional man which, in modern French literature, extends from Stendahl to Gide and in other literatures includes Dostoevsky, Nietzsche and Conrad. If he is not remarkable for his political sense, he is for his observation of men's conduct in extreme situations.

The above-named writers are in varying degrees Malraux's masters. Yet he is unique among them in the extent to which he makes history prior to invention and appeals to actual events in support of his ideas. If not the originator of the journalistic novel, he is probably its greatest practitioner. *The Conquerors*, with its vivid rendering of the Canton affair, is the perfection of that kind of novel. The strike and the attendant boycott of British goods are shown in their effect both on the British power in China and on the revolutionary power itself. Shameen, the thriving foreign settlement in Canton, is suddenly cut off from trade and communication; while nearby Hongkong, once the chief fortress of imperialism in the East, stands dark, idle and afraid on its rock. At the same time, faced with the possibility of assuming control, the revolutionary group develops alarming rifts. Chen-Dai, the liberal idealist and apostle of justice, is destroyed—whether by his own hand or that of the terrorist Hong is for some time in doubt. Meanwhile Chen-Dai's death is exploited by all parties without regard for the circumstances of it or for his own principles. And in this connection memories are evoked of the dying Lenin and of the fateful question of the Soviet succession. For the Chinese revolutionaries, the price of power is internal crisis: the failure of the center, the growth of extremism, the separation of the leaders from the people, the torturing and death of the devoted Klein, the grief of Klein's woman, the increasing illness of the two chiefs, Garine and Borodin, the final departure of Garine.

Malraux reproduces here many of the actual events and personalities of the Canton incident. But in making *both* of his heroes sick men, in the way he relates them to one another, in the selection and heightening of details, he is far more the novelist than the reporter. Borodin, who is of course an historical figure, is shown as the ruthless Comintern operator. Garine, an imaginary figure (though perhaps modeled to some extent on Malraux himself) is the revolutionary freebooter, the man with a mission of heroism to perform, a duty to himself to discharge. As such he must inevitably depart at last from a scene of action which is proving ever more unfriendly to individualism. *The Conquerors* (ironic title!) is not so complex in its organization as *Man's Fate* nor does it end with any scene of tragic resolution comparable to the concluding scenes of that book. A simpler performance, a kind of *tranche de vie revolutionnaire*, this story has nevertheless its own special vividness, its own kind of devastating realism. Malraux here carries into our time the high art and purposiveness, the great concern with human possibilities, of the classic French novel.

The Conquerors

ANDRÉ MALRAUX

1 Outward Bound

June 25th

A GENERAL STRIKE HAS BEEN DECLARED AT CANTON. This wireless message, underlined in red, was put up yesterday.

As far as eye can reach, the Indian Ocean, glassy, motionless, without a ripple. A sky of shapeless clouds seems to distill a hot-house atmosphere, wrapping us round in a blanket of warm, thick, damp air. And the passengers pace up and down the deck, counting their steps and keeping fairly close to the white notice-board on which the messages received during the night will soon appear. Through these daily radiograms the first act of the drama unfolds itself, growing steadily more and more actual, more and more threatening, until it obsesses everyone on board. Hitherto the hostility of the Canton Government had gone no further than words, now the wireless shows that it is proceeding to deeds. What impresses us all most profoundly is not so much strikes, rioting and street fights, but this unexpected determination, as tenacious as that of Great Britain itself, the determination to have done with mere words and to strike at the British Empire, by attacking what is dearest to it—its prestige and its wealth.

The boycotting of all British goods, even when offered for sale by Chinese, throughout all the provinces depending on Canton, the method of controlling first one market, then another, the destruction of machinery by the factory hands of Hong

541

Kong; finally this general strike—its effect on trade throughout the whole of this British possession, while, according to newspaper correspondents, the military schools are seething with unusual activity: all this seems to bring the passengers face to face with an entirely new kind of warfare, with a war waged by the anarchical powers of Southern China in conjunction with mysterious collaborators, against the very symbol of British domination in the Far East, that fortified rock of Hong Kong whence the empire of the sword surveys its subjects.

Hong Kong. There, on the map, is the Island—a clearly marked black spot, closing the Pearl River like a bolt. Along the river banks stretches the gray mass which is Canton, with dots indicating straggling suburbs, hardly more than a few hours away from the British cannon. Every day the passengers look—at first eagerly, now with an intense anxiety—at that little black spot as if they expected it to reveal something, as if they were trying to guess how that fortress on which their lives depend—how that richest rock in the world—would be defended.

If, sooner or later, it were to suffer some serious reverse, if it were to be reduced to the rank of a small port, if it were to be assailed in any way, then China, in her struggle against the white race, might be able to organize herself, in a manner hitherto impossible, and there might be an end of European domination. The dealers in cotton and horses among my fellow passengers are keenly aware of this, and the wondering look on their anxious faces—"how will it affect my business?"—is itself a reflection of the gigantic struggle being waged by the empire of disorder, hastily organizing itself, against a nation which stands above all others for strength, determination, and tenacity.

There is a stir on deck—passengers hurry, push and press: the wireless has appeared.

"England, Belgium, the United States," nothing of importance there—but what next? Russia? Ah! No, nothing worth noting. "China." At last!

"The President of the Republic."

What then?

"Canton."

The radiogram is long; and the passengers on the edge of the crowd push so hard that we are wedged against the partition.

THE CADETS OF THE WHAMPOA MILITARY SCHOOL, COMMANDED BY RUSSIAN OFFICERS, AND FORMING THE REAR GUARD OF A HUGE PROCESSION OF STUDENTS AND WORKMEN, HAVE OPENED FIRE ON SHAMEEN.* THE EUROPEAN SAILORS, WHO WERE PROTECTING THE BRIDGES, REPLIED WITH THEIR MACHINE GUNS. THE CADETS, URGED ON BY THEIR RUSSIAN OFFICERS, MADE SEVERAL ATTEMPTS TO STORM THE BRIDGES, BUT WERE REPULSED WITH HEAVY LOSS.

THE EUROPEAN WOMEN AND CHILDREN OF SHAMEEN ARE, IF POSSIBLE, TO BE REMOVED TO HONG KONG ON AMERICAN BOATS. THE DEPARTURE OF THE ENGLISH TROOPS IS IMMINENT.

A sudden silence falls.

The suspense is over. Not a single word is spoken. The passengers disperse in consternation. On the right, however, two Frenchmen meet one another: "Really, sir, whenever are the Powers going to make up their minds to take some strong measure, which . . . ?" And, as they move towards the bar, the noise of the engines drowns the end of the sentence.

Tomorrow, Singapore. We shall not reach Hong Kong for another ten days.

Five o'clock

An additional wireless message has most unusually appeared.

SHAMEEN. THE ELECTRIC LIGHT HAS FAILED. THE WHOLE CONCESSION IS IN DARKNESS. THE BRIDGES HAVE BEEN HASTILY FORTIFIED AND PROTECTED BY BARBED WIRE. THEY ARE LIT BY SEARCHLIGHTS FROM THE GUNBOATS.

* The European Concession at Canton. *Tr.*

Singapore: 7 *a.m.*
June 26th

Interminable delay—the stamping of passports. A long line of
motorcars for hire, some thirty of them, waiting behind the
docks. Malay children flourish newspapers—*The Straits Times*,
The Malay Gazette. They are instantly surrounded, the papers
seized and torn open; sheets falling to the ground are picked up
in a trice, while those who have not had the luck to get papers
look over the shoulders of their more fortunate companions all
to no avail; for the latest news in these evening papers is but a
repetition of the radiograms we have seen on board.

Jumping into the first car I can find, I fly through the deserted
oriental suburb, where the macadamized road winds round a
pagoda, the sides of which have been converted into hoardings
for advertisements. Crossing the bridge, I come on the blue and
green Chinese town, and on the *arroyo* with its sampans, packed
closely together like cattle. On the right is the English town—
banks, steamship companies' offices, vast sheds of reinforced concrete, housing some hundred offices, at the foot of hills surrounded by lawns and dotted with villas.

These bastions of British trade, brooded over by the arsenal
guns, would indicate that here at least for the present Great
Britain's strength remains unshaken.

Here is the junk port and the Raffles Hotel, with its stiff, bare
garden, its palms from the Botanical Gardens, its Sikh porter and
its Chinese "boys." Its lemonade with a shaddock flavor is the
best in Asia. Here perhaps one may be able to hear news.

The bar is crowded. Alone and lounging lazily at the middle
table, in a suit of cream-colored linen, is a big man whose mouth
I seem to recognize: his lips are full, slightly curved and protruding—sucking, babbling lips. Yes, it is Rensky, a Russian, who was
once a collector and who now travels at the expense of a Boston
museum, in search of masterpieces of Asiatic art.

He sits near the great square of green baize onto which the
radiograms are fixed with drawing pins. (A "boy" puts them up

as soon as they are received and, as on Test Match days, gives copies to anyone who has tipped him.)

I go up to Rensky. After the customary Russian effusions, he says, pointing to five little ebony elephants he has arranged pipe-wise on the table:

"As you see, my friend (I have met him about five times), I am buying little elephants. When we begin our excavations I shall put them in the tombs. Then the tombs will be closed; and half a century later, when they are reopened and these little things are discovered at the bottom, all encrusted and corroded, the archaeologists will wonder. I love the idea of puzzling pos-terity. On one of the Angkor-Wat towers I have engraved an obscene inscription, which I have carefully defiled. Finot will decipher it. These austere people must be scandalized a little. . . ."

I barely listen to him; for, from the opposite side of the table, I am reading over his shoulder:

HONG KONG. THE SITUATION IS EXTREMELY GRAVE. IN VIEW OF THE POSSIBLE DESPATCH OF A BRITISH EXPEDITIONARY FORCE FROM HONG KONG TO CANTON, THE CHINESE HERE, TO THE NUMBER OF MORE THAN FIFTY THOUSAND, HAVE BEGUN TO STRIKE.

"You are slandering the gods, Rensky."

"One must amuse oneself. And there are so few amusements for a man like me, my dear fellow. A medium here told me that the spirits of the dead are so bored during the night, when dark-ness prevents their watching those who are alive, that their only pleasure is to make, by moonlight, patterns out of the down of pillows, like hairdressers make out of hair. And it's quite true, my dear chap, quite true. Just open your pillow gently one morning and you will find in it all manner of designs in feathers—question marks, crosses, aigrettes, birds. . . I have arranged some myself, just to puzzle the spirits, which is much more thrilling than trying to puzzle scholars. Still, I can't spend my life in doing this. So you see I get as bored as the spirits. Only my night is longer than theirs. It seems unending."

"You are depressed, Rensky."

"No. But I miss love and irony. It is high time I returned to Europe, whither they have both of them fled."

The "boy" brings in a new sheet.

HONG KONG. THE STRIKE IS SPREADING TO THE STEAMSHIP COM-PANIES, BOTH COASTAL AND UP-COUNTRY. ALL THE BUTTERFIELD AND SWIRE BOATS AND THOSE OF THE HONG KONG, CANTON AND MACAO STEAMBOAT COMPANY HAVE BEEN DESERTED BY THEIR CHINESE CREWS.

"You do not like China?"

"I have no quarrel with her new gods—mirrors, electricity, phonographs. For that god with a trumpet, the phonograph, *is* a creature, you know. A light green pavilion insinuating itself curi-ously behind the altar of the ancestors, suggests strange thoughts. The idea that phonographs are spirits tormenting the dead might be worth preaching. . . . It would certainly be accepted in the North. . . . Look at that plan of Singapore hanging on the column to your right. Note the blue of the sea growing less and less marked from bottom to top. Time is like that in China. In the North, time does not exist. The map is a clean slate. It's a fine thing, my dear fellow, the indifference with which that hoary empire up here, just like a drowning man, has its eyes fixed on its necklace of cannon—its new fetishes—and at the same time on its bloodstained antiquity stretching far back into history. It is playing the game. That is enough. Have you ever noticed how it has put the world into its domino? Figure and flowers—and, above, both worth considering—happiness and wind. . . . "

Here comes the "boy" again.

HONG KONG. BRITAIN REPLIES TO THE CHINESE GENERAL STRIKE, BY PROHIBITING THE EXPORT OF RICE. NO CHINESE RICE IN HONG KONG WAREHOUSES IS ALLOWED TO LEAVE THE PORT. THE EXASPERA-TION OF THE CHINESE KNOWS NO BOUNDS.

Now Rensky has seen what I am looking at.

"Yes, the real game, the Game with a capital G, must be followed in the South—in the South where the blue is deep because time has passed rather too quickly. But you must notice the preliminaries—that droll Americanization of China with all its comforts and sensuality. . . . At Canton, where once were ancient pagodas, there are now California hotels, shops with thirteen stories, and those terrible skyscrapers, which have a cinema on the ground floor, a theater on the first, all manner of amusements on the second—automatic machines, bowls, acrobats, gladiators, dancers; on the third, a smoke-room; on the fourth, a tearoom; on the fifth, a select brothel; on the sixth, offices. Higher still, flats occupied by ladies of doubtful reputation, and higher yet, more offices. On the roof, a garden and a Russo-European restaurant. Four. . . ."

"What a marvelous description. You know it all by heart."

"That is what I do with my heart in Asia! But I was about to say 'four lifts,' when you interrupted me, showing that you are sadly wanting in curiosity."

"I await the sequel to your 'lifts' with ill-concealed impatience."

"The sequel to 'my lifts' is the Revolution. You know that the Canton Government depends for its existence mainly on the contributions of the poor. But many of the rich merchants also contribute, sending their donations in hard cash to the Kuomintang. That fat Chinese, sitting alone at a table near the bar, to whom the 'boy' is now taking the radiograms, is Koo-Chen, the President of the party here."

I recognize him; for I have his photograph in my pocket.

"He is worth several million dollars. He stakes his fortune on the Revolution, and, during the last few days, on war."

"The game may become dangerous."

"Do you think so? In a certain delightful street at Hong Kong, there are houses with closed shutters, surrounded by large gardens. . . ."

Another radiogram!

HARBIN. THE BOLSHEVIK DIRECTORS OF THE CHINESE EASTERN RAIL-
WAY HAVE ORDERED THEIR EMPLOYEES TO TAKE THEIR SHARE OF
THE CONTRIBUTIONS IN AID OF THE HONG KONG STRIKERS. THIS PREC-
EDENT WILL BE FOLLOWED SPEEDILY THROUGHOUT THE WHOLE OF
EASTERN SIBERIA.

HONG KONG. ALL BANKS ARE CLOSED.

"They are not boardinghouses—far from it; they are private
dwellings, to which the Chinese leaders used to send their numerous wives, when peace was threatened in China. Nothing thicker
than a partition wall separated the favorite wives or concubines
of certain revolutionary leaders. Sometimes they called on one
another, and when fortune favored the generals, the dictators,
driven out one by one, met in these bystreets. Sun Yat-sen came
here, and doubtless recalled memories of his college days."

"Those days are past."

"Who can tell?"

"Sometimes, Rensky, one can tell. One can tell, for example,
that this action of the Canton Government in venturing to attack
Britain is not within the realm . . ."

"Of pure fantasy?"

"Charming as that realm may be, and one through which you
yourself have just been wandering."

He was silent. Then he rejoined sadly:

"China is a country in which everything is possible. To attack
Britain! Since the Revolution of 1911, the Kuomintang has per-
meated China. Now it is reorganizing itself at Canton, from defeat to defeat or from victory to victory, much as budding Prot-
estantism reorganized itself at Geneva. With a strange blend of
stupidity and greatness, they have been endeavoring to establish
their Republic for the last fourteen years. . . . The real change
set in on the death of Sun, with the hold over the party and the
government acquired by the committees controlled by Bolshevists. Bolshevists! And yet a man like Garine is far from being a
true Bolshevist."

"In what way?"

"Well, my friend, if by Bolshevist you mean revolutionary, then Garine is a Bolshevist. But, if you mean, as I do, a particular type of revolutionary, who, among many other characteristics, is distinguished by a belief in Marxism, then Garine is no Bolshevist —at least in my opinion; but I am talking about things of which I really know very little. And, moreover, does anyone know Garine, does anyone know Borodin? Borodin's real name is Braun I-don't-know-what. He is a Lettish Jew. And Garine is no more Russian than he. His father was Swiss. He was almost entirely educated in France. That is all I know. (Strange that our information about the real opinions and character of the men who are set on rousing China against us, should be so meager. . . .) By the way, if such people interest you, there is a personage here, who is beginning to be talked about, and who seems to me very strange, very strange: he is a young Chinese, called Hong, one of the leaders of the terrorists. Have you heard of him?"

"Not yet."

"That is a pity. I don't quite recollect all that has been told me about him, but it is very interesting. Ah! what fun it will be to see the very persons whom the Bolshevists are now educating turning against them. . . ."

The "boy" serves us with cocoa, milk ice and at the same time with the latest radiograms from Hong Kong.

AT SHAMEEN THE POSTAL SERVICE IS SUSPENDED. THE TELEPHONE WIRES HAVE BEEN CUT.

Five o'clock

We shall be starting in a few minutes. Here are the newspaper boys at last. They rush across the gangway. Their newspapers, still damp, are bought up immediately. We read:

"Canton. The British steamboats in the harbor have been commandeered. The women and children still in the town have been evacuated to Hong Kong. Shameen is now nothing but a camp."

That will be good for British trade!

"The despatch of British and Indian troops to Canton is imminent."

What a mistake! Now for Hong Kong.

"Hong Kong. Trade is at a standstill. In private houses, hotels and hospitals, Chinese servants refuse to work.

"UNDER STRICT RESERVATION—The strike of employees on the big steamboats will be declared this afternoon."

One of the barmen is hurrying up and down deck, ringing a bell, which is the signal that we are starting. The Indian money-changers are leaving the boat, rattling the coins in their money-bags. At the end of the gangway, Japanese hawkers are calling out their wares—rattan armchairs, soap, ties, perfumes. Malay fruit sellers are landing awkwardly, encumbered with huge hampers bristling with plumes of banana leaves and filled with yellow mangosteens, kakis like tomatoes, and great green oranges.

There is a lull. A deep, deafening, rhythmic sound vibrates through the boat. It comes from the engines. Rensky hastily takes his leave. He has hardly left me when the gangway is pulled up.

Night falls. We can barely see that we are coasting along the shore of an inland sea, that we are passing the islands of the strait, crowned with Chinese shrubs. Soon we can discern nothing but lighthouses.

I am writing on the bar terrace. . . . The whole of that Americanized China, which Rensky was describing just now, with its islands dimly outlined and silent seems fading into the past. Another China is emerging, wavering and maladroit, animated by an unformed, self-tormenting soul. At Singapore, while monuments, names, landscapes, everything, dwindles into unimportance, there rises a new spirit, the spirit of the main body of the town, a spirit as clearly defined as the spirit of the past, a spirit which says: "Grow rich and grow strong." It would be hard to imagine a grander battle: British energy on the one hand, Chinese on the other, both fighting for money, and beneath, amorphous and yet active, the mass of revolution, flowing underground like a river. But, in this great business city, re-echoing with the constant screech of ships' sirens, all this is barely distinguishable. The old

Dutch gabled houses, the British Victorian homes, the squarely built dwellings seem planted like stakes in this warm red earth; but on the other side of this European and of this Russo-Malay scene of painted houses, I see a very different town: the native town inhabited by poor sordid creatures, a town of modest Chinese offices, the offices of the revolutionary committee of the island, of the committee of the Sultanate of Johore, of the committee of the Malay States, of the branches of the committees of Kuala-Lumpur, Malacca, Bangkok, Batavia, Sourabaya, Sumatra, Borneo . . . the syndicated union of rickshaw pushers, of restaurant "boys," of servants (not a single European without a servant), of dock laborers, all adherents of the town Kuomintang. All this is inert at present, almost asleep. No revolt as yet. But every day, dollars, bills and checks leave Singapore for Canton, while the half-naked fat old secretaries of revolutionary organizations sleep sanctimoniously in the equatorial heat, undisturbed by the whirring of the ventilating fans, their hands folded over their stomachs, under the very eyes of the police officers who have them under observation.

Five o'clock

HONG KONG. THE GOVERNOR'S DEPARTURE IS POSTPONED. LETTERS AND NEWSPAPERS ARE TO BE CENSORED.

SHANGHAI. AGITATION IS SPREADING THROUGH ALL THE SOUTHERN PROVINCES. FOREIGN CONSULS HAVE BEEN STONED.

HONG KONG. ADMIRAL FROCHOT, COMMANDER OF THE FRENCH NAVAL FORCES IN THE FAR EAST, STARTED FOR CANTON AT NOON YESTERDAY.

FURTHER ACTS OF VIOLENCE BY TERRORISTS. THE BRITISH VOLUNTEERS HAVE BEEN MOBILIZED.

The fête, which was to have taken place on board, has been canceled. Everyone is weighed down by anxiety, which is as pervasive as the heat. No waiters are to be seen. They keep out of the way in order to avoid the grumblings of the passengers at the slightest thing that goes wrong. It is only the women and men who do not avoid one another. Everyone points out irritably the poverty of the telegraph clerks' announcements, although we are all perfectly aware of it. Men, old and young, make the round of the boat, walking briskly, as if bent on tiring themselves out. Then, during the greatest heat of the day, they sleep in their deck chairs, waking with a start at the slightest sound, cross and peevish.

Ten o'clock

HONG KONG. MORE THAN TWENTY PACKET BOATS ARE LYING TO IN THE PORT. THE PROCLAMATION OF A STATE OF SIEGE IS BEING DISCUSSED.

In six days . . .

Saïgon
June 29th

A deserted, desolate provincial town, with long, straight avenues and boulevards, where grass grows under widespreading tropical trees. After a long drive we reach the Chinese quarter, where there are beautiful gilded signs inscribed with black letters, little banks and all kinds of agencies. Before us, down the middle of a broad, grass-grown avenue, runs a little railway. Numbers 37, 35, 33. Here we stop in front of a house like all the others in the quarter: a mere compartment. Apparently a business house. All round the door are plates bearing the names of obscure Canton companies. Inside, behind dusty, dilapidated counters doze two Chinese clerks: one corpselike, dressed in white, the other obese, of a terra-cotta complexion, naked to the waist. On the wall are chromographs of Shanghai, of girls with fringes plastered on their foreheads, monsters, landscapes. In front of me is a tangle of three bicycles. This is the headquarters of the President of the Cochin-China Kuomintang. I ask in Cantonese:

"Is the chief in?"

"He has not returned yet, sir. But go up and make yourself at home."

I reach the first floor by a kind of ladder. No one there. I sit down and look round lazily: a European chest, a Louis Philippe marble-topped table, a Chinese sofa in black wood, and two magnificent American armchairs, equipped with all kinds of devices. Stuck into the mirror above me is a large portrait of Sun Yat-sen, and a smaller photograph of the master of the house.

A sputtering sound and the strong smell of Chinese fat frying come in through the alcove.

The sound of steps on the ladder.

The chief comes in. With him are two other Chinese and the Frenchman, Gérard, whom I have come to meet. I am given green tea and told to assure the Central Committee of the loyalty of the whole of French Indo-China to those democratic institutions, which, etc. . . .

Finally Gérard and I go out. He is a special delegate from the Kuomintang to Indo-China, who has been here only a few days. A little man with mustache and beard growing gray, he suggests the Czar Nicholas II; he has his worried, hesitating look and his benevolent air; he is a cross between a shortsighted professor and a provincial doctor. He walks by my side with a dragging step, and far in front of him is a cigarette, fixed to the extremity of a long cigarette holder.

His car is waiting for us at the corner of the street. We get in and drive slowly out into the country. The movement of the air seems to transport us into another climate and to enable us to relax our strained and fatigued muscles.

"What news?"

He hesitates, not knowing whether to address me as "Sir" or "Comrade."

"Not much. Hardly anything beyond what you have read in the newspapers. The strike proclamation seems to have been obeyed implicitly by the various committees of workmen. . . And the English are apparently at a loss for any countermeasures. The organization of volunteers is a farce; all very well, perhaps, in case of a riot, but useless against a strike. The prohibition of the export of rice guarantees the food supply of Hong Kong for some time, but to starve out the town was never our object. What use would it be? For the rich Chinese who support counterrevolutionary organizations this prohibition is a staggering blow. . . ."

"But since yesterday?"

"Nothing."

"Do you think the Cochin-China Government has suppressed the radiograms?"

"No. The wireless employes are nearly all members of 'the Young-Annam.' We should have been informed. The reason is, doubtless, that Hong Kong has ceased to transmit."

A pause.

"And what about the Chinese stations?"

"The Chinese stations are all under the influence of our Propaganda department. That explains everything. The rumor that the Chamber of Commerce has asked its President to declare war on England, that the Cantonese have imprisoned English soldiers in Shameen, that very significant manifestations are in course of preparation—all this is nonsense. What is really serious and certain is that the English in Hong Kong see wealth escaping from them. The boycott was good. The strike is better. What will be the sequel to the strike? A pity we don't know anything! I ought to hear something soon. For the last two days not a single boat has sailed for Hong Kong. They are all there in the River. . . ."

"And here?"

"We are not doing badly. You can take six thousand dollars at least away with you. I expect six hundred more, but am not certain. And remember that those six thousand dollars I am going to give you come, almost all of them, from poor people: coolies, dock laborers, artisans."

"And they have good reason to hope. The Hong Kong and Shameen affairs. . . ."

"Certainly—this latent war against Great Britain and her lack of energy, intoxicate them. But all this is very un-Chinese."

"Are you sure of that?"

He is silent. Wedged into a corner of the car, with his eyes half closed, he may be reflecting or he may be merely giving himself up to the delicious sensation of the current of fresh air, which is as restful as a bath. In the blue evening haze, the rice fields whizz by, vast mirrors painted here and there or finely stenciled with clumps of bushes and pagodas, all dominated by the soaring poles of the wireless. Compressing his lips and pulling at his mustache, he replies:

"Have you heard of the Monad conspiracy that the English have just discovered at Hong Kong?"

"I know nothing; I have just arrived."

"Good. Well, the Monad is a secret society. You must know that at present the only connection between Hong Kong and Canton is by means of a little steamboat, the *Honan*. When the boat is in port at Hong Kong, it is guarded by a British officer and a few sailors. The representatives of the Society are shrewd enough to realize the importance of preventing the boat from leaving Canton when its cargo consists of arms, which the British are sending to the antirevolutionaries."

"Have we no one on this boat?"

"No; it was impossible. The boat takes up its cargo of arms at some lonely spot on the Pearl River—just in the same way as hashish is smuggled at Suez.

"But to return to our plot. Six of the conspirators—at the risk of their lives, as they well know—kill the British officer and the sailors in the night, take command of the boat, work on board for four hours, and are made prisoners at dawn, by a patrol of British volunteers, at the very moment when they were setting sail, carrying off—guess what?—one of those blocks of wood, painted with two eyes, which a Chinese boat carries at its prow."

"I don't quite understand."

"The eyes serve as a guide to the boat. A blind boat would be wrecked inevitably."

"Oh! I see."

"You are astonished, and so am I. But, this is the kind of society —more or less—that we have to deal with. Groups of fanatics—

brave—there is no doubt about that—of a few plutocrats out for notoriety or for security—and crowds of students and coolies."

"Is not such a society, like any other, at the mercy of a few energetic leaders?"

"Certainly. But that does not simplify matters."

"Energy is always energy."

"Not in the least. It is all a question of how it is employed. Would you, now, as a way of sinking vessels, go and capture a plank with eyes painted on it, at the risk of being shot in the attempt?"

"Were they shot?"

"No, the British did not go so far as that. But this is the type of energetic person with whom we can do nothing. Some of them, consumed with enthusiasm, are ready for any sacrifice. With them all is well. But woe to those chattering, idiotic students, who quote Marx as if he were Confucius! I don't know who the leaders of the Monad were. The Society was not in communication with us. But it counted among its adherents a large number of students who had returned from American Universities. . . . You must always remember that the most serious of these Societies, the one in which you place the greatest confidence, is capable at any moment of giving up everything in order to go off in search of an eye painted on a piece of wood."

And, seeing me smile, he exclaims:

"Ah! you think I exaggerate. But you will see, you will see. Why, Borodin and Garine could give you a hundred examples of such things."

"Do you know Garine well?"

"Why yes! We have worked together. What do you want to hear about him? You know how he behaved as Director of Propaganda?"

"I have heard very little about it."

"He. . . . It is difficult to explain. You know how innocent China used to be of any ideas tending to action. Now they have taken possession of her much as the idea of equality took possession of the French in '89. The same thing may have been occurring throughout the whole of yellow Asia. In Japan, when German lecturers began to preach Nietzsche, fanatical students cast themselves down from the rocks. Now at Canton, things were not so simple, but no less terrible. Of no kind of individualism had they the remotest idea. Today coolies are beginning to discover that they exist, simply that they exist. . . . Among the masses there is a certain type of ideology, as there is a certain type of art, which is not a popularization, but something quite different. . . . Borodin's propaganda said to peasants and workingmen: 'You are fine fellows because you are peasants and workingmen, and because in you reside the two greatest forces of the State.' Such an announcement had no effect whatever. They could not see how suffering blows and dying of hunger could constitute the greatest forces of the State. They were convinced that as peasants and as workingmen they were merely despicable. They were afraid that the Revolution would end and that they would be plunged back into that humiliation, out of which they had hoped to rise. Nationalist propaganda, as carried on by Garine, told them something quite different; it moved them, in a way quite unforeseen and extraordinarily violent, by teaching them to believe in their own dignity—their own importance, if you prefer the term. To realize the effect of this you should watch a dozen of these laborers with their sly little cat's faces, their rags and their wickerwork hats, drilling like volunteers, surrounded by an admiring crowd. The strength of the French Revolution and of the Russian Revolution, lay in the fact that they gave everyone his land. This revolution is giving everyone his life. Against such a revolution every Western State is powerless. . . . Hatred! people want to make hatred the key to everything! And yet how simple it all is! The revolutionary ardor of our volunteers arises from many things, but primarily from their craving for a life . . . a life in which they can do nothing but . . . spit upon the others! This Borodin has not yet understood. . . ."

"How do these two great idols hit it off?"

"Borodin and Garine?"

At first it seems as if he does not want to answer my question.

But no; he is thinking. At such a moment his expression is very acute. Where does he come from, this keen-witted person? The twilight is deepening. The only sound above the noise of the car is the rhythmic whistling of the grasshoppers. The rice fields fly past on both sides of the road. On the horizon the leaves of a palm tree wave slightly.

"I don't think they hit it off well," he said. "They hit it off; that is all. They complete one another. Borodin is the man of action; Garine . . ."

"Garine?"

"Is a man capable of action, at a given time. Listen! you will find two classes of people at Canton. Those who came in with Sun, in 1921, in 1922, to take their chances at the risk of their lives, and who were mere adventurers. For them the evolution of China was a drama, in which they were more or less involved. They were people whose attitude towards the Revolution resembled the attitude of certain militarists towards the army. They were people who had never been able to accept social conditions, who made great demands on life, who wanted to give a meaning to their existence, and who now, having discarded all this, *serve*. And then there are those who came in with Borodin, professional revolutionaries, for whom China is raw material. The former, almost all of them, you will find in the Propaganda department, almost all the latter in the strike and army departments. Garine represents and leads the former, who are not so strong, but much more intelligent."

"You were at Canton before Borodin arrived?"

"Yes," he replied with a smile. "But, believe me, I speak from an entirely objective point of view."

Where does he come from? The word "objective" must be rare on the lips of Cantonese revolutionaries.

"And before that?"

He is silent. I feel uncomfortable. Will he tell me that it is no business of mine? He would have a right to say so. But no. He is smiling again. And, placing his hand lightly on my knee, he replies:

"Before that, I was professor in the College at Hanoi."

His smile became more pronounced, more ironical, too, as, bearing rather more heavily on my knee, he continues:

"But I preferred other things."

Is there some story behind all this, or is he making fun of me?

He resumed the conversation quickly, as if to prevent my asking any more questions:

"Borodin is a great businessman—extremely industrious, brave, bold sometimes, very simple and absorbed in his work. . . ."

"A great businessman?"

"A man, who inevitably thinks of everything in this light: 'Can I make use of it, and how?' That is Borodin. All the Bolsheviks of his generation have been molded by their struggle with anarchists. They all feel the necessity of facing reality; they are obsessed by the difficulties in the way of government. And then he has memories of a youth spent as a young Jew in a little Lettish town, reading Marx, despised by everybody, and with Siberia in the offing."

The grasshoppers continue their song.

"When do you expect to receive the information to which you alluded just now?"

"In a few minutes. We are going to dine with the President of the Cholon section, who is the proprietor of a smoking-restaurant like that."

We are now passing restaurants adorned with huge characters and decorated with mirrors. We are in a quarter where life is nothing but glare and noise—reflectors, globes, crystals, the sound of mahjong and of gramophones, cymbals, gongs, and shrill singing to a flute accompaniment.

The lights grow closer and closer. Our driver gets annoyed and accelerates, trying to pierce through a white-clothed crowd, thicker than that on our own boulevards—workmen, Chinese of all professions loitering along, eating fruits and sweetmeats, hardly moving out of the way of the cars, which groan and grate while Annamite chauffeurs hurl insults. Nothing here is French.

The car stops in front of a restaurant—not one of those with iron-railed balconies like the restaurants we have just passed, but one less colonial, more like a private hotel. The entrance—above which, as usual, are two black characters on a gold ground—is nothing but mirrors. Mirrors to right and left, mirrors in front, mirrors on the vertical parts of the steps. In the countinghouse, the bare torso of a fat Chinese doing accounts half screens a long room, in the depths of which orange bodies and nimble fingers can be seen busy round a dish of mother-of-pearl lobsters and a pyramid of empty pink shells.

On the first floor we are received by a bulldog-headed Chinese, who ushers us into his private room and introduces us to three of his comrades. They are dressed in spotless white and wear military collars. Their white helmets lie on the black wood settee. Introductions follow. Impossible, of course, to catch a single name. On a little table, surrounded by wickerwork armchairs, and without a tablecloth, are dishes and little pots of sauce. Rays of light stream out from electric globes into the tumultuous night. A vague noise pervades the room, an undertone to the sounds of exploding crackers, the rustling of dominoes, the booming of gongs and, from time to time, the whining of a one-stringed violin, while whirling electric fans only partially dispel the gusts of hot air.

The bulldog, who is at once proprietor and interpreter, says in a low voice, with a strong accent:

"Monsieur, the Governor of the French hospital dined here this week. . . ."

He seems proud of the occurrence; but the most elderly of his comrades interrupts him, saying:

"Tell them that . . ."

But Gérard soon informs them that I understand Cantonese. Consequently they become much more genial and conversation begins: democratic chatter—"the rights of the proletariat," etc., etc. I feel firmly convinced that the only strength of these people resides in their vague emotions, and that all they are really conscious of is a sense of the wrongs they have suffered. I recall provincial societies in France, during the Convention. But then these Chinese are so perfectly courteous in spite of the horrible sound they make when they clear their noses in their throats. How they believe in words! And how powerless they must be in face of those executive committees to which they send their dollars!

Here is the medley of news that has rushed in on them today:

"In all inland towns, the British have been compelled to take refuge in the Concessions.

"The coolies' federations have resolved that each of their members shall subscribe five cents a day in aid of the Hong Kong strikers.

"A great public demonstration is being organized at Shanghai and Peking to protest against the violence and injustice of the foreign imperialists and to assert the liberty of the Chinese.

"In the southern provinces large numbers are joining the volunteers.

"The Cantonese army has just received a large consignment of munitions from Russia."

Then the following, printed in large type:

"The cutting off of electricity is imminent at Hong Kong.

"Five terrorist attacks have occurred here. The police superintendent has been seriously wounded.

"The water supply of the town is about to be cut off."

And then follows news of home politics, nearly all concerned with one—Chen-Dai.

After dinner, Gérard and I take our leave, amidst a fluttering of white sleeves and salamalecs. We decide to go for a short walk. The air is fresh. The hooting of sirens from the boats on the river not far away, lingering on the damp air, dominates now and again the clatter of the Chinese restaurants.

Gérard seems perturbed as he walks at my side. He has drunk deeply tonight.

"Aren't you well?"

"Yes, I'm all right."

"You seem put out."

"So I am."

But hardly has he answered when he seems to realize the curtness of his replies, and he adds immediately:

"I have good reason to be."

"But they all seemed delighted."

"Oh! they!"

"And the news is good."

"What news?"

"Why, of course, the news they gave us. The stopping of the Electric Light Works. The ——"

"Then you didn't hear what the man next to me was saying?"

"No, the man next to me was talking so much about the Revolution and about his father that I was compelled to listen. . . ."

"He was saying that Chen-Dai is certain to oppose us openly."

"And what then?"

"What then? Isn't that enough?"

"Perhaps it might be enough for me, if I . . ."

"Why! he is the most influential man in Canton."

"In what way?"

"I can't explain. But, never fear, you will hear plenty about him. He is the spiritual leader of the revolutionary right. His friends call him 'the Chinese Gandhi.' But in that they are wrong."

"What exactly does he want?"

"Exactly! Anyone can see that you are young. Exactly! Well, I don't know. Neither does he."

"But why are you so troubled about him?"

"Do I know? But you, because you have heard startling wireless messages, you think everything is going well. I assure you that the up-country is as important as the seacoast. It is not at Hong Kong merely, but at Canton that resistance must be organized against those military machinations which the British are constantly carrying on, and on which they rely. The only really good piece of news I have heard today is the wounding of the British police superintendent. Hong is cleverer than I thought. Hong is the Terrorist leader. The wireless refers to him occasionally. For instance. 'Two attacks were made at Hong Kong yesterday. . . . Three . . . Five.' And so on. Garine had great faith in him. . . . He worked with us and was Garine's secretary. Extraordinary idea! To make that midge his secretary! Hong has the ardor of youth on his side. But he will soon get over that. Still, he is a curious type. The first time I saw him was at Hong Kong last year. I learned that he had determined to assassinate the Governor with a Browning pistol, with which he was incapable of hitting a door ten paces away. He came to me at my hotel, waving his hands, too big for the rest of him, as if they were watering-pots. A kid—really nothing more than a kid. 'You don't approve of my project,' he says, in a staccato voice, as if his jaws were sawing his words. I explain to him that 'his project,' as he calls it, is not bad. He listens to me for a quarter of an hour, very bored. Then: 'Yes, but all that has nothing to do with it, because I have sworn an oath.' It was evident that my words had had no effect. He had sworn on the blood of his little finger in some wonderful pagoda. He was very annoyed at my reception of his 'project.' I could not help feeling a certain sympathy with him. Chinese of this type are rare. Finally, just before taking his leave, he wriggled his shoulders as if he had fleas, and grasped my hand, saying slowly: 'When I ha-ve been sen-ten-ced to ca-pi-tal pun-ish-ment, you must tell the young to fol-low my ex-ample.' For years I had not heard the term 'capital punishment' used for the death penalty. He had read books. But he spoke without the slightest emotion, as if he had been saying, 'When I am cremated.' "

"And the Governor!"

"Oh! he was to be struck down the next day during some public ceremony. I can still see myself, sitting on my bed, naked, with my hair on end, for the heat was the very devil, though it was only ten o'clock in the morning, listening to the shouting amid the clamor of horns and trumpets, wondering what it all meant, whether the end of the ceremony or of the Governor. . . . But Hong had been suspected and expelled that very morning. And through all the hullabaloo of cars and couriers, I could see his jaws sawing the syllables, and I could hear his voice saying:

" 'When I have been sen-ten-ced to capital punishment.'

"And I can still hear him. . . . Besides it was not bluff, you know. He really, with his extraordinary vocabulary, thought that

he would be sentenced to death. That will come. . . . Such a
kid. . . ."

"Where does he come from?"

"The lowest dregs. I doubt whether he ever knew his parents.
At any rate he never mentioned them to me. He had—by no
means to his disadvantage—substituted for them one of those creatures who sell curios and souvenirs at Saïgon—things like that.
. . . What a type! But here, won't you drink an absinthe, a real
absinthe?"

"Thank you. "

"Such things are not to be refused. We will go and see him
tomorrow. . . . And you will find in him one of those whom the
Terrorists have molded. They are growing rare. . . . Do you want
to go to bed?"

"No, not particularly."

He calls the chauffeur.

"To Ti-Sa's."

We start. A suburb dimly lit by a few lamps, here and there
arroyos reflecting large twinkling stars dimly visible. Out of the
darkness black masses loom now and again—Annamite booths,
where shopkeepers watch motionless among piles of blue bowls.
. . . Is Gérard really an ex-professor? Now that he is tired, his
character and vocabulary seem to change. I should like to know.

We are driving very rapidly; and I am almost cold. Shrinking
into my corner, with my arms folded to keep me warm, I still
seem to hear that democratic jargon of the dinner table, those
formulas which in Europe today sound so contemptible, but which
are employed here in much the same way as the rusty old steamboats that navigate the rivers of this country. I still see the grave
enthusiasm they arouse even in men who are almost on the verge
of old age. . . . And then behind all this there is the Canton Committee, directing everything and inspiring those wireless messages,
which Hong Kong is powerless to conceal and which appear one
by one like wounds.

Now we are passing high lamps, with clouds of insects buzzing
round them; we traverse sandy streets intersecting one another:

Saïgon. On our way to the native town we whirl along some French boulevards: grass, grass, damp grass, moldy walls, gardens, luxuriant vegetation, a few palms, a hothouse atmosphere, and here and there the lights of villas. Then the chauffeur sounds his horn again; for the passersby are numerous. By the lights from the ground floors of Annamite booths one can vaguely distinguish huddled forms; but here we realize we are in Southern Asia by the smell of pepper and fish, the dampness of the sultry air and the rattling of wooden shoes. Then once more we leave the town; and for about ten minutes we breathe the air of the forest. Now at length, at the crossing of two streets—mere tracks over the sand, without any sidewalks—our car stops. Immediately Anna-mite women flock around us. "Only ten *sous,* gentlemen." But, at the shadow and voice of an Arab policeman, they vanish. . . .

"Two dears! Two!" cries a woman as we enter.
"But, Gérard, do you think this is wise?"
"Oh! in Cochin-China, it doesn't matter."
It is a kind of café, frequented by prostitutes in white trousers and tunics. Two of them come to our table, but go away at a sign from Gérard. No floor, the bare earth, a roof of thatch, but, on the wickerwork tables, buckets of champagne. The mistress comes to shake hands with us. She is a beautiful young Annamite who looks consumptive, and who droops her eyelids while she is talk-ing to us. "You look tired, Ti-Sa?" . . . "Those wretches succeed always in cheating me, . . ." she replies, pointing feebly at some subalterns who are going out, laughing loudly. We order drinks. I don't think Gérard is drunk; but there is something strange about him; he seems to be vaguely enjoying pleasant physical sen-sations. Women go and come around us. Behind the room in which we are sitting are other apartments; and the humming of soldiers' songs comes to us over the partitions. . . . Our neighbors move away one after the other. When Gérard stops talking, the whole room seems dominated by the noise of the grasshoppers—no longer rhythmical, but monotonous, shrill, constant, like one long whistle.

Hong Kong
July 1st

ALL THE CHINESE NURSES IN THE HOSPITALS ARE ON STRIKE.

THE INDO-CHINESE NAVIGATION COMPANY'S BOATS ARE ALL AT
ANCHOR IN PORT.

THERE WERE MORE ACTS OF VIOLENCE YESTERDAY.

NO NEWS FROM THE SHAMEEN CONCESSION.

I am sad and bored and worried. For what is there to do here?
And yet I am obliged to wait till the boat's departure. And all the
while I am longing to be at Canton. Gérard joins me at the hotel.
We lunch early, almost alone in the dining room. He tells me,
more clearly than yesterday, the story of this Hong, who is now
actually causing the assassination of the heads of most British departments. He also tells me the story of the man we are going to
see this afternoon—who is more or less responsible for Hong. His
name is Rebecci. He is a Genoese who passed through the Chinese
Revolution like a somnambulist. On his arrival in China, years ago,
he opened a shop at Shameen; but he detested his European customers so heartily that he gave it up, and opened a Chinese shop.
That was where Gérard and Garine met him in 1920. To the
Chinese he sold all sorts of European wares. He also had automatic puppets—singing birds, ballet dancers, booted cats. They
worked by the insertion of a coin; and in this way he earned his
livelihood. He spoke Chinese fluently. His pretty native wife was
growing rather stout. About 1895, he had been a militant anarchist. He did not care to talk about that chapter in his life, for regret
tinged the pride within which he looked back to the vigor of
those days.

"After all, it can't be helped. That time is over."

Gérard and Garine would go to see him about seven o'clock,
when he had just lit up his great illuminated sign. They would
find him surrounded by a circle of kiddies, their hair in tufts, all
seated on the ground. Rays of waning daylight played on the

silks and spangles of the puppets; a clatter of saucepans came from the kitchen. Rebecci, reclining on a wicker couch in the middle of his shop, dreamed of glorious tours up country with new and numerous puppets. Chinese would line up in queues waiting for admission to the show. He would grow rich. He would buy a vast hall and furnish it with punching-balls, seesaws, Negroes in red velvet, electric guns, all manner of devices, perhaps even a bowling set. . . . When Garine arrived he would come out of his dreams as out of a bath, shaking himself. He would give him his hand and talk of magic. That was his King Charles's head. He was not really superstitious. But he was inquisitive. And, although there existed no proof of the presence of ghosts on earth, and especially at Canton, there was equally no proof of their non-existence, and so one might just as well invoke them. And—observing the proper rites—he did invoke many, from those whose names he discovered in an incomplete *Albertus Magnus* to those with whom beggars and servants were intimately acquainted.

Though he failed to discover many ghosts, he found directions for their discovery; and these he employed, with no small advantage, for the astonishment of his customers, and occasionally for curing them of certain slight ailments. He seldom smoked opium, so, when others were taking their siesta, his white silhouette might be seen crowned by a broad-brimmed hat, thin to the waist and thence bulging out in loose trousers, confined by cycling clips and swelling to the dimensions of a Zouave's breeches—as he sauntered along, dragging an old bicycle, seldom ridden, but always carefully polished.

He lived surrounded by little girls, his servants, whose chief duty was to listen to his stories, and who were well looked after by his Chinese wife. . . . Obsessed by the eroticism of his age and climate, he would read and reread certain French books, then awaking from a long reverie, would exclaim to Garine: "Sir, can you imagine what filthy things there are in love?"

"But no, old chap, why should I?"

"Oh! but they interest me. . . ."

In addition to such books, his library contained an edition of

Les Misérables and a few of Jean Grave's pamphlets, which he kept, but had ceased to admire.

In 1918, Hong joined the young Chinese who gathered to listen to his stories. Rebecci took a fancy to him, stopped telling him ghost stories, and taught him French (he had no Italian books and barely knew English). When Hong could speak French, he learned to read it. Then, thanks to the oriental gift for foreign tongues, he almost taught himself English, and read anything he could lay hands on—which did not amount to much. But his intercourse with Rebecci made up for lack of book learning. They became great friends, though Hong's bluntness and Rebecci's attempts at clumsy irony would hardly have conveyed that impression. Hong, brought up in poverty, had been quick to appreciate his old comrade's way of dispensing charity: he did not give alms, but would bring in beggars to drink a glass, until one day, seeing his shop invaded by a whole crowd of starving wretches, when he hadn't a penny, he kicked them all out. When his brother had been sent to Biribi, however, Rebecci had given up everything to take up his abode near the prison, in order to try and mitigate the horrors of his brother's detention, and to be in a position to go and kiss him occasionally on the mouth, while slipping a golden *louis* into his hand. It was Hong's broad grins at Rebecci's stories that had moved him at first. But he felt the youth to be inspired by a certain courage, by a strange indifference to death, and by a fanaticism that puzzled him. "You, if you are not killed too young, will do excellent things. . . ."

Hong read Jean Grave, and when he had finished asked Rebecci what he thought of him.

Rebecci did what was unusual with him; he reflected before speaking.

"I must think it over," he said, "because, my boy, that Jean Grave is more for me than individual, he is my whole youth. . . . Then one dreamed of things; now one winds up mechanical birds. . . . Those were better days than these. But all the same we were wrong. Because . . . listen to this . . . when one has only one life, one ought not to try and change social conditions. . . . The difficulty is to know what one really wants. If one throws a bomb at a magistrate and kills him, that is all right. But if one publishes a newspaper to propagate good doctrine, then everyone makes light of it. . . ."

His life was a failure. He didn't know exactly why. He couldn't return to Europe; he had grown incapable of any manual work, and yet he wouldn't accept any other. He was bored at Canton, though on the whole. . . . Was he really bored, or did he reproach himself with having accepted a life which was out of tune with the hopes of his youth? But wasn't that a fool's reproach? He couldn't tell. He had been offered the post of superintendent of a department of Sun Yat-sen's police. But he was too much of an anarchist to be capable of denouncing or watching anyone. Then Garine had asked him to work with him. "No, no, Mr. Garine, you are very kind, but, you know, it is, I think, too late now. . . ." Perhaps he was wrong. After all, though he might not be content, he was at peace at any rate with his ghosts, his books on magnetism, his Chinese wife, Hong and his automatic machines.

Hong pondered over Rebecci's vague ideas. The only thing that the West had indelibly impressed upon him was the unique character of life. One life, one only. . . . He had never felt fear of death—for he had never really understood what death was; and even today he could not conceive of death in the ordinary sense—it seemed to him like suffering to the extreme limit from some very serious wound. But what he did feel was a terrible fear of spoiling this one life which was his, spoiling it irremediably.

In this phase of incertitude, he became one of Garine's secretaries. Garine had chosen him because of the influence which his courage gave him, over a rather large group of young Chinese who formed the extreme left wing of the party. Hong was charmed by Garine; but he felt a certain mistrust of him; and he reported Garine's conversation and his orders to Rebecci every evening. The old Genoese, lying prone on his couch, would be turning a paper windmill or watching one of those Chinese globes filled with water, in which strange gardens can be seen. He would put down this object or that, fold his hands across his slim figure, knit his brows in puzzlement, and finally reply:

"Well, well, perhaps he is right, Garine, perhaps he is right."

Finally, as things grew more and more disturbed, and Rebecci more and more penurious, he had accepted a post at the General Information Bureau, after having stipulated that he should not be employed to spy upon anyone. Garine had sent him to Saïgon, where he was useful.

We had finished lunch, and were taking a stroll, oppressed by the heat, when Gérard stopped talking. This was apparently the time when one might discover Rebecci.

We enter a little bazaar: postcards, Buddhas, Annamite copper, cigarettes, a drawing of Cambodia, sampots, silk cushions embroidered with dragons, and, hanging from the wall, close up to the ceiling, well out of the light, strange things in iron. At the cash desk, a fat Chinese asleep.

"Is the governor in?"

"No, sir."

"Where is he?"

"I don't know."

"At Bistrot's?"

"Perhaps. Bistrot Nam-Long."

We cross the street—Bistrot Nam-Long's is opposite. A quiet café; little brown lizards are taking their siestas on the roof. Two servants carrying opium pipes and porcelain cubes for smokers to rest their heads on, pass one another on the staircase. In front of us, boys are asleep, bare to the waist, their hair in their folded arms. Alone, stretched on a settee of black wood, is a man, staring straight in front of him, and gently nodding his head. When he sees Gérard, he rises. I am rather surprised: I had expected a Garibaldian person, with heavy eyebrows and curly hair; but here is a withered little man, with gnarled fingers and sleek hair turning gray, cut soup-plate fashion—a regular Guignol figure.

"Here's a man who hasn't drunk absinthe for years," said Gérard, pointing to him.

"Well!" said Rebecci. "How are you?"

He goes out. We follow.

"Garine nicknamed him Gnafron," whispered Gérard, as we crossed the street.

We enter a shop and go up to the first floor. The Chinese woman looks up, watches us pass, and goes to sleep again. The room is large. In the middle is a bed under a mosquito net. Along the walls numerous articles covered with flowered linen. Rebecci leaves us. We hear a lock grating, a box being shut with a bang, water flowing from a tap and bubbling into a glass. "I am going down for a minute," says Gérard. "I must have a few words with the Chinese lady, if she is not too sleepy. It pleases her."

His minute is a long one. Rebecci is the first to return. He carries a tray, a bottle, sugar, water and three glasses. He says not a word, but sits down and, still in silence, prepares the three absinthes. After a moment:

"Well, you see, I have retired; you see . . ."

Not quite knowing what to say, I ask him if he knows Ti-Sa's, and tell him about our evening there.

"He goes there every evening—that fellow. I suppose he likes it. But only to drink. He also has retired."

"Rebecci!" cries Gérard coming up the stairs, stroking his beard, "the comrade wants to hear you talk about your spiritual son. Ah! I have been a long time. I rather thought you had gone. But I was mistaken."

He did not observe the change on Rebecci's face when he mentioned Hong.

"If I did not know you as well as I do, you would have my hand under your jaw. How can you joke about it?"

"What is the matter with you?"

"You choose a strange day."

"What day?"

Rebecci, furious, shrugs his shoulders.

"Didn't you go to the banquet at the President's this morning?"

"No."

"But what were you thinking of?"

"Our appointment is for five o'clock."

"Oh! Then you had better ask him for news of Hong. He will tell you that Hong is in the pig's paw. . . ."

"What, taken by the British? When?"

"Yesterday evening, they say. Two hours after the appearance of the radiograms, perhaps. . . ."

He taps his glass with his spoon, and then empties it at one gulp.

"Another day I will not refuse you. And the absinthe is there for pals."

Down River
July 2nd

One would have thought that our agitation would have increased as we approached our destination. But not so; dullness reigns on board. Hour after hour, as, in a dense, damp mist, we coast along the flat banks of the river, Hong Kong becomes more of a reality; it ceases to be a name, a place somewhere across the sea, a mere collection of buildings; everyone feels that it is becoming alive. Our acute anxiety gives way to a vague perturbation, mingling with the enervation caused by the regular beating of the engines and the consciousness of living one's last moments of liberty: our bodies are still our own; we are anxious about nothing in particular. Strange moments, during which the old animal powers take possession of the whole boat. A kind of numbness, an enervated indifference. As yet we see nothing; we only hear news; we are not in the struggle.

July 4th

The wireless is so strictly censored that one cannot even guess at anything. A real wartime censorship.

July 5th
Five o'clock

A GENERAL STRIKE HAS BEEN DECLARED AT HONG KONG.

Half-past five

THE GOVERNMENT HAS DECLARED A STATE OF SIEGE.

In Hong Kong Harbor
Nine o'clock

We have just passed the lighthouse. No one thinks of going to sleep. We are all on deck, men and women. Lemonade, whiskey and soda. On the water line, rows of glittering electric lights indicate the outlines of Chinese restaurants. Above them towers the mass of the famous, the formidable rock, widespreading at the base, gradually tapering into a double oriental boss, veiled with a light mist, and seeming to end in the stars. It does not give one the impression of a silhouette, or of a surface cut out in paper, but rather of something deep and solid, something like a black world. A line of lights (is it a road?) encircles the highest of the bosses, the Peak, like a necklace. The houses appear like a handful of lights incredibly close to one another, almost on the top of the twinkling outline of Chinese restaurants, dwindling like the rock as it ascends, until it is lost among the more substantial stars. In the bay are numerous steamboats, at anchor, with their stories of portholes shedding zigzag lights, which mingle with those of the town. All these lights in Chinese skies and waters do not suggest the power of the whites who made them, but rather some Polynesian scene, one of those feasts in which painted gods are honored by the scattering of clouds of glowworms into the darkness. . . .

Then there passes before us an indistinct screen, hiding everything, its only sound that of a one-stringed guitar. It is a junk. The air is warm and still. . . .

The land with its jets of light ceases to advance towards us. Stop. Anchors are let down with a grating noise. Tomorrow morning, the police will come on board. No one is allowed to land.

In the morning

The ship's crew carries our baggage on to the Company's tender. Not a single coolie has come to offer his services. We glide along the smooth water, the boat hardly rocking at all. Suddenly, just as we are rounding a little point bristling with chimneys and signal posts, the business quarter appears: high buildings towering along the quay, some London or Hamburg line, almost extinguished by a cone of luxuriant vegetation, and a sky in which the transparent air seems to tremble as if it were being belched out of a furnace. The tender puts in to the station wharf, the terminus of the Canton railway.

Still no coolies. The Company has asked the big hotels to send porters, we are told. But there is no one. The passengers, with the sailors' help, land their own luggage.

Now I am on the quay. It is deserted. I walk down a broad street, which looks as if it would lead to the center. Architecture half Flemish and half modern: gables alternating with flat roofs of reinforced concrete. At the ends of narrow streets, confined between eight-storied buildings, are the domes of Protestant churches which suggest that of St. Paul's in London. And above, everywhere, the vegetation of the rock and the Peak. From the ground, so soft that one's boots pass over it noiselessly, there ascends a strong odor of tar, asphalt and oil like that of Singapore. Petrol, golf clubs, all sorts of electroplated articles in cases, copper plates round door lintels, engraved with the names of different firms, English shops, tearooms, sweet-stores, bookshops displaying nothing but travel books and magazines; everything indicating a life of action. No trees, as at Saïgon, but lawns, as at Singapore— and stones. Energy. Dominion. No dwelling houses. But banks and offices—offices—offices—offices. Hoardings with advertisements. And over it all the peaked mountains of China hemming us in again in silence. The town might be in the clutch of some epidemic. It is an abandoned city, in which reigns a solitude as of night. And yet it hardly seems deserted, but rather the victim of some catastrophe. A great machine out of gear.

Beneath the notices indicating car and rickshaw ranks not a single vehicle. An English soldier crosses the street. Behind me, a Chinese clatters along in his wooden shoes as if to accentuate the silence.

Hong Kong Hotel. No one in the entrance hall. After I have rung the electric bell several times, an English servant arrives, tired and heavy-eyed. He does not understand a word of what I say. Then comes a Tonkin "boy." At the request of the Hong Kong Government, the Indo-China Government, in order to break the strike, has despatched a number of Tonkin and Anna-mite "boys," who have just arrived, and who will doubtless go out on strike, too, very soon. This Tonkin "boy" loses his way in his efforts to lead me to my room, which I find for myself. Having deposited my luggage in it, I go out.

I climb up Wyndham Street, narrow and precipitous. Here China begins: singers simply dressed, for it is early in the day, Eurasian girls on their way to lectures at the University, in white frocks, short hair and horn spectacles. No men. On the right, the newspaper printing offices are deserted. An overwhelming scent of narcissus comes up from the flower market as I look through the windows at the shining black presses, all motionless, and read the strike notice over the door. Scaffolding is in front of the *South China Morning Post*, but no one is working on it. Opposite, in the antique shops, are wonderful things—but all in gloom—for the electric light lamps have been removed. Here and there I discern vases of the Han period, severe, magnificent and doubtless fakes. But not a single customer.

Now here is the main street. The town lies at the meeting of rock and sea, built on the one, fringing on the other. This street intersected by all the roads leading from the quay to the Peak is like a hollow palm leaf. Here, normally, is the hub of the Island's activity. But today, here also, all is silence and solitude. Here and there, keeping close together and spying round like police-men, are couples of British volunteers, dressed like boy scouts, who are going to the market to distribute vegetables or meat. The sound of wooden shoes clattering in the distance. No white women. No motorcars.

Now I come to the Chinese shops: jewelers, jade sellers, dealers in all sorts of luxury wares. English houses grow fewer, until, round a sharp corner, they disappear altogether. The corner is so sharp that it seems almost to bar the road; and in this kind of blind alley one is surrounded by Chinese characters of all sizes, black, red, gold, inscribed on tablets, or over doors or hanging out in squares against the sky; they seem to surround one like a swarm of insects. From the depths of great dark caverns, surrounded by three walls, shopkeepers in long blouses, seated at their counters, look out into the street. As soon as I appear, they gaze up at things which look as if they had been hanging from the ceiling for centuries—dried cuttlefish, black sausages, *kalmars*, fish, glazed ducks the color of hams—or down at the sacks of seed or boxes of eggs, plastered with black earth, which lie on the floor, and are illuminated by thin rays of sunlight, dense with yellow dust. If I turn round after passing these traffickers, I find them looking after me, dark and malevolent.

In front of Chinese banks, adorned with gilded signs and railed in as closely as prisons, British soldiers are on guard; and occasionally I hear the tips of their rifles clinking on the asphalt. It is, however, but an empty symbol. British tenacity may have won this town, house by house, from the rock and from China; but now it is powerless in face of the passive resistance of three hundred thousand Chinese, who are determined that they will no longer submit. Weapons are useless. The British are losing something more than mere wealth.

Eleven o'clock. I buy some Chinese newspapers and return to the hotel.

No lunch is forthcoming. The Tonkin "boys," who arrived yesterday from Haiphong, are too few to serve all the passengers from the steamboats in the harbor. I am advised to go to the automatic bar, which is not far away. But that is useless; for the proprietor is Chinese; and the bar is closed. I return to the hotel. All the corridors are littered with trunks, thrown down anyhow, and among them the unfortunate Tonkin "boys" hurry in and out all of a flurry, called incessantly here and there. Throughout the hotel crowds of passengers push and press against one another. A child is crying in a corner. Surrounded by a noisy group, the proprietor and the manager, worried, exasperated, stop up their ears and shake themselves as if they were shaking off flies. Some things have already been stolen.

I might perhaps have lunched on board; but the tender has gone and there is no other boat. For some days there has been a fear of the electricity stopping. If the fans were to cease working, life would become almost unbearable for whites. Already—and it is not yet noon—the sultry heat renders it well-nigh impossible to keep awake. But European volunteers, who are working at the factory, have removed this danger. Everywhere one sees travelers rushing up and down, in search of a room, undecided and as bustling as grasshoppers, bag or helmet in hand, wiping their foreheads and throwing back their hair, wet with perspiration. The hullabaloo of our arrival has subsided. Now, strange to say, it has ceased altogether; and almost in silence these people, wearing the white of the tropics, move to and fro amidst the penetrating smell of leather which comes from the luggage. The child goes on crying. A man who is near me—a Frenchman from Indo-China, whom the strike has detained here for three days—begins to talk to me. In the town the situation is as bad as in this hotel. In this country, where the slightest physical exertion bathes one in perspiration, Europeans, women as well as men, are forced to do the humblest work. Clubmen, whose clubs are totally disorganized by the lack of servants, have to eat in canteens into which revolutionaries have penetrated, so that these unhappy bachelors go in daily fear of being poisoned. Nearly all the British shops, as I saw, are closed. A few, it seems, have reopened, being served by Eurasians and occasional whites from Shanghai.

But now the crowd is surging towards the bar. The brilliant idea has occurred to the barman of preparing sandwiches which the Tonkin "boys" are distributing—awkwardly, it is true, and at a loss, for they have to give change for coins of which they don't know the value, worried, too, as was the proprietor just now, by groups of clamorous, impatient purchasers.

Four o'clock. I have hardly slept at all. A restless siesta, partly
due to the intermittent action of the fan, for the electric light
works are not functioning regularly. It is terribly hot, and the
shining asphalt of the streets, which reflects the blue sky, radiates
air and sends up dust even hotter than the atmosphere. The assistant delegate of the Kuomintang is to give me certain documents. The delegate himself, who comes from the Baltic, has
just been banished. Perhaps I shall see the organizer of the strike,
the German Klein.

All that I know about this assistant delegate is that he is called
Meunier, that he was formerly a mechanic in Paris and a machine-
gun sergeant during the War. His appearance surprised me, as he
stood on the threshold of his colonial house, at the base of the
Peak. I expected him to be elderly; but he did not appear to be
more than thirty-five. He is a tall, robust fellow, clean-shaven,
whose upper lip, close to his thin nose, bright little eyes and stray
locks make up a head which suggests a facetious little rabbit. Sunk
into his capacious, wickerwork armchair, in front of two high
glasses of crème de menthe coated with vapor, he was set going
in two minutes.

"Ah! old chap, it's a fine sight: the bulldog of old England, the
only real bulldog, Hong Kong itself, rotting as it stands, worm-
eaten. You have seen the streets, haven't you, since you arrived
this morning? They weren't bad, eh? Rather amusing! But that's
nothing, old chap. That's nothing, I tell you. To be really appreciated, it must be seen from within."

His ironical tone and the creasing of his eyelids betray the
finesse of a man who is anything but naïve.

"And what do you see from the inside?"

"Ah! Any number of tricks! Look at the prices of things.
Houses which were worth five thousand dollars last year, are
offered for fifteen hundred. And even then it is not easy to sell
them. This price of houses is not without its importance, you
must know. And then there are the commercial firms; if they have
not all shut up shop, it is not because of the superb profits they
are making, you may be sure. It is on account of the banks, old

chap. It is because the banks lend them capital by the Governor's order. And it costs the bank something. If you would realize how things are, just go and buy a pencil sharpener or some ink-eraser in one of the big stores: at Whiteaway's, Jardine's or Yale's. They will rush to serve you, all those gentlemen. There will be three of them wanting to wrap up your purchase in tissue paper. Ah! now they have leisure. And they know how to use it. They are volunteers, all of them, butchers, greengrocers, stevedores. . . . It is quite gratifying to see the Director of Machinchose & Co., with a rifle slung over his shoulder. His leather coat is not uncomfortable now because he is a novice; but in a fortnight's time . . .

"What is really great, old chap, is to see them looking for strikers. They never find any. When, by chance, some miserable Chinese who has howled 'Long live China!' or something equally astute comes their way, who is he? Why, a member of the Monad! You know the Monad story?"

"Yes, Gérard told me."

"Well, old chap, they mowed them down with astounding rapidity. They were furious at having found no one for so long. They didn't know themselves. What stories they told of the efficiency of their police! That was how they came to spread abroad the story of Hong's capture. Hah! Hah!"

"Was it false, then?"

"What?"

"But every one at Saïgon believed. . . ."

"Oh, the simpletons! Fancy that! Why, Hong is at Canton, quite happy. But to return to the English: last week we made them lose 250,000 dollars. You can imagine how they liked it."

"But still, they must have the wealthy traders on their side, those who left Canton in opposition to the Kuomintang?"

"That does not take them far. You should see how many Chinese set out for Canton every day. Only yesterday a boat carrying eight hundred passengers was wrecked on the Pearl River. Just think how the English must have rejoiced. It must have reminded them of the good old Transvaal days. Well! Then ever so many plutocrats have rallied to the Kuomintang since it

has been victorious. Others rallied on account of an epidemic of
stabbing that spread like anything in that unhealthy atmosphere.
And then you must take enthusiasm into account. . . . This Garine
is anything but a bungler. . . . Over there, opposite, all along the
coast they seem to be suddenly taking courage. . . . I was at
Canton on the fourteenth, when Hsu Chiang Chi returned, after
having beaten the mercenaries of Yunnan, who had revolted. And
how? No one quite knows. It's one of those horrible tales of old
rags covered with blood, broken rifles, scraps of iron, and the
eyes of dead men. These are things one can't grow accustomed
to. . . . Living bodies buried in river mud. . . . I myself have seen
an officer impaled. Have you ever seen one? Let that pass. . . .
Speakers at every street corner. . . . And you should see the delight of the people. . . . All this slaughter seemed to bring them
a sense of relief. . . . What hatred! Ah! that military rule! They
are not likely to forget it. . . . Wherever civilians met a Yunnanese in arms it was quite simple: they cut him down and threw
his corpse into the river."

"And Hsu, how did they receive him?"

"With their fingers on their noses, and looking in the opposite
direction. With a certain reserve, as the Chinese would say.
One thing astounded them, that the victorious Red Army did not
plunder. When Garine and Borodin forbade pillage on pain of
death, I thought: 'Ha, ha! you will see.' I was wrong. The decree
was obeyed, as a similar decree was obeyed by the armies of our
own Republic. Besides, the soldiers are paid now. And then Russian officers have an eye. . . ."

"You know Borodin?"

"I imagine that Clemenceau must have been like that, at forty
or forty-five. Full of experience. The only reproach one can bring
against him is that he is too fond of Russians."

"And Garine?"

"He is clever, there is no denying it. Quite recently, he has
worked a regular miracle: he has converted the Canton strikers,
who lived on the allowances that he and Borodin succeeded in
obtaining for them from the Government, into a whole army of

propagandists. . . . But with Borodin, one knows where one is going to. Garine begins to look like a corpse. What it is no one knows; malaria, dysentery? Some say he neglects himself. His beard would bear that out. . . . At any rate, at Canton, gossips say that he ought to return to Europe, and that if he stays out East any longer he will leave his bones here. Naturally they are all more or less ill at Canton. I have heard that Chen Chun-ming has put a price of a hundred thousand dollars on his head, which the British have promised to pay. How impatient they are! But there may be nothing in the story. One thing, however, is certain: that the Secret Intelligence Department has promised thirty thousand dollars. That isn't bad. . . ."

"And what about you?"

"They seem to be cautious. If I didn't know them, I should marvel that I am not expelled. . . . They must be preparing something better for me. But, of course, I take the usual precautions."

"I was surprised at being able to come in."

"I might say the same."

"Perhaps they have been informed. At any rate, my papers are all right."

"What a mad child you are! Come and see."

We go up to the first floor. The windows are covered with mats. But through the chinks we look down into the street.

"Do you see two youths with the jaws of a cassowary close to that old woman selling soup and sugar canes? Well, they are for me. And the third Adonis in a domed helmet I give to you."

It is true. I recognize him. He is the Chinese whose shoes were clattering down the deserted street on my arrival. We go downstairs.

"Have some more menthe. One is best in one's armchair at this time of day. Oh! here are the papers. You had better have them now for fear of forgetting them. What an idea of the British to keep up the connection between Hong Kong and Canton by means of their men-of-war! Klein will be here directly; and you can start together. He was to stay a few days longer, but he is

marked, and he must get away at once, if my information is correct. My turn will come soon."

"Are you certain that I shan't be searched on my departure this
evening?"

"There is no reason why you should be. You are merely passing,
and they know your papers are all right. So to search you would
be of no use. But take every precaution all the same. If they
wanted to do anything, they would have to shut you up in prison.
But there is no danger in that direction."

"Strange!"

"No, it is quite simple. They don't want to risk taking a false
step. They prefer to rely on their Secret Intelligence Department.
And they are right; for they are in a peculiar position. You see,
they are not technically at war with Canton."

"They might have told the Navigation Company to say that all
the berths were booked."

"Ah! but I took your tickets five days ago. Klein had not yet
arrived; and you had not been actually denounced. They might
try to devise something. But they are not particularly anxious to
detain you: they look upon you as spies. . . .

"Tell me, you don't know Klein? No, of course you don't; you
have only just arrived."

The tone of his sentence makes me ask:

"What have you against him?"

"One must be just. He has done several years' hard labor for
the cause. He commanded in the Red Army which captured
Baron Ungern Sternberg (and Sternberg was lucky to fall into his
hands . . . he was merely shot). Klein is rather queer. But professionally he is good. I have just seen him at work. Well, my friend,
you can take my word for it, he really understands what a succession of strikes should be.

"By the way, there was something I wanted to tell you: at one
time Garine really surpassed himself, and that was when he organized the Cadet School. It was no joke. To turn a Chinese into
a soldier has never been easy, and a rich Chinese is especially difficult. He enlisted a thousand men, whom he made the *cadre* of a

little army. In a year that army will have grown tenfold, and then I can't see any Chinese force being able to withstand it. . . . Chang Tso-lin's perhaps; but I am not sure. As for the British, if they want to play their expeditionary corps game (provided our comrades over there are soft enough to let them start), well, let them try. . . . The recruiting of the army was nothing; but he has given his men titles and rank, he has made them respected. Even that, perhaps, others might have done. But he ended by inculcating them with a vice little known here and which is called courage. I take off my hat to him. He has achieved something I could certainly never have done. I know that Gallen helped him, and also the commandant of the school, Chiang Kai-shek. It was Chiang who, with Garine, formed the initial staff. He created it very much as the British created this town: man by man, courage added to courage, soliciting, exacting, making things go. To find out those grotesque little figures, with the nails of their little fingers as long as that, in order to persuade them to send their kids to be slaughtered. . . . I see it all as I sit here. . . . A great assistance to him was the despatch from Whampoa of a son of the former Viceroy. Then, perhaps, his own family. . . . It was all very well done. . . . And then he got it into his cadets' heads that they are not soldiers, but servants of the Revolution. That was excellent. The results were seen at Shameen on the twenty-fifth."

"Not very brilliant results."

"Because Shameen wasn't taken? but do you imagine they wanted to take it?"

"Have you any reliable information about that?"

"You will have over there. I think the key to the situation was Chen-Dai. He is one whom one must confront with something actually accomplished. It grows more and more necessary. We shall see. What we have seen already is that when the machine guns began to fire on our people, the mass ran away as usual, but about fifty—they were cadets—stood their ground and attacked. They were found lying, where they ought to have been, about thirty meters away from the guns. I have an idea that that day something in China changed."

"But why should the attack on Shameen have been directed against Chen-Dai?"

"I only said 'perhaps.' It is my impression that we are not on very good terms, and I don't feel sure about his friend, Governor Wou Hon-min."

"Gérard was anxious, too."

"There is no question about Chen-Dai's influence; but I doubt whether it will be on our side long."

"Why?"

"It is difficult to explain. . . . Once again you must bear in mind Gandhi and his Mohammedan chiefs. Chen-Dai thinks we are too violent, too much addicted to formulas, not attaching enough importance to justice."

"Is he as popular as ever?"

"Lately his popularity has been decidedly on the wane."

"But what is his office precisely?"

"He holds no office precisely, though he is President of Secret Societies. Do you remember, old chap, that when Gandhi, who also held no office, decreed the Hartal, commanded the people to go out on strike, why, they stopped work at once, in spite of the arrival of the Prince of Wales; and the Prince passed through Calcutta as if it were a city of the deaf and dumb. Many Indians lost their employment as a result, and more or less died of starvation. And here moral forces are equally active. Here they are just as real as this chair or this table."

"But Gandhi is a saint."

"So he may be—they know nothing about that. Gandhi is a mythological hero, that's the truth of the matter. So is Chen-Dai. You can't find people like that in Europe."

"And the Government?"

"The Canton Government?"

"Yes."

"It is like the bar in a pair of scales, oscillating, in its attempt to stay straight, between Garine and Borodin, who control the police and the syndicates, on the one hand, and Chen-Dai, who controls nothing, but who exists all the same, on the other.

Anarchy, old chap, occurs when the Government is weak, not when there is no Government. For there is always some kind of a Government, only when things go badly there are several, that's all. This Government Garine is prepared to involve up to the neck. So he wants it to issue his confounded decree. It will infuriate the British, of course! Hong Kong without ships in the harbor, Hong Kong closed against boats going to China, is no good as a port. The very idea was enough to make them demand military intervention here. Well! If that happens, then Garine will be happy. But we shall have our hands full."

"Why?"

"It's difficult to say. The Government, you must know, would like to go on side by side with us, even above us, if possible. It is afraid of being devoured—either by the British or by us—if it follows us at too great a distance. The British are so lucky. If it were merely a question of fighting against Hong Kong. But there is the interior. The interior. That's where they expect to have us. We must look into that. . . ."

He is silent. We drink our large glasses of menthe. Everything is quiet, strangely quiet for the tropics. Even the fan is still. Not a single street cry, not a Chinese cracker, not a bird, not a grasshopper. A very slight breeze, blowing in from the bay, makes the mats hanging over the windows flap a little, displaying a triangle of white wall, covered with lizards asleep, and bringing in from the street a smell of cooking asphalt. Every now and then one catches the distant call of a siren almost stifled, far out at sea.

About five o'clock Klein arrives. He is obviously tired, and falls at once, with his hands on his knees, into a wicker armchair, which creaks and cracks beneath his weight. He is tall, broad-shouldered, with a striking face, of a type oftener met with in England than in Germany: light eyes, beneath heavy eyebrows, a flat nose and a large, strong mouth, with deep lines from nose to chin, a thick neck, suggesting a bulldog, a boxer or a butcher. In Europe his skin would be red; even here, where it is brown, like that of all Europeans, the cheeks are still slightly mottled. He begins to converse in French, with a strong North German accent, which gives a singsong, almost Belgian, intonation to his rather husky voice; but, being extremely tired, the effort of speaking a foreign tongue becomes more and more marked till he lapses into German, while Meunier now and then gives the gist of their conversation in French.

The Canton general strike, aimed at strengthening the power of the extreme revolutionary leaders, at weakening that of the moderates, and at destroying the very fount of the wealth of Hong Kong—the riches of those Chinese merchants who trade with the British and oppose the Kuomintang—has now lasted a fortnight. All that time Borodin and Garine have had to support fifty thousand men out of the strike funds, that is, out of taxes collected at Canton and money sent by Chinese revolutionaries outside the town. Now the calling of a general strike at Hong Kong, depriving more than one hundred thousand workmen of subsistence, compels the Canton Government to allocate strike pay to such large numbers that the fund will be exhausted in a few days. Already the day laborers are not receiving their allowances. Now in this town, in which British detectives have hitherto failed to destroy revolutionary organizations, the city police, supported by volunteers with machine guns, have succeeded in holding the revolution in check. There has been nothing more serious than a little rioting. The employees are about to return to work, which is what the British expected.

Garine, who is at present head of the propaganda department, is as well aware as Borodin of the critical state of affairs: he knows that this colossal strike, which is nothing short of dumfounding to all the whites in the Far East, is on the eve of breaking down. Both of them possess other weapons against the British; for they have never regarded the Hong Kong strike as more than a provisional movement. But they cannot act save as leaders of their respective organizations (which are not unlike the Committees of the National Convention); and they are confronted by the Government's refusal to adopt the measures on which they had relied. Chen-Dai, says Klein, uses all his influence against them. At the same time the anarchist movement is gaining ground, as one might have foreseen; and various terrorist manifestations have occurred, even in Canton itself. Finally, the old enemy of the Kuomintang, General Chen Chun-ming, well supplied with British money, is raising an army with which to march on the town.

Six o'clock. On the quay. The brilliance has faded from the sky. At the extremities of the great curve of yellow land towering over the Chinese shops, the trim palm trees which had seemed to be shriveling all day, now begin to look as if they were alive. Opposite, in a forest of Kowloon chimneys, which have looked as if they were dead, a few begin lazily to blacken the sky with a thin trail of smoke. Two official fly-boats (manned by marines) slowly pass one another in front of the islet. All along the quay abandoned sampans lie motionless, while the great steamboats appear to be set eternally in the framework of the bay.

But all round our boat, what a hullabaloo! Hundreds of Chinese in white linen, shouting, pushing and hurtling against one another. Men with umbrellas overturning women whose tiny feet are shod with red shoes. Servants carrying wooden trunks and leather suitcases. Apart, near a pillar, a group of Chinese women in black trousers and light bodices, waiting to be taken on board. Above the clamor on the quay and the cries of women, the hooting of the siren.

After taking possession of my cabin, I go up on deck. The exhausted Klein has gone to lie down on his berth. Reclining in a deep armchair, I watch the Hong Kong twilight being gradually illuminated. Little by little the great rock begins to assume the appearance of a centerpiece in some grand firework display, its lights appearing side by side with the white stars in a sky rapidly changing color.

Once, so I am told, there were many more of these glittering signs. But one by one the flaming symbols of trade have been put out like footlights on a stage.

And this Chinese people, growing more and more active and influential, as, day by day, those lights disappear, this people who defend themselves with notices and words of command. . . . Is this beautiful darkening sky above me all I am to see of them? Their culture is not here, but far from capitals, like our own. Their revolution? . . . It is by virtue of their revolutionary instinct that their towns seem to live in my memory. Singapore, on the surface gay and placid, with its hundred thousand members of secret societies and its Chinese huddled together on the island as if in a prison; Saïgon and Cholon, suburban, with their sorry attempts at fashionable night life, their electric globes swarming with insects and that strange atmosphere of contending spiritual currents, torpor on the one hand, hostility on the other. Hong Kong definitely awakened from its sleep and showing how in a Chinese town hatred can be forged out of passivity, silence and indifference.

Canton remains to be seen.

All I can see of the Hong Kong Island now is a form outlined by a chain of twinkling dots, dwindling slowly as they stand out against the black sky, which seems to engulf them. The immense advertisement figures loom large: the publicity of all those great British firms, which those brilliant globes flashed over the town a month ago. Electricity has now become too precious to be used for their illumination; and their gleaming colors have died away in the darkness: machines grown rusty and out of gear. At a sudden turn, their place is taken by a bare wall of Chinese mountain, muddy, dotted with patches of short grass, rapidly growing invisible as night approaches, and swarming with mosquitoes, just as it did three thousand years ago. And so darkness covers this island, where intelligent ship brokers are doing their work, leaving it still looking imperial, though the once gleaming symbols of its wealth, now reduced to great black signs, no longer flare across the sky.

Silence. Unbroken silence, and the stars. Not far above us junks are passing, borne upon the tide which carries us all up river. Not a sound, not a face. The mountains, surrounding us with their dim outline, look unearthly, and so does the silent water, a kind of river of the dead flowing on into the darkness like one who is blind. There is nothing human about the boats we pass, except perhaps the lanterns at the stern, which burn so feebly as to be barely reflected.

"Even the smells are not the same."

Night has fallen. Klein is at my side. He speaks French, almost in a whisper.

"Not the same? Have you sailed up river by night before? In Europe, I mean?"

"Yes."

"How different it is, isn't it! At home the silence of night is peace. . . . But here one expects the crackle of machine guns every minute."

It is true. This night is a mere truce. This silence will soon be broken by the noise of firing. Klein points to twinkling jets of light, barely perceptible.

"Those are our people." He still speaks in a whisper. His tone is confidential. "Over there is nothing. The lights have gone out. But look here, on this bench. What an exhibition!"

On the deck behind us, some ten young Englishmen whose firms have branches at Shameen and who are going to help the volunteers, have gathered round two young women, who are said to be newspaper correspondents (but may they not be connected with the secret intelligence department?). Stories are being told: "He had asked Moscow to send a crystal tomb like Lenin's. But the one the Russians sent was only glass. [They are talking of Sun Yat-sen.] Another time . . ."

Klein shrugs his shoulders.

"They are not worth listening to. . . ."

He puts his hand on my shoulder and looks me in the face:

"During the Commune, a fellow who was arrested cried: 'But I have never dabbled in politics.' 'Precisely.' And his head was broken."

"That is to say?"

"It is difficult to explain, especially in French. It is not always the same people who suffer. I remember at some fête or other looking at people like these and longing for a revolver with which to shatter them . . . that smile. . . . What? Eugh! the sight of all those faces that have never been convulsed by any outburst of rage! Oh! if one could only make people like that realize that something called 'human life' exists. *Ein Mensch*, a man, is a rare creature. What?"

I take care not to reply. Is he talking because he must or in order to be sociable? Is he speaking to me or to himself? His voice is flat, sounding almost hoarse through the buzz of mosquitoes. His hands tremble. He has not slept for three days. He is half dead from fatigue.

Behind us and separated from us by a railing guarded by two turbaned Indian soldiers, rifles in hand, are the Chinese passengers, playing and smoking in silence. Klein turns round and looks at the substantial barrier.

"Do you know that, when one is in prison, one brings oneself to bear the most terrible, the most humiliating things? Well, I used to dream of poisoning the whole town. I could do it, I knew. I had only to go out to the reservoirs, when I was free, and to get a large quantity of cyanide, with which one of my friends, who was a chemist, would supply me. And when my sufferings became unendurable, I lulled myself with this thought. Then I felt better. The convict, the epileptic, the syphilitic, the wounded are not like other people. They cannot *accept*."

A pulley falls on to the deck, with a re-echoing noise. It makes Klein jump. Then he collects himself and resumes:

"I am too nervous tonight. Utterly dead beat.

"The memory of such things sticks. At the back of all wretchedness there is generally the soul of a man. And the man's soul must remain after the wretchedness has passed. . . . It is difficult. . . .

"What is the revolution for them and for the rest of the world? The essence of revolution is so important. What is it? I will tell you. No one knows. But it arises from the fact that there is too much wretchedness, not merely lack of money, but rich people living their own lives while others cannot."

His voice has grown stronger. Placing his two elbows on the taffrail, which is still hot, he moves his shoulders forward with a gesture almost like the shaking of a fist.

"Here, what a change! When the tradesmen turned volunteers wanted to restore the old conditions, their quarter blazed for three days. Women ran about on their tiny feet like penguins. And then there was nothing but corpses. Once again. . . ."

He pauses, lost in thought. Then he resumes:

"It is all too stupid. . . . The people of Munich, of Odessa. . . . Too stupid."

He utters the word "stupid" in a tone of disgust.

"They are there like rabbits, or like creatures in pictures. Is it tragic? No, it is stupid. . . . Especially when they wear mustaches. One has to tell oneself that they are really men who have been killed. One would never think it. . . ."

Again he is silent, leaning with the whole weight of his body against the taffrail. Denser and denser grow the clouds of mosquitoes and other insects, swarming round the veiled lights on deck. The banks and the river seem mere shadows reflecting the glow of the steamer's lights. Here and there, outlined against the darkness, loom tall shapes which may be fishermen's nets, or perhaps . . .

"Klein?"

"*Was?* What?"

"Why don't you go to bed?"

"What good would it do me? I am too tired. It is too hot down below."

I bring a deck chair and put it beside him. He sinks into it without a word. His head falls forward, he lies like a log, utterly exhausted. Except for the officer on duty, the Indian sentinels and me, everyone is asleep—the Chinese, on the other side of the barrier, on their trunks, the whites on deck chairs or in the cabin. In the intervals of the thumping of the engine, the only sounds to be heard are the snores of the sleepers and the ceaseless coughing of an old Chinese, irritated by the incense which the boys have set burning all over the ship in order to kill the mosquitoes.

I have slept for an hour. I awake still tired, with a parched mouth, eyelids glued together. It is impossible to sleep any longer, and yet I am not thoroughly awake. I rise heavily, and walk a few steps on deck. The silence, with the exception of the whirring of the engine, is now complete. I don't even hear that hacking cough, which interrupted my first attempts at slumber. The smell of the incense seems to be permeating the whole ship. Klein is asleep. A gust of fresh air seems to envelop me like a mist and makes me shiver.

I take refuge in my cabin. But I cannot shake off the heaviness which results from my interrupted rest: migraine, lassitude, shivering. I try to have a good wash (but with difficulty, for there is not enough water). I set the fan working, open the porthole. That is better.

Seated on my berth, by way of occupation, I take my papers out of my pockets, one by one: advertisements of medicines for tropical ailments, old letters, white paper stamped with the little tricolor flag of Les Messageries Maritimes. All this, torn into tiny bits, is thrown through the porthole into the river. In another pocket old letters from the man they call "Garine." I did not think it safe to leave them in my bag. And what is this? Oh! it is the list of papers confided to me by Meunier. Let me see. There are a great many. . . . But here are two which are marked on the list: the first a copy of a note relating to Chen-Dai, made by the Secret Service, with annotations by our agents. The second is one of the cards of the Hong Kong police and concerns Garine.

After locking and bolting my door, I take out of my shirt pocket the big envelope which Meunier gave me. The two documents I want are the last in it. The one referring to Chen-Dai interests me. Unfortunately the note is very short. In black ink. The heading written rapidly with a stylo—Chen-Dai: and in capital letters in red pencil: EXTRACT (doubtless an extract from some British detective's report):

EXTRACT

June, 1925

Confidential

Reply to your questions of the twenty-eighth.

I. Nothing doing. No man is more respected by the Cantonese.

II. Brave enough to get himself killed, but nothing more.

III. Will certainly oppose Borodin's forthcoming proposals.

IV. Yes, seems already surrounded and even threatened by the . . .

At the foot of the page, in our agent's handwriting, the same as that of the heading "Chen-Dai," these words: "The rest will follow without delay."

I am impatient to reach Canton. Now for the other note. It is longer and in cipher. At the top of the page is written: "Urgent. Pass on at once. The key to the cipher accompanies the document."

Curiosity and a certain anxiety possess me. I begin to translate. This man, whose most intimate friend I have been for many years, what is he like today? I haven't seen him for five years. Yet, ever since I have been out East not a single day has passed without my coming across some sign of him—a reference to him in conversation, or his influence at work in the wireless reports that reached us.

I seem to see him as he was at Marseilles during our last interview, but bearing on his face the trace of subsequent experiences: large gray eyes, hard, with barely any lashes, a thin, slightly curved nose—his mother was a Jewess—and his cheeks furrowed by two deep lines, giving that droop to the strong lips which one often notices in Roman busts. But the face derives its expression, not so much from these strongly marked features, as from the strong, muscular jaw moving a firm, energetic mouth.

In my state of nervous tension, my memories group and arrange themselves as I read: I seem to hear the voice. Tonight I am like a drunkard working out his dream.

"Pierre Garin, passing as Garine or Harine. Born at Geneva on the fifth of November, 1892. Parents, Maurice Garin a Swiss subject and Sophia Alexandrovna Mirsky his wife, a Russian."

He was born in 1894. Why does he add two years to his age?

"A militant anarchist. Sentenced for complicity in an anarchist plot in Paris, in 1914."

No, he never was a "militant anarchist." In 1914, at twenty, he had just completed his course in literature and was deeply impressed by the great conflicting forces in life. Are any books besides memoirs worth writing? Systems were nothing to him. He was ready to adopt any that circumstances might impose on him. It was an atmosphere more than anything else and the hopes that a general upheaval held out, that attracted him to advanced anarchists and socialists, in spite of the numerous police spies whom he found among the former. Many a time have I heard him speak in terms of irony and scorn of the men he had just met at some meeting, which, ingenuous youth! he had attended in a Barclay cap, men who talked of working for the good of humanity. "Those fools want to prove themselves in the right. But in practice there is only one 'right,' which is not a parody, and that is the efficient use of force." The idea was in the air; and it appealed to his own imagination, which was then occupied with Saint-Just.

On the whole, he was thought to be ambitious. But an ambitious man is one who conceives of definite deeds which have to be done. Now of desiring any course of triumphant action, or of preparing it, or of bringing his life into line with it, he was totally incapable. Neither in mind nor in character was he fitted for any such thing. Yet, like a disease, persistent, tenacious, he felt within him a craving for power. "It is not so much the soul of a man that makes a leader," he said to me one day, "but his achievements." "Unfortunately," he added ironically. And, a few days later—he was reading *Le Mémorial*—"It is achievement more than anything that sustains a leader's soul. Napoleon at St. Helena actually said: 'What a romance my life has been all the same!' Thus even genius rots!"

He knew that the vocation towards which he felt himself impelled was not merely one of the many which, from time to time, for a while attract the imagination of youth; and on that account he determined to dedicate his whole life to it, accepting all the risks that it involved. He craved power for its own sake, not for the wealth, notoriety or respect it might bring. If, in some moment of childish fancying, he ever dreamed of power, it was in a manner almost physical—not in the least romantic, but with a tension of his whole being, like that of a beast preparing to pounce upon his prey; and this led him to regard the actual exercise of power as a kind of relief, a deliverance.

Courageous and philosophical, he was prepared to risk everything. He realized that death can put an end to any situation; and, being very young, he had no fear of death. As for anything that was to be won, he had no clear idea of that as yet.

But, little by little, a definite resolve began to take the place of the confused aspirations of youth, though it did not as yet dominate a nature of which violence was still to remain the distinguishing characteristic; but it was a violence conceived with a lightness of heart, only possible in the twenties, when life is hardly more than an abstraction.

He was, however, soon to be brought up against life in all its brutality. One morning, at Lausanne, I received a letter from a comrade telling me that Pierre was involved in an abortion case; and two days later came a letter from Pierre himself, giving details.

Though Malthusian propaganda was actively at work in anarchist circles, few midwives would consent to bring on miscarriages on principle; but those who accepted payment while maintaining that they worked for "the cause," were less difficult to find. Pierre, either from conviction or from vanity, had from time to time contributed substantial sums which the young women themselves would never have been able to pay. He had inherited a considerable fortune from his mother—a fact which the police report had not recorded. It was known that an appeal to him would not be refused; consequently his assistance was frequently solicited. In this affair charges had been brought against several midwives; and he was accused of complicity.

His first feeling was one of bewilderment. He knew that his proceedings were illegal; but the absurdity of bringing such matters into court amazed him. He had no idea of what the sentence was likely to be. I saw him constantly at that time; for he had been left free on bail. The evidence of witnesses did not interest him in the least. As for the cross-examination carried on by a bearded judge whose one object seemed to be to make it a kind of judicial allegory, it seemed to him a struggle against an automaton, who was but a second-rate dialectician.

One day, in response to a question of the judge, he said: "What does it matter?" "It has a bearing on the nature of the penalty," replied the judge. This reply worried him. The idea of an actual conviction had never occurred to him. But now, though he despised his judges, he set to work to obtain the intervention in his favor of anyone likely to be of use. It seemed absurd to stake his life on a card so sordid, so ridiculous, on a card that he himself had not chosen.

Being detained at Lausanne, I could not attend the trial.

He told me later that the proceedings throughout seemed to him unreal, with the unreality not of a dream but of some strange comedy, something rather ignoble and quite beside the point. Outside the theater, stage conventions are only to be found in law courts. The sudden effect of the words of the oath to be sworn on the twelve placid shopkeepers who constituted the jury and who had heard them read by the presiding judge in the tired tones of a schoolmaster, did not surprise him: it had seemed to fill them instantly with a desire to render a just verdict, to judge with all diligence and not to make any mistake. The idea that they might not be able to understand the case evidently did not trouble them. The assurance with which certain witnesses gave evidence, the hesitation of others, the attitude of the presiding judge in conducting the examination—the attitude of an expert in an assembly of ignoramuses—the animosity with which he addressed certain witnesses for the defense, all convinced Pierre that there was practically no connection between the actual facts and the ceremony going forward. At first he was deeply interested; the conduct of the defense intrigued him. But after a while he grew weary of it all. And while the last witnesses were being examined it occurred to him that any passing of judgment implies a failure to comprehend. The attempts of the judge and the leading counsel to bring this succession of events home to the jury in the terms of an ordinary crime, seemed to him so complete a parody that he could hardly help laughing. In this court, the power of justice loomed so large, the magistrates, the police and the assembled crowd were so entirely at one that indignation seemed out of place. Forgetting his smile, Pierre fell into that state of exasperated powerlessness, contempt and disgust which any gathering of fanatics or any great manifestation of human foolishness will produce.

He found his super's part extremely irritating. He seemed to be a lay figure acting some drama, utterly wrong psychologically, but appealing to a stupid house. Sick and jaded, with an impatience mingled with resignation, having lost even the wish to tell these people that they were mistaken, he awaited the end of the play, which would also end his ordeal.

It was only when he was alone in the cell in which he had been confined on the day before the opening of his trial, that he began to realize the seriousness of what had been happening. Only then did it come home to him that it was a question of a sentence, that his liberty was at stake, that all this empty comedy might end in his being condemned to this vegetable life for some indefinite period. Actual imprisonment, now that he had experienced it, did not trouble him much; but the vision of spending his time—for a prolonged period, perhaps—in this way, no matter what alleviation might be introduced into his lot, filled him with a foreboding intensified by his helplessness.

"*Sentenced to six months' imprisonment.*"

But I must not exaggerate. Pierre telegraphed that a reprieve had been granted him.

In the following letter, he wrote:

"I do not consider society bad, in the light of being capable of improvement; but I consider it futile. That is a very different matter. If I have spared no effort to procure my acquittal by those dolts or at any rate to procure my freedom, it is because I revolt at the idea of imprisonment for so absurd a reason.

" 'Absurd!' No, I should say 'irrational.' The possibility of re-forming society is a question which does not interest me. It is not the absence of justice from society that strikes me, but something deeper; my incapacity for adhering to any social order whatever. I am a-social, just as I am a-theist. All this would not matter if I were merely a student; but I know I shall be up against society all my life, and that I shall never be able to enter it without being false to my inner self."

Soon after this he wrote again: "There is one passion which is more profound than all others, a passion for which any definite attainable object is as nothing: a passion that is sheer desperation, one of the strongest supports of force."

"Sent to the foreign legion of the French army, August, 1914; deserted at the end of 1915."

This is false. He was not *sent* to the legion, he enlisted. It was impossible for him to look on at the war as a spectator. About the early origin of the war he did not care. He regarded the German army's invasion of Belgium merely as a proof that they knew how to conduct the war. And if he chose the legion, it was only be-cause it was the easiest regiment to enter. What he asked of war was conflict: he found something quite different—millions of men passive and motionless in the tumult. The resolve to leave the army, over which he had long been brooding, was taken on the day when a new kind of weapon, designed for the clearing of the trenches, was distributed to the legionaries. Hitherto short swords, which looked like weapons of war, had been served out to them for this purpose; but on that day they received broad-bladed knives, with chestnut-wood handles, horribly, contemptibly like ordinary kitchen knives.

I don't know how he succeeded in deserting and getting to Switzerland. But for once he was cautious; for he was reported "missing." (Hence my surprise at the word "deserted" in the English police report. It is true that he has now no reason for keeping it a secret.)

"Loses his fortune in various financial speculations."

He was always a gambler.

"Owing to his knowledge of foreign languages, he is appointed manager of a pacifist publishing business at Zurich, and thus comes into touch with Russian revolutionaries."

The son of a Swiss and a Russian, he naturally spoke German, French and Russian. English he had learned at college. He did not manage a publishing business, but he was at the head of the translation department of a society whose publications were not necessarily pacifist.

As stated in the report, he had the opportunity of associating with a group of young Bolshevists. And he realized at once that he had now to do with experts rather than with preachers. The group was not very cordial; but his trial, which was not yet forgotten, gave him the right to admittance. However, he never actually joined the group; for he could not stand its hierarchical methods, neither did he believe in the possibility of a Russian revolution. Consequently his relations with the members were merely those of comradeship. The younger men interested him more than the leaders. Of the latter all he knew was their speeches, delivered in a conversational tone, in an atmosphere heavy with smoke, to a score of listeners, lounging round the tables of cafés, showing their lack of interest in their faces. He never saw Lenin. While the expert knowledge of the Bolshevists and their passion for revolution inspired him with admiration, the doctrinal trash which accompanied it exasperated him. For he was in fact one of those for whom the revolutionary spirit must come from a revolution in being, one of those for whom revolution is a state.

When the Russian Revolution actually occurred he was dumfounded. One by one his comrades left Zurich, promising to make it possible for him to join them in Russia. It seemed to him right and necessary that he should go to Russia. And every time he saw one of his comrades off, it was with a vague feeling of being robbed.

After the October Revolution, he longed to go to Russia more intensely than ever. He wrote to his friends. But the leaders of the party were too busy to reply to letters from Switzerland. Their neglect saddened and infuriated him. "God knows I have seen men passionately possessed by an idea," he wrote to me, "men devoted to their kids, to their money, to their mistresses, even to their own hopes, as they might be to their own limbs; men intoxicated, obsessed, forgetting everything save the object of their desires, defending it or pursuing it with the utmost zeal. . . . If I were to say that I desired a million francs, I might be considered avaricious, if a hundred million, I might be called a dreamer, though a clever one perhaps. But if I say that I consider my youth is the card to play, then they seem to regard me as a poor visionary. But this is the game I am playing, believe me, just such a game as any poor wretch at Monte Carlo plays, a game, after which he will kill himself, if he loses. If I could cheat, I would. To have a heart, the heart of a man—and to be unaware that one is laying it bare to a woman who makes light of it is quite natural. In such a case one is liable to error, as much as you like. But in staking one's life one can make no mistake. That is clear, though to fix one's mind on one's own destiny might appear less wise than to center it on one's daily cares, one's dreams and one's hopes. . . . But somehow I shall play my game, if only I could find for my first journey those means which I have so stupidly squandered."

"Sent to Canton by the International at the end of 1918."

That is absurd. He had, at his lycée, made the acquaintance of one of my friends, Lambert, who was slightly our senior, and whose parents, French officials, had been friends of mine. They were merchants at Haïphong. Lambert, like most European children in that town, had been brought up by a Cantonese nurse, whose dialect we both spoke. He had gone out to Tonkin in the beginning of 1914. Soon disgusted with life in the colonies, he passed on to China, where he became a collaborator of Sun Yat-sen. On the declaration of war he did not join his regiment. He had been keeping up a correspondence with Pierre and promising to arrange for him to come out to Canton. And Pierre, although he did not count on this promise, nevertheless began to study the Chinese alphabet, with no great success. One day in June, 1918, he received a letter from Lambert, in which he said: "If you have decided to leave Europe, let me know. I can bring you out here.

Eight hundred dollars a month." He replied immediately. At the end of November, after the Armistice, he received another letter containing a check on a Marseilles bank, for a sum slightly in excess of the cost of his passage.

I had a little money at that time, so I went with him to Marseilles.

We spent a day sauntering through the town. A Mediterranean atmosphere, in which all work seems easy; streets bright in the pale gleam of winter sunshine, here and there the blue cloaks of soldiers, who have not yet been demobilized.

My companion's features have not greatly changed. His cheeks bear the traces of war: they are thinner, more tense, furrowed with vertical lines, which accentuate the hardness of the cold, gray eyes, the curve of the thin mouth, and the depth of the two lines which prolong it.

We have been walking and talking for a long while. One emotion possesses him—impatience. Although he tries to hide it, it betrays itself in the jerkiness of his conversation.

"Do you really understand all the intensity of remorse?" he asked.

I stop, astonished.

"Real remorse," he exclaimed, "not the feeling you find in books or on the stage, but resentment against oneself, oneself at some other time.

"A feeling which results from some serious action, and such deeds are not done by chance. . . ."

"That depends."

"No. For a man who has finished with the experiences of youth, remorse comes only from failure to profit by a certain lesson."

And then, suddenly perceiving my surprise: "I refer to the Russians." For we had just passed a shop window filled with the works of Russian novelists.

"There is a flaw in all they have written. This flaw is something akin to remorse. There is something lacking in these writers because they have not killed anyone. If their characters suffer after having killed, it is because the world has hardly changed for them. I say 'hardly.' In reality, I believe they would find the world completely transformed, with all its perspectives changed, converted, not into the world of a man who has committed a crime, but into the world of a man who has killed. I cannot believe in the reality of this unchanged world, or 'hardly' unchanged, if you will. For an assassin there are no crimes, only murders, that is, of course, if he thinks clearly."

"That idea might carry one far in its implications."

"There ought to be no implications."

After a short silence, he resumes:

"However tired with oneself one may be, one is never so tired as one says. To concentrate one's mind on some great deed, to pursue it, to be haunted, to be intoxicated by the thought of it, is perhaps——"

But he shrugs his shoulders and leaves his sentence incomplete.

"It is a pity you are not a believer. You would have made a famous missionary."

"Oh, no! First because things that pass for vile do not humiliate me. They go to make up a man. I accept them as I do cold in winter. I do not want to make them subject to any law. For another reason I should have made a bad missionary. I do not love mankind. I do not even love the poor, the people, those for whom I am going to fight. . . ."

"You prefer them to the others, which comes to the same thing."

"Not in the least."

"What do you mean? That you don't prefer them or that it does not come to the same thing?"

"I do prefer them, but merely because they are the conquered. Yes, and because, on the whole, they have more heart, they are more humane than the others; they possess the virtues of the vanquished. . . . One thing is certain, that I utterly detest the middle class into which I was born. But, as for the others, I am well aware that as soon as we have triumphed together, they will become contemptible. . . . All we have in common is our struggle, that is the one thing which is clear."

"Then why are you going?"

This time it was he who stopped.

"Have you taken leave of your senses?"

"I should have been surprised if I had. Someone would have noticed it."

"I am going because I don't want to make a fool of myself again in a law court, and this time for a serious reason. My life is nothing to me. But this is clear, precise, definite: I do want a certain kind of power and I shall get it, or so much the worse for me."

"So much the worse if you fail?"

"If I fail, I will begin all over again, either there or elsewhere. If I am killed, the problem will be solved."

His luggage had been taken on board. We shook hands warmly. He went to the bar, where, failing to get served, he began to read, alone. I hailed a taxi. Some young Italian beggar girls were singing on the quay. As I drove away their song pursued me, mingling with the smell of varnish, which came from the newly painted steamboat.

"Engaged by Sun Yat-sen with the title of 'Judicial Adviser,' and a salary of eight hundred dollars a month, commissioned, after our refusal to provide the Canton Government with experts, to reorganize and manage the Propaganda Department. (A position he now occupies.)"

It was true that on arriving at Canton, he learned with pleasure that he was to draw a monthly salary of eight hundred Mexican dollars. But after three months he discovered that the pay both of soldiers and civilians employed at Sun Yat-sen's Government was very uncertain. They all had to depend on commissions and bribes for their livelihood. By distributing among opium importers cards which enabled them to pass as secret agents of propaganda, and so to escape police investigation, he acquired one hundred thousand gold francs in seven months. Although it did not amount to very much, this money gave him a certain independence. Three months later Lambert left Canton; and Garine became head of the Propaganda Department, which was by no means a sinecure.

In his independent position, Pierre tried to transform the Propaganda Offices, hitherto more or less of a comic opera, into something serious. He took the finances under his control, dismissed almost the whole of the staff, and exacted strict loyalty from all whom he appointed. But, in spite of the promises of Sun Yat-sen, who was taking a deep interest in these reforms, the Government did not pay the new officials, and every day Pierre had to devise some way of remunerating them. Having annexed the Government Police Department to the Propaganda, he proceeded to take control of the town and secret police also. And, in defiance of the Government's decrees, he provided the Propaganda Department with funds by levying secret taxes on opium importers, keepers of brothels and gambling houses.

Hence we find the following statement in the police report:

"*Chose clever collaborators, all in the service of the International.*"

The facts are not quite so simple. Realizing that he was succeeding in creating the very instrument of which he had so long dreamed, he made every effort to save it from destruction. He was well aware that, however amiable he might appear, Sun Yat-sen would not hesitate to throw him over whenever it suited him to do so. So Pierre gathered round him young members of the Kuomintang; they lacked adroitness, but they were fanatics; and he succeeded in training them, with the help of a steadily increasing number of Russian agents, ex-soldiers whom hunger had driven out of Siberia and Northern China. Before the meeting of Borodin and Sun Yat-sen at Shanghai, the Moscow International had sounded Pierre, reminding him of the Zurich negotiations. Moscow found him prepared to collaborate. For in Moscow alone could he find the means of organizing Canton for the revolution and of substituting some permanent policy for the fluctuating desires of the Chinese. Consequently any influence he possessed over Sun Yat-sen was used to bring him into relations with Russia, and he inevitably became the collaborator and ally of Borodin, when the latter went to Canton.

From Pierre's letters I gathered that for some months after Borodin's arrival, he was extremely pleased, and that a definite

course of action had been decided on. Then his letters grew few
and far between; and it was with surprise that I learned that the
ridiculous little Government of Canton had launched upon a
struggle with England, with the object of establishing the unity
of China.

When, after my collapse, Pierre gave me that opportunity of
going out East which Lambert had given him, my only information as to the struggle between Canton and Hong Kong came
through the wireless; and it was in Ceylon, from a representative
of the Kuomintang at Colombo, that I received my first instructions. We had put into port. It was raining, as it can rain only in
the tropics. While I was listening to the old Cantonese, the car
was flying along beneath low clouds, brushing the dripping palm
leaves with her misty screen as we rushed past. I was endeavoring
to persuade myself that the words I was hearing did indeed represent realities—struggles, deaths, anguish. Back again on board, I
went into the bar, and still under the spell of the words of the
Cantonese, I took Pierre's most recent letters out of my pocket.
Rereading them, I began to realize the leader's part that he was
playing. There they are now—those letters—lying open on my
bunk. And, as I look at them, now, in my white cabin, I seem to
see a cloudy image of my friend, mingling with memories, some
clear, some vague, and rising from the background of an ocean
beaten by torrential rain and bordered by the long gray line of
the high plateaux of Ceylon merging into dark, motionless clouds.

"You know how ardently I long for your coming. But do not
expect to find here a life in accordance with the aspirations that
filled me when we parted. The power which I dreamed of and
which I exercise today, requires for its attainment a peasant's
diligence, unflagging energy, and a determination to add to what
we already possess, just that man or that element that is wanting.
That I should write this may surprise you. But the perseverance
which I lacked I have found here in my collaborators, and I believe I have myself acquired. My strength comes from my being
absolutely unscrupulous in the service of something other than
my own immediate interest."

Every day, as we approached Canton, I read the radiograms which were such excellent substitutes for his letters.

This part of the police report is extraordinarily incomplete. At the foot of the page are two big exclamation marks in blue pencil. Perhaps the note is an old one. But of quite a different order are the contents of the second page:

"Has placed the Propaganda on a sound financial basis by allocating to it a certain percentage of the donations sent by the Chinese outside Canton and of the subscriptions of the trades unions. Seems to be largely responsible for the enthusiasm with which the idea of war with the British troops is welcomed here. By dint of the persistent advocacy of his agents, has succeeded in getting compulsory trades unions recognized here.

"On the importance of this there is no need to insist. Borodin had demanded their foundation before organizing his strike pickets. Has organized seven different departments of police (detectives and ordinary) and as many departments of Propaganda. Has connected with the Political office and thereby with the International, the Commissionership of Justice (here again I need not insist) and the Commissionership of Finance. Finally, I inform you of a matter which is of the highest importance—that he is at present promulgating the decree the mere suggestion of which caused us to ask for the military intervention of Great Britain: the decree forbidding any ships which had put in to Hong Kong to enter the harbor of Canton, a decree of which Lord Sheppard said most truly that it was as certain to kill Hong Kong as cancer. This sentence is posted up in several Propaganda offices."

Beneath are five lines twice underlined in red pencil.

"I venture to lay special stress on the following: this man is seriously ill, suffering from severe malaria and from chronic dysentery. Some say his case is hopeless. In any event he cannot stay much longer in the tropics."

I am not so sure of that.

2 The Powers

Sнouts, cries, policemen giving directions—all the hullaba-loo of yesterday is beginning again. Now we are actually land-ing. Hardly anyone looks at Shameen with its little houses sur-rounded by trees. All eyes are fixed on the bridge, protected by trenches and barbed wire, and especially on the British and French gunboats close to us, with their guns turned on Canton. A motor-boat waits for us, for Klein and me.

Here we are in old China, China without Europeans. The boat glides slowly over the yellow, muddy water as if it were in a canal, between two rows of sampans, which with their wicker-work roofs suggest large gondolas. In the bows are women cook-ing food on tripods giving forth a strong smell of burning fat; behind them frequently a cat, a cage, or a chained monkey. Flit-ting from one to the other are the children, yellow little naked bodies, shaking their fringes of straight hair, more lively and animated than the cats though their little stomachs are bulging with nothing but rice. The babies, bundles of black linen tied to their mothers' backs, are asleep. The golden sunshine playing round the sampan awnings makes the women's blouses and trou-sers stand out boldly in blue patches against the brown back-ground, while the children climbing on the roofs look like yellow dots. On the quay the irregular line of American and Chinese houses; above, the sky, colorless in the dazzling brightness; and everywhere, over sampans, houses, water, light as froth, the gleam-ing sunshine into which we sail as into a mist.

Now we are alongside the quay. A car, which was waiting for us, carries us off at a fine pace. Our chauffeur in military uniform, constantly sounds his horn, and the crowd falls back instantly as if before an avalanche. Our flight is so swift that I can barely catch the vision of a blue and white multitude, of robed men set in a frame of sunblinds, inscribed with huge black letters and broken constantly by hawkers and laborers, who walk with agile gait, bent bodies and shoulders bowing beneath the bamboo rod, from two extremities of which dangle heavy loads. For a second one catches a glimpse of narrow lanes with worn pavements, ending in a grass plot in front of some horned erection or moldy pagoda. Then in a whirl there flies past us the car of some high official of the Republic, with two soldiers, parabellums* in hand, standing on the footboard.

Emerging from the commercial quarter, the car passes along a tropical boulevard bordered by houses with gardens; the boulevard is almost deserted; only now and again is the whiteness of the road broken by the silhouette of some soup-seller hobbling along and soon disappearing down a narrow lane. Klein, who is going to see Borodin, leaves me in front of a colonial house with overhanging roof and verandahs, surrounded by a railing, such as one sees round chalets near Paris. I pass through a little garden gate, which is open, then through a door, kept by two Cantonese soldiers in gray linen uniform. One takes my card and goes off. I wait, studying the remaining soldier. With his flat cap and parabellum at the waist, he reminds me of an officer of the Czar. But he wears his cap on the back of his head, and his shoes are made of straw. The other comes back. I may go up.

A narrow staircase leads to the first floor, where I find one fairly large room communicating with another in which men are talking rather loudly. Absolute silence reigns in this part of the town. Now and then through the broad palm leaves which darken the two windows, one catches faintly the distant sound of motor horns. Hanging in the doorway leading to the other room is nothing but a mat, and I can easily overhear the conversation, which is in English. The soldier points to the mat and leaves me.

". . . let Chen Chun-ming's army be organized. . . ."

On the other side of the mat, a man's voice goes on talking, but indistinctly.

"I have been saying this for more than a month. Besides Boro is as determined as I am. You must understand that this decree

---

* A parabellum was the particular kind of pistol used in Canton at this time. *Tr.*

alone [it is Garine's voice, a fist thumps the table, punctuating the words], this decree alone will enable us to destroy Hong Kong. This confounded Government must decide to move. . . ."

.   .   .   .

"Whether it's real or not, it must decide to move. We have need of it."

.   .   .   .

"And those who are over there, they will have to take thought; for they know as well as I do that this decree will smash their port like . . ."

The sound of steps. People are coming in and going out.

"What do the Committees propose?" There is the rustle of sheets of paper being turned over.

"Nothing much . . . [a fresh voice is speaking]. Most of them have nothing to suggest. Two ask for an increase of strike pay and for the allowance to laborers to be continued. Another proposes the execution of the workmen, who were the first to resume work. . . ."

"No, not yet."

"Why not?" (Chinese voices in hostile tones.)

"You can't use the death penalty like a broom."

I feel embarrassed. If anyone were to come out, I should look like a spy. But I can't very well blow my nose or begin to whistle. The only thing to be done is to push aside the mat and go in.

Gathered round a desk are Garine, in officer's khaki, and three young Chinese in white coats. While I am being introduced, one of the young Chinese mutters:

"There are people who won't touch a broom for fear of soiling their hands."

"There were not a few who regarded Lenin as hardly a revolutionary," replied Garine, turning round for an instant, with his hand on my shoulder. Then, addressing me:

"You don't look any younger. You come from Hong Kong?" And without waiting for my reply: "You have seen Meunier? Have you brought the papers?"

"They are in my pocket." I give them to him. At that moment, a soldier comes in, bringing a bulky envelope. Garine gives it to one of the Chinese, who translates:

"Report from the Kuala-Lumpur section. It calls our attention to the difficulties it is experiencing in raising funds."

"And in French Indo-China?" inquires Garine.

"I bring you six thousand dollars collected by Comrade Gérard. He says the militants are more enthusiastic than ever."

"Good. Come along."

He takes up his cap, puts his arm in mine, and we go out.

We are going to Borodin's. He lives quite near.

We pass along the silent, deserted boulevard, with its sidewalks of burnt-up grass. The glaring sunlight on the white dust dazzles one's eyes. Garine asks me a few rapid questions about my journey, then, as he walks, reads Meunier's report, bending back the leaves so as to keep them steady. I look at him: he has not aged materially; but I notice how every feature, overshadowed by the green lining of his peaked cap, bears the trace of illness: the hollows beneath his eyes stretch down on to his cheeks; his nose has grown thinner; the lines on each side of his mouth have deepened and broadened into furrows; and when he grows animated the nervous tension of his face, the result of fever and fatigue, has completely changed its expression. Around that head, bent forward, with eyes fixed on the paper, the air seems to tremble, as it always does at this hour in the haze of the dusty palm leaves which border the road. I should like to talk to him about his health. But he has finished reading, and making a little roll of the papers, he leans his chin upon it and says:

"Over there, too, things are beginning to go badly. Our sympathizers are growing cold. The servants are going back to their employers. And here, all we have to rely upon are young fools for whom a revolution is like the third act in a Chinese comic opera. . . . It is quite impossible to increase strike pay. And it wouldn't help if we did. The best remedy for a sick strike is victory."

"Has Meunier nothing to propose?"

"He says that the general feeling is not bad as yet: the weak

are wavering because England is browbeating them, with her detectives and her terrorist methods, the resumption of flogging, for
example. On the other hand, he reports that the Chinese committees are proposing to carry off some two or three hundred brats,
children of the guilty or of the suspected. 'They could be brought
here,' he says, 'and treated well, but only restored to their parents
when they came to fetch them. So they would not be likely to go
back to Hong Kong tomorrow. . . .' 'For this,' he adds, 'is the
time when people are taking their country holiday. This would
give the others food for thought.' But such measures will not
carry us far."

We reach Borodin's house. It is like Garine's but yellow. As we
cross the threshold, Garine stops and salutes an aged little Chinese
who is coming out. He shakes hands with Garine, and says slowly,
in French, in a feeble voice:

"Monsieur Garine, I came here hoping to meet you. I think it
would be well for us to have a talk. When can I see you?"

"Whenever you like, Monsieur Chen-Dai. I will come to you
this . . ."

"No, no," he cries, waving his hand as if to calm Garine, "I
will come to you, I will come. Will five o'clock suit you?"

"Certainly. I shall expect you then."

As soon as I heard his name, I scrutinized him carefully. Like
the faces of most of the old lettered class of China, Chen-Dai's
was corpselike, no doubt because, seen from a distance, it seemed
nothing but teeth, prominent cheekbones overshadowing the
sunken orbits of the eyes, and a barely perceptible nose. Drawing
nearer, however, one became aware of animated, almond-shaped
eyes and a smile at one with the extreme courtesy of his words
and the distinction of his voice, all this considerably mitigating
his ugliness. He plunges his hands into his sleeves like a priest and
moves his shoulders slightly forward as he speaks. This makes me
think of Klein, for he also, while conversing, moves his whole
body; but Chen-Dai appears finer, older, subtler. He is wearing the
trousers and the white linen military coat with a stiff collar, affected by the leaders of the Kuomintang. His rickshaw man—he

has a private rickshaw man, who is black—is waiting for him. Taking short steps, he goes towards him, enters his rickshaw and drives off slowly and solemnly, sitting well back in his seat, gravely shaking his head, as if he were weighing certain arguments that occurred to him.

After we have watched him for a while, we pass by the guards, and, without being announced, traverse a large empty hall, where we meet another sentinel in khaki embroidered with orange (is this a mark of distinction?). It is no mat this time that faces us, but a closed door.

"Is he alone?" Garine inquires of the sentinel, who nods his reply. We knock and enter. The room is spacious. A full-length portrait of Sun Yat-sen, about two meters high, hangs in the middle of a whitewashed wall. At a desk, covered with papers carefully classified and arranged, sits Borodin, with his back to the light, blinking as he watches us enter, looking rather surprised (at my entrance, no doubt). He rises and comes towards us. Now I can see his face in miniature beneath the massive, wavy hair, thrown back from his forehead, which was all I could perceive when he was seated bending over his desk. With his half-closed eyes, his drooping mustache, and his prominent cheekbones, he suggests an intelligent wild animal. He may be about forty.

During his conversation with Garine his attitude is almost military. Garine introduces me and summarizes Meunier's report, which he has placed on the desk. Borodin takes up the paper and adds it to a pile of documents, beneath an engraving, another portrait of Sun Yat-sen. One special detail seems to interest him particularly. He makes a note of it as he talks. Then in animated, anxious tones the discussion continues.

"Which was the point that he noted?" I asked Garine as we took our leave.

"The threat of flogging. That must be passed on," he said.

We go back to Garine's house for lunch. My companion walks with an anxious air and eyes cast down.

"Things are not going well?"

"Oh! I am used to that."

In front of his house, an orderly is waiting for him to give him a report. Garine reads it as he goes up the steps, signs it at a wicker table on the verandah, and gives it back to the orderly, who goes off, running. Garine appears more and more worried. After some hesitation, I inquire the reason:

"Well?"

"Well. That's that."

His tone is enough.

"Things are going badly?"

"Rather. Strikes are all very well. But they are not enough. Something more is necessary: the execution of the decree forbidding Chinese ships to touch at Hong Kong as well as all foreign boats bound for Canton. The decree was signed more than a month ago, but it has not yet taken effect. The British know that the strike can't go on forever; and they ask what we are going to do next. Do they expect any great result from Chen Chun-ming's expedition? They provide him with arms, instructors and money. When the decree was signed the Hong Kong residents were so alarmed that they telegraphed a demand for military intervention to London. The decree has remained in its drawer. I am perfectly aware that its execution would give ground for war. Well, and what then? If they couldn't face war? If Hong Kong were to be . . ." He makes the gesture of turning a screw.

"Only think, that by depriving the Hong Kong port of the custom of the Cantonese companies alone we should reduce its revenue by one-third. That spells ruin."

"Well?"

"What do you mean by 'well'?"

"What are you waiting for?"

"Chen-Dai. We are not yet the Government. And this policy of ours will fail if that old stupid should take it into his head to oppose it."

He ponders for a moment.

"Even when one is very well informed, it is impossible to get at the whole truth. I should like to ascertain whether or no he is

concerned in what Tang and those swine of his are preparing
for us. . . ."

"Tang?"

"He is only one of the generals, and of no great importance.
But he is preparing a coup d'état. He wants to thwart us. That is
his concern. He himself is of no account. He merely represents a
risk we must run. The risk is unavoidable. What matters is the
support he can rely upon. British, of course. British funds are now
at the disposal of all who oppose us. No doubt every soldier in
his regiment is in the pay of the secret intelligence department.
And, unfortunately, Hong Kong is near enough for Tang and the
others to take refuge there when they are beaten. And then there
is Chen-Dai, the honest Chen-Dai, whom you saw just now. I am
sure that Tang, were he to be victorious, which he will not be,
would offer to place him at the head of the Government, being
himself quite content to rule in Chen-Dai's name. Chen-Dai, and
Chen-Dai alone, could replace the Committee of Seven. The societies, both public and secret, would accept him; there is no
doubt about that. And for our policy he would substitute moving 'appeals to the peoples of the world,' like the one he has just
made and to which Gandhi and Russell have replied. Oh! this
paper age of ours is grand! I see it all—compliments, claptrap,
return of confiscated British goods, the English smoking their
cigars on our quays, the destruction of everything we have done.
All these Chinese towns are as soft as jellyfish. We are the only
backbone. I have just been talking to Borodin about it. He is
obviously anxious. I am writing for more reports. . . ."

Just as we are sitting down to table, another orderly arrives,
bearing a document. Garine takes a knife from the table, cuts
open the envelope, sits down and reads:

"Good. That's all right."

The orderly goes.

"You wouldn't believe what a number of toads there are crawling round Chen-Dai. The day before yesterday, the creatures,
who pose as being out for ideas, held a meeting. They assembled
on a square near the river. He was there—weary and dignified as

you saw him just now—of course not to speak. And you should
have seen those stump orators mounting tables and declaiming
over the heads of a not very enthusiastic crowd, against a background of corrugated iron, pagoda horns and ends of twisted
zinc. Chen-Dai stood a little apart, but not too far away, surrounded by a respectful circle. A few roughs attacked him; for
he is hated by all the Terrorists. With him were a few chosen
disciples by whom he was defended. The police superintendent
had both assailants and defenders locked up. And today his de-
fender in chief—this is his cross-examination—asks the examining commissioner to give him an appointment even in the police.
What do you think of that? Now, look at this other paper. . . ."

He gives it to me. It is the copy of a list drawn up by General
Tang: Garine, Borodin, Nicolaïeff, Hong, and some Chinese
names. At the top of the page, these words: "Have them arrested
without delay."

During the whole of lunch the talk turns on Chen-Dai, the
enemy. Garine can't think of anything else.

Just before he died Sun Yat-sen said: "Borodin's word is my
word." But Chen-Dai's word is his also; and there was no need
for him to say so.

His public career began in Indo-China. What did he go to
Cholon for? Surely that great town can have had no attractions
for such a scholar. . . . He became one of the organizers—nay,
more, the prime mover—of the Kuomintang there. Whenever the
Government of Cochin-China, prompted by the wealthy guilds or
on its own initiative, intervened against one of the members of
the party, Chen-Dai appeared—giving work or money to those
whom the police were trying to reduce to starvation, raising
funds to send exiles and their families home to China, founding a
hospital for the members of the party, against whom the doors of
the regular hospital were closed.

He was at that time president of the Cholon section. Finding it
impossible to raise the necessary funds by subscriptions, he appealed to the Chinese banks, who refused him a loan. Then he
offered his property at Hong Kong, a third of his estate as se-

curity. This the banks accepted; and the building began. Three months later, as the result of wire-pulling during an election, he was deprived of the presidency of the party, and at the same time his contractors informed him, that, owing to certain alterations in the plans, they were obliged to increase their charges. The banks refused any further overdraft, and, worse still, threatened by the Cochin-China Government, which had it in its power to expel their managers at twenty-four hours' notice, they began to put difficulties in the way of paying the sum promised. Chen-Dai sold the property he had pledged as security, and the building was proceeded with, but further funds were needed. Meanwhile a secret movement against him was going on in the heart of the Kuomintang. Chen-Dai was aware of it. It grieved him, but he went on with the work; and while electoral agents in white sweaters were busy in Chinese cafés after the siesta, insinuating to artisans, half awake and dazed by the heat, that his attitude was, to say the least of it, strange, Chen-Dai was selling the old family house at Canton. Even when the hospital was finished, various commissions had to be paid; and, after having consulted Grosjean, dealer in antiques at Pekin, he parted with his painted scrolls and famous collection of Sung jade. What remained to him? On what could he depend for his modest livelihood? He was the only member of the party who did not drive a motorcar. That was why I had seen him driving in his rickshaw, nothing loath to display a poverty which proved his highmindedness.

For though sincere, this highmindedness is tinged with a certain shrewdness. Like Lan-Yit, like General Hsu, he is a poet. All the same, it was by him that the boycott which a few clever merchants originally directed against the Japanese alone was converted into the effectual weapon which we know today. It was he who applied it to the British, it was he who, being conversant with Western trade (a pupil of the Jesuit Fathers, he reads, speaks and writes both English and French with ease), so directed Sun Yat-sen's propaganda as to give confidence to the British; it was he who gave the information bureau control of the prohibitions

to purchase, allowing the British to accumulate goods with which
the Chinese world suddenly refused to have anything to do.

But the authority he exercises is spiritual, above everything;
Garine says it is quite right to compare him to Gandhi. His influence, though less extensive, is of the same order as a Mahatma's.
It is above politics, it touches the soul, it is not of this world. But
though they may exercise much the same influence, the men
themselves differ widely. At the heart of Gandhi's mission is the
passionate, all-consuming desire to teach men how to live. There
is nothing of that in Chen-Dai. He wishes to be neither leader
nor example, but adviser. The death of Sun Yat-sen, at which he
was present, was the saddest hour of his life. But he held himself
entirely aloof from politics; and when invited to succeed the dictator as leader of the party, he refused, not because he was afraid
of responsibility, but because the part of arbitrator seemed to
accord with his character better than any other. Moreover, he
would not allow himself to accept an office which would absorb
all his activities and convert him into something entirely different
from what he aspired to be: the guardian of the Revolution. His
whole life is a moral protest, and his hope of victory is the nearest
approach to strength attainable by that profound unconquerable
weakness which is so common in his race.

Possibly in this very weakness may be found the key to his
present attitude. Has his passionate desire for years really been
the deliverance of Southern China from British domination? Yes.
But having spent years in defending and directing an oppressed
people whose cause was unquestionably just, he has grown accustomed to the rôle, and today he has—unconsciously, of course
—arrived at the position of preferring that rôle to the victory of
those whom he is defending. He thinks more of his protest than
he does of victory. To be the soul and the expression of an oppressed people is a part for which he is eminently suited.

He has no children, not even a daughter. He married; his wife
died. He married again. In a few years, his second wife died childless. When he dies there will be no one to perform his anniversary
rites. His sorrow at such a situation is calm, persistent, incon-

solable. He is an atheist, or believes himself to be; but this solitude in life and death obsesses him. It will be to a reborn China that he will bequeath the inheritance of his glory. Alas! . . . He who was once rich will die almost poor; and the grandeur of such a death will impress millions of men. In the end solitude. . . . Everyone knows this; and they know also that this solitude binds him closer to the destiny of his party every day.

"A noble figure of a victim preparing his own biography," said Garine. He would regard any attempt to fulfill his wishes as nothing short of betrayal. Swayed by temperament and by habit, he has forgotten the very possibility of drawing any logical consequences from his attitude. To undertake and control any decisive struggle no more occurs to him than the idea of becoming Pope would occur to a Catholic. One day, when Garine was concluding a discussion on the Third International with the words: "But the Third International has actually *made* the Revolution," Chen-Dai's only response was to place his two hands on his heart with a gesture at once evasive and restrictive. "And," said Garine, "I never realized more clearly the immense distance that separated us."

He is thought to be capable of energy; but in reality he is only capable of one particular kind of energy—that which leads to a man's conquest of himself. His success in building a hospital and overcoming such formidable obstacles was entirely due to his disinterestedness. He was driven to impoverish himself; and he did it, possibly without any effort, proud to think that few would have been capable of such self-sacrifice. In his case, as in that of the Christians, charity is his main motive, but while with Christians charity is pity, with him it is solidarity: members of the party alone are admitted to his hospital. The grandeur of his life proceeds from that contempt for temporal things which characterizes all his public actions. But this contempt, sincere though it be, is not incompatible with a sense of its utility, and Chen-Dai is not averse to his disinterestedness being recognized throughout China. Indeed it becomes the center of his whole being, giving him a sense of superiority over other men. His self-denial is the expression of a calm and conscious pride, which accords with the sweetness of his disposition and with his literary culture.

Like all those who dominate the masses, this courteous old man with his dignified gestures, is possessed—possessed by Justice; that Justice, which he feels himself called upon to maintain and which he almost identifies with his own ideas. The problems with which this defense of Justice confronts him, occupy him in the same way as pleasure and ambition occupy others. He thinks of nothing else. Justice is the noblest of all human aspirations, the god who must be worshiped above all others. He believes in Justice as a child believes in a statue, in a pagoda. He had always experienced a profound, absorbing craving for Justice. Now it possesses him like a fetish. It may always have been his heart's desire, but now it is a guardian divinity, without whose approval nothing must be attempted, to forget whom would be to court some mysterious vengeance. . . . The greatness of his divinity has grown old with him; it has become pale and deformed. But it still possesses him, and, concealing it beneath sweetness, smiles and mandarin graces, he withdraws from the daily revolutionary round, which absorbs the rest of us, and moves in the dream world of a monomaniac, which is strewn with the relics of aristocracy. It is this mono-mania which enhances his influence and his prestige. In China the sense of justice though it has always been strong, has been also passionate and confused. Chen-Dai's life—growing into a legend already—and his age make him a symbol. The Chinese are as anxious to see him respected as they are anxious to obtain recognition of their racial virtues. He is for the moment almost sacred. And for the present the anti-British propaganda must follow the direction he has marked out for it, carrying everything with it. As yet it is too soon. . . .

As the meal proceeds, report after report is brought in. Garine, growing more and more perturbed, devours the contents of each and places them on the floor by his chair.

The whole of that world of aged mandarins, smugglers of opium and of obscene photographs, of scholars turned bicycle dealers, of Parisian barristers, of intellectuals of every kind, pining for advancement, who gravitate round Chen-Dai, the whole of that world is well aware that in reality the present state of affairs depends absolutely on the Representatives of the International and the Propaganda, that they alone maintain this great attack on British power, that they alone stand between a return to the old conditions, to a republic of bureaucrats and mandarins, and the new republic of doctors, lawyers and engineers. "We are the backbone," Garine said just now. And the reports would seem to show that all, though perhaps Chen-Dai, who disapproves of any military coup d'état, is unaware of it, are gathering round General Tang, hitherto practically unknown in Canton, but who is their superior in point of courage. In Chen-Dai's circle there are a number of British agents. . . . When I express my surprise that such a movement can go on without Chen-Dai's knowing of it, Garine thumps on the table and says:

"He doesn't want to know. He doesn't want to undertake the responsibility; but I believe he is willing to suspect."

Two o'clock

At the Propaganda Office with Garine. On the wall of the room assigned to me, is a portrait of Lenin and one of Sun Yat-sen. Other decorations are two-colored posters: one represents a Chinese giving a good kick to the rounded back of John Bull, whose arms and legs are in the air, while on the horizon stands a Russian in fur cap, radiating beams of light like a sun. The other represents a British soldier with a machine gun, firing on a crowd of Chinese women and children, who raise their hands to the sky. On the first, in European characters, is the year, "1925," and in Chinese the word "today"; on the second "1900," and the word "yesterday." A yellow blind saturated with sunlight is drawn over the large window. On the ground is a pile of newspapers, which an orderly is coming to fetch. The departments' secretaries cut out all political articles, and classify them carefully. On the commandeered Louis XVI desk lies a caricature, a duplicate, doubtless, which has been forgotten: it is a hand, and printed on each finger are the words, "Russians, students, women, soldiers, peasants"; in the palm is "Kuomintang." Garine crumples it up and throws it into the wastepaper basket. Is he growing cautious, too? A set of cardboard drawers stands against the wall, in which is a door leading to Garine's room. This room, too, is full of the yellow light coming in through the blind. There are no posters on the walls, and a safe takes the place of the drawers. A commissionaire stands at the door.

Nicolaiëff, commissioner of police, lounges in an armchair. He is a fat man, one of those fair, stout people, to whom a slightly *retroussé* nose gives an air of affability. He listens to Garine with his eyes closed and his hands folded over his stomach.

"Well," said Garine, "you have been reading all these reports that have been sent to you?"

"Busy with them till this minute."

"Good. And what is your opinion? Is Tang going to oppose us?"

"Without a doubt. Here is the list of the Chinese he intends to have arrested."

"Do you think Chen-Dai knows of this?"

"They want to make use of him, that is all."

The commissioner speaks in French with a very slight accent. The tone of his voice—in spite of the clearness of his replies, one might almost think he was speaking to a woman and expect him to add "my dear"—the calm on his face, the unction of his attitude suggest some venerable priest.

"Are there any members of the secret intelligence department that you can make use of?"

"Nearly all of them."

"Good: about half of the town is ready to proclaim that Tang, who is in British pay, is preparing a coup d'état which will transform Canton into a British colony; the working-class quarters, of course. Then we can rely on about one-fourth of the trades union officials. They are excellent and very important. For our remaining supporters we must go to the unemployed with those

numbers of the *Canton Gazette* which declare that Tang's friends
have demanded the suppression of the strike pay which comes
from us."

"Let us see, how many registered unemployed are there?"

"Don't trouble to look at the report. There are twenty-six
thousand."

"Right. We shall have enough."

"And, in addition, a few picked men, who, after the meetings
of the party this evening, will vaguely insinuate that Tang is
about to be expelled, that he knows it, and is looking for support
elsewhere."

"Agreed."

"You are absolutely certain that there is not a shadow of evidence, and that it is impossible to have Tang arrested?"

"Alas!"

"What a pity! He will lose nothing by waiting."

The fat man takes his leave, his documents under his arm.
Garine rings. The orderly brings in several visiting cards which
he puts on the table, while helping himself to a cigarette out of
Garine's case, which lies open.

"Show in the delegates from the trades unions."

Seven Chinese come in, one behind the other, silently. They
are in white linen suits, with high buttoned up collars. Young and
old, they range themselves in a half-circle round the table. One
of the oldest half-sits on the desk. He is the interpreter. They all
listen to Garine.

"There will probably be a coup d'état against us this week. You
know as well as I do the opinions of General Tang and his friends.
There is no need for me to remind you of how often Comrade
Borodin has been obliged to intervene with the Council to prevent the suppression of strike pay at Canton. You represent those
unemployed who made every effort to prove their real worth at
the recent trades union meetings. I know I can rely upon you.
Here is the list of those who are suspected by Tang or by Chen-
Dai and who are to be arrested at the outset."

He gives them a list. They read it and look at one another.

"You see that your names are included. Consequently from the moment of your leaving this office . . ."

The interpreter in a monotonous voice translates each sentence as it is spoken. The others respond with a murmur. It is a litany.

"You must not go home. Each of you will stay at the office of his union and will sleep there. As for you——" He points to three Chinese. "Your offices are too far away to be defended. You will fetch your papers and bring them here. I have had offices prepared for you. You will give definite instructions to your strike pickets. We must be in a position to assemble all our men within an hour."

As he spoke he passed round the cigarette case. When it returned to him, he closed it with a slight click and rose.

The Chinese go out one after the other as they came in. They shake hands with him as they pass. He rings.

"Ask this person to write down what he is calling about," he says to the orderly, giving him back one of the cards. "And then show in Lo-Moi."

Lo-Moi is stout, clean-shaven, his face covered with pimples. He stands respectfully in front of Garine, with eyes cast down.

"During the recent phases of the strike, at Hong Kong and here, there has been too much talking. If our comrades think they are in parliament they make a mistake! Now, once and for all, such speeches must be accompanied by deeds: if the employer's house is too far away or too difficult they can always take possession of his motorcar. I say again, your spouters must have no doubt as to what they are attacking. Don't let me have to repeat this."

The little Chinese bows and goes out. The orderly returns with the card Garine had given back to him, and handing it to him, says:

"About tanks."

Garine raises his eyebrows.

"That is Borodin's business."

He writes Borodin's address on the card and a few words (of introduction, doubtless). Two knocks at the door.

"Come in."

A tall, strongly built European, with Roman features and an American mustache, wearing an officer's khaki uniform like Garine's, opens the door.

"Good morning, Garine."

He speaks French, but he also is Russian.

"Good morning, General."

"Well, and has he made up his mind, this Monsieur Tang?"

"You know?"

"Vaguely, yes. I have just seen Boro. He is really ill, the poor fellow. The doctor says he is afraid of an attack."

"Which doctor: Myroff or the Chinese?"

"Myroff. And Tang."

"Two or three days longer."

"He has only his thousand men."

"Yes, and the additional ones he can buy with their money and England's. Fifteen to eighteen hundred in all. And what is the shortest time that it will take the Red Army to get here? Six days?"

"Eight. Has the Propaganda been at work among Tang's troops?"

"Not much. Most of his men are Honanese or Yunnanese."

"That is a pity. How many machine guns have they?"

"About twenty."

"You may have between five and six hundred cadets in the town, Garine, but no more."

"Our forces will increase as soon as we open hostilities."

"I agree. As soon as Tang's troops are on the alert, you will send the cadets which are at your disposal, with the machine gun section and the police bringing up the rear. We shall come from the opposite direction."

"All right."

The man goes out.

"Tell me, Garine, is that your chief of staff?"

"Yes, Gallen."

"He looks like an officer of the Czar."

"So do the others."

Another Chinese comes in, his short white hair brushed up. He walks up to the desk, touches it with the tips of his fingers, and stands waiting.

"You have all your unemployed well in hand?"

"Yes, sir."

"How many could you assemble in half an hour?"

"How, sir?"

"With the greatest possible haste and without calculating means of transport."

"More than ten thousand."

"Good. Thank you."

Thereupon the Chinese with the beautiful white hair goes out.

"Who was that?"

"Our paymaster. A scholar. An ex-mandarin. Quite a story. . . ."

He calls the orderly.

"Send all those who are waiting to the Commissioner of Police."

But another Chinese has calmly entered through the half-open door, knocking twice as he passes. Stout like Nicolaïeff, clean shaven, with a heavy mouth and an almost featureless face. He smiles a broad smile, displaying teeth stopped with gold. He holds an enormous cigar. He says in English:

"The Vladivostok boat has come in, Monsieur Garine?"

"This morning."

"How much gasoline on board?"

"Fifteen hundred . . ." (then follows a word indicating a Chinese measure, with which I am unacquainted).

"When will it be delivered?"

"Tomorrow. Here is the check, as usual."

"Would you like me to sign it now?"

"No, everything in its time."

"Then, good-by, Monsieur Garine. We meet tomorrow."

"Tomorrow."

"He buys the supplies that we obtain from the U.S.S.R.," Garine whispers to me in French, while the Chinese is going out. "The Kuomintang is not rich just now; and we need all kinds of things: gasoline, petroleum, weapons, teachers."

He gets up, goes to the door, looks out. No one is there. He returns to his desk, and begins to read a packet of documents: the latest reports from Hong Kong. From time to time he hands me certain papers, that he wants me to classify separately. To get a little air, I turn the handle which controls the ventilator, and the sheets of paper fly away immediately. Garine stops the ventilator, gathers the sheets together, and goes on underlining sentences with red pencil. Reports, reports, reports. While I am making a summary of those he has selected, he goes out. Reports.

The strike that is paralyzing Hong Kong cannot last more than three days in its present form.

Supposing that the employees who no longer receive strike pay wait another ten days before resuming work, making thirteen in all; then, unless Borodin has thought of some new course of action within the next fortnight, British ships will be in the port of Canton. Hong Kong will revive, and the whole lesson of the strike will be in vain. Hong Kong has received a stunning blow: the banks have lost and are still losing heavily. Moreover, the Chinese have perceived that Great Britain is not invulnerable. At present, our agents and those of the British banks are supporting a town of three hundred thousand inhabitants, in which no one is working. Who will be the first to grow tired of this game? We shall, inevitably. And, over by Wai-Chow, Chen Chun-ming's army is preparing to take action.

As for the refusal to allow any ships bound for Canton to put into Hong Kong—if such a prohibition is to be effectual there must be a decree; and as long as Chen-Dai is in power the decree will not be signed.

Hong Kong: the British Empire. Behind Chen Chun-ming's army: the British Empire. Behind the cloud of locusts surrounding Chen-Dai: the British Empire.

On the desk are a few books: the Chinese-Latin Dictionary of the Jesuit Fathers, two medical books in English, one on dysen-

tery, the other on malaria. On Garine's return, I inquire whether
it is true that he neglects his health.

"No, it is not true! Of course it isn't! I may not always have
been as careful as I ought, but that was because I had other
things to do; and it is of no great importance. I am perfectly
well aware that if I considered my health I should return to
Europe. But I should stay there as short a time as possible. And
how could I possibly go now?"

I did not insist; for I saw that the subject irritated him. And
the orderly had just brought in a letter, which he was reading
attentively. Then he passed it to me, remarking merely: "The
words in red pencil have been written by Nicolaiëff."

It is another list, like the one given to Garine when we sat
down to lunch, only longer: Borodin, Garine, E. Chen, Sun-Fo,
Liao Chong-hoi, Nicolaiëff, Semioneff, Hong, numerous Chinese,
whose names I do not know. Nicolaiëff has written in a corner
of the paper in red pencil: *"Complete list of persons to be arrested
and executed on the spot"*; and at the end of the list he has
scribbled in ink: *"They are having proclamations engraved."*

At five o'clock, the orderly brings in another card. Garine
rises, goes to the door and draws back to let Chen-Dai pass. The
little old man enters, sits down in an armchair, stretches out his
legs, plunges his hands into his sleeves, and looks at Garine, who
has returned to his desk, kindly, but with a certain irony. He
says nothing.

"You wanted to see me, Monsieur Chen-Dai?"

He nods assent, slowly takes his hands out of his sleeves, and
says in a feeble voice:

"Yes, Monsieur Garine, yes. I do not think I need ask whether
you are aware of the acts of violence which have been occurring
lately in rapid succession."

He speaks with great deliberation, raising his first finger.

"I have too high an opinion of your ability to think you can be
ignorant of them, considering the constant relations you must be
in with M. Nicolaiëff, by virtue of your office.

"Monsieur Garine, these acts of violence are too frequent."

Garine makes a gesture which implies: what can I do?

"We understand one another, Monsieur Garine, we understand one another."

"Monsieur Chen-Dai, you know General Tang, do you not?"

"General Tang is a loyal and just man."

And, slowly putting his right hand on the desk, as if to emphasize what he says:

"I depend on the Central Committee to take effective measures to suppress violence. I believe that the best plan would be to accuse publicly all those who are known to be leaders of the Terrorist groups. Monsieur Garine, I want to know what attitude you will assume, you and your friends, towards the proposals I am about to make."

He withdraws his hand and puts it back into his sleeve.

"It cannot be denied, Monsieur Chen-Dai," replies Garine, "that for some time the instructions you have been giving to your friends have been absolutely contrary to all our wishes."

"You have been misinformed, Monsieur Garine. You must have had some bad advisers, or perhaps your information is derived from an unreliable source. I have not given any instructions."

"Should we say 'suggestions'?"

"Not even suggestions. . . . I have explained my way of thinking, given my opinion, that is all." He smiles more and more. "I can't think that you can take objection to that."

"I set great store on your opinion, sir, but I should like—we —the Committee—would like to receive information concerning it in a different way."

"Than through its police, Monsieur Garine? So should I. Your Committee might, for example, have sent me one of its members, a well-authorized person. There is no reason why it should not, and the proof of that is that we are together."

"A few months ago, there was no need for our Committee to appoint me to ascertain your opinions. You yourself kept them informed. . . ."

"Then the question is whether you or I have changed. Now,

if it is you . . . I am no longer young, Monsieur Garine, and perhaps you will admit that my life . . ."

"No one dreams of attacking your character. We all have the greatest respect for it. We know what China owes you. But . . ."

He had bowed, smiling. On hearing that "but," he draws himself up and looks anxiously at Garine.

". . . but you can't doubt the rightness of the course we are taking. All the same, you are trying to thwart us."

Chen-Dai does not reply, hoping doubtless that Garine will feel uncomfortable and be constrained to speak. After a moment's silence, however, Chen-Dai continues:

"Perhaps it would be advisable to make our position clear. . . . Your ability, Monsieur Garine, and that of certain members of the Committee cannot be denied. But you act in a spirit of which we cannot altogether approve. For example, what importance you attach to the military school of Whampoa!"

His gesture recalls a Catholic priest deploring the sins of the faithful.

"I cannot be suspected of being too fond of the ancient Chinese customs, which I have helped to destroy. But I believe, nay, I am firmly convinced that no policy the Party may adopt can be worthy of it and of that which we expect from it unless it be founded on justice. You want to attack?"

Then, in a voice still feeble:

"No. . . . Let the imperialists assume all the responsibility. A few more assassinations of unhappy wretches will do more for our cause than all the cadets at Whampoa. . . ."

"You do not value their lives."

As he throws back his head and looks Garine in the face, he has the air of an old Chinese schoolmaster moved to indignation at some question put by a pupil. I believe him to be very angry; but he does not show it. His hands are still in his sleeves. Is he thinking of the firing at Shameen? At length, as if stating his final conclusion, he says:

"It is better than sending them to be shot down by Hong Kong volunteers, don't you think?"

"But that is out of the question. You know as well as I do that there will be no war, that the British will not make war. Every day proves to all Chinese—and the Party endorses the proof—how stupid this European bluff is, this power that relies on bayonets hanging on the wall and cannon which are not fired."

"I am not so sure as you appear to be. War would not be unwelcome to you. It would give you an opportunity of demonstrating your skill, which is remarkable, it would enable Monsieur Borodin to display his organizing powers and General Gallen his military gifts."

(With what contempt he utters that word "military"!)

"Is not the salvation of the whole of China a just and noble cause?"

"You are very eloquent, Monsieur Garine. But we do not look at things in the same light. You are fond of making experiments and of using for them anything that comes to your hand. Here it is a question of the people of this town. Frankly, I should prefer them not to be employed in this experiment. I like to read tragedies. I admire them. But I do not like to see them happening in my own family. If I were to venture to express myself in too emphatic a term, in a term which would exaggerate my idea, I should use one which is often on your lips, and I should say that I cannot without regret see my compatriots made into 'fodder for cannon.'"

"To me it seems that if any nation has been experimented on for the sake of the whole world it is not China but Russia."

"That is true. . . . But perhaps she had need of it. You and your friends, you feel this need. And certainly if danger were to present itself, you would not run away."

He bows.

"But, Monsieur Garine, this does not appear to me to be a reason for seeking the danger."

"I should like—I ardently desire—the Chinese to be tried by Chinese courts, to be actually, not merely theoretically, protected by Chinese policemen, to possess in fact, and not merely in principle, the land of which they are the lawful rulers. But we have no right to attack Britain in any overt manner or by any act of the Government. We are not at war. China is China; and the rest of the world is the rest of the world."

Garine is nonplused. He makes no reply; and Chen-Dai resumes:

"I know only too well what would be the tendency of such an attack, how it would serve to keep up that fanaticism which came in here with you. Fanaticism the value of which I do not question, but which, to my keen regret, I myself cannot accept, Monsieur Garine. Foundations should be built on truth alone."

Parting his hands, he makes a gesture of apology.

"Do you think, Monsieur Chen-Dai, that Great Britain cares so much about justice as you do?"

"No; and for that very reason, we shall end by conquering the British without recourse to violence, without fighting. In less than five years nothing coming from England will be allowed to enter China."

He is thinking of Gandhi. Garine, tapping the table with the end of his pencil, replies deliberately:

"If Gandhi had not intervened—and he also in the name of justice—to break the last *Hartal*, the British would be out of India today."

"If Gandhi had not intervened, Monsieur Garine, India, which now offers us the noblest example of our time, would be nothing but an Asiatic country in rebellion."

"We are not here to offer a noble example of defeat."

"Thank you for a comparison which honors me more than you realize, but of which I am not worthy. Gandhi knows how to redeem the errors of his compatriots by his own sufferings."

"And by the lashes which his virtues procure for them."

"You are angry, Monsieur Garine. And why? China may choose between your ideas and mine."

"It is for us to make China what she ought to be. But can we if we do not agree among ourselves, if you teach her to despise that of which she stands in greatest need, if you refuse to admit that the first thing she has to do is to exist."

"China has always conquered her conquerors. Slowly, it is true. But always."

"Monsieur Garine, if China is to become anything but the China of Justice, that China which I have humbly tried to create; if she is to resemble the United States . . ."

(A pause, in which "or Russia" is understood.)

"I do not see why she should exist at all. Let her remain a great memory. In spite of all the abuses of the Manchurian dynasty, the history of China is worthy of respect. . . ."

"Then you regard the pages of her history which we are now writing as indicating a decline?"

"Fifty centuries of history must contain some very sad pages, Monsieur Garine, pages sadder doubtless than those to which you refer will ever be; but at least it was not I who wrote them."

He rises, not without difficulty, and, taking short steps, goes towards the door. Garine accompanies him. No sooner is the door shut than he turns to me:

"Great God! Deliver me from saints!"

The latest reports come in: Tang's officers are in the town. But for tonight, there is nothing to fear.

"We are not defenseless against Chen-Dai, even in the realm of ideas or rather of passions," explained Garine to me at dinner. "All Asia is entering on a phase of individualism and discovering death. The poor have understood the hopelessness of their condition; they are realizing that a new life has nothing to offer them. When lepers ceased to believe in God they poisoned the wells. Any man who has cut himself adrift from the old Chinese life, from its rites and its vague beliefs, and who rebels against Christianity, is a good revolutionary. You will find this exemplified in Hong, and in any Terrorist you may happen to meet. With the new idea of a death which involves nothing, neither compensation nor atonement, has been born the idea that every man has it in his power to overcome the collective life of suffering and to attain to that individual, independent life, which is in some way re-

garded as the greatest treasure of the rich. It is to such ideas as
these that the few Russian institutions Borodin has introduced
owe their success. They, for example, have given the workmen
the idea of insisting on electing their own shop stewards. Their
motive is not mere vanity or foolishness but a desire to attain to
an existence which is more actually human. . . . Was it not in some
such impulse as this, in a desire to attain to some distinct individual life in the eyes of God, that the strength of Christianity
lay? That there is but a step from such impulses to hatred and
even to fanatical hatred I see every day. . . . If you show a coolie
his master's motorcar, any result may ensue; but if the coolie has
his legs broken . . . ? And there are many broken legs in China.
. . . The difficulty lies in transforming the vague wishes of the
Chinese into resolutions. We have had to try and give them confidence in themselves gradually; and we have had to try and prevent their losing that confidence when gained. We have had to
show them a long line of victories before engaging them to fight.
The struggle with Hong Kong, which we launched for various
reasons, affords an excellent way of doing this. The results have
been brilliant. We have made them more brilliant still. They all
want to take their part in the destruction which they see threatening this symbol of British power. They see themselves as conquerors, and conquerors without having to submit to those experiences of war which mean nothing to them but defeat. For them,
as for us, it is Hong Kong today, Hankow tomorrow, Shanghai
the day after tomorrow, and later Pekin. . . . It is the impulse derived from this struggle which must and will sustain our army in
its conflict with Chen Chun-ming, as it will sustain our expedition
to the north. That is why we must be victorious, that is why at
any cost we must prevent popular enthusiasm, which is on the
verge of becoming heroic, from being extinguished in the name
of justice or of any other fairy tale."

"Can such a force be so easily destroyed?"

"Destroyed, no. Annihilated, yes. An ill-timed speech by
Gandhi (just because Indians had got rid of a few Englishmen!)
sufficed to break the last *Hartal*. Enthusiasm can't bear hesitation,

especially here. Every man must feel that his life is bound up with the revolution, that it will lose all significance if we are defeated, that it will become nothing but a rag. . . ."

After a pause, he added:

"Not to speak of a resolute minority."

After dinner he went to inquire about Borodin. It is as the doctor feared; Borodin, in the grip of an acute attack of malaria, can neither read nor discuss anything. Garine is very anxious; and this anxiety for a moment turned our conversation on himself. To one of my questions he replied:

"In the depths of my heart is a strain of the old rancor which influenced me when I threw in my lot with the Revolution."

"But you had had very little experience of poverty."

"Oh, that is not the question. My deep-rooted hostility is not so much against the property owners as against the stupid principles on which they defend their possessions. And there is another thing; when I was a youth, I did not think clearly, and a mere trifle sufficed to give me confidence in myself. Today I still have confidence in myself, but in a different way; today I must have proofs. The bond that unites me to the Kuomintang . . ."

Putting his hand on my arm, he continued:

"The bond is habit, of course, but above everything it is the desire for a victory in common. . . ."

The next day

Terrorist violence continues. Yesterday, a rich merchant, a judge and two ex-magistrates were assassinated, some in the street, the others in their own houses.

At the meeting of the executive committee tomorrow, Chen-Dai is to demand the immediate arrest of Hong and of all who are suspected of being the leaders of anarchist and Terrorist societies.

"Tang's troops have assembled."

We have hardly begun lunch when we are obliged to start. The car flies along the river bank. Nothing is to be seen in the town as yet. But inside the houses where we stop, companies of machine gunners are ready. No sooner have we passed than the regular police on the quay and the strike pickets disperse the crowd and close the bridges, near which they establish batteries of machine guns. Tang's troops are on the other side of the river.

At the Propaganda, which is opposite Garine's office, are awaiting us Nicolaïeff, and a young disheveled Chinese, rather handsome; this is Hong, leader of the Terrorists. Only when I hear his name do I remember that apelike length of arm of which Gérard spoke. There are already several of our people in the passage: posted in front of the houses of such of our friends as were suspected by Tang, they have been charged to inform us of the arrival of patrols to make the arrests. They say they have seen soldiers forcing their way into the houses and carrying off women and servants in their rage at not having found those whom they were seeking. . . . Garine silences them. Then he inquires of each one the scene of his observations and marks on a map of Canton the places visited.

"Nicolaïeff?"

"Yes."

"Come down. A message to Gallen. You will take it yourself, won't you? Then, send someone in a car to each of our offices; let every union despatch fifty volunteers for every patrol. The patrols will be going towards the river. The volunteers will be on the quay. Companies of cadets must command them, each with a machine gun."

Nicolaïeff sets out in all haste, puffing and panting to such an extent that the whole of his big body quivers. In the passage is a crowd being intercepted on their way to Garine by the questions of a Cantonese officer and a tall European (Klein, I think, but he is in the shadow). Another Cantonese officer, very young, is pushing his way through this mass of people, some in robes, others in white linen suits.

"I am starting, Commissioner."

"All right, Colonel. You will receive the messages when you get as far up as bridge number three."

He gives him a plan on which the places where the patrols are stationed are marked in red, also Tang's point of departure and the route he is likely to follow. The blue line of the river intersects the town; there, as always at Canton, the battle will be fought. I remember Gallen's words: "Those forks. If they can't cross the bridges, they are done for."

A young secretary comes in, running. He brings reports.

"Stay, Colonel. Here is the police report. Tang has fourteen hundred men."

"And I only five hundred."

"Gallen said six."

"Five. You have posted scouts along the river bank?"

"Yes. There is no danger of our being outflanked."

"Good. Then we shall hold the bridges."

The officer goes out, without saying another word. Through the hullabaloo we hear the wheels of his motorcar beginning to turn and then the perpetual sounding of his horn growing less and less loud as he whirls away into the distance. The heat, the heat! We are all in our shirtsleeves; our coats are thrown into a heap in the corner.

Here is another report: a copy of one from Tang.

"Objectives: banks, the railway station, the post office," Garine reads aloud. He goes on reading, but to himself, then resumes: "But they must cross the river."

"Garine, Garine! Feng Liao-dong's troops . . ."

It is Nicolaiëff. He has returned, mopping his big face with his handkerchief, his hair dripping and his eyes rolling like billiard balls.

". . . have joined Tang's. The Whampoa roads are blocked."

"Are you certain?"

"Certain." Then, in a low voice: "Never shall we be able to hold out alone."

Garine looks at the plan open on the table. Then he shrugs his shoulders nervously and goes to the window.

"There are not many courses to choose from."

"Klein," he calls. Then, in a low voice: "Hong, go to the chauffeur's station and bring along some fifty of them."

And, returning to Nicolaïeff:

"The telegraph? The telephone?"

"Cut, of course."

Klein comes in.

"Well, what?"

"Feng has played us a dirty trick. He has cut us off from Whampoa. Take a patrol of red guards and police. Commandeer all the cars you can lay hands on. Put a policeman and a chauffeur in each. You will find chauffeurs down there. Hong has gone for them. Let them drive right through the town, without crossing the bridges, and send as many unemployed and strikers here as possible. Then go on to the stations and tell those who are posted there to send us all the men they can spare. Also contrive to reach the Colonel and ask him to give you a hundred of his cadets."

"He will grumble."

"Let him grumble. A hundred. You understand. Bring them along yourself."

Klein goes. The sound of firing is heard in the distance.

"Now. Take care not to get bottled up. If we had only three thousand to begin with."

He calls the cadet who had been with Klein just now, questioning the police in the passage.

"Send an orderly to the coast station. Thirty coolies immediately."

Another car starts. I glance through the window and see a dozen cars waiting in front of the office, with their chauffeurs. Each orderly takes one, as he comes out. It emerges from the shadow of the building, groaning, and disappears in a cloud of

sunlit dust. The sound of firing has stopped; but while I am looking out, I hear a man's voice saying to Garine, behind me:

"Three patrols have been captured. The three emissaries from
the sections are waiting."

"Shoot the officers. And the men, where are they?"

"At the stations."

"Good. Disarm them. Handcuff them. If Tang crosses the
bridges, shoot them."

As I turn round, the man is going out; but he comes back:

"They say they haven't any handcuffs."

"The devil! Haven't they?"

Our private telephone bell rings.

"Hullo! Captain Kovak? The Commissioner at the Propaganda
Office, yes! There is a fire? How many houses are burning? On
the other side of the river? . . . Let them burn."

He hangs up the receiver.

"Nicolaiëff, what guard is there round Borodin's?"

"Forty men."

"That is enough for the present. Is there an ambulance at the
house?"

"I have just sent one there."

"Good."

He looks out of the window for a moment, wrings his hands,
and again addresses Nicolaiëff:

"They are all in a muddle. Go down. The cars must draw up in
a rank, one behind the other. Anyone going out takes the first.
Then bar up the approach with the unemployed."

Already Nicolaiëff is downstairs, ordering and gesticulating,
his face flaming beneath his white helmet. The cars are moving
and getting into position noisily. In the shade, two or three hundred ragged men are crouched, waiting. Newcomers are constantly arriving. With a dazed air they question those already
there, and crouch down behind them, trying their best to get into
the shade. I hear a voice behind me:

"The first and third bridges have been attacked."

"Were you there?"

"Yes, Commissioner, at the third."

"Well?"

"They couldn't stand against the machine guns. Now they are getting the sandbags ready."

"Good."

"The Colonel gave me this note for you."

I hear the envelope being torn open.

"More men? Yes, yes!" mutters Garine angrily. Then, in a whisper: "He is afraid he will not be able to hold out."

Outside, the ragged crowd is growing. From the edge of it, in the shade, there come sounds of quarreling.

"Garine, there are five hundred at least down below."

"But no one yet from the coast station?"

"No one, Commissioner," the secretary replies.

"What a pity!"

He draws up the blind and calls through the window:

"Nicolaiëff!"

Garine throws out to him a bundle of armlets which he has taken from a drawer in his desk.

"Take thirty of your chaps, give each of them an armlet, and begin the distribution of arms."

He turns away from the window.

Nicolaiëff's voice is heard below:

"But the keys, good God!"

Garine detaches a little key from the bunch and throws it out of the window. The fat man catches it in his two hands. At the end of the road stretcher-bearers appear, carrying wounded.

"Send two red guards down the road. No wounded here just now."

I turn round for a moment to rest my eyes from the glare of the sunlight on the walls and dusty road. Within, everything—Garine's form walking to and fro, and the blotches of color, the posters on the wall—is blurred and confused. Then, as my eyes grow accustomed to the gloom, these posters seem to come to life. . . . Garine returns to the window.

"Nicolaiëff, nothing but rifles."

"Good."

A spur of the crowd of unemployed, which is growing larger and larger, framed by policemen in uniform and a strike picket, sent doubtless by Klein, advances towards the door. The rifles are in the cellar. The mass in the shade grows denser and denser. Some twenty men, wearing armlets and led by an orderly, emerge into the sunlight.

"Garine. Here are some more of them with armlets."

He looks.

"Ah! coolies from the coast station. That is all right."

Silence. As soon as we are in suspense the burning heat tortures us like a wound. Down in the road there is a confused sound, made up of murmurs, anxious cries, a hawker's rattle and the shout of a soldier, who is driving him away. In front of the window nothing but the terrific glare. It is a hush palpitating with anxiety. Then the rhythmic sound of men marching begins to grow clearer and clearer; a sudden clack as they halt. Then silence again. Vague noises. The sound of a man's footstep on the stairs. The secretary.

"The coolies from the coast station have arrived, Commissioner."

Garine writes, and folds the paper. The orderly holds out his hand for it.

"No."

Garine crumples it and throws it into the wastepaper basket.

"I am coming."

But now more orderlies come in with papers. He reads: "Hong Kong, later!" and throws the papers into a drawer. A cadet enters.

"Commissioner, the Colonel asks for more men."

"In a quarter of an hour."

"He wants to know how many he can have."

We look out of the window. The crowd now stretches right down the street, always keeping in the shade and swaying with a motion like the ebb and flow of the waves of the sea.

"Fifteen hundred at least."

The aide is still waiting. Garine again takes up his pen; and this time he gives the order to the aide.

The private telephone bell rings again.

.   .   .   .

"But, plague take them, which rebels?"

.   .   .   .

"You must know!"

.   .   .   .

"Well! Yes! But how did they come?"

.   .   .   .

"Several banks? Good. Let them attack."

He hangs up the receiver and goes out of the room.

"I follow you?"

"Yes," he calls from the passage.

We go down. The men with armlets, whom Nicolaiëff has just selected, are coming up from the cellar bringing rifles, which their comrades on the doorstep are distributing to the unemployed, who are falling into rank. But meanwhile the coolies from the coast station have been bringing up boxes of cartridges. The armed men mingle with the others, who are pushing forward and trying to get cartridges before they have been given rifles. Garine shouts in broken Chinese. No one listens to him. So he comes forward and sits on an open cartridge case. There is a pause. What is happening? is being asked in the rear. He makes the unarmed men fall back and give way to those who have rifles. The latter, in groups of threes, and with exasperating deliberation, pass by the cartridge cases and receive their cartridges. From the cellar comes up the noise of hammers and screw drivers opening cartridge cases. Outside is the sound of distant marching. We can see nothing through the crowd. Garine leaps on to the steps and looks:

"The cadets."

Yes, here are the cadets led by Klein. Coolies are coming up from the cellar, panting beneath the crushing loads of cartridge cases hanging from bamboo poles. Klein stands before us.

"Two cadets to support you," Garine says to him. "All who have munitions twenty yards in front. Those who have rifles and no munitions ten yards further back. Between them a case and three men to give out cartridges."

When all this has been done silently, in a thick cloud of sunlit dust:

"Now, rifles first, munitions three meters away. Cadets well in front. The men in tens. One leader for each row, a soldier, if possible, if not, the first in the rank. Each cadet take one hundred and fifty men and march to the quay for the Colonel's instructions."

We go back into the house; and the first thing we do is to look out of the window. The street is crowded. Everywhere, in sunshine and in shade, are speakers, borne on their comrades' shoulders, howling at the mob. From the distance comes the sound of the firing of machine guns. Down below the first group starts off, marching regularly, commanded by a cadet.

Then begins the wearing tension of suspense, of passive waiting. Under the window, one by one, the sections form and march off in step. Papers relating to Hong Kong are brought in. Garine merely glances at them and throws them into a drawer. The rasping sound of machine gun firing continues, and from time to time the isolated noise of the discharge of a rifle. But it is all very remote, almost merging into the salvos we heard yesterday. . . . We still hold the bridges. Five times Tang's troops tried to pass, but failed to cross the bridgeheads, on which our machine-gunners kept up a constant cross fire. Whenever a cadet brings in a report it is, "Attack on bridge number . . . repulsed." Then our suspense begins again, Garine walking up and down the room or covering his writing pad with heavily drawn curves, I looking out of the window at the perpetual formation of sections. Two informers have come in, having swum across the river. On the opposite bank they are burning and plundering. A slight trail of smoke over the street softens the blinding glare.

Garine and I are flying along in a car, on our way to the quay. All the shutters of the big shops are down; the booths are barred with planks. At the windows, as we pass, immediately behind mattresses or pieces of linen stretched across, faces appear and disappear. At a street corner is a woman running along on tiny feet, with one child in her arms, another on her back.

In order to escape the enemy's fire, directed against the opposite bank of the river, we stop a few yards from the quay, in a street which runs parallel with it. The Colonel has taken up his station in a house not far from the main bridge. In the courtyard are officers and children. On the first floor is a table over which is extended a plan of Canton. Three wooden bedsteads placed in front of the windows create an obscurity only broken by a sunbeam, the shaft of which alights on the General's knee.

"Well?"

"Have you received this?" asks the Colonel, holding out a paper.

The note is in Chinese. Garine and I read it together. He seems to understand it partly. But I translate in a whisper: General Gallen is attacking Feng's troops which are between us, and is marching towards the town. The Commandant of the Cadet School, Chiang Kai-shek, with the best sections of our machine-gunners, will attack Tang's troops on the flank.

"No, it must have arrived after I had started. Are you sure you can hold out here?"

"Certainly."

"Gallen will make short work of Feng. One can rely on his artillery. Do you think Feng's troops will fall back on the town?"

"Probably."

"Good. Have you enough men now?"

"More than I need."

"Can you let me have ten machine guns and a captain?"

The Colonel is reading reports.

"Yes."

"I will have the streets barricaded and station groups of machine guns at the corners. If the defeated troops attack them, they will reply."

"Of course."

He gives an order to his artillery officer who goes out, running.

We take our leave, the sunbeam glancing through the loophole plays upon us as we go. The firing outside has died down.

Outside, twenty cadets have descended like a cloud of flies upon our two motorcars, huddled together on the seats, hanging on to the mudguards, sitting on the hoods, standing on the steps. The Captain comes with us. The cars start at a flying pace, jolting the cadets at every crossing.

More reports are waiting for Garine on his desk. He hardly looks at them. He puts the Captain in command of the sections which are still being formed. In the street, the setting sun is casting shadows, and one can see nothing but heads.

"Commandeer material for the barricades."

Leaving Nicolaïëff to organize and arm the sections, Klein goes down into the cellar, followed by the twenty cadets. Then the group re-emerges and appears in the passage, confused and lit up here and there by the brilliant shafts of light reflected from the barrels of the machine guns. Once again the cars set off with the groaning of engines and the hooting of horns, overflowing with jolted soldiers, and strewing a khaki cap here and there on their track.

Two hours of suspense. Now and again a report comes in. . . . Only one incident: about four o'clock the news that the enemy has carried the second bridge. But almost at once, our line of armed workmen at the back of the quay, arresting the advance of Tang's division, gave our machine-gunners time to come up, and the bridge was retaken. Then there was firing in the streets running parallel to the quay.

About half-past five the first fugitives from Feng's division begin to come in. But the machine guns soon drive them back into action.

Garine and I make a tour of inspection of our outposts. The car stops some distance off; and we, with a Cantonese orderly, walk down the streets, barricaded with beams and wooden bedsteads. Behind the barricades, machine-gunners are smoking long Chinese cigars and peeping through the loopholes now and again. Garine looks on in silence. A hundred yards away from the bar-

ricades, the workmen we have armed are crouching, talking or
listening to the talk of our improvised noncommissioned officers,
the soldiers of the syndicates who wear their armlets.

Then, back again to the suspense of waiting at the Propaganda
Office. But our anxiety is relieved: at the last outpost we in-
spected, an orderly came in and brought Garine a message from
Klein: Commandant Chiang Kai-shek had forced Tang's line,
and Tang's men in confusion were trying to escape into the country. The rifle firing near the bridge has ceased, but it rattles like
a shower of hail on the other side of the river, whence now and
again comes the sound of an explosion, like that of a bomb—the
bursting of grenades. As night falls, the noise of battle fades away
rapidly in the distance. While I am at dinner in Nicolaïëff's office,
classifying the latest reports as I eat, lights are lit; and now through
the darkness one only hears occasional explosions, almost lost in
the distance. . . .

When I go down the first floor, the sound of talking and the
rattle of arms come up from the dark street. The lamps of the
motorcars reveal the black forms of the cadets and their weapons,
streaked with rays of light. One of Chiang Kai-shek's divisions is
already in the street. It is difficult to distinguish anything in the
blinding glare of the motor lamps, but one is conscious of a crowd
animating the darkness, and filled with that craving to make itself
heard which follows fighting.

Garine at his desk is munching a large slice of toast, crackling
it between his teeth as he talks to General Gallen, who walks up
and down the room while he listens.

"I cannot arrive at any definite conclusion now. But, according
to the few reports I have received, there are islets of resistance
everywhere, and there is the possibility of another movement like
Tang's."

"Has Tang been taken?"

"No."

"Is he dead?"

"As yet I don't know. But today it is Tang. Tomorrow it may

be someone else. British money is always there, and the Secret Intelligence Department also. One struggles or one does not. But . . ."

He gets up, blows the dust from his desk, shakes the crumbs from his clothes, goes to his safe, opens it and takes out a pamphlet, which he gives to Gallen.

". . . this is what really matters."

"Ha! the old wretch!"

"No. He is doubtless quite unaware of these pamphlets."

I look over Gallen's shoulder: the pamphlet proclaims the constitution of a new government, of which Chen-Dai is invited to become president.

"They know that he is the man to oppose us. In all our propaganda we have to reckon with his influence."

"Have you had this pamphlet long?"

"An hour."

"His influence. . . . Yes, I see. He acts as a magnet. Don't you think that all this has gone on long enough?"

Garine ponders.

"It is difficult."

"All the more so because I am beginning to mistrust Hong. . . . He is now taking it upon himself to get rid of those who have contributed considerably to the party. . . ."

"Put someone else in his place."

"That requires thinking over: he has great gifts, and this is hardly the time. Besides if he ceases to be with us, he will be against us."

"What then?"

"He can't do us any permanent harm; Terrorists are always unwise, always badly organized . . . but for a few days . . ."

The next day

"Of course," said Garine, coming into his office in the morning and seeing huge piles of reports. "This is always the way after any incident. . . ." And we set to work. These reports, which we now classify as if they were dead things, palpitate with wild energy —with the desires, the resolves of yesterday, with the violence of men who today may be corpses or fugitives—we know not. Then there are the hopes of the others who want to attempt to-morrow the very thing in which Tang has failed today.

Garine works in silence, gathering all his papers together. There are a great many of them, especially those relating to Chen-Dai. Sometimes, as he puts some particular paper aside, or marks an-other with red pencil, he exclaims in a half whisper: "Again." All our enemies seem to be centering around this old man. Tang, who thought he would cross the bridges quickly enough to capture the army gathered round the Propaganda Office, wanted to place the Government in his hands. All who are averse to any action, who live on lamentations, all who gather round the presidents of secret political societies, old men who once collaborated with Chen-Dai, form an incoherent body to which Chen's life gives a kind of solidarity. . . .

Here are the reports from Hong Kong. Tang has taken the town. Britain, well aware of the emptiness of the Propaganda purse, takes courage. Now, even better perhaps than when I was at Hong Kong, do I understand this new war, in which words of command take the place of cannon, in which a captured town is not laid waste with fire but delivered up to the vast silence of an oriental strike, to the alarming emptiness of a town which seems deserted by its inhabitants save for some fugitive form vanishing rapidly, breaking the stillness for an instant by the clattering of wooden shoes on the pavement. It is no longer the name of a battle that indicates a victory, but these writings, these reports, the fall in the prices of houses, the rows on office doors of plates which are blank and which used to be engraved with the names of com-mercial firms. . . . But the other kind of war, the old-fashioned kind, looms up also: Chen Chun-ming's army is being commanded by British officers.

"Money, money, money!" This is the gist of all the reports. "We shall be obliged to stop strike pay. . . ." As he turns these

requests down, one after the other, Garine draws a big capital D:
the decree. The idea of the decree obsesses him: a number of Cantonese firms, for whom this decree would spell hopeless ruin and
who once offered Borodin huge sums, have now turned to the
friends of Chen-Dai. . . . About eleven o'clock he goes out.

"The promulgation of this decree is absolutely necessary. If
Gallen comes, you will tell him that I am at Chen-Dai's."

I go on working with Nicolaiëff. Our police superintendent
was once one of the agents of the Okhrana. Borodin and Garine
know his record, which is now in the hands of the Tcheka. Before the war he had joined the Terrorists, and had had several
militants arrested. He was thoroughly well informed, not only
through his own observations but through those of his wife, who
was a very sincere and highly respected Terrorist. Her death is a
strange story. Certain circumstances made him suspected by his
comrades, though they did not supply sufficient evidence to warrant his execution. Henceforth the Okhrana regarded him as done
for and stopped his pay. Incapable of any regular work, he fell
from one humiliating employment to another, was by turns guide,
dealer in obscene photographs. . . . From time to time he appealed to the police, who would dole him out a little money. He
lived in disgust with himself, down at the heels, hanging on to the
police through some kind of *esprit de corps*. When begging for
fifty roubles in 1914—it was his last request—he informed against
his neighbor, an old woman who was hiding arms, as a way of
paying his debt.

The war saved him. He left the front in 1917, found himself at
Vladivostok, then at Tientsin, where he took a job as scullion on
board a Canton boat. At Canton he returned to his old trade of
informer, and so distinguished himself that four years later Sun
Yat-sen made him one of the most important officials of his secret
police. The Russians seem to have forgotten his former occupation.

While I classify the Hong Kong papers, he is studying the reports of the suppression of yesterday's rising.

"Then, old chap," he says, "I select a large room. It is really

spacious, very spacious. I sit there in my presidential chair, on a
platform, alone, quite alone, do you understand? No one is present except a clerk in a corner, and behind me six red guards, who
don't understand Cantonese, armed with revolvers, of course.
When my man enters, he clicks his heels (some men are brave,
as your friend, Garine, says); but when he goes out it is in a very
different manner. If the public had been admitted I should never
have discovered anything: the accused would have defied me.
But when we are alone together. Alone. Ah! you don't know
what that means. When we are alone!" And with an inveigling
smile, like that of some licentious old man looking at a naked
child, he adds: "You can't think what cowards they become."

When I come back to lunch, I find Garine writing busily.
"One moment, I have nearly finished. I must make a note of
this at once, or I should forget it. It is my call on Chen-Dai."
In a few minutes I hear the sound of a line being drawn; and
Garine pushes away the papers on which he had been writing.
"He seems to have sold his last house, and to be lodging with
some poor philosopher. No doubt that was why he preferred
coming to see me the other day. I was taken into a dark little
room. He gives me the armchair and sits on the divan. Somewhere,
down in a courtyard, a lantern-seller is hammering tin; so we
have to shout at one another. As for what we said, you need only
read this."
He gives me his papers.
" 'Begins to . . .' 'But of course . . .' C.D., that is he. 'G' obviously is I. But, no! I will read it to you. There are so many
abbreviations that you would never decipher it."
He bends over the paper; then, just as he is about to read it:
"I will skip all the compliments at the beginning. He was as
mandarinal and distinguished as ever. But when I brought him to
the point and asked whether he would vote for the decree—yes
or no:
" 'Monsieur Garine,' he said [Garine mimics the feeble, meas-
used, somewhat pontifical tones of the old man], 'will you permit
me to ask you a few questions? I know it is not the custom. . . .'

" 'Please do.'

" 'I should like to know whether you remember the time when you were founding the military academy?'

" 'Very well.'

" 'In that case, you may not have forgotten that when you were so kind as to call upon me and to explain your plans, you said—you maintained—that the object of this academy would be to enable the Kouang-Ton to defend itself.'

" 'Well?'

" 'To defend itself. You may possibly recollect that I went with you and the young Commandant, Chiang Kai-shek, to call on certain prominent persons. In some cases I even went by myself. I was insulted on the public platform, decried as a militarist—I! But to persons worthy of respect and consideration, who put their faith in me, I said: "You know me to be a just man. I ask you to send your child—your son—to this academy. I ask you to forget all the wisdom taught us by our ancestors: the disgrace of the military profession." Monsieur Garine, did I say this?'

" 'Who denies it?'

" 'Good. One hundred and twenty of those children are dead. Three of them are only sons. Monsieur Garine, who is responsible for those dead? I.'

"With his hands in his sleeves, he bows low and then, drawing himself up, he continues:

" 'I am an aged man. I have long ago forgotten the hopes of my youth, of a time before you were born, Monsieur Garine. I know what death is. I know that some sacrifices are necessary. . . . Three of those young men were only sons, Monsieur Garine—and I have seen their fathers. Every young officer whose death is not for the defense of this province, dies in vain. And I advised that death.'

" 'Your argument is convincing. I regret that you did not put it to General Tang.'

" 'General Tang knew it and forgot it, like so many others. . . . Monsieur Garine, factions are nothing to me. . . . But since the

Committee of Seven, since a certain section of the people attach some importance to my ideas, I will not conceal them.'

"Then he adds with great deliberation:

" 'In spite of any danger in which their divulgence may involve me. Believe me, I am sorry to speak thus, but it is your fault, Monsieur Garine. I shall not support your policy. I shall even go so far as to oppose it. . . . I do not consider you and your friends to be good shepherds of the people.' "

(Resuming his ordinary voice, Garine reminds me that it was the Jesuit Fathers who taught Chen-Dai French.)

" 'I even regard you as dangerous, extremely dangerous, because you do not love the people.'

" 'And whom would you have a child love best,' I ask, 'the nurse who loves him and lets him drown himself, or the nurse who does not love him and teaches him to swim?'

"He thinks for a moment, then looking me straight in the face, replies respectfully:

" 'That may depend, Monsieur Garine, on the contents of the child's pockets.'

" 'Well, you, at any rate, you ought to know that, since, after helping him for twenty years, you are still poor.'

" 'I never sought . . .'

" 'As for me. Look at the holes in my shoes (I lean against the wall and show him the sole of my shoe). You can see how rich corruption has made me.'

"It was disconcerting but of course absurd. For he might have retorted that however low our funds were, they would have permitted us to buy new shoes. Whether it did not occur to him, or whether he merely wished to put an end to the discussion, which alarmed him, I do not know. Like all Chinese of his generation, he was afraid of emphasis and irritation, which he regarded as signs of vulgarity. So he took his hands out of his sleeves, stretched out his arms and rose.

"There!"

Garine puts the final sheet on the table, crosses his hands over it, and repeats:

"There!"

"Well?"

"I think the matter is settled. The only thing to be done now, is to delay pushing the decree until we have finished with him. Fortunately he does everything to help us."

"In what way?"

"By demanding the arrest of the Terrorists (and he may demand it; for if he succeeds in getting them charged, the police will not find them, that is all). Hong has hated him for a long while."

The next morning

Entering Garine's room, as I generally do when he is late, I hear cries and discover two young Chinese women, who jump up howling and rush behind a screen. Garine, who is putting on his officer's uniform, calls "the boy" and tells him to pay them and show them out when they are dressed.

"After one has been here for some time," he says to me as we go down, "Chinese women upset one, as you will see. And the best way to rid oneself of the obsession is to take them and think no more about it, and set one's mind free for more important matters. With two at once the cure is certain."

.   .   .   .   .   .

Nicolaïeff is waiting for us downstairs. As soon as he sees Garine, he shouts:

"Yes, yes, it is still going on. Listen to this."

He takes a paper from his pocket; and, as we walk to the Propaganda—for it is not very hot yet—he reads as quickly as his corpulence will allow:

"The men and the foreign women in the mission stations have fled before an inoffensive crowd of Chinese. Why? if they were not guilty? Ever so many bones of little children have been found in the mission garden. This proves beyond a doubt that in their

orgies these depraved creatures have cruelly massacred innocent
little Chinese children."

"This is Hong's, isn't it?" inquires Garine.

"Of course, as usual: dictated, since he doesn't know how to
write. . . . It is the third of these papers."

"Yes, I have already told him not to exaggerate like this. I am
beginning to have enough of Hong."

"And I believe he means to go on. At the Propaganda he never
seemed to be working with real zest except when he was drawing up anti-Christian communiqués. He says the people like
them. . . . Perhaps. . . ."

"That is not the question. Send him to me, when he comes."

"He wanted to see you this morning. I think he is waiting."

"Be careful not to question him as to his intentions with regard
to Chen-Dai. Get your information about that elsewhere."

"Good. Tell me, Garine——"

"What?"

"You know that the banker, Shia-Chow, has been killed?"

"A knife?"

"No, a bullet in the head, after we had crossed the bridges."

"And you think that Hong . . . ?"

"I don't think, I know."

"You had told him to leave him alone?"

"Yes, I had told him that you wished it, and Borodin, too. By
the way, Borodin is getting better. He will soon be here, I expect.
Hong is set on having his own way."

"He knew that Shia-Chow was supporting us?"

"He knew very well. But he did not care. Shia-Chow was too
rich. . . . No loot, of course. . . ."

Garine's only rejoinder is to shake his head.

Here we are at the Propaganda.

I go up to Nicolaïeff's room with him, take a packet of the
latest reports from Hong Kong from his desk and go down again.
On entering Garine's office, I find myself up against Hong, who
is taking his leave. He is talking emphatically, in a low voice,
which betrays a rage that is ill-controlled.

"You may censor what I write. But you shall not censor my opinions. Torture—to my mind—is just. Because a poor man's life is one long torture. And all who teach poor men to bear it —all, the Christian priests and everyone else—ought to be punished. They don't know. They don't know. Then, in my opinion [and he makes a gesture as if to emphasize the word] they must be made to *know*. I am not to let the soldiers loose on them? No? Take lepers. A man's arm putrefies and falls off: that man comes and talks to me of resignation: all very well for him. But *this* man says something different. . . ."

He smiles as he goes out, a smile which shows his teeth and suddenly makes a face which is gleaming with hatred, look almost childish.

Garine remains rapt in anxious thought. When he looks up, his glance meets mine. . . .

"I have warned the Bishop," he says, "of the danger his missionaries are running. Their departure is necessary, but not their massacre."

"And what then?"

"All proper precautions will be taken," he replies. "As for the rest, God will grant or refuse us martyrdom. His will be done. A few missionaries have gone already."

While he is talking his eyes wander over his desk. One of the pieces of white paper, with which it is strewn, arrests them.

"Hah! hah! Chen-Dai has left his philosopher's and taken up his abode in a villa, which an absent friend has placed at his disposal. . . . And yesterday evening our sage obtained a military guard. Ah! how I wish we could substitute for the Committee of Seven something more autocratic, a kind of Tcheka, so that we were not obliged to rely on people like Hong. . . . There is still a great deal to be done."

"What, someone else? Show him in."

The orderly brings in a roll of silk from Shanghai. It has been sent by one of the delegates. Written on it in Chinese ink are congratulations. And then at the foot, in a kind of postscript, written in a lighter and muddier ink, is the following:

"We [four names follow] have signed this with our blood, having each of us cut off one of our fingers to testify our admiration for our compatriots of Canton, who have made such a magnificent stand against imperialist England. Wherefore, we express our respect; and we count on the struggle being continued until the final victory is won. Signed by (numerous signatures follow, representing sections)."

"Until final victory," repeats Garine. "The decree, the decree! Everything depends on it. If we can't prevent Hong Kong boats from coming here, then in spite of anything we may do, it is all up with us. The decree must be promulgated. If not, what are we doing here?"

He takes up a bundle of papers from Hong Kong.

"Nothing but demands for money. There is but one solution: to give up the general strike. All Asia is watching us. For Hong Kong to be paralyzed is enough. The strike of sailors, marines and coolies, directed by the trades unions, will suffice. Hong Kong disarmed is as good as Hong Kong deserted; and the International is in sore need of money, sore need. . . ."

He begins to write a report. For it is Borodin who takes decisions which involve the International. His pinched, wrinkled face stands out in the strong light. The Orient and its ancient power loom before me: those Hong Kong hospitals full of patients and forsaken by nurses; and here, scribbling on this paper yellow in the sunlight, one sick man writing to another. . . .

Two o'clock

Hong's new attitude alarms Garine. He relies on him to save him from Chen-Dai; but, while he knows by his informers' reports that Hong will not wait to be charged before acting, and that his knowledge that the police are not against him yet, moves him to act promptly, he has no idea what course the Terrorist intends to pursue. For some time, he tells me, he has discerned a new strange personality in Hong: from beneath a veneer of culture derived from books and conversation, there has been emerging the uneducated Chinese, a man who cannot even read Chinese characters. This new personality which threatens to dominate the reader of French and English books, is at the mercy of the strain of violence in Hong's character and the influence of the only experience he has ever made his own —the experience of poverty. . . . His youth was spent with those whose horizon is completely shut in by poverty, he had lived in those slums of the great Chinese towns, which are populated by the diseased, the aged, weaklings of every kind, people dying of hunger and a much larger multitude, those who, from living on the food of wild beasts, have fallen into a state of perpetual apathy and weakness. These last have been too enfeebled, too occupied with procuring some pittance, to be capable of hatred, of thought, or even of feeling. Only now and again do impulses of revenge and despair pierce through the rags, gleam through hollow eyes and animate bodies which have rolled in the dust, and which lean on staves, the gifts of the missionaries.

But there are others, others who occasionally become soldiers or brigands, who are still capable of some kind of feeling, who plot and plan to obtain a handful of tobacco. For them hatred exists, tenacious and unifying, their daily companion, awaiting the day when a faltering army shall call plunderers and incendiaries to its aid. Hong has risen out of this wretchedness; but he has never forgotten the lesson it taught him or the impression it gave of a world ferocious and possessed by impotent hatred. "There are but two races," he would say: "the poor and the others." The experiences of his youth have rendered him so utterly disgusted with the powerful and the rich that he desires neither wealth nor power. Little by little, as he left behind him *la Cour des Miracles*, he discovered that what he hates is not the happiness of the well-to-do, but their self-esteem. "A poor man cannot respect himself," he would say. He might have been content to accept such a condition if he had believed with his ancestors that his existence was not bounded by this life. But having been led to concentrate on the present by his discovery of death, he has ceased to accept, to wonder or to discuss: he merely hates. Poverty for him has become a kind of wily demon, set upon convincing man of his baseness, cowardice, weakness, decadence. Without a doubt Hong hates above all others the self-respecting man, who is sure of himself. No one could be a more complete rebel against his own kind. It was his loathing of respectability, that Chinese virtue par excellence, that induced him to join the revolutionaries. Like all who are fired with passion, he expresses himself forcibly. This gives him a certain authority; an authority which is enhanced by his bitter hatred of idealists—of Chen-Dai in particular—a hatred which is wrongly ascribed to political reasons. He hates idealists because they claim to introduce order into things. And he does not want order. He will not exchange his present hatred for any uncertain future good. He is furious with those who, forgetting that this life is all we have, speak of sacrificing themselves for their children. Hong does not believe in having children, or in sacrificing oneself, or in putting oneself in the place of another. He would like to see Chen-Dai reduced to seeking his food in sewers and then caring to listen to some venerable old gentleman talking of justice. He won't see anything in this agitated old chief but the frustrator of his vengeance. And recollecting Rebecci's confidences, he arrives at the conclusion that too many allow some shadowy ideal to divert them from following their proper vocation. Hong does not intend to end his days making mechanical birds, or to be imposed upon by old age. When he heard the following lines, written by a poet of Northern China, he learned them by heart:

> I fight alone and win or lose.
> I need no one to win my freedom for me.
> I need no Jesus Christ to think that he died for me.

Garine's influence, added to Rebecci's, has intensified his craving for reality, with its undercurrent of hatred. Hong regards his life in much the same way as might a consumptive who knows there is no hope and yet feels in full vigor. Hong's passion of hatred, which seems almost a duty to him, imposes a kind of savage and brutal order on the confusion and agitation of his emotions.

Only by yielding to this impulse can he escape from lying, cowardice and weakness. This passion of his is the very antithesis of mere empty words. It is this craving for action that has brought him to us. But the International is too slow for him. It is too indulgent. Twice this week he has had men assassinated whom the International wants to protect. "Every murder," says Garine, "increases his self-confidence; and he is gradually coming to realize that he is an anarchist at heart. A break between us is imminent. I only hope that it does not happen too soon!"

After a brief silence:

"There are few of my enemies whom I understand better."

The next day

Just as we are leaving, two American journalists arrive and ask for an interview with Garine. They wear the armlet of the Commissariat and the town police, and they have written on their cards that they are introduced by the Kuomintang of California. Garine tells me to receive them; and I spend an hour regaling them with alcoholic drinks and cigarettes and expounding various ideas, of which they take notes in all seriousness. Only now and again is any question asked, and then always by the elder of the two, a clean-shaven Anglo-Saxon with long teeth, who smokes a pipe. What interests him more than anything is the struggle of Canton against Great Britain. He comes from Hong Kong and was amazed to see the town almost deserted. At last I contrive to get rid of them.

When I enter Garine's office, Klein and Borodin are talking, sitting opposite one another near the door. They are looking out of the corners of their eyes at Hong who is standing in the middle of the room, arguing with Garine. Borodin is out of bed for the first time this morning; emaciated and yellow, he looks

almost Chinese. The attitude of the men, the atmosphere of the
room, suggests disagreement and hostility. Hong stands perfectly
still, talking emphatically in a staccato tone. All his sinews seem
tense as if he is about to hit out at his interlocutors. His glance
and the tone of his voice express the violence of a temper over
which he is losing control. Observing the brutal movement of
his jaws (he jerks out his sentences as if he were snapping at
something) Gérard's words suddenly occur to me: "When I am
sentenced to capital punishment."

"In France," he was saying, "they did not dare at first to cut
off their King's head? Well, they did, in the end. And France did
not die of it. One should always begin by guillotining the King,
always."

"But not when he pays."

"When he pays. And when he does not pay. What does his
paying matter to me?"

"To us it does matter. Listen, Hong: any Terrorist movement
must reckon with the police, who are opposing it. . . ."

"What?"

Garine repeats the sentence. Hong seems to have understood,
but he does not stir, and stands, bending forward, his eyes fixed
on the floor.

"Everything in its time," adds Garine. "Revolution is not so
simple."

"Oh! Revolution!"

"Revolution," says Borodin, turning round, "involves paying an
army."

"Then I lose all interest in it. I am to choose? Why? You are
the most just? I leave such ideas to our respectable Chen-Dai.
His age excuses them. They suit that pernicious old man. Politics
don't appeal to me."

"There you are!" cried Garine. "Words, mere words! Do you
know what the heads of the great financial houses in Hong Kong
are doing at this moment? They are standing in a queue at the
Governor's asking for overdrafts, and the banks are refusing
them the sums they demand. On the quay, grand personages are

shouldering their own luggage. We are ruining Hong Kong; we are forcing five hundred thousand British working men to come out on strike; we are transforming one of the wealthiest possessions of the British crown into an insignificant port—not to mention the example we are setting. And you, what are you doing?"

For a moment Hong is silent. But from the way he looks at Garine it is evident he is about to speak.

"No social order is anything to me. Life, our one and only life! Not to lose it. There!"

But this is only preliminary.

"Well, go on," said Borodin.

"What am I doing, you ask?"

He has turned to Borodin; and now he looks him in the face.

"What you don't dare to do. To make poor men die of work, that is shameful; to have the enemies of the Party killed by miserable wretches, that is good. But to take care not to soil one's own hands by doing such things, is that good also, eh?"

"I am afraid. Is that what you mean?" asks Borodin, beginning to get angry.

"Not of being killed, no."

Then, nodding violently:

"But of the rest, yes."

"Everyone to his part."

"Hah! And that is mine, eh?"

He becomes more emphatic as his anger increases.

"Do you think I like doing it? I? It is just because it hurts me that I do not always make others do it, do you understand? Yes, you are looking at Mr. Klein. He got rid of a great noble, I know. I asked him. . . ."

He stops short in the middle of his sentence, looks first at Borodin then at Klein, and laughs nervously.

"There are other *bourgeois* besides owners of factories," he mutters.

Then suddenly he shrugs his shoulders violently and goes out almost running, slamming the door.

Silence.

Then Garine says: "Things are as bad as ever."

"What do you think he will do?" Klein asks.

"With regard to Chen-Dai? Chen-Dai has almost asked for his head."

And, after thinking for a moment:

"He understood when I said that any course Terrorism pursues must reckon with the police who are opposing it. So he will try to get rid of Chen-Dai as soon as possible. . . . And he may do so. But from today he will have us in mind, too. We shall be among the first."

Borodin, biting his mustache and buckling his belt, which is uncomfortable, gets up and goes out. We follow him. There is a large black mark on the wall, the reflection of a big moth which has flown on to the electric light bulb.

Klein and I go down together.

"One day," says Klein, "Hong asked me what I felt like when I executed Kominsky. . . . I told him that my one thought was that I wished I had taken a revolver instead of a knife. That's why he was grinning like an idiot when he went out. Do you think it funny? . . . It is true that I wished I had had a revolver. Because then I could have killed him without touching him. It would have . . . hurt me less. . . . And then I shouldn't have been so afraid of making a mess of it. Ah! Hong doesn't know what he is talking about. No doubt those he has dealt with were shot. To shoot one's enemy is nothing. It is . . . impersonal. I had taken a hunting knife to make sure. But I had to try it first. And I did —on a rabbit, dead, of course. Oh! its ribs! . . . When I saw Kominsky, I could only think of one thing—perhaps I shall miss him. I felt sick. I had even forgotten that I was executing justice. Another thing that troubled me was that I knew he must be carrying a watch on his left side. Then I felt my own side before striking. One's bones are hard. . . . I might have plunged the blade into his stomach, but I could not bear to do that. . . . So, like an idiot, I threw the knife with all my strength, and Kominsky fell under the force of the blow."

"Did he die at once?"

"I believe so."

"And then?"

"Oh, that doesn't matter."

When I returned, Garine's doctor, Myroff, was waiting for him.

Nine o'clock

Myroff must have said something to make Garine anxious, because, for the first time, he mentions his illness without my questioning him.

"Disease, old chap, ah! no one who is not ill can have any idea of it. They think it something that can be striven against, something outside oneself. They are wrong: disease becomes one's very self. . . . Well, as soon as this matter of Hong Kong is settled . . ."

After dinner, a telegram was brought in: Chen Chun-ming's army has left Wai-Chow and is marching on Canton.

On waking the next morning, I hear that Garine has had an attack and has been taken to the hospital during the night. I may go and see him after six o'clock.

Hong and the anarchists are announcing meetings for this afternoon, in the halls of the chief syndicates—Hong himself will speak at a meeting of "The Junk," the most important society of Canton coolies, and he will also address some of the other meetings. Borodin has chosen an aged and celebrated orator, Mao Ling-wou, to reply to him.

Tomorrow, our people will proclaim the cessation of the general strike at Hong Kong. At the same time, in order to keep the town in a state of alarm, our spies will inform the English police that the Chinese, furious after the failure of the general strike, are preparing an insurrection. During the last few days, certain English firms have tried to organize, at Swatow, a series of boats for the despatch into the interior of goods landed at this port. But yesterday, by our order, the trades unions of

Swatow declared a strike of the coolies, and this morning ordered the seizure of all goods of British origin. Finally, the decree has gone forth that all traders accepting British goods shall be arrested and condemned to pay a fine of two-thirds of their estate. Those who fail to pay within ten days will be executed.

Five o'clock

I have been kept very late; and the meeting of "The Junk" must have begun.

We, that is Nicolaiëff's Yunnanese secretary and I, arrive at a kind of factory. We enter a garage, full of Ford cars, and, passing through it, come to another building, a plain roof, a great white wall down which the rain has fallen in broad green splashes, as if buckets of acid had been thrown at it. Here is a door, and in front of it is a commissionaire, sitting on a case, wearing straw shoes and showing his automatic pistol to a group of children, the smallest of whom are naked. My companion gives him a card. He gets up to look at it, pushing back the pigtailed children, overturning some of them. We go in. We are greeted by a muffled roar from which fragments of phrases come towards us out of a dense bluish haze. At first I can see nothing but two broad sunbeams, riddled with atoms, falling from the windows in two great bars of light, stretching from corner to corner of the hall; an atmosphere dense with dust and waves of tobacco smoke. Gradually the vague sounds we heard on entering clarify into the measured utterances of a speaker who stands in the shade, and who is constantly being interrupted by the yes, yeses or the no, noes of the crowd, resounding like a refrain.

Little by little my eyes grow accustomed to the gloom, and I perceive a bare hall, with three platforms, one for the officers, the president and two vice-presidents, who sit at a large table on which letters are engraved (Sun Yat-sen's will, perhaps—they are too far away for me to read); another on which is standing the speaker, whom we can hardly see or hear; and a third on which, more plainly visible, in a kind of little pulpit, sits an aged Chinese, with a fine arched nose and gray hair brushed up. He is listening attentively, leaning forward on his two elbows.

Now I begin to discern the crowd. It is quite still, not a single gesture—some four or five hundred in this small hall: near the officer's platform are a few short-haired women students. Beneath the ceiling great ventilators are beating the heavy air. The audience wedged tightly one against the other—soldiers, students, small shopkeepers, coolies—give signs of approbation by jerking their heads forward, without moving their bodies, like dogs barking. Figures perfectly upright and rigid, as if dead, no arms crossed, no elbows on knees or chins in hand, but faces thrilled, jaws protruded, jerking or barking out applause.

Now I begin to hear clearly enough to understand: it is Hong's voice, not hesitating as when he speaks French, but hurried and voluble. He is at the end of his speech.

"They say they have given us liberty! We have been smashing the Empire like an egg for these last five years, while they have been crawling on hands and knees under the lash of their military mandarins!

"They are making their paid agents, 'their boys,' say that they have taught us how to make a revolution.

"Had we any need of them?

"Had the Tai Ping leaders Russian advisers?

"Had the Boxers?"

All this, expressed in the commonest Chinese, but with intense passion and interrupted more and more frequently by the guttural yes, yes of the audience. At each sentence, Hong raises his voice, until with a shout, he cries:

"When our oppressors were about to butcher the proletariat of Canton, was it the Russians who threw cans of vitriol in their faces? Who was it who threw the swine, the shopkeepers who had volunteered, into the river?"

"Yes, yes, yes!"

Mao, still leaning forward on his elbow, neither stirs nor speaks. The whole audience is obviously on the speaker's side; and it would be useless to tell them that they did not beat the volunteers unaided.

Hong has produced the desired effect. He must have been speaking for some time; and now he comes down from the platform, and, amidst a roar of applause, goes off to another meeting. Mao has begun his speech; but his voice is drowned in uproar —impossible to hear a single word. Hong has packed the meeting; and it is obvious that the instigators of all these shouts and protests are seven or eight Chinese scattered through the hall. The mass of the audience, though hostile, would evidently like to listen; for Mao is famous and venerable. But he does not raise his voice. He goes on speaking through all the hubbub, looking fixedly at those parts of the hall, in which the opposition is strongest. He must see how few they are who are leading the tumult. Then suddenly, in a clear, strong voice, moving his arms as if he would reap the hall, he cries:

"Look at those who interrupt me with their insults; they are afraid to listen to me."

The audience wavers. Mao has won. The eyes of all turn to one of the anarchists. Mao's only opponents are now the few ringleaders.

"Those who live on British money while our strikers are dying of hunger are worse than . . ."

The end of the sentence is inaudible. Mao is leaning forward, his mouth wide open. Torrents of abuse, poured forth on every note of the Chinese scale, come from all parts of the hall. It is like the barking of a pack of hounds. In this confused volume of sound one catches every now and then the words: "Dog! Sold! Traitor! Traitor! Coolie!"

Mao may be speaking. I cannot hear him. Meanwhile the hullabaloo dies down; and in the midst of a few isolated interruptions, Mao recaptures the attention of the audience, and, with uplifted hands, raising his voice, cries:

"Coolie? Yes, Coolie! I have always gone in and out among the unfortunate. But not in order to shout out their names, as you are doing, coupled with those of thieves and traitors. When I was hardly more than a child . . ."

(There are tussles in the hall between the interrupters and those who want to listen, but Mao is making himself heard.)

"I swore to identify my life with theirs, and no one shall deliver me from that oath, for those to whom I swore it are dead."

And with open hands and outstretched arms:

"You, the roofless, you, the riceless, hewers of wood and drawers of boats, dock laborers, you who are nameless, whose only identification mark is the wound on your shoulders or the bruises on your hips, listen to those who glory in the shedding of your blood. Hah! how glibly they utter that word 'coolie'— the fine gentlemen!—in the very same tone as that in which I called them 'dogs' just now!"

"Yes, yes!"

And again that approving refrain:

"Yes, yes."

"Death to those who insult the people."

Who shouted? No one knows. The voice was weak and wavering. But instantaneously the cry is taken up.

"De-a-th— to . . ."

A growl, a groan which waxes into a roar. The word is barely distinguishable. The tone is enough.

The anarchists push towards the platform. But Mao has not come to the meeting unaccompanied; and his men, with the help of the crowd, defend him now. One of the anarchists, hoisted on his comrades' shoulders, no sooner tries to make himself heard than he is assailed, thrown to the ground and beaten. In the tumult, we go out. At the door, I turn round: through the thickening clouds of smoke I catch a confused vision of white robes mingling with the blue or brown rags of the dock laborers, of agitated forms and clenched fists, dominated by dead-white helmets.

In the street I see Mao going away. I try to catch him up, but fail. Perhaps he does not wish to be seen with a white man today.

I go to the hospital, alone and on foot. The way in which Mao saved the situation does credit to his skill. But had not that idiot shouted "coolie" what would have happened? Such a chance victory means nothing. Besides, Mao defended no one but himself. As my Yunnanese companion said, when he left me: "Had Hong been there, Monsieur Mao might not have triumphed so easily."

"Triumphed?"

By the time I reach the hospital night has fallen. Soldiers with parabellums are stationed under the palms at the four corners of the bungalow. I go in. No one in the passages at this hour, except for a man nurse asleep on a settee of carved wood in the vestibule. He awakes at the sound of footsteps on the tiles and takes me to Garine's room.

Linoleum on the floor. Whitewashed walls, a ventilating fan, a smell of drugs and of ether. The mosquito curtain is partly drawn up. Garine appears lying on a bed shrouded with gauze. I sit down at his bedside, laying damp hands on my wickerwork chair. I relax, worn out with fatigue, while the eternal mosquitoes are buzzing outside. Below the roof a still, metallic palm leaf is outlined against the soft and formless darkness. Borne on the warm night air which comes in through the window, is an odor of decay, exhaled from the ground, and the sickly fragrance of flowers from the garden mingling with the smell of tar, iron, and stagnant water. In the distance, the sound of mahjongs, like a storm of hail falling, the crackling of crackers and the hooting of motor horns. When the breeze blows in as if from a stagnant pool, but really from the river, if we listen attentively, we can catch the sound of a one-stringed violin; it must be some traveling theater or some craftsman playing, half asleep in his half-shuttered booth. A reddish light glows behind the trees, suggesting the close of some great fair: it is the town.

As soon as I enter the room, Garine, with pinched face, half-closed eyes and hair dripping over his forehead, asks me eagerly:

"Well?"

"Nothing of any importance."

I give him the news. Then we are silent. The lamps in the room and passage, veiled by clouds of insects, burn, burn as if they would burn forever. The nurse's steps die away in the corridor.

"Would you like to be left alone?"

"Oh, no! I don't want to be alone. I can't bear to think of myself now, and, when I am ill, I always do think of myself. . . ."

The weariness of his voice—generally so clear, but tonight trembling a little, as if his mind had lost control over his words—is all of a piece with everything else: with the dim lights, the silence, the smell of perspiration, more pungent now and then than the smell of ether, and the scents from the garden, where soldiers are marching; with this hospital where the only living things seem to be the swarms of insects buzzing round the lamps.

"It is strange. But after my trial I was obsessed by the vanity of life and of humanity as a whole. It seemed a prey to blind forces. Now this obsession recurs. . . . It is idiotic, of course, and comes from my illness. Yet it seems to me that in doing what I am doing here I am struggling against this vanity of life. . . . And that it is reasserting its rights."

As he turns over in his bed, I breathe the acid smell of fever.

"Ah! that intangible something which makes a man feel that his life is dominated by some force. . . . How strange the power of memory is when one is ill. All day I have been thinking of my trial. I wonder why. It was after my trial that my impression of the futility of the social order came to include everything human. . . . I don't see why it should not. . . . And yet . . . At this very moment, are there not many who are dreaming of victories which they would have thought impossible two years ago? I am responsible for that dream. I have created that hope. I don't want to preach; but it is hope that makes men live and die. And then? But when one's temperature is high one ought not to talk so much. . . . It is foolish. . . . Yet to lie thinking of oneself all day! . . . Why is my mind fixed on that trial? Why? It was so long ago. . . . How stupid fever is. . . . But one sees things. . . ."

The nurse had just shut the door noiselessly. Garine turns over again; and again the human smell prevails over the smell of ether.

"At Kazan, on Christmas night, '19, that wonderful procession.

... Borodin was there, as he always is. . . . What? They are bringing all the gods to the front of the cathedral. Huge figures like those carried in carnivals, even a fish goddess in her siren's sheath. . . . Two hundred, three hundred gods. . . . Luther, too. Players muffled up in furs make the devil of a row with any instruments they can lay hands on. A pile heaped high is flaming. The gods borne on men's shoulders round the square stand out black against the background of fire and snow. . . . A roar of triumph. . . . The exhausted bearers of the gods throw them on to the flames. A terrific blaze cracks the heads open and shows up the cathedral, white against the darkness. . . . What? Is it the revolution? Yes, and this continues for seven or eight hours! I should have liked to have seen the dawn! . . . Corruption, decay! What things one sees! But one cannot cast the Revolution into the fire; all that is not the Revolution is even worse; one has to admit it, even when one is disgusted. It is just the same with oneself. Neither for nor against. I learned that at the Lycée . . . in Latin. It will all be swept away. What? Perhaps there was snow, too. . . . What?"

He is on the border line of extreme lucidity and delirium. Agitated by the sound of his own voice, he has spoken in loud tones, which resound throughout the hospital. The nurse whispers in my ear:

"The doctor said that the Commissioner must not be allowed to talk too long. . . ." And aloud: "Would you like to have some chloral to send you to sleep, sir?"

The American adviser to the Government left Canton yesterday evening. For some time he had only been consulted about unimportant matters. He was aware of it. He may have thought his position unsafe. If so, he was right. . . . Borodin takes his place as official adviser to the Government, with control over land and air forces. Consequently Gallen, who is chief of the Canton general staff, will now be responsible to Borodin alone, which means that the whole army is in the hands of the International.

3   *The Man*

THE BRITISH at Hong Kong live in fear of an insurrection. Their wireless announces to the whole world that the town has resumed its customary activity, but adds: *the dock laborers alone have not returned to work*. They will not return. The harbor is still deserted. The city is more and more like that great hollow black figure which stood out against the sky as I came away. The British will soon have to find some kind of occupation suitable for an isolated town. . . . The chief source of its wealth—the rice market—is leaving it. The big producers are dealing with Manila, with Saïgon. "Hong Kong," writes a member of the Chamber of Commerce whose letter we intercepted, "will in one year become one of the most unsettled ports in the Far East, unless the British Government decides on military intervention."

Bodies of volunteers parade the town. Many motorcars belonging to shopkeepers have been armed with machine guns. Tonight, the main telephone—without the telephone no defense is practicable—has been barricaded with barbed wire. Trenches are being dug round the reservoirs, the Governor's palace and the arsenal. And, in spite of its reliance on the militia, the British police, taken by surprise, is sending messenger after messenger to urge General Chen Chun-ming to march on Canton.

"My dear chap," Nicolaiëff said to me in his pontifical manner, "don't you see that the best thing he could do would be to go away? . . . Myroff has been talking to me about him. If he stays another fortnight, he will stay a great deal longer than he likes. . . . Oh, of course, one might as well be buried here as anywhere else. . . ."

"He says he can't go now. He has too much work to do."

"Yes, yes. . . . We have plenty of sick here. . . . With our way of living no one can escape from the influence of the Tropics."

He points to his stomach, smiling.

"I prefer this. . . . And then, when what he regards as most important is not at stake, Garine is rather flabby. . . . Like everyone else."

"And you don't think that life is dear to him?"

"Not very."

Today, there is consternation at the Police Station. One of Chen-Dai's "boys," an informer, has just sent in a report. Chen-Dai knows that the Terrorists want to assassinate him. He has been advised to flee and refused. But the informer heard him say to a friend: "If my life cannot stop them, perhaps my death may. . . ." And it was to suicide, not to assassination, that he referred. If Chen-Dai, famous and respected as he still is, were, in the oriental manner, to kill himself for the cause, he would give that cause a strength against which it would be difficult to contend. "He is incapable of it," said Nicolaïeff. All the same we are alarmed.

Garine has just left the hospital. Myroff or the Chinese doctor will come and inoculate him every morning.

The next day

Chen-Dai's conduct is not the only cause of Nicolaïeff's anxiety: Chen Chun-ming took Chao-Chow yesterday and is marching on Canton after having beaten the Cantonese troops. Borodin regards these troops—mercenaries who were once in Sun Yat-sen's service—as of no importance, being utterly incapable unless reinforced by the Red Army and the cadets. But the cadets, commanded by Chiang Kai-shek, remain at Whampoa; and the Red Army under Gallen is still in its cantonments. The Propaganda sections alone will leave the town tomorrow; and they may prepare victory but not obtain it. "Let the Committee of Seven decide," says Garine. "Now it is either the Red Army and the decree or Chen Chun-ming; and Chen Chun-ming for them means the execution platoon. Let them choose."

That night

Eleven o'clock at Garine's. We are waiting for him to return, Klein and I, and looking out of the window. Beside Klein, on a little table, is a bottle of rice spirit and a glass. A police orderly has brought in a blue poster which lies there partly folded on the table, which the boys have forgotten to clear. There are similar posters all over the town.

It is the first paragraph of Chen-Dai's will.

I, Chen-Dai, have voluntarily killed myself in order to convince my compatriots of this: that PEACE, our greatest treasure, must not be destroyed in that confusion into which evil counselors are about to lead the people of China.

And who are putting up these posters, which may do us more harm than all Chen-Dai's preaching?

Has Chen-Dai killed himself? Or has he been murdered?

Garine has been to the police station and to Borodin's. At first he had tried to get confirmation of the rumor of Chen-Dai's death, the rumor having doubtless reached the station; but he had come away without waiting for a reply. Now the reply reaches us: Chen-Dai died of a knife wound in the heart. Impatient, all on edge, battering our thighs with our fists at the slightest mosquito bite, we wait. I am so perturbed that I hardly distinguish Klein's voice; it seems to come through a veil, as he says:

"I maintain that it is impossible. . . ."

I have just said that I think suicide not improbable; and Klein protests with a sudden vehemence, which he seems trying to suppress. I have always thought there was something strange about this man, who is really extremely cultured, though he assumes the air of a military boxer. Garine, who is a great friend of his, when I questioned him about Klein, replied in the very same words that Gérard had used: "Here it is practically the same as in the Legion, and I know no more about his private life than anyone else."

As he leans heavily on the arms of his chair this evening, Klein seems to find it difficult to express himself, and this not because he is speaking French. His closed eyes and swaying body give one the impression that he is struggling with his words. He is drunk, but lucid in his intoxication, and his voice is harsh and shrill.

"It is not pos-sible."

The humming of the ventilator is like a singsong, which obsesses me as I look at him.

"You have no idea! It is . . . No, I can't explain. You must know people who have tried. One puts it off. One says at first: 'In an hour—in half an hour'—then one is at peace. But after a while one thinks: 'I must do it now.' And, with eyes fixed on the light, one drops into a kind of stupor. One is glad to see the light; one smiles like an idiot and one thinks it is over. But not quite. The idea comes back. It masters one this time. Not the act, but the idea. One says to oneself: 'Why do I make all this fuss?' "

I ask, as if accidentally:

"Then you think the love of life returns?"

"Life, death, you don't know what they are. Only you feel you must do the deed. My elbows were pressed against my ribs, my two hands grasped the handle of my knife. And then! Would you believe it? I shrugged my shoulders. How stupid it all is! My motives—why, I had even forgotten them. I had to do it, because I had to. That was all. I was stupefied. Ashamed of myself, ashamed. . . . I felt I was good for nothing but to be thrown into the canal. It was foolish, wasn't it? Yes, foolish; and it lasted a long while. Daylight ended it. One does not kill oneself in daylight. At least, not deliberately. One might perhaps suddenly, almost without thinking. But . . .

"It took me some time to recover myself."

He laughs; and his laugh rings so false that I go to the window and look out to see if Garine is coming. Through the noise of the ventilator I hear Klein's nails tapping on the wickerwork of his chair, as he talks to himself. . . . Then, obviously in order to set me at my ease by showing that he is considering the whole matter sanely he continues sententiously:

"It is difficult. . . . Of course for those who want to quit life because they have had enough of it, there are ways in which one hardly realizes what one is doing. But our Chen-Dai kills himself for something he holds dear, dearer than anything else. Moreover, if he succeeds it will be the noblest action of his life. For that reason he cannot employ such means. No, it would not be worth the trouble. . . ."

"But surely the example would be the same?"

"Ach! You cannot understand! . . . You, you speak of 'an example.' How difficult it is to explain! Don't you see, it is something like the Japanese? Chen-Dai does not do it to remain worthy of himself. Nor to live—how do you say it in French?—'heroically,' Yes, that is it, Chen-Dai does it in order to remain worthy . . . of his mission. Consequently he cannot, so to speak, take his life by surprise!"

"And yet . . ."

But all at once he is silent, he is listening. A car stops. There is a hum of voices.

"Come back at six o'clock." The car goes off.

Garine!

"Klein, Borodin wants to see you."

He turns to me. "Let us go upstairs." Hardly has he sat down when he says: "What was he saying to you?"

"That Chen cannot possibly have committed suicide."

"I know. He has always said that Chen would never play us such a trick. We shall see."

"What do you think, yourself?"

"At present I don't know what to think."

"And what about him?"

"Whom do you mean? Borodin? No. You need not smile. We have nothing to do with it. I am certain. Not even indirectly or accidentally. He was as astounded as I."

"No, but . . . what about the tips given to Hong?"

"Oh! that is another matter. But, according to the first report, it is not certain that Hong is implicated in any way: the military guard was always on the alert, and no one went in. But that matters little. We have other things to do. First of all, the posters. Write this down and translate it:

"We must never forget that a man respected throughout the length and breadth of China, Chen-Dai, was vilely murdered yesterday by the agents of our enemies.

"And then for another which must be put alongside the first. (Make that clear.)

"Shame on England. Shame on the Canton and Shanghai murderers.

"Put in a corner of the second and in smaller letter the dates: May twenty-fifth—June twenty-fifth (the Shanghai and Shameen incidents).

"Good. It will be understood. Now for the communiqués to the sections: *Chen-Dai did not commit suicide. He was murdered by men in British employ. Nothing will prevent the political bureau from executing justice.* Eloquent but concise."

"So you are giving up the Terrorists?"

"We must think of Hong Kong first. And this affair may make the decree possible."

He sits down. While I translate he is drawing strange birds on his blotting pad. Then he rises, walks up and down, returns to his desk, begins to draw again, throws his pencil away, examines his revolver attentively and finally becomes lost in meditation, with his chin in his hands. I give him the two translations.

"Are you quite sure they are correct?"

"Absolutely. But perhaps you wouldn't mind telling me what you are going to do with them?"

"Surely that is obvious."

"No, I don't understand."

"Why, of course. They will be posted on the hoardings."

I look at him in bewilderment.

"Come," I say, "before your poster is printed, all the Chinese will have read the other."

"They will not."

"You are going to have them torn down? That will take a long while."

"No, I shall have them covered up. The troops who are on our side will be employed in various ways and will not enter the town before noon. At five o'clock the irregulars will go about firing rifles. The police have been warned. No one of the educated class will dare to come out for several hours. The others do not know how to read. Besides, by three o'clock all their posters will have been covered up. Tomorrow at eight—or rather today, for it is already one o'clock—five thousand of ours will be on the walls. We shall print another five thousand in leaflet form. And the whole police force, mind you, will set to work. Perhaps a score or even fifty posters may be forgotten and not covered up. But we cannot help that, and they will not be read before ours."

"Supposing they make Chen-Dai's death the pretext for a movement?"

"No, they won't. Not yet. They have hardly any troops. By themselves they wouldn't dare. As for the people, they may not perhaps believe us implicitly, but at any rate, they will hesitate. And no popular rising was ever made by people who hesitate. No, it's all right."

"If he happened not to have killed himself?"

"If he had, we should be faced with problems of a very different nature."

". . . You must admit that it is those who think they will benefit by the blue poster who represent him as having killed himself?"

"Those who drew up that poster are in the same position as ourselves. They received their information before us, that is all. And they used it as quickly as possible. Oh! we shall soon know where we are. But for the moment we must deal with what is most pressing. Chen-Dai's death may have important consequences."

We go downstairs, almost running.

"And Borodin?"

"I looked in on him as I passed. He is ill. Each in his turn. I wonder whether they haven't been trying to poison him. His 'boys' can be relied upon—besides . . ."

He suddenly stopped short; for, rushing down after me, he had missed a step and only escaped falling by catching hold of the banister. For a second he pauses, takes breath, pushes back his hair, and begins to tear down as quickly as ever.

"Besides, they are well watched."

"To the printers."

We place our revolvers on the seat, close to our hands. The town seems quiet. As we fly by, the electric lights look like mere sparks in the darkness and we can barely distinguish the booths with their planks put up, showing a feeble gleam of light through the chinks. No brightness in the sky, no moon, no houses standing out against the darkness. The only sign of life is on the ground: lanterns, hawkers, cook-shops, lamps blazing in the still hot air, fleeting shadows, motionless forms and gramophones, gramophones. . . . In the distance—the discharge of rifles.

Here is the printer's. Our printer's. A long shed. . . . Inside, the light is so dazzling that we have to shut our eyes. The workmen belong to the Party and have been carefully chosen. All the same, the doors are guarded by soldiers. They are expecting us. A very young lieutenant, a cadet, comes to take Garine's orders. "He is not to admit anyone." The work in hand is suspended. I give the manager, a Chinese, my two translations. He cuts them into vertical lines and gives one to each compositor.

"Correct the proof," says Garine to me, "and bring me the first leaflet when it is printed. I shall be at the police station. If I am not there, wait for me. I will send a car for you."

The copy does not take long to set up. The manager pastes the lines side by side and gives me the proof. Not one of the workmen knows the sense of the poster he has helped to print.

Two of the machines stop, while those who work them wait for our corrections. There are not many; and in two minutes the sheets are on the machine, worked by hands and bare feet.

I take the first page that is printed and go.

A car is there. It whirls me at full speed to the police station. A few rifle shots are heard in the distance. A cadet is at the door. He takes me down deserted passages dimly lit by occasional lights shrouded in haloes, where our steps re-echo in the silence of night, to the office, where Garine is waiting for me. I begin to be conscious of a vague uneasiness mingled with exultation, and to feel that parched sensation in the throat one has after a sleepless night: fever and spirits. . . .

A large well-lighted office. Garine is pacing up and down, looking worn, with his hands in his pockets. Against the wall, a Chinese bedstead in carved wood on which Nicolaïëff is lying.

"Well!"

I give him the poster:

"Take care; the ink is wet. My hands are covered with it."

He shrugs his shoulders, unfolds the poster, looks at it and sucks in his lips as if he were nibbling. (Not to know Cantonese, not even the letters, or rather to have but an imperfect knowledge of them both, exasperates him, and he has no time to learn.)

"Are you sure it is all right?"

"Don't worry. Do you know that they are beginning to fight in the streets?"

"To fight?"

"Well, I don't know. But I heard shots as I came along."

"Were there many?"

"Oh, no! few and far between."

"Good. That is all right. It must be our men shooting those who are posting up the blue bills."

He turns to Nicolaïëff, who is lying on his side, resting on his elbow.

"Come, let us go on. Do you know anyone among them who is not very brave, but who is likely to know things?"

"I think I understand the sort of person you mean when you say 'not very brave.' "

"Yes."

"In my opinion no one is very brave under such conditions."

"Oh, yes, they may be."

Garine's arms are folded, his eyes closed: Nicolaïëff looks at him in a way that is strange, almost hostile.

"Yes. Hong would not tell."

"One might try."

"Useless."

"You think well of your former friends. That is as it should be."

"As you wish."

Garine shrugs his shoulders.

The other is silent. We wait.

"Ling, perhaps."

"Ah! no, not any 'perhaps.'"

"But it is you who make me say 'perhaps.' For my own part I should say there is not the slightest doubt. When one has seen fellows in the evening, after a fuss, looking for their parents or their wives among the corpses, when one has seen Chinese examining prisoners, one begins to know whom one can rely upon."

"Ling, isn't he a trades union leader?"

"Of the harbor coolies' union."

"Do you regard him as well informed?"

"You will see. But in my opinion he is."

"Good. That is agreed."

Nicolaïeff stretches, leans on the arms of a chair and gets up, not without difficulty.

"I think we shall have him tomorrow. . . ." And, half smiling, in a curious attitude of deference and irony:

"And then, what are we going to do?"

Garine makes a gesture as if he did not care. A slight expression of contempt passes over Nicolaïeff's face. Garine looks at him with protruding jaw and says:

"Incense." (Incense being a means of bringing people back to life after strangulation.)

The fat man closes his eyes by way of assent, lights a cigarette and lounges out.

The next day

I leave my car in front of the market place. In the soft light the long buildings look like streaks of plaster drawn across the sky. All the drinking booths are crowded with men wearing the brown or blue linen suits of dock laborers. As soon as the car stops, shouts are heard, long and resounding, borne upon the transparent air as if on that of a river. The men pour out of the booths, howling and pushing one another, and noisily putting into their pockets the change for the coins they have just taken out. One by one they climb into the buses and wagons, which have been commandeered and which wait for them at the end of the white street. The leaders shout again. Some men have not yet arrived. But here they are, shouting also, and with little sausages between their teeth. . . . One by one the vehicles roll noisily away.

The second section of the Propaganda, preceding the Red Army, has gone.

Our posters are on all the walls. Chen-Dai's forged will—now covered up—had come too late. It had been printed in the hope of a popular rising; but no preparations had been made. Had Tang's defeat been a lesson? Had the fear of Chen Chun-Ming's arrival at Canton prevented any new attempt at rebellion?

The cadets are parading the town. All the morning one long procession of agents files through Garine's office. With his hollow face worn even more hollow by his sleepless night, Garine leaning over his desk with his head in his left hand, dictates or gives orders, with nerves strained to the utmost. He is having more posters printed:

The End of Hong Kong. The British, he announces, are leaving the town in crowds: the banks are finally closing their branches. (It is false; the banks, acting on orders from London, are still assisting British enterprises as far as they can, somewhat glumly, it is true.) At the same time, in order to compel the Committee of Seven to follow him, he gets our agents to announce the fall of Chao-Chow and the failure up till now of the Red Army to get into position—this is the only army to which the people are attached.

At noon, special editions of the newspapers, posters and huge calico placards carried through the town proclaim that the shopkeepers and manufacturers of Hong Kong (almost the whole European population of the town), assembled in the Grand Thea-

ter yesterday, telegraphed to the King, asking for the despatch of
British troops to China. This is true.

Borodin has told the Committee that he has no objection to the
promulgation of the decrees against the Terrorists, proposed by
Chen-Dai, and that these decrees will be executed from today.
But our spies tell us there will be no meeting of the anarchists.
Ling has not yet been arrested. As for Hong, he has disappeared.
The Terrorists have decided to confine themselves to direct ac-
tion, which means executions.

Later

Chen Chun-ming is still advancing.

At Hong Kong, there are telegrams with enormous headlines:
"The Rout of the Cantonese Army." In the halls of hotels and in
front of telegraph offices, the British are anxiously waiting for
news of the war, but, in the harbor, where the water is quite still,
save for a slight swell in the wake of slowly moving junks, the
steamboats at anchor, as motionless as if they were mere wreckage,
sink further and further into the water.

The Chinese in power here are seriously alarmed. For them
Chen's entrance into Canton means torture, or execution at the
street corner, by one of the platoons, whose officers are in too
much of a hurry even to identify those they shoot. Everyone
talks of death. Every look suggests it. It is as all pervading as light.

Garine is preparing the speech that he will deliver tomorrow at
Chen-Dai's funeral.

The next day
Eleven o'clock

The roll of drums and the beating of gongs in the distance,
broken by the notes of a flute and a one-stringed violin, modu-
lated at first, then shrill, then soft; a screeching of bagpipes, thin
and fine, though sharp, and beneath it all the muffled clattering of
wooden shoes on the pavement and the sound of conversation

punctuated by gongs. I lean out of the window to see the procession passing at the end of the street. A whirlwind of children, looking behind them as they run, with necks outstretched like ducks, a shapeless cloud of dust advancing and shrouding a mass of white-clothed forms, on to which seem to be grafted banners of silk—red, crimson, purple, cerise, rose-colored, vermilion, carmine; every shade of red. The crowd hedges the procession round and almost hides it from my view, but not quite: two high poles are passing, they support a horizontal band of white calico. Waving like a ship's masts, they seem to keep time with the roll of the big drums, which dominates everything. I contrive to make out the letters on the banner and read: "Death to the English. . . ." Then the procession moves on, and there is nothing at the end of the street, but the crowd, the rising dust and the music interrupted by the beating of gongs. Now come the offerings: first, heaps of tropical still life, over which float scrolls covered with writing, carried by men, and waving and tossing as if they were about to fall. Then comes the catafalque, the traditional long pagoda of carved wood, red and gold, hoisted on the shoulders of thirty bearers. They are very tall. I can just see their heads. They give me the impression of a few steps of rapid advance, then a halt, then another advance, making the enormous dark red structure pitch and toss like a vessel in a storm. What is this that comes after it? It looks like a house made of calico. . . . Yes, it is a house of linen stitched over a bamboo frame. This also is borne on the shoulders of men who advance in jerks. . . . I rush into the next room and take a pair of field glasses from Garine's drawer. When I return the house is still at the end of the street. Huge figures are painted on its walls. Chen-Dai is represented—dead—with an English soldier standing over him and transfixing him with his bayonet. There are words round the painting in bright red letters; and just as this strange representation is disappearing round the corner of the street, I succeed in deciphering the legend: "Death to the English brigands." Now there is nothing to be seen but multitudes of small placards following in the wake of huge moving symbols like a flock of birds flying after a vessel, all of them proclaiming hatred of England. Then there are lanterns, staves, glittering helmets, and then . . . nothing. . . . The human hedge at the end of the street breaks up, while the sound of drums and gongs dies away in the distance, and the golden dust rises slowly until it is lost in the daylight.

A few hours later, long before Garine's return, fragments of his speech begin to circulate from orderly to orderly, in our stations at the Propaganda. These sentences are brief and concise; for Garine, like Borodin, can only address his audiences through an interpreter. So the chance office talk reports phrases like these: "Hong Kong, the turnkey"; "Hong Kong displaying the ill-gotten wealth of a prison warder in the face of our famine." "Those who talk as distinguished from those who act." "Those who merely protest and those who drive the British out of Hong Kong like rats." "Like an honest man cutting off the hand of the burglar who is trying to open his window, you will have in your possession tomorrow the hand of the British burglar, the hand of British imperialism, of Hong Kong ruined."

A crowd of workingmen is pouring down the street. They flourish banners, on which I read: "Long live the Red Army." They press round the windows of the hall, in which the Committee of Seven is sitting. Like a herd of cattle they draw together and disperse, then come together again, and the street is filled with their cries of "Long live the Red Army," now a solo, then in unison. In these cries I seem to distinguish a China that I am beginning to know; a China in which a wild idealism is imposing itself on the vileness and meanness of the masses, just as in the smells coming in through my open windows from the seething town, the scent of pepper dominates the odor of decomposition. As I watch the funeral procession of Chen-Dai, as I listen to the shouts of "Long live the Red Army," there seems to float up to me, out of all those confused reports, a cloud of mean ambitions, of craving for personal advancement, of electoral wirepulling, of secret gifts to the Party, of bribes, of opium smuggling, of blackmail—a world which lives by exploiting the principles of San-Min as it might have done those of the mandarins. A section of that very Chinese bourgeoisie for which the revolutionaries express such contempt has insinuated itself into the Revolution. "You must pass through all that," Garine once said to me, "just as a kick passes through a pile of filth."

No news from the Terrorists. Ling, the man to whom Nicolaiëff referred, is still at liberty. Since Borodin's nomination (he is not better and is still confined to the house), six of our people have been murdered.

And Hong Kong is holding out. The Governor has appealed to Japan and French Indo-China. In a few days coolies will start from Yokohama and Haiphong to take the place of the strikers. On their arrival at Hong Kong, the coolies, who have been despatched at great expense, must find mountains of rice without buyers, and merchants driven to despair. "Canton is the key with which the British have unlocked the doors of Southern China," said Garine in his speech yesterday. "And now it is for us to use this key to lock them up, and so securely that they can never again be opened: boats that have put in at Hong Kong must not be allowed to anchor at Canton. . . ." Already, in the minds of foreigners, Hong Kong, the British port, Crown territory, is beginning to be regarded as a Chinese port, which is in a perpetual state of agitation, and foreign boats are tending to ignore it. . . .

Mail boats and vessels with large cargoes, when they do enter Hong Kong Bay, stay only a few hours. They unload at Shanghai. In the native town there, the British, by means of Chinese agents, are trying to do what they failed to do at Swatow: to create an organization which will distribute in the interior goods ordered from England by Hong Kong firms. Many commercial houses are reducing their staffs at Hong Kong and transferring them to Shanghai. We shall see. . . .

The Committee of Seven is again taking steps to bring the Red Army into the field and to secure the execution of leading Terrorists. The Committee's representative asserts that the decree Garine is demanding will be signed in three days. . . . All day, outside the house where the Committee is sitting, a threatening and well-organized crowd has been crying out for the Red Army.

The next day

Ling was arrested yesterday. This afternoon we shall no doubt receive the information we expect him to give us. The advance of the enemy's troops is making the Propaganda office extremely busy. Our agents who precede the army have received minute instructions, their leaders from Garine himself. I saw them, one after the other, pass down the passage, smiling. We have given up distributing leaflets. For we have so many helpers that we can rely entirely on propaganda by word of mouth, by far the surest method, though the most dangerous and the most costly in lives and money. Liao Chun-wei, the Governor's Commissioner of Finance (whom the Terrorists want to murder), has succeeded in raising large sums, thanks to a new system of collecting taxes, invented by the International experts, so that the Propaganda is once more in funds. In a few weeks the enemy's commissariat and his whole administration will be disorganized; and you cannot get mercenaries to fight for you without payment. Then a hundred of our men, whose leaders answer for them, are about to enlist in Chen Chun-ming's army. They know full well that they run the risk of being shot, either by him as traitors, or by our men as enemies. The day before yesterday, three of our agents were discovered and strangled, after having been tortured for more than an hour.

All the office doors were ajar when the leaders of the Propaganda sections in Chen's army started. Lenin's bears, as they are called, affected young Chinese in sack coats and broad trousers, who scorn native dishes and speak English, who have just returned from American or Russian universities, watched our agents setting out to enlist in the enemy's army, with supreme contempt.

Everything in its turn.
News from Shanghai.
The Chinese Chamber of Commerce, acting under the influence of the Kuomintang, decrees the confiscation of all British merchandise in Chinese hands. And from July thirtieth, for the space

of one year, it forbids the purchase of all British goods and the transport of any goods by a British ship.

Shanghai newspapers declare that this measure will reduce British trade by eighty per cent. This trade for last year (without reckoning Hong Kong) was valued at twenty million pounds! Hong Kong's one remaining hope is in the army of Chen Chunming.

Nicolaïeff has received the following, written in capital letters: "IF LING HAS NOT BEEN SET AT LIBERTY TOMORROW, THE HOSTAGES WILL BE EXECUTED."

Do the Terrorists really hold hostages? Nicolaïeff does not think so. But many of our men have been sent off on various errands for several days; and we have no means of ascertaining what has happened to them.

Six o'clock

An orderly from the prison brings Garine some papers. They are Ling's cross-examination. He reads them. When he has finished, I go up to him.

"Has he said anything?"

"Once again Nicolaïeff proves to be right. Ah! there are not many who can hold out against torture. . . ."

"Did it last long?"

"What do you think?"

"What is going to be done with him?"

"In the devil's name, what would you have us do?"

"One does not set a Terrorist at liberty."

"What then?"

"The prisons are full, of course. And then he must be tried by a special court. Yes, as Nicolaïeff said, everything is coming to light. First, Hong's whereabouts; second, that he intends to get rid of me—that, of course, I knew—third, that it was by Hong's order that Chen-Dai was killed; the murderer was one of his 'boys.' "

"But we had informers in his house."

"Only one; and he was serving both sides. He has tricked us, but not for long. Needless to say, he is now in prison. And soon, we shall be using him as a witness, if there is a trial."

"Would not that be rather risky?"

"Oh! he is an opium addict. If Nicolaïeff deprives him of the drug for a few days and promises that he will not be executed, he will say what we want."

"Can there be people who still believe in such promises?"

"In any case, it would be quite enough to cut off his supply of opium."

He pauses; then, slowly shrugging his shoulders, says:

"It is terribly easy to deal with a man who is about to die."

And then, a few minutes later, as if thinking aloud:

"Nearly all the promises I have made have been kept."

"But how can they distinguish?"

"How can I help that?"

Hong was arrested yesterday evening, in a house where he was hiding.

At Hong Kong, the British are gradually gathering together as many dock laborers as they need for the resumption of work in the harbor. When they have enough—and even now the men, Annamites and Japanese, are in the sheds, awaiting orders from the Governor—they will reorganize the work, and suddenly the trade of the town will go on as before. If we were to waver for a moment, a regular town of boats, laden with cargoes, would sail up to Canton, and the great carcase of the island would come to life again—unless the decree we are expecting should be signed. But this decree is the recognition of the war of the trades unions, the affirmation of the will of the Canton Government and of the power of the International in China.

The next day

Garine is sitting at his desk. He looks worn out. His back is bent, his chin in his hands, he is leaning his elbows as usual on bulging masses of papers. His belt lies on a chair. On hearing steps, he opens his eyes, pushes his hair from his forehead and raises his head. Hong comes in, followed by two soldiers. He has not been captured without a struggle; and on his face, in which his little oriental eyes gleam sadly, there are marks of blows. As soon as he enters the room, he halts with his arms behind his back, his legs apart.

Garine, dropping with fatigue and in the kind of stupor which is the effect of his fever, looks at Hong vaguely and waits, his head drooping slowly from right to left as if he were about to fall asleep. . . . Suddenly he draws a deep breath; he has pulled himself together. He shrugs his shoulders. At this moment Hong looks up, frowning. He perceives Garine's gesture, and, freeing himself from the soldiers, starts forwards, then falls, struck by the butt end of a rifle. He had seen Garine's revolver lying in its case on a chair and was about to pounce on it.

He gets up.

"That is enough," said Garine in French; and then, in Cantonese: "Take him away."

The soldiers go off with him.

Silence.

"Garine, who is going to try him?"

"When I saw him there, I felt inclined to get up and say: 'Now what have you done?' as if he were a naughty child. That was why I shrugged my shoulders, and he thought I was insulting him. Another of his follies!"

Then, as if he had only just heard my question, Garine replied hurriedly:

"The special court. He has still about twenty-four hours of life."

The next day

Garine is giving a watchmaker photographs of Chen-Dai and Sun Yat-sen with anti-British inscriptions; and he is looking at samples of cases when our orderly brings in a sealed note.

"Who has brought this?" asks Garine.

"Someone from the office of the sailors' syndicate."

"Is the comrade there?"

"Yes."

"Bring him in, at once."

A coolie comes in, wearing the armlet of the sailors' syndicate.

"Did you bring this?"

"Yes."

"Where are the bodies?"

"At the office."

Garine hands me the note, which he has opened.

The bodies of Klein and three murdered Chinese have been found in a brothel near the river. *The hostages* . . .

"Where are their things?"

"I don't know."

"But surely their pockets have been emptied?"

"No."

Immediately, Garine rises, takes his helmet and signs to me to follow him. The coolie gets up by the chauffeur and we start.

In the car:

"Tell me, Garine. Klein lived here with a white woman, did he not?"

"Well, and what has that to do with it?"

The bodies are not at the office, but in the meeting-hall. A Chinese, sitting on the ground, is watching at the door. Near him is a big dog, which is trying to go in. Whenever the dog approaches the door, the Chinese stretches out his leg and gives him a kick. The Chinese watches us coming up, and when we reach him, he leans his head against the wall, half closes his eyes and pushes open the door with his hand, without rising. The dog, some little way off, walks round and round him.

We enter. A bare hall, with a well-trodden earthen floor, heaps of dust in the corners, the glare hardly softened by the blue-tinted skylights. As soon as I raise my eyes, I see the four bodies, *standing*. I was looking for them on the ground. They are stiff already. They have been placed leaning against the wall, like posts. At first sight I was almost stupefied; for, in the silence and the light, these straight bodies are not in the least ghostly, but, on the contrary, excessively real. Now I can breathe again; and the air that I inhale is infected by an odor, unlike any I have experienced before—an animal smell, strong, but not pungent: the smell of corpses. Garine calls the watchman, who rises slowly and unwillingly and comes in.

"Fetch some sheets."

The man leans against the door as if dazed. He does not seem to understand.

"Fetch some sheets!"

Even then he does not budge. Garine goes up to him with clenched fists and then stops.

"Ten taels if you bring me sheets within the next half-hour. Now do you understand?"

The Chinese bows and goes out.

My tense muscles relax; for Garine's words seem to have brought a breath of humanity into the hall. Then, turning round, I perceive Klein's body—I recognize it at once. There is a large mark in the middle of the face: the mouth has been slit by a razor. My muscles contract again. I grip myself convulsively, and have to lean against the wall. I turn away from the open wounds, the great black splotches of congealed blood, the eyes turned in. All the bodies are alike. They have been tortured. One of the flies, buzzing round, has alighted on my forehead; and I cannot raise my arm to brush it away.

"But we must close his eyes," says Garine almost in a whisper as he goes towards Klein's body.

His voice rouses me; and with an awkward, swift and violent movement I brush away the fly.

Garine puts his two fingers, stretched apart like scissors, on to the white eyeballs. Then his hand falls.

"They must have cut off the eyelids!" he exclaims.

Then he fumbles in Klein's tunic and takes out a pocketbook, the contents of which he examines. He puts a folded paper on one side and looks up. The Chinese comes in trailing awnings. They are all he can find. He begins to lay the bodies side by side. But we hear steps; and a woman comes in, her arms hanging close to her body and her back bent. Garine roughly takes me by the arm and drags me away.

"It is she," he whispers. "What idiot can have told her he is here?"

She takes no notice of us but goes straight to Klein, knocking up against one of the bodies as she passes. . . . She is opposite to him, looking at him. She neither moves nor cries. Nothing. Flies buzzing round her head. Such a smell! Close to my ear Garine's hot, panting breath.

Then, suddenly she falls on her knees. She is not praying. With parted fingers she is clasping his side. She seems to be kneeling in worship before these evidences of torture, the wounds and the mouth, on which her eyes are fixed, all gashed and slit down to the chin by a knife or razor. I am sure she is not praying. But her whole body trembles; and, just as she fell on her knees, with a movement as convulsive, she puts her arms round the body, with a motion of the head and breast expressing infinite anguish. . . . Then, with a tenderness which is heart-rending, she rubs her face against the wounds, against the blood-stained clothes, wildly, without a sob.

Garine, still holding my arm, drags me away. The Chinese has resumed his seat at the door. He does not even look at us, but he has pulled at a lappet of Garine's coat. Garine takes a note out of his pocket and gives it to him.

"When she has gone, cover them all up," he says.

In the car he does not utter a word. He has sunk down on the seat, his elbows on his knees. He grows weaker every day. The starting of the car makes him jump; and he stretches himself out to his full length, his legs stiff and his head almost on the hood.

Leaving the car in front of his house, we go up to a little room on the first floor. The blinds are down. He seems more tired and ill than I have ever seen him. The large violet marks under his eyes are bordered by two deep folds, running parallel to those which extend from nose to chin; his features, set in these four furrows, seem to be already decomposing as if in death. "If he stays a fortnight longer," Myroff had said, "he will stay longer than he wishes." The fortnight is more than over. He is silent for a while, then in a low voice, as if he were questioning me:

"Poor old chap. . . . He used often to say that life is not what one thinks it. . . ."

"Life is never what one thinks it."

"Never."

He sits down on his camp bed, his back bent, his fingers on his knees trembling like those of a drinker.

"I loved him as one man loves another. . . . To find that his eyelids were gone and that one could touch his eyeballs . . . !"

He has clenched his right hand involuntarily. He has fallen back and is now leaning against the wall, his eyes closed. His mouth and nostrils grow more and more distended; and his eyebrows seem to cast a blue shadow halfway down his cheeks.

"Often I succeed in forgetting—often, but not always. And less and less frequently. What have I done with my life, I? But, good God, what could I do? . . . Never to see any results! All these men whom I control, whose souls I have helped to create, how do I know what they will do tomorrow. . . . There have been times when I should have liked to carve it all like wood, and to be able to say: 'This is my work.' To build with time in front of one! How strange one's desires are, eh?"

His fever is increasing. As soon as he became excited he took his right hand out of his pocket, and gesticulated in his usual way, with his forearm, keeping his fist closed.

"What have I done? What have I? There! There! I am reminded of the emperor, who, you remember, put out his prisoners' eyes and sent the captives back in bunches to their native land, led by one-eyed guides. The latter soon became blind also, through fatigue. An excellent illustration of what we are doing here, far more apt than the little pictures our Propaganda issues. When I think that all my life I have been seeking liberty! Who is free here, the International, the people, I, all the others? The people can always resort to sacrificing their lives. That is something. . . ."

"Pierre, you have so little faith."

"I have faith in what I do, in what I do. But when I am not faced by . . ."

He pauses. Between us are Klein's bloodstained face and white eyeballs.

"What one does when one knows one must cease doing altogether."

He remains for a while rapt in thought, and then resumes bitterly:

"Service is what I have always hated. . . . And yet who has served more and better than I? For years, many years, a craving for power has obsessed me; and yet I have not even been able to invest my own life with it. Klein was at Moscow when Lenin died. You know that Lenin had written an article in defense of Trotsky, which was to appear in—*The Pravda*, I think. His wife had taken it to the office herself. In the morning she brought him the newspapers: he could hardly move. 'Open it,' he said. His article was not there. His voice became so confused that no one could understand what he said. He was looking so intently that everyone followed the direction of his glance and it fixed on his left hand. It lay flat and open, like that, on the sheet. He wanted to take up the paper, but could not. . . .

"Then he opened his right hand with a jerk, stretched out his fingers, and, while he was speaking, slowly bent his fingers and looked at them.

"While his right hand was still, the left began to close its fingers, like a spider folding its tentacles. . . ."

"He died soon afterwards."

"Yes, Klein said 'like a spider.' Ever since he told me that, I have never been able to forget that hand and that article—refused. . . ."

"Would you like me to get you some quinine?"

"My father often used to say to me: 'You must never let go of the earth.' He had read it somewhere. He also used to bid me remain attached to myself. His Protestant origin counted for something. 'Attached to oneself!' The little ceremony in which a living body was bound to a corpse was called a republican marriage, wasn't it? Yes, that's it, 'republican.' I used to think it would mean liberty. . . . The other told me . . ."

"Who?"

"Klein of course! How when he was in some town where the Cossacks were forced to clear out the population, one of the idiots paused for more than twenty seconds with his sword raised over the head of some kids. 'Come, hurry up,' howled Klein. 'I can't,' replied the other. 'Poor little things! I must take my time!' "

He looks up at me with a strangely hard expression.

"What I have done here few could have accomplished. And what has it all led to? Klein, his body covered with wounds, his mouth slit open with a razor, his lip hanging. . . . I say nothing of myself, but the others. Not to mention the women. We have seen one of them who, in her despair, can do nothing but rub her head against the wounds. . . . What? Yes, come in."

It is an orderly from the Propaganda, who brings a letter from Nicolaiëff. The Cantonese troops re-formed, after their defeat at Chao-Chow, have just been defeated for the second time by Chen Chun-ming; and the Committee makes an urgent appeal to the Red Army. Garine takes a blank sheet of paper out of his pocket, writes the word "decree," signs it and gives it to the orderly.

"That is for the Committee."

"Aren't you afraid of annoying them?"

"That is not the question now. I have had enough of discussions. Their cowardice, their fear of finally compromising themselves exasperate me. They know that this decree, once promulgated would be irrevocable; the people, not to speak of ourselves, have their minds fixed on Hong Kong. And if they are not satisfied . . ."

"Well?"

"Then, with the help of all the sections which we have left armed, we can, in case of necessity, play the part of Tang. I have had enough of it all."

"But if the Red Army were to be beaten?"

"It will not be."

"But if it were?"

"When one gambles, one must run the risk of losing. But this time we shall not lose."

And as I go out to get the quinine, I hear him muttering between his teeth:

"All the same there is one thing that matters in life, and that is not to let oneself be beaten."

Three days later

We are on our way home to lunch, Garine and I. Four revolver shots: the soldier at the chauffeur's side rises. "That's it!" exclaims Garine. I look and start back, for a fifth bullet has just struck the door. It's our car that is being aimed at. The soldier fires back. A score of men take flight, their sleeves flying in the wind. Two bodies lie on the ground. One of them the soldier has hit by mistake, the other is the man with the revolver. A parabellum fallen from his hand lies at his side, glittering in the sunlight.

The soldier alights and goes up to him. "Dead," he cries. He has not even leaned down. I call for bearers and an ambulance to carry to the hospital the other Chinese, who is wounded in the stomach. The car jolts over the curb.

"He was a brave fellow," says Garine as he gets out. "He might have tried to escape; but he was still firing when he fell. . . . He certainly sacrificed his life. . . ."

As he leaves the car Garine half turns round, and I see that his left arm is covered with blood.

"But . . ."

"Oh, that is nothing. It hasn't reached the bone. And the bullet has passed through. Come; this time it was a miss."

It is true there are two holes in his coat sleeve.

"My hand was on the back of the driver's seat. The worst of it is that I am bleeding like a calf. Will you go for Myroff?"

"Certainly. Where is he?"

"The driver knows."

While the driver is turning the car round, Garine mutters:

"Perhaps it was a pity. . . ."

I come back with Myroff. The thin, fair doctor with a head like a horse, can talk no language fluently except Russian; so we are silent. Before he can bring his car up to the door, the chauffeur has to scatter a group of idlers, which has gathered round the dead man.

Garine is in his room. I wait in the little antechamber.

A quarter of an hour afterwards he comes to the door, with his arm in a sling, to show Myroff out. Then he goes back into the room and lies down on the black wooden bedstead opposite me. He makes a grimace, turns round and settles himself in the bed. As he lies there in the shadow all I can see of his face are the hard lines on his cheeks, the straight mark of his eyebrows, the thin outstanding ridge of his nose, and the movements of his mouth, which droops downwards when he speaks.

"He begins to exasperate me."

"Who?"

"Myroff. He says it is serious.

"This." He points to his arm. "You know whether I care. But he says it is absolutely necessary for me to go away."

He closes his eyes.

"And the stupid part of it is, that I believe him to be right."

"Then why do you stay?"

"It is rather complicated. Oh, the devil! how uncomfortable this camp bed is!" He gets up, then sits down, his chin in his right hand, his elbow on his knee, his back bent. He is thinking.

"During these last days, I have often been driven to look back over my life. I was doing it just now, while Myroff was playing the prophet. That bullet might have been fatal. . . . You see my life has been one emphatic affirmation; but when I think of it thus a certain picture comes before me. . . ."

"Yes, you told me about it at the hospital."

"Oh, no! I am not thinking of my trial now. I am thinking of something else. . . ."

He remains plunged in thought.

"It is not altogether irrelevant to my impressions during my trial. There is a certain association of ideas, though it is remote."

He throws back his hair, which is falling over his face, and gets up, as if he were shaking himself free from something. The scarf in which his arm is slung comes undone, for the pin has fallen onto the ground. He bites his lips: and, while I am looking for the pin, he says slowly:

"I must be careful. When my conduct seems to be something apart from myself, when it begins to recede from me, it is just as if I were shedding blood. . . . In the past, when I did nothing, I used to wonder what my life was worth. Now I know that it is as good as almost . . ."

He does not finish his sentence. I look up as I give him the pin, and see that sentence terminate in a long smile, expressing a certain pride tinged with bitterness. . . . No sooner do our glances meet than he resumes, as if he had suddenly been recalled to reality, "Where was I?"

I also have to think:

"You were saying that you often looked back over your life."

"Ah! yes. Well . . ."

Then he pauses, seeking for words.

"It is always difficult to speak of these things. But come. . . . When I used to give money to midwives you don't suppose that I had any illusions as to the importance of 'the cause'; and yet I knew I ran a great risk. All the same, I continued in spite of warnings. Good. When I lost my money, I almost allowed myself to be won over by the very system that ruined me. And my ruin had something to do with my coming here. My conduct renders me indifferent to everything apart from it, and, to begin with, to its own results. If I readily threw in my lot with the Revolution it was because its results are remote and uncertain. At bottom, I am a gambler; and, like all gamblers, my whole mind is concentrated on my play. Today I am playing for bigger stakes than in the past; I have learned how to gamble; but it is still the same game. How well I know it! There is a certain rhythm in my life:

a kind of urge, if you like to put it so, from which I cannot escape. I cling to everything that gives me strength. . . . Another thing I have learned is that though a life is worth nothing, there is nothing that is worth so much as a life. . . . For some days I have been under the impression that perhaps I am forgetting the main thing, that something else is at hand. . . . I anticipated being tried and ruined, but vaguely. . . . And if in the end we were to destroy Hong Kong, I should like . . ."

But he stops, and, suddenly drawing himself up, mutters with a grimace: "Come, enough of this."

He sends for the telegrams.

The next day

THE DECREE IS PROMULGATED. We sent word at once to the Hong Kong sections. And the vanguard of the Red Army, which was sixty kilometers from the front, has just been ordered to advance into position. There is nothing but Chen Chun-ming between us and power.

August 15th

A fête day in France; and not long ago, there would have been a fête in the cathedral of this town also. But today the cathedral is transformed into a place of refuge, guarded by Red soldiers: Borodin has decreed the confiscation of all religious edifices by the State. Nothing in Europe can convey the slightest idea of the utter wretchedness of that crowd in the cathedral; the bestial misery of an animal suffering from some skin disease, with dazed, leaden eyes in which there is no appeal, no hatred even. As I look at these men an emotion, as gross, as vile as they, takes possession of me: I feel ashamed and horrified, but also glad not to be like them. For all these skeletons, these limbs like mandrakes, these rags, these scars as large as one's hand on the greenish skin, these eyes already glassy, agonized, when they are not closed, I feel no pity until I have turned away from them.

I tell Garine on my return.

"It is merely because you are not accustomed to such sights," he says. "The remembrance of a certain depth of misery is like the thought of death: it puts human things in their proper places. The best in Hong comes from that, as also did the courage of the fellow who fired at me. . . . Those who have fallen to the lowest dregs of wretchedness never rise from them: they decompose in them, like lepers. But the others are the most excellent, if not the most reliable, instruments for carrying out certain secondary tasks. They have courage, and they have no feeling either of dignity or of hatred."

"You remind me of those words of Lenin which Hong had had tattooed in English on his arm: 'Shall we ever take possession of a world which has not bled to death?' Once Hong used to admire Lenin fervently, but afterwards he hated him just as fervently. Probably it was because of his hatred that he left them. . . ."

"Also because tattooing cannot be effaced."

"Oh! but he would have burned them out. He is a fellow who hates fanatically. . . ."

"Hated. . . ."

He looks at me gravely.

"Yes, hated. . . ."

And after a moment's pause, gazing at the green palm leaf which bars the window, he adds:

"To think that for Lenin hope was of that color!"

I look at him, as he sits at his desk, his profile in the sunlight. Seen thus he does not appear to have changed. And this profile, not unlike what it was when I first arrived here, almost two months ago, and not very different from that of many years earlier, lends an intensity to the tones of his voice. Ever since that evening when I saw him in the hospital, he has seemed to be something apart from his own conduct; his deeds are drifting away from him with his health and his hold on life. Those words he has just uttered stick in my mind: "The remembrance

of a certain depth of misery, like the thought of death, puts
human things in their proper places." He is always comparing
things to death now. . . .

The manager of the Propaganda cinematograph department
comes in.

"The new cameras from Vladivostok have come, sir. And our
films are ready. Would you like to see them?"

Immediately Garine's face resumes its expression of hardness
and decision. And almost in his old tone of voice he says:

"Come."

August 17th

One division of the enemy's army has been beaten near Wai-
Chow by the Red advance guard. We have recaptured the town:
two cannon, machine guns, tractors and a large number of
prisoners have fallen into our hands. (The machine guns are
British.) Three English prisoners have already been sent to Canton. The houses of important persons, who were on friendly
terms with the enemy's officers, have been set fire to.

Chen is reforming his army; there will be a battle before the
week is out. The Propaganda is employing every means at its
disposal. The heads of corporations have been ordered to set
their men to stick up our posters: and there are posters everywhere—on the corrugated iron roofs, on the shop windows of
the wine merchants in all the bars, in all the shops, in all the
public vehicles, on all the rickshaws, on the posts in the market
place, on the parapets of the bridges: they are stuck on to the
punkas in the barbers' shops, they hang from bamboos in the
lantern shops, they are pasted on the glass windows in the bazaars,
folded fan-wise in the restaurant windows; every motorcar before it leaves the garage has a poster stuck on to it somewhere.
The whole town joins in the game; and the posters are to be
seen everywhere, in the hands of all the passers-by, just like

the morning newspapers in Europe. Only the smaller posters for the present—the large ones are not printed yet. They represent proud victorious cadets with their Cantonese soldiers in rays of light looking at the fleeing, emaciated English and Chinese, who are green with terror; and then underneath are the smaller figures of a student, a peasant, a workingman, a woman and a soldier hand in hand.

After the siesta the excitement of the people grows more serious. Soldiers in disordered uniforms parade the festive streets. All the people are out of doors; a dense crowd winds slowly and gravely along the quay, silent and exalted. With fifes, gongs and placards, processions defile, followed by children. Bands of students, waving little white flags, appear and disappear like white sea foam above the serried phalanx of robes and white suits. This compact mass advances quietly and solemnly, opening to admit processions, and leaving behind it a vague swell from which rise arms waving helmets and panamas. On the walls are our posters, on the roofs immense placards, pictures of victory, hastily painted. Beneath a low white sky, the procession advances in the heat, as if it were bound for a temple. A number of old Chinese women follow it, each carrying a bundle of black linen on her back containing a sleepy child, with its lock of hair standing on end.

The distant tumult of gongs, crackers, and shouts and the playing of musical instruments mingle with the sound of footsteps and the clacking of countless wooden shoes. Clouds of dust rise as high as a man, acrid and parching, whirling down the narrow streets, which are now deserted save for some latecomer, hastening along as fast as the festive garb he has donned in honor of the victory will let him. The shutters of nearly all the shops are closed or partly closed, as on days of high festival.

Never have I experienced more keenly than today that isolation to which Garine referred, that solitude which comes from the distance separating everything that is fundamental in us from the emotions of this crowd, even from its enthusiasm.

The next day

Garine returns from Borodin's, furious.

"I do not say he is wrong in making use of Klein's death as he might make use of anything else. But what exasperated me and seemed idiotic was his insistence on my speaking at Klein's grave. There are plenty of other speakers. But no! Once again he is dominated by this insufferable Bolshevik mentality, this stupid glorification of discipline. That is his affair. But I have not cast off the dust of Europe from my feet, at the risk of ending like some Rebecci, to come here either to teach, or to learn the word 'obedience.' 'In the face of revolution, no half measures are possible.' Just think of it! Why, there are half measures wherever there are men and not machines. . . . He wants to manufacture revolutions as Ford manufactures cars! It will all come to a bad end and that soon. In this thick-haired Mongol head of his, the Bolshevist is wrestling with the Jew; and if the Bolshevist wins, woe to the International. . . ."

As soon as the promulgation of the decree became known in Hong Kong, the British assembled in the Grand Theater and sent another telegram to London, demanding military intervention. The reply telegraphed back was that the British Government is opposed to any military intervention.

The cross-examination of British officers who have been captured has been recorded by phonograph and large numbers of the discs have been distributed among the sections. But every officer protested that he was not fighting against us by order of the British Government. This passage had to be deleted from the report of the cross-examination. As several of us spoke English without any foreign accent, more edifying discs were prepared. As Garine says, you may question a newspaper article in a newspaper, but the only effectual reply to a photograph or to a sound is by the cinema and the phonograph, and of such retorts British propaganda in the Far East is not yet capable.

"He is doing well before he leaves," Nicolaiëff said to me this morning. "He is Garine."

"Before he leaves?"

"Yes, I think he is really going this time."

"That is said every week. . . ."

"Yes, yes. But this time he will go. You will see. It is decided. If the British Government had sent troops, I think he would have stayed. But he knows London's reply. I hardly think he will wait for the result of the next battle. . . . Myroff says he will never reach Ceylon."

"And why?"

"Why, old chap! Simply because it is all over with him."

"It is very easy to say that."

"But when Myroff says it?"

"He may be mistaken."

"Dysentery and malaria are diseases that are understood. They can't be played with, old chap. If you suffer from them, you must take care. If not, you will regret it. . . . And after all, perhaps it is just as well. . . ."

"Not for him."

"His day is over. There was a time when such men were necessary. But now the Red Army is prepared. Hong Kong will be finally defeated in a few days; and we must have people who know how to forget themselves better than he does. I bear him no grudge, believe me. Whether I work with him or another. . . . All the same he has certain prejudices. I don't reproach him, but he has. . . ."

Then, smiling in his cheek and crinkling up his eyelids:

"It is human, all too human," as Borodin says. "This is what neglected maladies lead to."

I recall Ling's cross-examination and those remonstrances of Garine which Nicolaiëff calls "prejudices."

"And then, you know, he exaggerates! He really does exaggerate. Now why did he refuse to speak at Klein's funeral? It was—well, how shall I describe it?—it was absurd. . . . Surely if, as he maintained, he was Klein's friend, he owed it to his memory."

"I think it was precisely for that reason—because he was his friend—that he refused."

"But why? once again! If everyone began to choose his own work, the work that he likes . . ."

"After all, you know, he is not the only one here. There are others who could speak as well as he."

"Believe me, six months ago he would not have refused."

He pauses. Then, putting his finger on my chest, he resumes: "He is not a Communist. That is it. Of course, it does not matter to me; but all the same Borodin is logical: communism has no room for those who want to be themselves first, and to lead an independent life."

"Does not communism admit of the individual conscience?"

"It demands more than that . . . Individualism is a *bourgeois* malady."

"But, at the Propaganda, we have seen Garine to be right: we have seen that to renounce individualism here is to prepare for defeat. And all who work with us, whether they are Russians or not (Borodin perhaps excepted) are as individualist as he!"

"You know that Garine and Borodin have had a serious quarrel—at least it is said to be serious? Ah! that Borodin!"

He puts his hands in his pockets and smiles, but not malevolently.

"Much might be said about him."

"If Communists of the Roman type, if I may say so, if those at Moscow, who are defending the acquisitions of the Revolution, will not accept revolutionaries of the . . . what shall I say—type?—the conquering type, which China is giving them, they . . ."

"Conquering? Your friend Garine would consider that a bitter word."

"Will impose dangerous restrictions. . . ."

". . . but that does not matter. Your distinction is not a bad one.

Do you know what it will lead to? It will lead to the employment of your 'individualist revolutionaries,' supported by two
resolute Tchekists. Resolute. What is the use of this restricted
police force? Borodin, Garine, all that. . . ."

He makes a languid gesture, as if he were mixing liquids.

"Borodin will end like your friend. Don't you see that an independent conscience is a disease in a leader? What we want here is
a real Tcheka. . . .'

Ten o'clock

Splash, splash! The sound of junks bumping against one another. The moon, hidden behind the roof, brightens the warm
clear air. Two bags are leaning against the wall on the veranda.
Garine has decided to start tomorrow morning. For some time
he has been sitting rapt in thought, his arms hanging loosely, his
gaze lost in space. But when I get up and reach for a red pencil
with which to make notes on the *Canton Gazette* I have been
reading, he rouses himself.

"I was thinking once more of my father's words: 'You must
never let go of the earth.' Whether one lives in one absurd world
or another . . . There can be no strength, there cannot even be
any *real life* without the conviction, without the obsession of the
futility of everything. . . ."

I know that for him the true meaning of life resides in that
idea, that the strength of his personality lies in this profound
conviction of the vanity of things: that if the world is not
absurd, then his whole life has been wasted in vain gestures, vain
not with that fundamental vanity which exalts, but with the vanity
which drives one to despair. From this comes his craving to
impress his ideas upon others. But tonight everything in me rebels
against him; I protest against this attitude of his, which is all the
while gaining on me, and to which the imminence of his death
lends a sinister significance. But it is an inclination rather to
revolt than to protest that I feel obsessing me. . . . He lies in
wait for my reply as if he were an enemy.

"What you say may be true, perhaps. But your manner of saying it makes it false, absolutely false. If this real life can be set in opposition to the other, it is not in the way you mean, the way of desire and of rancor."

"Rancor? What rancor?"

"There are things here which ought to bind a man who has such proofs of strength behind him as you have, things . . ."

"To have proofs of strength, that is worse. . . ."

"Things which ought to bind him for his whole life, for . . ."

"So I am to rely upon you to instruct me!"

His irony was almost vindictive. For a while neither of us spoke. I should have liked to say something to unite us. For I was afraid, afraid like a child, that this friendship might be broken, this friendship with a man whom I have loved and whom I still love in spite of what he says and thinks, with a man who is at the point of death. . . . But once more he was stronger than I. He laid his right hand on my arm, and, with a caressing deliberation, said:

"No, listen. I am not trying to be right. I am not trying to convince you. I am simply loyal to myself. I have seen many men suffer, many. Sometimes abjectly. Sometimes horribly. I am not easily moved. Yet it has happened to me to feel pity, a pity which almost chokes me. Then, when I have been left alone with myself, that pity has always melted away. Suffering merely intensifies life's futility, rendering it despicable. Klein's life sometimes fills me with something like—like . . ."

His hesitation does not come from lack of words, but rather from a certain constraint. However, he goes on, and, looking into my eyes, says: "Like a kind of laugh. Do you understand? Deep pity is impossible for anyone for whom life has no meaning, for anyone who lives a walled life. For he sees the world as a grimace, reflected as in some distorting mirror. This may be the real aspect of the world. What does that matter? But this is true: no one, no one, do you understand? can bear it. You may live believing in the vanity of all things, but you cannot live in that vanity. Those who want to let go of the earth find it sticking to their fingers. You cannot escape it, but neither can you find it if you set out to do so. . . ."

Then, striking his knee with his fist, he continues:

"The only way is to create. Borodin says that nothing constructed by men such as I can last. And what about anything constructed by such a man as he? Ah! How I should like to see this China in five years' time!"

"Whether anything can last! Is that the question?"

We are silent, both of us.

"Why did you not go away before?"

"Why should one go when one can do otherwise?"

"It would have been prudent."

He shrugs his shoulders and says nothing. Then, after a pause:

"One does not live according to one's view of life."

Another pause.

"And the best in us clings. . . ."

Again he pauses. A strange, vague, undefined sound, almost muffled, is heard in the dim distance. . . . It begins to attract his attention as well as mine. Then we hear the grating of pneumatic tires on the gravel outside: a cyclist has ridden into the courtyard. There is a sound of steps coming up the stairs; and a messenger enters carrying two envelopes and preceded by the "boy."

Garine opens one and gives it to me: ALL CHEN CHUN-MING'S TROOPS AND THE MAIN BODY OF THE RED ARMY NOW AT THE FRONT ARE ENGAGED.

The decisive battle is beginning.

While I read, he opens the second envelope, shrugs one shoulder, rolls it up in a ball and throws it away. "What do I care, what *do* I care? Let them do as they can. All this . . ."

The messenger goes out. We hear his footsteps dying away and the gate being closed. But Garine has gathered himself together. He stands at the window and calls him.

The gate reopens. The messenger returns. Standing under the window, he talks to Garine. But the latter is coughing and I cannot catch his words.

The messenger goes off again. Garine paces up and down. Now he is furious.

"What is the matter?"

"Nothing."

Good. One can easily see there is something. He picks up the ball of paper, unfolds it, smooths it out with his right hand, not without difficulty owing to the rigidity of his left arm. Then, turning to me:

"Let us go down."

As we go, he mutters—to himself or me? "Why, a thing like that might have destroyed ten thousand of them!"

As I refrain from asking any questions, he is constrained to add, as we go downstairs:

"Two of our people, Propaganda agents, taken with cyanide in their pockets just as they were going up to the wells, used by our troops. Spies, no doubt. They couldn't explain their presence there. They have said nothing, confessed nothing. And Nicolaïeff tells me he will resume their cross-examination tomorrow."

He is driving the car himself, and at full speed. The chauffeur is asleep. His right hand only is on the wheel; and twice we narrowly escape running into houses. He slows down, and gives me the wheel; then with his head quite still, sunk into his shoulders —the hollowness of his cheeks accentuated by a streak of light that we fly through, he seems to have forgotten my presence.

As we go down the passage, at the police station, I notice the pink bills I had caught a glimpse of as we flew through the streets; they are the Decree, which we have had posted up.

The sharp, military click of our heels, as we approach Nicolaïeff's office, sounds almost ominous in the dead silence of the night. There at his desk sits the superintendent, his elbow on the arm of his chair, fixing two prisoners with his clear pig's eyes. Both of them are clothed in the blue linen of dock-laborers. One has a drooping mustache, black and fine. The other is an old man, with his hair brushed up from his round head, and with bright, gleaming eyes.

I begin to grow used to these nightly sessions at the Propa-

ganda and the police station—to the silence, the smell of sickly
flowers, mud and petrol, to the warmth of the night, to drawn,
tired faces, eyelids almost gummed together, backs bent, lips
loose—and to that parched sensation in the mouth which follows
a drunken night.

"Have you any news of the battle?" Garine asks as he enters.

"Nothing, it is proceeding."

"And those men of yours?"

"You saw the report, my dear chap. That is all I know, at any
rate as yet. Impossible to get a word out of them. But it will
come."

"Who stood surety for them?"

"N. 72, according to the report."

"You must inquire into that. If it is correct, N. 72 must be
brought back, tried by the special court and executed immediately
after his conviction."

"You know he is a police officer of the first rank?"

Garine looks up.

". . . and one who has often rendered good service. . . . He is
loyal."

"He need not take the trouble to be so any more. As for his
services, they are nothing to me. You understand, don't you?"

Nicolaïeff smiles and nods his sleepy head, which looks like the
porcelain figure he has ironically placed on his desk.

"Now for these men."

I take my stylo out of my pocket.

"No, you need not take any notes. It will not be long; and
Nicolaïeff will write down the replies."

"Who gave you the poison?"

The first prisoner, the younger, begins an absurd explanation:
he had been charged to give the packet to someone whose name
he does not know, a woman who was to recognize him by the
description given to her, but . . .

Garine only vaguely understands; so I translate sentence by
sentence. The Chinese, with a nervous gesture, lays his hand flat
on the long forks of his mustache, then realizing that this prevents

his being understood, takes it away, then puts it back again. Nicolaiëff, utterly worn out, gazes at the lamp round which clouds of insects are buzzing, and smokes. The ventilators are not working, so the smoke rises straight.

"Enough," says Garine.

He puts his hand to his belt.

"Good. I have forgotten it again."

Without another word, he opens my case with his one free hand, takes out my revolver and puts it on the desk, on one of the shining metal corners.

"Make the first prisoner clearly understand that if, in five minutes' time, he has not given us the necessary information, I shall fire a bullet into his head, *I* shall."

I translate. Nicolaiëff has almost imperceptibly shrugged one shoulder. All our spies know that Garine is a great leader and that his methods are those of a child.

One minute . . . two . . .

"Ah! That is enough. Now let him reply at once."

"You said he was to have five minutes," remarks Nicolaiëff, respectfully and sarcastically.

"Don't you interfere."

He has taken the revolver from the desk. His right hand is steadied by the weight of the firearm, his left, emerging from the white sling, trembles. Once again I tell the Chinese to reply. He signifies that he cannot.

The bullet is fired. The body of the Chinese stands rigid, a dazed expression on his face. Nicolaiëff has started; he leans against the wall. Is the prisoner wounded?

One second . . . two. The man droops loosely, his legs half bent; and his blood begins to flow.

"But," stammers Nicolaiëff, "come, Garine! What about the court . . ."

"Don't you interfere."

In such a tone as to silence the fat man immediately. His smile has vanished. His mouth droops, the line of his jaws stands out. His hands are folded over his chest, like an old woman's. Garine stares at the wall in front of him. A trail of light, a kind of transparent smoke, ascends from the half-lowered pistol.

"Now for the other. Tell him, too, that . . ."

It is unnecessary. The terrified old man is already talking, talking, talking, his little eyes rolling. Nicolaiëff has seized his pencil and is taking notes with a trembling hand.

"Stop," cries Garine in Cantonese. "Warn him before he says anything more, that if he tells us any nonsense he will suffer for it. . . ."

"He understands."

"His death penalty might be even more severe."

"How can I tell him that?"

"You must find some way."

(It is easy to talk! But I do make him understand.)

While the prisoner speaks in halting tones, Nicolaiëff is blowing the dead bodies of insects off the paper on which he is writing. . . .

The man was in the pay of Chen Chun-ming's agents. That is obvious. At first he spoke rapidly, but said nothing of importance. Then, seeing the revolver was being lowered, he hesitated. Suddenly he pauses. Garine, exasperated beyond control, looks at him.

"And if . . . if I tell everything, what will you give?"

In an instant he falls, flapping his arms, and rolls along the floor. Garine in his fury has struck him a blow on the jaw. With his fist still clenched, he bites his lips and sits down on one corner of the desk. "My wound has opened," he says. The prisoner on the ground is pretending to be dead.

"Ask him if he has ever heard of incense."

Again I translate. The man opens his eyes slowly, and, still lying on the ground and without looking at either of us, says:

"They were three. Two have been taken. One of the two is dead. The other is here. The third may be at the wells."

Garine and I look at Nicolaiëff, who proposed resuming the cross-examination tomorrow. His face is expressionless; but the muscles of his cheeks contract and expand, as if they were trembling. He writes while the prisoner explains.

"Now we know."

"Is that all?"

"Yes."

"If you have not told us everything . . ."

"I have told everything."

The prisoner appears completely indifferent. He can do nothing more to defend himself, so he must give himself up to fate. . . .

Nicolaïeff rings, shows us a paper, then gives it to the orderly.

"Send a cyclist to the telegraph office immediately."

He turns round to us.

"Under these conditions . . . under such conditions as these . . . there may be others, you know. . . . Don't you think . . . one ought to try a little . . . ?"

As an excuse for his horrible negligence, this man who was prepared to postpone the conclusion of the cross-examination until tomorrow, is now proposing to have the prisoner tortured . . . just "in case . . ."

"He is impossible," muttered Garine between his teeth.

Then, aloud:

"And why? Simply in order that he may tell us falsehoods and set us on the wrong track . . . ? He cannot have any general information. In this matter of wells, there are usually not more than three. Three, you understand? Not two."

Now it is Garine's turn to ring. He does so, four times. Two soldiers answer. They take away the prisoner. Nicolaïeff has not replied. He seems absorbed in brushing away the dead insects which are still falling on to the desk, as if he were smoothing his paper, like a good child.

In the passage we meet an orderly from the War Commissariat, who is bringing a dispatch. Garine takes it and reads: "CHEN'S TROOPS ARE BEGINNING TO FALL BACK."

There is no light on Garine's staircase; the lamp is broken. Outside, too, darkness reigns, and over my own nerves also. . . . My eyelids burn and I feel wide awake. I shiver slightly, as if I were a little drunk. While I stumble up the stairs, groping with my toes for each step, my eyes close, and in a strange blend of confusion and lucidity, I behold a distorted vision: the two prisoners, one prisoner dead (on the ground), Nicolaiëff, the light from the street, Klein's mutilated face, and a splash of pink made by the posters. . . . The sound of Garine's voice makes me jump, as if I had been suddenly awakened:

"I can't get used to this darkness. It always makes me feel as if I were blind."

But here is light. Now we are in the little room again. The two bags are still on the veranda.

"Is that all you are taking?"

"It is quite enough for a few months."

He had hardly listened to what I said. For his attention is fixed on a dull roar which fills the house, and which was already puzzling me before we left.

"Do you hear?"

"Yes . . . I heard it before."

"What do you think it is?"

"Listen."

There is something mysterious in that muffled, remote, mechanical rumbling. It is a kind of dull, gnawing noise, almost like that made by rats. It is regular and seems to proceed at once from sky and cellar. At intervals there are noises like the bursting of bubbles and the cracking of wood, prolonged, as are all sounds, in the darkness, and merging into the more continuous roar. Garine stands still. He looks anxious; he holds his breath, contracts his shoulders, tries to be as noiseless as possible. The creaking of his shoes deadens the sound, which, after a few seconds, is heard again, wavering and uncertain, then increasing in volume— remote and inexplicable. Finally he relaxes; and making a gesture which implies that it is nothing to him, he stretches himself out on his wooden bedstead.

"Will you have some coffee while you are waiting?"

"No, thank you."

"Perhaps it would be better if you took some quinine and changed the dressing."

"All in good time."

"Three months, six perhaps?"

Still worried, he is biting his cheek.

"After all, it would be rather stupid to stay here because I refused to leave in time."

By "stay" he means "die."

"My old friend Nicolaiëff insinuates that it is almost too late. . . ."

Hitherto he has seemed to be talking to himself. Then his voice changes. Once more he raises his right shoulder.

"What a fool! . . . If I had not gone there tonight . . . Who can Borodin put in my place? Chen for Propaganda in the sections, but in the other departments . . . ? A few fellows like Nicolaiëff, disciplined, highly disciplined, would suffice to end everything. . . . Klein is dead. What will it all be like when I return? One single blunder at the police station is enough to bring me back to this Canton life; and yet at this moment I feel as if I had left it already. Ah! if the end were to come while I was at sea what a pretty label might be pasted on the sack. . . ."

His lips are thinner than they were just now and his eyes are shut. The shadow cast by his nose, which now appears very prominent, merges in the circle round his left eye. He looks ugly, with that disquieting and offensive ugliness of corpses.

"To think that when I arrived here in Lambert's time Canton was a comic opera republic. And now, today, there is Britain! Trying to conquer a town, to destroy a town! The town is the most social thing in the whole world, the very emblem of society. There is one town at least that the lousy Cantonese are getting into a fine state! This Decree. . . . The effort of all those who have converted Hong Kong into a clenched fist is at last . . ." He puts his foot down and leans forward, as if he were crushing something, slowly, heavily. At the same time he sits up straight from the waist, takes out of his pocket a little round mirror with a celluloid back and looks at his face. (It is for the first time.)

"I think the hour has struck. . . .

"It would be really too stupid to die here like any other colonist. If men such as I are not murdered, who will be?"

Something in all that he says makes me anxious and ill at ease. He resumes:

"What in the devil's name can I do in Europe? I shall probably go to Moscow. . . . I have no faith in the International's methods, but one ought to see. . . . Shanghai in six days. Then the Norwegian boat and the impression of alighting at the porter's lodge. I shall be shadowed by two detectives, which is always an honor. Provided I do not find everything I have done smashed to bits on my return. Borodin is very strong; but he can be very maladroit. Ah! one can never go where one would like to."

"Wherever would you like to go?"

"To England. Now that I know what Empire is—one tenacious, constant act of violence. To direct, to determine, to constrain. That is life."

Then, I suddenly understand why his words are so disconcerting. It is not I whom he wants to convert. It is he himself who does not believe what he says, and with his nerves strained to the uttermost, he is trying to convince himself. . . . Does he know there is no hope for him? Or does he know nothing? Confronted with the certainty of his death, I feel his hopes and affirmations driving me to an agony of exasperation. I am sorely tempted to say to him: "Enough, enough, you are dying." But his very appearance renders such words impossible. Disease has hollowed his face so terribly that it requires no effort of imagination to see him dead already. And it seems to me that if I were to speak of death I should conjure up before him that picture of himself, those drawn features which perpetually obsess me. I feel also the danger of any reference to death, for fear lest I should seem to be confirming his own suspicions. . . . He has stopped talking for a moment. And during the silence that strange sound that had puzzled us just now recurs. It is no longer a dim roar, but a distinct reverberation of successive shocks, remote and muffled as if in a dream. It seems as if someone were beating the ground with some heavy implement covered with felt. And now those shriller sounds, like wood cracking, that one heard before at intervals, have grown more distinct, have become almost metallic, like the clearing of a throat, punctuated by the rhythmic fall of hammers.

Again these noises mingle with the sound of pneumatic tires bounding over the gravel. The "boy" comes up, followed by a cadet. He brings the reply from the telegraph office. Now the noise, though still in the distance, is filling the room.

"Do you hear?" Garine asks the "boy."

"Yes, sir."

"What is it?"

"Don't know, sir."

The cadet, with a gesture of pride, says: "It is the Army, Comrade Garine."

Garine looks up.

". . . The rear guard of the Red Army taking up its position."

Garine draws a deep breath, then reads the dispatches and gives them to me.

THIRD SPY ARRESTED, WITH EIGHT HUNDRED GRAMMES OF CYA-NIDE ON HIM.

ENEMY ROUTED. SEVERAL REGIMENTS PREPARED BY OUR PROPA-GANDA COME OVER TO US. COMMISSARIAT AND ARTILLERY IN OUR HANDS. HEADQUARTERS DISORGANIZED. CAVALRY PURSUING CHEN, WHO IS IN FULL FLIGHT.

He signs the receipt for the telegram and gives it to the cadet, who goes out, again preceded by the "boy."

"He won't see my signature again for some time. . . . Chen's army scattered. Shanghai before the year is out."

The noise of the approaching army rises and falls, borne on the hot breeze. We can now distinguish the groaning of tractors, the vague shaking of the ground beneath the tramp of the soldiers, and, at intervals, wafted in by some sudden hot gust, the sound of horses' hoofs and the metallic ring of the axles of gun-carriages.

As Garine listens to this distant uproar a vague sense of exaltation comes over him. Is it joy?

"I shall hardly see you tomorrow morning among all those fools who will come to see me off."

Slowly, biting his lower lip, he takes his wounded arm from its sling, and raises it. We embrace. A strange melancholy springs in me, deep and desperate, inspired by the futility of things and the presence of death. As we separate and the light shines upon our faces, he looks into my eyes. I search his for the joy which I imagined I had seen gleaming there; I see nothing of the kind, nothing but a hard and yet a fraternal seriousness.

PERMANENT LIBRARY BOOKS

The Permanent Library makes available to the general reader those works of the world's great writers which have long been out of print, or which are not readily obtainable. They give a better understanding of the wide range of the talents of these masters of literature. The volumes are carefully edited, durably bound and tastefully designed. The average length is in excess of 700 pages.

GREAT FRENCH SHORT NOVELS
edited by F. W. DUPEE *$5.00*

GREAT ADVENTURES AND EXPLORATIONS
edited by VILHJALMUR STEFANSSON *$5.00*

SHORT NOVELS OF COLETTE
with an introduction by GLENWAY WESCOTT *$5.00*

GREAT RUSSIAN SHORT NOVELS
edited by PHILIP RAHV *$5.00*

THE GREAT SHORT NOVELS OF HENRY JAMES
edited by PHILIP RAHV *$5.00*

THE SHORT NOVELS OF DOSTOEVSKY
with an introduction by THOMAS MANN *$5.00*

GREEK PLAYS IN MODERN TRANSLATION
edited by DUDLEY FITTS *$5.00*

GREAT AMERICAN SHORT NOVELS
edited by WILLIAM PHILLIPS *$4.00*

THE PERMANENT GOETHE
edited by THOMAS MANN *$5.00*

THE SHORT NOVELS OF BALZAC
with an introduction by JULES ROMAINS *$4.00*

THE SHORT NOVELS OF TOLSTOY
edited by PHILIP RAHV *$4.00*

THE SHORT STORIES OF DOSTOEVSKY
with an introduction by WILLIAM PHILLIPS *$4.00*

THE BOSTONIANS
by HENRY JAMES *$3.00*